Copyright © 2021, Dianna Love Snell
All rights reserved.

ISBN 978-1-940651-12-5

By payment of required fees, you have been granted the *non*-exclusive, *non*-transferable right to access and read the text of this eBook. No part of this text may be reproduced, transmitted, downloaded, decompiled, reverse engineered, or stored in or introduced into any information storage and retrieval system, in any form or by any means, whether electronic or mechanical, now known or hereinafter invented without the express written permission of copyright owner.

**Please Note**

This is a work of fiction. Names, characters, places, and incidents either are the product of the author's imagination or are used fictitiously, and any resemblance to actual persons, living or dead, business establishments, events or locales is entirely coincidental.

The reverse engineering, uploading, and/or distributing of this eBook via the internet or via any other means without the permission of the copyright owner is illegal and punishable by law. Please purchase only authorized electronic editions, and do not participate in or encourage electronic piracy of copyrighted materials. Your support of the author's rights is appreciated.

Cover Design & Interior Format

© KILLION
THE
GROUP, INC.

# DIANNA LOVE

# TREOIR DRAGON CHRONICLES

## OF THE BELADOR WORLD

# VOL. 3

### BOOKS 7 - 9

# DEDICATION

This entire series is dedicated to my amazing editorial team, beta team, and audio team as well as the Killion Group Inc. services. Everyone stepped up to go above and beyond in helping me to deliver the best Treoir Dragon Chronicles series possible to my readers. Any errors are mine.

Thank you to content editor Jodi Henley, copy editor Judy Carney, proof editor Stacey Krug, plus top beta readers Tina Rucci and Sherry Arnold for your wonderful attention to detail and multiple reads from everyone.

Thank you to narrator Stephen R. Thorne, plus audio editors Stacey Krug and Joyce Ann McLaughlin, for the beautiful audio productions.

An additional thank you to the Blackstone Audio team for superior work in the final digital and hard copy audio creations and distribution.

Thank you to Kim Killion for all the great covers and Jennifer Jakes-Goodbar for terrific formatting of every version.

# PRONUNCIATION GUIDE

Note: A complete guide of unusual names, places and terminology for the Belador series is located on any Belador book page at *www.AuthorDiannaLove.com,* but below are from this book.

**Ainvar** – AIN var (AIN rhymes with rain)
**aiteann** – ah chin
**Apsu** – AHP soo
**Brynhild** – burn HILD
**Casidhe** – CAH sih duh
**Cearcall na Sìorraidheachd** – SEHR cull nah SEE ur RYE eecht
**Chaakir** – shah KEER
**Cúpla Dearg** - COOP luh JAIR eg
**Dagda** – DAHG duh
**Dhraoidhean Dorcha Elite** – GREY geen DOOR chuh
**Eesumor** – EE sue more
**Eógan** – OH un
**Garwyli** – gar WHY lee
**Gruffyn** – GRUFF in
**Hawdreki** – haw DREK kee
**Immortuos Grimoire** – im MORH tue ose gruhm WAAR
**Imortiks** – im MORE ticks
**Jennyver** - JENN uh vir
**Joavan** – joh uh VAHN
**Josue** – hoh ZOO eh
**Ketche** – KETCH uh
**Lann an Cheartais** – lahn nah KAIR tus
**Lann Saoirse** – lahn SEER shuh
**Lakyle** – luh KYLE

**Lorcan** – LOR can
**Luigsech** – LOO gi sehk (g is hard like 'egg')
**Mac Seáin** – mac SHAWN
**Maistir** – MY stir
**Marduk** – MAHR dook
**Maze Mortis** – MAVE MOR tis

**Medb** – MAVE
**Mulatko** – moo LOT koh
**Noirre** – NOIR ay
**Phoedra** – FAY druh
**Renata** – REY not ah
**Ruadh** – ROO awn
**Scamall** – SKAH mull
**Scáth Force** – SCATH (like bath) Force
**Seanóir** – SHAWN ore ee
**Seilbh a ghlacadh ar chumhacht** – SHEN ith  uh hu lacha air hohcht
**Skarde** – SKARD
**Sùilean** – SOO lun
**Talamh Dearmadta** –TAHL am DUR mah tah
**TÅµr Medb** – TOWER MAVE
**Tiamat** – TYAH maht
**Timmon** – tim MAHN
**Tír na nÓg** – TEAR nah nowg
**Tzader** – ZAY der
**Uruk** – OO rook
**Wang Mu Niang Niang** – wong mew nee AHNG nee AHNG
**Zeelindar** – ZEE lin dar

# DIANNA LOVE

# TREOIR DRAGON
# CHRONICLES
### OF THE BELADOR WORLD
## BOOK 7

*"LONG AGO, I WAS OFFERED an arranged marriage to gain a powerful ally for our kingdom and declined. My father understood, but asked for a promise in return if I found the mate of my heart. He said I must agree to fight for this love match no matter what tribulations might arise.*

*With one look into your eyes, I am willin' to go to war."*

~ Daegan, Dragon King of Treoir.

*L*YDIA STONE WITH ATLANTA NEW *Millennium News* stared at something she never thought she'd see in Atlanta. She whispered to Al, her cameraman, *"You getting this?"* When Al nodded, she said, *"No editing. We run it raw or no one will believe we filmed a ... what are we calling that yellow thing?"*

*"Hell if I know. Let the viewers tell us. Looks like a demon ..."* Al's calm demeaner went ballistic. *"Call the cops. It's chasing a human being."*

*"It's a little girl!"* Lydia called Atlanta PD on her mobile phone as she started running and screaming, *"Stop, you monster!"*

# CHAPTER 1

*"I BELIEVED I WAS FAMILY!* I did everythin' you asked of me and you used me like a lamb staked for a wolf. I will *not* be punished for *anyone's* mistakes and never for yours."

Herrick's eyes bulged, staring at Casidhe as if she'd turned into a demon. "Do not think to condemn me when you brought the red dragon *here* to my home. *You lost Skarde!* You *failed* the only task I gave you."

Fury flooded her and raced beneath her skin, a wildfire rage. She held his crazed gaze with her determined one. "I am ashamed to have had a role, even unintentionally, in your unforgivable deceit. You imprisoned a woman for thousands of years and kept her from bein' at her dyin' father's bed to barter for your selfish wants. You should be ashamed to face your people."

All around, she heard gasps and prayers.

Herrick's face distorted, warping his head. Eyes glowing hot as blue flames held no humanity. He lifted massive hands above his head as his body twisted into an unnatural shape. Tremors shook his arms and chest, then ran down legs thick as tree stumps now ripping out of his leather pants.

He roared a prehistoric sound, rocking the castle.

Casidhe held her sword up, preparing for whatever he did.

Herrick flung a hand at her, but no energy flew from him. He shouted, "I am only ashamed of you and the danger you have brought to the clan."

His words cut and her heart bled, but Casidhe would grow a thicker shield for her heart and new emotional muscles to protect her from ever blindly trusting again.

Her voice took an edge capable of slashing through his lies. "You said *the* clan. Not *our* clan. You only confirm every word

I've spoken here today."

She'd struggled and fought for the life she'd built, having foolishly believed this man had cared for her.

Lowering her free hand, she lifted the backpack, but it would not fit across her back with the shoulder pads of her new armor.

Herrick took a step toward her, but it landed as a heavy thud. She'd never seen him in a half shift. His eyes glittered with predatory intent. Sharp fangs of his dragon struggled to break free of his misshapen mouth.

His voice couldn't sound any more inhuman. "What do you think you are doing?"

She steeled her voice to come out strong. "I am done with all of this. Do not try to stop me from leavin'."

"Take a step toward that door and you shall regret it!"

Sliding her sword back into the sheath inside her pack, she slung a strap over her shoulder. Without another word, she headed for the door.

A loud growling noise from a creature who had ruled the skies long ago blasted the air.

She had no idea how she knew, but she realized the second he lunged at her from behind.

Energy rolled down her arm as she spun and shoved a hand at him. Power crackled then punched him square in the chest.

Herrick's big body flew backward, hit the floor, and slid against the wall knocking over a candlestand. Stones cracked and buckled, debris raining down on him. His body returned to a fully human shape, but he didn't move.

Kleio hurried over and dropped to one knee. The seer checked for a pulse then turned to Casidhe. "He'll live."

Good. Casidhe felt sick and frozen. She hadn't intended to kill Herrick, but he had better never try to put a hand on her again.

When Kleio stood, she gave Casidhe a deep bow of her head and lifted upright again. The woman's eyes gleamed with something Casidhe wanted to call admiration.

Giving the seer a brief nod, she turned again to leave. When she reached the door, she grabbed the thick metal handhold and whipped the massive entrance door so hard it slammed the wall.

She looked at her hand. Huh.

Stepping forward, she continued out into the cool night and drew in a deep breath of freedom that cleansed her soul.

One of Herrick's men still tended the fire. He watched her intently as she took the steps down.

This was no time to crumble or show weakness.

Herrick had crushed her heart, but he no longer held her every thought in his grip. She now knew the truth of her position here.

She had no position.

No significance.

Her eyes burned with tears she refused to give into. Not here. Her chest physically hurt as if she'd been clawed open.

Crackling fire off to her side tossed shadows in the dark night.

One foot in front of the other. Keep doing that and she'd cross two hundred yards to make it out of here.

Look at the positive. No more questioning where she stood with Herrick or what action she could take without upsetting him or the fear of failing at her duty.

She'd spent her life trying to be worthy of Herrick. She'd never questioned if Herrick had been worthy of her.

Had it all been a sham?

Pain burst behind her eyes, turning her vision red as she grimly forced her feet to move faster.

*Who was she? Where had she come from?*

She had vague memories of her time as a small child before a man snatched her up, covered her head, and delivered her to Herrick's castle. She only knew what the castle lord had told her along with the MacConnaugh squire family.

Was it all lies? Had any of it been true?

For the first time in many years, she tried to reach back in time before her arrival at the castle, searching for something she could cling to, and found ... nothing. Just blurred memories.

*Herrick had lied to her.*

He'd had her captured just to twist and use for his own purposes. Where had she been? Who had birthed her?

Pain built inside, gnawing at her with jagged teeth until she burst forward, running and screaming at the heavens over a life that had never been hers. Power churned and rolled through her until she felt like a fireball about to explode.

Energy raked over her skin, jarring her. Then she was through the barrier and gone from Herrick's land.

She slowed, gasping for breath.

Tears dampened her lashes. She wiped a hand over her eyes. If she gave into the ache clawing her chest, she'd crumble to the ground. She stumbled away from the ward.

Don't look back. Ever.

This was her moment to stand on her own, find a way home without any support.

What home? Wrapping her arms around her middle, she shoved the pain behind walls. After all she'd survived, she would worry about all the unanswered questions once she found a way out of these mountains.

Still, home had no meaning.

There would be no Daegan waiting for her.

His words had hurt, too. He'd shredded her heart as if it had been made of paper. How could he believe so easily that she'd hide his sister from him?

*Maybe because you hid your entire life from him.*

"Shut up," she muttered, in no mood for a noisy conscience. Sure, the circumstances were damning, but hey, he clearly hadn't cared enough to ask questions or give her a chance to explain.

He obviously didn't care for her as much as he said.

How could he make a vow and walk away that easily?

So many questions, but for once she had no other duty but to herself. She'd find answers.

At least the ones she could research, but where had that blast of power come from within her to send a dragon shifter flying backward? And what about this armor covering her body? That showed up when she'd grasped her sword.

Even *Lann an Cheartais* knew more than she did. She'd feared not being able to pull the sword from its sheath and facing Herrick's wrath.

She'd had no lifeline to hold onto in that turbulent moment where she'd lost all, then a female voice spoke in her head. *Honor my sword. It will honor you.*

A calm settled over Casidhe. She called the sword to her with reverence and confidence. *Lann an Cheartais* came to her aid immediately.

She hadn't paused to question anything. She simply went on instinct she'd never experienced so deeply until the moment when she truly took possession of this weapon.

With the journey ahead of her, she hoped the sword did not forget they were now besties.

She had to cover as much ground as possible, to get as far from here as she could before her legs would carry her no more.

A dark valley between towering mountains lay ahead with the western ridge clinging to a thin line of light. She dug out her trusty LED flashlight key ring and managed not to fall in a hole as she covered the first quarter of a mile from the castle.

The backpack strap on her shoulder wouldn't slide off the ornate armor made of something that felt like flexible steel, but she had to change shoulders. Maybe by dawn she'd have an idea of how to remove the armor. That was a long eight or nine hours away.

Wind barely moved through the canyon, but she caught an out-of-place whooshing sound.

Wings flapping behind her.

Approaching fast.

Had Herrick sent Stian, that damned vulture?

Herrick would not think her worth the effort to come himself. She'd be damned if a griffon vulture thought to drag her back to its master.

As the sky lost all light save for a partial moon, she looked around to find the ghostly dark shape of the griffon vulture flying toward her. No other bird out here should be that large, not even another griffon vulture.

It flew too high to be attacking. She arched her head, dropping it back as she watched the bird race past without stopping.

Guess she scared the vulture, too.

A second later, the louder sound of a large creature flying in from behind yanked her chin down.

"I'll be damned."

Herrick's dragon bore down on her with claws extended.

She waited as air rushed around her. No power climbed her

arm. Uh-oh.

No, no, no! She flipped to her right at the last second, hitting the rocky ground hard and rolling. She caught the strap of her backpack at the last second, dragging it with her. Pain stabbed her shoulder.

That hadn't been her best idea.

Still, she was alive. She stood and rubbed her aching shoulder muscles.

His dragon flew over the empty spot she'd left, roaring in anger and blowing out ice.

Her power growled and rumbled in her chest.

Lowering her hand, she pulled her sword out. Energy sizzled up her arm to her fingers around the hilt. The silver blade flashed as if a powerful beam of light had struck it.

Herrick's dragon banked around hard and came back at her.

Grasping the hilt with both hands, she lifted the blade vertically in front of her. She'd been torn about harming Herrick when he threatened her.

Not anymore.

Anyone who attacked her from now on was not her friend. That made for a simple rule to follow when deciding who faced her sword.

She'd never faced down a dragon and never this dragon.

Angry tears streamed down her cheeks.

He intended to blast her with frozen water. She couldn't avoid the ice and falling down would end with her being buried alive.

The closer his dragon came to her, the tighter she gripped the hilt. Her arms quivered.

His dragon opened wide jaws with gleaming fangs hanging down.

She stood her ground with the razor-sharp blade pointed forward.

Glowing blue reptilian eyes narrowed on her and a thunderous load of ice gushed out of that dark maw.

He was going to kill her.

The freezing water blasted at her full force, then split apart on each side of her blade. Goosebumps lifted over her skin from the freezing air as his dragon flew past again.

Shocked out of her skull, she couldn't move.

Ice piles surrounded her with one way out. Her knees threatened to buckle from surviving that attack. How had she not been buried? Turning the sword, she watched energy race up and down the blade, sizzling.

Then the glow died and she had a normal sword once more.

She lowered the tip to the ground and turned, walking through a narrow path in the ice mountain. She searched for Herrick's dragon.

A giant black silhouette flew high then slowed and angled back her way.

What now?

Her arms had turned to jelly, but she picked the sword up again. No glow this time. She murmured, "Come on, *Lann an Cheartais*. It's not time to quit."

Evidently, her sword was done.

She still held the blade in front of her, feet apart, ready for whatever Herrick's dragon did next. If he blasted her again, the sword would be only as good as a giant ice pick to chip a way out. She wouldn't survive that long.

The dragon swooped low and landed a hundred feet away. Herrick shifted into his human form, complete with furs, boots, and a billowy white shirt.

He stalked over to her.

She had no idea if the power she'd wielded would return or not, but when he reached twenty feet from her, anger gripped her hard. She ordered, "Stop right there."

He halted with eyes churning blue flames.

"What do you want, Herrick?"

"I want you to find Jennyver!"

The sound of her jaw dropping could probably be heard two mountains away. "Are you mad? Why in the world would you think I'd help *you* find her?"

"I do not wish to capture her."

"Oh, sure." She screamed, "You just tried to *kill me!* Why should I believe anythin' you say?"

He sighed a rumbling sound. "I was angry."

"That's *it*? You were angry. Well, here's a news blast. I am *furious* and I will *never* trust you again."

"I speak the truth," he argued, seeming unbothered by her words. Thick-headed, self-serving man. "I only want Skarde back. I ask you to help me find the woman to offer the red dragon for my brother."

Unbelievable gall. Even now he came to drop a duty at her feet.

Taking a deep breath, Casidhe forced her shoulders down. It would feel so good to throw all he'd done to Jennyver, and to her, in his face, then walk away. But he had knowledge she needed. For that reason, she took a moment to think.

He needed her, again.

If she did anything for him, this time it would be on her terms, but she would not hand an innocent woman to Herrick.

That also meant she was unwilling to offer any deal yet. "I will *consider* this, but only if you give me somethin' right now."

He snarled and his chest rumbled.

"Screw this," she snapped and headed for her backpack.

"What do you want to know?" he growled.

Her pulse pounded and questions flew through her mind. She angled around, eyeing him with suspicion. "Does this mean you're not goin' to continue tryin' to kill me?"

"Had I wanted you dead, you would not be uttering any questions."

She might have believed that at one time, but not after just surviving a deluge of ice from his dragon.

She let his boast go for now, opting for the more important win. "I no longer believe you just happened to choose me off the streets to have brought to your castle. You don't operate that way, Herrick. How did you find me?"

He crossed his arms and stared over her head for so long she considered walking away again. "I had scouts in Pakistan watching for someone with unnatural gifts."

She'd never believed in coincidences and this confirmed he knew exactly where she came from or had enough information she could use to find out everything. "Why me?"

It dawned on her she probably hadn't been the first person taken. He might have done this over and over for centuries. How many other people had he hunted who had possessed her skills or some other unusual abilities?

A tiny jaw muscle pumped in and out as he studied her. "I give my word I will tell you all if you find Jennyver and help me gain Skarde. Do not dare to insult my word." He turned his back on her, took two steps, and shifted. His dragon pushed up and flew away.

At that same moment, her armor withdrew, slowly disappearing until leaving her in the loose shirt and jeans she'd worn for two days now.

Her stomach growled and ached.

She hefted the backpack into place across her shoulders, latching the straps, then pulled out a half-bottle of water she had left. With another search, her fingers landed on a pack of peanut butter crackers. Her mouth actually watered in response.

After being drugged, then driven cross-country in a food truck, she'd had no chance to eat last night before Herrick showed up to fly her to the castle.

Her anger dissolved into a drive to eat, stay strong, and reach safety. Then she'd figure out her next move.

Moonlight fought its way through clouds to float free. Long shadows played over the rugged canyon floor as she picked her way up and down the uneven ground.

What felt like two miles in, adrenaline had worn off, leaving her body drained. She nodded off while walking and had to give herself a break.

Just a quick power nap would do a lot right now.

Scoping out the area with her LED light, she hiked over to where she could sit with her back to boulders piled higher than she stood. Dropping the backpack to the ground, she sat down with her knees pulled up, then moved the pack between them. That provided a place to lay her head over her crossed arms.

She had almost fallen asleep when a tingle across her neck woke her. She sensed someone watching her.

Moving carefully, she lifted her head until she stared at the intruder twenty feet away.

Stian stood tall, larger than any natural vulture she'd ever seen. The bird's black eyes shined with intelligence that creeped her out.

How long had Stian been there?

How long would Stian stay?

The bird opened its vicious beak and let out a hiss, then lowered its head with black eyes still locked on her.

She didn't dare fall asleep with that demonic vulture watching her. She barely moved her hand toward the sword.

Stian took a step forward.

Even if the sword flew to her again, it would not reach her hand before that beak ripped her neck open.

# CHAPTER 2

DAEGAN APPEARED ON THE TREOIR grounds right behind Tristan.

He bunched his shoulders and let out a muffled roar. His fangs shot down, stabbing in his oversized jaw and threatening to strangle him.

*Liar!* Sweet-smelling, sinfully addictive *liar!*

How could Casidhe have been part of keeping Jennyver from him?

How had Herrick kept Jennyver all these years?

Casidhe had stood right there with Herrick, proving she had been part of that unconscionable crime.

How had he not realized her true nature? Even now, his heart refused to accept what his mind demanded. He'd survived many wounds in battle.

This wound would fade, but never truly heal.

Tristan turned to him with worry claiming his face. "Boss?"

Hell, the guards walking the grounds had paused along with those surrounding the castle. All eyes were on Daegan.

He had to force words through his blocked throat and get a grip on his pain for the good of his people. Difficult didn't begin to describe yanking control of his emotions.

Daegan's head returned to normal shape and Treoir's energy aided his healing from the battle. The venom from Imortiks remained, interfering with his teleporting and feeding the headache beating his head.

He slanted a look at Tristan. "Did ya return the ice dragon to the dungeon?"

Tristan blew out a harsh breath and ran his fingers over his hair, clearly working to hide his relief. "Yep. I couldn't put Skarde in the warded area you created for him though."

The castle grounds shook hard.

Tzader's voice came into Daegan's head. *Are you back, Daegan?*

*Yes. Just arrived.*

*Do something about that damned ice dragon. The whole castle is quaking. We have glass breaking and the babies are crying.*

Daegan fisted his hands, done with these ice dragons. *I shall handle it immediately, Tzader.*

*Thanks.* With Tzader gone from his mind, Daegan announced to the guards, "Return to your stations." Then he quickly informed Tristan, "I am teleportin' into the dungeon."

When he reappeared, Tristan stood beside him with a matching fierce expression.

Skarde had shifted into his dragon with one wing still bent at a bad angle. The ice dragon roared and stomped around the area in back where Daegan had allowed his dragon a lair.

No more appeasing Skarde.

Daegan shifted into his red dragon.

Ruadh scorched a line across the ground to the ice dragon. Skarde's dragon had been so worked up he'd failed to realize Daegan and Tristan were present until his wing caught fire.

The ice dragon jerked around and blew ice water across the damaged wing.

Daegan spoke out loud through Ruadh. "Change back to human or ya shall burn where ya stand. Ice dragons have used up all the mercy I have to spare."

Skarde spoke in Daegan's mind. *Let me heal first.*

*Why should I? What one thing have ya done for me or my people since I saved ya?*

*You do not understand my anger, Daegan.*

*I do not care about your anger. Change back or burn.*

After a few seconds of silence, Skarde began shifting back to human, but the change came about slowly.

Daegan returned to his human form quickly, which was due to being in Treoir. Ruadh fought well in the mountains, but the Imortik venom in their body prevented Daegan from regenerating his powers as quickly after a battle as he had in the past.

Skarde leaned forward, holding his bad arm with one hand. That arm would never heal properly if not attended to soon, but Daegan had given Skarde aid time after time.

To gain any more, he would have to earn it.

A pair of loose pants covered Skarde's lower half, but only a minimal attempt at covering himself. The ice dragon shifter did not possess all his power either.

Limping forward, Skarde made it to the area with a chair, table, and bed.

With a flick of Daegan's hand at the closest wall, both torches already mounted there burst with flames. He wanted to see the face of this bastard.

Skarde sat heavily. Sweat poured off his head and his arm bled from new damage. "I need to rest. I must heal."

Daegan's fury grew to a new level. "Ya say that as if I am goin' to just overlook all ya have done. I gave ya a chance to reunite with your family and your brother betrayed me just as ya have done. I come back and ya are shakin' our castle, disturbin' newborn bairns. Do *not* ask any more of me when ya stand so close to your final hours."

Skarde's head hung. He talked to the floor in a voice filled with shame. "Please tell the mother of the babes I am sorry. I will not disturb the small ones again."

Daegan cut his gaze at Tristan who shrugged. Neither of them had heard this contrite Skarde and neither were willing to accept his words as truth.

"Why did your brother show my sister then pull her back?" Daegan recalled that Herrick had claimed she'd been stolen from both of them. Those words neither absolved Herrick of what he'd done or carried any truth in Daegan's mind.

Tears streamed down Skarde's cheeks. He lifted his head and agony stared out from his red-lined eyes. He whispered in a raspy voice, "I had no idea she lived. I could not speak the truth in front of my brother."

Daegan roared at this disgusting dragon shifter talking about Jennyver as if he knew her. As if he cared. His dragon ripped out of him.

Ruadh lowered his head. "Daegan shows mercy. I am not

merciful."

Skarde showed no fear. He held his head, moaning, "I wanted to die until today."

"You may have your wish, ice dragon."

Skarde stood up, grimacing in pain. He barely had room with Ruadh's head so close.

Tristan watched his every move, but would not interfere with Ruadh in charge.

"You do not understand." Skarde gritted his teeth and cried out, "*I thought she was dead, too, all this time!* I went to save her, but as the dragon flew to attack King Gruffyn's castle, I was taken to Scamall realm by your father's steward."

*What?* Daegan whispered in his dragon's mind. *How much more does Skarde know?*

Ruadh said nothing at first as smoke curled from his snout. *This one deserves death. All still hidden in his head would die with him.*

There was the help Daegan needed. He had never allowed his emotions to rule his actions, but seeing Jennyver for seconds then ripped away still gutted him.

His dragon had given him honesty. Ruadh believed Skarde deserved death and would execute the ice dragon shifter upon Daegan's order. But the wise old dragon knew Daegan wanted answers, so many answers, and never seemed to find someone to provide those.

Ruadh lifted his head high. Power flooded the room as Daegan returned to his human form wearing jeans and a dark pullover.

Skarde started talking the minute the red dragon vanished and Daegan stood there. "I am sorry for all I have done before. I ... will not fight you anymore. I was in pain and crazy in my head when you brought me here from Scamall realm. Then just now when I returned, my dragon took over while I was upset ... I did not try to stop him from shaking this place. But I will do better. I will not disturb the castle again. If you decide to kill me, I have no reason to expect less." Skarde sat heavily, grunting in pain every time he moved his arm.

Daegan ordered, "Explain everythin'. Did Herrick steal my sister upon your word?"

"*No!*" Skarde claimed with great furor. "I would have fought him to the death tonight to free her from his hands."

Tristan sneered, "You want us to believe you would have fought *and killed* your own brother tonight? Do you think we're that gullible?"

After that outburst, Skarde sounded as if all the energy escaped his body. "Think what you will, but yes, I would have killed Herrick to have freed Jennyver."

"I do not believe ya," Daegan stated, losing patience.

Skarde sat back hard and admitted in a whisper, "I would have killed anyone to protect her. I love Jennyver."

# CHAPTER 3

D AEGAN SHOUTED, "JENNYVER WAS *BOUND* to the father of her babies. Do ya dare claim she was unfaithful?"

"No, never her." Skarde glanced up, shaking his head fervently. "She was a good mother and tolerant wife."

Tristan made an aggressive step toward Skarde. "I think you need to start talking fast, ice dragon, unless you're done living."

Skarde breathed in and out, gathering himself. "Almost a year before you were captured, I ran into Jennyver during a meeting at your father's castle between you and Herrick. You remember that meeting about the Vikings?"

It took some effort to dredge up old memories, but Daegan recalled Herrick coming to discuss their cattle and lands being attacked by what the ice dragon clan had believed to be small groups of Viking raiders.

Daegan stood with his feet apart and hands at his hips. "Aye. 'Twas before your family claimed I had started the Dragani War. I agreed to help Herrick hunt them. We found no raiders from other countries. It left us thinkin' the attacks were from within our own groups, but ya would do yourself well to not accuse me of startin' such a heinous war again."

Skarde stared at the table. He nodded and sniffled. "I hate politics. Never wanted to rule. While you two spoke that day, I wandered around and found Jennyver crying in the chapel. We ... talked and talked until my brother called to me telepathically. I saw her two more times when she came to visit your father and I was there to trade our wares for wool sheared. My brother showed up one time unexpectedly and beckoned me from the chapel. We had words over it when he accused me of looking for more than friendship. I straightened him out and we never discussed her again. Jennyver sent word to me through a messenger each time she would be visiting King Gruffyn and praying in the chapel."

Daegan warned, "Do not twist the truth, Skarde. Not about my sister."

Clearing his throat, the ice dragon shifter said, "Never. She is an angel. Her mate had a liaison. He was the unfaithful one. Jennyver knew about his transgression."

Daegan's words stalled in his throat.

Had his sister been going through the blackard's betrayal alone? Daegan tried to recall the last time he saw Jennyver. She had seemed reluctant to return to the Treoir realm. He'd thought she just needed some time to herself without caring for children, the castle, and dealing with Macha, which could exhaust anyone.

He hurt to think of Jennyver bound to an unfaithful husband. King Gruffyn would have had the man dragged through the streets and placed in the stocks for public humiliation. Then he would have beheaded that scourge on humanity.

That would have been far nicer than what Daegan would have done to the unfaithful cur.

Tristan interjected, "So you're trying to say you went to King Gruffyn's castle when she was there and hurting from a worthless husband, but you had no thoughts of taking advantage of a woman in distress."

This time, Skarde's eyes glowed a crazy blue and his voice dropped to the inhuman grit of his dragon. "*No!* Do *not* speak of our friendship that way. I believe she needed someone to listen to her who would hold her confidence. We became friends. That was all."

Daegan corrected him. "Ya just said ya loved her."

Losing his angry edge, Skarde seemed to pull back into himself. "I did. I never told her. I cannot explain, but I held her in my heart. It would have been wrong to have expected anything more. I had decided to be there for her no matter what. I admit I would not have mourned her mate's death, but neither would I have harmed him just to gain her freedom and affections." Skarde inhaled deeply through his nose and said, "I do have honor. I have not shown it here, but I would never dishonor *her*."

One revelation after another struck Daegan between his eyes.

Jennyver still lived after two thousand years and Skarde had been in love with her.

Daegan struggled to hold those two thoughts in his head.

In the silence that followed, Skarde closed his eyes and leaned back in his chair. He held his arm and breathed in a tired way. "I was wrong to attack innocent beings the day we flew in this realm." He opened his eyes, slow to look up. "I wanted to die. I had lived two thousand years locked in a horrible realm for eternity while my family and Jennyver had passed. I had nothing to live for. The pain of just being alive in a world without them was too great. My actions are inexcusable."

Daegan walked around, running his hands through his wind-lashed hair and trying to think. So many things he had not known.

So many years lost.

But Jennyver lived.

He would find her. As he thought on that, he stopped and considered what had led up to her being alive today. Whipping around, he strode back to Skarde. "How did Herrick come to capture her?"

Wiping tears from his eyes and cheeks, Skarde considered the question. "I mentioned how Herrick once saw me talking to Jennyver and questioned me. I told him we were friends. He told me not to lust after a married woman. That was the only time I shouted at Herrick and told him to shut his filthy mouth."

Daegan waited to speak unless he had to push Skarde. It seemed the ice dragon shifter had held a lot inside and the words were now pouring out freely.

Skarde squirmed on the chair and grimaced. "Our castle fell when we lost our last bloody battle. My parents and sisters were dead. I thought they all died, could swear I'd seen Brynhild's body. I don't know how she escaped her fate." He stared off into nothing.

Tristan said, "Cathbad kept her trapped underwater in an ice pond inside a remote mountain cave for all this time. Who knows? He might have grabbed her when she was unconscious and left an image of her dead."

Lifting his sad gaze, Skarde nodded. "Very possible. Herrick walked the castle grounds where the stench of death hovered in the air. He roared like a madman. I left him a message and flew to King Gruffyn's castle. I rushed to find Jennyver, thinking she would be there."

"Why?" Daegan asked.

"We all knew you were captured and word had leaked out that King Gruffyn had fallen ill. I surmised her selfish mate would go to his mistress. I believed Jennyver would leave her children in Treoir and go to be at her father's side or in the castle chapel praying for him."

Emotion clogged Daegan's throat at hearing what actually happened while he'd been imprisoned in TÅµr Medb. Queen Maeve shared no details. Whenever she came to her private quarters, she'd gloat every time she saw his dragon in the shape of a throne.

Then one day, Queen Maeve walked in laughing wildly. "They're all gone, Daegan. Your father, Jennyver, the clan is wiped out. That bitch, Macha, has the Treoir children and control of the realm. Damn your father for allowing her to have Treoir, but ... I have you."

His heart shattered all over again, just as it had that long-ago day.

"Hold up, Skarde," Tristan said with his hand lifted in the air. He turned to Daegan, "You need to hear this, boss."

Daegan had drifted off with Skarde's low voice droning in the background. He shook off the dark cloud that had settled over his mind and heart. "What?"

"Tell Daegan what you were saying." Tristan instructed.

Skarde frowned at him then addressed Daegan. "You once offered to share a meal with me. I am not healing. If you will feed me, I will share all I know while we eat."

Tristan scowled. "You should share information freely."

Daegan struggled to make a decision. If he granted Skarde's request, he would betray his decision to treat this ice dragon shifter as an enemy. On the other hand, the man was sharing more than he had his entire time here.

More than anyone had.

And his words made sense.

Daegan asked Tristan, "Would ya ask the cooks to prepare somethin' simple?"

Tristan nodded and blinked out of sight.

Lifting a hand, Daegan called up two more chairs, placing them on the opposite side of the table. He studied Skarde's damaged arm. "Ya may shift to heal your arm. If ya try to cause trouble again, Ruadh shall decide your fate."

"I will be quiet." Skarde stood and limped far enough away to shift. Once he completed the transformation, his dragon stood calmly as the damaged wing began to mend.

Daegan watched Skarde's every move, but the dragon shifter had not lied.

With so much quiet time by himself, Daegan's thoughts circled back to Casidhe, stalling when her face smoked through his mind.

The last place he'd seen her had been as he and Herrick shifted to battle.

When he'd shouted at her for tricking him, she'd stood frozen with heartbreak in her red-rimmed eyes. For a second, he'd struggled in a crazed moment, torn apart and lost.

His mind had taken over, warning him women lied with their tongues and their emotions. Had she thought he'd accept any excuse for her part in all this? To go to her in that moment would have only opened the door to more lies and heartache.

What had happened after he left?

Should he care?

Damn his soul, he did, and not knowing she was safe wore on him. How long would it take to carve out all these feelings ripping through him?

He had been too accommodating with her. He'd lowered his drawbridge, allowing her to breach his defenses with little more than a smile and a kiss.

Skarde came walking up dressed again in his clothing. "I thank you."

Daegan shook himself back to the present. He had failed to keep an eye on the ice dragon, a dangerous slip on his part.

Tristan appeared with a platter of chopped pork, cheese, and fruit. He placed the food on the table with forks and napkins.

The succulent smell brought a rumble from Skarde's stomach.

Daegan had no appetite, but he supplied cold mugs of ale. He waited to see if Tristan would join them. Sighing, Tristan took a chair next to the one Daegan sat on.

Once they were all settled and Skarde had eaten a bit, Daegan asked, "What were ya sayin' before?"

Skarde finished swallowing his last bite and said, "I was speculating on how Herrick might have ended up with Jennyver. I will not know for sure if I am correct until we speak to her as I do not see Herrick telling the truth, but when I arrived at King Gruffyn's castle, it was in turmoil. Your father's clan was rushing to gather family and whatever they could carry. Screams carried over the noise of carts and bodies trying to leave. They ran for the forest."

"Why?" Daegan did not understand. "Our Beladors would have protected them."

"Your father had lost over half his army, including many of the nonhumans," Skarde explained quietly. "Word had preceded my arrival that our king's lands had fallen and your father's castle would go next."

Shaking his head, Daegan crossed his arms. "'Tis another reason why it made no sense to accuse my red dragon of startin' the war."

Skarde lifted his good hand to stall Daegan. "The earth dragon and his army attacked us because of our alliance with the red dragon. He was headed to your father's lands next. As I arrived and rushed to hunt for Jennyver, I heard screams that a dragon approached in the distance. Many yelled it was *not* the red dragon."

The idea that Fadil would have harmed Daegan's people was almost too much to take in one day on top of everything else. Fadil had been angry the last time Daegan saw him, but ... his friend had never murdered innocent people.

"I see in your face you doubt my words."

Daegan spoke with honesty. "Fadil and I did not always agree, but I have difficulty believin' he would attack innocent people, especially those under my father."

"But Fadil did *not* lead the attack. His youngest brother

brought an army of bespelled warriors to our land."

"What?" Daegan pushed his untouched plate away and leaned forward on the table. "They had no such warriors and Fadil's only siblin' was his sister."

Eyebrows lifted in resignation, Skarde admitted, "That was what all the dragon clans thought. You do recall when Fadil's father almost died fighting the giant trolls two years earlier before everyone showed up to help?"

"Aye. King Anasch lost a leg. 'Twas a terrible blow for Fadil and his family." Daegan had spent time with Fadil hunting and flying their dragons any time he could to give his friend a break from stepping into his da's role. Fadil and his sister were just in their early twenties. The clan went into a dark time as if the king had died. Many warriors would rather die in battle than live without a limb. Fadil's da had always been hard on him, but he turned mean after the injury. His sister pulled into herself and became a recluse, dealing with grief in her own way.

Skarde sounded sincerely sad when he added, "Fadil's mother had a baby, a boy younger than Fadil, by another dragon shifter. None of us knew anything about it, including Fadil and his father. To this day, I have no idea who fathered the child. Our mother told us of Queen Anasch's adulterous act and that she feared the day this false earth-dragon-shifter prince would come into power. Being jinn, my mother sensed things with her gifts. Fadil's mother hid her illegitimate child with her family's clan to raise the child in secret far from the kingdom of King Anasch."

"That would explain Queen Anasch's long visits alone to see her people in another land over all the years I knew Fadil," Daegan mused to himself. Fadil often spoke in angry tones about his mother, but if he knew of her infidelity, he never shared it with Daegan.

That part Daegan understood. Who would make family shame public?

Not ready to accept anything easily, Daegan prodded, "How would this information slip out?"

Skarde chuckled. "You, Herrick, Fadil, and Brynhild were gone so much fighting invaders, you may not have realized how the clans all had spies in the other castles. Informants lived well back in our time."

"Yes," Daegan admitted. There was much truth to his words. Daegan knew about those who skulked in the shadows to steal secrets, but he had never been one for gossip. Looking back, he'd been too arrogant about the strength of his father's kingdom and fear of the red dragon. Any power could be toppled with a well-executed plan.

Picking up where he had left off, Skarde said, "In Queen Anasch's time after Fadil's father became crippled, it was rumored she might have been losing her wits. The best we could tell, once she believed the red dragon had attacked King Anasch's clan and his health had deteriorated even more, she sent for this son when Fadil refused to lead an army against any of us. I do not know Fadil's actual thoughts, but I heard he would not attack your father's castle with you captured in TÅµr Medb and unable to mount a defense."

That would be the friend Daegan had always believed Fadil to be. Even after he and Fadil had parted on bad terms that last day, Fadil had a core of honor. "How did Jennyver become entrapped in all this?"

"Ah, back to what I was trying to sort out. When I went to find her, I headed to the chapel first. That's when your father's steward captured me."

"How, Skarde?" Daegan asked, trying to make sense of it all. "Ya said Germanus used majik. My father's steward possessed some supernatural power while in the Scamall realm where he held ya, but he had been a human in this world with no majik." Daegan wished Germanus had died a slower death for what he'd done to King Gruffyn, Evalle, Skarde, and many other flying creatures. Germanus had secretly, and against King Gruffyn's orders, worshipped the god Abandinu.

Skarde explained, "Abandinu had given the steward a short stick loaded with majik to capture flying creatures Abandinu would take into the realm. But that god never expected a dragon."

Daegan nodded. "'Tis exactly as I thought when I went to Scamall. Abandinu had never been known to pick battles he might lose."

"True. But Germanus had enough majik left in the stick for one last capture when he found me looking for Jennyver. He thought to surprise Abandinu with a dragon shifter. I had no idea until waking in Scamall that Germanus had made a deal to become immortal." With Skarde's injured arm now healing, he leaned his elbows on the table to prop his chin. "The only joy I received from any of that time was watching Germanus lose his mind when he realized Abandinu had granted his wish to live forever by imprisoning him in Scamall with the rest of us."

Tristan had finished his food and now toyed with his mug. "You still haven't told us how Jennyver got screwed over in all of this."

"I clearly did not reach Jennyver *that* day," Skarde clarified. "But if I had, I would have made sure she returned to Treoir where she would have been safe even if I never saw her again."

Leaning back, Daegan crossed his arms behind his head, stretching tight muscles. "How could ya expect her to leave our da with him sick?"

"I had expected for Macha to teleport Jennyver and your father to Treoir, but I also harbored doubts about Macha protecting your father with you not around. Jennyver did not trust the goddess. If Macha would not teleport your father to safety, I planned to remain and protect him against the earth dragon and any other threat."

That put Daegan on his back heel. To hear someone else claim to take on the duty to protect his family while Daegan had been imprisoned flipped his stomach.

He could not so easily accept Skarde's words. Did the ice dragon think to feed him pretty lies with no one present to counter his words?

Tristan came into Daegan's head. *Do you believe him?*

*My first thought is no, but I have so little information about what happened durin' that time. I wish to know if he lies or not. If not, then he possesses details I may find nowhere else.*

*What if he does lie?* Tristan asked.

*I shall ward him into a spot the size of the chair he sits upon.*

*Sounds fair to me, boss. Want me to find out if Storm could pop in?*

Daegan nodded. *If we can make this quick.*

When Tristan left, Skarde sat up, alarmed. "What is happening? I have done nothing wrong."

Daegan could see no point in pretending otherwise and explained, "Tristan will bring someone who is capable of determinin' a lie from truth. I wish to know if *all* ya say is true."

"I swear on my honor, I tell the truth."

"Your honor is tarnished."

"What if I do not agree with this person's decision about my words?"

Daegan stood and leaned on the table. His voice came out rough as the pain clawing his insides. "It does not matter what ya think, because *I* know this man's ability to ferret out the truth." Daegan lowered his head until his face was no more than a foot from Skarde's. He wanted the ice dragon shifter to hear the conviction in his voice. "Ya had better have been tellin' the truth with every single word. If not, ya shall never have another chance for freedom and shall remain here forever, locked in a ward too small to shift in."

# CHAPTER 4

"I COULD HAVE *KILLED* THE RED dragon!" Brynhild raged in Joavan's hotel room. She could not be more disgusted with herself for allowing her emotions to sidetrack her plan.

Her ice dragon had rammed Daegan's dragon, knocking that red monster to the ground, but did she follow through?

No. She'd been too crazed over Herrick's lack of interest in his own sister when Daegan told him she lived.

So much for family blood.

Herrick only cared for Skarde.

She shook her fists and yelled, *"You bastard, Herrick!* You will pay for that just as Daegan will for his crimes."

She slapped a bottle of wine off the table where she and Joavan sat to eat meals. It flew twenty feet and crashed against a white wall, splattering the red liquid.

Joavan came running from the bedroom with a towel wrapped around his waist and his fingers holding the ends together. He stopped short at the sight of the streams of red dripping down the wall as if the wall had been massacred.

Jerking his head up, he stared at her with disbelief. "What are you yelling about?"

*"Herrick,"* she snapped. "He is as bad as Daegan. Maybe worse. He is family and turned his back on me. He never looked for me once the Dragani War ended. Did he not wonder what happened to *me* with my other two sisters lying in their own blood with their heads no longer in place?"

Speaking carefully, he replied, "Maybe your brother thought you were somewhere else when he came back to the family house."

"What?" She stared at him as if he spoke in a language she could not understand. "I would *never* have left my family during a battle. I would have stood to my last breath fighting to protect our home and my people."

Dropping his head in defeat, Joavan said, "I have no idea what you want me to say."

"Nothing. I want *nothing* from any man." She stomped out to the balcony where the lights of Paris twinkled late at night. She should bathe after that battle in the mountains, but she could not stand still to wash her skin when she wanted to rip Herrick apart.

Joavan's feet padding over the carpet preceded him before he joined her on the balcony. He stood next to her for a quiet moment, taking in a view of the Notre-Dame cathedral brilliantly lit and reaching to the sky.

"So now you want nothing from me, dove?" he asked.

She rolled her eyes and snapped a look at him. "Do not make this about you. I have been wronged by every man in my life."

"Wait a minute." He stood up straight, taking offense. "You include me in that list? Had I not placed a simple tracking spell on Tristan when I glamoured him to rescue that woman from TÅµr Medb, we would never have found Daegan in the mountains with Herrick. I think I have more than carried my part of our arrangement."

Male egos bruised so easily. Why did she have to appease them to get what she wanted? When this was done, she would have no need for any man's services except to please her in bed.

Joavan smelled fresh from his shower and she found his body enjoyable to look upon. He managed her needs in bed well enough, but he took too much to heart.

She leveled him with the closest she could offer for a consoling gaze. "Yes, you did much to find Daegan. I give you credit for good thinking." She told the truth. Had he not gotten them close to the mountains she knew well, she would not have been able to shift and cloak her dragon for the chance to attack Daegan and Herrick.

Her chest lifted with a long breath. On the exhale, she admitted, "I am angry at my brother for not thinking I might have survived. He never looked for me, but he was willing to make a deal with the red dragon. Who does that?"

Joavan had a moment of guilt pass through his face.

Yes, he had made a deal with Daegan. He believed he would make another deal to get his diamond back, but only if he could do so before she killed Daegan.

Still, between being a Faetheen and moving through the human world as smoothly as a fish through water, he had many skills and gifts she could use.

He leaned over and kissed her.

She allowed it and gave him a half-smile.

Shaking his head at her stubbornness, he said, "We should rethink killing Daegan right now."

She bristled at him. "Do not think to tell me what I will do if you do not wish to be on the list with those other men. Do not get in my way either."

"I know better than to tell you what to do, Brynhild. I am merely making suggestions. You know I must retrieve the amulet with the powerful diamond for my people."

Not allowing her face to reveal her thoughts was a trait she'd brought with her from the past. She did not care about his people, but by not arguing the point, she allowed him to think she agreed with his words.

That served her well at the moment.

Joavan waited until she lifted her eyebrows to get him talking again. "Tell me this so I can understand. What is the benefit of you killing Daegan?"

Just like that, she wanted to strangle Joavan, too. "Do not make me repeat myself all the time."

"Wait." He put a hand on her shoulder. "What I'm saying is, wouldn't it be better to let the Beladors think someone *else* had destroyed their precious dragon king?"

"*No!* I want to hold up Daegan's bloody head for all to see that he died at my hand!"

Turning around to lean against the rail, Joavan secured his towel and propped his elbows on each side of him. "But what about *after* the red dragon is dead?"

"I will celebrate." She held her chin up and smiled at the vision.

"The Beladors are very loyal to him. They will come for you

again and again, Brynhild."

"I will kill all who are stupid enough to challenge me."

Joavan scratched his head. "You're not getting my point."

Her smile fell, ending in a growl. "I do *not* care. Daegan pretends to be so honorable. Always he carries on that he did not start the Dragani War. His dragon struck villages at night, burning them to the ground and killing their animals. Those people stopped looking to him as if he were a god." She hated the pain those awful memories wrenched from her.

"I understand."

She argued, "You do not. I had a wonderful life. *The best!* I was revered and loved by many." She strode back into the living area. "If not for Daegan, I would not be here in this new world. Daegan and Cathbad. I want that druid's head, too." She turned to Joavan, who followed her in, then stood with his arms crossed, waiting for her to finish.

"I would have lived and died with my family, Joavan. I protected my father's clan every day. We lost all when the red dragon came as a lowly thief in the night, attacking innocent people. Then the earth dragon came and destroyed what was left, but Daegan's greed for power cost me all. My parents and sisters were slaughtered."

Joavan remained quiet. Now he showed wisdom.

Pinning the Faetheen with a pinched gaze, she asked, "Can you find this so difficult to understand? Daegan *destroyed* my world. Cathbad put me in an ice pond for two thousand years. Now, I find Herrick has been in our many-times-great-grandfather's ancestral lands, waiting for *Skarde*. Even when Daegan told Herrick I still lived, Herrick wanted *only* his brother."

Joavan's words held a genuine sadness. "You may have what you wish and I will help you just as I vowed. I only hoped to point out that you should consider this world after you have gained your revenge. You could accomplish the same thing, Daegan's death, yet prevent other supernaturals such as powerful ones allied with Daegan, Loki, and others in what is called a Tribunal from coming after you. Deities are not fans of any dragon shifters, after all, since you are one of their greatest threats. If the one who kills the red dragon remains anonymous, there is power in being unknown in this world."

Brynhild took in his words. Much as she did not want to admit it, Joavan gave valid reasons for his suggestion. She tired of this conversation and changed the subject. "I must find a place for my hoard."

Excitement glowed in his eyes for only a moment before he turned serious. "How big a space will you need?"

Glancing around her, she mused, "Maybe ten times this entire hotel room."

He gave her words consideration. "We could find a cave and I would be happy to ward it for you so no one entered without your permission."

She withheld her thought that he would have no access to her treasure as she would never allow another person to have control over the protective wall surrounding it.

When she said nothing more, Joavan changed the topic. "We should eat." He walked past her, flicking his hand to clean up the wine mess, then stopped and placed his hands on the shiny wood table. "I have a thought on a place for your hoard. You could accomplish the same if we found a building in this area where your hoard would be easy to reach when you need it. We'd also have a comfortable residence to stay in when not hunting Daegan."

She'd followed him with her eyes and considered the structures she'd seen in this city. "These buildings are too easy to breach. Too simple to destroy."

"Ah, but the buildings I'm thinking about are part cave."

That piqued her interest.

She did appreciate the way this Faetheen thought. Her people had often built castles up against mountains. "Yes. We will find this cave-building."

Twisting up one side of his mouth, he rubbed his jaw. "I am not able to touch my funds hidden in my home world, not until I regain possession of the amulet again and return it."

Did he always have to return to his missing jewelry?

Shrugging, he said, "I can negotiate a terrific deal, but you will have to pay for the building until I can cover my part."

That's what he worried about? He must think it would be

expensive. "How much gold?"

"We should find something for ten or twenty pounds." His tone suggested he was digging to learn how much treasure she had.

"You find house with cave. I will buy." She dismissed it with a wave of her hand. "I must see houses first."

He rubbed his hands. "This will be fun. I can't wait to show you these places. I've already showered. Soon as you are ready, we'll go out and walk around. I'd like to show you some of the areas. You can point out things you like."

Brynhild took little time showering and dressing. She still enjoyed towel drying her short hair. She used majik to adorn her face with kohl after using creams she'd bought while shopping with Joavan.

He did have the paper money, but that must not hold enough value to buy a house in this world.

As soon as she came out of the bedroom area, Joavan waited for her with a glass of wine.

She took the fine glassware and sipped, then lifted it in the direction of a bed on the floor across the room. "What about her?"

Joavan turned to glance. "That's not Daegan's sister."

"What do you mean?" She narrowed her eyes. Had Joavan dared to trick her after all she'd told him?

"That woman is only an image of his sister. If anyone touches her, I will know immediately and return to catch them."

"You do not worry Daegan will locate her?"

He grinned. "He won't come here. He can't find her. I hid his sister with a friend in my people's world."

Suspicion crawled up her neck. How trustworthy could Joavan be?

He did not have to pull Daegan's sister back into this world until he had the amulet. This time, she did not lose her temper. She had to stop allowing her emotions to reveal so much about her. To do so only made it easier for Joavan to read her and try to manipulate her.

He'd promised to deliver Daegan. She would give him the chance to do so. He'd been the one to find Daegan, and Herrick as well, on this last trip.

She should have thought about those mountains where the oldest ice dragon shifter had built a castle. She'd always heard the castle and lair in that mountain held powerful majik. She'd believed her mother had bestowed a special gift on all of them, something from her jinn blood line. They were told to not share the gifts with anyone, not even each other.

Brynhild had been the only one with cloaking.

What had Herrick gained? Some form of immortality from living inside the old family castle and grounds?

Did Herrick believe all of that land and castle belonged to him?

She would show him differently one day.

But not today.

For now, she would find a building, then have Joavan take her close to the cavern holding her treasure. He would want to accompany her all the way there, but she did not trust him to return later without her to steal her treasures.

That would require killing Joavan sooner than necessary.

Once she had moved all her hoard, she would have a place to live, the skills to maneuver among humans, and the ability to plan how to kill Daegan.

Joavan now had her thinking about life after Daegan died.

But if not her, then who would drive a sword through Daegan's cold heart? That reminded her, she needed to find her sword. In the meantime, she could kill Daegan over and over in her mind.

She laughed at that thought and Joavan turned to her with a smile. "What has made you happy, dove?"

"Power."

He clinked his wine glass with hers. "We should celebrate how we caught Daegan unprepared today. We will do more planning for the next time."

"Yes, it was good to surprise his red dragon," she agreed. Daegan must have been shocked to see her in the mountains while he fought Herrick.

To catch the red dragon unprepared made her very happy. Just as rewarding had been when she shifted and cloaked her dragon, which allowed her to listen in on Daegan and Herrick talking.

Joavan deserved some credit. She'd thought he waited where she'd left him when she flew cloaked in dragon form. But Joavan had used his secret way to travel and snatched Daegan's sister from under their noses.

She would make him bring the sister out of his world soon if he wished to live long enough to regain his amulet.

# CHAPTER 5

*Sweetwater Creek Park west of Atlanta, Georgia*

QUINN WANTED BLOOD. NOW.
His team stood perfectly still, waiting through the standoff.

Even the wind rustling leaves through surrounding trees earlier had silenced when I-zubrrali showed up.

Reese sat on his shoulders where she'd been when they'd battled demons with her blasting power fastballs. He clutched her shaking legs tightly.

Rabid demons and Imortiks didn't faze her.

All of the predators attacking had been frozen in motion the minute I-zubrrali had shown up.

That bastard had raped her mother and condemned Reese to being a demon magnet for life. Dark-blue eyes stood out against his cadaver-white skin, but the silver eyebrows and matching shoulder-length hair put him into major creep league. He stood fifty feet away, calmly waiting for her permission to take an unborn child from her womb.

Quinn and Reese's son.

I-zubrrali's voice bounced with confusion. "Did you not understand my generous offer, daughter? I will allow you and your friends to survive *and* give a blood oath to disappear from your life, along with my demons ... for one *thousand* years. Just give me the baby. He's of no use to you. How is this difficult to understand? That baby won't survive without me."

Reese's voice shook. "Let me down, Quinn."

With his Belador strength, he easily lifted her over his head and to the ground in front of him.

Evalle and Casper kept their attention on the enemy, paying

no attention to the sixty or seventy demons and Imortiks now imitating statues in motion all around them.

I-zubrrali held the ignition switch to turn the predators loose. Reese swallowed hard.

Quinn spoke softly to her. "Let me get Evalle and Casper out of here. We'll face whatever he throws at us."

"Don't you dare," Evalle warned both of them under her breath.

Casper stepped closer as well in a protective way.

Shaking his head and appearing entirely dumbfounded, I-zubrrali asked, "You would kill everyone here, knowing your baby will not live past birth?"

"Fuck, yeah, you piece of dirt," Casper replied first in a deep voice packed with southern fury.

Reese lifted her hand, telling her group, "Let me go to him and see if I can trade myself—"

"*No!*" boomed in a chorus of three voices.

Quinn put a hand on Reese's shoulder. "Looks like we're stuck with Hector."

Reese spewed out a tearful laugh. "That name won't fly."

Evalle suggested in a tight voice, "You should name him Moonspin like the celebrities do."

"Hell, no!" Reese said, never taking her eyes off her father who watched them with amusement and perplexity.

Quinn censored himself. Calling that monster a father was a travesty to real ones.

These were his people, standing strong in the face of potential death, loyal to a fault.

I-zubrrali started forward, weaving between demons and Imortiks ready to attack when released. "I can take the child from you," he admitted. "I thought you would welcome the choice to be a hero."

"You're a piece of work." Reese stretched her neck. "Your death will be the best baby gift ever."

Evalle stomped her boots, releasing blades in the heels of her boots. "Let's do this."

"Hell, yeah. Here comes my crazy half again," Casper added, referencing the highland warrior who also shared his body.

"You four think this is a joke?" I-zubrrali asked with true shock. "How have you lived this long with no better survival skills?"

"Grit and talent." Evalle unbuttoned her shirt. She was partial to her BDU clothing. Her body started enlarging with her battle form Quinn hadn't observed in a long time. Muscles stretched and bones cracked.

I-zubrrali's eyes went from deep blue to blaze-red. Needle-sharp teeth dropped inside his mouth. A horn pushed out the back of his head with three spikes on it. His voice deepened to the fitting sound of a demon. "I will enjoy your deaths." He lifted his hands and shouted, *"Attack!"*

Demons and Imortiks came alive and rushed forward, screeching and howling in a bloodcurdling cacophony.

Quinn yanked Reese to the side. He knew better than to push her behind him. He shoved kinetic blasts at everything in the half circle he and Reese faced, knocking demons into Imortiks.

Reese must have regenerated her power while talking. She rolled energy balls the size of baseballs and hit multiple demons and Imortiks with each strike.

They exploded into fire. The Imortiks stunk of sulfur and the demons turned into ashes, drifting to the ground.

Evalle slashed kinetic hits at a demon closing in on her fast, slamming it back into two others. All of them hit the ground. She shoved up an invisible wall and hissed at Quinn, "We're running out of energy."

"I've tried calling Trey to find Tristan to teleport us out of here. No luck." He groaned when a mix of five demons and Imortiks rushed his kinetic wall.

Reese's last hit didn't have as much punch in it.

He didn't want to lose her any more than he wanted to watch Evalle and Casper fall beneath a pile of demons and Imortiks.

Diving into I-zubrrali's mind would be suicide.

Quinn had enough experience to know when to use mind lock and when not, but ... he might give his people and Reese a chance to escape.

"Don't, Quinn," Reese begged more than ordered.

This woman knew him too well.

He had no time to waste with pretending he would not use mind lock. "We're running out of options, sweetheart. I-zubrrali—" Quinn took a hit to the center of his kinetic field and bent back. He roared, shoving his power forward again. Hurrying, he said, "I-zubrrali is waiting on his first strike to knock us off our feet. He won't allow them to kill us until he gets what he wants. I'm not watching you die at that bastard's hands."

"I'm not watching you die either ... *shit!* They're piling up to climb over the kinetic walls," Reese shouted.

As the words left her mouth, the demonic-Imortik pile had grown until a predator at the back of the pack came rushing up to jump high enough and land on the four of them.

Not just a demon, but a glowing yellow demon.

Quinn struggled to hold the wall and lean forward over Reese to shield her.

As the Imortik-demon went airborne, a blast of blue light ignited its body into a fireball. Streaks of yellow arrowed away, shooting in all directions.

The bright-blue power zinged around them, blasting demons and Imortiks.

Quinn hugged Reese close and looked over his shoulder to see Isak and his team sighting in on every threat. When Quinn glanced back to see if Isak's men had gotten I-zubrrali, there was no sign of that disgusting being. He'd like to think Isak had turned the monster into ash, but seriously doubted I-zubrrali would risk being hit.

The battle was over in a minute.

Evalle dropped her arms and bent over with her hands on her knees, supporting her body. She sucked air and heaved out breaths.

The ancient highlander disappeared again and Casper looked as if someone had stretched his body out as far as it would go then released it to yank back into shape.

Quinn caught his breath.

Reese hugged him with her face on his chest. He kissed her head. "How's Bucephalus?"

She sniffled and muttered, "Can't use that. You'll never find trinkets with his name spelled right."

He patted her on the back and led his team through disintegrating bodies and stench as those things ceased breathing.

Isak gave a hand signal and his men lifted up from where they'd been kneeling with blasters ready. His team immediately formed a perimeter with half of them facing toward Quinn and his group. The rest faced away, watching for new threats.

Somehow, Isak had returned with twelve black op soldiers.

Evalle fell into step on Quinn's right. Casper did the same to the left of Reese whose arms now fell loose at her sides.

Just like his men, Isak's face had black marks and he held his weapon at the ready across the tactical vest covering his chest.

Quinn broke free and strode quickly to reach him and offer his hand. "I don't know why you came back, but thank you. We would not have gotten out of that alive."

"Thank you, Isak," Evalle added.

Teared up, Reese wiped her nose on her sleeve. "You saved all of us."

Isak shook Quinn's hand then Casper's and nodded at the women. "I came back to tell you I calmed down and realized I can't waste any chance of saving Adrianna."

From everything that had happened before, Quinn understood the amount of backbone required to admit that in front of all of them, including his men. No wonder Isak's men appeared ready to step off a cliff if he told them that was their only hope to survive.

Evalle pushed loose hair off her face, then retwisted her ponytail band. "We *will* find Adrianna, with or without Sen. But I have a feeling we need to find him, too. I'm convinced that supernatural being came for Sen and that Adrianna just happened to be in the same proximity."

Another short nod from Isak. His steely gaze swept around. "Who was that guy in all white?"

Reese glanced up. "My miserable father. Did you kill him?"

"No."

"*Dammit!*" She held a fist to her forehead.

Isak huffed a dark sound. "No love lost there, huh?"

Quinn shook his head. "It's a long story, but we all agree he has to die. He's creating many, if not all, of the demons flooding this region. He also wants the baby Reese is carrying inside her."

Frowning, Isak eyed Reese's stomach where nothing of a baby showed beneath her loose clothing. He asked, "What happened? You didn't send him an invitation to the baby shower?"

Chuckling a watery sound, Reese dropped her fist and gave a relieved smile. "I-zubrrali didn't want to wait on a shower. He intended to take the baby today with or without me."

"Damn. That's a new level of monster." Disgust wrapped Isak's voice. "If we see him, we'll kill him on sight."

His men standing nearby glanced Reese's way. Hardened expressions echoed their leader's words.

Quinn put his arm around Reese. "We would deeply appreciate it, Isak."

Reese muttered, "Yesterday wouldn't be soon enough."

Isak looked around as if he planned to head out, then stopped. "By the way, did you hear about the dragon sighting in south Russia?"

"No, not a word," Evalle replied, looking around to see if anyone else had heard.

Quinn shook his head along with the other two. "Was it identified as a red dragon?"

"No. You might only have heard from your supernatural resources. I receive intel from a satellite report. If the dragon had been flying at night, I doubt anyone would have made out the shape. But it flew during the day and appeared silvery."

"Ah, hell. There are *more* dragons?" Casper asked with no small amount of shock.

Isak shrugged. "Sounds like it."

Six Beladors from Quinn's perimeter team slowly filled in around him.

Where were the other four? He'd find out as soon as he finished with Isak Nyght.

"You need anything else right now?" Isak asked.

Quinn thought quickly. "We should be good. I plan to advise the teams on what happened here and then come up with ways to avoid being caught in another I-zubrrali attack. We'll be in touch with anything we learn on Adrianna and please do the same."

"I will." Isak gave another hand signal and murmured into his comm unit. His men retreated to their trucks. Isak had arrived with only one Hummer the first time.

As they drove out of Sweetwater Creek State Park, Quinn wheeled around to the Beladors who had been patrolling a wide perimeter before joining them. "What happened to the other four Beladors?"

The team leader, a middle-aged warrior who had plenty of experience, said "We beat back the demons and Imortiks, but as we headed here to check on your group, four just ... disappeared." His gaze had flooded with disbelief of that being possible even for a nonhuman living in a supernatural world.

"*What*?" Evalle wiped sweat off her face. "Did someone show up and teleport them?"

"We have no idea. No one in our group saw anyone else. Our Beladors were there one minute and gone the next."

Quinn could not keep sending patrols out if someone invisible or cloaked was snatching them up. "Everyone stay in this group. From this moment on, we stick together until we get out of here."

Casper asked, "What about keeping humans out of this park?"

Evalle jumped in. "We have additional law enforcement, some of which are our Beladors, with patrol cars out at the main entrance to stop anyone from coming in. Most will avoid even turning in with the lights on their patrol cars running."

Reese whispered, "Quinn, uh, we have new company."

He twisted to face the same direction she was looking.

Evalle moved into action with hands lifted, ready to defend. Casper stood with his arms hanging loose, but not to be underestimated.

Buzzing sounded just before a hologram glowed and wavered into the shape of a translucent being who then turned solid.

Evalle swore and murmured, "That's *him*."

"Who?" Quinn asked as he took in a being whose black hair and bloodless skin should have dark-red lips to go with all that, but no. His lips were thin lines and two orbs of swirling white where he should have eyes. That changed in an instant when the centers glowed red. Dark energy swam around his copper-brown robe as if in awe of his body.

Reese cleared up Quinn's confusion. "That's the guy I saw when I did remote viewing from Adrianna's car. He's the one who took Adrianna and Sen."

"Grand-Damn-Central station today for supernaturals." Quinn stepped ahead of his group, ordering his people to stand back.

Reese stayed with him, grumbling, "I'm re-energized."

Evalle and Casper disobeyed as well. Quinn could feel the rest of his Beladors coming forward in solidarity.

He had no time to waste and demanded, "Who are you?"

"Tenebris. Thank you for asking. It's so nice to be appreciated."

That bastard. Quinn asked, "Did you take four Beladors just now?"

"Is that what you are? Beladors? How quaint. I didn't realize they still existed. I don't have time to be bothered with any of you at the moment, but I will keep that suggestion in mind for a later date."

Quinn swallowed the curses when he wanted to roar at this being and everything else attacking his people. Hopefully, his missing Beladors were still alive, but for how long?

Speaking in a powerful voice his people needed to hear as much as for the benefit of Tenebris, Quinn said, "If you give us Adrianna and Sen, we will leave you alone. If not, my people and our dragon will hunt you down."

When Tenebris spoke, his voice had a smooth tenor. "I am not here to listen to foolish statements, but I am glad I visited today. I was able to rescue an Imortik I found nearby before you and your people dared to harm it." Lifting his hand, he blew on his open palm and a slip of pale-yellow paper floated through the air.

Quinn, Evalle, and the other Beladors threw up a massive kinetic shield.

Tenebris had blown a piece of parchment the size of his palm at them. The scrap bumped against their kinetic field and fluttered to the ground.

He scowled. "How disrespectful. I suggest you retrieve the parchment before it disappears."

The shadow of a glowing yellow figure standing eight feet tall moved through the woods far behind him.

Tenebris lifted a negligent hand as if to signal to the yellow monster. "I must be off. You would be wise to follow those instructions." Tenebris spun into a swirling mass of energy that buzzed into the woods, scarfing up the giant Imortik, then both of them vanished.

Quinn shouted, "Drop the shields." He bent down to lift the parchment, read it quickly, and filled them in. "If the dragon king delivers a grimoire volume to the Imortik master before sunset in Oakland Cemetery tomorrow, he may choose to save either Sen or Adrianna."

"That's it?" Evalle asked with deep concern. "We need to save both of them."

"Unfortunately, there is more." Quinn drew in a labored breath. "The last part warns once the grimoire is delivered, one captive will walk free and the other will become an Imortik."

Reese sounded haggard when she pointed out, "Time is spiraling out of control. We don't have a thing to negotiate with and Daegan can't give them a volume even if he has one."

Evalle rubbed a hand over her forehead. "This is insane." She lowered her hand and turned to him. "Don't get me wrong. I'm here until this is done and so is Storm. Turning either Sen or Adrianna into an Imortik would be ... like creating a supernatural nuclear bomb. *And*, once Loki finds out Sen is missing, there's going to be hell to pay. Even if Daegan finds a grimoire, he can't give it to that Imortik master."

"I know." Quinn had rarely felt so helpless as a Maistir. It was time to bring Daegan in to strategize and regroup.

Power boiled around them.

Casper muttered, "Oh, hell. Is there an off-switch for this day?"

The powerful being now standing before them had two curved horns growing out of thick black hair. His face and body would compete with an Adonis and win. His blue eyes burned with fury. A long black duster billowed around him, moved by furious swirling energy.

Loki.

# CHAPTER 6

*Tuatha Dé Danann realm*

THE BOUNTY HUNTER SCREAMED AND pleaded for his life.

Macha listened with a half ear as she mapped out her next step, studying holograms of different beings spread across the floor. She hadn't used this space inside her mother's realm for thousands of years. She'd only returned to this realm recently after Daegan invaded Treoir and pushed her out.

Stupid, stupid Queen Maeve's fault.

That bitch had been a nuisance since she and Macha manipulated King Gruffyn into giving them each a child. Everything had turned out well, at first, and would have continued perfectly if Queen Maeve had not imprisoned Daegan when she should have killed him.

Macha's gaze fanned over the holograms half her height, pausing at a new one. What was it about that female with a library in Galway full of old tombs that interested Daegan? Macha's secret scouts in the human world were doing their best to bring her answers, but none of them had the ability to teleport.

She was *never* giving a supernatural the gift of creating bolt holes again, not after the last one lied to her about how he used that majik. He'd been forced to confess in the worst possible place.

Never lie in a Tribunal.

The majik used to create that realm activated immediately and turned the liar bright red from head to toe.

Once that happened, death followed close behind.

No one would interfere with Macha's plans this time. She pointed a finger at another female hologram and moved it across the space to stand next to the one of Quinn. He had a protective interest in this female, but the same woman had also been seen in the company of Daegan and Tristan.

What was her name? Reese.

That might be useful. Less important followers of the red dragon often became the best resources. Still, if Macha found no better way to bring the dragon to a place where he would be vulnerable, she would choose Quinn or Evalle for baiting her trap.

With the human world falling into pockets of chaos, she had an opportunity, a window of time. Daegan would have to be around—

In the distance, a bloodcurdling scream from the arena went on and on.

She paused. Was that one ready yet? Crazed yelling and shouting erupted.

No, not yet.

Where was she? Ah! With Daegan running around trying to save humans from Imortiks. He would end up exposed at some point.

She had to prepare an ironclad way to destroy Daegan when the opportunity presented itself, while ensuring Queen Maeve could not use her scrying wall to interfere or to pin the death on her. She didn't care, but taking over Treoir and the Beladors again would be much simpler if they thought she was saving them and not that she'd killed their dragon king.

Macha tapped a long ebony-and-silver nail against her chin. If Queen Maeve's next desperate attempt to drag Daegan back to TÅµr Medb succeeded, it would take him out of Macha's reach again.

"Your highness?"

She lifted her gaze to the servant who oversaw all minion activity in this realm. Her mother chose them well. "Yes, Tuubok?"

"I believe this one is ready to speak."

Her mother took pride in her captives. His pants, known as *dhoti*, were the color of red wine, which fit him snug at the waist and tight around his ankles, blousing out between. Beyond that, the rest of Tuubok's exposed body showed off sleek brown skin over toned muscles.

"Wonderful." She teleported to the arena used for entertainment. An easy area to clean afterwards, which did not require her power.

Tuubok rushed in, not even out of breath. He waited with an anxious expression in his brown eyes.

She smiled at him. "Are you worried?"

Muscles in his face relaxed. "Always. I wait with anticipation to learn if I have served you well."

"I am pleased." She had to admit how life here had been far more relaxing than she'd expected at first. Nodding at the bloody figure strung with chains from above, she said, "Hold his head up. He needs to breathe to answer my questions."

"Yes, goddess."

Tuubok rushed to grab a hand full of black hair matted with dried blood and lifted an unrecognizable face.

When the bounty hunter did not open his eyes, Macha snapped her fingers.

Both swollen eyes struggled to open.

She didn't care if he was blind at this point as long as he answered her questions. She would have compelled him to speak if his majik had not interfered. He seemed to possess a mix of supernatural and human blood, which gave him a few gifts. Nothing that had stopped her minions from finding and containing him.

On occasion, she had met a being she could not compel.

This one had taken work from VIPER recently and had joined up with a Belador team patrolling the city of Atlanta for Imortiks.

Unlike the bounty hunters who had remained independent and cared nothing for the Beladors, a few had shown poor judgment by allying with them.

"You may die quickly if you do not strain my patience," she announced. "Tell me how to find Daegan, where he meets his people in the human world, and where is the best place to ambush him."

Split lips tried to move. A moan drained out of him.

She rolled her eyes and hit him with a jolt of power.

He jerked and twisted then shook his head. His face healed enough for him to open his eyes and speak, but his battered body had not changed. "Water, please."

Tuubok growled and popped the bounty hunter's head with the back of his meaty hand. "Answer her questions now or I will make you wish you had not annoyed her."

Tears rolled down the bounty hunter's face and his shackled hands trembled. "The ... the dragon hunts for grimoire volumes." His eyebrows drew tight as if he struggled to pull a thought together. He mumbled, "Dragon sees Quinn, maybe Evalle." His entire body started shaking. "I don't know where they meet." He whimpered. "Please, kill me. I have no more for you."

Glancing up, Tuubok waited for her decision.

She frowned. "He has nothing more. Do with him as you will."

"You said a quick death," the bounty hunter's raspy voice pleaded.

"No, I said you may die quickly, but I am not the one burdened with killing you." She teleported to her private quarters where she dispensed with her gown, leaving her naked to take a soothing break from all this. She strolled across the cool slate floor to a waterfall tumbling from a wall of golden stones. Sparkling blue-green water rushed across sizzling coals the size of goat heads. A luscious scent of lavender rose to her nose.

She'd had a sorcerer take a prized lavender plant from the human world and turn it into one which floated on the water. The delicate flowers and vegetation clustered in a three-foot-wide band around the perimeter of the pool.

She'd just stretched out with her body submerged and her back supported by a silk cushion when Loki's disgusting voice rode through her mind.

*Your presence is requested in the Tribunal.*

Did he really think asking nicely would make a difference? She said, *I think not.*

*Do not be that way, Macha!* Loki replied with a sharper tone.

Annoyed at this interruption, she replied, *I have been in the realm of Ernmas since the last time we met. I have bothered no one in spite of my mistreatment.*

*If you recall, I said we requested your presence. I have not accused you of any misdeed, Macha. Is there a problem with leaving your mother's realm?*

That prick thought to insult her as if she did not have permission? She smoothly told him, *If that day ever arrives, I shall ask Ernmas to answer your question in person.*

Nothing came back.

Her lips curved up with smug happiness at the sudden silence. Loki often stirred up trouble anywhere he could, but he had not survived this long by making an enemy of someone as old as Ernmas.

Macha resided here whenever she chose. She answered to no one.

He finally said, *I intended no insult.*

She sat up. That had been dangerously close to an apology, which would never pass his lips. Unconvinced, she poked at him more. *The last time I visited the Tribunal, you favored the red dragon.*

Sounding exasperated, Loki countered, *How can you fault me for the position I was in when your bounty hunter kidnapped Evalle? On top of that, your man announced you would make him immortal. None of us wanted that to become common knowledge.*

*Do not try to convince me you believed him, Loki. You act as if you have never manipulated a lesser being with a few twisted words.* She studied vines trailing down the golden wall and loaded with ruby flowers.

Would this be a missed opportunity for her? To be honest, she didn't care. *Call that dragon for his help.*

Loki made a hissing noise.

Her attention perked up. Loki truly needed something? How often did that happen?

Never.

Lifting a fluffy bathing cloth to drag water over her arm, she asked, *Will Daegan be there?*

*No, this will be a meeting of Tribunal deities only.*

She stilled. What could the Tribunal want?

More important was what were they willing to trade in return?

Daegan stood in her way of taking over the Treoir realm again. As the last of King Gruffyn's original family members, once Daegan was truly gone forever, she could walk in and rule Treoir without question. Brina might be queen, but her position could not overrule a vow King Gruffyn had made as part of the deal for giving Macha a child many centuries ago.

As long as no immediate member of King Gruffyn's family lived, Macha ruled Treoir.

She still found it funny how King Gruffyn had thought he'd outfoxed her by agreeing to provide a baby in trade for protection when his queen had been unable to birth live children.

Macha had taken care of that small issue.

That bitch Queen Maeve slipped into the king's bedroom and used the same majik to ensure a child for her, which resulted in two female babies, but not twins.

*Macha?* Loki pressed, though not with the fury he was known for when being ignored.

He definitely needed her.

*I am thinking.* She smiled and stood, stepping out to the flat slate area surrounding her bathing pool. She lifted a crystal bottle of helianthus annuus oil infused with tonka bean and began hydrating her skin.

How far could she push Loki's patience?

He still owed her for that last debacle in the Tribunal.

But maintaining a degree of alliance with Loki in particular could be beneficial. She replied, *I shall come to the Tribunal. Allow me time first to finish what I am doing.*

*How soon will you be here?*

There was the irritating trickster god who often stepped on her nerves. *I will be there when I arrive, Loki.*

He jerked his presence from her mind so fast she felt the snap of his anger and laughed.

As if she would just drop what she was doing and go to a Tribunal?

He knew better than to expect such a fast response.

She called up a gown beaded with tiny emeralds and diamonds to compliment today's shade of her ginger-red hair no one could match. When she turned to view herself in a full-length gilded mirror floating above the ground, she admired what no one could do better.

The sound of small bells chimed in Macha's area. That would be her mother's only signal before her presence began to take shape with a gentle push of energy.

"You are leaving," Ernmas declared in the lilting voice of a child as she came into view. Glistening hair of a deep aqua-blue color stolen from the Aegean Sea fell in waves across her pale shoulders. This woman had lived an adventurous life to date. She'd once inserted herself inside the royal family of a sultan during the Ottoman Empire era when women of stature, known as sultanas, held significant power.

All well and fine if not for her lingering attachment to harem clothing. For Macha's mother to prance around dressed as a servant was beneath her.

Ignoring what she could not change, Macha responded, "Yes. I may be gone the time it takes you to enjoy a bowl of cherries or ... longer."

"I thought you would not return to the human world for at least a few hundred more years. What pulls you from me?" Ernmas conjured up a plush silk-covered bench and glided down to relax. The gray-skin legs with black hooves supporting the bench had been cut from a centaur Ernmas defeated in a long past battle.

Avoiding a long conversation, Macha waved her hands around her head, directing her hair to arrange itself. She suddenly wanted to teleport to the Tribunal. "Loki has a problem he must be unable to solve on his own."

Not beautiful or plain by choice, Ernmas had a captivating nature, which drew in those who underestimated her. "Why aid those who have given you much trouble in the past?"

Macha lowered her hands and toyed with a strand of hair falling to her breast. She smiled, amused by her mother. "You say this as if I make a foolish decision and risk placing myself vulnerable at the hands of others."

Laughter burst from Ernmas.

Macha enjoyed that sound.

When Ernmas calmed again, she covered her mouth with a

delicate hand until she could speak calmly. "You have never been vulnerable to other beings, daughter. I merely am curious. Is this related to the annoying dragon who outplayed you in Treoir?"

That doused Macha's smile.

There were times when her mother should remain quiet.

Macha stepped closer and spoke softly, avoiding discussion of Daegan. "I do not enter this meeting unprepared. I have always had sources in many places. The human world is in turmoil from Imortiks."

Now *her mother's* joy blinked out of existence. She crossed her slender legs covered in sheer purple material and placed her hands on the cushions at each side of her, waiting for more.

"That Loki called me for help at all is one thing, but he was ... pleasant," Macha added, still perplexed.

Angling her head with a frown as she did when something in the new world did not make sense to her, Ernmas asked, "Why?"

"That is the question, is it not?" Macha enjoyed a bit of thrill at the upcoming encounter, much like she used to feel going into battle.

Her mother waved her off. "Go. Enjoy yourself, child. I shall see you when you are once more bored."

Macha dipped her head once in acknowledgement then teleported away.

Ernmas had mentioned recently how she missed visiting the human world.

Macha asked her mother to wait until she discovered the identity of Daegan's unknown goddess mother before returning. The second Macha found out who joined with King Gruffyn to birth the last red dragon, she would know how to destroy Daegan and possibly need her mother's additional power to do so.

Without the true identity of Daegan's mother, Macha chanced walking herself and Ernmas into a trap they might not survive.

Finished teleporting, Macha stood in the Tribunal realm where the huge space had a feel of being inside a giant half globe in the black of night. Stars twinkled in the sky stretching across from side to side all around the ground covered in plush grass.

Loki with his smirk, Justitia with her scales of justice, and that irritating Hermes with his tortoiseshell lyre stood on the platform.

Who had given that idiot an object with which to make noise?

The trio looked up as one when Macha appeared.

"Why have you *requested* my presence here?" She wanted everyone clear that this group had nothing to hold over her and owed her answers.

Loki got right to the point. "We have a situation getting out of hand. As you likely know, we are dealing with Imortiks. Your insight would be valuable."

She stared at him with derision. Did he really believe she would offer her aid without gain of some kind? Only a fool would expect that of her.

At least he had not insulted her by pretending to inform her of the Imortiks first.

Calling up a throne, she seated herself.

Justitia's nose twitched at the slight.

As if Macha cared? "Yes, I am aware of Imortiks escaping a rift in the death wall. Which dragon house failed to uphold their vow to protect their grimoire volume?" With enough deities, she would consider joining in a war against a dragon clan. If only they would target Daegan, but his clan's grimoire volume sat in the VIPER vault.

Justitia lifted her voice. "We do not know as yet *which* grimoire opened a rift, but a second one is also now circulating."

"*Two?*" Macha could not fathom two dragon clans having been so careless, or stupid, to have hidden their volumes in easy places to locate. "How could two volumes have been exposed? Putting those Imortiks behind the death wall *last* time was no simple task."

Justitia heaved a long breath. "The second volume was stolen from VIPER's vault."

Macha eyed the goddess of justice for a long, heavy moment. She began speaking in a normal tone, which ratcheted up with her building anger. "I warn all three of you not to make the mistake of questioning any involvement I might have had with that theft after *I* was the one who brought that volume here twelve hundred years ago! I was there when we put them behind the death wall. I would not have done so if I wished them to be free."

Loki released a growl.

Justitia angled her head away from him.

As the de facto leader of this Tribunal, he said, "No one is accusing you of such a grievous offense. Imortiks attacked VIPER and stole that volume from our vault, which means an Imortik has the ability to teleport."

"That is ... interesting." Macha wanted to say impossible, but evidently the theft had happened. She detected what was odd about the group today. Their enforcer was not present. "Where was Sen when this attack happened?"

The blindfolded Justitia would not be shut out of the conversation any more than she'd put down that set of scales or wear a gown with color. "Sen had been tricked into receiving what he believed to be Beladors possessed by contained Imortiks ready to be locked away in cells below VIPER. What he teleported into VIPER was an Imortik and demon war party."

"Did you bring in the Belador who dared to do this?" Macha raised her voice without care of who she insulted.

She could stand upon that same dais where they stood any time she wished, but she had little interest in dealing with trivial issues.

Thankfully, there had been no need for her to take a turn up there.

In fact, most of the deities allied with VIPER had not been here in too long to recall.

Not with Loki, though, who enjoyed tormenting nonhumans. If he wanted to be entertained by those foolish enough to speak a lie here, then he had to put up with the nuisance cases.

Justitia's firm chin slanted in Macha's direction. "Sen had venom in his body after an Imortik stabbed him, which required healers to work on him. The healers could not remove all of it, but once they had him capable of functioning again, Sen teleported to the human world. He went to the location from where the suspected prisoners had teleported."

"What did he find?" Macha would have caught a power

signature and so should have a demigod.

She'd directed that question at Loki, but Justitia was no one's pushover. She continued without giving the floor to anyone. "Sen found no sign of a nonhuman. Someone aware of the Belador system had mimicked the voice of their team and VIPER coordinator, known as—"

"Trey." Macha wanted them to realize they were speaking to the goddess who had held sole power over the Beladors for many centuries. She knew every one of them.

"Correct." Justitia sounded miffed at being cut off. "The point is that any power signature or scent had vanished without a trace. Sen brought Trey to a Tribunal meeting where the Belador denied knowledge of the attack or the person who pretended to be him."

That sounded as if there was no new direction to take. As a very powerful telepath who coordinated teams and communication over great distances, Trey had known the consequences of lying here.

Macha got to the real question. "Why am I here?"

"While on another trip to retrieve a possessed Belador, Sen was taken by an unknown being," Loki said, watching Macha closely.

This might turn out to be more interesting than she had first thought.

She cocked her head at him. "You *lost* your pet demigod? Who would dare take him? No, let me rephrase my question. Who has that level of power, yet is unknown to any of you?"

Hermes strummed three sharp strokes, then stopped all sound. "Why would we ask you here if we knew who this being could be?"

Macha stared at Hermes with his shaggy brown hair sticking out wildly from his skullcap and a robe that looked to be made of weeds and tree bark. She hadn't seen him in that attire before.

Hermes would always be safe from kidnapping unless his captors were deaf.

Loki shifted his glowing gaze to Hermes. "Unless you wish to stand here for an eternity, leave the questions to me."

"*Us!*" Justitia amended in a tight voice.

Shaking his head, Loki returned to the point. "We must find Sen. He has been privy to much here over the centuries. If he is compromised, it might be an issue for ... *all* of us."

Macha held up a hand to allow her a moment to think as she stood and walked to one side. She stared out into a black void. During the past thousand years or so, Sen had been involved in terminating a few problems for her as well.

She walked back over to face the trio on the dais. Tired of staring up, she floated to eye level with her arms crossed.

Hermes had begun strumming again and slowed to frown at her, but knew better than to utter a word.

She had more say than others here. "I helped infuse the energy required to build the Tribunal and VIPER," she started, reminding them of her investment. "We needed this organization at that time."

Justitia huffed out, "We are aware of the service this provides for nonhumans."

Loki added in a dry tone, "I think everyone here understands the need for followers to maintain our power and strength."

"We did not form VIPER *for* nonhumans," Macha countered, bringing them to specifics. "We created this justice system to prevent nonhumans from joining forces and powers to attack *us*. While we are at the top of the power food chain, we took precautions when Evalle showed up as an unknown quantity, did we not?"

No one replied.

Macha took that as a sulking agreement since none of those three wanted to admit a threat of any kind existed. A fool's approach to survival in the supernatural world.

She continued, "Once the Beladors had expanded their force to other countries, we used that army to manage the world *for* us. What about now? In truth, we only need the humans. They'll worship the being, or beings, who saves them."

Clearly irritated, Loki snapped, "Make your point."

"It is simple. You are reacting when *we* are the power. Stop making knee-jerk reactions when it's time to take decisive action."

Justitia's face twisted into disbelief. "Are you suggesting we enter the mortal realm to dispense with Imortiks and find Sen?"

Macha hated dealing with beings who had little battle experience. "Of course not. You need Sen returned first, then we can work on the Imortik problem. Can you not see the simplest way to have Sen found?"

Silence slapped back at her. The trickster god never remained silent for long though.

Loki's eyes brightened and his lips formed a smile. "I believe I know where you're going with this and agree it is time for action. What you do not know is that we already have Daegan in a difficult position."

Finally, Macha sensed something of value coming out of this. "Oh? In what way?"

"Daegan negotiated for the lives of his possessed Beladors to remain locked up in VIPER and for us to spare them while he hunts for the grimoire volumes and closes the death wall."

She took her time to appear as if she considered that for a bit and not give away her hand. "And if Daegan fails?"

"His people die," Loki replied cheerfully. "But more important is the last part of our deal."

"I'm listening."

Loki sighed, letting her know he did not care for anyone to interfere when he was having a good time. "Daegan must tell us the name of the person behind opening the rift or deliver that person to us. Before you ask, I shall tell you what he will forfeit. If he fails, he must admit the identity of his mother."

It had been a long time since Macha's heart raced. Excitement filled her to the core.

Justitia, pissy now, sniped, "So what is this great plan you hint about, Macha?"

Macha shoved a hand, palm out, in Justitia's direction. "Silence." She wanted a moment to enjoy this. Her heart fluttered with the wings of a thousand bats.

Daegan would have to share the name of his goddess mother. This was ... too good to be true.

Loki leveled a dark glare in her direction, pressing her to give to him in return.

Macha explained, "Finding Sen is simple. Make it too painful for Daegan to ignore."

Lines formed on Justitia's forehead with her exasperation. "Loki just explained that we already hold the life of Daegan's possessed Beladors over his head."

Loki dropped his head back and stared up as if searching the black sky for patience.

Justitia turned her blindfolded face his way but held her thoughts.

Toying with all of them, Macha asked, "Is that all Daegan has to lose, Justitia?"

The goddess of justice must have realized she was being patronized and quieted. She returned to facing straight out as if her covered eyes stared at nothing.

Lowering his chin, Loki's tone shifted into a more serious one. "Everything is on the table. You would not come here if you saw no way to benefit, Macha. What do you want?"

"First of all, Daegan is best suited to hunt Sen. Threatening Beladors who will likely die anyhow is not enough to force him to use his resources immediately. Place significant pressure on him and you should see results."

Justitia interjected, "Loki brought in four healthy Beladors and will continue to collect more until Sen is returned."

"All well and good, but still not enough pressure." Macha tapped a long black fingernail that sparkled with tiny lights against her cheek. "This is what I will do. As long as I have the full support of the Tribunal with no one getting in my way or tying my hands, I will search for the grimoire volumes and close the death wall once I have them." She paused when a thought hit her. "Does Daegan know what is required to close the death wall?"

Justitia's eyebrows pinched together. "Why is that of importance?"

Macha hissed out a sigh. "You would know why had you been present the last time that wall was closed, Justitia. I, however, *was* there."

The prim truth speaker shut down again, which worked for Macha.

Loki interjected, "I do not think Daegan knows all involved in closing the wall." He smirked.

For Macha, that smirk was a more definitive answer than his words. "As I was saying a moment ago, I will hunt for the volumes. If I am successful, I will know the identity of the being behind opening this rift and hand that one to you if he or she survives. Assuming all of this comes to fruition, it would result in Daegan's failure to uphold his agreement, correct?"

Nodding slowly, Loki's eyes twinkled with evil as he grasped what she had on her mind. "At which time you wish to be given the name of Daegan's mother."

"What?" Justitia gasped. "That deal was *not* struck with Macha!"

Loki snarled, "Do you wish to take Sen's place?"

Justitia had a decent snarl of her own. "Do *not* speak to me with condescension. We are not *all* intimidated by you. I merely remind you we may have to work with the red dragon to end this Imortik problem."

Macha enjoyed this conflict. "But that is why you asked me for help, Justitia, is it not?"

Taking time to answer, Justitia's tone turned brittle. "We asked for your advice, not to make a dangerous situation worse. What do you propose we do when Daegan fails then later discovers we have revealed his mother's name? Do you think he will just continue on without retaliating?"

Macha had only heard Justitia become so engaged a few times in the past. Floating closer to the dais and at eye level with them to speak in a more intimate way, she quietly told the goddess of justice, "There will be no delay in him learning what has occurred. I expect to be standing here when he is forced to reveal his mother's name if I am the one to solve these problems and close the wall. I will also hand you a world of compliant followers. At that moment, we would hold all the power to join together and tear that dragon apart. Never forget he is not one of us. Dragons are our enemies."

# CHAPTER 7

DAEGAN WOULD GIVE THE ICE dragon shifter one last chance. No more.

Skarde nervously twisted his hands where they sat upon the table in the Treoir dungeon. "I told you the truth. I admitted what I've done wrong. I am trying to work with you."

"Perhaps ya should have thought to do so sooner, Skarde." Daegan clung to a thin strip of patience. He feared Skarde had truly lied and Daegan would not discover the truth of what happened to all of his family. "Ya act as if I told ya an executioner is on the way. Storm is an unusual Skinwalker with the ability to tell truth from lies. 'Tis simple if all ya have said is true."

"I said—"

"*Silence!*"

Tristan appeared with Evalle's Skinwalker mate, Storm, teleported here from the human world.

Storm had cuts and bruises across his nut-brown skin. His black hair normally pulled back with a leather tie fell loose as if he'd just left a battle.

Daegan stood. "I am sorry to pull ya away from Atlanta. This shall truly take no more than a moment to determine if this one has spoken the truth. To learn the truth matters greatly to me."

Storm's dark-brown eyes latched onto Skarde. "Repeat what you told Daegan and make it fast."

Skarde asked, "Why? Who are you?" The panic in his voice undermined his demand.

Daegan powered up his voice. "He is an ally of mine. I have already told ya what he can do. If ya are not lyin', then tell him what ya told me so he can make a determination and return to the human world. Our people are bein' overrun by Imortiks. We have no time for lies or delays."

Gaze flicking around with concern, Skarde started relating all he'd said to Daegan. When he stopped, he looked pointedly at Storm with a worry-laden face. "Tell Daegan I speak the truth."

Storm angled to Daegan. "All he said *just now* is true."

"Thank ya, Storm. Any word on Adrianna or Sen yet?"

"Not as of the last time I spoke to Evalle before we split up to patrol with different teams."

Nodding, Daegan asked Tristan to take Storm back.

Tristan returned in less than a minute.

Thankful for one positive surprise, Daegan took a seat again and waved a hand at Skarde. "Continue."

Sitting a little taller in his chair, Skarde commented, "My honor has been restored a bit, agreed?"

"We shall see." Daegan would allow no more. He would still take Skarde's words at face value for now.

Tristan flipped his chair around and sat with his arms crossed over the back.

Skarde heaved out a tired sigh. "I had intended to return to Herrick as soon as I could but I had to know Jennyver was safe. Before leaving the devastation of our lands, I instructed our clan to hide and left a message for Herrick. I said I was going to see if King Gruffyn would accept our people until we could rebuild if we helped protect his kingdom."

"Why would ya say that when ya believed my father and I to be at war with every other clan?" Daegan still seethed over being condemned by the ice dragons, and others, for the bloodshed.

Skarde began moving his hands around as he talked now that he had use of both arms. "The truth is I did not understand why you would start a war. I accepted what my brother and Brynhild told me, because I could not live in the ice dragon clan and be disloyal. My other two sisters also went along with the family. But the last time I spoke to Jennyver, she swore you had not been behind the attacks and pointed out how many of those attacks she had heard occurred after sunset and before sunrise when it was difficult to see clearly."

Sitting back, the tension in Daegan's shoulders loosened for the first time in many years.

Not everyone had believed he would start a war.

To hear Jennyver had spoken up for him warmed his heart. That sister had always been supportive, but he'd thought her too meek to speak out.

Clearly, he had not known her as well as he'd thought.

"I believe Herrick came to your clan's castle and could not find me or talk to me through our minds. Herrick probably believed I had been captured and took Jennyver then with the expectation of trading us."

Tristan tapped a thumb on his arm. "Why would he take Jennyver?"

Skarde frowned when he admitted, "I told you Herrick had seen me talking to Jennyver more than once. After our argument, I thought he'd dismissed both of us as unimportant." Washing a hand over his face, Skarde stared at the floor. "If I am correct in believing he kidnapped her when he could not find me, I must find Jennyver and beg her forgiveness. I would never have put her in jeopardy."

More pieces of the broken images from Daegan's past began to fit together. This meant his father had died without knowing Jennyver had been captured.

Daegan still questioned if Queen Maeve had poisoned his father. He'd heard enough for now and stood.

Skarde jumped up quickly. "Where are you going?"

"I have more duties than this. I shall return when I have time, but the Imortiks still run loose in the human world and I have grimoire volumes to locate." Daegan paused and cocked his head at Skarde. "Do ya know where any of the Immortuos Grimoire volumes are hidden?"

"No. If I did, I would take you to them. I do not want those creatures to survive with Jennyver in this world."

Daegan struggled with hearing this ice dragon shifter speak so personally of his sister as if Jennyver held more importance to him than to Daegan. He would overlook Skarde's interest in her for now. He might need more information from this ice dragon shifter to find her again.

Tristan stood and rounded the table to Daegan's side. "Where you gonna leave him?"

Skarde took immediate exception. "Do not speak of me as if

I am a dog."

Tristan replied in a sincere voice, "I would never insult a dog that way."

Before this broke into an argument, Daegan said, "Ya wish to regain your honor?"

Skarde had a moment of looking annoyed, but nodded.

"I shall trust ya to remain here without the ward so ya may shift. But ... if my people call me back because ya have disturbed them again, I shall bring the young lass here. She will wrap ya in a way ya will not be able to speak to me even mind to mind. You will stay that way until I have time to deal with ya again."

Mouth open in shock, Skarde said, "No, please. I will be quiet. I only ask you not to leave me alone for months. My dragon ... is damaged and feels trapped again as we were in Scamall."

In spite of all the things Skarde had done to anger Daegan, he would not want to leave Ruadh in this dungeon for months and months either after they escaped TÅµr Medb. "I shall have my people bring ya food and whatever else ya need. They pass through a ward I placed for them to enter, but they stopped comin' when ya terrorized them. I warn ya they cannot aid ya in passin' through the ward. If ya treat them well, they may talk to ya. 'Tis up to each one, but my people report everythin' that happens here to me. Ya should know by now what the penalty would be if ya harm any of them."

Skarde hurried to claim, "I will give them nothing but good things to report. I destroyed your trust my first time out. I wish to regain that trust and be freed again at some point."

Daegan said, "The more information ya share that aids me, the closer ya shall come to leavin'. But I do not lie when I say ya can go nowhere until I regain my sister."

"Fair enough." Skarde sat again with a hopeful look in his eyes. "I would not wish to leave until I know Jennyver is safe unless you asked me to go somewhere and help you. I would do anything to save her."

Daegan could not listen to Jennyver's name on this man's tongue any more today. He teleported outside the dungeon at the end of the building.

Tristan showed up right behind him. "Where are we going

now?"

"To see if Lanna can use her gift to find Jennyver and offer any suggestion on how to locate the oracle. We have little time to track down another grimoire volume."

"The last time Luigsech found the oracle through that professor. Should we try to contact him?"

Daegan's long strides ate up ground as he headed toward the castle entrance. He considered Tristan's suggestion about the professor, then shook it off. "Luigsech indicated the professor will not talk to anyone who is not invited. Also, he must be nonhuman. He knew we were outside his house while she was inside that night."

"Hmm." Tristan frowned as he kept up with Daegan. "Do we need Luigsech?"

"I hope not." Daegan had barely managed to utter those words. He couldn't bring himself to admit out loud that he wanted to go find her for reasons not connected to locating grimoires. She would not leave his head no matter how hard he tried to think of anything else.

He had this nagging feeling she needed him.

Or was that only his heart making excuses?

What kind of leader would he be to worry over someone who had betrayed him? He had to consider more than his ravaged emotions.

His people came before his needs. He knew this, but logic helped little to wipe her from his thoughts.

Tristan asked, "What do you think happened to make Jennyver disappear in the mountains?"

Daegan had tossed that question around in his mind more than once. At first, he hadn't questioned how she'd vanished, only that she had.

Now he wanted answers. He sorted through possibilities out loud. "Herrick does not possess the ability to teleport. I do not think he cloaked her. I never saw him use cloakin' or teleportin' back durin' the times we battled together when such abilities would have been useful."

Tristan took the steps to the entrance with Daegan. "I've run that moment when she vanished through my mind over and over, as I'm sure you have. Jennyver seemed to jerk sideways to her right. Luigsech and Herrick both appeared seriously shocked. I'm not forgiving either of them for what happened to Jennyver all these years. I'm saying what if those two were not responsible for her missing right now?"

Following Tristan's logic, Daegan agreed, "Perhaps someone else was involved." He paused on the landing at the top of the steps. "And what about Brynhild? How did she find us? Her anger at Herrick not lookin' for her sounded sincere, which leads me to think she had only just discovered her brother's location and that he still lived."

Tristan opened a door for Daegan. "Based on what I saw in the cavern where Cathbad kept us imprisoned, Brynhild had not been outside that cave since breaking free of the ice pond. She would have no resources or support in the human world. Having her find us doesn't make sense."

Inside the castle, Daegan lead the way to Garwyli's area and slowed as he reached the door. "'Tis not realistic for her to have discovered Herrick without followin' us in some way. With no other place to go, she would have gone to those mountains where we found Herrick if she had known about the location. To have not gone there sooner seems she must have found him through us."

"That would be logical," Tristan agreed.

Daegan expected the old druid or Lanna to greet him at the door to Garwyli's area.

When neither popped out first, he knocked.

Lanna pulled the door open, looked over her shoulder, and stepped out, closing it softly. She carried a book tucked in the crook of her arm. "Garwyli is resting. Do you need him?"

Daegan shook his head. "I wish to ask for your aid in findin' Jennyver."

Lanna appeared unsurprised. Had she been expecting him? "Brina is not leaving her family quarters for now. She has offered me her sunroom whenever I wish. We would be private there."

"Good idea." Daegan turned to Tristan who lifted a finger in a sign he was ready. In the next moment, they stood inside Brina's sunroom where chairs with cushions covered in blue and silver material woven with the Belador triquetra emblem added color to the room.

Lanna walked over to take a place on the window seat where a tall wall of stained glass stood at her back. Sunlight sent a rainbow of colors dancing over the peaceful space. She placed the book facedown beside her and clasped her hands in her lap.

Before Daegan could say a word, Lanna asked, "Did you go to the Luigsech woman?"

"Why would I do that?" Daegan snapped, then regretted his sharp tone.

Not the least bit affected by his irritation, Lanna asked, "How will you find more grimoires?"

Daegan didn't know for sure, but he brushed off the question with, "I shall go to the oracle. She should be willin' to tell me how to find more volumes just as she did before. Besides, Luigsech is inside a warded castle. I cannot break through the ward there any more than Herrick could enter Treoir without my permission."

"Ah. I did not understand you find oracle on your own."

"I did *not* find her alone last time." There was the rub. Not only did Daegan have to battle his worry for Casidhe and disappointment over her betrayal, but he had not had time to think through how he would find the oracle without her help.

He only knew he did not want her with him on this next hunt.

Lanna's dainty eyebrows lifted at his conflicting words.

Unable to talk about Casidhe without feeling as if his insides were being slashed again, he moved on to what he needed from Lanna. "I would like ya to see if ya can locate my sister with my half of her ring."

As normal, Lanna replied with another question. "What if Luigsech woman still holds other half? I may find her."

Muscles in his jaw tightened. "It belonged to my sister first." He glanced at Tristan who appeared to find Lanna's questions normal. Had Tristan not told him about Lanna being a busybody, determined to help, especially if she felt they needed help finding happiness?

This was not the time for Daegan to fantasize over happiness.

He had a duty and no time left for saving his people. He'd even have to put finding his sister second, but would like to know if she could be found again. Casidhe was not so much personal as important to his locating the oracle, his conscience argued. The headache that never completely went away with venom in his body began pounding.

Something must have shown on his face. Lanna quickly said, "I will try." She took the ring from him and clasped it between her hands, then closed her eyes.

While she sat that way, Daegan's mind wandered back to the last time he visited Treoir realm before being captured and imprisoned in TÅµr Medb.

He'd spoken to Jennyver in this very room.

Had her mate been unfaithful the whole time? She never complained to Daegan or his father, at least not that he knew of. In thinking back, Jennyver had more often had a smile when Daegan found her at their father's castle.

Had he been so busy fighting battles and watching the land that he missed threats to his family? While her mate would have been insane to physically harm the daughter of King Gruffyn, protected by the red dragon, breaking her heart would have been just as damning. Daegan could not go back and fix any of those things, but he would be a better protector if he could just get his sister back.

Tristan walked around the room, taking in the furniture, paintings, and earthen vases painted with details. The minute Lanna stirred, Tristan returned to Daegan's side.

Lanna opened her eyes. "I see two things. Do you want both or only what I see of your sister?"

Daegan wanted every bit of information she could share with him. "Both, but my sister first."

"Your sister hides from me again, but not in same way. I sense she is alive and ... close to human world, but protected from view again. Strange majik hides her. This half of ring is calm as if it does not look for her."

An odd observation, but Daegan realized Lanna was correct. The ring no longer vibrated after he saw Jennyver in Herrick's mountains. "'Tis correct. I do not understand why the ring would stop huntin' my sister."

Tristan broke in to ask, "Do you have a continent or anything for us to go on, Lanna?"

"Yes, but not much. I see Europe map in my mind. Tip at far west glows. Maybe France or Spain. Is why I believe she is still near human world."

"Well, that's a starting point, boss."

Daegan wanted to accept the hope in Tristan's voice, but the fact that Lanna could not see Jennyver disturbed him. This young woman had incredible sight.

What could be blocking her view of Jennyver?

Lanna watched him solemnly as he struggled with not being able to spend time tracking Jennyver. To not go looking for her physically hurt, but he had to protect his people. In doing so, he hoped to protect her wherever she might be.

One thing he felt certain about.

The being who had Jennyver wanted something from him.

Sighing softly, Lanna suggested, "Best way to find sister is to first find person who takes her."

"'Tis an excellent point, Lanna, and one I realize, but I have no idea who has her since she disappeared before my eyes," Daegan admitted.

"What do you remember?"

Tristan spoke up. "I told Daegan I recall Jennyver standing there then sort of falling to one side."

Daegan shook his head. "If she was pulled to that side, someone was cloakin' their existence." He closed his eyes to see it all again. "I should have been payin' closer attention to her and not Luigsech."

"Who was person closest to Jennyver?" Lanna asked.

Opening his eyes, Daegan replied, "Ya were standin' there too, Lanna. Ya know full well Luigsech was next to my sister."

"Yes. Is correct," Lanna noted as if he'd passed a test. She tapped her cheek a moment. "You should ask Luigsech what she saw when Jennyver vanished. She would know more than anyone."

Trying not to be short with Lanna, Daegan allowed, "I shall consider all ya have said, but I do not know if Herrick lied and still has my sister somewhere else. What else do ya have?"

She lifted her shoulders.

Tristan pointed out, "Herrick wanted Skarde. He had no reason to hide Jennyver again."

Lanna pointed at Tristan and nodded with a smile.

Daegan understood the round path she had taken him on to bring him back to her original point. He asked both of them, "Ya think I need to talk to Luigsech?"

Lifting his hands in surrender, Tristan said, "I'm not pushing you to do that, but I am willing to go hunt her to see if she knows anything about what happened to Jennyver. That might give me a chance to get my hands on that scepter."

Another problem for Daegan. He needed the scepter to pay back the oracle for her help finding the first grimoire volume. He paced around, furious at his predicament.

"Maybe find Luigsech to get answers," Lanna prompted again.

Daegan had just begun to realize he had few options to make any move without Luigsech.

"What's wrong, boss?"

"I am angry with myself. She betrayed me, yet I require her aid with the oracle and the grimoire volumes."

Sounding frustrated, Lanna stood and spoke her mind. "You *must* go to her."

Shoving his hands to his hips, Daegan stepped over to her and looked down at the tiny powerhouse. "I have already said I cannot enter Herrick's property." Fool that he was, he worried what Herrick would do to Casidhe. That should not be his problem. He reached up and cupped his aching head.

It might help if he stopped calling her Casidhe.

If Luigsech stood in front of him right now, he would be relieved to see her safe, but unable to trust her.

He had to push her out of his mind and get busy with his many duties. When he found her again, he'd negotiate for the scepter and how to deliver it to the oracle.

"Luigsech is not at castle," Lanna announced.

Daegan dropped his hands. "What are ya sayin'?"

Tristan stepped up beside him, both of them towering over Lanna, who seemed unconcerned. She had a stubborn look in her eyes. "You need help. Luigsech has left castle. You must go to her."

"How do you know this, Lanna?" Tristan asked.

She twisted around and picked up the heavy book she'd brought with her. When she faced them again, she showed the cover of the book she'd taken with them to find Luigsech at Herrick's castle.

"Oh." Tristan crossed his arms. "Okay, boss. What do you want to do now?"

Trying not to sound anxious to find Luigsech and expose his internal battle, Daegan calmed his voice when speaking to Lanna this time. "Do ya have any idea if Luigsech is on foot or flyin' with the dragon?"

Lanna nodded. "She walks. No dragon around."

"In that case, we have plenty of time to find her." Daegan's heart thumped faster at the thought of seeing her again.

Then he blasted himself mentally to stick to what was important.

Ready to move on, Daegan found his manners. "Thank ya for your help, Lanna. We shall talk more when I return."

She twisted her lips into a grimace. "You should talk to Luigsech."

Daegan snapped, "Why?"

His sharp tone rolled off Lanna. She angled her head to study him. "You must find grimoire volumes."

"I intend to move forward without her." He had no idea how he would find the blasted oracle, but he'd find a way.

Both of Lanna's eyebrows rose at that claim.

Mentally tired from all that had happened and feeling as if he'd never patch up his insides again, he said, "I cannot risk workin' with someone whom I am unable to trust again. Can ya understand my position?"

She shrugged.

He sensed she wanted to tell him something and knew better than to dismiss her. "Why do I need Luigsech?"

"To read the grimoire volumes when you find them."

Hell. How could he argue with that?

He hoped Garwyli would be able to translate the volumes so

they could find the information for stopping the Imortiks and put them behind the wall.

But Lanna had a point he'd have to think on later. "I shall give that much consideration. Do ya have anythin' else to tell me?"

Holding the half-ring inside her fisted fingers, Lanna replied, "Luigsech is alone in mountains."

That was not news. Daegan had to get moving. "As she has clearly made that trip before, she knows how to find her way home."

"Maybe," Lanna muttered. She handed the half-ring back to Daegan.

He slipped the partial ring into a pocket and started to ask Lanna another question, but Trey's voice came into his mind. *You're needed in Atlanta, Daegan. Quinn asked for you.*

Quinn would not call to him unless he had a critical issue.

Daegan's shoulders slumped under a weight that continued to grow. There were not enough parts of him. *Give me Quinn's location, then let him know I shall be there very soon.*

Trey gave him the location of a building in Atlanta Daegan knew, then withdrew from his mind.

Tristan turned to Daegan as if he sensed a problem. "What's going on, boss?"

"Once we finish here, I must go to Atlanta to see Quinn right away."

Giving Daegan a quick nod, Tristan waited silently.

Daegan returned to Lanna, disturbed by her cryptic comment. "What did ya mean about Luigsech *maybe* findin' her way home?"

Lanna cocked her chin up. "You are busy. You do not want to be bothered with Luigsech's problems."

He had no patience to drag something out of Lanna. *"What* problems?"

Tristan said, "Just spill it, Lanna."

"Luigsech walks alone through canyon and stopped to rest."

"Understandable." Daegan's gut twisted with worry over Luigsech being alone. Why should he worry about someone who had traveled there without his help? The same person who betrayed him.

If only he could purge her from his mind as easily as she had him.

When Lanna said nothing more, his impatience came out with an abrupt, "*And?*"

Anyone else would be backing up when Daegan's anger climbed this fast.

Not the least daunted by his tone, Lanna raised her calm face to his. "Herrick's large vulture stands over Luigsech ... waiting."

His stupid heart started bouncing around like a frantic ball in his chest, wanting to jump out and race to those mountains. "Waitin' for *what?*"

"To die, I would think."

# CHAPTER 8

A FLY BUZZED AROUND, LANDING ON Adrianna's nose. She blew air straight up, disturbing the annoyance, and blinked her eyes open. Her next inhale dragged in damp and stale air, confirming she still sat on a filthy floor in some dungeon-like place Tenebris had taken her and Sen.

Just her for now.

Tenebris had taken Sen somewhere to torture.

She swallowed hard, unable to stop recalling how someone as powerful as Sen had screamed over and over.

Had Sen survived?

What level of power could Tenebris possess to hold a demigod captive and possibly kill him? She doubted Sen was dead. Tenebris could have killed him, and her, at any time. What could Tenebris want badly enough to torture a demigod in the service of VIPER as a liaison?

Did he not fear the Tribunal deities coming for him at some point?

Nothing stayed a secret forever with supernaturals.

Tenebris had better have an exit strategy from this if Sen did escape.

Otherwise, he would face far worse than what he was inflicting upon Sen.

The silence now bothered her just as much as Sen's screaming.

Her arm muscles cried at being held above her head with majik-infused manacles rubbing her wrists raw. She moved her fingers, glad they still worked.

Who would have thought standing too close to Sen would result in being captured? As much as she did not want to be here, she was glad Evalle hadn't been snatched with him instead. She hoped her best friend had found somewhere to hide from the sun. Had Evalle been able to call Storm to find her before daylight?

Oh, yes, Sen would have loved making Evalle's life even worse had they been kidnapped together.

Adrianna shook her head over what she'd learned. Sen should have petitioned to be released from the Tribunal long before now.

Looking around the dismal cell for the hundredth time, Adrianna saw no way to escape without teleporting. Not one of her powers or talents.

She'd never been so glad to be wearing sturdy jeans and a cotton shirt, though covered in grime. Shaking off the groggy feeling from coming out of crashing from exhaustion, she licked her dry lips.

She should never close her eyes in a place like this.

Evidently her body had given up at some point and demanded she rest. With no window to allow light or darkness to pass through, she had zero idea how long she'd been out or how long she'd been in this place.

She had even less of an idea on how to escape.

What specific majik had Tenebris used to prevent Sen from teleporting and to disturb her Witchlock power?

Speaking of that power ...

She opened her fingers, calling up Witchlock to come alive above her palm.

Normally she'd see a white spinning ball of energy the size of a golf ball to start off. At the moment, the energy had a sickly pale-green cast and spun in a wobbly blob the size of a goose egg.

Calling it egg-shaped would be a generous description.

But the center was not shooting out points in all directions this time.

What had her majik jumping around crazy or was it just agitated?

She closed her fingers.

She had not possessed Witchlock very long and had never intended to pull the ancient power to her. Had she not, Veronika, a crazed witch with ancestral roots tied to the first witches to possess this power, would have taken ownership. The minute that happened, Veronika intended to turn all the witches in this era, white or dark, into slaves, and that was just to start.

Adrianna leaned her head back and shifted her shoulders, trying to loosen stiff muscles. She rarely activated Witchlock without thinking of her sister and their family, the heartless Sterling dynasty of witches who had traded her sister to Veronika's family to protect their dark souls.

Her sister's blood was on their hands.

In the end, Adrianna had to take control of Witchlock to save her sister from a hellish perpetual existence where Veronika was siphoning off her twin's powers.

Adrianna had suffered along with her sister for months. Her sister's cries for help screamed in her head nonstop back then. She'd had no way to free her until Witchlock spun down to earth.

She'd swallowed the bitterness of saying goodbye as her sister thanked her for death, the only way out of the energy cocoon she'd been trapped in. There had been many days since then when Adrianna struggled to work with this power.

No matter how difficult it became, she reminded herself how her sister had survived much worse while a slave to the energy.

As she studied the wobbling energy, she had to admit she'd avoided truly bonding with this power, unsure of what it might do if she failed to hold control.

Her past hesitation to become closer to Witchlock might cost her life now.

From this moment on, she would stop testing and start believing in Witchlock if she hoped to survive. Even if Sen came back, he'd made it clear he would not help her escape.

Adrianna opened her mind to different possibilities of what affected Witchlock right now. Was it reacting badly to the majik in this place or to her emotions?

What if Tenebris came to drag her to his torture chamber?

She needed to know what would happen if she had to tap the energy.

What better time to try a little test than now?

If she could call upon the power without harming anyone else, except Tenebris, she might be able to find a way out of here.

The fly returned and landed on her nose. Really?

She scrunched her nose, but the little critter held tight.

"Okay, buddy, you're on your own." Opening her hand, she waited until the misshapen ball of energy began to steady.

She'd have more confidence in a perfect sphere over this odd blob shape, but when imprisoned she had to take whatever she got.

Twisting her wrist against the metal cuffs and grimacing at the bloody cuts, she turned the hand holding Witchlock toward the far corner of the room and pointed her fingers. Large brown and gray stones cut with primitive tools were stacked like bricks. The corner had a jagged seam where stones had broken apart.

That should be easy to pierce.

With her mind quiet, she focused on knocking a hole where the stones met. She sometimes gave firm orders to her power, but those were moments when she was in a wide-open field or on top of a mountain where she could test her limits with the energy.

She concentrated harder to drive the power into that corner.

Energy trickled out and floated in a loose cloud.

Not even a chip fell from the wall.

This should not be that difficult.

She called up a little more power. Witchlock grew from the size of a fat golf ball to an odd-shaped tennis ball. She could call up more, but she'd once unleashed something just a bit larger than a cantaloupe in an attack.

The results of that had been terrifying.

Clearing her throat, she spoke in a solicitous tone meant to encourage teamwork. "Witchlock, I wish to strike that corner and drive through the stone."

Energy churned and spun, building up.

She debated on backing it down. Before she had a chance to speak, power lashed out, slapping the ceiling then the walls. It bounced back and forth, knocking chunks of stone loose everywhere it struck.

Rocks and debris rained down and pinged across the room.

She tucked her head and tried to close her fingers. Her digits wouldn't fold into a fist. She might as well be trying to force the jaws of Daegan's dragon closed.

She shouted, *"Stop, Witchlock! Stop!"*

Spears of energy still shot out of her hand, hitting all over the room, making a loud crackling noise.

*"Don't do this, Witchlock! Come back to me! Now!"* she ordered, done with being polite.

The shooting daggers of energy ceased. The powerful ball slowed and shrank in size until it sucked back to her hand.

Her fingers closed into a trembling grip. That had never happened. She couldn't depend upon Witchlock to break out of here. Not without knowing if she'd kill Sen or herself.

All bets were off with Tenebris.

She'd put him in her crosshairs if she got the chance.

Speaking of the monster, Tenebris appeared. "Have you been enjoying yourself? I heard some noises."

She answered with a blank stare.

"Oh, come now, witch. This is far more fun when you participate."

"Where's Sen?"

Tenebris smiled as if she'd given him something special. "Do you miss him?"

She sighed heavily for his benefit. "I'd like to turn him into a two-legged hedgehog for dragging me into his problems, so no, I don't miss him. I miss making him miserable for me ending up here." She had to be careful not to arm Tenebris with anything he could use against her or Sen.

"He's busy at the moment. I intend to have another discussion with him soon." Tenebris toyed with the edge of his robe that shifted from a copper to gold color when he moved. The strange emblems would help identify him if she could get that information to her Belador friends.

He had answered one question. Sen still lived.

She couldn't gamble with Witchlock while she and Sen still had options. Not very good ones, but better than going Armageddon and killing Sen along with her in the process.

Tossing this monster a bored glance, she asked, "What do you want from me, Tenebris?"

"I have put some thought into that and come up with what

to do with you." His eyes held a secret reinforced by the smug smile.

She scoffed, "You're just now figuring out that I'm of no real use to you? You should just let me go." Not the best bluff, but she hoped it would cause him to react and share something she could use.

If she did find a chance to escape, she'd take it only because she'd have a better chance of returning with others, maybe even Loki, to rescue Sen.

Sen didn't deserve her consideration, but she was not him. She wouldn't leave anyone here no matter how disgusting that person had acted to her and others in the past.

Tenebris took a step, paused, and took another step as if considering which way to go. "You are just as guilty as Sen of destroying Imortiks."

She didn't argue the point since he'd likely gotten a lot out of torturing Sen, who would kick her under the bus right away.

For the first time since being captured, she suffered the vile feeling of vulnerability.

But she refused to let any thought of it show.

She'd love a cup of water, even a thimble full. Didn't matter. She knew better than to ask. Neither did she want to give Tenebris the idea she would be easy to break. "I have nothing to say on Imortiks. Believe what you will. I won't argue with someone unable to listen. So, tell me, what have you decided to do with me?" She mentally braced herself for his next words.

"I need one of you in your current state. Sen is the greater prize, so that means you could replace one of my Imortiks."

A dizzy feeling swamped her before she could shut down the weakness. He'd hit on the quickest way to knock her off her game, and frankly it was working.

# CHAPTER 9

DAEGAN APPEARED ON A ROOFTOP near Five Points in downtown Atlanta with Tristan next to him. Rain fell steadily over the area where five roads merged into one intersection. He pushed up a kinetic cover over the two of them.

"Watch out for a trap," Daegan warned the friend he'd never thought to find. Pride filled him at Tristan's confident stance, always ready for whatever they faced. "If anythin' threatens, leave immediately. Protect yourself first."

Tristan opened his mouth then closed it again before abruptly nodding. "Will do, boss." Then he blinked out of view, teleporting in search of Luigsech.

That should ease Daegan's mind, but now he worried about Tristan *and* Luigsech.

"Daegan!"

Daegan's North American Belador Maistir stood at the edge of the roof in a rain jacket with a hood, staring down at the intersection where lights shined through the rain-soaked night. He called up a poncho, a plastic garment Tristan had introduced him to during another storm.

As Daegan approached, his Maistir said, "I am sorry to call you back here."

Stepping up next to Quinn at the short wall surrounding the roof, Daegan shook his head. "Do not apologize, my friend. It pains me to not stand alongside my people when they fight. We have Imortik outbreaks in other countries. Not as bad as here, but 'tis spreadin'." Then he saw all of the scene below. "What is goin' on, Quinn?"

"Many things, but those are what this country calls the National Guard, warriors who protect humans on American soil. This state and other parts of this country are under a curfew now."

"Curfew?" Daegan turned a frown to him.

"All people are to be off the streets from eight at night to six in the morning."

"What about our people patrollin'? Without them, there will be no one to protect humans from Imortiks or other supernatural predators."

"That's the point, Daegan. The humans want to catch any nonhuman roaming at night to make killing them easier."

What had one supernatural unleashed on the human world?

Daegan wanted to gather up all his people and keep them somewhere safe, but Treoir realm could not contain the multitudes of Beladors living today. Also, many of his Beladors had human partners and family. They were unwilling to abandon their families in this world as he would be in their places.

Running only protected the one fleeing, not the greater group.

Gripping his jaw, Daegan could not take his eyes off the armed men and women below in matching pale brown uniforms. They were likely most, if not all, humans. "We must find a way to speak with their leaders. To show them we are protectors of humans and want to work together."

"I wish that was the most pressing issue." Water drizzled off the front edge of Quinn's hood.

Daegan called up his cloaking, glad when it required little effort. He had no idea when all of his power would return, but he always enjoyed more right after leaving Treoir.

Quinn pushed the hood off his head and turned to sit on the wall.

Daegan sat and propped his hands on his knees. "Perhaps 'tis time to share all with the humans."

"The National Guard is now impeding our work, though, through no fault of their own," Quinn explained. "We've also encountered a rogue paramilitary group similar to Isak Nyght's operation running the streets. But ... this new bunch is being led by a wizard called Palaki."

"Are they willin' to work with our people?"

A sad chuckle slipped from Quinn's lips. "No. In fact, they are *actively* hunting all nonhumans." He lifted a hand to squelch Daegan's next questions. "This wizard believes he is above all nonhumans and we do not deserve to exist. The humans with him must have decided Palaki could live as long as the rest of us are wiped out."

Daegan seethed at the arrogance of that supernatural. "I shall deal with him myself."

"I feel the same, Daegan, but we are sorely outnumbered at this moment and you still have venom in your body, correct?"

"Yes. Tristan teleported me here to save my energy, but I am able to teleport a reasonable distance if I do not test it often. Bein' in Treoir aided my body in buildin' back my power, plus the new Treoir babies boosted all of ours."

A true grin lit Quinn's face. "I felt the rush of power as did our people here."

Daegan stared at the dark rooftop where fat raindrops slapped loose gravel. "I shall withhold any plan of action until I know all."

"Sadly, there is more. We found the being who has been producing demons as fast as you can eat a cookie. Actually, Reese figured out *who* he is, but I have no idea *what* he is."

Arching a questioning look at Quinn, Daegan waited for more.

"He's called I-zubrrali. Have you ever heard of him?"

Daegan thought for a moment. "I have not, but I shall ask Garwyli when I am able."

"None of us had any idea who he was either until Reese spoke to him and realized he's her father."

This Imortik problem was bringing the worst of nonhumans out of their holes. Daegan wondered how Quinn had managed this well so far. "Is he a danger to Reese?"

"Yes. He claims he'll destroy all his demons, not harm anyone else here, and go away for a thousand years if she'll hand over our baby."

Daegan roared, "*No!* She did not believe him, did she?"

Appreciation filled Quinn's tired gaze. "Whether she did or not, everyone around her voiced the same support for her and our baby." Quinn smiled weakly at that, but his eyes told a story of deep hurt. "We know she can't birth a live baby, but she and I have decided to treat her pregnancy as if we had that chance. We're discussing names. Both of us were humbled by others willing to stand strong in spite of I-zubrrali's offer."

"I would expect no less from Beladors and our allies." Daegan had no words of comfort for a man whose child had no hope of surviving outside the womb. Upon mentioning allies, he asked, "Any word on Adrianna? Tristan told me what he could when he returned from openin' her car for Reese to use her remote viewin'."

"Ah, I have not finished the litany of issues." Quinn rubbed his forehead and sighed. "Tenebris, the being we now know kidnapped her and Sen, showed up after I-zubrrali disappeared earlier this evening." Quinn's forehead creased with strain and worry. "Now that I think about it, Tenebris might have been watching to capitalize on the result of our battle with I-zubrrali's demons, which were joined by Imortiks."

"I have no idea who Tenebris is, but my father might have known," Daegan grumbled, but in truth there were multitudes of different supernaturals he also had no knowledge about. Perhaps Garwyli would be able to offer more information on this one as well. "Any idea what sort of bein' Tenebris is?"

Quinn lifted a finger to wait. "I can't tell you that as yet, but he gave us a note with his demands. Based upon Evalle's first encounter with him, he is in league with the Imortik master. This new being may be some sort of protector for Imortiks. He was enraged with Sen over killing an Imortik-possessed Belador Evalle and Adrianna had been battling to hold in place until Sen showed up to transport him."

"Tenebris," Daegan murmured, hoping some bit of history would aid him in identifying that being. "What are his demands?"

"He has given us until sunset in Atlanta tomorrow for you to deliver a grimoire volume to the Imortik master." Quinn paused before adding in a tight voice, "Tenebris says if you do that, he will allow you to choose to save Adrianna or Sen. The one left behind will be possessed by an Imortik. Before you think that's it, Loki appeared as we were packing up."

"He came *here* to the mortal world?" Daegan couldn't recall the last time any of the deities who attended Tribunal meetings lowered themselves to visit the human world.

Macha might have, but as far as he knew she had not been

seen in this world since he had banished her from the Treoir realm. Jennyver had been placed in Macha's care to protect since his sister could walk.

How had Jennyver ended up captured at his father's castle?

The sole time Daegan called the Blood Law on Macha during a Tribunal meeting to hand over his sister's remains, Macha had acted as if she had not known what happened to Jennyver.

Everything with Macha was a lie, but she had not turned red in the Tribunal, which meant she could not deliver Jennyver's remains. That in no way absolved her of any blame.

She just knew how to dance around the truth without blatantly lying.

Quinn explained, "Yes, Loki showed up. Evidently, he had just figured out Sen was gone. It would be an understatement to describe him as enraged."

Daegan crossed his arms, wondering how he was going to save Adrianna and Sen. "I take it ya informed him of who had Sen."

"Not really. Loki made his demand, said he would put healthy Beladors into cells with possessed ones below VIPER if Sen wasn't returned, then disappeared. He gave no specific timeline."

"Is he *mad*?" Daegan roared. He stood, unable to sit calmly as Loki threatened warriors already battling an impossible threat.

"Don't ask me that, Daegan. Of course, I think he's insane, but that doesn't change the fact that Loki has already taken four perfectly healthy Beladors to hold in VIPER. I only hope Loki waits to speak with you before sticking them in the cells with Devon and the other possessed Beladors."

Daegan paced several steps, remaining inside the cloaking. He turned to Quinn. "Has Loki forgotten why puttin' these Imortiks away permanently is important to all of us? Even gods and goddesses? I must talk to Loki. He needs to realize Imortiks are beginnin' to slip through the rift in greater numbers and even in other countries."

"They're being battled in other parts of this country as well," Quinn added. "The news stations on televisions are trying to one-up each other on calling us *all* predators." Quinn stood. "I keep sending as many of our warriors as I can, but ... we are running out of Beladors. I can't ask those to come here from other countries when they have families and communities of their own to protect." Quinn's gaze wore the burden of doing his duty while unable to protect his warriors.

As a warrior from the day he drew his first breath, Daegan understood the difficult task of sending men and women to battle with no idea if they would return home at night. He'd moved many Belador families to Treoir. Warriors missed their defenseless human families, but wanted them safe more than anything.

Quinn cleared his throat, ready to move ahead. "I need those four Beladors Loki took, which I know you realize. Just as I realize that even if you have a grimoire volume, we are not giving it to the Imortik master. Either way, I have no idea what to do about any of that when we can't even find this Tenebris." He wiped a hand over his mouth during the silence.

Daegan had to help his Maistir, who carried more on his shoulders than he should, and all due to Daegan not being able to stay and fight with him.

But Daegan could help Quinn with strategy. "I think we should hand the rogue military group problem to Isak, but make sure he understands about the risk of dealin' with the wizard leadin' them." Daegan's people fought on too many fronts. "Isak has demon blasters and other weapons to use against a powerful bein'. Perhaps he can convince this group to not attack our people, which should be possible knowin' how he feels about Adrianna."

Quinn listened intently. "I see your point. I will contact him, Daegan, but I'll be shocked if Isak can convince that wizard to stop hunting nonhumans."      .

"Isak is wise," Daegan said, thinking out loud. "He should allow the wizard a chance to make the right choice or suffer the consequences. Tell Isak if he has no other choice but to use his weapons on a powerful bein' harmin' our people or his, he does so with our backin'."

"Understood. We barely convinced Isak not to go off on his own to hunt for Adrianna. We need his intel and he needs our supernatural powers."

"This task shall keep him in touch while everyone hunts Adrianna."

"True."

Daegan continued, "Also, he would be our best person to speak to the human government and convince them to allow nonhumans on their side to continue patrollin'."

Quinn's shoulders still drooped with all he carried. "If trolls and demons had not been attacking humans as well, the human government would probably listen. Right now, I don't know."

Disgust soured Daegan's thoughts. Nonhumans needed to learn to band together or they would all be ground under in this fight. "Put the word out with our people, our allies, the Nightstalkers, anyone and all, that any nonhuman who attacks a human shall be put to death immediately. If they harm a Belador, they face the red dragon. These predatory nonhumans are comin' out of holes, thinkin' to take advantage of easy prey."

Quinn lifted his head and his eyes filled with the light of hope. "I will handle that immediately."

"Good. Ya have taught me how we have many resources in this new world. We shall have them help us put word out to the humans of how they have nonhuman friends. We need our supernaturals to make it understood we intend to deal swiftly with any nonhuman caught harmin' a human." Daegan wished he could offer more. "'Tis time the nonhumans who wish to be protected step up and give aid."

"That's a solid idea, Daegan. We need to start a campaign of getting humans on our side or at least willing to speak to our representatives." Quinn's renewed drive to tackle this head-on rippled with power in his voice. "I will take Reese with a contingent of Beladors to tackle eliminating I-zubrrali, which will severely reduce demon production in this world. Evalle has performed well as Maistir whenever I have not been available. She's an excellent leader, no matter how much she hates it."

Daegan chuckled. Quinn now sounded strong and ready to thrash these problems. His Maistir could not carry this load alone forever.

Quinn held up a finger, indicating he spoke telepathically. He lowered his hand. "Trey informed me a number of Imortiks have been seen moving together, as if a unit. I must go there next. I'll call Isak on the way."

"I shall go to the Tribunal and force sense upon Loki."

"Should you go to the Tribunal without Tristan to back you up?"

Daegan could not admit he had a concern of entering a hostile realm when he was not at his strongest, but he had no choice. It wasn't as if he could deliver Sen with a snap of his fingers. "I shall be fine. I have enough power to teleport to VIPER and Tristan shall return soon."

Thankfully, Storm was not present to call him on the lies.

Daegan did feel he could teleport to the mountain housing VIPER headquarters where he would be teleported inside. But he had no idea if he could truly leave on his own.

# CHAPTER 10

WIND WHISTLED THROUGH THE DARK canyon where the temperature continued to drop into the forties. Casidhe gave silent thanks that it was summer and not winter in the Caucasus Mountain range.

That was all she could be thankful for right now huddled on the ground against a boulder at the base of a mountain with no coat. Jeans and a long-sleeved T-shirt offered little defense against the cold.

Even less against a dangerous bird stalking her from fifteen feet away. That griffin vulture was no longer a natural being after Herrick had befriended it. She didn't know what Herrick had done to Stian, but the bird stood as tall as her.

*If* she were standing and not sitting on the ground.

Herrick's massive pet had paused, not moving a muscle, oblivious to the wind lifting the tips of its feathers. It stared down at her with obsidian eyes, daring her to move.

The occasional moonlight breaking through clouds dusted the bird's dark outline, lighting up a few spots of white. Its thick and sharp beak could rip a mountain goat apart.

No telling what that vicious beak could do to smaller prey like her.

She couldn't maintain this standoff forever. She'd lifted her hand to call up her sword, which brought Stian a foot closer.

In spite of her arm muscles already complaining, she would be happy to try to stay in this frozen position for hours if it meant not being killed, but nothing in Stian's black gaze indicated the bird would wait much longer.

Flexing her fingers slowly, she kept her vision pinned to the vulture, watching for any reaction.

That empty gaze had flicked to her hand, noting her movement.

Stian hopped a step closer. A couple more hops and it could peck a hole in her skull with one sharp strike from above.

Weren't vultures supposed to wait for something to die?

Natural ones maybe, not one shot full of majik.

That huge beak opened and hissed. Stian hopped forward.

Spit dried up in her mouth.

Blood roared through her ears. Her heart might explode from the pressure alone. Adrenaline rushed through her body, keeping her alert and powering a drive to get out of this canyon. She'd never reach Stian's head with one swing. Those wings could swat her sideways first.

Hold everything. She'd blasted Herrick with power when he tried to grab her to drag her to the dungeon.

Confidence squeezed in between panic and fear.

Lifting her free hand, she shoved it forward and shouted, *"Back!"*

Wind lifted white tufts around the vulture's collar, but Stian didn't budge.

Ah, crap. Why should she think her new power would show up just because her sword had decided to be a team player?

She glanced at the wall of rock behind her, then to each side. With this canyon dark as a bottomless pit, she might get away from Stian unless that bird had powerful night vision, but she'd have to run exposed through barren land.

It didn't matter at this point.

She couldn't survive trapped here. She'd have to distract Stian long enough to race past. That meant leaving her backpack. Any move in that direction would give Stian the perfect opportunity to attack and draw blood with its first strike.

Could the bird be here just to take her back to Herrick?

Stian's beak opened wide and fangs dropped down.

Nope. That did not look like a retriever. What had Herrick done to this creature? Did he even realize his attack bird was going to kill her?

Stian lifted its wings in a predatory move and hissed a loud sound. A battle cry.

Time had just run out.

She hoped the new mojo with her weapon remained and called

in a quiet, but firm, voice, "Come to me, *Lann an Cheartais.*"

Everything happened at once.

The blade hissed out of the sheath inside her backpack.

Stian opened wings that stretched fourteen feet wide and headed for her.

Her sword flew up in the air and down in front of her. She gripped the hilt and leaped to her feet.

Now was the time to run one way to trick the bird then race the other way to escape, but Stian moved faster than she could have imagined.

Its wings blew dust and grit into her face.

She shut her eyes and turned her face. Damn. She would never see the bird's head to cut it off.

Screeching wildly, Stian's flapping grew louder as it went airborne but didn't fly off. Wind whipping down from where the giant bird hovered above her shoved her to the ground. She yelled obscenities and fought to stay afoot, slashing her sword blindly at empty air. Her eyes burned and blurred.

She had to see to strike even a giant bird.

A dark form filling the cloud of dust dropped closer.

She swung her blade wildly and hit a solid part of the body. But not fast enough to prevent the bird's sharp claws from slashing her shoulder.

She cried out at the burning pain and sidestepped. *"Bastard!"*

Stian hissed, flapping just enough to stay above her like a flying tornado looking for a spot to land and rip the world apart.

She gripped her sword with two hands, swinging back and forth to protect her head. She jabbed upward and her sword hit a solid wall. She yanked it back down.

The bird made a pained noise.

This was her opening. She ran out from under the bird, trying to watch her steps on the rugged and half-lit ground. Tears streamed from her abused eyes.

Hissing closed in on her.

She spun to face Stian.

Its black eyes now glowed blue, so much like Herrick's. Wings stretched wide and beating rapidly drove the monstrous bird at her like a fighter jet.

She called up power to her hands.

Energy sizzled along her arms and down the sword. She'd get one shot at the bird, but Stian had the advantage. Fingers locked tight on the hilt, she lifted the tip, pointing at the vulture's soft belly.

Stian flew straight, not the least bit of fear in its glowing eyes.

At the moment she could see the black centers, Stian vanished.

Wind and the hissing giant bird gone.

Her arms trembled and her eyes burned. She blinked, trying to clear her vision to take in the empty landscape.

Where had Stian gone?

How had that bird just vanished when Herrick had never possessed the ability to teleport?

She didn't care as long as she got out of this canyon before the vulture showed up again.

Or the dragon.

Maybe Stian had known to avoid her power.

She didn't think so, but couldn't care right now.

Her shoulder ached where the claws had caught her. Warm blood leaked down her arm and back. Adrenaline still pumping through her body gave her the energy to get moving.

She stumbled over to her backpack and stabbed the tip of the sword to stand it against the boulder she'd been using for a backrest. Her body hadn't finished shaking. She took several deep breaths, trying to calm down and listen for any approaching sounds, like giant wings flapping.

When her legs felt steady again, she lifted her backpack and gritted her teeth getting the injured shoulder through the strap. She dug out a shirt and wrapped it around her shoulder, using the strap of the backpack to hold the cloth in place.

Did she need stitches? Probably.

Walking would not be a good idea, but staying put was worse.

After latching the straps, she reached for her bad shoulder, pressing on the padding to stem the bleeding.

"Let's go," a male voice ordered.

She jumped, reaching for her sword and knocking it over. Tristan stood where Stian had before attacking her.

Grabbing her head, she wheezed out, "Thank goodness it's

you."

Tristan said nothing. She took one look at his rigid pose and went on immediate alert.

Why wasn't he talking to her?

She tried again, keeping her voice as steady as she could manage. "Did you teleport the vulture away?"

Tristan nodded. No muscle twitched in his face and she'd never seen that flat look in his eyes.

"Why are you here?" she asked, trying anything to communicate with him. It didn't escape her notice that Tristan made no move to carry her backpack this time when she would have gladly given it to him.

"Do you want to leave or not?" he asked, sounding worse than impatient. Hostile, in fact.

Fine hairs lifted on her arms, but her heart jumped at the idea of seeing Daegan. "Sure. I'd appreciate it if you'd teleport me to ... wherever Daegan is."

"Make another choice." Tristan lifted his hand. "If you ask me to take you to Daegan again, I'm leaving."

She gulped down her next breath, pain wracking her from more than the shoulder injury.

Daegan and Tristan had been her friends. Daegan had vowed to give her and him a chance if they all survived the Imortiks. Tristan's cold demeanor and Daegan not coming here with him crushed the glimmer of hope she'd had for Daegan after walking away from Herrick's castle.

Sending Tristan here alone spoke volumes.

Daegan really did not want to see her again.

It was all she could do not to fold to the ground and bawl at the unfairness of everything. But if she uttered the wrong word now, she'd be stuck taking a week or more to get back home.

She couldn't call Galway home anymore, but that was the only place she knew to go.

Sucking her broken heart back into her chest, she ignored the searing pain of her clawed shoulder and squatted to grasp her sword. Once she shoved it back into the sheath, she stood, never taking her eyes off Tristan.

For a tiny moment, he grimaced.

She was sure of the small change in his face, but a blink later his face returned to unemotional.

Did that involuntary reaction to her bleeding mean somewhere inside his stone-cold reserve he still thought of her as a friend?

She hoped so. She needed one badly.

Now wasn't the time to ask.

Giving her throat a chance to open up, she said, "I'm ready to go to the hotel in Galway, if you—"

Everything blurred then stopped as she finished her sentence. "—don't mind."

Her head ached from no food or sleep in too many hours. She fought a moment of vertigo, grabbing the back of the chair in the hotel room to steady herself. Her fingers clutched the wooden rolling chair shoved against a narrow desk with a lamp. A padded chair in floral material sat on the other side of the bed next to a window hidden by sheer drapes.

The double bed had been dressed out with white linens. Five decorative pillows stood against a wall with a picture of the cliffs in County Clare.

Cozy under different circumstances.

Her gaze danced around the room more as she unlatched her backpack. This place looked familiar. "What hotel is this?"

"Same one you had before you left Galway," Tristan explained in a voice devoid of emotion if someone failed to pick up the anger seething beneath his words. "I set it up before I teleported to pick you up on the mountains. The room and expenses for food are paid for five days."

"Wait," she shrieked, sure he'd disappear any second then she'd never find him again. Or Daegan.

"For what?"

She let the backpack fall to the floor and did her best not to whine at the pain in her shoulder. "Come on, Tristan. Give me a chance to talk for a moment."

Arms crossed and shoulders squared, he had negative body posture nailed. "I don't have time."

"I can explain everythin'—"

"No, you can't." He stared her into silence and added, "You could have. You had plenty of opportunities, but you never said one freaking word. Now, after you're caught in your lies, you want someone to listen and understand. I'm not that person."

Tears burned her eyes. She had lost so much after all the years of devotion and hard work. Her voice quivered. "You can believe what you want, but I had no idea Herrick had Jennyver. Never crossed my mind that he could have anyone hidden in his lair."

Tristan's eyes flickered with something she couldn't identify, but she kept going. "Yes, I was raised in Herrick's clan, but I could not tell Daegan while I was tryin' to figure out if he had come to me huntin' for Herrick."

Shaking his head at her words, Tristan blew out a rush of air. He didn't believe her.

She was losing him. Hurrying ahead, she explained, "But I never told Herrick about me meetin' Daegan either. I didn't want those two to fight."

"Well, you failed. They did."

The finality in his voice said she could not keep him longer. "Please take a message to Daegan."

His face hardened. "No."

She walked over and placed a hand lightly on his forearm. "Please at least tell him I'm sorry."

Tristan stepped back, freeing his arm from her touch. His throat moved with a slow swallow. "I am the *last* person who will speak on your behalf. No one cared for Beladors, especially Alterant-gryphons, until Daegan showed up. You have no idea what he means to us, what he means to *me*. You're on the wrong side in this battle. I only teleported you here because Daegan was too honorable to leave you in danger. If I had not come for you, he would have lost important time needed to save our people, but in spite of that and how badly you hurt him, he would have still come. I did not want him to suffer another minute in your presence. Don't fool yourself by thinking he's weak and will overlook this betrayal. Ever."

Her heart beat painfully faster with each crushing blow of his words.

She had no way to reach Daegan if Tristan blocked her. She'd never been a hand-wringing type of woman, but her hands were balled up now. "I'm pleadin' with you, Tristan. If I can have one chance to talk to Daegan and explain my side then … " She had to stop, hating to finish that sentence. Catching a breath, she forced the words out. "If he never wants to see me again, I will walk away without another word. I swear it. Just tell me what I have to do for a chance to speak with Daegan one more time."

Tristan breathed slowly several seconds, which she took as an encouraging sign. "Find his sister. He'd talk even to you to get her back." He lifted the scepter that had been in her backpack. "I'm taking this with me."

Her mouth opened to protest she had no idea what happened to Jennyver, but Tristan had teleported away.

# CHAPTER 11

DAEGAN TELEPORTED TO THE BEATEN-DOWN ground outside VIPER headquarters in the North Georgia mountains. A human might find this odd with no entrance of any sort to indicate this was more than a clearing next to a rock face.

Rain drizzled unlike the storm he'd left Quinn in on a rooftop.

Daegan called out, "Loki, I—" The irritating god's name barely left his mouth when his world spun out of view.

"*Now* you come here?" Loki shouted from the dais where he, Justitia, and Hermes stood in their usual order. "We do not exist to be subservient to your schedule."

Too tired and mentally spent for these antics, Daegan countered, "What is goin' on, Loki? I hear ya have taken my people from the streets. Warriors who are puttin' their lives at risk to keep humans and nonhumans safe. We had an agreement that my people would not be harmed while I hunt for the grimoire volumes. Or have ya decided to give the mortal world to the Imortiks?"

"I want Sen back *now!*" Power roared from Loki's voice, blasting across the Tribunal realm so hard the ankle-deep grass bent over then returned to stand up straight again.

Even Justitia stumbled sideways, bumping into the musician, though calling him such stretched the definition.

The goddess of justice sniped at Loki, "Was that necessary?"

Loki grew in size and fury, staring down at her while horns protruded from his head and a long black coat formed from his shoulders to his knees. "*Do not think you are my equal. Ever!*"

Justitia's jaw dropped, then she closed her mouth in a hard line. "Keep in mind that I am *not* alone." That was all she said and turned her blindfolded face to Daegan.

Twisting around, Loki snarled at Daegan, "Your Beladors are

becoming more trouble than help."

"Ya would not say such a thing if ya spent more than a few seconds in the human world where they fight the Imortiks *every minute!*" Daegan shouted right back. "Takin' my people off the streets only weakens our ability to win this war with the Imortiks."

Loki silently returned to his human form with a fancy suit and no horns. "I have a hard time getting your attention unless it involves your people."

Daegan had no argument there. He would not be here now if Quinn had not needed him. "I have spoken to my Maistir. They have determined the name of the person who took Sen, but not one of us knows more than that."

"Who is it?"

"The bein' called himself Tenebris." Daegan watched for any recognition and saw none.

"Why didn't Quinn tell me?" Loki demanded.

"'Tis difficult to speak to someone unwillin' to listen." Daegan would not be arguing at the moment if others would simply discuss an issue. "'Twas not Quinn's fault at all. Do ya know of this Tenebris?"

Loki clamped his thumb and forefinger on each side of his jaw and stared at the ground in front of Daegan. He shook his head as he lifted his gaze. "I do not. What about you two?" Loki glanced to his left.

Justitia said nothing. She'd quieted after his earlier rebuff when she'd asked why he had to lose his temper and push power around.

Loki seemed amused, enough so that he waited silently.

Hermes strummed slower until he paused. "I have not heard of Tenebris."

When Justitia finally decided to speak, she said, "I should have, but I do not recognize the name. If I had a description, I might be able to sort through my memories of someone connected to this person." The frown Loki had put on her face relaxed after that statement.

She lowered her scales of justice a bit while she seemed to think more on the person.

"Oh?" Loki asked. "How would a description aid us?"

"I take note of everyone and any beings connected to them when I have been asked to decide the truth in difficult conflicts. Details remain with me forever." Her last words were spoken with supreme confidence meant to put Loki back in his place.

Daegan expected a reasonable conversation now that Loki had calmed down. He was wrong.

Loki lashed out, "That does not change the fact of Sen missing, dragon."

"I feel duty bound to ask how any of this is *my* problem?" Daegan would do all in his power to get Adrianna back. If Sen was close by during a rescue or if his freedom could be negotiated along with Adrianna's, then he would benefit as well. But Loki needed to work with Daegan if he wished for the return of his demigod servant.

As one in perpetual movement, Loki moved around while he answered. "Sen was taken with Adrianna La Fontaine, the Sterling witch who is allied with you and your Beladors. Additionally, Sen had been called to retrieve a possessed Belador, which resulted in his capture."

"Sen *killed* our Belador after claimin' ya had no room here for that one." Daegan still ground his jaw over that action. "Had he not been usin' time to aggravate our people, he might have been gone when Tenebris showed up. Then Adrianna would still be here to aid us with her Witchlock power."

Strolling around on the dais and staring up at the endless dark sky with twinkling stars, Loki heaved a big sigh and returned to his initial position. "I do not care what started all of this. I need Sen back. Every time I am forced to visit the human world, I will return with Beladors who can do my bidding."

"'Tis not a wise move, Loki," Daegan warned. "I have told ya all that I am doin' to get rid of Imortiks. Ya three could accomplish more than fifty of my Beladors if ya were there."

A collective gasp rippled across the dais.

Hermes wouldn't look at Daegan.

Justitia's face reshaped into disbelief.

Loki just stared at him as if he'd been told to feed the red dragon grapes. "I will not even acknowledge such a ridiculous comment. I did all of you a favor to travel to the human world myself."

From what Quinn had said, Daegan doubted his Maistir considered the visit from Loki a favor. "In spite of all your threats and yellin', it so happens my people are doin' all they can to track down Adrianna and Sen. We are puttin' every person we have available on findin' them. If ya wish me to return Sen, then put my people back on the street and do not put them near the other possessed Beladors."

Hermes smiled and said, "I don't think being possessed is contagious. It's like being pregnant. You either are or you aren't."

Justitia lost her patience with Hermes. "You know this from experience?"

Hermes thrummed his fingers fast over the strings of his instrument, creating a demonic sound.

Daegan didn't reply or smile. Nothing about any of this amused him.

Loki said, "Do be quiet, minstrel, and I use that title loosely."

That set down sent Hermes to snuggling his instrument plunking one string at a time.

"Will *you* be hunting Sen?" Loki asked, pinning Daegan down just as it seemed they might have been getting somewhere.

"If I stay here, I can do no more than my people. 'Tis a better plan for me to keep huntin' the grimoire volumes. If my people need me or my dragon, I shall return immediately."

Justitia shrugged daintily. "He does make a valid point."

Loki slowly turned a ferocious face on her, eyes glaring and mouth opening to likely yell again.

She didn't spare him a glance. "If you lose your temper again around me, you will be left to find another deity to take my place, who will likely know nothing about Tenebris. I am not here as a way for you to vent."

Daegan enjoyed seeing Justitia stand up to Loki.

She had the trickster god since the goddess of justice might be the only person in this bunch to figure out the identity of Tenebris.

Pulling himself back together, Loki ignored her and addressed

Daegan again. "I need confirmation that your people will succeed, unless they are hiding something."

"What makes ya think my people have a demigod tucked away somewhere?" Daegan's temper had a boiling point and Loki pushed dangerously close to the red line. He decided to shove Loki in a different direction. "Why don't ya bring in Macha? She has not been seen or heard from since all this started with the Imortiks."

Loki arched a dark eyebrow. "Do you accuse Macha of being behind the Imortik rift?"

Daegan sidestepped that trap easily. "I accuse no one until I have proof. I only say she was around durin' the time of the last Imortik outbreak and played a role in securin' the grimoire volume placed in VIPER's vault, or is that not true?"

Justitia answered, "It is true."

Tired of standing there, Daegan crossed his arms and took a couple steps to the side, then paced back until he gave them his attention again. "Macha could offer details to aid in findin' the volumes. She might have an idea who took the one from the vault. The point is, ya brow beat my people and waste precious time I need for findin' these grimoire volumes. I am not the only one ya can call when ya have a problem."

"I have asked Macha to come to the Tribunal and made it clear she would be safe and welcome. For that reason, you must not be here when she is present. She has not gotten over the last time you two faced off in our presence."

Maybe if Macha had not given a leader of the bounty hunters she'd taken to her bed the ability to open bolt holes, she might have left happier.

Justitia's calm expression had changed when Loki spoke. She seemed annoyed.

Now that Daegan thought back on Loki's words, something bothered him. If Macha had been assure of her safety, why had she not been here yet?

What if the rule of consequences for lying in a Tribunal did apply to a being on that dais?

More suspicious than usual in this place, Daegan asked, "When is Macha to be here?"

Loki lifted a shoulder in disregard. "As I said, Macha is not in conflict with our Tribunal. She travels when she chooses."

Daegan could solve nothing by questioning Loki's truth, not at this moment. "I would like to have any information she shares, which might aid my search."

Whenever the trickster god smiled, as he did now, that normally would only bode well for Loki. "I will consider passing along information, but you have yet to give us a satisfactory agreement for the time of Sen's return."

Daegan thought he'd talked his way around that and dropped his arms to think. "I am only able to promise we shall do all in our power to help, but my Maistir needs the four Beladors back ya took."

"Always asking for something, yet you offer nothing in return, dragon." Loki eyed him with the same disdain given a beggar. "Since you continue to dance around a reasonable agreement, I will make the terms. I will allow you time to find Sen until not having him creates an issue for us."

There was no way Daegan would leave here without knowing what Loki had in mind. He needed exact terms spelled out. "What is to happen if ya need Sen before my people are able to locate him?"

"The bounty hunters we brought in when the Beladors abandoned us the last time—"

"My Beladors did *not* abandon VIPER," Daegan cut him off, arguing in a deep voice that should warn Loki to take care with accusations. "'Twas in truth the other way around."

"It's in the past," was all Loki would allow. "Anyhow, the bounty hunters will be tasked with duties."

Loki sounded too smug by far. He was hiding something, but if Daegan lived two thousand more years he would not figure out Loki's secrets.

Daegan shook his head at the obstinate god. "After all the problems the bounty hunters created in the past, ya would open VIPER to them again?"

Justitia's head swiveled to Loki, clearly just as curious as Daegan to hear the answer.

"Oh, no. The bounty hunters will not go to VIPER. They'll

be given bounties for bringing in Beladors until Sen is here to take over his duties again. I have returned your four. That is generous of me, don't you think?"

Daegan had no move against Loki when he wanted nothing more than to allow Ruadh out to teach that god about playing with people's lives. "No, 'tis *not* generous. I have clearly wasted my breath tryin' to be reasonable if ya believe such."

"I disagree, dragon. If I want to be *truly* unreasonable, I could send out bounties on Quinn or Evalle first. Or both." Loki paused staring up at the dark sky and smiling. "Actually, that is an excellent idea," he crooned to himself.

Seething at Loki's sick gloating, Daegan snarled, "Do not dare—"

With a stroke of Loki's hand, Daegan teleported away in a cyclone of power with no idea where that god had sent him.

# CHAPTER 12

R ENATA ACHED EVERYWHERE. IT FELT as if acid ran
through her veins. Every breath hurt her throat. She'd been
screaming at times then blacking out. Her heart barely beat one
thump, then waited two or three seconds to thump again.

She hated to admit that she hoped her heart would quit.

Humans were falling victim to Imortik takeovers more quickly
because they lacked nonhuman strength.

She had spent her life protecting humans from preternatural
threats but could not save herself or anyone else. Would she be
able to move when Timmon called her up to join the army he'd
been creating?

Against her will, her gritty eyes opened. She'd kept them
closed often during her time in captivity to avoid seeing what
Timmon, the Imortik master, did.

If that were not difficult enough, she now played tug-of-war
with the Imortik inside her body day and night. The miserable
presence grew stronger as she grew weaker.

She'd named her Imortik Minos after the King of Crete who
built a labyrinth and filled it with a minotaur, which killed
everything dropped in there. Minos liked to torture people. She
tried to think of an even more disgusting person, but none came
to mind.

Her Imortik was so stupid it thought the name had been a gift.

That gave her reason to smile when she said Minos in her
mind. Sort of like telling someone they smelled like pig shit and
that person inhaled deeply every time.

What did Minos want her to see now? That had to be why
her eyes were opening. She blinked a couple times to wash her
dry eyes and lifted her head. More captives had been taken off
horizontal poles like the one she was draped over.

The air smelled nauseating and sickly.

Speaking of stink, her body must be slowly dying. She hated the stench of this place.

Had bodies missing from the poles died or been turned into zombies like the ones she'd seen Timmon compel to do his bidding and send out?

*We will go soon*, Minos said in her head with his squeaky voice. How old was her Imortik?

She asked, *Where?* As usual, she tried to gain any information she could. She'd found talking mentally to the creep kept Minos busy and allowed her to hold onto some thoughts.

*The master will show us.*

While her eyes were open, she scanned the room, searching for anyone she might recognize much as she'd hate for more Beladors to be here.

Wretched screaming warped through the room.

Timmon was on another emotional bender.

"Where are you?" he shouted. "You promised this would end soon." Then Timmon's voice changed from the high-pitched human pleading to the demonic one of the Imortik ruling his body. "He has abandoned us. Stop calling for the traitor."

Human Timmon cried, "No, no, no ... " He grabbed his head, shaking it back and forth. He wore jeans and a long-sleeved light-gray pullover. His face had begun aging past the smooth thirtyish attractiveness he'd possessed when she first saw him. A pretty monster in the beginning, but he clawed his face more often and failed to heal, leaving long bloody streaks. His hair had begun to fall out in chunks and his eye sockets were shrunken.

She had no sympathy for the hideous being.

When Timmon devolved into a whining puddle again, she searched the room. Her gaze paused on a male who held his head up. Tired brown eyes stared back at her. Was he human or nonhuman?

His lips moved, but she couldn't read lips.

She silently mouthed, *What?*

He looked to his right.

A female three bodies away draped over the same pole lifted her head. With some rest and a bath, that one would be a pretty woman even with the ratty blond hair.

Hell, with rest and a bath, even Renata with her plain looks could be a supermodel compared to what she must look like now.

Half of the guy's gray shirt had been ripped away, revealing a fit body covered in walnut-brown skin.

Those two people hadn't been here long, not to look healthy in spite of their grooming.

The female turned to the man who kept his eyes on Renata.

Then he nodded, as if answering someone. Were they communicating?

Now the female stared at her.

Renata whispered, "I don't understand."

Minos climbed into her mind and shouted, *Do not talk to others!*

She dragged one heavy arm up to grip her head. She told Minos, *I'm not talking to anyone. I'm practicing using my voice for when we go to do the master's work.*

The anger bubbling from Minos calmed, then her Imortik seemed confused.

She met the gazes of the other two watching her and frowned.

The woman struggled to lift her hand to her head just as the man did. They tapped their foreheads. The man mouthed the word, *Link.*

Could that be right? Were those two Beladors suggesting to link with her to join their powers? Would it even work?

Renata's heartbeat picked up from its normally sluggish thump to beat once a second. She must have gotten a shot of adrenaline. Her other arm came up. She had taught sign language to native children in South America to give them a universal language.

Would those two know how to sign?

Her fingers were stiff from lack of use. She flexed them in and out from her palm then sent a simple question. *Are you Beladors?*

The female smiled and nodded, but the guy glanced between them, confused. When the woman tapped her chest with her knuckles, his eyes widened with understanding.

Minos remained quiet, which had Renata believing it had no

idea what she was doing. Did that mean Imortiks were all like hers or were some more developed than others?

She hoped hers was truly an idiot she could work around.

Timmon's mania erupted again. He walked across the open area at one end of where the long poles pointed. Timmon carried on his one-sided conversation again. "He told me not to call her. She'd destroy us both, but I can't do this anymore. *I can't. I can't. I can't.*"

Crap. He already sounded like a broken record as it was.

His alter ego voice said, "I tire of waiting."

Moving around frantically, Timmon moaned, "I'm tired, too. He said he'd be back in a couple days."

Renata glanced at her two new best friends who frowned in Timmon's direction. Did they know something? Was Timmon about to go nuclear on all of them?

Timmon wailed and sobbed, falling to his knees and pounding his fists on the floor. "My life was good! I ruled my world. You bastard. You tricked me with a stupid debt." He muttered to himself then lifted his head and raised his fists. "I never owed you *this*!" he shouted in a wild voice.

Renata watched her friends who had also stopped moving. No one wanted to draw Timmon's attention.

The Belador woman slowly tapped her head then pointed at the male Belador. He made the same motion but pointed at Renata.

She had no idea what they wanted her to do. Her palms dampened with anxiety. She didn't want to screw up, but she needed to know specifically what they were asking of her.

While she kept them both in sight, the woman closed her eyes then the man jerked a little and took a breath. He opened his eyes and turned that tired gaze on Renata.

A hit of energy rocked her body. She jerked.

Her breathing picked up as her muscles began to strengthen.

*We can talk,* a raspy female voice said in her head. *I am Gretchen.*

Then a male voice just as rusty sounding added, *I am Kaiser.*

Tears poured from Renata's eyes. She sobbed while trying to send back, *I am Renata. Thank you. I have been so alone.*

Minos flared in her mind. *What are you saying? Who are you talking to?*

She carefully only spoke to Minos. *I am telling you I am glad to not be alone anymore.*

That sensation of confusing the Imortik filled her mind, then its presence receded once more. Still, the pain sizzling through her body remained as a constant reminder she was not free. She sniffled and clamped her jaws tight to stay quiet.

Then she used sign language to tell Gretchen her situation with the Imortik hearing her thoughts sometimes. Not consistently, but enough she had to be careful.

Before she could say more, Gretchen tensed as if someone had pulled a muscle from her neck to her feet. She shook, struggling with the internal attack. Blood ran from her eyes and her mouth opened in a silent scream of horror.

Renata's tears fell again. She was helpless to do anything for her new friend.

Kaiser stared at Gretchen with pain creasing his face.

Then Gretchen flopped forward, her limp body drooping over the pole. She stayed that way for maybe ten minutes before forcing her head up and looking as if she'd been twisted into a pretzel. Sweat poured off her face and dampened her shoulder-length blond hair.

Renata looked at Kaiser as if he could help her, but he couldn't without drawing deadly attention to Gretchen and himself.

In a voice suffering from not enough air, Gretchen said, *I'm okay. Finish what you were telling me, Renata.*

Relieved to see Gretchen lucid again, Renata moved her fingers, adding that the Imortik inside her had not noticed Gretchen or Kaiser's words in her head.

Tilting her head in Kaiser's direction, Gretchen must have explained telepathically to him. He gave a sign of acknowledgement, then started explaining to Renata, *We have to link all three powers to—"*

Timmon jumped up and yelled, "This has to end! *Now!* He told me to wait. Unfair! He keeps telling me to hang on. He has no idea how bad this is."

His Imortik side replied, "He is not master. We are."

In a whiny voice, Timmon complained, "He said not to call her. Who can help me? Where is he?" He doubled over at the waist and moaned, "Do not call her. Do not call her. Do not."

His other voice instructed, "We are the master. We do as we please. He is the servant. Not us. Rise and show him who is master."

Silence blanketed the room with a frightening suddenness.

Timmon calmly stood upright and announced, "Fuck him. *I am the master.*"

But that had been a nasty blend of his and the Imortik's voice.

Did that mean the yellow monster inside of him was fully taking over?

Renata's gaze skittered to Kaiser and Gretchen, whose gazes swung from Timmon's one-man crazy show then back to her.

Kaiser spoke to her telepathically. *Gretchen and I have been here less than a day, but we're battling the Imortiks inside us. We saw what this master is doing. He's building a hellish army. He's taking Belador-Imortiks who have become fully possessed, wiping what is left of their minds, and sending them out to find other Beladors.*

Renata had been here since she and Devon were captured. She'd heard of no others before them in the Atlanta area. The ones Kaiser spoke of might have come from other areas of the country and beyond.

Gretchen spoke to her this time. *Kaiser and I believe we can escape and battle our Imortiks for control. Our monsters can't hear our thoughts yet.*

Renata used her hands to ask, *What do you want me to do? I don't know how compromised I am, but my Imortik feels a bit dense.*

Gretchen explained, *We have linked with you, but we need you to link with us.*

Renata sent back, *My Imortik has possessed me longer. What if it harms one or both of you?*

Still receiving Renata's messages via Gretchen, Kaiser replied, *We have to take that chance. The longer we are here, the less chance of breaking free. With the two of us stronger, we should be able to keep your Imortik from killing anyone.*

Renata wanted out more than she could put into words, but she did not want to harm anyone. Should she risk it or tell them to go without her?

Gretchen shouted in Renata's head, *Play dead! The master is coming toward you!*

# CHAPTER 13

CASIDHE STARED AT THE EMPTY spot Tristan had left. *"Damn it!* Damn you all!"

What had she done so wrong in her life to be in this spot? She slapped the pillow off the bed and pounded her fists, then dropped to her knees, hugging the bed. Her choppy breathing shook with anger.

Tristan could have taken a message to Daegan.

Daegan could have talked to her in the mountains.

But the one who deserved the lion's share of blame was Herrick.

She'd had two friends when battling her way to face Herrick and call him out for his deceit. He managed to take even that from her.

Had he cared about what he'd cost her?

No. He had the gall to expect her to still help him with gaining Skarde. "Hold your breath on that one, Herrick," she muttered and climbed to her feet.

How had everything important to her disappeared in a fleeting moment?

Daegan's handsome face bloomed in her mind, but not smiling. He stared at her as if she'd gutted him.

She shook her fists at the universe. Pain built from the bottom of her soul, gained power, and burst from her in a scream. The curtains blew about and lights flickered.

She dropped her arms, heaving air in and out. What now?

Time to figure out her next step. Galway no longer called to her as home. No place did.

If she walked out the door and kept moving, maybe she could outrun her mistakes.

Not possible.

The mistakes were hers to own regardless if she'd been given corrupt information.

She walked around the end of the bed toward a window where the grayish-brown curtains had stilled. Outside the window, lights glimmered along the quiet street in the darkness. Dawn wouldn't come for a few hours. A couple huddled close as they moved along the walkway on the other side of the street. They passed under a streetlamp with the light catching them smiling at some private moment.

"Why didn't I get that life?" Her chest heaved and thudded heavily. She slapped the window with her palms.

The couple startled, looked up, then rushed away.

She had no one else to turn to once Tristan shut her last door.

Without Tristan, she had no hope of getting in touch with Daegan. She dropped her forehead to the smooth glass. Nothing would ease the crushing ache of losing the one man she needed above all else.

Not for his power or place in the world.

She wanted Daegan for the way touching him gave her something she could find nowhere else in this world.

To feel cared for. To be wanted. To be cherished.

Her heart curled up inside her chest, shaking with loss.

All of her future dreams gone in a moment.

Daegan was just as hurt and angry.

She understood, but she harbored anger, too. "He should have given me a chance to explain, dammit. Once I told him everythin', he could have still walked or flown away. What would it have cost him for *ten freakin' minutes?*" she demanded.

"You should have told Daegan all of that when you last saw him."

Casidhe jerked around, eyes burning from unshed tears and pissed off all over again. "*Where the hell did you come from?*"

Zeelindar's translucent form swayed back and forth in the open space near the door. "Why do you ask the room important questions and only offer me stupid ones?"

Leaning forward and energy stirring inside her, Casidhe shoved her hands on her hips. "If you've been here long enough to hear me workin' through my problems, then you should know that I don't need any more *crap* dropped on my ass."

The oracle's skin still showed fine black lines drawn on every inch, including her smooth face. Her clothes hadn't changed from the sheer material draped at her shoulders and held there by tiny gold clasps, but Casidhe could see through all of that, too. Zeelindar's form funneled together past her hips, appearing much like a smokey snake being charmed by someone with a flute.

Not even Casidhe's meltdown affected the oracle. Zeelindar continued staring as if waiting for an answer and not the other way around.

What the heck did that oracle want? Casidhe sighed, releasing the fury like steam from a tea kettle. "I'll try for a question worthy of you, Zeelindar. Why are you here?"

"I could ask you the same thing."

Casidhe grabbed her head with her hackles jacked up again. "Argh! Everyone in this world is makin' me crazy!"

Zeelindar corrected, "I am not currently in your world."

Why continue to feed the oracle more opportunities to bait her? Casidhe walked around the other side of the bed and sat on the edge to face the annoying oracle. She breathed deeply during the ensuing silence.

When she had a better grip on her thoughts, she said, "I would like to hear why you are here and what I can do for you."

Slanting her head with a half nod, Zeelindar replied, "I do not possess the staff owed to me."

Casidhe's throat ached with the need to shout. "If you'll recall, I tried to give the staff to you last time we talked. You couldn't take it in this ... " Casidhe fluttered a hand in the oracle's direction to indicate her holographic-type form. "Astral state."

"I *travel* in astral projection. I am *not* in an astral state."

After a couple beats, Casidhe said, "I'll be honest with you. I am way past arguin' syntax. I don't even have the scepter anymore. Daegan's second-in-command brought me here and snatched the scepter before he teleported away."

Casidhe had expected the oracle to go ballistic.

Instead, Zeelindar quietly weaved from side to side for a bit longer. "I do not care who has the staff at this moment. It was *yours* to protect. You came to me for help. I provided aid you and the dragon needed. You have yet to fulfill your word. I find that dishonorable."

Sitting up sharply, Casidhe lifted her chin and felt steel infuse her backbone. "Do *not* call me dishonorable. I am not all powerful to snap my fingers and get whatever I want. If I was, I wouldn't be in this position."

"You are not being held captive, therefore, you are in the position you choose," Zeelindar argued with force.

Every word from the oracle's mouth punched Casidhe's chest, but she was not going to fold to this spectral being. "If you're so damned smart and all-seein', you know what hell I've been through since before I found you the first time and since then. How can you chastise me when I've been doin' all I can to find grimoires, rescue that staff, and stay alive?"

Holding her palms together in a prayerful way, Zeelindar countered, "And after all you have done, you question why I regret gifting you with knowledge another could have put to better use?" The oracle's odd eyes filled with disappointment. "What happened to the woman who scaled a mountain and braved other dangers to gain information? Where did *she* go?"

Standing, Casidhe's body shook with the urge to wreck everything she could get her hands on. She'd had enough of everyone telling her how she could have done better.

Vibrating with the effort to hold back from taking the room apart, Casidhe spoke in a lethal tone. "You want to know where *that* woman went? I discover the woman I considered my closest friend was only with me to do Herrick's biddin'. As for Herrick, he used me and lied to me all these years I have given my life to find answers about his brother. I was attacked while travelin' a long distance to confront him only to find out he had kept a woman hostage for two thousand years. That woman happened to be Daegan's sister from the life he lost at the hands of Queen Maeve. Then Daegan sees me standin' with his sister."

The oracle's eyes narrowed and darkened.

"What, Zeelindar? Are you preparin' to zap me into another world? Do it. I don't care. Anythin' would be better than this one. Daegan shows up and sees me with his sister before I can explain I'd gone there to sever ties so I could be with him. He. *Hates*. Me. The man I love believes I *betrayed* him!" Pain poured out along with hot tears. She shouted, "I would have carried his sister on my back by foot through those mountains to hand her to Daegan."

With narrowed eyes still on the oracle, Casidhe stomped over to snatch up a wad of tissue to wipe her face and blow her nose. Her hands trembled and her heart raced from adrenaline still pumping through her.

How was there a step forward from this?

Just one step that made sense so she could figure out a way to survive all she'd lost.

As she began taking in slow breaths, the angst and deep hurt remained, but with less of an edge. She stayed there another few seconds as a calm came over her.

This world had drained her of all she could give right now.

She might bawl her eyes out again tonight, but she could breathe a little right now.

When she turned back to Zeelindar, the translucent woman's eyes were closed and her palms still steepled in front of her chest.

Casidhe asked quietly, "Is there some other way for me to repay you and at least take care of *my* debt to you?"

Zeelindar ceased weaving, opened her eyes, and lowered her hands to her sides. For the first time since arriving, her voice turned sharp as a honed blade. "Our agreement is *not* to be treated as one with a street vendor where choices are made as casually as sipping water. I told you both my price and you *both* agreed."

"Then I'm all ears on whatever you think I should do." Casidhe saw no point in trying to have a normal conversation with someone on the other side of the world from normal.

Mouth thinning more with every word, Zeelindar declared, "*Nothing* has changed about your obligation. You and Daegan must bring me the staff. I will not accept it from either of you without the other."

Casidhe held her tongue. Better to allow the oracle to get all of her unrealistic demands out of the way.

Maybe *then* they could have a real conversation.

Oddly, now that Casidhe had released all that emotional gunk, she felt lighter and better focused. Her chest still ached, but that would not go away any time soon. It wasn't as if she could get over losing Daegan with one good cry.

Every thought of him held her heart hostage.

As if Casidhe's silence had been taken as agreement, Zeelindar nodded. "Once you two deliver the staff, then I shall give you directions on locating a second grimoire."

"Is it in another crazy world?" Casidhe muttered.

Instead of answering that question, Zeelindar said, "The next grimoire volume will be found where it is."

That made as much sense as a brick sandwich.

Now that Casidhe thought about it, what had Daegan done with the grimoire volume she'd helped him rescue?

Zeelindar returned to swaying like a human cobra enthralled by music only she could hear.

Was the oracle about to take off in her astral travel?

In fact, where did she exist?

Casidhe smoothed the buzz-saw edge out of her tone, hoping to reach an agreement before Zeelindar disappeared. How could the oracle expect her to show up with Daegan when she had no way to even reach him?

To be honest, Casidhe had no idea exactly what her next move would be. If she allowed her heart to weigh in, the advice would be for her to go to Daegan and beg him to hear her out.

The idea of begging anyone soured her stomach.

Much as she wanted to be with him again, she couldn't overlook that broken trust. She was just as hurt he never even asked her to explain herself.

Hadn't they run up against this wall before? Not exactly in the same way. She had jumped to the wrong conclusion about him based on believing Queen Maeve's twisted lies.

Daegan might argue this wasn't the same after seeing Casidhe standing with his sister. That did smack of betrayal. But he owed her the chance to give her side. If not, he was making the same mistake she'd made in TÅμr Medb.

Exhaustion dragged at her. "What do you want from me,

Zeelindar? I'm not arguin' the point of a debt to you. I just have no idea what you think I can do."

The woman's gold-and-black molten gaze studied her for a drawn-out minute.

Casidhe's exhaustion fell away as her skin tingled with warning. The last time Zeelindar became upset, energy flew all over Tristan's hotel room.

A muscle in the oracle's smooth cheek twitched. She spoke in a terse voice, but one reeking of regret. "I never chose this role. I lost everyone who mattered to me when I was *forced* to be an oracle. I have no say over my life. I lost all I loved by no choice of my own. I am stuck here forever." She paused, her gaze carrying the heartache she'd lived. "Would you rather take *my* place right now?"

Just hearing all that made Casidhe cringe. Her skin crawled at the thought of someone having imprisoned Zeelindar into an oracle's role. "No, I wouldn't," Casidhe admitted in soft words. "I'm sorry—"

Zeelindar held up her slender hand. "Do not apologize for what is not your doing. If I had freedom to do as I wished, which you should realize is a power in itself, nothing would prevent me from reaching any goal. You ask questions you should be able to answer on your own."

"Look, I tried—"

Zeelindar's loud voice filled the room, pushed by her power. "If with all your knowledge, skill, and *freedom*, you cannot accomplish this one goal, it was never that important to you. Saving thousands of innocent lives and having a world worth living in must not be of significance either. The window to locating *both* missing grimoire volumes is closing. In six days, the Imortiks will take over and the venom in Daegan will destroy him. Live with your conscience, if you can."

Zeelindar's energy swirled and poofed out of existence.

Casidhe leaped up and reached for her. Her fingers grasped air. *"Wait! Stop! I do care!"*

# CHAPTER 14

CATHBAD TELEPORTED INTO THE CAVERN this time, but only inside the passage from the cliff.

Just breathing in the cool air reminded him of the mistake he'd made. One he'd regret if he failed to find Brynhild again.

He'd thought to keep her captive until she'd served her purpose. A simple plan, which had been working fine before he left Tristan shackled here with her free to roam the cavern.

He'd had no reason to believe those two would be able to escape together.

Underestimating any foe could be a deadly mistake. He rarely made that error, but he had this time.

Walking ahead slowly, he listened for any sign of life.

With the ward no longer protecting the entrance, she could return at any time to move her hoard. Not a simple task for someone who did not teleport to accomplish. That would not prevent her from finding someone who *could* teleport, but who would that be?

Tristan or Daegan?

No, he didn't see Brynhild befriending them based on Tristan's blood she spilled. That dragon shifter had been brutal in gaining Tristan's acquiescence, which Cathbad admired.

Cathbad reached the end of the narrow passage to where the cavern bloomed before him. The damp air carried smells from time long gone. He'd learned of this cave centuries before he brought Brynhild here and had feared another dragon showing up, the one who originally used this lair. None appeared while he'd kept watch. After that, he'd felt confident to hide her in the ice pond.

Stopping inside, he took in the high ceiling, tall enough for a dragon to fly overhead. Plenty of space in here for the frigid pond where chunks of ice still floated across the surface and more area stretching to the far-left wall where her hoard still sat. Gold, jewels, and other treasure shined in the torch lights still burning.

Nothing seemed disturbed.

Why hadn't she been back?

He had to capture her again, and soon. He could not have those Tribunal fiends discover he'd kept a dragon alive all these centuries. They would not be concerned about her treatment, only that he'd introduced another dragon to this world. Having Daegan here rankled them enough, but Daegan held a hammer over their heads as long as no one knew the identity of his goddess mother.

Deities might be all powerful, but every group of beings had a pecking order. In the case of gods and goddesses, the most powerful tended to be reclusive.

The Tribunal did not want to face off with a being they could not kill for sure, even as a trio.

One day, they would all know the secret of who birthed Daegan. When they did, the red dragon faced the end of his days.

For now, Cathbad had to stay on good terms with powerful beings. All but one, to be specific.

Queen Maeve had earned her death as soon as Cathbad had time to plan it. He would not kill her until the timing was right where he could benefit in more than one way.

When he reached the foot of Brynhild's hoard mountain, he called over the chair he'd repaired with majik last time and sat.

Had she been here and left him a trap?

That female dragon shifter thought as strategically as any notable leader in a military conflict. And she'd hidden her cloaking gift. Did she possess more gifts?

He hated disturbing the pile, but he could do so with his majik and put everything back in its exact spot. First, he kinetically moved her shield, which she had left as a Do Not Touch sign. He continued moving pieces to each side until he reached the gold tray used for feasts when all her family lived.

A treasured family piece.

Crooking a finger, he called the plate to him and grasped it from the air. He ran his fingers over the fine details of her family's dragon crest carved into the gold tray highlighted with black.

Holding opposite edges with his hands, he called up the spell that he'd placed on the serving dish.

No energy buzzed.

No sign of her having put her hands on the family treasure then leaving. He wouldn't be able to go right to her if she did not have the tray, but he could still use information from a touch to find her.

"Brynhild, ya shall pay for puttin' me through so much trouble to find ya." He beat down the urge to throw this into the hoard and blast the pile apart.

To this day, patience remained one of his greatest assets, so he carefully replaced every item.

Standing, he glanced around, seeing nothing else had changed. He sent the chair back to its place.

When she did return, she'd see how he'd rebuilt the destroyed chair. His message to her that she could not outrun him.

He teleported to Newgrange where the skies were dark with yet a few hours to go until sunrise. The half-finished moon sent soft light over the ancient mound.

Large kerbstones, many engraved with art, ringed the mound.

So much power hidden within a humble exterior.

No humans were in the area. They came during the daylight hours when his druids would not be around. Humans traveled here out of curiosity and for spiritual reasons, none of which were related to his dark druids.

That's why choosing a secret chamber far beneath the mound where no one would stumble in had been the perfect meeting place back when Ainvar had been in control.

Cathbad only wished he'd found confirmation of Ainvar's death and not rumors. But if that druid lived today, would he not be here at this moment?

The dark druids answering Cathbad's call would arrive with no fanfare nor by any human means. They were all capable of teleporting or using bolt holes to travel.

Energy would build once two or more powerful beings entered the chamber far below the surface pathways in the mound. As they gathered in *seomra rúnda*, which simply meant *secret chamber*, the mound would emit an aura across the curved top from edge to edge.

While he observed the mound from this distance, a thin glow of green began to stretch over the wide surface.

He smiled and strolled across a distance which would cover a human football field in many countries.

Halfway there, power burst in front of him.

Queen Maeve appeared, her face distorted from years of hate.

"What do ya want?" he asked, glad no humans were here, but neither did he wish for druids to witness him and Queen Maeve together.

She glowered at him, stretching each second thin. "*Return the girl!*" she demanded, arms crossed and braided hair swirling into loops then slithering away from her head.

He had his own version of Medusa. "I have no idea what ails ya, Maeve. I suggest ya go on about your business and stay out of my way."

"Do not think to dismiss me, druid. *Teleport her here this minute!*"

"Who are ya speakin' of?" He did not want to teleport into the meeting. He had a reason for walking inside the entrance, then joining the other druids. He could not allow Maeve to best him if any attending this meeting showed before he rid the land here of her.

He needed them all at the meeting to respect his power and obey his orders.

"You disgust me." Maeve's golden braids changed colors going to a vibrant green, then orange, then deep red, a bloody color that suited her. All spectrums of the rainbow fit with her black pointy nails.

He realized what did not fit. Maeve wore pants and a jacket. She dressed similar to human females, which she had never done in the past. Was she trying to fit in with humans in this world? Why?

Time dripped away. "If ya want someone I might know about,

ya need to start with a name and save us both time."

"I am not entertained by you acting confused. Return the *Luigsech* woman I captured."

His jaw almost hit the ground at his feet. How could Maeve know about Casidhe? "I know nothin' of ya capturin' her. 'Tis a surprise by itself. What would make ya think I have her?"

Maeve lifted her hands, railing, "If I did not need her back, I would kill you!"

Clouds formed and began gathering in what had been a perfectly clear sky moments ago. The swirling weather event rumbled with threat as her anger took on shape.

"I warn ya, Maeve. First ya accuse me of somethin' I had no part in and now ya threaten me. How many times do ya think I intend to overlook your antics?"

Her voice sharpened. She shrieked like a harpy, continuing to screech nonstop. Damn her.

"*Stop!*" he ordered, glancing around to see if any of his druids were watching. None. They'd been informed to teleport or use a bolt hole to enter the chamber immediately. Not to walk through the entrance.

Eyes glazed with insanity turned on him. Queen Maeve seethed, "You think to convince me you did not teleport her out of the TÅµr Medb library?"

Lightning sparked from the dark clouds. If she turned that energy on him, he'd have to teleport or kill her. At the moment, he considered being late to his own meeting to terminate this major nuisance.

Extending his hands with palms facing down, he waited for her gaze to notice. He would not shout at her unless he was ready to unload a blast of majik. "What the devil gave ya the idea I have been back to TÅµr Medb since our last lovely meetin'? I have been busy. None of what I have been doin' affects ya in any way."

Queen Maeve was clearly torn between choosing to believe him or attack him.

He shook his head and angled it at his palms still pointed down. "This was always our sign of comin' in peace. I have not entered TÅµr Medb since our last encounter and I do not have this Luigsech woman. Why would I even want her?" He could talk his way around Queen Maeve without admitting he knew who Casidhe was. He had done so for many centuries before they went into a deep slumber then awakened in this new world recently.

He'd made the transition just fine.

The mind of this woman, on the other hand, had been corrupted at some point after waking up.

She drew her arms in, crossing them again. "That sounds like the truth."

"'Tis the truth. What point would there be in lyin' to ya if I had someone ya wanted? If I wanted this woman, I would have captured her before ya and not allowed her to escape." He'd certainly tried hard enough, only to have this crazy being get her hands on Luigsech at some point.

Queen Maeve's exceptional beauty no longer glowed. Whatever ate at her mind and power had begun to dull her looks. Her face showed serious lines a being of her power should never allow.

"What are you doing here?" Queen Maeve demanded as if she spoke to one of her servants.

Cathbad gave up and lowered his hands. "I have again been patient with ya when ya do not deserve it. What I do is my business. Ya stay out of my way and I will do the same for ya. Stayin' in TÅµr Medb is the safest place for ya."

The tenor of their conversation had been tolerable until he made that suggestion.

Her eyes glowed with a crazy shade of red. She pulled her lips back to snarl then flashed her hand at him so fast, he failed to move.

Power struck him in the chest. He shot backward, hitting the ground and sliding. He should have a hole in his chest the way his body felt. Smoke sizzled from the spot where she'd hit him.

He pushed to his feet.

She had already grown to seven feet tall and might get even taller. Her head was half again the normal size, looking like a larger version of her face except for her lips, which had thinned and stretched wide with jagged fangs. Her black fingernails grew as long as his fingers. Her hair turned into a coarse black color intermingled with drab gray.

That had never been her color.

The jacket she'd been wearing shredded at the shoulders. One breast hung free and truly hung. Not the firm ones she'd enjoyed her entire life. What was left of her pants fell in torn strips.

"Get ovah heah yah pissy drude." Her words were garbled from that mouth.

He'd intended to kill her when she wouldn't see it coming, but she was most vulnerable right now outside of TÅµr Medb and when she couldn't control her power.

Also, he could not risk a druid having witnessed this encounter and see him fail.

He wiped dirt from his hands as if that bothered him. No, he just needed a moment to generate more power, enough to heal his chest fast and take down one as old as her.

Still dusting off his clothes, he strode back to her, pretending not to watch her when he never let her out of his sight. Fury rode him hard, but he would not lose control. Not when he could ill afford a mistake.

It wasn't as if this would be an easy battle.

They knew each other too well.

His gaze tracked past her to the Newgrange mound. No one stood out there unless they'd cloaked their appearance, but he'd still see their glow.

That was another reason for meeting here.

Hard to hide a nonhuman on these grounds, especially at night. That had to be why this bitch had found him so quickly on her scrying wall.

That wall would belong to him as soon as this was done.

The closer he stepped toward her, the more her body grew, now reaching nine feet. Her head no longer appeared human. She made a deep growling sound belonging to a feral animal.

Slowly, he moved his hand from his jacket to distract her then teleported behind her in an instant.

The moment he reappeared, he struck out with a shaft of energy to cut her head off.

But she disappeared, too.

His blood rushed fast through him. He listened with his supernatural hearing for any sounds of her coming at him. Had she cloaked herself?

Claws slashed across his face, then his chest, digging deep. He latched his hands onto hers, calling out a string of words to unmask her.

What he saw when she appeared would give even him nightmares. He jammed his hand into her chest and pushed his power into her.

She arched back, yanking away to roll in the air, landed, and wailed in pain with arms wrapped around her chest. Blood spewed from her mouth and leaked from her eyes.

The bitch's arms shifted into long ribbons of blue flames with snake heads at the ends she whipped at him.

He shoved up a kinetic wall and roared, running at her. The snake heads tangled attacking each other.

She teleported away.

Heaving deep breaths, he did something he'd never expected to do. He cloaked himself and moved twenty feet away, waiting for her to come back. Everything inside of him went against hiding, but this fight was to the death.

A minute passed.

No sign of the heathen.

She would not come back until she'd gained control of her power, better prepared to battle. He would have liked to finish this now just to get her out of his world.

With a last glance around, he held his cloaking and moved toward the mound.

He'd made ten steps when something heavy hit the ground, causing him to step sideways. He looked around to find a two-headed beast with jaws the size of a vehicle. It made a pissed-off jungle cat sound if the cat was a megamonster, its voice deep as a lion's roar.

But this thing couldn't see him.

He'd smash her toy to pieces, then he'd ... his gaze dropped to the ground where she had covered it with pale-blue dust. Sparkling footprints ended at his feet, televising his location.

He tried to teleport.

It didn't work.

What had Queen Maeve done to lock him in this place with no way out?

He'd never experienced terror, ever, but blood rushed through his body faster than a brush fire doused in gasoline.

Slobbering jaws from two heads dove at him.

# CHAPTER 15

TRISTAN TELEPORTED TO DOWNTOWN ATLANTA, reappearing in Piedmont Park where everything was still wet from a recent downpour. It had slowed to a drizzle he could ignore. Once his eyes adjusted, he eased out and swept a look around. A few people were east of him and heading away. Not citizens. National Guard.

Had Quinn's team run into issues here? Trey had given Tristan the park for the closest place to teleport near Quinn's last reported location.

Tristan searched the area. No sign of Quinn or his team.

Yelling and gunfire erupted. He pinpointed the area as west of him and called to Quinn telepathically. *Tristan here. I'm in Piedmont Park. Where are you?*

*Halfway to the interstate from you.* Quinn gave him details on where they were being attacked. *You may not be able to reach us without drawing fire from a black ops group killing everything that isn't human. There's a curfew in effect from sundown to sunrise. Anyone out at this time of night is considered nonhuman.*

The time had to be closing in on midnight. Tristan sent back, *I heard about the curfew. I'm gonna teleport close and check it out.*

He wasn't concerned for himself, but for all the Belador teams out patrolling. They were in even more danger.

He teleported to the roof of a one-story business he knew about near the location Quinn described. A military-like unit moved around as one, closing in on the area where Quinn and his team should be.

Before Tristan could call to Quinn and nail down an exact spot for him to teleport over to, Quinn's team raced away from where they'd been hidden by a parked van to the back corner of the tall building anchoring that city block.

Four of the six black ops shooters lifted up, activating blasters very similar to Isak Nyght's weapons.

This group might have weapons comparable to Isak's team, but that's where the similarities stopped.

Isak and his people were allies.

Quinn and Evalle threw up kinetic fields to shield the team, but that would not last forever. As they backed up to the end of the building, the other two on the team ducked into an area behind the structure.

One of those two had moved too slowly as if injured.

Tristan teleported behind Quinn and Evalle. He yelled, "Back up faster. Quinn, you get to whoever is injured. Evalle and I will follow while we hold the kinetic wall."

Tristan stepped up and shoved his invisible barrier in place, allowing Quinn to drop beneath his arms and take off.

Evalle informed Tristan, "I'm starting to feel the hits."

"Move back faster. We just need to get out of sight."

Her boot steps matched his, splashing puddles until they ended up shoulder to shoulder. She continued backward into the alley.

Tristan entered last and turned to take in the group, all of them wet from head to toe. Quinn and Reese wore rain jackets. Getting soaked in warm weather would be no big deal to this group, but add that to running hard and he could feel the exhaustion wrapping them.

The team was stuck in a dead-end spot. This alley served as a place to unload delivery trucks with a gray cinder block wall separating this building from the next. No way out unless they tried using their kinetics to catapult to safety. They couldn't pull that off without exposing themselves.

As soon as he knew everyone's condition and Quinn determined a safe place to go next, Tristan would teleport them out.

A coppery scent stung his nose. "Who's hurt?"

"I took part of a blaster hit," Casper grumbled from where he squatted against a wall with his arm tucked against his chest. "I can heal, but it won't be quick."

"That's the most serious injury," Quinn explained. "You ready to teleport, Tristan?"

"Absolutely. Where do we go?"

"How about the park?" Evalle suggested. She often looked like she'd been through a combat zone on a normal day, but she was beat down. Water dripped off the bill of her cap. "Somewhere that's big enough for us to see a threat coming while we catch our breaths and share information."

"Should be good," Tristan agreed. "I didn't see any serious activity when I teleported in."

"Agreed." Quinn pulled Reese to him, a blatant show of protectiveness. "Casper, you good?"

"I'm fine. Let's get out of this hole."

Tristan said, "Quinn, you and Evalle link with me so we can get out of here faster."

Evalle called out, "Done."

Quinn said, "Do it."

Energy from a demon blaster struck behind Tristan, blowing a hole in the wall. He teleported all of them at once before someone took a chunk of cinder block to the head.

When they reappeared, Tristan had them near the underpass of the Park Drive Bridge where graffiti artists had left their creations.

Just as he'd expected, no one was hanging around this place at this time of night with the inclement weather, but they'd have to keep an eye out for the National Guard, too. Beladors supported law enforcement and had to avoid tangling with the human good guys.

Tristan led the way to the underpass of a bridge over vacant land just as rain started coming down again in a steady flow.

Quinn and Reese stopped at one of the thick support structures for the middle of the bridge. Hair plastered to her head, Reese dropped down to sit on the ground. Quinn pulled off his rain jacket and laid it over her against her protests.

Evalle leaned back on the closest graffitied wall with her feet apart. Wet strands of dark hair had broken free of her ponytail.

Casper picked a spot two steps from her and sat hard on the wet ground where finger-thick streams of water cut grooves in the dirt. He let go of his injured arm and dropped his head against the wall.

Tristan had rarely seen that cowboy without a hat, but water leaked from his wet hair, too. With all of them safely in one place, Tristan shoved his hands from his face back like a squeegee to wipe water away.

"What are you doing here, Grady?" Evalle asked, her forehead furrowed in concern.

Tristan turned to find her Nightstalker standing between the two of them.

Quinn glanced over and dismissed Grady to finish speaking to Reese.

Casper didn't stir.

Grady had been old when he died in downtown Atlanta during a bad weather event and normally stayed near Grady Hospital, which is why Evalle started calling him Grady. His flannel shirt and pants hung on the bony frame he'd had at death. Evalle said her favorite Nightstalker could switch from sounding like he'd lived in the hood his whole life to speaking with the clarity of a professor who understood every word in the dictionary. He could do a great impression of Morgan Freeman with his voice.

Arms crossed, Grady pouted, "You never came to see me."

"I'm sorry, but we're running crazy in the city," Evalle explained. "Did you find out anything on Adrianna?" She leaned forward. "Wait. We have a name. The being that took her—"

The old ghoul waved a hand to stop her. "I know, I know. They call that sorry piece Tenebris around the city." Grady's body slowly turned solid, blocking Tristan's view of Evalle. Taking corporeal form normally would not happen unless a Nightstalker traded supernatural intel for shaking hands with a powerful being. Even then, they'd only remain in solid form for ten minutes.

Evalle admitted extending the handshake in the past to allow Grady to stay solid much longer as he hid inside a church to watch his granddaughter's wedding.

Quinn called over to Grady, "Does anyone know what Tenebris is and how he's involved with the Imortiks?"

"Nah." Grady's gray head shook. "But he's been around the city for the last month. All the Nightstalkers avoid him. That one's mean and never offers a handshake."

Sounding disappointed, Evalle said, "That's okay, Grady. Thanks for checking around."

"Hush, now. I ain't done." Grady had turned sideways to Evalle where Tristan could see his grizzled face and skinny arms crossed. "One Nightstalker thinks she saw Tenebris around Gresham Park."

Evalle stood up straight. "How recently?"

"Been about two weeks and she ain't the best with intel," Grady admitted. "But I also heard this Tenebris been seen over by where they mined dirt in that area."

Tristan knew the Gresham Park area was southeast of the city, but couldn't place those pits.

Quinn frowned in deep thought, then asked, "You mean those excavation pits?"

"Yep. That's them."

Tristan had missed running the streets with Evalle and the others.

"Can you keep an eye on those areas and let me know if you see anything else?" Evalle asked.

"I plan to do that. We need our witch."

Tristan could hear the worry in Grady's voice for Adrianna. The old guy cared about Evalle and everyone he considered her friend.

"Can you change back or not?" Evalle asked Grady.

In answer, he became ethereal again and gave her a cocky grin. "I got all kinds of tricks these days."

She laughed as Grady vanished then leaned back on the support beam again.

Tristan would update Daegan on all this when he saw him. He stepped over and propped a hand against one end of the colorful wall of urban art, waiting for Quinn, who still spoke to Reese. She nodded, waving him off.

As Quinn spun around slowly, his gaze bounced over Evalle and Casper before he headed over to Tristan, rubbing his eyes.

Tristan had rarely seen Quinn not put together in a slick suit and with a car waiting, but this Maistir had been a warrior long before he donned a suit from what Evalle had said. Right now, that warrior was running on fumes.

They were all exhausted.

Tristan hadn't been sitting around on his duff, but he felt bad about not being here to help them.

"I'm glad you showed up, but why are you here?" Quinn asked with thanks in his voice.

"I came looking for Daegan. Trey caught me up about Daegan being in a Tribunal meeting where I can't enter uninvited. Then Trey told me your team might welcome my help."

Crossing his arms, Quinn explained, "I hadn't called him yet for backup so I'm glad he sent you to us. As for Daegan, he went to the Tribunal alone after we spoke."

"Why? What happened?"

Quinn lifted the edge of his T-shirt and wiped his face, then let it fall back. "Many things are happening, but I'll answer that one first. We must find Sen and Adrianna, and not just because of the obvious reasons. Tenebris appeared at another location and made a demand." Quinn went on to fill Tristan in on the entire confrontation. "We still do not know what type of being Tenebris is specifically, but he appears very powerful and protective of Imortiks. Daegan hopes Garwyli will be able to help us with the few details we have on Tenebris."

"I can't bring Garwyli here," Tristan mused out loud.

Shifting his stance, Quinn explained, "I'm waiting for Daegan to return before doing anything else beyond tapping our local resources, because Loki also came to the last place we fought the demon maker—"

"Wait. Loki came to *this* world?"

"Yes. Right after Tenebris showed up to deliver his demand."

Tristan couldn't begin to imagine either Sen or Adrianna as an Imortik. Just more reason to find them as soon as possible. "What was Loki up to? I'm sure it was not anything good for us."

Quinn let out a dark laugh. "Hell no. He took four of our Beladors and demanded Sen be returned. Getting those four back is the main reason Daegan is in the Tribunal right now."

Tristan stomped around, disgusted at how hard Daegan fought to save everyone. What a thankless job when it came to the self-centered deities at the Tribunal. He shook his head. "Why do we even deal with the Tribunal? They sure as hell are never willing to offer help."

"Ditto," Evalle agreed.

Casper's light snoring followed. The cowboy wasn't in this conversation.

Sighing as if he made that sound often, Quinn said, "I feel the same most days, but Daegan went to negotiate for our people and make it clear to Loki we are already searching for Sen and Adrianna. Knowing Daegan, he'll point out how Loki and Tribunal allies could lift a finger to wipe out a small army of Imortiks."

Evalle snorted. "I want to see that day."

Tristan turned back to Quinn whose gaze had flicked over to check on Reese again. She stared at the ground with her elbows on her bent knees and her hands wrapped around the back of her neck.

Casper had dropped into a dead sleep, his arms flopped loose at each side of him and his mouth half open. That must be his healing mode. He trusted this group to watch him while he was asleep.

Quinn gripped his neck, rubbing muscles. "If Sen and Adrianna are still in the city, Lanna might be able to find them. I don't want her here until someone can protect her, though."

Tristan gave that a thought. "You might not need her here. Do you have something of Adrianna's she could hold?"

Evalle pushed off the wall. "Good idea. I do." She stepped across the opening to face Tristan and Quinn while digging a set of keys out of a pocket of her jeans. "The keys aren't as important as the woven key chain. Her sister made it for her."

"That should do it," Quinn murmured.

Tristan took the key chain, which showed wear, meaning Adrianna used it often. Strings of different color had been twisted in a specific way with tiny charms of different shapes. Some were silver, some were stones, and some might be bones.

Putting the keys and ring in his pocket, Tristan offered, "I'll stick around until I hear from Daegan. The minute he's out of the Tribunal, I need to teleport to him. Then I can take us both to Treoir and talk to Lanna. Daegan wouldn't allow her here either unless both of us could guard her."

Sounding surprised, Evalle asked, "Are you two saying Daegan *teleported* to the Tribunal on his own? I didn't know that."

Tristan nodded, but replied to Evalle telepathically. *I don't want to talk about the venom still in Daegan's body out in public, but he's got some power back after spending time in Treoir and the babies being born. He just can't do it often or for long distances.*

*Ah, that makes sense.*

Reese lifted her head. "What about ... ah, shoot. I shouldn't ask that out loud." She shook her head, mumbling to herself.

Quinn waved Tristan and Evalle to follow. When he reached Reese, Evalle stepped over to one side and squatted next to Reese.

Casper was still out cold.

Taking in each of their faces, Reese whispered, "Where are we on locating the missing grimoire volumes?"

Tristan replied, "He and Luigsech found one. We have it secure inside Treoir."

Quinn twisted to him with an appalled expression. "In Treoir realm?"

"Uh, huh. I took it there after asking Garwyli where we could hide it for now and he said he had a place to store the volume safely."

"I suppose that's better than another volume being in this world," Quinn admitted.

"Ziggy," Casper said in a groggy voice.

They all turned to him. Evalle asked, "What are you talking about?"

Lifting his bad arm and moving it around, Casper pushed himself up to a better sitting position and cleared his throat. "A baby name. Ziggy."

"That's an awful name unless he's a ukulele player in a street band," Reese replied with a hint of amusement in her voice.

Quinn took up the light-hearted suggestion. "I don't know, sweetheart, it does have a certain panache."

She glared at him, but Quinn's chuckle gave him away. He admitted, "I would never name our son Ziggy."

"Good." She let out a loud sigh and smiled.

"Not when Ackley would be far superior."

She cocked an eyebrow at him. "That sounds like someone coughing."

Tristan felt tension release from the entire team for the first time since he'd found them. He knew Reese and Quinn's child could not survive birth and was pretty sure everyone present understood the future of their unborn baby thanks to the monster that had cursed her. It warmed his heart to hear the team playing Reese and Quinn's name game.

There would be plenty of time to mourn later if they lived that long. He respected how those two wanted to celebrate the baby for as long as they could.

Thinking on what they faced hurt his chest after all both of them had been through.

Daegan's voice boomed in his head. *Tristan, where are ya?*

*With Quinn and his team in Piedmont Park. Where are you?*

*I am atop a very tall buildin' in Atlanta.* He gave Tristan a description of his location.

*I know where that is and can't wait to hear what you're doing up there.*

*Loki teleported me away without notice.*

Of course Loki would treat the dragon king with so little respect. *Let me inform Quinn that I'm leaving, then I'll be there in half a minute.*

Tristan filled in Quinn and asked, "Will you be okay if I go to Daegan now then on to Treoir?"

Quinn quickly agreed. "Yes. Finding out something from Lanna could make the difference in saving Adrianna and Sen. We desperately need actionable information."

Reese pushed herself up to stand with Quinn quickly cupping her arm. "We're all good to roll, right?"

Evalle and Casper agreed.

"Be careful." Tristan brushed a quick look over the group before teleporting to the building to snag Daegan, then continued to Treoir.

They arrived in the middle of the groomed grounds leading up to the castle at twilight. Time and weather were never the same here as anywhere else, but not as jarring this time since it had been dark in Atlanta.

Tristan sensed Daegan's concern and asked, "What's up, boss?"

Daegan cleaned up his wet appearance in a blink. "Loki is bein' more unreasonable than usual."

"That's hard to imagine for someone with his record of transgressions." Then Tristan felt clean and dry clothes on his body as well. "Thanks."

Daegan grunted an acknowledgement. "Our first priority is to speak with Lanna and determine what she needs to help us find Adrianna." He headed for the castle where every guard outside had snapped to attention. "Be at ease."

Even though they relaxed, the guards loosened their stance, they still held themselves with evident pride in their dragon king.

"Evalle gave us something for Lanna." Tristan dug out the key chain as he took the steps to the castle entrance alongside Daegan. "She said Adrianna's sister made the key chain for her."

Daegan paused at the landing. "Well done." He took in the guards all watching them and murmured, "'Tis been difficult for me to be away from my people huntin' grimoire volumes and unable to stand with Quinn and his teams in Atlanta." He lifted a serious gaze to Tristan. "I am blessed to have a strong second-in-command and the support of Beladors again as well as our allies."

Tristan didn't see it the same way. "I don't think you understand how fortunate all of us feel about having you show up after years and years of being screwed over by Macha, Sen, and the Tribunal. Everyone is pulling for you to find the grimoires."

Nodding with humility Tristan had never witnessed on Macha or the Tribunal leaders, Daegan opened the doors and hurried ahead to Garwyli's quarters where they normally encountered Lanna.

Garwyli stepped out of his room. "What is it ya need, dragon?"

Tristan muttered, "Does he have like an alarm that tells him you're here?"

"Do not be insolent, boy," the old druid snapped back.

Tristan made a mental note. *Never talk out loud within a mile of Garwyli.*

Smothering a smile, Daegan said, "I wish to speak with Lanna."

"She be in Brina's solarium."

Tristan asked, "Is she alone so we can speak in private?"

"If she was not, I would have said so," the grumpy druid replied.

Even Daegan frowned. "I apologize for disturbin' ya, druid."

Garwyli lifted a gnarled hand and sent them away. "'Twas not restin'. Go on about yar business." He turned, leaning on his cane and hobbled back inside.

Daegan made an about-face and headed toward the solarium.

Tristan whispered, "Is he okay?"

"The druid is agin'." Daegan gave that off-handed reply in a light tone, but worry lines creased at his eyes.

Tristan let it go. When they reached the solarium, the door was open.

Lanna sat on the window seat. She closed the book she'd been reading and stood up. "Please, come in. I wish to help."

Tristan entered on Daegan's heels, commenting, "You and Garwyli must have the same gift for knowing when someone is coming to see you."

"We do not." She sat on the edge of the window seat again. "We are same in some ways, very different in others."

As if that cleared up any confusion for Tristan? Nope.

Daegan picked up two chairs from a nearby table and plopped them down to face Lanna, taking one for himself.

Tristan sat and waited for Daegan to speak.

"We need help findin' Adrianna."

She frowned. "Why is she lost?"

Daegan said, "She was arguin' with Sen while on top of a parkin' deck in Atlanta when a bein' named Tenebris showed up. Tenebris took both of them."

"Oh, no. Is bad." Lanna's face paled.

"Yes. But Reese sat in the last place Adrianna had and followed her with remote viewin'. She thinks both of them are still in Atlanta, not another realm. Evalle had somethin' important of Adrianna's she sent for ya to hold."

"Yes. Is good. Very good, if is something Adrianna holds dear."

Tristan produced the keys and key ring, explaining how Adrianna's sister had made it for her.

Relief spiked through the room from Lanna. "To make a gift with hands is always most important. Is filled with love." She extended an open palm to accept his offering.

Wrapping her fingers around the key ring specifically with the keys poking out, Lanna closed her eyes. After a few seconds, her breathing calmed significantly.

Tristan and Daegan made no sounds as she remained that way for two minutes.

When she drew in a deep breath and opened her eyes, she said, "Very powerful majik hides her."

"You can't find her?" Tristan asked, unable to hide his disappointment.

Her glare scolded him. "You must learn more patience."

Tristan blew out a hard breath. "Sorry. I'm in a hurry for all of this to be done."

"I understand, but does not change what I can or cannot do."

"I get that," Tristan grumbled. "I just keep hoping something will break loose."

Addressing both of them, she said, "I do not know exact location, but I feel it is not far from place for watching movies. Sometimes a place like market where people have tables."

"Did you see a name on the theater?" Tristan asked since he might know the location better than Daegan. He didn't understand the market part.

"Something about stars. Is not inside. Movies shown outside on big screen. People sit in cars."

Daegan turned to Tristan, but did not push him.

"I haven't had a chance to tell you, boss, but Evalle's Nightstalker said he'd heard Tenebris had been seen by the ghouls around Gresham Park, but none of them mentioned a theater." Tristan searched his mind for that area. He snapped his fingers. "Starlight Theater. They have flea markets there sometimes, too."

"'Tis a start," Daegan said, though still sounding deeply worried.

Lanna sighed softly. "I do not know those places in Atlanta. Is good everyone works together." She stared at nothing for a moment, then continued, "What I sense is much power around Adrianna. Not *her* power. Also, Witchlock is not happy."

Tristan glanced at Daegan who seemed no happier than when he'd entered. "Boss?"

"I appreciate all ya can share, Lanna. Do ya have any idea if we will see Adrianna soon?"

She slowly shook her head. "Everything in vision stops fast, then nothing. I do not know what that means. I may have more if I sleep and a dream comes to me, or maybe nothing again."

Tristan sent to Daegan telepathically, *What if we take Lanna close to the location?*

Daegan turned sharply to Tristan. *No.*

Lanna grumbled, "I tell everyone is rude to talk in heads in front of me."

Tristan smiled at her. "You just don't like that we can do it and you can't."

She gasped. "Not true."

"Yes, it is." Tristan laughed then turned serious again. "But I agree. I was rude. I wanted to ask Daegan something without having to leave and come back just to be polite because we're in a hurry."

Daegan explained, "He wished to know if we should take ya to the area in Atlanta ya mentioned to see if that would help ya figure out more. I would prefer ya not to be in that city unless we have no other choice."

"Is not bad idea, but I would tell you if I could do more there," she admitted.

"Fair enough." Standing, Tristan asked, "What now?"

Daegan lifted up, too. "I just sent Quinn the information Lanna gave us. We can do no more than him and his team to find Adrianna. I must return the staff to the oracle before continuing to hunt grimoire volumes."

Lanna jumped up and angled her head at Daegan. "Did you find Luigsech?"

"Yes. She is safe."

Tristan appreciated the fact that Daegan trusted him to have done his job even when Tristan had yet to inform Daegan of all that had transpired once he went for Luigsech.

"Will you take her to hunt with you?" Lanna asked.

Daegan's mood visually darkened. It wasn't enough that he carried all the problems of his people on his shoulders. Tristan had seen the emotional damage now piled there, thanks to Luigsech.

Daegan sounded polite, but everyone in the room knew he was irritated. "No. That woman betrayed me, Lanna. I do not trust someone once they have proven unworthy of such a gift as trust."

Lips pressed together, she stared at him until Daegan asked, "What? What is it ya are achin' to say?"

"Is not my business." She shrugged.

Daegan sounded close to the last of his patience slipping from his grasp. "I am comin' to realize ya say that when ya feel I am not fully informed. Why should I speak to Luigsech again?"

"To take her with you to find grimoire volumes." Lanna made that sound as if it should be clear to anyone.

Daegan scratched the back of his head, acting ready to get the hell out of there.

"I shall think on it," Daegan muttered.

Not believing a word of that, Tristan said, "Thanks, Lanna." He turned for the door.

"Yes, thank ya, lass. I am always glad for your help." Daegan walked away with Tristan.

"You ask for information you do not always use," Lanna replied with an edge of irritation

Shoving a look at Daegan, Tristan wished he could yank the frustration from his boss. He offered, "Want to teleport from here?"

"No. I wish to walk a moment." Without turning, Daegan again called over his shoulder, "Thank ya again."

"You are welcome, but you are not understanding my words."

Dropping his head in defeat, Daegan asked, "What else do ya wish to say?"

"Nothing."

When Tristan glanced at her, Lanna lifted her chin in a prim look. "Garwyli tells me I must allow others to find their way. You will figure this out yourself."

Hell. Even Tristan had no idea what she was getting at, so Daegan had to be close to losing his mind in this conversation. He continued walking and Daegan caught up.

Once they were outside, Daegan strode down the steps and out toward the trees.

Did he want to teleport from out there?

Tristan left him to his thoughts until Daegan asked, "Am I bein' difficult with Lanna?"

"Nope. I didn't get what she was saying either. Whatever it was, Garwyli must have drawn the line for conversations with you in particular. The druid knows her best by now and I'm thinking he's trying to get her to stop putting her nose in where it doesn't belong."

Tristan got a telepathic message from Trey. He held up a hand. "Wait a second." He replied to Trey. *I was talking to someone. Start again.*

*I've got a woman who has to talk to you. Says her name is Casidhe.*

Just what Tristan did not need at the moment. She must have remembered Trey's number and used the hotel phone. Before leaving her, he'd found a smashed mobile phone of no use in her backpack when he snatched the scepter. Daegan sure as hell didn't need an upset female on his case right after talking to Lanna. He sent back to Trey, *Tell her I can't be reached. I'm busy.*

Clearly not happy to be in the middle, Trey grumbled, *She said to expect you to say that and to tell you if Daegan does not recover the next grimoire volume, it was on you.*

Tristan cursed, drawing Daegan's attention. "Luigsech is trying to get in touch with you."

Daegan's chest rumbled with what sounded like Ruadh's displeasure. His dragon couldn't be happy about what Casidhe had done. "Why? What does she want from me *now*?"

Someone once told Tristan to be angry meant you still had feelings for the person who had wronged you. No matter what he thought, Casidhe still mattered to Daegan and the betrayal was tearing apart his boss ... his friend.

The best Tristan could do was explain the situation and support the man he admired in any decision. "Luigsech claims it's about finding the next grimoire volume. I haven't had a chance to tell you how she begged me to convince you to talk to her. I think she'll say anything to plead her case to you about being secretly attached to the ice dragon clan. I can have Trey let her know we're out of reach." Tristan hesitated. He couldn't make Daegan's decisions.

Daegan's jaw twitched with anger he would not shed any time soon.

Swallowing past a tight throat, Tristan pushed the words out. "What do you want to do, boss?"

# CHAPTER 16

PREPARING FOR WHATEVER TENEBRIS DID to her, Adrianna stretched her fingers slowly on the hand where she could call up Witchlock. She silently apologized to Sen, but maybe a demigod could survive unleashing her power. She wouldn't bet on it. Without ever having called upon the full power of Witchlock, she could only make a wild guess.

Tenebris did his little two-step walk again and turned to her. "You aren't concerned about becoming an Imortik?"

"Are you waiting on theatrics?" Adrianna offered what she hoped sent the message she was not impressed.

He wondered if she was concerned?

Her heart wanted to climb out of her chest and hide in the corner at the thought of being restrained while an Imortik was dropped on top of her. But she had no intention of giving him the pleasure of knowing she sat here contemplating how to end her life and spare the world an Imortik empowered with Witchlock.

If only she'd had one more hour to talk to Isak. To kiss him goodbye. To hold him and tell him how much he meant to her. To say goodbye to her friends.

She drew in a ragged breath, fingers ready to open and turn Witchlock loose when all hope was gone.

Tenebris cocked his head as if she'd just shown him something he wanted to see.

What had she done?

He crossed his arms, never taking his eyes off her. "I am not just going to bring an Imortik in here to take you."

Did he think that sounded reassuring?

"No, no, no." He chuckled. "If you knew me, you'd know how much I enjoy a hunt."

She stilled, trying to read between his words. "What are you talking about?"

"I will release you to run and do your best to outwit the Imortik."

She studied him, waiting for a punchline to this joke. "Besides that bit about enjoying a hunt, which I don't buy, why would you do this and risk losing another Imortik?"

His next laugh came out sounding as if she'd said something clever in a polite conversation. "I really do enjoy a hunt, but this would additionally allow me to observe an Imortik going up against an equal opponent. The more I learn from a match such as this one, the better I can plan for how our future army can defeat the enemy."

She lifted a shoulder to shrug, but suffered a spike of pain for her effort with hands shackled above her head. "Or you'll see how easily they can be destroyed."

"I do like your attitude, witch. It will make this exercise so much more enjoyable."

"But you're not going to give me any chance to escape, so why should I fight hard at all?" She would, though. If he uncuffed her, she had a chance of escaping.

Not much of one, but she'd take one over none.

"Killing the Imortik is possible, though not probable," he mused out loud. "But you are incorrect. I understand the drive to survive creates the best motivation in a battle. For that reason, I will give you a chance to escape if you can reach a specific point. You will be far more powerful outside these walls. For that reason, I would not pursue you right away."

She huffed out a breath. "You think I'm going to believe that after you popped in once before and captured me?"

"Of course. I will have gained all I need from this experiment and require a new test subject. I'd just pick up that human named Isak, which Sen informed me about."

She yanked forward hard against her chains. Her throat tightened with emotion and threatened to strangle her. "Touch him and I will kill you slowly and painfully."

Tenebris stepped back quickly then caught himself and moved forward again. "I had not believed Sen when he told me of your relationship with a human. That made no sense if your power is as great as he claimed, but ... I have come across stranger pairings."

Her eyes burned. She had to get out of here now. This insane being would go after Isak regardless of what happened. Her power pooled in her chest and spread to her limbs.

"Do not use your power or the chase is off!" Tenebris shouted.

She'd like to think she'd heard fear in his voice, but that had to be her mind playing tricks. She'd managed her emotions the entire time she hunted for her sister while Veronika had held her twin captive. She'd kept her head together when she had to take Witchlock, knowing her sister would die.

After all that, her heart screamed like a crazed animal at the idea of losing Isak. She had to look as rabid as she felt.

Isak's endearing face filled her mind.

She couldn't allow Tenebris to get near him. That was the only reason she started taking deep breaths, determined to jump on any opening he gave her to run.

Tenebris held himself with arrogance, but wariness drifted into his gaze. Then gone again.

She hoped he feared her, regardless of how unrealistic that might be with her power acting erratic. "I thought you wanted a hunt. Changed your mind already, Tenebris? Don't think your Imortik can win?" she taunted, hoping she'd be able to stand if given the chance.

His mouth twisted into an incensed smile. "This will be more fun than I had anticipated. Pay attention, witch. When I release you, I will open a passage from this room. You must find your own way to a tall mirror, which can be used to pass through to the human world again. Finding the mirror will be obvious *if* you make it that far."

"What about Sen?" She had to ask.

"You should worry about your own skin. Sen would."

"I'm not like Sen to turn my back on someone else."

This time, Tenebris offered a genuine smile. "I would. Everyone is like me when given a choice to live or die. Still, you will not die, but become a powerful soldier in our Imortik army once you lose."

Before she could come up with any witty reply, Tenebris

lifted a hand and spoke muffled words toward a wall where an opening appeared a foot taller than him. The cuffs fell from her arms at the same moment.

Tenebris had vacated the room.

She had this vision of jumping up and running, but merely lowering her arms took some work. Then she massaged them to bring feeling back. It finally happened, stinging her arms with needles of pain.

When she finally reached her feet, she stepped through the opening on shaky legs to find a dark hallway. A stingy light burned maybe thirty yards away. No right or left turn choice, so she moved carefully.

Had Tenebris set traps for her?

Would it stop her from moving? No.

She called up her cloaking. Nothing around her changed. Everywhere she looked was still in sharp focus.

No cloaking. What else could she not do in this place?

Drawing in a deep breath, she choked on the stagnant air.

Why would there be a mildew smell as well as an odor of past bodies staining the air in this place?

She'd reached halfway down the passage when a deep-throated growl rumbled behind her. Turning to sidestep allowed her to see ahead and behind while still moving.

Growling echoed louder.

Taking one step after another, she glanced to each end. On the next look behind her, three glowing eyes at the height of her shoulder peered out from the black shadows and were advancing on her.

Stay and fight or run?

If she ran, she might end up in that open area with something worse.

Hot fetid breath blew past her nose.

Opening her hand, she flicked a look at Witchlock. The power spun as if bouncing in an uneven blob the size of a golf ball, but one that would not roll. She brought her hand around to point at the beast.

A hideous howl shook the air.

Red eyes lunged at her.

Adrianna called out a spell she'd been practicing with Witchlock and closed her eyes.

Light flashed bright.

When she peeked, the creature was frozen in midmotion, standing on four legs with dingy yellow fangs in stark contrast to the black maw holding them. Glowing eyes filled a hairless head and shoulders wider than a rhinoceros, both of which had probably been covered in the coarse gray fur still jutting out from behind the shoulders to its hindquarters.

The spell was supposed to kill whatever chased her.

Would it make any difference if she upped her mojo next time?

How long would that monster remain stuck?

She was in new territory with corrupted Witchlock.

Every breath she released came out in noisy exhales. With a glance, she risked a look at the end of the hall. The puny light had not extinguished. This place smelled of stale food, body odors, and ... death.

Moving forward again, she got within ten feet of the room at the end when a horrid wail erupted behind her.

Pounding loud as a stampeding elephant pushed her to move faster on aching legs.

She rushed into the room and searched for a way out. Nothing. She stood in a forty-foot-square space surrounded by strange blurred walls the color of dirt and dead leaves as if an artist had lost interest and smudged a drawing.

The room smelled of more rot and bodily fluids. What was this place?

Heavy thudding from the hallway increased.

Three stationary odd-shaped objects stood along the far wall and in the corner. Was that furniture waiting to be designed or carved?

A rusted black steel door that had been bashed in repeatedly and clung to corroded hinges offered her the only way forward.

She took a step.

One inanimate blob began to move and flex.

The putty-colored shape turned into a squatty being with the body and head of a two-hundred-pound troll. Tall ears stuck out each side and pocked greenish skin covered the creature.

Could it be a golem?

With those empty eye sockets, she doubted a real troll had just come to life. The downturned mouth opened wide as a car hood, showing off two rows of fangs. The creature made the noise of a wounded grizzly caught in a trap. Four fingers on each hand grew sickle-shaped claws. Dragging one leg then the next, it moved toward her.

Guttural growls rounded the corner.

Adrianna flipped around, backing up and opening her Witchlock hand.

The three-eyed beast lunged for her.

Screeching, the eyeless troll dove forward at the same time.

She could only strike one. Stabbing her hand toward the open jaws of the larger threat, she shouted words from her practice with Witchlock.

The troll bellowed, "Mine," right before it landed on the three-eyed monster, slashing claws to open bloody gashes.

At the same moment, Witchlock's power streamed from her hand and raced over both threats.

Energy sizzled and brightened, then fizzled.

Again, not what she needed from Witchlock.

What had happened to her deadly ancient power? She limped on the ankle she'd injured in one of the last attacks and considered how much longer she could survive.

Mixed noises of howls and screams pummeled the air.

Witchlock had not destroyed either one.

While the troll and super-sized beast fought each other, she hurried across the room and yanked the door open.

# CHAPTER 17

BRYNHILD WALKED ALONG COBBLED STREETS beneath early morning light peeking through trees on her left. The stone buildings and stone paths on her right were part of what Joavan called the Loire Valley. This area filled her with a sense of home where some villagers lived a simpler, if not more primitive, way of life.

Though she had seen exquisite hotels and homes once Joavan brought her here using his majik, she was not interested in those places. Had he not used his Faetheen way of traveling, he claimed the trip would have taken over an hour, maybe longer.

She did not want to stand out, but neither did she wish to live among so many people in the finer areas.

"I think you're going to like this next place a lot," Joavan said, sounding overly enthusiastic. He wore casual gray slacks and a white button-down shirt open at the neck with long sleeves turned up at his wrists.

The white showed off the golden skin on his muscular forearms.

He tossed her a look full of question.

"I *might* like something if this place is of greater size than the last one." Though she had to admit she appreciated this new area they'd entered away from the main flow of traffic and people.

He held his hands out, always moving them when he spoke. "I could have found you many spectacular locations, but that will not suit your purpose. Keep in mind, I have never shopped for a residence in this human land before and it is still very early. I must wait for more property owners to wake up if you do not care for this one. But I truly think you will be nicely surprised when you see it."

"Mm-hmm." She could understand his thinking, but she did

not find searching for a place enjoyable. She had lived in her father's castle since birth and had never considered finding another home. Her sisters talked of going to start a life with a man worthy of their rank, which would have required their mate to own a castle as a minimum.

Not her. She'd been content to take her fun with a man who interested her for the night, then leave running a castle to her parents and sisters as she practiced and battled with warriors.

"We're getting close," Joavan murmured, his gaze anxiously rushing over the rough stone wall on her right, which stood as high as three men stacked. He announced, "This is the one."

She followed him up a brief incline with rectangular stones arranged in a smooth walkway that had been here many years, but not for as long as the cave houses.

Workers had carved some of the stone exteriors with interesting entrances.

"Yes. This one is very nice," he encouraged as they walked between the raw mountain exterior with bushes and vines growing across the top. On her left, a knee-high stone wall stretched for twenty feet then opened into a larger space in front of a tall entrance. A black iron gate had been installed four feet deep, allowing an arched opening tall above her head.

She could see little except darkness beyond the gate, but a deep breath told her flowers grew nearby and someone baked bread.

This was nothing like her father's castle, but she ran her hand over the stone, feeling comforted by that small similarity. So much better than hotels and buildings in the city, which had no meaning to her.

She put a hand on Joavan's arm as he lifted a key for the door. "This is nice, but small as well."

Gifting her with a smile of bright white teeth, he said, "Just wait."

She released his arm. "Go ahead."

When he unlocked a tall gate of hammered iron, the metal squealed in protest when he held it open. She walked past him into a dark area where the ceiling dipped too close to her height for comfort. "Joavan, you waste time I must use better."

"Patience, dove. I really think you shall love this one."

She grumbled, "I truly believe you overestimate your power of persuasion."

He tipped toward her and kissed her cheek. "I do enjoy surprising you."

Unconvinced, she followed him through the low-ceiling area as light shined from the other end. The ceiling began to rise above her and the space opened out. Ground beneath her sandals reached out past the covering, extending twenty feet in a half circle which ended at a drop-off.

Passing through into sunlight again, she continued to the edge of the cliff where the land fell away for hundreds of feet. More stunning was the bowl-shaped mountain location this cliff perched within three stories below the peak. The mountain walls curved away from her to the right, continuing around until meeting her on the left again. Over to the far right, a waterfall fell from an opening halfway down the mountain into a pool of water covering a third of the bottom. That connected to a narrow creek, which took a crooked path and disappeared either in the ground or into the base of the mountain.

"I admit this is a beautiful view, but where is the house?" she asked.

He had that smug look as the cat who finally caught a bird it had stalked all day. "Do you see any way for someone to observe you standing here, dove, unless they are flying over?"

Taking her time to search all around, she shook her head. "No."

He turned and pointed at another ledge of similar height from the valley as the one where she stood. "See that ledge? It's as large as the one we stand upon." He angled back to her. "Think you can shift into your mighty dragon, then cloak and fly us there?"

She had to admit he'd piqued her curiosity and she saw no harm in taking flight in this hidden spot. "Stand back."

Hurrying away, he waited near the cave they had walked through.

Her dragon could not wait to fly again and burst from her body quickly. Swinging her big head to Joavan, she spoke in her dragon's voice. "You will not fly on my back."

Dejection hit his face. "You will not take me with you?"

"Why can you not travel there the way we traveled to the mountains?"

His eyes strayed from hers in embarrassment. "I do not like to admit this, but I must not use that ability often." He dropped his head back to stare up at her. "This is why the amulet and diamond are so important. I have not been back to my world often enough. I could not stay long when I took Daegan's sister there. I can use my gift to travel there, but we may need me strong to travel greater distances at some point."

That might be a lie, but she would test him soon to find out. "Walk to the edge of the cliff and turn to face where we are going. Then open your arms out to each side."

He didn't seem excited over that idea. "What do you plan to do?"

"My dragon will not allow you to ride. We will fly out and circle around to pick you up. I will be invisible. Do not move once you find a spot to stand."

He chewed on his thumbnail while taking in what he had to do.

"If you wish to join me, go now." Her dragon hopped and took off with wings wide to catch the air as her cloaking fell into place. She flapped slowly, making a wide arc around the quiet area. Her dragon approved of this, which meant a lot to Brynhild.

She and her dragon had to both be happy.

As her dragon came around, Joavan's slender form stood rigid as a corpse with skin just as pale. His arms were sticking out straight as arrows.

Her dragon swooped down, snatching him up.

He yelped and clutched the huge claws holding him. He also rattled off many words, which sounded like a frantic prayer born of terror.

Joavan passed his first test to prove his trust in her.

The question was if she could ever trust him.

At the next cliff landing place, her dragon slowed and gently dropped Joavan as far from the edge as possible. The power of flying sent him to his knees and rolling a bit, but he jumped up grinning and waving.

Such a strange man. He was beginning to grow on her.

As her dragon slowed to land, Joavan realized he was in the way and backpedaled into a dark hole.

On the first step, Brynhild dropped the cloaking then shifted into her human body. She clothed herself again in the comfortable dark-blue pants of silk and a filmy yellow top with sleeves ending at her elbows. The sandals she liked very much came last. Women from her time would be awed by clothing today. She called up her new favorite bone necklace.

Where had he gone? "*Joavan!*"

"I am here." He came striding out of the dark shadow, dusting off his clothes, and kept coming until he pulled her to him for a real kiss.

Feeling generous, she allowed it and had to admit she enjoyed the pleasure of having someone with her to do so much.

Stepping back, he rubbed his hands together. "Now, I will show you a home unlike any other out here."

He walked over and lifted a box he flicked a button on and light bloomed from the end.

"What is that?"

"Flashlight. Once we are inside, we'll have light fixtures you can turn on easily like you do at the hotel room." He led the way up a soft rise to another heavy-iron gated opening. After producing a key for this one, he walked her through a narrow hallway to yet one more gate.

Her eyes adjusted to the dim lighting, allowing her to see past this second gate.

A giant room on the other side appeared to be larger than the cavern where Cathbad had held her prisoner. That bastard.

Lights hanging on wires from the ceiling and cut off at different lengths charmed the stone interior. Several pieces of furniture were shrouded with material. She saw many possibilities for this room.

She asked, "How do the lights work? You said the hotel uses ... " She held up a hand, stopping him from filling in the word. She would not fit in if she failed to learn the language. "Electricity."

It sounded like majik to her.

He nodded and smiled with pride at her determination to learn everything. "I engaged an onsite generator, which feeds the electricity. I can show you all of those things when you want, but I am thinking you will have someone handle the everyday household functions."

"Yes."

When they reached the center of the room, Joavan spun around with his arms out. "Is this not spectacular?"

"It is very nice, Joavan. So far, I am impressed."

Dropping to his knees in a dramatic way, he held his hands up in the air. "Thank you, universe, for allowing me to live long enough to hear those words."

She swatted his head gently. "Do not pat yourself so much on the back. You may hurt your arm."

"It would be worth it." He stood, a wide grin in place. "Now, I will show you the rest of the rooms and kitchen, then we go down to your treasure room."

Following him from one spot to the next, she admired the fine work done by craftsmen with an artistic heart. Now she began to think strategically about servants and managing this place. As wonderful as it seemed, this place was of no use to her if she had to do everything herself.

She needed a squire family of her own, but not one that lived here with her. They must go home at night.

"What, dove?"

"How would a human reach this house?"

"There are two tunnels, one short and one long, to the outside world. Both are protected by gates."

She complained, "Why so many gates? I do not like opening doors. I had people for that duty at one time." She crossed her arms.

"I specifically searched for somewhere with iron gates. If you have majik to use, you could put protective spells or wards on them, but leave the rest of the area free. That way, if you open a gate and leave it open for you, all is fine. But once you infuse it with majik to work as you wish the gate will prevent anyone else except you from coming in."

Once again, Joavan proved his value. He had a wise thought. "That would not stop you, Joavan, if you used your travel majik."

"I will tell you how to ensure even I cannot enter."

She found that surprising and refreshing, but not necessarily believable.

As if he'd read her thoughts, he said, "I see you have doubts, but I will show you. We must be honest to work together. I have tried to prove my trust. I will not betray you and try to steal from you. I do not need your hoard, only your help in retrieving my treasure."

She found it difficult to argue with his simple terms. She would have to think on all he had said and done so far. "Show me this last room."

Wise man to realize she no longer wished to talk on the trust subject. He opened the gate and walked a few steps before lifting a torch from the wall to light with his majik.

As he began descending, he would light other torches on the way. Every ten steps, they would turn and go down another ten.

She counted eleven sets of steps before he walked away from the stairs. She saw parts of the room, but much of it was very dark.

He paused, staring into the darkness. "This will be simpler with a few changes. Please take this and stand still." He handed her the small torch.

Then he walked into the room and called out strange words. They were not of any language she had heard, nor did they sound French.

Light burst from flames in fifty places along the walls and at different heights from six to thirty feet above the floor. The ceiling was even higher.

She sucked in a breath. "This is exceptional."

The massive room went much deeper as lights appeared along the far walls. She strode across the wide expanse, taking quite a few steps to reach the other side before the floor dropped four steps to another large area.

Joavan followed. "There are pockets of areas way up you'll find as you explore. Some are twenty feet deep. Many places to hide things. Will this hold your hoard?"

She took her time tapping a finger on her cheek.

"Brynhild?" Joavan prompted in a worried voice.

He had been tortured enough. She spun to him and dropped her hand on his shoulder. "You have done well."

He put his arms around her, drawing her closer to hug and share her joy.

And she was happy.

She had felt untethered from this world since waking up in that miserable ice pond. She might never have wanted to leave her father's castle, but at this moment she liked the idea of her own stronghold.

That selfish Herrick had taken over their ancestral castle, but it did not belong to him. Or Skarde.

This place would belong to her. She pulled away from Joavan and stepped down into the next area where wooden casks had been stacked on their sides and piled four-high against a wall. "What is in there?"

"Oh, fine wine, dove. The last owner lived here long ago and enjoyed different wines from all over the world."

"He did not take them with him?"

"Evidently not. He may have died while away. He left and never returned, then five years later a woman who cooked for him and lived nearby received a letter giving her authority to sell the house. As nice a gift as that was, this is not an easy house to sell. Not many people wish to go to so much trouble to walk the tunnels."

Excited to move her hoard, she asked, "How soon can I have this?"

"I used my persuasive powers you mocked earlier and took possession of it today for you. We need to pay the woman, but right now she believes she convinced me to move in and give it a try for a week."

This man had to be watched, but she had doubts about his persuasion working on her only because her dragon would attack anyone trying to use majik on her after Cathbad.

"I want to go to my hoard now."

"With me?" He sounded truly surprised.

"Yes. You must take me close enough, then I will fly us in."

"In your dragon claws again?" he asked with hesitance.

She sent him a censoring glance. "Do not be such baby."

It had to be true about how much he needed her help, because he said, "Fine. Where are we going?"

When she described the location and how to find it, his eyes widened. "That's a long way to use my travel majik. It took me many hours to regain energy after our trip to the Caucasus."

She started to tease him then recalled that trip. "How did Daegan and Tristan find Herrick's mountain?" She had been so anxious to go when Joavan told her he could locate Daegan, she'd wanted to leave immediately.

"Daegan has people with special gifts. I will guess that young woman with him in the mountains had something to do with locating Herrick's land."

"Do you speak of the woman standing with Herrick?" Brynhild's voice burned with anger.

"No. That's the woman I helped Daegan rescue from TÅµr Medb by glamouring Tristan. I meant the younger woman standing *with* Daegan and Tristan."

Pondering all he'd said, Brynhild asked, "We may need her."

"What for? We already have Jennyver."

These were the moments when Brynhild lost patience. "Jennyver is of no help in locating something. I need someone who can find ... something important to me if it is in this world."

"I see what you're saying." Jovan cupped his chin while thinking. "That could be difficult if Daegan keeps gifted followers in Treoir realm to protect them. Allow me to do some snooping and find out who would be best for what you need. It would help to know exactly what you're missing."

She saw no risk in sharing this with him. "I have a shield with my hoard. My sword should have been with that shield. I need someone who can find the sword."

He walked a few steps and suggested, "Give me a day before we go for your hoard and I will find out who this person is with the majik gift you need and how Daegan uses him or her, or if there is more than one who could help."

Stopping in mid-stride, she warned, "I do not want to be seen around Daegan's people. He would set a trap for me."

"Not you, dove." Joavan stopped and gently grasped her upper arm, pulling her to him. He kissed her slowly. "I would never put you in danger. I will use less majik to travel alone and move on my own. If I find this person, I will bring him or her to you once I am sure their majik is not a danger to either of us."

She enjoyed the heat he stirred and moved closer to him. She ran a hand over his hair. "Do this and I will reward you in more ways than a man has ever imagined."

He grinned. "I warn you, I have a powerful imagination."

# CHAPTER 18

DAEGAN HAD NEVER FELT SO undecided.
     A single bulb thirty feet away cast enough light to brighten this walkway of the hotel. He'd prefer the darkness beyond where he stood.

He had to do what was best for his people and the world. That was the only reason he stood outside the hotel room where Tristan had left Luigsech in Galway after teleporting her away from the griffon vulture.

Or was it?

She could have been ripped apart. She could have died.

He pounded on the door.

After the sound of a lock being unclicked, the door opened. Luigsech leaned to her right, her full lips parted in shock and hair in damp waves. The fresh scent of her bath wafted to him.

Damn his heart for the traitorous fast beating. He had to keep this all about the grimoire volumes.

Nothing else.

"Daegan?" Surprise gave her voice a hitch.

Determined to get through this, he forced his face to remain stern and give away nothing. "Do ya have the location for a second volume or not?"

He seriously doubted she had such information, since he had one volume tucked away in Treoir and the other two were most likely in Atlanta.

Pink tinted the smooth skin on her face. She nibbled her lip and her forehead tightened with worry. She started, "Not exactly, I—"

"Lyin' again." He started walking away from the door.

"*Daegan!*"

He spun around and confusion banging around inside his

head brought out a snarl. "I have no desire to play this game. Ya call me here then have nothin' to offer. I will not waste another second dealin' with ya."

She stepped out with fisted hands set at her hips. She wore dark pants and a tan long-sleeved pullover, none of which hid her shapely body. She warned, "Walk away before you hear what I do have to say and you'll have to figure out what to tell your people when you fail to deliver those volumes."

His insides shook, fighting to keep the anger trapped there, struggling against the need to touch her, and forcing himself to not foolishly pass up a chance for a volume. The betrayer with a sexy mouth had a point. He would shove his pride aside any day to protect his people.

Standing out here speaking of the grimoire volumes in raised voices was beyond foolish.

He walked back to her door, not slowing.

Her eyes widened. She backed up quickly as if a raging bull barreled toward her. In truth, his frame of mind fit that description.

As soon as he stepped inside, he kicked the door shut and crossed his arms. "I shall hear ya out if your next words convince me I did not make a mistake to travel here."

Holding stubbornly still, her ferocious gaze shouted she would not be pushed around. She combed agitated fingers through her wild curls, drawing his attention to where he should not be focused. Did he still want to touch her? Yes.

Would he? No.

"Let me get this out, then we can talk," she started. "The oracle came to me—"

"She came to ya? Why should I believe this when we climbed a mountain to find her last time?"

Luigsech's lips flattened with a fierce expression. "This will go *much* faster if you can hold your tongue long enough to hear all of it, which will answer your last question."

They locked into a staring contest he held as long as he could before glancing past her to look through the window. "I shall wait. For now."

"How generous of you, your highness," she snapped at him.

His lips twitched, but he ordered his mouth to behave. To be honest, he had missed her sharp tongue.

"Now, as I was sayin'." She fidgeted with her hands rubbing her forehead then scratching her arm as she walked back and forth. "The oracle has come to me *twice*. The first time was in the hotel room Tristan set up for me." She paused and shot a glance at Daegan. "I did not get a chance to tell you about that before we separated again."

He grunted just to let her know he was listening even if his gaze strayed from her.

She mumbled something he would call a curse. The termagant still had a temper.

"The oracle came to me the second time in this hotel room earlier today." She stared at the wall, muttering, "Hadn't thought about that similarity." She shook her head. "Can't make any difference."

Daegan's heart calmed down to a normal pace as he allowed her to sort through her thoughts out loud.

Luigsech explained, "The oracle appeared both times in a holographic or ethereal type of form. I'm not sure that's exactly right because she said she was travelin' by astral projection."

Daegan knew of how one could appear in holographic form as Garwyli and Lanna had when they came to him in the Ghost Castle. He'd never heard it specifically called astral projection. Perhaps it was the same.

Turning to walk back across the short distance Luigsech had claimed as her territory, she explained, "The oracle is upset with us for not continuin' to hunt the grimoire volumes."

"Why?" Daegan asked before he could stop himself from showing interest.

"I honestly don't know. I asked her that and she just got mouthy with me. On the second visit here, she pretty much said we must not care about people and the world, because in her eyes we had quit."

"What has that to do with the staff? Does she know we recovered it?" he asked.

"I have no idea why she has such an interest in the grimoire volumes. Yes, she knows we have the staff. I had it in Tristan's hotel room when she came to see me in Atlanta. I offered it to her then. She snapped at me that she couldn't carry it in astral form or whatever ... cranky woman."

Daegan had to look down to hide the amusement in his eyes. His chest felt stretched too tight from the pain of Luigsech's betrayal while his heart kept telling him to give her a second chance. He'd never done so when betrayed in the past.

Living inside his mind right now was torment. He missed this woman more than he could put in words. Just being close to her and not touching was driving him insane.

This had to end. Soon.

If not, he might drag her to the bed and toss her on her back to ...

"Are you even *listenin'*?" Luigsech demanded, sounding ... hurt.

By the gods, why would he be made to feel sorry? He'd done nothing wrong. He groused, "I am listenin'."

She shoved her bottom lip up hard against her top lip in an angry frown. "Then tell me what I just said."

He'd walked into that trap by lying. Much as he wanted to tell her she made no sense, he admitted, "I might have missed the last part."

He could take her anger better than the look of hope clinging to her gaze. If he spoke a word, it would betray his mixed feelings so he said nothing, pushing her to continue.

She quickly glanced away. "I was sayin' that the oracle will not accept the scepter or share more information unless we are together. I promise you, that was *not* my idea. She claims we have six days left to prevent the Imortiks from takin' over the world. Does that time frame mean anythin' to you?"

Lowering his arms, he took in Luigsech more closely. She spoke the truth about the oracle. He heard it in her voice and saw it in her body.

Six days.

That was the time he had left to save Devon, Renata, and the others who had been possessed at the very first. He still held hope that Renata had not succumbed during her capture.

He had no choice but to lower a wall and find out more. "Yes, six days is important."

Luigsech made a noise that sounded like relief. She clearly had not been sure he would meet with her or listen to her. When they first went hunting for the grimoire volumes, she had only done so to find her friend, Fenella.

The one who betrayed Luigsech, according to Tristan.

Luigsech no longer had that reason to help hunt the grimoire volumes. That meant she was offering to do so when she could simply walk away and leave all this behind.

Daegan could sympathize over someone close having hurt her. Were all those involved with Herrick enemies?

Was betraying each other part of who they were?

She snapped her fingers. "*Hey!* It's time to decide, Daegan."

He jerked his head up. "Decide on *what*?"

Luigsech clenched her jaw hard enough for muscles to flex. "On if you are willin' to work with me to save your people and this world from Imortiks." She held her arms loose at her sides, ready for battle.

Telling her no would be the correct answer if he only considered his peace of mind.

Daegan had to come to terms on all of this. Hadn't he been raised by a king who said to never bring an enemy inside the fortress while at war? To never trust anyone once they betrayed him?

What would his father think if he stood in Daegan's boots at this moment?

His father had always put the safety of his people first. His father had never backed away from a battle and had been a brilliant negotiator, who had maintained peace for all the years he'd ruled prior to Daegan being born.

His father believed if people followed him that he had to be willing to lay down his life along with his followers to defeat an enemy.

If Daegan were honest with himself, his pride had been greatly injured over being duped about his sister. He could set aside his pride and join up with this female, but he would have to keep a close watch on her the whole time.

Plus, he hoped to ask the oracle about locating Adrianna and

Sen.

First there had to be rules. His rules. "I shall agree to take the scepter to the oracle together. That is as far as I will commit until I speak to Zeelindar myself."

Luigsech did not appear as pleased as he would have expected based on how much energy she put into gaining his agreement.

She turned away, remaining there a moment as if gathering her thoughts, then turned back. "Well, that's settled. Now we just have to find Zeelindar."

"Will she not come here to speak with us?" Daegan asked.

"Maybe, but we have to go to her in person to hand over the staff." Casidhe frowned over something. "Where is the staff? Tristan took it with him."

"He is nearby. The scepter is safe. How do we find the oracle?"

Luigsech's gaze danced around, hunting a place to land. "I ... I don't know. I contacted the professor the first time and accidentally called to Zeelindar in Tristan's hotel room. I was just talkin' to the room, but she claimed I called her. She *might* appear again if I did the same thing, but to be honest, I think she's contrary and shows up on her own."

"Zeelindar gave ya no direction durin' this second visit?"

Her angry gaze jerked to his. "If she had instructed more than the two of us to be together with those items, I would have said so, Daegan."

Hearing his name on her tongue gave him pause. He had a moment of guilt over badgering her, then mentally shook his head at twisting this around. He had been honorable with her since their first meeting.

She had lacked honor when she stood with Jennyver and Herrick in the mountains.

As if she'd caught his thoughts, Luigsech said, "About Herrick and—"

Daegan lifted a hand. "Do not start with new lies."

"This isn't a lie," she argued. "I want to explain."

"Ya had ample opportunity the many days we were together. That time has come and passed. Ya said to make a decision. I did. Now, ya must decide if ya truly intend to find another grimoire volume or admit this is only a ploy to bring me here."

Her eyes narrowed with threat and her words held a warning. "I am *not* without honor. I'm gettin' damned tired of mine bein' questioned. One day you will realize the truth, but I begin to think *you* don't deserve the truth. Yes, I will find the next grimoire volume."

Daegan stretched his shoulders, wanting out of this conversation. Standing close to this woman had him questioning if he was being unreasonable, but he'd been trained to deal with enemies and betrayal. Why was it then his upbringing and head warred with his heart over what to do about her? He had always kept emotions out of important decisions.

He had to get her back on track about this being a duty to perform and nothing more before she breached his dam. "In all your talkin' to Zeelindar, did she not tell ya how we find her?"

Luigsech had returned to walking about. She muttered, "Let me think. The first time Zeelindar came to me in the other hotel room, I asked how to find her." She nibbled on her thumbnail, paused, then kept moving.

Daegan had no choice but to wait her out, which meant watching her shapely body move around like a fairy flitting through a meadow. That one could not be still.

She had energy and drive that called to him.

"Wait!" Casidhe's eyes flashed with an idea. "I remember what she said durin' our first meetin' when I asked how to find her. She said we had to be together with both the scepter and the grimoire volume. She was explicit about not reachin' out to her again until then. Based on that, I'm thinkin' we need to have both of those in hand and be standin' together for her to come to us."

He did not like the idea of bringing out the volume he had hidden in Treoir. What if this were a trick for Herrick or some other person to grab that grimoire volume? Anger at being unsure what to do next boiled his blood.

"*Daegan!* Can you dial back your power? It's suffocatin' me. What is wrong now?" She had a hand on her chest. "Oh, wait, let me guess. You're irritated because you don't want to work with me or you need more control or ... oh, I have it." She'd sounded sassy until her voice lost energy at the end and dropped to a whisper. "You don't trust me. You think I'm goin' to betray you."

How could she make him feel as low as a snake's belly when he had done nothing to her?

"That's it, isn't it?" She dared him to deny it. "I am willin' to risk everythin', *again*, to do this with you, but I would be a fool to trust *you*, wouldn't I?"

"I have done nothin' to cost your trust." He'd spoken honestly, but the words felt empty.

"Yes, you have. We talked about not believin' others. You were supposed to ask me to explain what was goin' on when we met in the Caucasus Mountains."

Hurt and anger drove the bite in his voice. "I do not need someone to convince me my eyes lie!" He had nowhere to walk in this small and cluttered room. An idea came to him on how to settle this. "I have a question. Dependin' on your answer, I will listen to what ya have to say."

"Ask it."

"Do ya know where my sister is right now?"

Her lip trembled. She closed her eyes. "No."

The word no crushed him.

He spoke in a low tone. "I have no choice but to do whatever I can to find these grimoire volumes. I shall make this vow. If ya go with me to the oracle and she can convince me where the next volume is, I shall offer to go alone and spare ya from any more time in my company."

She closed her eyes very slowly. If he did not know better, he'd say she died, because all the life drained from her.

Her lips tightened into a hard line.

She folded her arms and lifted her firm chin with glistening eyes stabbing him.

He pulled his energy back and swallowed hard before softly suggesting, "Let us have a truce to not discuss that subject and show respect to each other. I can do this if ya can."

Her calm gaze never moved from him.

He had the sick feeling something precious was slipping from his grasp.

She nodded, then cleared her throat. "I agree. Since Tristan took the scepter, he should be able to get his hands on it quickly. Where is the grimoire volume we rescued?"

"Both are in another realm."

Shouts and screaming rose from outside the window. Casidhe spun around and raced around the bed to yank the curtains apart. "An Imortik is chasing a small boy!"

Daegan ordered, "Stay here!"

She dove for her backpack. "No!"

# CHAPTER 19

"**Y**OU GOOD, BOSS?"

"Aye." Daegan leaned back against a wall on a side street where he and Tristan had chased down an Imortik. They'd driven it away from a child Daegan could still hear screaming even this far from where the mother hugged and rocked the little one.

"I'm good too, Tristan, just in case you wondered," Luigsech called over with plenty of sarcasm.

Stepping away from the wall, Tristan leveled her with a glowing green gaze. "If you'll recall, Daegan and I drew the Imortik away from that kid by getting it to chase me into this alley. Then *we* battled it to the ground when you showed up and swung your guillotine blade. I knew you were fine."

"It's not a guillotine blade."

Tristan opened his arms. "Hey, all I've heard you do with that thing is cut off heads."

She grumbled out a curse.

Daegan had experienced a moment of terror when she came running up to the Imortik as if she had no qualms about the yellow monster jumping into her body.

That had been damn close.

Tristan had told him about the vulture clawing her, but Luigsech did not favor that shoulder. Was she able to heal herself?

It didn't matter. He still shook with fear for her being so close to the Imortik and ordered, "Ya need to learn some constraint for the next Imortik may not be so easy to kill."

She lowered her backpack to sit next to her feet. "You two have the worst way of sayin' thank you."

"She doesn't get it, boss."

She stabbed her sword in the ground. "I'm standin' *right here*, Tristan."

He sent her a bland glance. "Your point?"

"Don't talk about me as if I don't exist."

Tristan murmured, "We should be so lucky."

"Okay, fine." Luigsech put her sword away and pulled the backpack straps over her shoulders, jabbing the buckles. "Be a jerk. I'm gettin' tired of riskin' my life for no appreciation. Daegan and I made a deal to show each other respect. Why is that so hard for you?"

Daegan heaved out a long breath. He had to find a way to hunt the grimoire volumes without her. He could not take watching her battle an Imortik or the friction her presence created, which would not end between her and Tristan.

Arms folded over his chest, Tristan said, "If I have to explain why, you're not as intelligent as you want people to think, Luigsech."

Her silence drew Daegan's gaze. Something Tristan said had upset her and Daegan doubted it had anything to do with questioning her intelligence. The little termagant could hold her own in any verbal battle.

Tristan had called her Luigsech.

The moment he did, she lost all her spirit to argue.

"We must leave here," Daegan announced, standing away from the wall.

"Where to, boss?"

Luigsech piped up, "Yeah, where to, *boss*?"

Before Tristan could pop off again, Daegan said, "We go to Treoir."

"Really?" Luigsech practically bounced on her toes at the idea of traveling to Treoir.

Tristan's desire to snap at her again sat squarely on his face, but he held his tongue.

Eyes darting from Tristan to Daegan, her excitement drained out from her face, leaving her gaze wary. "What's up? Are you takin' me with you or leavin' me here to ... kill more Imortiks?"

He would not leave her alone now and she knew it. Daegan said, "Ya go with us."

Her smile returned.

Daegan's chest loosened at what that smile did to him, but realizing the mistake sharpened his tone. "But ya stay with Tristan the entire time or he will teleport ya away. Let's go, Tristan."

He had to look away from her or suffer guilt at how quickly he'd dashed her happiness. The world spun with Daegan hoping he was not making a huge mistake in taking Luigsech with him.

When they reappeared, Luigsech spoke in a hushed voice. Her face filled with awe as she stared at the castle and grounds. "Oh, my. This is ... incredible."

Daegan started for the castle.

"Wait." She ran a couple steps and clutched his arm.

This would not do. Not here in front of his people.

He pulled her hand off and instructed, "Do *not* touch anyone here, includin' me. Do not speak to others here. Ya are only to stand with Tristan while I retrieve the scepter and grimoire volume."

In her usual caustic way, she snapped, "Since you didn't say don't *talk* to *you*, I have a question."

This day would not end. Daegan sighed. "Speak your question."

Now she turned shy. "Uhm, I was wonderin' if Skarde was here."

Fury ripped through Daegan in a wave of fire. "Ya come here to see an ice dragon? Is that what this is all about?"

She stepped back. "No. I wanted to ask him a few questions."

Tristan stepped up. "So you can go back to Herrick and tell him all you've learned about Treoir and exactly where Skarde is?"

Her eyes blazed more like the termagant Daegan knew.

She stepped toward Tristan, glaring him down. "I have *no* ulterior motives! I want to find the *real* ice dragon chronicles. Some or all of everythin' Herrick and his squire families told me were lies. I'm tired of people I believed in lyin' to me." Inhaling deeply, she raised red-rimmed eyes to Daegan. "When we hunt another grimoire volume, I fear usin' faulty knowledge I've depended upon my whole life to make decisions."

Her energy swirled and reached for Daegan's as his rushed toward her.

Again, her words sounded truthful.

Daegan pushed his gaze to Tristan whose face remained stony. He sent his second a telepathic message. *I am considerin' allowin' her a few minutes with Skarde just to hear what is said between the two.*

Tristan stared up at the dark sky and replied silently. *I will do whatever you ask, but I'm going on record that she can't be trusted and every word from her mouth might be a lie.*

*Understood.*

Luigsech normally complained when she noticed them speaking telepathically, but not this time, even though her gaze had traveled from Daegan to Tristan and back.

"We shall go to Skarde first and only for a brief visit," Daegan announced. "Be forewarned if ya try to gain information on me, my clan, or this realm, ya shall receive my wrath."

"I won't," she promised quickly. "I know you two don't believe me, but I have no one who cares for me, so I have no one to share any of this with even if I were inclined to do so, which I'm not."

Daegan had a weak moment of feeling for her. No one should be entirely alone in the world. He had been that way for thousands of years, but he'd had Ruadh with him.

Tristan had a point about spending time around her being risky. Not for the reasons Tristan thought. Daegan's walls were not as sturdy as he'd thought. He would have to do a better job of protecting himself or he'd make a mistake such as agreeing to listen to her story about Herrick.

The minute he opened that door, she'd slide inside him again. Too many powerful men had been brought down by women who knew how to twist them around their finger.

He could not fail his people by trusting unwisely again.

Nor could he go through the loss still tearing him apart twice. "Teleport us to the dungeon, Tristan."

In the next moment, Daegan, Tristan, and Luigsech stood in Skarde's area where the dragon shifter sat in the old chair at the wooden table with room for six. Tristan called it a folding chair. Two torches on the wall nearest Skarde brightened his humble area and bed.

Skarde got up slowly and turned. His face went from calm to crazy the second he saw Luigsech. "What did you do with Jennyver?" He started for her with his hands up.

She backed up. "I had nothing to do with all of that."

"*You lie!* You had Jennyver." He sounded both furious and close to tears. "Where is she?"

Daegan grabbed Skarde's arm and warned, "Do not."

The ice dragon shifter turned on him. "Why would you stop me? Do you not care?"

"Of course, I do. She knows nothin'."

Shaking, Skarde lunged for Luigsech. "She will tell me."

Before Daegan could say another word, Luigsech held her hand out and ordered, "Come to me, *Lann an Cheartais.*"

The sword immediately flew out of her sheath from inside the backpack, up in the air, the hilt slapping against her open hand.

"What the hell?" Tristan murmured in shock.

Daegan had not seen her perform such an act either. Had something changed after she went to Herrick's castle?

Skarde stepped back, holding his chest. "How dare you touch my sister's sword?"

Ah, now Daegan understood why he'd felt ancient majik on that sword the first time she pulled it out in her cottage.

"It is now *my* sword," Luigsech claimed, still holding the blade upright in front of her.

"That cannot be," Skarde argued, but his voice quivered with indecision.

She arched a delicate eyebrow at him. "We both know this sword would not go to someone unless it chose to do so."

Tristan tossed a questioning look at Daegan who shook his head. He had no idea what happened within the ice dragon family and their swords.

Her claim must have confounded Skarde. He stood there unable to speak or move.

Tristan cupped his hands behind his neck, giving Daegan a what-are-we-going-to-do-now lift of his eyebrows.

Daegan shrugged, then said, "Skarde, take a seat so we might speak." He hoped Skarde recognized his polite words were spoken as an order. "Tristan, bring us another chair."

His second didn't question why Daegan would not use majik here in Treoir to call up one more chair where his power increased. While Skarde shuffled back to the table, Daegan pointed for Luigsech to follow.

She put her sword away and moved toward the table.

Tristan returned, dropping the additional chair into place then moving all three seats in a half circle across from Skarde.

"How can you bring her here, Daegan?" Skarde had his elbows on the table and his head propped on his fists. The book he'd been reading had worn edges and yellowed sheets as if it might be one of Garwyli's.

Luigsech placed her backpack next to the chair she chose, which seated her between Daegan and Tristan.

Did she think to push Tristan away?

Once everyone had taken a seat, Daegan explained, "She is helpin' us find the missin' grimoire volumes and had some questions for ya."

"I am not talking to someone who tortured Jennyver."

Luigsech jumped up. "Do *not* include me in your brother's unforgiveable actions. Herrick kept her presence secret from everyone. The minute I found out, I wanted her handed over to Daegan immediately." Her head angled his way a moment before returning to face Skarde. Just long enough for him to see her concern.

She wanted to know if he'd heard her words.

How would he not?

He gave no reaction, but he would keep what she'd said in mind for later.

"Then where is she?" Skarde cried out. "What did he do to her?"

Glancing away, Luigsech said, "I don't know exactly what Herrick did. He had Jennyver hidden in somethin' like a special ward in his dragon's lair." Luigsech moved her gaze to stare over Skarde's head. "Not exactly a ward, but some majik that kept her body static for all this time. A seer lives at the castle and she actually discovered what he had done in a vision. I walked in as she was tellin' Herrick he had to act or lose his secret treasure. Then Daegan showed up with you. The seer and I followed Herrick to a place deep in his lair and watched Jennyver wake up. We did all we could to help her understand where she was and that I was takin' her to her brother."

A tear ran down Luigsech's face and dripped on the floor. "That was the worst day ever."

Skarde appeared torn between believing her and wanting to rage at her more.

Daegan suffered the same conflict.

Had Luigsech just told the truth? Even so, she still had a lot to explain about keeping her connection to the ice dragon clan secret from him.

Skarde asked in a strained whisper, "Why did Jennyver disappear?"

Sitting back down, Luigsech swiped a hand over her cheek and sniffled hard. "I wish I knew. One minute I was holdin' her up and the next she just leaned to the side and vanished." Pulling herself together, Luigsech asked Skarde, "Where have you been all this time?" Then she tensed and twisted to Daegan. "If that question is not acceptable, say so."

"He may answer."

Skarde slumped back. "I was captured at King Gruffyn's castle after we had been defeated in the Dragani War. I went there to check on Jennyver, because we were ... friends." His eyes would not support that lie.

Whether Daegan liked it or not, there may have been more going on between this dragon shifter and his sister. As for Luigsech's words, he was not so ready to easily accept them. He'd been tricked by words in the past, which had cost his freedom and left his family to face death and kidnapping without his protection. He could not make that mistake again with so many lives depending upon him. If the opportunity arose later, he might have Luigsech make her claim of innocence again when Storm could be present, but that would not happen any time soon.

Still explaining, Skarde said, "King Gruffyn's steward tricked me and used majik given to him by a god named Abandinu. He captured me and took me to the Scamall realm where I was added to their menagerie of flying creatures. I stayed there the whole time until Daegan and his people came for a captured Alterant-gryphon who belonged to the Beladors. Abandinu destroyed that realm. Daegan teleported me here and ... brought me back to life." His lifeless gaze drifted to Daegan. "I have had time to think on much. Thank you for what you did."

Daegan could not take Skarde out any time soon again, but it did warm his heart to see the ice dragon shifter finally understand that Daegan was not his enemy.

Tristan leaned forward, propping his forearms on his thighs. "I don't mean to interfere, but Daegan and Luigsech have to get moving soon."

"'Tis true," Daegan agreed. "I shall allow her questions then we must leave."

Drawing in a deep breath, Luigsech said, "I do not think Herrick and his squire families gave me the truth on the dragon family history. In fact, I'm quite sure they did not. Do you know where the true ice dragon chronicles might be kept?"

Skarde took a moment to answer. "I do not. I am sure either our father, mother, or both would have had those records. The MacConnaugh were our squires."

She nodded. "That's correct, but I don't think I've ever seen the real chronicles based on what I've learned recently. Would there be anything else written I could search for?"

He clasped his hands in his lap, appearing interested. "Some of the siblings kept journals. Herrick was not as dedicated, but he did keep one. I did. Brynhild never considered writing down a thing. In fact, of my three sisters, only Shannon kept many journals."

Excitement rolled through Casidhe's voice. "Where would I find these journals? I would give them to you once I had a chance to read through each one in hope of findin' answers."

"Mine was hidden behind a loose stone on the window wall in my room. Shannon always put out more effort to protect her secrets. She would have kept hers hidden somewhere in the castle, possibly her room, but I do not know the location. We were very close as twins and knew each other's thoughts at times, but I never would have searched for her private journals."

Luigsech smiled as if she'd just received a gift. "I understand and would feel the same way if I had lived in that time. If I find a journal from that time, I might better understand why this sword comes to me as well as many other questions I have about the era of ice dragons. I have had this sword with me a long time, but only recently lifted it to carry."

Shaking his head to himself he explained, "I do not deny you have control of the blade, but it makes no sense."

Her narrowed gaze pinned him in place. "Why?"

"No one can wield a family blade except the person it was made for or a descendant. Shannon had no children before she died."

Daegan kept watch on Luigsech's reaction.

Her eyebrows drew together with a ferocious expression. "I'm told I was born to human parents who tossed me aside. That doesn't make sense."

"Ya know this for sure, Skarde?" Daegan asked.

"As I said, we were very close." He spoke more gently to Luigsech this time. "You see now why I question your holding my twin sister's blade? Our swords were struck from the same metal and given power at the same moment. Mother pressed our hands on each other's sword so they would cross imprint. I could lift her blade to protect her or myself, and the same for her with mine. No one else should have that ability. If you find her journal, I would very much like to know what you learn as well."

Daegan sensed Luigsech had taken a blow from what Skarde told her, which confirmed she had not been given the true ice dragon chronicles or she'd have known that about the sword.

To give her a moment to recover, Daegan asked Skarde, "How is it that Herrick is still alive now? I understand Brynhild bein' here after Cathbad kept her in a frozen pond all this time and ya bein' in Scamall, but not Herrick. I did not think any of ya were immortal."

"We are not immortal, but I believe Herrick has the ability to remain in this world indefinitely as long as he spends enough time in that castle during the year."

Luigsech came to life again. "What do you mean?"

"Shannon once told me she overheard our parents discussing who should have the castle built for the first ice dragon. My mother said the castle had to go to the oldest whose duty it would be to protect the others if my father's castle fell in the Dragani War."

Tristan huffed out a laugh. "Herrick didn't care about Brynhild. He only wanted to get you."

"My brother and Brynhild never got along. She wanted to be the oldest and most powerful of our kind."

Daegan had not received his answer. "Is the castle keepin' Herrick alive?"

Skarde sat up, frowning. "I think what Shannon told me is that our father said the energy in that castle, the lair, and lands would continue to renew power of the ice dragon who lived there, but even the oldest I knew of only lived eight hundred years. I believe our mother gave each of us a different gift from her jinn bloodline. Shannon told me she once asked our mother where she went when she was gone for weeks at a time and came home exhausted. My mother told her because she shared more with her than she did the rest of us."

"Why?" Luigsech asked with genuine interest.

"I always felt my sister received more jinn than dragon shifter in her blood, plus she could keep a secret from anyone. Mother said she traveled to the castle of our dragon-shifter ancestor in those mountains to infuse additional jinn power so an ice dragon shifter who took possession of the land would live much longer than others had in the past."

Tristan commented, "I wonder if that played a role in keeping Jennyver alive so long."

Daegan hadn't considered that possibility. "But is she still at the castle?" He'd been told otherwise. Still, he turned his frustration on Luigsech, demanding an answer with his stern look.

"No, she's ... gone."

# CHAPTER 20

AINVAR SAT CROSS-LEGGED ABOVE THE walking entrance to Newgrange mound and cloaked from view. He grinned at the battle before him.

What could be more enjoyable than watching Queen Maeve's two-headed monster rip Cathbad to pieces on a beautiful night?

Cathbad's insane partner had played this well by casting a ward over the druid's body to prevent him from teleporting away.

Ainvar made a mental note to remember Queen Maeve's sly trick.

Shouts and roaring destroyed the peaceful setting. Cathbad beat back the beast, but was losing ground.

That druid really deserved to die screaming.

If only Ainvar had the luxury to allow Cathbad's death to proceed.

He stood and began calling energy to him.

Cathbad shouted something at his monstrous opponent, but the ward blurred his words.

Two giant heads reared back, both jaws opened wide then they lunged at Cathbad.

Ainvar snapped energy across the space, slashing both heads off the beast. Then he struck the ward.

Power burst in an explosion, knocking Cathbad backward. His clothes caught fire. He yelled and moved his hands, causing everything he wore to disappear, then dropped to his knees.

The monster crashed over on its side with both heads landing nearby.

Leaned over with his hands on the ground, Cathbad cursed, "Ya bloody miserable bitch. Do not die before I have a chance to kill ya." Spitting out some blood, he struggled to his feet.

Cathbad shoved his hands in the air, shaking them at his absent opponent. He stayed there until his breathing calmed. He muttered curses, then pointed a finger at the carcass, which erupted in flames. Once he finished burning the heads as well, he swirled his hands and called out a spell Ainvar hadn't used in a while.

Every bit of the beast and heads turned into black chips, which spun into charcoal dust and flew away.

Pinching his nose, Ainvar turned up his nose at the acidic smell left behind.

Cuts across Cathbad's body were closed and healing, no longer oozing blood. He called up water to douse his body clean, then flicked a hand in the direction of his head. His black hair fell into place. All water droplets were gone and he donned a fresh dark suit, purple tie, and white shirt, resembling the well-groomed men of this new age.

*This* was the druid who dared to take Ainvar's place as Seanóir, the Elder of seven dark druids?

Ainvar had taken note of the aura rising over the mound, which indicated others had joined in the dark druid meeting place below. Cathbad would not see Ainvar's aura. He'd destroyed his personal aura a long time ago while experimenting with majik to provide himself immortality.

Possessing no aura around his body allowed him a measure of invisibility.

Waiting until Cathbad entered the mound below, Ainvar floated to the ground, comfortable in his robe. Cathbad's narcissistic need to compete with modern men from clothes to hairstyle only reinforced a lack of internal strength.

Ainvar had empowered very old majik to remain here for far longer than he should have with his original human body. To arrange an attractive facial and body appearance was not such a chore.

Cathbad's strength visibly returned as he moved more smoothly down the passage, no longer trying to hide a limp. Ainvar floated behind, careful to contain his power and not reveal himself tonight with even a whispered noise.

After another minute, Cathbad reached a room with bones.

He took care with his steps to avoid touching any of them. The scent of years past assaulted him, but the bones had been here too long to hold a smell. He moved his boots until he found a place to stand which suited him.

Ainvar floated closer to Cathbad while keeping his energy pulled deep inside. It would be interesting to discover how Cathbad accessed the meeting place for dark druids.

Would he dare to use Ainvar's code?

Cathbad held his arms out with palms up. "As one of its own, I call to the power of Newgrange for passage to the conclave of *Dhraoidhean Dorcha Elite.*"

Wise on Cathbad's part to not tempt fate by using the words Ainvar originally put into place for allowing the leader to pass through.

That could only mean Cathbad did not know for sure if Ainvar lived or not.

Otherwise, he would have taken ownership of the code. With no follower nearby to question Cathbad's entrance, he could pretend to be the leader.

Over the next few seconds, Cathbad's body lost its solid form, changing into a filmy shape, which slowly descended below ground.

With him gone, Ainvar spoke his code and followed.

When Ainvar's body became solid again while still hidden, he inhaled deeply at the sweet putrid smell of the crypt he and five of the first members created down here. That had been when people of his time lived a simpler way. Not with all the technology and other problems interfering with accessing power in some cities today.

Ainvar took note as Cathbad addressed each of the mature druids already seated around a small fire sending up a smoke trail from the shallow bowl. The wonderful scent of sage floated in the air.

This room would allow no more than a total of seven, regardless of him being cloaked.

Cathbad spoke to five followers.

Was there not a sixth?

Had Cathbad killed the sixth just to avoid not being allowed passage should Ainvar still live?

Ainvar lifted his legs to cross beneath his robe, emulating those also in robes, as he slowly lowered himself to the cool marble surface.

Did the other five not find Cathbad's clothing odd?

When Cathbad finished addressing each druid, he took a spot opposite of Ainvar, which allowed him to keep everyone in view.

Cathbad started off with, "I called ya here today to preserve our future and that of followers, who will one day take our places. I would hope ya know the human world is changin' quickly with supernaturals bein' exposed."

All heads nodded, many with grim expressions.

"These humans do not know the difference between us and other supernaturals."

Three chuckled at the absurdity, one rolled his eyes, and the last one showed no reaction. If anything, that one's serious expression intensified. He wore a simple gray robe similar to the others and would be considered in his fifties, if described using human age.

Holding his arms folded inside the deep sleeves of his gray robe, the serious one asked, "Do ya suggest we should be concerned about human threats?"

Cathbad slashed a look at what seemed to be the youngest of the druids present. "I do not, Lakyle. 'Tis not the point of why I am here. Ya should consider the gift of silence when bein' instructed."

Even at his age, Lakyle's ruddy cheeks deepened in color.

Any druid in this place had earned the right to join this circle. To invite one not at the top of his majik would be foolish, but to speak down to any attending stepped into the area of dangerous.

Silence fell quickly after that dressing down.

Nodding appreciatively, Cathbad continued. "We have no reason to fear any humans. We should take care to consider the many powerful weapons they have constructed, though, as some be capable of disintegratin' any of us by simply pressin' a button." His dark-blue gaze swept around the room where all five faces wisely showed nothing this time.

Ainvar frowned. This group had not been well managed. There was no sense of cohesion in the group. Certainly no trust flooding the room as had been when he'd last addressed the dark druids of years past.

Perhaps that indicated what some, if not all, of these druids believed about Cathbad's claim to the role of *Seanóir*.

"The world is fillin' with Imortiks from a rift," Cathbad said, turning to a new issue. "We have an opportunity to place ourselves atop of the power structure among supernaturals while takin' a spot between those and humans."

Leaning forward, Ainvar tried to discern if Cathbad played a game with his words or if he really meant them.

When no one dared to interrupt, Cathbad kept laying out his plan. "The humans in charge believe their weapons will save them from anythin'. A foolish thought from uninformed mortals. Soon, they will realize they need help from nonhumans. If we allow others to step into that role, we will have lost a great opportunity to rule both worlds. If we join forces with humans, but only when it benefits us, we will hold control in this world movin' forward."

Those seated did not raise their eyes to Cathbad.

Ainvar enjoyed a smirk.

Cathbad had always been too arrogant to pay attention to those beneath him. The desire to rule long ago had been plain in Cathbad's words and gestures. He'd awakened from his great slumber with Queen Maeve believing no other druid alive stood above him.

Thankfully for Ainvar, Cathbad had failed to be an alert student, instead thinking if he lived the longest he could rule this order.

Clearly pleased at the silence, Cathbad explained how they needed all three grimoire volumes to wipe out the Imortiks and prevent any others from escaping the death wall.

After another pause, Cathbad announced, "I have excellent news. I know the person who can locate these grimoire volumes hidden thousands of years ago *and* ... read them."

That brought up every set of eyes.

To be honest, even Ainvar listened closely with interest.

"I request the aid of our order to locate one known as Casidhe Luigsech, a descendant of the red dragon squire family, and bring her to me. Now, what be your questions?"

"What of the red dragon? Does he truly fly again?" Lakyle asked.

"Yes, he does."

Pressing his luck, the youngest druid asked, "Is he aligned with the humans?"

"The dragon king has secured no position with the humans," Cathbad replied carefully. "Even with the red dragon, the humans and other supernaturals cannot stop the Imortik invasion without those volumes. 'Tis why we must hold that power."

Murmurs of doubt scuttled around the circle. Energy buzzed the air in chaotic tension.

"You doubt me?" Cathbad asked in a chillingly quiet voice, which immediately silenced the room.

Eyes fell, their energy shrank back.

Cathbad's satisfied face said he'd received his desired reaction.

Fingers curling tight, Ainvar wanted to shout, *"Liar!"*

Cathbad either did not know what it took to stop the Imortiks or he did and purposely lied. Ainvar would bet on lack of knowledge.

Now smiling, for some unknown reason to Ainvar, Cathbad put his hands together, appearing pleased with himself. "In the interest of time, I shall make this an adventure. The one who brings Luigsech to me first shall be named my successor."

Now energy rushed across the room churning with excitement.

Ainvar knew exactly how to punish Cathbad for claiming the lead of this order.

# CHAPTER 21

BLOOD AND SWEAT RAN DOWN Adrianna's face. She lifted a torn sleeve and yanked off enough for a rag to wipe her eyes.

She leaned against a nasty wall with a blurry surface, but it felt solid and flat like bricks or cement block.

Why couldn't she see this place clearly?

Had Tenebris glamoured walls, floors, and ceilings?

Loud rattling and crashing called to her from up ahead. She'd figured out quickly that she could not go backward when those areas had shown her no way to escape.

Going forward was her only choice.

Tenebris would not give her another chance to find a way out of here. He'd only done so this time to entertain himself. Was there really a mirror where she could pass through as an exit point?

What was on the other side of that mirror?

All good questions. None of which could be answered from standing still.

Pushing away from the wall, she took a step and clamped her lips against making a noise. Her ankle had not healed yet. If she couldn't step without pain, she couldn't run. Her majikal healing had been slowed significantly. At this rate, she would eventually not heal at all.

More noise headed her way from behind.

She tried again to cloak herself. Nope.

Opening her hand, Witchlock crawled around in a shape that defied description. It was as if a wad of energy had three marbles inside shooting back and forth. Witchlock would go from the general size of a golf ball to fatter than a navel orange.

A loud hiss raised the hair on her arms and neck.

Turning to look would not help her fading confidence, but she had to know what she faced now.

She blinked to clear her vision. Nope, it wasn't her vision. A bulbous head hosted drooping eyes with black centers and orange where white should be, plus two holes for nostrils sat upon tentacles thick as her body next to the head. The tentacles narrowed to thin strips at fifteen feet with bumps that blinked open and closed.

"Come on, Witchlock, it's time to power up," she whispered and hobbled away toward a new location. Pain stabbed her ankle with every step. She kept moving and checking her power.

Until this place, she and Witchlock had reached a mutual agreement to support each other. At least that had been her take on their relationship.

A tentacle shot out like a whip and slapped her sideways.

She fell and rolled, then scrambled up. Her skin stung where puckered spots on her arm matched the bumps on the tentacle tip.

She scrambled backward and hit a wall.

The gushy monster crawled through the last opening and into the vast room, moving smoothly on six legs.

Not a type of octopus. What else had that many legs?

She could think on that as she would die soon if she didn't hobble faster. Gutting out the pain, she raced back and forth across the space, dodging that leading tentacle trying to play whack-a-mole with her body.

Her hand warmed excessively.

Was Witchlock powering up?

She opened her hand and flinched at the shape and pale-green cast of the normally bright white energy orb. Turning to face her multiped attacker, she stalled when the head split horizontally to display a double row of serrated fangs.

A mouth of death and pain coming for her.

Glancing over her shoulder, she had maybe forty feet to reach … *the mirror! Yes!* The mirror existed.

The tentacle slapped just short in front of her.

She jumped and whipped her hand forward. She begged, "Come on, Witchlock."

Energy wobbled and half fell off her palm, but pulled back together.

The monster crawled forward.

She called up power and sent a stream at that gaping hole full of daggers for teeth. Energy hit the monster, then crackled and raced over the body, flowing down the tentacles.

Creepy monster froze in place and whined like an engine that wouldn't turn over.

All at once, the tentacles broke free of the majik and flew drunkenly in her direction.

She might have a minute or less before that thing pulled its wits back together.

"Not enough power last time," she whispered to Witchlock as she backed away. Time to try for the size she'd experimented with on a mountain top that had caused her not to practice it again.

Desperate times and all that.

She bumped into something on the ground, a blurred shape, and kept moving before it turned into another threat. Pushing her will into the energy to grow, she said, "Let's do this, Witchlock."

Energy began to turn faster, tumbling like a giant pale-green misshapen tire, bouncing up and wobbling all over her palm.

Tentacles began moving in sequence again. One shot out fast and Adrianna dodged, slamming her shoulder against a wall.

Whatever Witchlock had would have to do.

She forced her hand out and ordered, "*Kill it*, Witchlock!"

Gray-green energy blasted as the monster's mouth opened again. The power struck inside, spiking power in different directions before ripping that blob apart. Huge pieces zoomed away in every direction.

She ducked to avoid getting hit in the face. Not fast enough. She still ended up slimed with some of the tips stinging her. Even after all that, severed tentacles kept moving.

Gross. She heaved a deep breath and immediately regretted it.

The stink of burned guts gummed up her lungs.

Something pounded the floor above her.

She had to keep moving. Her ankle felt a little better or terror had replaced the pain. Spinning around to check, she found the mirror still waiting, oddly enough.

The mere fact that nothing stood between her and that mirror sent a shiver down her spine and screamed trap.

Moving forward a step, then another, she took off at an uneven jog for the glass offering escape. Maybe. She split her attention between the moving tentacles and her destination coming closer. Fifteen feet left to go.

She felt a wash of energy flood around her.

Where was that coming from?

Don't lose focus. The mirror was still there.

Whoa! Why couldn't she see her reflection in the mirror? She took another three steps and the power circulating around her pressed against her chest, halting her six feet from the mirror.

The wall to the right of the mirror opened up and Tenebris stepped through and closed it behind him. "You are surprisingly difficult to kill and quite determined."

Curses flew through her head. She shouted, "You said if I made it to the mirror, I could pass through it and leave."

He waved his hand casually toward the mirror and it disappeared, replaced by an Imortik twice her size. Far greater than any Imortik she'd confronted before now.

The monster slammed against an invisible wall separating them.

Why? Not that she would complain, but why would Tenebris put up a kinetic field to stop the Imortik?

Tenebris mused, "Much as I've enjoyed your entertainment, it is time for you to accept your destiny."

She took a step back. "You are such a lowlife even for a whatever you are."

"If you knew me better, you might like me," he taunted.

"If I knew you better, I'd have already figured out how to kill you." She could not let Witchlock fall into the hands of an Imortik. She took another step back.

Tenebris found her amusing. "Where are you going? You've lost the contest. There is nowhere else to go. You are too dangerous to keep shackled. You may enjoy this new form of life."

"Don't do it, Tenebris. You'll regret this decision." She opened her hand and lifted Witchlock into sight. Sadly, her energy wobbled all around, barely the size of a fist.

He broke out laughing. "Don't humiliate yourself anymore. I was born of a god. You are no match, not even for this Imortik."

"Now is the time to be great, Witchlock," she urged. The energy increased in size and shaped as a warped melon.

Tenebris chuckled as if someone tickled him. He waved two hands at the invisible wall.

The Imortik shoved again and stumbled forward, pushing its hands down to stay on its huge feet.

A bodyless tentacle slithered around her leg and squeezed, holding her in place.

She'd run out of options. Opening her hand wider, she pushed power harder. The blob of energy enlarged more.

Tenebris laughed like the lunatic he was and gave her a finger wave, then passed back through the wall.

His Imortik monster roared and stood upright, then stomped forward.

# CHAPTER 22

BEFORE DAEGAN COULD HAVE TRISTAN teleport them out of Treoir's dungeon, Skarde pleaded, "When will you find Jennyver?"

If only Daegan knew the answer to that himself. His chest ached at now realizing she could be out there dying away from the majik at Herrick's castle. "Soon, Skarde. I must find these grimoire volumes first or no one will be safe."

"*Free me!* I will hunt for her."

Daegan felt the other two sets of eyes on him. Tristan would think he'd lost his mind if he freed Skarde. Luigsech likely thought he was no better than Herrick for keeping a family member locked up in the dungeon.

Some days there were no good answers.

"I thank ya for the offer, but I would rather ya stay here for now."

Surprisingly, Skarde nodded quietly and returned to his seat. "I understand."

Daegan wanted to say more, but Adrianna and Sen were still missing. His days to locate the volumes were dwindling and his sister's frightened face had taken residence in his mind. He could not bend for Skarde again, but the ice dragon shifter was showing signs of humility Daegan could work with later.

"'Tis time, Tristan."

Outside the dungeon, Daegan told Tristan, "We shall wait here. Bring me the scepter, then go back for the grimoire volume. Tell Garwyli I hope to return it to his safe keepin' soon."

"Got it."

Luigsech adjusted her backpack and stuck her hands on her hips. "Why make him go twice? Surely Tristan can carry those two things."

"Do you not think there is a reason for everythin' I do?"

She scratched her neck. "I do. It's just sometimes I'm not sure what those reasons are."

"'Tis because they are not your concern."

"Why won't you allow Skarde to leave?"

He tensed at the accusation in her voice. "Once again, ya do not have all the information. I shall try to enlighten ya. Skarde spent weeks not shiftin' into his human form or speakin' to me in my mind. I felt he could do both, but the damage done from so many years imprisoned in the Scamall realm could not be chipped away in one day. When he finally spoke and shifted, he attacked my gryphon village, harmin' a woman. Tristan's sister, in fact."

She lifted a hand to her mouth. "Oh, no. That's ... awful."

He was glad to hear disappointment in her voice, which was not directed at him for once. "I am doin' Skarde a favor by not just allowin' him to live in spite of his attack, but by tryin' to help him adjust to livin' again in today's world. 'Tis no small adjustment for anyone."

She made a move toward him and acted as if she wanted to speak, but Tristan popped back into view.

His second-in-command gave her a look of warning. "Here's the scepter, boss. You won't be able to carry both."

She snorted. "First he insults your strength, now you insult his."

Ignoring her, Tristan suggested, "Maybe you should let her carry this since she has so little to offer at the moment."

"'Tis a good idea."

Swinging the staff around and holding it out, Tristan said, "Take it."

She cocked an eyebrow at him. "If I don't?"

"Then stop wagging your tongue if you're not going to help."

She snatched the scepter from his hands, forgetting how heavy it was and having to grab the treasure with two hands.

Tristan vanished again.

Daegan could not fault Tristan for his attitude toward Luigsech. They had both trusted her and shown her friendship only to be deceived.

When Tristan reappeared, he held his palm out with the grimoire volume as a bronze box floating an inch above it. He used kinetics of one finger to push the volume over to Daegan's open palm where the box floated again.

"Ah! Now I get it," she said, stepping closer.

"Always good to know you can catch up," Tristan quipped.

She rolled her eyes at him. "Are you goin' to be this irritatin' forever?"

"No."

"Really?"

Tristan added, "Sure. Once you leave, I'll be content again."

Daegan broke up their sniping with, "Where do we meet the oracle this time? 'Twill be difficult to carry this grimoire volume while climbin' a mountain."

Luigsech swung her attention to his question. "No kiddin'. My best guess is to return to the hotel where you found me. Zeelindar's criteria was for us to be together and she visited both times while I was in a hotel room." She paused and sent a pointed look at Tristan. "The oracle stated she wanted to see *only* the two of us along with both the grimoire volume and staff."

"I thought ya said when she travels in this astral way she would be unable to receive the scepter," Daegan said, bringing up their past conversation.

"That's what she said, but I have no idea what will happen when we meet her this time, Daegan. She's as much a mystery as everyone else in my life." She moved the staff from the crook of one arm to the other one.

Tristan worried on something with his silence. "You said she came to you in *my* hotel room. What about going there? It's better protected than the one in Galway."

Daegan waited on Casidhe to weigh in.

Not Casidhe. He could not fall backward with her. Not now with so much at stake. She would be Luigsech from here on out.

She offered a polite smile. "I know this will surprise you, Tristan, but I think that's a great idea."

Daegan fought amusement over Tristan's dilemma. He'd never seen his second intentionally be rude to someone without cause.

Tristan clearly was not ready to lower his walls either, but he didn't have a response for her easy agreement.

"You ready, boss?" Tristan asked, his voice less aggressive.

"Aye."

In the next stretched moment of the world swirling, Daegan stood in Tristan's hotel room in Atlanta once again. Luigsech immediately unhooked her backpack and placed it at her feet, then sat upon the sofa while Tristan walked over to peer out the window.

Daegan would have liked to put this grimoire volume away, but he had to be ready for when the elusive oracle arrived.

Stepping away from the window where the city remained dark, Tristan said, "I'll be close by. Just call me when you need me."

Daegan started to agree, but Luigsech said, "I don't want to get yelled at, but the last time we met with the oracle she sent us catapultin' through space to another place."

"We were in her world when she used her power," Daegan clarified.

"True, but I thought she was goin' to blow somethin' up *here* when she got irritated and her power fanned out."

Tristan crossed his arms. "Why does it not surprise me that you'd piss off an unknown being while here?"

"*Annnd* the jerk is back." Luigsech crossed her arms, too, and leaned against the cushion.

"Go ahead, Tristan. I shall do my best to inform ya if the oracle sends us somewhere without notice." When Tristan vanished, Daegan decided to sit on the other end from Luigsech. This way they could both talk to the oracle.

He wished he had not sat upon this thick sofa. His body sunk into its softness. He wanted to lean back and close his eyes, just take a break from all that was going on.

He felt her eyes on him.

All he could do was continue to remind himself why his attraction to her had been disastrous for him and could be now for his people. He had no idea what the future would bring with Herrick knowing he had Skarde or once Daegan met the oracle again.

"Don't you have any questions for me, Daegan?"

He shook his head without looking at her.

"You don't want to know everythin' that I couldn't tell you before?"

Another head shake.

After a long silence, he cut his eyes to the side to see what she was doing.

Her elbow rested on the end of the seating. She had her chin propped on her fist, looking away from him. None of that bothered him until he saw her lip tremble.

Please don't let her cry.

He'd seen many tears in his life, but he could not watch hers. Regardless of all that had transpired, her distress still bothered him. He still fought the urge to pull her to him and hold her.

That would last until his mind brought up the image of her standing with Herrick and Jennyver.

Power flushed through the room.

Daegan went on alert.

Luigsech sat up straight.

In the open area on the other side of a low table from Daegan, a knee-high iridescent swirl began to enlarge until it became as tall as him when he stood. Muted blue, green, and orange colors meshed until a translucent form took shape.

Now he understood why Luigsech could not describe the oracle's presence beyond being similar to a hologram.

A filmy powerful image.

Zeelindar's upper half had defined shape, but the lower half seemed to have joined together into one part and blurred as it fell to the floor. She moved back and forth with hands clasped in front of her chest, weaving in a calm way.

"Hi, Zeelindar," Luigsech started.

The oracle dipped her head in answer then turned her strange black-and-orange swirling eyes to Daegan. She snapped, "Why did you bring that grimoire box here?"

He frowned at Luigsech, expecting her to answer.

Luigsech quickly explained, "The last time you showed up, you told me we had to be together and to bring that box as well as the scepter."

Now that angry gaze burned black and swept over to Luigsech. "Those were *not* my words. Do not dare to argue with me. My parting words to you were specifically 'When you are together and possess both the grimoire and scepter, you will receive my message. Do not reach out to me again.' Anyone would understand to *only* bring the scepter for this meeting."

Luigsech's jaw dropped then she closed her mouth and glared as if she would like to breathe fire. "Fine. I did get the last part right about not callin' you."

Daegan asked Zeelindar, "Since we do not need this box to be present, I wish to send it back to where I had it safely hidden."

"I would prefer that as well."

"I shall return in a moment." Daegan called telepathically to have Tristan meet him in the hallway.

As soon as Daegan stepped out, Tristan appeared. He took a look at the box. "What's wrong?"

"Nothing. 'Twas a misunderstandin' about bringin' this with us."

"That fits," Tristan groused. "Want me to take it back to Garwyli?"

"Aye. Ya may return, but I have no idea if I am to still be here or not. If we end up sent somewhere, I shall call to ya as soon as I can."

They did the box transfer. "I wish I could go with you, boss."

"I would welcome your company, but I must do whatever it takes to fulfill my duty. Maybe if I am successful, we shall have the volumes needed to stop all the Imortiks and possibly free Adrianna and Sen."

Tristan puffed his cheeks and blew out a slow breath. "That would be ideal. I'll be amazed if we get that opportunity, but I'm pulling for you." He met Daegan's gaze with one of devotion. "Don't let your head get twisted around with *her*."

"Luigsech will not be a problem." Now if only Daegan could convince himself of those words.

Tristan left as Daegan stepped back inside the room.

He felt the negative tension immediately. While he stepped over to sit again, he asked, "Is anythin' amiss?"

Luigsech said nothing, just stared at Zeelindar.

The oracle continued to move slowly with her hands in a prayer position. She wore the same sheer material as before, but her legs were not bent. In fact, all below her waist blurred into a single misty shape.

Zeelindar's dark-red lips moved again. "There is no problem if you are prepared to hunt for the next grimoire volume."

"That's not all you said," Luigsech interjected.

Daegan held his thoughts and waited out both of them.

Zeelindar took her time speaking, as usual. "I also said there will be a cost for this trip."

"I expected as much," Daegan said, not confrontationally, just confirming.

Luigsech sat forward and rubbed her eyes. "Here's the long and short of it, Daegan. We have to find a stone *first*, then she'll tell us how to find the next grimoire volume."

He found that unacceptable as well. "We have made good on our original agreement, Zeelindar. We rescued the scepter. Do ya not trust us to fulfill our agreement this time?"

"That is not the issue, dragon. I am not able to share everything at this time. All will be made clear when you locate a brilliant onyx stone carved in the shape of a small hand closed around a pulsing red stone." She turned her severe gaze on Luigsech. "Once again, you misstate my words. I said you must find the stone first and I will then tell you how to find the grimoire."

"Is that not what I said?" Luigsech challenged.

"You failed to understand that I did not indicate the necessity to return to me for that information."

Luigsech's mouth dropped open in confusion then she closed her lips and held her silence.

"Who is the original owner of this stone?" Daegan asked with no little suspicion.

The oracle pushed her power in his direction and swung her disturbing gaze to him. "I will share all when you have the stone and grimoire volume in your possession. Once you hear my words, you may choose what you wish to do with the stone next. Regardless of your decision at that point, our agreement will have been met in full."

He didn't take the time to argue about a treasure hunt. The last time he had, she'd only lost her temper. He did have a question. "From what I understand, one volume has been in this city of Atlanta from the beginning of the rift. A second one was stolen from the vault of VIPER, which is—"

"I know of this VIPER and the Tribunal," Zeelindar said.

Daegan continued, "Good. If the second one was stolen from VIPER, are you sendin' us to search for a stone that is in the same place as a grimoire volume?"

She closed her eyes and lowered her head for one nod. "You will place the scepter on this small table."

Luigsech sent Daegan a frown of confusion, but deposited the staff on the glass top. As soon as she did, the scepter vanished. "What the heck? You told me last time you couldn't carry that with you in astral travel."

"Do you see me holding the scepter?" Zeelindar asked.

"No, but, uh ... never mind." Luigsech pulled the backpack onto her lap and put her arms around it the way someone would hold a pet for comfort.

"A wise choice of words I thought to never hear you utter," the oracle commented, ignoring the sound of irritation Luigsech made under her breath.

Daegan returned to what he considered an unfinished conversation. "Back to the grimoire volume ya shall inform us about once we locate your stone. Are we to be huntin' in this city? Atlanta?" That might be helpful if he could bring Storm and some of his Beladors to track the volume without weakening the teams patrolling.

"Do you agree to what I have told you?" Zeelindar asked, still not sharing the actual location of the stone.

Daegan had never made so many one-sided agreements in his life, but the last time paid off. He wanted to move ahead and ask about Adrianna and Sen. "Yes, we agree."

"*I* didn't agree," Luigsech said, clearly angry with everyone.

Zeelindar said, "Very well, I wish you luck hunting."

"*Wait!*" Luigsech cupped her forehead. "I agree. I'm just ready to get this done."

Zeelindar's power spun up and began expanding. *Search for Mulatko.*

Daegan felt the energy slam his chest. Ruadh roared to break free. They both wanted out of here.

Luigsech called out, "*Stop! Stop it!*"

Lunging toward her, Daegan tried to grab Luigsech's arm, but her body sucked backward into a dark hole where she spun out of sight, clinging to her spinning backpack.

He was pulled in right behind her. *Stay put, Ruadh. I do not know what is ...*

Power unlike anything he had experienced dragged him inside a tornado, throwing him around and around. The power pushed around for what seemed a long time when it was likely only seconds. When it all stopped, he landed facedown on a smooth but hard surface and grunted.

He coughed and fought for air.

A moan reached him.

Turning to his side, he squinted in the twilight to find Luigsech flat on her back and struggling to get to her feet. His fingers moved over the slick surface, catching a straight edge. Was he inside a place with so little light?

Pushing up, he stumbled over to Luigsech and hooked a hand beneath her arm, lifting her to her feet.

She stilled, eyes fixed on something behind him.

"What is wrong, lass?"

Her lips moved, but no words came out.

He turned to see what held her in its grip.

# DIANNA LOVE

# TREOIR DRAGON
# CHRONICLES

OF THE BELADOR WORLD

# BOOK 8

# CHAPTER 1

DAEGAN HAD SEEN A LOT of things in two thousand years, at least when not imprisoned, but nothing like these strange carvings and marks. Light slowly glowed brighter from two long glass tubes in the lower corners of the pink stone wall.

Luigsech had yet to find her voice. She just stood there like a statue.

Had she hit her head when they landed? "Are ya hurt? Can ya hear me?"

She still did not answer him. Her body started trembling.

He fought the urge to grab her to him and hold her safe. To do so would be to mislead her. He had to keep his head on straight, but watching her in distress was killing him.

Stepping in front of her, he put his hands on her shoulders and immediately regretted the feel of her energy humming at his hands. Damn everything, he missed her. What kind of fool did that make him?

He'd worry about that later. For now, he feared her reaching a point she could not breathe at all. "Take deep breaths and calm down. 'Tis not the time to panic."

She blinked and looked up at him as if she just realized he stood there. "Do you know where we are?"

How could he? That blasted oracle had said nothing more than search for Mulatko, whatever that was. Beyond the pink wall with carvings and smooth square-cut gray stones covering the floor, he had no idea. "Feels as if we are inside a buildin'."

Tears glistened in her eyes. Her voice shook when she whispered, "Uhm, yes, sort of, but there's no *door* out of here."

This time, he took in the entire room all the way back to where it was dark behind her. Only solid walls and no air movement.

Ruadh rose up inside him, alert.

Daegan had only one way to escape, but how could he teleport out without knowing what lay beyond these walls? He was done with the oracle after this.

If they survived.

Luigsech's labored breathing continued. She gasped for air.

*Bad place*, Ruadh warned.

It wasn't as if Daegan could do anything yet. He gave her shoulders a little shake. "We shall get out of here." He had hoped to sound more convincing than he had to his ears, but she sounded worse. Then he came up with an idea he hoped would not end with him headless.

"Listen to me," he ordered. When her gaze lifted to his, he said, "Ya are behavin' like a child for someone who spent much time in tunnels."

Her mouth rounded.

Had he injured her feelings? That had not been his intent. Only to find a way to calm her before she suffocated.

She glanced at his hands on her shoulders and jerked backward. "Oh, really?" Anger spread from her face to her fisted hands. She shouted, "We. Are. Trapped! *Do you not get that!*"

To be honest, Daegan fought his own battle with a sick feeling in his gut at being locked inside anywhere. He'd sworn to Ruadh they would fight to the death before being imprisoned again. Now that she trembled with fury instead of fear and had begun breathing again, he would not admit his reservations when it would undermine her calming down.

"Aye, we are in a sealed room, but we shall find a way out," he said with confidence, in spite of his own trepidation.

"How? Wait. Where's my backpack?"

Daegan stepped past her to retrieve the bag from where it had landed. He handed it to her.

"Thanks," she muttered, showing her manners even when irritated with him.

Daegan sniffed at the stale air. This place had been closed up a long time. "Ya never answered me. Are ya hurt?"

That brought her around to him. Her eyes shined briefly with surprise, then a fleeting hopeful expression appeared before she shook herself free. "No. I'm fine. I was just unable to get over bein' in a room with no exits."

Why would she be surprised at him caring if she had been injured? He was not a monster.

*Betrayed you!* Ruadh reminded him.

True and he had to continue thinking of her as Luigsech and keep his hands to himself or he'd slip up and make another big mistake. Had his father not drilled it into him one betrayal always leads to another? Never lower his guard once someone had broken his trust.

Daegan could adhere to that rule, but he would not mistreat her. He noticed Ruadh seemed off and asked, *Did ya have trouble from the teleportin'?*

*Dark energy*, was his dragon's answer. *Leave now.*

Between the stale air and the sensation of pressure from being locked in a room with no doors, Daegan agreed but still had no way out. He asked Luigsech, "Where do ya think we are? Ya spoke as if ya know."

"Based on those images, I, uh ... " Luigsech paused. Why did she hesitate? "I think we could be somewhere in Egypt."

That word stirred a memory, but Daegan could not bring it forward. "What world is Egypt?"

"It's a country in the human world. If you look at a map and start with Ireland up north, this land would be way down southeast of Ireland."

Not a country that Daegan could place in his mind. They wasted their time even coming here. The other two grimoire volumes had to be in Atlanta. Zeelindar had been accurate about finding the first one, but anyone, even an oracle, is not infallible.

He couldn't stop himself from declaring, "This was a mistake."

"Are you serious? We haven't even tried to search yet. How can you dismiss bein' here so easily?"

He sounded angry and had every reason to be. "'Tis simple. One grimoire volume is in the Treoir realm. The other two are in Atlanta. There are only three. How do ya explain Zeelindar sendin' us *here*?"

Luigsech shifted all the way around to face him with one hand on her cocked hip. "I can't explain *any* action Zeelindar takes, but how can you be *positive* the other two are in Atlanta?"

He was in no mood to be taken to task. "The first one brought to the city opened a rift. Days later, VIPER headquarters was attacked and the second one stolen from their vault. That one was locked away in VIPER when the rift opened again for a short time twelve hundred years ago. 'Tis why I asked the oracle about huntin' in Atlanta."

"Well, she must know somethin' you don't. It *is* possible." Luigsech ignored him to inspect the wall again.

Daegan wanted to argue, but not as much as he wanted to find a way out of here. "'Tis possible I know more than the oracle this time. Has *that* possibility not crossed your mind?"

"Of course you do," Luigsech said, sarcasm dripping. "You're the dragon king. How can anyone know more than *you*?"

"'Tis not what I am sayin'."

"Really?" She opened her arms wide. "Please tell me because I'm standin' in an unknown place in an unknown location lookin' for somethin' to help stop Imortiks from takin' over the world. From where I'm standin', looks to me like she knows somethin'. Are you truly willin' to abandon this before searchin'?"

"Never mind. We do not see any of this the same way." He was not thinking clearly and paying attention to potential threats as he should be when in an unknown place.

Ruadh pressed hard against his insides, pushing to get out.

Daegan grunted, but held his human form. *Be calm, Ruadh. I need time to find a way out of this place.*

His dragon calmed and withdrew.

Two-foot-thick round columns of the same pink stone supported the ceiling. Similar images were sculpted there, too.

What the devil did all these carvings mean?

Daegan tested reaching out to the most powerful Belador telepath. *Trey, this is Daegan. Can ya hear me?*

No one answered.

He tried teleporting from one side of the room to the other. Energy ground inside him, but his body never moved.

Luigsech lowered her hands, her gaze focused on a lower corner of the wall. "Where did those lights come from? They turned on after we appeared." Walking forward, she squatted for a closer look.

Daegan followed her and dropped to a knee to figure out what had her curiosity.

The two bright lights were the length of his hand and oblong with one end fatter than the other. The larger round end was as thick as his fist. "Why does that surprise ya? I have seen similar lights in Atlanta."

"No." She shook her head vehemently and waved her hands as she spoke. "There are no cords to the wall and it looks as if the entire globe is the entire fixture with no obvious electrical mechanism for makin' the light function. I don't even see a place for a battery. That long squiggly thing in the middle might be a filament, but ... this still makes no sense."

Confused at what she was talking about, Daegan stood. "Ya make no sense."

Her lips parted, drawing his attention to the one place it shouldn't be. "You don't realize where we might be, do you, Daegan?"

"'Tis a buildin' of some sort," he replied, annoyed at how he allowed himself to be distracted. She also tested his patience with talking in circles. "Just say what ya have figured out. I tire of havin' to guess."

She glared at him, then returned to studying the wall. "It does feel like a buildin', but not the way you think. I believe we might be *beneath* a pyramid or some other ancient structure in Egypt."

The word pyramid shook loose thoughts Daegan hadn't encountered since he and Fadil were young men. He now recalled how he'd heard of Egypt from Fadil, whose family of earth dragon shifters originated there. Fadil's father went against his family to mate with Queen Anasch, a woman from an unacceptable dragon-shifter bloodline. Fadil never shared details, because young men fighting battles and having fun rarely discussed anything personal.

One thing Fadil had shared with Daegan had been his father's warning to never return to Egypt or he might not survive.

Fadil's mother could not shift into another form, but her blood allowed Fadil's father to sire dragon-shifter children.

Thinking back on what Skarde had shared about Queen Anasch's infidelity had Daegan wishing he'd known more of her ancestors as well as the paternal side of Fadil's family. That might have helped in this moment.

The oracle had said to look for Mulatko. With recalling Fadil, Daegan half remembered his friend mentioning that word, or maybe a name.

Now he understood why he stood in a place called Egypt.

Zeelindar had sent him and Luigsech here to hunt for the grimoire volume hidden by the earth dragon shifters. If that volume was truly down here, how could there be two in Atlanta?

Ruadh had the right of it. They should leave this place, but now Daegan had to see this through.

He felt a glimmer of satisfaction from his dragon.

"Are ya sure we are *beneath* the ground?" Daegan managed to sound calm at the disquieting possibility of being trapped.

Luigsech took several steps back, her eyes moving as she followed the carvings across one row. "I can't think where else we might be with hieroglyphics all over the walls and no windows."

"High row *what*?"

Luigsech drew in a deep breath as if he tested her patience. She explained, "Hieroglyphics are considered an ancient language of the Egyptians, though I've heard of it found in other places. Designs carved into the wall are called reliefs, which are sometimes painted and sometimes not. This place could be a thousand or more years older than you." Her eyebrows drew together in thought. "Lot of debate on pyramid datin', construction, and such so who knows how old this place is? Now you understand why I question the lights? I've heard of these tubes, but not enough to believe they existed."

Daegan stepped back, his gaze skimming over the odd shapes and images ... none of which he understood. He asked the most important question first. "Do ya have any idea how we escape from here?"

She propped an elbow on the arm around her stomach and propped her chin on her hand. She wore a troubled expression, which offered little confidence. "I'm not a buff on pyramids, but if we are beneath the Great Pyramid, which is the largest one in Egypt and above ground, I recall somethin' about a narrow passage into the king's tomb. Maybe the queen's tomb, too, but again, that's not my area of study. We might even be beneath another structure and I have no idea how far down we are. I'm guessin' we may have to teleport out."

Ruadh snarled inside Daegan. *Trapped.*

Daegan agreed, but he could not get them out yet. Interestingly, the venom did not bother him in this place. Instead of admitting to her he could not teleport at all, he said, "I am not sure how far I am able to teleport. I shall need to know how far beneath ground we are and in which direction to go before tryin'. To teleport blindly could end with death."

Her face lost a shade of healthy color.

She hadn't panicked yet, which he now realized had been due to thinking he would teleport them out. He struggled with his anger over seeing her with Herrick who had captured his sister, but he had to put that aside and give Luigsech encouragement. "We shall figure the way to escape when the time arrives."

"I keep tellin' myself that," she grumbled in a quivering voice. "Freakin' Zeelindar could have given us a little more information." Luigsech stepped toward the wall again, stopping an arm's length away.

Ruadh banged Daegan's insides. *Free me. Escape.*

He told his dragon, *I shall not risk ya and this woman without first searchin' for the safest way to escape. If we find none, I shall free ya to do your best to break out of here. We must be careful, Ruadh.*

*Bad place.*

*I agree, but if we shift, we might bring down the entire structure on our heads. I do not wish for any of us to be buried here.*

His dragon was not pleased, but the banging around ceased.

Luigsech rubbed her arms where goose bumps had risen.

Daegan had an unexpected desire to rub her arms and comfort her. He shook his head at his weakness.

When would his body understand this woman could not be trusted? He had to remind himself over and over to heed his father's teachings. To be betrayed once was dangerous. To allow a second chance was to welcome death.

Daegan would behave honorably just as he would around anyone in this situation, nothing more. He sensed her anxiety building and decided to distract her. "Have ya figured out what any of those pictures mean?"

"Not yet." She frowned, lowering her arms and squinting at the wall. "From what I understand, only a tiny number of people can actually decipher hieroglyphics."

"Ya mean the shapes are words and ya can read them?" Would she finally admit her gift?

She tossed him a pointed look full of accusation. "I have no idea if I can read *these* shapes until I try, but you already know it's possible. You snuck up behind me readin' one of my books on that mountain in Spain and saw me use my gift, didn't you?"

He had not intended to ruffle her feathers and might as well admit he'd caught her trying to read in secret. "Aye. How did ya make the letters change into gold and lift off the page? 'Tis one of the most unusual abilities I have ever witnessed."

She fidgeted with her hands. "To be honest, I can't explain how I do it. I never realized I possessed this ability to translate any text with my fingers until I went to college and started researchin' *very* old books with languages I was told could not be read. I have never found another person similar to me, which is strange enough. I wish I knew just who and what I am, anythin' that would give me a sense of wholeness and peace." She shrugged. "Everyone has issues to deal with. One day, I'll find answers."

Daegan admired how once again she stood up and accepted her circumstances, not whining or carrying on even when thrown into an underground prison.

He should feel guilty for poking at her. His anger chewed at him and he could not shake it.

Starting now, he would avoid asking questions that were not important at the moment and allow her to concentrate on using her gift. That should keep her fears at bay.

Stepping over close to the interesting designs, he asked, "Are ya ready to try?"

She nodded. "Yep, here goes nothin'."

What the devil did she mean by that?

Standing with one hand propped on her hip, she studied the wall before stepping even closer. Lifting her right hand, she pressed two fingers together and positioned the pads an inch away from the carved shape. She swiped her fingers as far as she could without moving.

Nothing happened.

She moved three steps to her left and repeated the same motion.

He kept his deep disappointment at their first failure to himself.

Luigsech made a grumbling sound, scrubbed her left hand on her jeans, and placed that hand on the wall. She then moved her right fingers above the drawings again.

Gold symbols began to lift and twist into new shapes.

He stood back, arms crossed, and tried to figure out how her gift worked. "What does it say?"

"I don't know yet. I can't make sense of ... wait a minute." She kept her left hand in place but pulled her right hand down. "Some languages are read right to left, which is what I tried, but I thought I once read that some hieroglyphics were translated accordin' to the direction a human or animal image was facin'."

He took note of the flat birds staring left. "What are ya sayin'?"

"I think if the head of a bird or a person points to the left or right, that's where the person who made this began creatin' their story. Like these birds are pointed to the left so I'm goin' to start on that end." She moved all the way across and started once more, this time moving her translating hand from left to right. Her voice brightened. "Okay! I'm gettin' some words but not like sentences. This is all still weird. Give me a minute to translate more to see if I can make sense of what I'm seein'."

While she worked across the wall from end to end muttering to herself, he turned his attention to the rest of the space. The room had no hallway or door. How was someone supposed to enter or leave if they did not teleport?

In his mind, if this had been intended as a tomb, there should be a coffin.

He found another set of shapes running on a wall that met the one where she continued reading, but these shapes covered less area. He could stretch his arms wide and touch both ends of one row. The tallest section of carvings was eye level to him.

Using a finger and no pressure, he traced the odd shapes. Nothing came to him, but he had no gift or expectation of reading these odd shapes. He started to turn away when a flying creature on the far left caught his eye.

Before he could touch that one, Luigsech said, "*Ah ha!*"

"What did ya find?" Daegan walked over to her.

She wheeled around with a grin. "I think this is a story of how this spot was created as a secret room."

"I commend ya on translatin' any of this, but how does that story help us? Did it mention anythin' about Mulatko?"

"No, it doesn't." She muttered something unintelligible and turned back to the wall.

"I did not mean to insult ya."

Flapping a hand at him, she said, "You didn't. I would love a chance to read all of this, but that's not why we're here. Give me a minute to see if I can find anythin' useful."

She went to the left end and stood on her tiptoes.

He rolled his eyes. Stepping close, he grasped her at the waist and lifted. Now she could reach the top row.

She sucked in a breath. "What are you doin'?"

"Do I need to explain?" he asked, but in truth he asked himself the same question. Just touching her brought up the last time he'd had her in his arms. His hands were the only happy part of his body right now. Much as he wanted to pull her to him and feel her warm body against his, he had to remind himself one touch would lead to another.

He had to hold his defenses strong or he'd pay a price for letting her back in. He would also be misleading her, which would be dishonorable.

After another grumble, she put her left hand against the wall and began translating with her right fingers.

He kept an eye on her progress and sidestepped to his right slowly.

Luigsech claimed to have not been a part of Jennyver's imprisonment, but she'd spent her life with the ice dragons. How was he supposed to just overlook the fact she'd never said a word about them the whole time they'd spent together? How could she not tell him when she'd awakened in his arms in Tristan's hotel room?

His conscience reminded him she had agreed to come here to help stop the Imortiks, but he countered that any family fought from time to time then made up and kept going. He had no way to know for sure if she was here on someone else's behalf or to convince Daegan to hand over Skarde.

Herrick wanted Skarde and knew Daegan held his brother captive. Thinking so hard with too many unanswered questions made him want to slam a fist into a wall.

Why did she have to smell so good? He wanted to bury his nose in the small of her back.

She stopped reaching for letters. "I'm, uh, done. You can put me down."

He lowered her quickly to her feet and released her, backing away. His hands couldn't be trusted. They had no more sense than the lower half of his body.

She spun around and stared for a long stretch, opened her mouth as if to speak then snapped it shut. "Whatever." She shrugged and turned to read the last line of figures at her knees.

Why had she taken offense after he'd made it easy to read the wall? Or had it been due to his releasing her so quickly after him picking her up? He had said nothing.

Women had never confused him so much many years ago.

Long ago, they smiled or yelled, spoke their minds.

He thought about freeing Brynhild of a forced mating. She had taken exception to what he'd thought an honorable action on his part.

Perhaps women had not changed so much after all.

Not meeting his eyes, Luigsech flipped a hand in the general direction of the entire wall. "My best guess is this sounds like the carver was involved in plannin' this area. I get the feelin' if this underground structure had an entrance, we would be standin' in it."

"'Tis not much of an entrance when it goes nowhere."

"Exactly." She looked past him. "I'll take a look at the columns."

"I found more carvings on the far end of this other wall." He pointed toward the less-bright area he'd been inspecting.

Rubbing her eyes, which made them even more red, she said, "Show me."

At the short block of rows, Daegan stepped past and waited to see what she might figure out.

She leaned in, squinting.

He decided to bring one of the lights over. When he pointed at the nearest bulb and tried to lift it using kinetics, the light didn't budge.

No kinetics. What other powers would not work here?

His father had taught him worry devoured energy. Better to focus on what he could to solve a problem. In this case, he would focus on hunting a way out of this room. One of these rows of sculptures might hold the key.

To offer her some light in this dark area, he opened his palm and called up a small flame. That should put a smile on her face.

She swung around to him. "Fire will burn up oxygen we need to breathe. We'll suffocate."

Closing his hand into a fist, he lowered it to his side. When they last hunted a grimoire, he was busy the entire time. Not standing around waiting.

She seemed unable to decide where to start this time.

Reaching to the side of her, he said, "I found this shape with wings. Could be a dragon or gryphon type of creature." He touched the shape with two fingers this time, moving it across the image.

"So you're readin' text now?" she smarted off.

"I do not claim to do such a thing. I only wish to give aid in this search."

She stood away from the wall and crossed her arms. "Maybe if you'd find somewhere to sit down and give me time, I might get lucky."

Unable to hold back his irritation, Daegan opened his hand and leaned on the wall. "'Tis not a good use of—"

A squealing sound cut him off.

The room shook and the wall beneath his hand turned into a large block that flipped open as a door would. With his weight leaning on it, he fell into the opening and banged his shoulder before landing on the ground.

He cursed and stood up.

"What did you do?" Luigsech exclaimed.

She accused him of that happening? "I did not tell the wall to open." He turned to search the area, but this space had no light.

"Come back out here."

He listened to her with half an ear. "Not yet. I wish to see what this room might be."

"*Daegan!*"

He jerked around.

She had both hands pushing against the block of stone that had opened and was now slowly closing.

He rushed forward and gripped the stone to hold it open. "Grab your backpack!"

"No. We don't know which room we need."

Leaning back with all his weight, his booted feet slid an inch, then another. "This may be our only way out. *Hurry!*"

Lights in the room behind Luigsech went dark. She made a high-pitched noise then ran across the room, yelping when she ran into something. Probably a column.

"*Get over here!*" he shouted.

She pushed through the wall, dragging her backpack. "Don't yell at me! I'm not the one who did this."

His fingers slipped off as the door closed and the wall turned whole again. "We may need to be here."

"I don't trust blind logic," she snapped so close to him her warm breath brushed his chest.

"Ya trust little," he complained more to distract himself from how her warm breath reminded him of how soft and willing she'd been in Tristan's hotel room.

"And you're at the top of that list."

Why should it pain him for her not to trust him when he had the same lack of trust for her? He hated this internal arguing. He'd always been decisive and had no patience for this conflict of heart.

And now was not the time.

He started to ask if she had her small LED light in the pack when she sucked in a deep breath. Daegan could not see her face. "What is wrong?"

She whispered, "You don't hear that?"

He dragged his focus off her and opened his senses. A shirring sound of something moving reached him.

"Don't make a sound," he whispered, reaching out until he bumped her arm, grasped it, and eased her behind him.

# CHAPTER 2

ICE SLID OVER ADRIANNA'S SKIN.

Seven feet of glowing yellow abomination came at her, pausing to rage and shake its clawed fists in the air. A predator driving fear in its victim. Its thick gray tongue slithered past three-inch fangs when a wide maw opened.

The bodyless tentacle holding her ankle tightened like a barbed wire, holding her in place.

Witchlock continued to rotate erratically on her palm like a melon bouncing down a rocky hill.

She'd faced plenty of monsters, but not one capable of diving into her body and possessing her. She hadn't believed such a thing possible, not with her Sterling witch blood and wielding Witchlock.

Adrianna prided herself on keeping her emotions hidden, but she flinched when the Imortik shouted, "*Mine!*"

It could speak?

She held her shoulders back, determined to face the end with dignity. She would never quit fighting, but she had always been realistic about her survival chances. For the first time, she had no last minute idea on how to overcome this threat.

She closed her palm, pulling Witchlock back inside. The power had to stabilize. She dug deep for a Sterling curse she'd never intended to use and shouted the words with a flick of her hand at the monster.

Black sparks hit the Imortik in its face. It started slapping at its hideous head and howling. That might not last long.

She had no answer for the bodyless tentacle shooting hot pain up her leg.

While spilling his guts to Tenebris, Sen should have also told this creep he would be a fool to expect her to give in and plead for her life. She might die screaming, but she would inflict as much pain as she could.

Was Sen still alive? She shouldn't care about that heartless demigod, but hadn't heard any more after his initial screams. That had probably been due to her being too far from where Tenebris had him locked up and not because Sen had succumbed.

Unfortunately for Sen, as a demigod, his body wouldn't easily succumb where a human had zero chance of surviving this place.

If Sen was a demigod, what did that make Tenebris? Who cared?

The Imortik had spun around, trying to get away from the stinging black sparks and slammed into a wall. It pounded fists and yelled unintelligible things. Maybe *mine* was the extent of its vocabulary.

If she was in a realm, then Isak wouldn't come charging in to save her and he would. The possibility of him facing an Imortik or Tenebris terrorized her. She'd never have a chance to sort things out between them. To never feel his warm gaze holding her safe even when they were not touching.

This soul-crushing pain at never seeing him again to just say goodbye and give him the truth of how much she cared for him squeezed her heart in an iron fist. She fought past the ache in her chest for a breath.

As long as she checked off regrets, she'd add a big one.

She should have learned more about Witchlock. She should have bonded with her power. The last time she opened her hand a few minutes ago, it hurt to watch Witchlock's misshapen energy wobble around on her palm.

Was this place killing an ancient energy?

She clenched her hands, drawing shallow breaths. She could not allow Witchlock to fall into the hands of an Imortik, but she honestly had no idea how to prevent it from happening.

Still trying to bat away the sparks, the Imortik pushed off the wall, coming toward her blindly. Not good.

She tried to back up a step, yanking against the tentacle.

Lifting her hand, she opened her fingers. Witchlock rose above her palm, spinning off course. Her poor energy quivered and bobbed about, barely the size of a fist.

She lowered her head and whispered at her palm, "It's time to power up, Witchlock." The energy increased in size to that of a warped melon shape.

She'd run out of options.

Opening her hand wider, she pushed power from her core as hard as she could toward Witchlock.

The blob of energy enlarged more, but just as deformed.

The Imortik monster roared, batting bright yellow arms back and forth as it staggered for her.

Heart thundering in her chest, Adrianna called out an old incantation meant to destroy. The energy above her palm bloomed to the size of a basketball, then a beachball, then ...

Shouting unintelligible words, the Imortik wildly slapped a clawed hand at Adrianna's head.

She ducked with her palm still up.

The glowing claw missed her and struck Witchlock.

Power shot out in all directions.

Yellow skin peeled back from the Imortik, then its body exploded.

A white-hot explosion engulfed everything.

# CHAPTER 3

EVALLE KEPT SWEEPING A LOOK all around as she, Quinn,
Reese, and Casper covered ground in the dark. After receiving Lanna's information on where Adrianna might be and
adding that to Grady's intel, Quinn and the team began the hunt
at Starlight Drive-In Theater southwest of the city. They now
headed eastbound toward Gresham Park.

She'd searched her part of the outdoor theater quickly. Not
much going on there at three in the morning. With the ambient
light, she could see well enough out here even wearing her
special dark sunglasses.

No one was supposed to be outside from sundown to sunup
due to the curfew. Human law enforcement and military were
hunting nonhumans.

With one look at her glowing green eyes, she'd expose her
whole team as supernaturals.

Crickets cranked up a loud clicking Evalle could do without.

She'd rather fight a demon than have a small critter jump on
her skin.

Metropolitan Atlanta was only ten minutes away by car, but
being in the woods anywhere felt like a different country to her
where nothing was familiar. Night boasted a different kind of
quiet out here.

*All good with you, Evalle?* Quinn asked her telepathically.

She glanced up to where the glow of a flashlight bobbed ahead
of Quinn and Reese walking together. Evalle sent back, *No
boogie men, yellow or otherwise.*

The moon hadn't managed to fill out a round shape yet, but
with most of the rain clouds gone, she could just make out Reese
and Quinn in camo clothing.

Only for Adrianna would Evalle wear Isak's stupid camo

outfit. Dressing like Isak's black ops team had been a stipulation to searching together this morning.

Still, if not for Isak working out a deal with his military connections to allow his teams to help protect the city, Quinn and his people would be targets right now.

She yawned, rubbed her eyes, and squinted, looking around for Casper.

He could shift into a shadow and hide himself when he chose, but he emerged at the moment from the trees and came into view on her right. The cowboy had spent time in the military and looked at home in fatigues. He adapted as easily as a chameleon, going from wearing broken-in boots, a Stetson, and talking smooth as whiskey to the man now in military clothes ready to take down an enemy faster than a thought.

Tristan appeared next to her, walking in step.

She jumped and cursed. "Not funny."

"Wasn't trying to be funny, but quiet."

"You need sunglasses or you're gonna out all of us." There had been a time when they'd battled as enemies, then he came to the Belador side and stayed. She'd had a front-row seat to this tawny-haired misfit going from an angry male screwed over by the goddess Macha to becoming Daegan's right-hand man.

Tristan dug into a pocket and pulled out a pair of sunglasses to hide his bright green eyes, which were a mark of being a Belador Alterant-gryphon.

Cold air brushed up against Evalle. Out here? She stopped and told the Nightstalker, "We know Tenebris was seen in this area. If you don't have more than that, I don't have time to shake hands."

A translucent sad face came into view. Like Grady, these were ghouls who died here during a disaster and provided nonhuman intelligence for the right price. The filmy old woman drifted away.

"Nightstalkers have been wearing us out for handshakes," Casper commented as he stepped up to join them.

Tristan suggested, "Might be worth shaking with a few more."

Evalle held up a hand. "Quinn and I each shook with a total of five different Nightstalkers only to end up with similar information to what Grady had already given me." She hoped between Lanna and Grady's information, someone in Quinn or Isak's bunch would find a lead to Adrianna and Sen.

*Tell Casper that Reese feels energy coming our way,* Quinn sent to Evalle telepathically.

She shared that with Casper and Tristan, then replied, *Got it. By the way, Tristan just teleported in. We'll head your way.*

Tristan and Casper changed direction, following her when she angled to the right toward Quinn's flashlight beam.

"Do you think an Imortik can take you in your shadow or highlander form, Casper?" Tristan asked, his head moving constantly as he kept watch.

"Hell if I know."

"Let's not find out," Evalle muttered, having recently seen the highlander warrior that shared his body. She had faith in everyone out here tonight if they faced off with Imortiks, but she harbored a sliver of fear one of them might make a mistake.

She didn't want it to be her and cost the life of a friend.

She closed the distance to where Quinn and Reese stood. "Why'd you stop here?"

Quinn pointed east into the vast darkness in front of him. "With Isak and his team starting at the boundary for Gresham Park and working back this way, we're both going to run into this quarry."

"What quarry?" Evalle leaned forward, trying to see into the black void.

Reese had taken over handling the flashlight. She shined the beam so everyone could see the steep drop-off.

Evalle heard a whisper of sound and turned to face Tristan. "Where's Casper?"

"I don't know. He said sit tight, then he was gone."

She searched for any sign of Casper's shadow. Had he decided to float down into the pit to take a look?

Evalle stepped away, looking for Casper in one of his alternate forms. She called out in a sharp whisper, "*Casper!* Where are you? I told you Reese feels demons. Some could be yellow."

A tall shadow coalesced between her and the group, then merged with Casper's body, all of it taking shape at the same moment.

Casper asked, "Did ya sight one of them there vermin?"

The only thing missing from the cowpoke dialect was a spit of tobacco. Evalle kept that thought to herself. Never give that cowboy any ideas.

Everything quieted.

"Do you hear that?" Evalle asked softly.

"What?" Tristan stared at her.

"No cricket sounds. In fact, no sound," she explained, feeling a little cocky at having a frontier moment.

Reese lifted her free hand to cover her stomach in a protective way. "The energy I felt has stopped. I'd say I'm baffled because demons never walk away from trying to suck the demon energy from my body, but this happened last time I-zubrrali was involved. He's probably actively hunting me as much as we are him."

Quinn called over, "We need to move away from this pit. I don't want to battle demons or anything else backed up to this drop-off."

"Wouldn't we see the yellow ones?" Casper asked.

"Sure, if someone hasn't cloaked them," Quinn pointed out. "This pit could stretch several thousand feet from end to end and almost that wide across at this point."

Evalle actually liked one point of being out here. The small chance of encountering humans, which meant they could use their supernatural powers.

Quinn lifted a hand to his ear. When he lowered his hand, he asked Reese for the flashlight, which he switched to a different function and flashed three short blasts.

With that done, he explained, "Isak just crossed Intrenchment Creek on the other side of this hole. He asked me to send a signal with the tactical flashlight to confirm our location and that we're heading toward each other. We're not quite in position to be across from his team. Let's turn south and stay ten feet off the edge of the pit. We'll meet up with Isak's team at the southern end of the pit."

Evalle preferred Quinn wear Isak's comm gear to keep in touch with the black ops human team. She didn't like people talking in her ear. Plus, Isak got his back up when she didn't speak in acceptable radio jargon.

"I would never have found this hole," Evalle grumbled as they headed out.

Tristan opened his phone and showed her a glowing map.

"See? I don't need that in Atlanta, only out here in the boonies."

He laughed. "This isn't the boonies. We're still in the metro area."

With Quinn and Reese taking the lead, Evalle, Tristan, and Casper fanned out as they covered the rear. Moonlight danced over the landscape, silhouetting trees. Quinn and Reese reached a narrow stretch of open space they all had to cross with the pit on their left and forest on the right.

Good ambush spot.

Evalle sent her thought to Tristan and Quinn, who both acknowledged their agreement.

Casper would likely already have figured that out before her. From his many human years of experience in the military before being struck by lightning in Scotland and gaining an ancient highland warrior who shared his body sometimes, he had great operational skills.

Demons, Imortiks, or both could attack from the trees and push her people down the ravine.

She called to the minds of Tristan and Quinn again. *Maybe we should pick up the pace and high foot it to—*

Quinn cut her off, calling out loud for everyone's benefit, "Demons coming up from the pit!"

A howling noise rushed up the ravine on Evalle's left.

She spun around to face a glowing yellow demon on all fours, clawing its way to her. Whipping up an underhanded slug of kinetic power, she unloaded her fastball, hit the strike zone, and sent the demon sailing through the air. Yellow glow bounced down the hill into the dark hole.

Tristan said, "Casper, you fight with Evalle. I'll watch our backs."

Evalle glanced at Quinn who had an arm around Reese tucked in front of him, her usual position when those two battled together. He kept looking around at the trees at his back. He was allowing Reese to smack demons with her power as long as he could snatch her away if too many charged them.

Two more demons scrambled out of the black abyss.

Was I-zubrrali down there pumping them out? How many would he have created? He had to be cloaking them or the bright yellow Imortik demons would be glowing at the bottom of the hole.

Blasters lit up on the opposite side of the expanse from her, illuminating part of the quarry.

That was one ginormous hole in the ground.

Evalle caught movement out of her peripheral vision. Her gaze locked on mouths filled with sharp fangs, horns on heads, spiked tails, and sinewy muscular bodies with patches of hair clamoring up from fifty feet below her.

When the demons got close enough, they would turn to head for Reese.

Energy whizzed around her and a highland warrior stood near her. Casper's other half looked nothing like him. The Scottish warrior stood six inches taller and had another fifty pounds on Casper, who was pretty built himself. This guy wore a kilt. She couldn't imagine fighting in a skirt, and he probably would take offense at her calling it a skirt.

He swung a huge sword that made her spelled dagger look like a toothpick.

Her toothpick had destroyed plenty of demons, dammit.

Blasters going off repeatedly lit up the pit bright as daylight for a few seconds.

Evalle's jaw dropped at the sheer number of creatures crawling around the bottom like freaking roaches. Some glowed yellow and some did not. Could I-zubrrali control the Imortik demons?

She said, "Must be seventy or eighty."

"Aye, lass. We shall fill the hole with their blood."

At that gruesome image, she pointed out, "The demons should turn to ash instead of bleeding out." She added, "Don't call me lass."

He grunted a sound she took to mean he ignored her.

Tristan alerted them from behind, "Yellow glowing shapes coming through the woods. I've got 'em."

She hoped so since she couldn't turn around to help.

She smacked the demon closest to her with another upper cut, but ... that one did not go flying. In fact, it shook off the hit and kept coming. "*Shit!*"

The other demon launched at Casper's highlander. He swung his sword across the middle of the demon as if he sliced a sharp knife through butter. The top half went flying, then both parts disintegrated into ashes.

Evalle was holding back her demon with a kinetic wall.

"Free him, lass!"

"*Don't call me that!*" She backed up a step and dropped her shield for the crazy warrior to take the head off another demon. More ashes flew around. "Watch my back," she shouted and turned to join Tristan.

Three Imortiks, two tall creatures and one that failed to grow into its big feet, blasted out of the trees.

She ran over next to Tristan.

He suggested, "Let's pick them all up together and slam 'em down."

"Okay, three, two, *one!*" Evalle used her kinetics to lift the yellow monster closest to her and latch onto the one in the middle as Tristan mirrored her actions. It wasn't smooth at all, but they came down at the same moment hard enough to knock out the creatures.

"That's not going to last long, Tristan."

"Stand back."

She sidestepped away as he stripped down, turned into his gryphon, and blew fire at the three demons trying to get up. He melted them into a stinking sulfur puddle. It finally dried into ashes.

"What the hell?" she asked no one in particular.

Tristan shifted back and quickly dressed. "I can't do it often. Another side effect of the witch highball that gave me the ability to teleport. I say we use it now."

She'd find out more later. "Teleport Quinn and Reese somewhere safe first, then come back." When Tristan vanished, she backstepped to stand next to the highlander where she could watch all around them.

Over her shoulder, she glanced in time to see him swing that blade to take down two demons at a time.

Not bad even if he was annoying.

The black hole belched out three more demons.

Why was I-zubrrali not sending his army of demons at once? She didn't want that, but she feared he was keeping them distracted to attack another way.

She threw kinetic hits, knocking two glowing demons out over the hole where they fell to the bottom.

Sling-Blade-in-a-kilt took out the third one.

Tristan returned twenty seconds later. "Isak's going to unload on the pit. Let's go."

"Get Casper out of here and I'll start your way so I can watch our backs."

"No. Take the lass," the highlander shouted.

"Call me that again and I'm gonna hurt ya!" Evalle's world spun in a flash of colors. When her head stopped spinning, she cursed and snarled, "Little notice next time."

Tristan snapped right back, "I did. Pay attention."

Next to him stood the highlander, Quinn, and Reese.

"Sorry. You know I hate teleporting, but thanks." Evalle shoved hair out of her face, then yanked her elastic band out and smoothed her hair back into a new ponytail.

Isak's team dropped something in the hole that blasted fast and sucked back into itself.

Nice. Evalle looked around. "Anyone hurt?"

Reese said, "No. We're all good, but I-zubrrali has to be down there."

"Yep, I saw him during one of the big blasts from Isak's team," Evalle admitted. "Wouldn't it be nice if they took out Daddy Dearest at the same time?"

"What is Daddy Dearest?" the highlander asked.

Evalle had lost the ability to carry on a conversation with Casper's other half. "Will you let Casper come back?"

Eyeing her as if some wench had refused to serve him a mug of ale or whatever medieval warriors drank, the highlander became translucent, lost shape, and reformed as Casper.

The cowboy looked around. "How'd we end up this far along?"

Tristan filled him in.

Evalle added, "Have a talk with your highlander and tell him to stop calling me *lass* like some damsel when we're battling."

"I have no idea what he says most of the time," Casper said, sounding not happy to admit that point.

To lighten the mood, Evalle teased, "Better be careful or you might wake up in a Las Vegas Elvis chapel married to some *lass* he actually charmed."

Casper frowned. "Hell, I don't need another reason to worry about him takin' my body."

"Listen up, group," Quinn said, getting them back on track. "Isak is working his way to us. We'll be stronger as a larger single unit."

"He needs to hurry," Reese announced.

Evalle asked, "Demons still coming from the pit?"

"Yes." Reese stood here with all of them ready to battle monsters, but it didn't change the worry in her voice. She had a baby to protect regardless of said child being cursed to never live.

"Tell little Wonkerdink to be cool. We got this." Evalle forced a smile for Reese, who snorted a laugh, breaking the tension.

Casper scowled. "That's not even a name, Evalle."

"Who says?"

Quinn had his arm around Reese. He whispered close to her, "Keep an eye on our backs so nothing sneaks up."

She reminded him, "Don't start pushing me to the side. You need my power to fight these things."

"True, but not until we've used our power first. Agreed?"

After letting out a long sigh that sounded like a teapot releasing steaming air, she muttered, "Fine."

Evalle smiled at Reese, who swung around to face the pit just as three demons raced up from a sea of black. "*Incoming!*"

"Oh, hell," Casper grumbled. "Not sure how much juice I have."

"Why don't you watch over Reese and take a minute to regain your energy?" Evalle suggested quietly.

"I'll do that."

She, Tristan, and Quinn worked well as a team of Beladors

blasting demons. They could communicate faster telepathically when Quinn didn't have to ensure Casper and Reese heard his orders.

One short-legged demon with black holes for eyes and a big head covered in scabs raced up on Evalle's unprotected left. She called up her spelled blade, took a step, and pushed off the ground with kinetics to flip in the air. She came down behind the demon that dropped its head back as it watched her fly over him.

She rammed the blade into its back, stabbing deep to hit the heart, then yanked out her blade.

The demon imploded and turned into a cloud of dust.

Blaster strikes hit twenty feet below her.

She stood too close to the edge when power blasted dirt away. Her feet slid out from under her. She stabbed her blade to slow her fall.

Tristan lunged forward, grabbing her wrist. She latched onto his wrist and then he flipped her over his shoulder.

She landed on her feet with knees bent, jumped around, and caught sight of Isak's men closing a short distance to reach them. They took out demons every step along the way.

Isak reached them first. "Seen any Imortiks other than what's coming out of the pit?"

Quinn pulled Reese closer to him. "Yes. We had a couple attack from the woods."

"Three, in fact," Evalle added.

"The ones in the pit scattered after our big strike." As he spoke, Isak gave a hand signal to his men. Three split off from his team with their badass blasters up and ready as they headed into the tree thicket.

"Did you get I-zubrrali?" Reese asked hopefully.

Shaking his head, Isak glanced at the pit then back to her. "I saw him the first time we unloaded hard to the bottom of the pit, but he blinked away."

"Dammit." Reese stared at the dark hole as if she could conjure I-zubrrali up for target practice.

Blasters fired in the trees. It was over in seconds.

"That might be all of the Imortiks near us for now," Isak

said. His stoic face revealed nothing, but Evalle had known him longer than the rest of this group. His eyes held so much disappointment. She wished they'd found a building or some unexpected energy that might indicate a lead to Adrianna.

With the exception of a few small buildings they'd checked out near Starlight Theater, there had been nothing but land between the drive-in and Gresham Park area.

A large helicopter flew overhead with loud thumping, then circled back to make another pass north of them. Everything about it screamed military.

Evalle asked, "Is that one of your people?"

Without glancing up, Isak said, "Yes. I had him wait until we cleared out all we could up to this spot. He's running the FLIR to see if any undetected warm bodies show up."

"Forward-looking infrared," Casper muttered. "I don't think Sen is warm-blooded."

Isak gave the cowboy a dark smile. "Exactly."

The helicopter kept making passes, moving away from them.

As soon as Isak's three men returned from the forest, he used hand signals to turn his team south. "Let's see what else is out here."

Quinn fell into step with Isak, keeping Reese next to him.

Evalle, Tristan, and Casper caught up. Evidently Isak's men knew to hang behind and watch their backs.

"Where is Daegan right now?" Evalle asked Tristan in a low voice.

"Oh, man. We were—"

An explosion sounded a millisecond before a surge of power hit Evalle hard as a steel bar across her middle, sending her flying backward with Tristan.

She saw and heard nothing else before she blacked out.

# CHAPTER 4

HIDDEN BY CLOAKING MORE THAN the black cover of early morning, Macha perched on the small roof of a mausoleum in Oakland Park Cemetery. Humans living or visiting Atlanta found this cemetery fascinating because of its age and occupants.

How amusing. This place was not even three hundred years old yet and many who toured the sprawling cemetery had no idea just what slept here.

Mutterings below her had been going on for the last ten minutes. Five warlocks of Queen Maeve's Scáth Force unit milled around in anxious quiet, all wearing clothes more suited to young humans rambling through the city at night.

Or there would be if not for the humans having established a curfew. All to kill nonhumans running free.

These humans had no idea what they were going up against.

If Queen Maeve did not show soon to meet with her elite warriors, Macha would be forced to get her hands dirty to find out what information this bunch had for their crazy leader.

No, she would be patient.

Killing this group would mean starting over trying to find Queen Maeve and observe her people in secret. It had taken Macha handshakes with three Nightstalkers to learn where these warlocks had been today. The last ghoul had seen the men heading into Oakland Park Cemetery.

What were these warlocks searching for that Queen Maeve could not discover from her scrying wall?

Perhaps the wall in TÅµr Medb no longer functioned.

An owl flew up and landed on the corner to Macha's right and hooted as if trying to out her position.

Two warlocks glanced up sharply and squinted.

One flicked on a flashlight, turning the beam on the owl.

Could that Scáth Force warlock not produce light with his hands?

A loud blast south of here shook the ground and drew everyone's attention.

The Scáth Force leader told his men, "Doesn't concern us. Stay alert."

The bird departed and Macha sighed, once again waiting while the men returned to kicking stones and grumbling.

She leaned back against the tall pinnacle rising above the narrow mausoleum roof and stared into the dark skies as she had long ago when this land had been known as Atlanta Graveyard. A desolate place before the ostentatious markers were added. Mausoleums like the one beneath her came later.

Vehicle horns blared nearby. Not many. The sound of Atlanta traffic a stone's throw away on the interstate rarely moved so fast. With the curfew, many roads had been reduced to no traffic at all.

A swirl of energy and dark crystals spun into view below. The form of Queen Maeve took shape.

Her men snapped to attention.

She stood over six feet tall with hair tumbling past her shoulders to her waist, though disappointing. Why was her hair so dull when it should have been vibrant with life? The locks failed to lift and float at will, almost a signature look for Queen Maeve. Even her gown lacked any dazzle.

Had she come here incognito or had she lost some of her shine?

As if Macha cared?

That bitch was responsible for Macha being pushed out of Treoir realm by the only being who could do such a thing, one of King Gruffyn's children. Why couldn't Queen Maeve have killed Daegan while she had his dragon trapped in her realm?

Arrogance and overconfidence would be that fool's downfall, but not before Macha got what she wanted.

What she deserved.

She would rule Treoir realm again and this time she wouldn't be so nice to those who had welcomed Daegan and turned their backs on her.

A woman should always learn by her mistakes.

When Macha learned a lesson, she made sure others paid the price.

The warlocks dropped their heads in deference at the presence of their queen.

"What news do you bring me, Erath?" Queen Maeve asked the one who appeared to lead her Scáth Force warriors.

"The Beladors are wearing down and they're now being hunted by human military forces out to kill any nonhumans. I've spread my unit out to monitor Beladors, the human military, and other nonhumans. Vladimir Quinn comes and goes as the Belador Maistir with Evalle filling in when he's not around. He's been here longer than normal, which appears to be due to a woman named Reese as much as the Imortik problem."

Queen Maeve nodded slowly. "I have seen those two together on my scrying wall, but paid them little mind. What is going on?"

Macha had received a report long ago that the Beladors had broken the scrying wall when they rescued the dragon throne.

Evidently Queen Maeve had a new one.

Erath continued reporting. "A being is creating demons fast. A lot of them. When we were able to draw information from Nightstalkers, we learned the being is called I-zubrrali and that he wants the baby this Reese is carrying."

Queen Maeve's physical change from irritated to calm indicated his news had pleased her. "Is there a problem gaining information from Nightstalkers?"

"Not if we can find them. Someone has been killing Nightstalkers after shaking with them. The ghouls who observed this have pulled back into the dark and word is getting around. That person has shut down what we can find out quickly."

Macha grinned. A benefit she hadn't expected from killing the three Nightstalkers whose hands she'd shaken. She'd only intended to cover her tracks.

Queen Maeve floated a foot off the ground.

Every warrior stared at her in horror.

What did they expect to happen next?

When their leader glanced down, she scowled. "Why are you staring?"

Every set of eyes turned downcast. Erath said, "We are merely in awe of your power and greatness, my highness."

That one knew how to appease his crazy queen. She floated back to the ground and began issuing orders again. "Pay attention. I still need a grimoire volume and not one of the two moving around this city."

Erath cautiously said, "We are prepared to do your bidding, your highness. We merely need direction and intel."

Her hair finally began moving, though chaotically. "Once Daegan and Tristan are not around to teleport their people, capture Quinn. If not him, then this Reese. That will provide leverage."

Erath performed an impressive job of hiding his reservations. "Yes, your highness," he started off carefully. "How will we know the dragon and gryphon are not around to kill us?"

At one time, Queen Maeve had been as attractive as any goddess should be, though no match for Macha. At the moment, even when Queen Maeve smiled, her lined face could no longer be called attractive or even plain.

Dark Noirre majik had chewed away at her prior beauty. Poisonous majik practically bled from her pores. Her terse voice would slash off an arm if used as a weapon. "I shall ensure the dragon is not in the way. When you hear reports of the red dragon flying in Mongolia, that will be the time to hunt Quinn. It might be tonight or tomorrow. I go there next."

Erath began instructing his men on how they were going to regroup and focus on Quinn's team to be ready for their queen's signal.

"One more thing, Erath."

"Yes, your highness?"

"Bring me an Imortik-human. I do not want a possessed demon or Belador."

Not a sound came from the appalled guards until their leader spoke up again.

Color faded from Erath's face. "How, uh, how do we stop the monster from grabbing one of us?"

"You just bring one to me," she snapped. "I will pull the Imortik from the body then use that Imortik to gain a grimoire volume."

Macha blinked at that claim.

How could Queen Maeve do such a thing? Macha tossed it around in her mind. Queen Maeve had been known to use necromancy, a disgusting habit. Could this crazy queen withdraw an Imortik from a human body after it died? Or would she be able to kill the human while keeping the Imortik alive?

Was that even possible?

Macha seriously doubted so. Queen Maeve had continually shown signs of deterioration after she and Cathbad reincarnated in this time, or what they called reincarnation.

"You have your orders, Erath. I shall return after I have dealt with the red dragon." Queen Maeve vanished in a blaze of sparks and energy, nothing impressive for those who expected more of a being with her powers.

Macha seethed. She would not allow that whacko bitch to screw her again by trapping Daegan.

While Queen Maeve lived up to the rumors of her insanity, being crazy did not diminish her power or ability to upend Macha's plans.

She considered what to do while the Scáth Force warriors filed out, whispering about how they feared bringing in an Imortik.

But they had no choice if they did not wish to face a horrid death.

She'd heard their plans and knew where they were going. If she followed them, she might end up with a grimoire volume after all.

But if she showed up in Mongolia, she would be there to kill Daegan and anyone else who dared to stop her, including Queen Maeve. That would provide someone to point a finger at for the death.

Decisions, decisions.

Maybe she could have both.

# CHAPTER 5

FEAR TAPPED DOWN CASIDHE'S SPINE, trying to provoke a reaction.

"What is it?" she whispered against Daegan's back, too tired to protest his caveman action.

She'd normally squawk at any man who pushed her behind him as if she couldn't protect herself. After tangling with Herrick's vulture, arguing with Zeelindar, then ending up trapped underground, she was a quart low on give-a-shit.

Daegan had dragged them into this dark room. Let him deal with whatever was making that swooshing sound. She could see nothing in this inky darkness.

Heat rolled off him like a furnace.

She struggled not to lean forward against his wide form and soak up his warm strength. Every inhale reminded her of being up against his hot body in the hotel bed. Seemed like ages ago.

"I do not know what 'tis yet." Daegan spoke low, having turned rigid as a statue when he went on alert.

"Huh?" She startled, having zoned out, drunk on her memories.

Good way to be caught off guard.

She waited for him to snap at her, but his hand reached around, bringing her closer to him. One touch and her hormones stopped playing cards and took note.

Her senses sharpened, trying to pick up any hint of what shared this space with them.

She didn't hear the shirring noise again, or any noise.

Now the quiet bothered her.

Where had the owner of that swooshing sound gone? Or was the thing still in the same room with them in stealth mode?

"Hand me your wee LED."

Daegan's whisper jolted her into action. She had a grip on

the strap to her backpack but had hesitated to make noise by bringing out her sword. Leaning over to one side, she fumbled for the correct pocket and found the zipper pull. No matter how slowly she tugged it, the zipper teeth made a ripping sound. She cringed, hurrying ahead to find the key ring flashlight.

When she had the marketing trinket in hand, she caught his hand and opened it, clamping her hand down with the light sandwiched between them.

Energy buzzed between her fingers and his hand.

He jerked as if she'd shocked him.

She curled her fingers away from him. They were connected, dammit, if only he'd admit it. Something about her energy called out for Daegan's. She'd give anything to know why. Damn Herrick for keeping her past secret. There was no way she'd ever give him Jennyver, which meant there was no way she'd ever know who she was or where she came from.

She made a pissy face at the irritating man only inches away. How could she be such a fool to crave Daegan's touch, to want him, when he refused to discuss the issue between them and act as if he didn't want her touch?

Hardheaded dragon shifter.

"Thank ya." Daegan's deep voice had a small hitch in it.

When he flicked the light on, she held her breath and looked around his left side. The wide beam from such a small gadget illuminated walls on each side of her, but disappeared into the darkness straight ahead.

Was this a corridor?

"Nothin' on these walls. 'Tis not another room but a passage." He moved the light side to side then above them to the ceiling.

She hadn't even considered some creature clinging to the ceiling and should have. She'd seen her share of scary movies.

Thankfully, nothing dropped down on them.

The hall was twelve feet wide and as tall as the last room. She asked, "What do we do now?"

"Ya stay here. I shall search farther and come back for ya."

"Are you serious? *No!*" she hissed quietly. "A wall may open and close again. You're not leavin' me here. We're together until this is done."

He said nothing.

Why did being with him now have to feel so awkward? Because he would not just talk about what happened in the Caucasus Mountains and clear the air.

He had to meet her halfway for any hope of going forward.

Daegan finally said, "We shall go together, but stay behind me and do as I say."

"Of course, your highness," she snapped back at him.

Turning to her with the LED glow pointed down, the ambient light outlined his angry features. "I am not your king to order ya around. I wish only to keep ya safe, not to offend ya."

Not what she had expected.

Exhaustion pushed at her body and mind. She didn't want to sound crabby when they had to locate a rock for Zeelindar and the grimoire volume plus, just as important, find a way out. They could be many levels underground and she'd read that some underground structures in Egypt had no access between levels.

Rubbing her eyes, she shook off her weariness. "No insult taken. I'm just tired. I'll follow your directions."

Muscles in his face loosened. His mouth moved as if his lips were going to smile, something she'd been missing. The moment stretched and stretched.

His deep gaze held her in place. He tilted his head down.

Her heart danced around, sure he was going to kiss her. She lifted up. She would meet him halfway.

A loud clacking noise erupted sounding like a gun blast.

She jumped back.

Daegan's words were quick and precise. "Do ya have your backpack on?"

She snapped the buckles. "Got it."

"Draw your sword. Should I go down, I want ya armed."

No! They would find a way to escape together. She grasped the hilt of her sword and slid it free.

If they faced something that could defeat Daegan, she would go down fighting to protect him.

He took several steps forward and paused. His voice was gentle when he said, "Grasp my jeans so I know ya are close."

She extended her free fingers, then hesitated. "What about how our energy reacts, Daegan? Will me touchin' you be a distraction?"

He grunted something that sounded like a curse, but said, "I shall be fine."

She arched an eyebrow in challenge at his back and slid her fingers over the top of his waistband at his back, curling them into a solid grip. She tried to come up with something clever or teasing to say to lighten the moment, but her hand warmed so close to him she couldn't think.

*He* was going to be a distraction to her. "Ready."

Daegan moved slowly on light steps, keeping his stride short, which allowed her to stay on pace with him. She laid her blade over her shoulder to avoid accidentally slicing off a part of his anatomy.

Every ten to fifteen feet, she angled her head to see what he saw. Nothing but more of the dark hallway.

What if they could find no emblems or carvings that said Mulatko? Was that a person, place, or thing? Zeelindar could have given them more. What if that information had been in the first room and they hadn't found it?

She could see no way for them to return to that room.

They'd covered about seventy steps when Daegan stopped.

She'd been so lost in thought she bumped into him and murmured, "Sorry."

"Shhh."

All grogginess fled at being hushed. What had he seen or heard?

She kept her breathing shallow, listening for any indication of a threat.

There was the swooshing again.

And a little crackling sound, too.

Daegan's upper body moved with deep breaths. "We have nowhere to go but forward."

He was telling her they couldn't stand in this hall and find the grimoire or a way out.

"I understand." She did. There was only one choice. Face whatever was down here with them.

When he made another twelve steps, light bloomed ahead of him, which had nothing to do with her LED. She released his jeans and stepped up beside him.

He gave her back the key ring light and kept moving until the passage had funneled them into another room.

It stretched over forty feet long and maybe thirty feet wide with a copper sculpture in the center.

The most elegant bird she'd ever seen had feathers that flowed away from its body in a way that reminded her of beautiful betta fish with sweeping fins. Long tendrils trailed from the wing feathers and its tail fanned behind with different-length streamers as if it stood in a pleasant wind. Even its head had a tuft of swirly ribbons in tall curls.

She studied the shape beneath the bird. It perched on a stack of different sized silver globes piled three feet high.

"I wonder what that bird represents?" she murmured.

"I do not know. It looks nothin' like the simple images on the walls."

She angled her head back and forth, searching for some marking on the globes, but saw none. "We may not be in Egypt. I've never heard of a giant bird sculpture like that found by archeologists, but then again, we may be the first people to walk through this area in a millennium or more."

Daegan said nothing, seeming deep in thought.

"What made the lights come on again?" she asked more for herself, not expecting him to provide an answer.

He told her, "I feel we must have caused that to happen by enterin' the rooms."

She looked up at his profile. Deep worry lines cut away from the corners of his eyes. "You mean like a trip wire, somethin' that we stepped on or touched to activate the lights?"

"No. I feel 'tis more along the lines of this structure choosin' to light an area or not for us."

If she wasn't already creeped out, the idea that the walls, floors, and ceilings were sentient would do it. She rubbed her arms at the cool air circulating around as if this place had an air conditioner.

No noise. No vents.

There had to be some way to bring oxygen here, right?

Four tube lights like the ones in the first chamber glowed at each corner again. These were larger but still shaped with one round end fatter than the other.

And the same snake-shaped filament.

"We should search the images on the walls while we have light," Daegan pointed out as he moved deeper into the room.

She agreed, but stepped forward cautiously. When she was halfway to the bird statue, she turned slowly to assess the walls.

Her gaze dropped to the lights.

She couldn't get past those being down here. Having been around supernaturals for so long, she'd have better understood candles or a torch blazing to life.

She'd heard about what appeared to be filament lights found by archeologists in Egyptian structures with the bulb still glowing as if it had done so continually since the structures were built in 2500 BCE.

That sounded unrealistic. She'd dismissed it out of hand the first time she'd heard it. There had been some argument about no soot from candles or torches inside those structures, which begged the question of how the people had carved and painted so many intricate designs, people, and animal shapes if there had been no light.

At the moment, she wished she'd researched more. With all the ancient information jammed in her brain, why hadn't she spent a little time researching hieroglyphics?

Because Herrick would have thought she was wasting time?

She couldn't use that excuse moving forward. Every decision from now on was on her. A familiar scent tickled her nose. "You smell somethin' like frankincense?"

"I do not know of this scent."

"It's an incense and, uhm, I think an embalmin' material used on the bodies." *Way to up the creep factor, idiot.* She slipped her sword into her backpack and focused on the wall to the left of what appeared to be the exit hallway.

If she tried to translate that she wouldn't think about mummies chasing them down a corridor with no exit.

Walking around the copper centerpiece, Daegan took a spot

in front of the dark hall. "Read what ya are able to reach while I keep watch at where the passage continues beyond this room."

She stepped up to the wall and studied it.

Of the eight horizontal rows, she chose one in the middle at eye level. She wiped the damp palm of her left hand on her pants. Old habits never die when it came to touching anything this old. Placing that hand on the wall to steady her as much as make a connection, she moved her right hand across just above the relief.

The letters flipped up and down. Had to be because her reading hand trembled. She paused and took a couple deep breaths to calm her insides. How long would it take to find something useful? What if they didn't?

Daegan asked, "What is wrong?"

She stiffened her backbone. "Nothin'. Just gettin' settled into translatin'."

His long stare argued the truth of her words.

Too bad. She turned back to the wall. This time the letters moved more smoothly. By the time she reached a row at her knees, she had gleaned enough to believe this was not what they needed.

Speaking without turning to Daegan, she explained, "This is talkin' about how this space was constructed for celebratin' someone or somethin'. That might be in the images higher up. I read it as dancin' or movin' in some ritual way that brought pleasure. I'm goin' to try a different wall." She walked toward the one on Daegan's right.

He extended a hand, stopping her.

She lifted an annoyed glance at him. "What?"

"All ya must do is read what ya can figure out. Do not fash over bein' unable to find the answers this minute. I have a sense this could be a large place. It may require a bit of patience for our search."

Her anger bubbled and deflated.

Had that been what was eating at her? It was her nature to take responsibility for every task, knowing those around her held high expectations for her gift.

Daegan would place high expectations on himself, too, which

was probably why he figured out what had her on edge.

They had to work together. To do that, sniping and arguing had to stop.

She blew an errant lock of hair off her forehead that returned immediately. "Thanks."

Before he dropped his hand, he lifted it to her face and brushed her hair back. Of course, it stayed this time.

The small touch stomped the accelerator on her adrenaline.

She didn't know where to go from here. He'd asked for a truce.

Touching her felt like more than a truce.

Would he talk now? Her gaze stayed on his long enough to read the conflict there, answering her question.

He cleared his throat and stepped back, turning to keep guard over the dark hall she hoped was an exit.

Moment broken, she continued to the wall, feeling less stressed over figuring out the hieroglyphics, but more tense about being with Daegan, yet not being with him.

Two rows into this side, she backed off. "This one makes no sense. Sounds like it may be talkin' about someone comin' here or comin' to the land. I may have to start at the top to see if there is any reference to what we need."

Daegan came to her. "Ya wish to go higher?"

His deep voice so close started her hormones rabble-rousing. The bunch of little traitors wanted to climb up against him, get as close as possible. Kissed, lifted, laid down, mounted ... touched everywhere.

A trickle of sweat ran down between her breasts.

"Up or not?" he asked impatiently.

That's right. He waited for an answer.

"Up," she choked out. This place was doing strange things to her. The air felt cool one moment and hot the next.

Those large hands clamped firmly around her waist and picked her up to eye level with the top line. Daegan showed no strain to hold her in the correct location. He understood exactly how fast to move her from right to left, the direction she'd chosen this time as a starting point based on the birds facing to the right.

She spoke as she read even though each image did not equate to a word or a sentence. "Okay, this helps. The time of ... somethin' like power risin' began in this land. Uhm ... Eesumor," she said slowly, pronouncing the name phonetically, which was likely wrong.

Daegan paused from moving. "E su what?"

"*Ee-su-mor*," she said louder. "It appears to be the name of the bird, the statue. The bird came to honor Amentet, which I think was an Egyptian goddess. Huh."

"What?"

"There's an image of a creature with wings like the one you found. Amentet is lookin' at it in one image. I haven't found a word to go with the winged creature, but it does remind me of a dragon or a gryphon. Hard to say. Like I said, this unfortunately was not my area of ancient studies, but if I recall correctly, Amentet was one of the nicer deities."

Continuing to carry her along the wall, Daegan asked, "I recall that name, but nothin' else about it. The face on the woman looks like a cat or lion."

"Evidently she is associated with a lion as well as some other forms. It's interestin' how jewels wrap the lion's neck, but the rest seems to be human from there. I'll definitely look into her history if I ever get out of here." Fat chance of that happening. Nothing they had tried did any good. They were trapped and might die here.

He lowered her to the floor and turned her. "We shall escape this place. Ya shall study many more books."

Daegan said that with such conviction, she decided to believe him even if he only said it to give her confidence.

Trying harder to smile, she said, "Thanks for the pep talk." When he frowned, she added in a wry voice, "Pep talk is like encouragin' your soldiers before they battle."

He lifted an eyebrow at that. "I would say far more and in a stronger voice to bring my soldiers up to battle ready."

"Well, what you said works for me right now. Please put me back up to the third line. I feel like I'm startin' to make some sense of this."

When he had her in place, she skipped forward, explaining rather than trying to read the words and terms that appeared. She did recall that hieroglyphics did not read as text in a book would.

Back on track, she resumed translating. "Best I can figure, Eesumor came to meet Amentet and honor her. The giant bird delighted Amentet. As a guest, the bird flew throughout the, uhm, buildin', no." She stretched her hand to catch more information. "Palace, maybe? While doing so, Eesumor found a thief and ripped the thief apart. Eww."

"Sounds as if the bird reacted as a guard or soldier."

"I suppose so. I can read the rest standin' on the floor."

Daegan put her down, but his hands remained around her waist. Heat flowed from his fingers. Her crazed energy buzzed where he touched.

If he didn't pull away soon, she'd melt back against him and that was no way to retain her self-respect.

She stepped forward and to the side, pulling away from his hands. She could not give in to her longing, no matter how nice a few minutes in his arms again might be. Not until he was willing to hash out what happened with his sister and clear the air.

She had to know where she stood. Nothing would change between them otherwise.

She desperately wanted to go back to a time when they were in sync, but only if they were on equal footing again.

Right now, he didn't trust her and would not listen to her explanation. For that reason, she didn't trust him with her emotions, her body, or her heart.

She hurried to the right end of the wall and began reading again as Daegan drifted over to guard the hallway leading out of here. She kept her voice steady, pretending she was not emotionally off-balance inside.

"This part talks about how those restin' here are honored, but it mentions none by name except Amentet. This area seems like a general statement of some sort. Based on that, there may be many others entombed here. Maybe. I can't say anythin' for sure."

When she could read no more, she stood upright and stretched her back muscles from leaning forward so much. "If I'm decipherin' correctly, Eesumor vowed to remain with Amentet as a guardian, even after death, to protect her and her treasures. That would explain the statue."

Daegan's deep voice rumbled. "If the statue was made to represent lifelike, the bird was of great size."

She caught him glancing her way for only a second then turning his wide back on her again. He had his arms crossed, a normal look for him, but he seemed drawn into himself.

Was he trying to *not* look at her?

To *not* touch her? Major fail on that one.

Probably wrong of her to feel a little happy about him being moody, but she was tired of dealing with all these jumbled feelings alone. Why should *he* be content when the stubborn man wouldn't give an inch?

Daegan scratched his chin where his beard had begun growing then folded his arms again.

She'd seen him with a clean-shaven face and beard. She liked the scruffy uncivilized look in direct contrast to the modern jeans and T-shirt he wore. Modern clothes would never change that man. He struck an imposing silhouette of muscles upon muscles, all gained by battling and training to battle. His strong chin led the way when he spoke, letting an opponent know he meant every word and warning.

She didn't want to be his opponent, dammit.

"We may need to go deeper into this structure," Daegan announced.

Resigned to keep moving, she took in the only hieroglyphics left for her to review. "All that is left for me to read is a single row at the top of the walls on each side of the hallway we entered from. Makes me think they might represent some information about that first room."

Daegan glanced behind him. "Zeelindar may have dropped us in the first room to start the search. If we continue goin' this way in the same direction, we may find Amentet's tomb. Perhaps somethin' there will point us toward Mulatko."

That hinky feeling of being watched crawled up her spine. She slowed her step, searching all around. She even looked up at the ceiling this time.

Nothing here except her and Daegan.

And the statue.

She heard a brief swooshing sound again.

Daegan became very still. His arms unfolded slowly to fall loose at his sides.

An electrical buzz charged the air. Fine hairs stood up on her arms.

"Come here," Daegan said so quietly, Casidhe had to convince herself he'd even spoken. He hadn't turned around.

Her heart slammed her chest. She took two calm steps toward him when she wanted to run. That deep primal fear of something in the dark alone with you when she'd been a kid returned.

She wasn't in the dark.

Or alone.

Daegan turned. His face morphed into a fierce warrior. He held his hands out and called forth something by name.

She'd bet he had called up his ancient sword.

Nothing appeared. Shock rode his face. He rushed to her, yelling, "*Runnn!*"

She tried. Her legs struggled as if running through quicksand.

A high-pitched scream and loud swooshing flooded the air. She looked over her shoulder as she reached the dark exit

Daegan faced Eesumor, but not the statue.

The bird stood ten feet tall. Vibrant orange, blue, and gold energy glowed along every feather on wings stretched wide.

Smoke trailed from the bird's eyes now bright as brake lights at night.

Daegan backed up quickly and tried to hit it with kinetics.

Nothing.

Did that mean Daegan had no powers?

Casidhe had frozen at the exit, unable to plow forward and leave him.

Eesumor flapped those wild wings. Sparks flew off the tendrils streaming from the feathers. When the long wings slapped the silver balls on the stand, one exploded with bright light.

Daegan shouted, "*Run, dammit!*"

# CHAPTER 6

KLEIO FINISHED HER MORNING ABLUTIONS and hung the damp washcloth over the edge of the basin. The woodsy and crisp scent of myrrh incense permeated the room. She inhaled deeply, saturating her being with the best armor she had against the negative energy building in the castle.

Herrick roared in the main hall.

She placed her hands on the basin cabinet and leaned forward, staring at the dark circles beneath her eyes in the mirror.

And the rage continued.

Herrick was losing his mind. In looking back, he might have been deteriorating slowly over the past year. He'd become more crazed over finding Skarde as she'd shared visions about his brother. She might have withheld some had she known Herrick would throw Casidhe into danger as he grasped for anything to find his brother.

He'd thought nothing of holding Daegan's sister for thousands of years to trade for Skarde.

Kleio's heart ached every time she thought about how long she'd lived here with no idea of what he'd hidden in his lair. She'd had odd visions she couldn't translate of heavy darkness in his cave at the rear of the castle. She'd written those off as Herrick struggling to live this long without family.

That had been so far from the truth.

Stepping away from the mirror, she walked anxiously around the room, trying to clear her mind. If Daegan had left with Jennyver and Skarde had remained here, Herrick might have begun to heal.

Screams from below climbed the stairs to the second floor, destroying any hope of peace today.

She did not believe he would physically harm his clan, not yet, but those docile and kind people did not deserve his wrath.

He demanded visions from her as if she could harvest them on demand. She'd hoped for a few hours in meditation to open herself up to visions she needed to guide her forward, but she couldn't in good conscience stay in her private area.

Not if she could go down and quiet Herrick to offer the rest of the castle folk some peace.

Once she finished dressing in her gray wool gown, her normal unadorned clothing, Kleio went downstairs to the main hall.

Not a serving person moved through the great hall. No one tended the fire. No one performed daily cleaning.

She followed the smell of fresh baked bread to the dining table set with the sliced loaf and apricot jam in an earthen jar. Arranged on a round platter were pakhlava rolls and qatik, a sour cream type of cheese she hadn't cared for her first year. Funny how she'd become accustomed to the odd foods, much like learning how to deal with an overbearing dragon shifter. She spooned the jam on a piece of warm bread.

Herrick had provided well for everyone all the years Kleio had spent here. He had not been a tyrant until recently.

The heavy entrance door banged open.

"*There you are!*" Herrick shouted.

Kleio finished her bread, wiped her hands on a napkin, and turned to greet him. "I have been in this castle since yesterday morning when I last saw you."

He stomped across the distance, pausing three strides from her.

She refused to be intimidated by him. "What did you want?"

"I want my brother."

"I think everyone in this castle is aware of that desire. I am not a magician to snap my fingers and produce Skarde."

Lines in Herrick's face sharpened with his voice. "Do not get mouthy with me today. I have not rested since watching Daegan's witch steal Skarde from me. I want answers."

"I do not think she is a witch."

"Do not argue with me!"

Not sleeping certainly attributed to Herrick's nonstop fury. Kleio avoided mentioning that observation as he never welcomed advice on his mental and physical health.

She moved ahead, hoping conversation might help. "I have had no new visions on Skarde. This makes me think he is in Daegan's realm."

Wiping a hand over his mouth, Herrick turned away, muttering to himself. He made a fast spin, circling back to her. "I have no bargaining chip to force the red dragon to bring back Skarde. You *must* find Jennyver."

Herrick had hounded her nonstop for any vision. She'd had several and had put off as long as she could to share them while she decided her next move.

Her mentor god, Janus, had told her, "Your vision will change your path and your path will change the course of the human world."

She'd dwelled on that late last night. When she arose this morning, she still was not sure when her path would change or why. "You must be careful with your next actions, Herrick."

"Do *not* tell me what to do!" he shouted.

"If you allow me to finish what I have to say, you'll realize I have something of importance to share."

He strode over to the fireplace, stewing over her words. "Speak."

"I merely am saying if you harm anyone connected to the red dragon, be that Jennyver or Casidhe, you risk harming Skarde."

"Casidhe betrayed all I did for her," he argued in a menacing tone.

Kleio no longer engaged with him about his twisted view of Casidhe. To do so only wasted her breath. "Have you considered that Skarde may not wish to come here?"

That brought Herrick's head up. Eyes wide, he acted as if she'd cursed him in tongues. "Of course he wants to be here. He is my brother. Where else would he go?"

She might have agreed at one time, but after one specific vision she'd been holding back, she believed Herrick would be disappointed to learn the truth. Skarde cared for Jennyver. That being the case, Skarde would likely be furious over her treatment. At least, she would hope so.

Kleio shrugged. "Everything changes with time. Even family.

You were not happy to see Brynhild."

"That sister always fought me for first place in the family even knowing it was mine by birthright. I will eventually speak to her, but I want no one else until Skarde is here where he will be safe."

Kleio lifted the napkin, folding it to take a moment and prepare her next question. She'd noticed small signs of aging appearing recently in Herrick's face. What was going on with him? "I now understand why you were limited in how long you could be away from the castle in the past, but why do you stay here and not take a nice break with your dragon now that you are free of Jennyver depending upon you?" She braced for his reaction at having Daegan's sister brought up again.

He surprised her by lifting a poker and pushing logs around casually. "I am waiting for Skarde's dragon to fly with mine."

Kleio acknowledged the sadness as sincere, but only that part. She could not put her finger on why his words sounded untrue, but she did not believe he stayed here only for that reason. Unease had filtered through his voice and movements more than anything else.

She seriously doubted he suffered a lick of guilt over his sin with Jennyver.

What did he still hide?

Putting the poker down, he turned a calmer expression to her and crossed his arms. "I thought you had something significant to share with me."

"I have pieces of visions, not my normal ones with clear meaning. That is why I'd like you to be careful as I pull together everything. One vision was of you never seeing Skarde again."

Herrick's jaw dropped and his arms fell loose. "What? *That is wrong!*"

"I told you the vision is not complete. I am having to guess at some of it."

"I do not *accept* that vision. *Go back and do better!*"

She clamped her teeth hard to keep from yelling at him. "I feel a complete vision would come to me if there was *peace* in this castle. You shout all day and scare everyone. If you give me time and harmony in my surroundings, I will have more success."

His blue eyes darkened to black pits. "This should be a simple request, one you've always been able to provide in the past. Find Casidhe. That should be simple. I wish to speak with her."

Was he that thickheaded? "Why? The night Casidhe left, I had a vision of your vulture attacking her in the valley."

Herrick would not meet her eyes. "Unlike some around me, Stian is loyal and thought only to bring her back."

"That is not true."

On a hair trigger to strike at anyone, he shifted a deadly gaze at her. "You *dare* to call me a liar?"

Yes, she did dare, but sidestepped that question by answering, "I meant that is not what I saw in the vision. How do you expect her to ever return or to help you again when Casidhe had to fight your vulture?"

He dismissed the question with, "Stian did not bring her back. The girl escaped."

Kleio's fingers curled at him calling Casidhe a girl. That young *woman* had bested this dragon shifter right here in his castle. "Casidhe escaped only because she had help once more from the red dragon." Daegan's gryphon, to be exact, but the result was the same.

Herrick shook his fist. "Casidhe constantly betrays me and you encourage her!"

"How do I encourage her?" Kleio asked rather than admitting she had done just that. "She is not here. She has visited less times in the past ten years than I can count on one hand."

His face flushed with crimson. Herrick's head might explode if she pushed him too far.

He shouted, "*You want time?* You have *one* day to find Casidhe, Skarde, or Jennyver. If not, you will walk out of this canyon alone, too."

Kleio stiffened at yet another threat. She would tolerate no bully. "I told you in the beginning to never threaten me."

Stepping forward quickly, Herrick brought his face close to hers and warned, "Do not think to go up against me as Casidhe did. Had she not carried Shannon's sword, she would not have slipped through my fingers that day."

Kleio moved away from the onslaught of all that anger and walked to the middle of the room.

"Do not leave until I have dismissed you!"

She turned, taking in his hulking form with every rigid muscle bulging and ready for battle. "You were the one who always said Shannon's sword would not bond with Casidhe until she proved herself worthy. From what I saw, the sword made a decision. By tomorrow, I will have made a decision as well."

One Herrick would not be happy about.

# CHAPTER 7

AFTER THE SILVER BALL EXPLODED, Daegan staggered back, hands over his eyes. Casidhe! She hadn't made a sound.

Had anything happened to her? Where was she?

The sound of wings flapping approached.

He lurched around, bumping into Casidhe.

She shrieked. "*I can't see!*"

Already moving forward, he tossed her over his shoulder and shoved a hand forward to protect her.

"Where are you goin'?" She flopped around behind him.

He ordered, "Stop talkin'. The bird follows."

Wings made no sounds, but wind whistled over the massive bird's body, which was likely gliding behind them.

Daegan's hand glanced off what felt like a column.

Hideous sounds erupted from the bird, closing in on them, then the wings flapped.

Had they entered a room?

He blinked three times and his eyes cleared.

Still in the dark, he lunged to the right and hit nothing. They had to be out of the passageway. He took two more steps in the same direction, didn't hit anything, and dropped Casidhe off his shoulder.

He whispered, "Stay here and make no sound."

"Why? What are you doin'?"

Did she not understand a simple order? Daegan had turned to watch for the bird now easy to follow with energy sparking off the feathers with every flap.

He watched for red eyes to know it had turned this way.

The room they'd rushed into seemed much larger than the last two with an even higher ceiling, based upon flashes of light from the bird. It kept bellowing long screeches, but had not circled around toward them yet.

Just as he'd thought they might be safe for a moment, he heard, "Come to me, *Lann an Cheartais.*" The snick of Casidhe's sword sliding from its sheath followed, then a glow lit behind him.

He demanded in a hushed voice, "What are ya doin'?"

Stepping up beside him she snapped, "Tryin' to save your butt. Just once, you could act happy about it."

The bird swooped around quickly and came right for them.

"I am *not* happy to be found!" he growled out.

"You will be if I get a chance to cut its head off," she countered. "I have had it with birds attackin' me and this one would have found us if we were quiet or yellin'."

How would he keep her safe? "Give me the sword. I am taller."

"No! My sword only answers to me," she shouted, sounding determined and terrified.

Shooting sparks of light trailed the bird as it angled down toward them.

Daegan looked around quickly, hoping for anything he could use as a weapon. With the sword's glow offering some light, he squinted to make out a wall ten feet behind them. With a quick check over his shoulder, the red eyes were almost on them.

He ordered, "When I tell ya, jump to the side."

"No."

The bird dove fast.

Seconds before it reached them, Daegan shouted, "*Now!*"

Casidhe swung her blade with the skill and daring of a Valkyrie, then leaped away.

She struck something solid.

The bird screamed then hit the wall with a loud whack.

Glowing tendrils floated to the ground around them. She may have only managed to catch a wing, but it had been enough to distract the bird from banking away at the last moment.

Daegan got to Casidhe and dropped down to his knees beside her. He pulled her to him and around to protect her so his back faced the bird. He called telepathically to Ruadh. He had not felt his dragon since back when they'd arrived in the first room. There was plenty of space to shift in this area and his dragon saw better than his human eyes.

All he heard in return was a dull rumbling inside.

Daegan couldn't shift? What had happened to Ruadh?

Panic climbed his throat, threatening to strangle him. How would he keep Casidhe safe? Lowering his mouth close to her ear, he whispered, "The bird does not seem to be movin'. We should go but quietly."

Her voice shook. "Agreed."

He stood first. He hoisted her up from her knees then gripped the backpack to keep her upright. When he took a step, lights brightened around the room.

Not four, but eight this time. One at every corner next to the floor and two more on each side at the base of the long walls stretching from right to left.

The instant lighting caused spots in his gaze.

Wrenching around, he blinked to clear his eyes and checked on the bird. A small mountain of blue, gold, and orange feathers lay in a pile, but that mound of feathers moved with breathing.

"Daegan, this place looks to be some kind of tomb room." She started forward.

He grabbed her pack, snatching her back to him. He didn't really care about the room, only keeping her close enough to protect.

"Hey!" She wrenched away.

"'Tis safer together."

That must have sunk in. She nodded.

The longer they spent here hunting, the more chances to die. He still was not convinced he'd find a grimoire volume in this place.

Zeelindar might only want that hand-shaped black stone clutching a red pulsing center. Had he yet again trusted the wrong person and put Casidhe in danger? He wanted to get her out of here, far from this underground death trap, but how?

Speaking softly, he informed her, "The bird is alive."

"Are you surprised if it's here to guard a goddess?" Trembling, she still held her sword ready to battle.

He had never known another woman like her. His admiration for her grew. She'd asked him to listen to her about being with the ice dragon clan and standing with Jennyver.

His mind had been locked tight, just as he'd been taught when dealing with someone who betrayed him.

Rules of the old world might not fit perfectly in this new one. What would it cost him to listen to her? Was he not strong enough to still walk away if he did not accept her words?

Nay. He had never allowed anger and emotions to drive any decision in the past, but he had this time. He had also never cared so deeply in a very long time, and no woman had ever turned his insides into knots as Casidhe had.

How could he deny her anything when she stood here at his side, ready to face whatever came at them? As soon as they found a safe spot, he would hear all she had to say with an open mind and heart.

Keeping a grip on her backpack, he led her into the middle of the room. Now he saw what she was talking about. There were ten recessed rooms, each with a gold, blue, and black tomb shaped as a body. Above the openings were similar carvings as the other rooms, but these possibly identified the tomb.

Large, shiny squares of black marble with gold veins covered the floor.

Noises from behind pulled Daegan and Casidhe around quickly.

Eesumor stood slowly, shaking its head.

Casidhe wheezed out, "Oh, crap,"

Daegan had found no exit from this room. "If it moves—"

"Too late," Casidhe murmured.

The bird pushed off and flew, rising to the ceiling, which had to be fifty feet up or more. The walls were the pink stone he'd seen in the first room, but these rose to a peaked ceiling.

Casidhe's lethal sword came into view as she lifted it high, ready for an attack.

He stepped ahead of her.

"Stop, Daegan. Eesumor might slice your arm off with its claws or bite a chunk from your head."

"I shall block it toward your blade."

"Damn, you. No! I don't want to watch *you* die!" She abruptly cut off a snuffling sound.

The concern in her words warmed his chest. She still cared? She didn't hate him for being angry with her and refusing to listen to her explanation about Herrick? Humbling, as he had not been as generous with his feelings for her since meeting up again in Galway.

"I do not plan to die," he claimed, though he had every intention of leaping up to grab the bird when it came close again. Where the devil was Ruadh? What in this place affected his dragon? His hands shook. Terror welled inside him. He had to stop that bird from tearing Casidhe apart.

Eesumor picked up speed as it reached the tall ceiling and circled around to face them, turning downward again.

Daegan had doubts about defeating the bird by hand, but if he could fight it to the ground, Casidhe had a chance to lop off its head. Even that could be a disastrous decision if a power in this place took offense at harming the bird.

He would do whatever it took to protect her and face the consequences.

Casidhe sucked in and blew out deep breaths, gripping the hilt with both hands. "This place smells like a flower shop."

Daegan smiled at the return of her grit. He sniffed the air, catching the overly sweet scent. He kept his arms loose, ready to react. One second could make the difference of keeping her alive and preventing the bird from slashing her to pieces.

Eesumor barreled down at a sharp angle.

Daegan began to believe the bird might crash into the floor. At the very last second, it made an impossible hard turn to the right, disappearing into the hallway, which led back to the room where it had been a statue.

Ruadh could not have executed so sharp a turn at such a high speed and the red dragon was unmatched in flying.

Daegan hurried forward to see what happened to Eesumor.

The bird landed gently on the base of the stacked silver balls, settled into its original pose, and returned to being a copper statue. Hadn't one of those balls exploded?

Casidhe joined him. "I don't understand."

"Neither do I."

A deep voice behind them shouted strange words Daegan had

never heard.

Casidhe's terror-filled eyes lifted to his face. She turned with him. He took her hand and walked toward the figure.

They had nowhere to run.

A filmy figure standing twelve feet tall with a long, thin body possessing small breasts, human hands, human legs, and human feet faced them. The head appeared to be both feline, possibly lionish, and human with eyes outlined black. Narrow black braids fell past her shoulders. She wore a band around her forehead of gold and jewels. Rubies, diamonds, and emeralds sparkled as she became fully corporeal.

Was this the goddess Eesumor guarded?

Her rigid appearance matched that of a similar carving above a tomb room behind her. The floor of it turned into water the same level as the floor in this room. Bright blue flowers with vibrant gold centers began appearing on the water.

The sweet smell from before increased.

He watched for a serpent to climb out of the tomb lagoon, but none so far.

Daegan hoped to soothe this being before she took insult at their presence and battling Eesumor. "We did not mean to disturb ya or the bird. We would not have harmed the bird had it not attacked us."

The filmy woman held hands up to each side of her head as if concentrating while she stared straight ahead, not blinking. When she lowered her hand, she replied in words he could understand.

"You cannot harm Eesumor."

Her words were stilted as if she had to figure out each one before the word left her tongue. Had she used majik to understand Daegan's words to now speak them?

Casidhe asked, "Are you Amentet?"

"You abuse my name with poor linguistics. Yes."

Casidhe ground her jaw hard enough for Daegan to hear.

Amentet lifted delicate arms and crossed them. Her dark eyes stared down at them as if she watched small bugs. "You have entered where you are not welcome."

Jumping in, Casidhe said, "We apologize. We were teleported

here by a powerful person with no idea where she sent us."

"The end result is the same."

Daegan caught the sound of termination. "We shall leave if ya are willin' to point us to the way out."

"You ask of me when you have earned nothing."

He didn't like the sound of that, but as this was her area, he would take care to remain peaceful.

"You wish to leave." Amentet made that announcement as if it should already be obvious, then she turned her dark gaze on Casidhe. "Step forward twice."

Daegan leaned forward as if to move.

Amentet warned, "Not you. The woman."

Casidhe released his hand but hesitated.

Daegan could feel her fear and wanted to stay beside her. If he knew for sure he would not put her in further danger, he'd grab her hand again to keep her close, but knowing Casidhe she would take his head off. She'd tell him he'd been foolish to make a knee-jerk reaction when they had no idea if Amentet, who appeared calm, might allow them to leave.

At Casidhe's delay, Amentet's eyes glowed gold and red, bright as a sunrise.

Damn the consequences. Daegan reached for Casidhe.

She shook her head, warning him off. She stepped once, then twice. "Is this where you—"

The marble floor opened and swallowed her then returned to a solid form.

Daegan roared, calling up his dragon.

Ruadh answered with battering and sounded far away. Energy tried to surge in Daegan's body, but couldn't break through.

Furious, Daegan roared, *"Give Casidhe back to me!"*

*"No!"* Amentet began to grow and expand in a room accommodating her twelve-foot-tall size. Her voice deepened into a threatening sound. *"Leave!"*

The floor beneath Daegan slid apart and energy sucked him down.

# CHAPTER 8

EVERYTHING GLOWED BRIGHT WHITE, BLINDING Adrianna. Thunder pounded against her chest. She had no control of her body. Power shot into her chest and out her back. Her legs lost feeling. Her arms flailed and her ears roared with the noise in her head.

Energy buzzed around her body with the sound of a giant bee, scorching her skin wherever the blast touched.

She flipped and tumbled, her body yanked this way and that.

High-pitched squealing and cries filled the typhoon whipping her through a furious electrical storm.

She tried to squint, but could see nothing. Yelling didn't work either.

The spinning slowed suddenly.

Her body began to fall while still flipping end over end. If she wasn't dead yet, she would be the minute she struck something hard. Why hadn't the explosion torn her body apart? Probably a bad question right now.

Maybe she was in pieces and only her mind remained intact ... for now.

All the turmoil around her decelerated along with the speed of her tumbling. She continued descending but not as violently. When she rolled onto her back, she floated until she stopped moving, now held up by a cushion of air.

Why did that not reassure her?

Limp from head to toe, she struggled to move a trembling hand to her face to touch her skin and eyes. She still had both. With an awkward struggle, her fingers pushed hair off her face. Was it still blond or maybe white now? Allowing her arm to fall back to her side, she focused on opening her eyelids enough to peek.

Light seeped through one slit. Her vision adjusted. Pearl-white air swirled around her, glowing softly.

Humming? Yep, the air hummed.

Was she dead?

If so, why did every inch of her hurt?

Opening both eyes gave her a tiny push of hope. She rolled her head left then right and looked up.

She was inside a white globe of energy.

Her heart dropped.

No. Was she trapped inside Witchlock's energy as her sister had been before her eventual death?

Power stirring around her stopped humming and became very still. Too still.

Her heart thumped faster. At least she thought she still had a heart.

What happened to that Imortik?

What happened to Tenebris and Sen?

Had she destroyed the realm or alternate world she'd been in? Had she killed everyone, including herself? Maybe not her, but this didn't feel like life either.

She tried to make herself sit up by sheer force of will. Not happening. One arm did not want to move at all and the other had muscle failure just from touching her face.

But at least she could feel her arms, unlike other parts of her body.

Time passed without any reference to go by.

After a little bit, she forced her arm to lift again. That took the kind of effort she'd expect to need for pulling a car one-handed. Propping her elbow at her side, she gazed at her hand.

Cuts crisscrossed the skin on her palm and down her arm. She needed to see the rest of her body and tightened her core muscles to sit up.

That didn't work, but she did manage to pick up her head.

Pain stabbed her and stars shot across her gaze for the few seconds she managed to catch sight of her shredded and bloody clothes. She could feel blood trickling down her arm and across her chest, but no such sensation lower.

What about her legs? She couldn't lift either one or wiggle her toes. A tear leaked from her eye and streaked down her face, stinging where the salt met a cut.

Her body felt as if she'd been beaten with a hammer then slashed with a filet knife.

Time to ask the only question left, the only one that mattered. Her raw throat burned and sounded raspy. "Witchlock? Are you still with me or did I blow you up, too?"

Silence had never been so loud.

"Witchlock?" she squeezed out in a choked breath.

What had she done?

She closed her eyes and gave in to the tears. She'd had the most powerful witch majik ever known to exist. She'd taken great care to keep the ancient power safe from evil just as she'd spent hours learning how to protect the world from Witchlock.

But in the end, she'd failed.

One last time, she begged, *"Witchlock?"*

Quiet surrounded her. She'd stopped an Imortik from taking Witchlock, but condemned herself to a slow lingering death.

# CHAPTER 9

QUINN SHOOK HIS HEAD, TRYING to clear his hearing from the explosion. He lifted up from where he'd covered Reese's body as they went airborne.

She had cuts on her face and arms. Nothing the two of them couldn't heal, but ... what about the baby?

"Reese." He brushed his hand over her hair. "Wake up, sweetheart."

Fingers on one of her hands moved.

He grasped that hand, cringing at how cold her skin felt. He called to her more urgently. *"Reese!"*

Her lips moved and she mumbled, "Truck hit me. Get the tag." Her eyelids fluttered then she squinted at him. "No shouting."

Hell, she might have a concussion. He raised up on his knees. "Are you hurt?"

"Headache."

"What about the baby?"

Reese came fully awake at that and moved a hand to her stomach. After a few more seconds, she whispered, "I think he's okay. I don't feel pain and I still feel his warm energy."

"His energy?"

She wheezed out, "Help me sit up."

Quinn moved to the side and lifted her to a sitting position. He glanced around where everything was dark as a tar pit. "Hold on a moment and let me find my people."

She leaned against his chest. "I'm good."

No, she wasn't, but he'd take care of her soon. He called out telepathically, *Evalle and Tristan. Where are you and are you injured?*

Evalle sounded groggy when she sent back, *I'll live.*

Tristan replied, *I'm up. Casper's with me. We're hunting*

*Evalle. Wait ... I see her.*

After a pause, Evalle came back with a stronger voice. *Where are you and Reese? Oh, hell, are you both okay? What about the baby?*

*We are all three fine. Reese might have a concussion, but that should clear up soon.* Quinn gave them directions.

As soon as those three teleported close and walked over, Quinn asked, "What about Isak and his men? I don't have the comm unit to call him. Must have lost it after the blast."

"They have to be in this area, too," Evalle mused. She had one nasty gash on her arm, but the blood had stopped oozing.

Casper's hair stuck out everywhere. He asked Tristan, "If Isak's alive, he's up and will probably have a tactical light on. Think you could teleport to the top of a tree and take a look?"

"Yeah. Be right back." Tristan disappeared.

Evalle dropped to her knees and ran her hands over her face, shoving a mass of dark brown hair back she twisted into a knot. She propped her hands on her thighs. "What do you think caused that blast?"

"I don't know," Quinn admitted. "The first thing that comes to mind is a meth lab, but that doesn't fit."

"Why not?" Reese sat away from Quinn and grimaced when she touched her head. Then she blinked a couple times as if to clear her vision.

Casper offered an explanation. "Because that blast was huge with a shock wave. I think of meth lab explosions being more like a gas explosion. Big fireball, some shock wave, but not enough power to send us all flying seventy to eighty feet in the air."

Quinn nodded. "I agree with your logic."

Tristan's voice came into Quinn's head. *I found Isak and we're headed your way on foot.*

After sharing that with the group, Quinn checked Reese again who fluttered her hand. "I'll be fine. Just a headache. Go do your job."

This woman knew him well enough to read his thoughts, but she had to know he would not move far from her.

Two helicopters roared overhead, flying north to south. They sounded larger than the first one, which had been searching with thermal imaging. What had happened to that one?

Quinn stood to meet Isak, who strode up limping. Must have landed bad. Carrying a body as wide as a refrigerator, Isak kept his flashlight turned down to the ground to avoid blinding everyone, but it gave their circle some light.

Blood ran a trail down the side of his head from a gash in his close-cropped hair. He still had his tactical vest on and his mono night-vision headgear, leaving one bloodshot eye peering out. "I've called in more choppers to make passes over the explosion zone to visually search for any bodies. The thermal unit will only register survivors."

Evalle pushed up to stand. "What are the chances of finding survivors, especially humans?"

"Not much." Worry pushed deep into Isak's face. He stared into the darkness.

"What, Isak?" Evalle asked.

"Your intel has been that Reese thinks Adrianna and Sen might be in the human world. You said Lanna and Grady narrowed it down to this general area. What if ... " He stopped and took a couple breaths. "What if Adrianna had been in that explosion?"

Quinn's heart hit the ground. He hurried to interject, "It's possible, but she's more than human. Let's not make that leap until we determine what actually caused the explosion."

Isak gave a small dip of his chin, acknowledging Quinn's point, but not necessarily accepting it. "Two of my men were closer than me. They were on this side of the road. Sounds like the explosion happened on the other side. I called in medics who are taking care of them and my bomb techs have just arrived at the detonation site."

"How'd you get all those people here so quickly?" Casper asked.

"I staged teams close by," Isak replied, as if that should have been expected. "Is anyone here in need of a medic?"

"Not me," Reese quickly replied, giving Quinn a look that said he better not argue.

Now that Reese looked and sounded better, Quinn answered for the group. "No. We can heal our bodies, but thank you."

Looking around, he asked, "Ready to go?"

Heads all around nodded.

Isak must have noticed that Quinn had little left of his equipment and handed him another flashlight.

Reese lifted a hand for him to help her stand. Once she was on her feet again, Quinn kept a hand on her arm in case she became dizzy while they walked with the group.

As they neared the explosion site, trees had been laid over and stripped of leaves like a category five hurricane had swept through.

He shuddered to think what might have happened had the teams been closer to the detonation point.

Loud whomp, whomp, whomps of helicopters flew overhead slowly. The sound of all three helicopters in the general area offered a backdrop to the grim search.

Bricks, debris, and cement blocks were strewn in every direction.

Quinn swept his flashlight beam over a large chunk of wall covered in graffiti.

No body parts or blood.

So far.

As they approached a paved road, the blast location was clearly obvious on the other side. Beams of light moved quietly through the smoking wreckage. Isak's men worked in stealth mode. Some parts of what appeared to have been a building were still on fire and smoldering, but oddly the forest surrounding that spot had no flames.

How could that be with an incredible force that flattened a hundred feet out in all directions?

Evalle slowed before crossing the road. "Hey. That's the uh ... " She wiggled her fingers, trying to come up with the rest of her thought, then snapped them. "The Old Atlanta Prison Farm building."

"That's right," Isak confirmed from up ahead.

Sirens cried miles away. Based upon the direction of the sound, the emergency vehicles and police cruisers moved quickly on the major north and southbound interstates through Atlanta.

Quinn swung his gaze back to the narrow road cutting through this area. Two black Hummers were parked on a shoulder forty feet away with men moving around efficiently.

A van pulled up and parked quickly, then the rear doors opened. Two stretchers were carried out by more men dressed in camo like the rest of Isak's black ops team. They had the injured soldiers loaded in less than a minute and drove off.

Isak issued orders to the rest of his team. "Load up before LEOs arrive. Stay close."

"Yes, sir," rumbled practically as one voice.

The first Hummer left. The second one appeared to be waiting on Isak.

He started to walk over, but paused and held a hand against his ear.

With Belador hearing, Quinn picked up the chatter from one of the helicopter pilots. He explained how he'd left the other two choppers to cover a one-mile radius around the explosion site while he'd been circling in wider bands.

Sounded like the smaller chopper with thermal imaging found something.

Could a heat signature mean someone survived that blast?

Isak asked, "How many?"

His man sent back, "Only one. Could be nothing since the area appears to be a park." The pilot gave specific directions.

As soon as the pilot said he'd keep circling, Isak started for his truck.

Possessing the same sensitive hearing as Quinn, Tristan said, "I can teleport you there faster."

All the time Isak had been an ally of Beladors, he'd never teleported with anyone that Quinn knew about.

Isak turned to Tristan and snapped, "Do it."

Tristan and Isak disappeared.

Evalle mentioned, "We aren't going to be able to figure out much if this place is covered up by law enforcement. I know they need to do their job, but something is off about this explosion."

Quinn had the same gut feeling. "I'm calling our Beladors in law enforcement to see if they can divert Atlanta PD long enough for us to do a quick search." Using telepathy, he reached three Beladors. They'd redirect the police for as long as possible.

This location was far enough from downtown and no homes nearby for police to not easily drive straight here without someone calling in the coordinates. They had Beladors in dispatch, too.

Leading the group, Quinn crossed the road with Reese walking better on her own.

When Quinn and his team reached a spot two hundred feet off the highway, Evalle said, "I was here a long time back hunting a troll. This place was in ruins but still had a lot of structure. It stinks but it never did smell nice here."

Casper picked his way across the rubble. "Whatever blew this thing apart had nothing to do with chemicals. I don't even smell residue of bomb-making materials."

Reese walked around part of a wall, pausing to stand in spots, then kept moving across a slab so clean it could have been pressure washed. "Looks like someone took a mega blower here." She meandered, hesitating again before moving on.

Quinn waited silently to see what she was trying to do.

After six spots, she went dead still.

"Reese?" He walked over to her.

She lifted a hand.

Evalle and Casper noticed, both joining Quinn where he waited a few yards back from Reese.

"Is she doing what I think, Quinn?" Evalle whispered.

He lifted both shoulders. "Maybe."

"Casper and I will keep watch for demons." Evalle nodded at Casper to go one way and she went the other. Both of them took up a position with their backs to Quinn and Reese.

Quinn stepped closer in case she began talking. She sometimes did not recall all she said when using remote viewing.

The only sound that interrupted the silence was the steady thrashing of helicopters moving all over the place.

Tristan called to Quinn. *We're back. The warm body we found was a drunk passed out in Gresham Park.*

Quinn felt disappointment for everyone, especially Isak, deep inside. He sent back, *We're on a slab in the explosion area.*

*Be there in a minute.*

Reese angled her head and leaned forward as if trying to see something.

When Tristan walked up, Quinn turned to find Isak talking to his men on his comm gear. Isak must have changed his mind about having his men around if the Atlanta PD showed up. It sounded as if he was bringing in an army to search.

Quinn walked over to meet them and kept his voice down. "I have Beladors holding off law enforcement from coming here for now. Bringing in an army of your men is going to draw unwanted attention when we haven't determined if Adrianna is even here."

"I'm not waiting another second."

Quinn could sympathize. Isak got his hopes up only to have them crushed at not finding Adrianna, but Quinn needed Isak to hold off bringing in more bodies. Turning the slab beneath Isak's boots to water would be simpler than getting that soldier to wait.

Tristan suggested, "Hang on, Isak. I can do some teleporting around to check from high points first."

Isak washed a hand over his tired face. "I appreciate you teleporting me to that park. It saved time, but my helicopters have covered more than a square mile by now. If the thermal imaging doesn't pick up a body by itself, then you won't see it."

Quinn argued, "But we still do not know where Adrianna is, which might be miles from here. We have a better chance of sneaking up on a location with a smaller team."

"Every minute we wait is another minute she could be dying if she was in this blast," Isak argued in an unyielding tone.

What was Quinn to say to that when he would be just as out of his mind to find Reese? He sure as hell wouldn't point out the miniscule chance of anyone, even Adrianna, surviving if she'd been here.

Reese walked up to them. "I think Adrianna *was* here."

That dumbfounded Quinn a second before nausea burned its way up his throat at this news. He swallowed hard, unable to say a word to help Isak.

Tristan found his voice first. "Do you know if she's ... alive?"

The devastation on Isak's face at the possibility of Adrianna having been blown to bits ripped Quinn's chest apart. Quinn quickly suggested, "She might have been here, then moved before the explosion."

Isak sucked in a deep breath of relief. "That could be true."

Reese put her hand on Isak's arm. "I can't say what shape she's in, only that in my remote viewing I saw her lying in a very small park by a lake."

Isak froze at those words. "She's there now?"

"I think so."

All Isak could do was nod. His throat moved with a hard swallow.

Before Quinn could ask Reese where they were going, Evalle and Casper walked up. Evalle asked, "What are we doing?"

Reese repeated what she knew.

"*Let's go!*" Evalle had that ready to attack anything to reach Adrianna look on her face.

"How about I take Isak first?" Tristan asked, his gaze skipping from face to face. "It's easier for me to teleport one person."

"I don't care. I just want to go *now*," Isak said, cutting off conversation.

Evalle frowned at Tristan who stared back with a don't-push-it look. She tensed, then nodded and let it go.

Quinn trusted Tristan's reason and would wait to find out what it was later.

Reese pointed to the southeast from where she stood. "There's a lake shaped like a roll of salami with a cemetery on the north end and a small, wooded area on the east side."

"How far?" Tristan had turned to look in that direction.

"Two miles," Isak snapped out. He had his mobile phone display open and turned it to Tristan with a map showing. "Can you find that?"

"I can now. Ready?"

"*Do it!*"

They disappeared again.

Quinn pulled Reese against his body. "Thank you for that."

She whispered, "I might have only found Adrianna's body. Doesn't mean she's alive."

Scratching his chin, Casper said, "I'm tryin' to figure out how a body goes that far in anything less than a tornado and comes out alive as well."

Evalle had been quiet since she'd had that staring match with Tristan.

Quinn asked, "What were you and Tristan discussing silently?"

"I asked why we couldn't link and teleport everyone to Adrianna?" She lifted pain-filled eyes. "Tristan said Isak was clearly upset when the person in the park was not her. If Adrianna was in this building when the blast happened, Tristan has a hard time believing she could have survived because she's more human than not. He thought taking Isak alone would be better if ... you know."

If Adrianna was dead.

# CHAPTER 10

CASIDHE SCREAMED, FALLING IN A surge of air with arms straight up. Amentet had shot her down into a bottomless hole. Wind whistled loud in her ears. Her shirt stood up, flapping against her face. Her backpack bounced against walls she couldn't see.

She fell in a torrent of black. Her heart beat its way up to her throat, trying to get out before the big splat.

She gasped for air and stopped screaming.

Who would listen?

Harsh wind blistered her skin. Tears burned her eyes.

What had happened to Daegan? Had that bitch sent him down here, too?

Or had she done far worse to him?

He'd been right. They should have hunted a way out right off the bat and left.

All at once, her body's descent slowed a little, then more until she began floating down feet first.

As if that made being dumped in a hole better?

Her shoes landed on a solid surface, hammering her knees she had not known to bend. "Ouch!" She caught her balance, but still saw nothing.

Where were one of those bulbs?

Dropping to a knee, she ran her hand over the smooth floor, which reminded her of the last one she'd stood on.

A consistent detail yet nothing to comfort her.

Raking hair back into place as much as her mess would go, she straightened her clothes, all simple actions in an effort to calm down. Hard to be calm when she still could not see her hand in front of her face.

What now? Walking away would be insane. She had no

idea where she stepped. She dropped her head back, could see nothing above her any more than in front of her.

She listened.

No sound of Daegan falling.

She sat down and crossed her legs. Was she stuck here forever? Would she never see Daegan again? Would she die slowly?

The panic attack she'd been keeping at bay hit. She wheezed and dropped her head down, closing her mind to everything except slowing her breathing. Her chest hurt from trying to draw air into her lungs.

Finally, she drew a long breath and lifted her head. "No panickin'!" she ordered just to hear a sound. Her hands shook and her heart thundered along.

A tiny light glowed at what seemed like fifty or more feet away. She had no sense of distance without enough information.

As the light brightened more, a path forward came into view.

"Light is good." She got back up to her feet, straightened the backpack, and started toward that glow.

A beacon of hope when she had none.

By the time she'd covered half the distance, everything around her came into view.

She slowed, taking it all in as she walked through a towering hallway twenty feet wide and twenty-five feet tall. One-foot-thick, rough-cut wooden beams ran up the walls on each side six long steps apart and were tied together by another gray beam stretched across the top. All that created sections.

Every area had different reliefs in pink sandstone. That was her best guess at the material used for the walls.

Most of these images had been painted.

On her right, carvings of men her height with skin painted a deep rose-brown took up most of one area. They wore knee-length white wraps around their waists and carried buckets, spears, and other items she couldn't make out.

No head covering or sandals.

What a contrast to the images on her left, which were smaller and painted ochre, dark ruddy-brown, and deep blue against an almost white background in some sections. Had the white areas been painted or had the pink surface turned chalky with age?

One male image sat on what appeared to be a throne where smaller men, in comparison, attended to him. Had that male been a giant? He wore a tall headdress and had a smooth face except for the chin beard, which could have been braided to look that narrow and long.

At the end of the hallway, she stood at a tall wooden door in conflict.

What if Daegan came to this first place and she left? Would she be able to return through this door or could he follow?

She knocked.

No one answered.

Fine, she could try to read these images while she waited for Daegan to show up. The possibility of him not making it back to her was not a thought she could entertain and remain sane.

At the closest wall, she placed her left hand on it, then moved her right hand. No symbols or letters lifted up, gold or otherwise. She tried three other spots down the hall.

Nothing happened. Why?

She had serious doubts that anyone here would answer that question as she was an uninvited visitor.

When she reached the door again, she chewed on her lip. What now? While she deliberated on a plan of action, she heard a voice on the other side of the door.

A male voice.

Or was she imagining the sound because she wanted to hear another living being? What if it was Daegan looking for her?

Grasping the wooden handle, she dragged the door open only two feet, but that was enough for her to slip through with her backpack.

The next area continued as another hall, but smaller and with no art on the walls.

She called out, "Daegan?" Had he landed on this side of the door?

A noise came back to her from farther down the hall.

What if he had fallen and been hurt?

She lifted her chin and squared her shoulders, forcing her backbone to buck up. Daegan wouldn't hesitate to hunt for her. She continued forward.

The ancient bulbs came on as she approached them, lighting her way. Every time she reached a new light, the last one went dark.

Far down the passage, she encountered a split.

It wasn't as if she had a yellow brick road to follow.

"Eenie meenie miney moe. It's to the left I go." She stepped forward on the left side and ran into an invisible barrier, hitting her nose. "*Ouch!*"

That deep voice sounded again, but from the right.

This was no time to start second-guessing herself. She took off down the right side, picking up her pace and forcing the lights to flip on and off faster. After hurrying for a minute, she came to the end of the hall, which dumped her into another cavernous room, but nothing like the previous ones.

Flaming torches were tucked in holders around the room.

Water flowed through the middle from her left to right in a stone-cut channel with a wooden bridge across the water to the other side. Along this side were places to sit on benches of thick stone slabs. Floral and butterfly designs carved into these might translate, but they seemed more decorative than informative.

The sitting area seemed to go forever to her right. How long was this room?

On the far side of the bridge, statues stood in groups around circular benches. Some were well-built men wearing nothing, not even a fig leaf. Statues of each female had the body draped with a single piece of material that flowed around the torso in different ways. More benches were scattered along that side of the waterway.

Did someone come here for lunch or to read?

She shook herself loose from that crazy thought.

"Casidhe?"

She froze at the sound of Daegan's voice. "Where are you?"

"Over here."

She could see no one. "Across the bridge? Are you hurt?"

"Yes."

Which question had he answered? She walked over inset stone tiles cut in rectangles and stepped up on the wooden bridge that creaked. *Please don't break.*

She made it across the bridge and searched. "Daegan?"

"Over here." He stood next to an archway behind a seating area. Where had that archway been before? She should have noticed it.

Walking quickly to him, her irritation broke free. "Why didn't you meet me at the bridge? How'd you get here?"

He shrugged. "I thought ya would come to me. I am glad to see ya."

While that sounded nice, it irked her that he thought she should come to him.

Weren't they both in this stupid place as a team? "What do we do now? I tried readin' the walls in the hallway and my gift didn't work there."

He frowned, walking past her and moving his head as if he searched the room. "I do not know where to go next, but there are two more passages out of this room."

Sighing hard, she caught up to him. "Where are they?"

He stopped and pointed with both hands. "Those."

She hadn't seen those either at first. "Which one do you want to take?"

"I shall take the one ya do not choose."

"You want to split up *again*?" she shouted. "What the heck? We may not find each other next time."

Daegan turned to her with a pained look on his face. He crossed his arms. "I did not mean to upset ya, Luigsech. Ya are unlike other women. Ya do not back away from a challenge, so I thought we might try to do this as quickly as possible by each takin' a different path."

He was telling her he trusted her skills and ability.

That meant a lot, but he also called her Luigsech, reminding her she was not Casidhe to him. Daegan clearly no longer held her dear in any way or he would not consider splitting up.

She swallowed to hold back the emotion threatening to overwhelm her. She'd thought he'd been opening up to her a little in those first couple of rooms, enough to give her hope of more.

Not now.

Forcing her words to sound strong, she said, "Fine. I'll take the right side. How far do you want to go before we come back here to meet?"

"What seems like thirty minutes should be enough." He smiled at her. "I am very proud of your ability to navigate this place."

A compliment she might have taken to heart earlier when she could swear Daegan had almost kissed her in the chamber with the bird.

No longer. She had to stop assigning character based on what he *might* do. He'd had plenty of time to talk about what happened with his sister in the mountains and still had not brought it up.

Now he acted as if he had no worry she would show up again.

If he wanted to be all business about this, so could she.

Without any other word, he walked to the left passage, which lit up as he entered.

She strode over to the right and started forward. The lights were spaced farther apart, too far for her to see well. She pulled her LED from her backpack and flicked it on.

That was better.

Ten or fifteen minutes into the hall, she passed a door. Then another ten steps, she passed another door. She stopped and pushed it open since there was no handle on this one.

Stepping inside, she shined her LED light around, finding rows of reliefs in different places, more like the first batch she'd been able to somewhat translate.

Moving deeper inside must have triggered the small tube lights in different areas. Now she had a better look at the domed-shaped room with many more large images of people standing, sitting, eating, holding swords, and one held what appeared to be a purse.

Probably not a purse.

Four lights glowed up above, too. That was different.

Stuffing the key chain LED away, she walked over to a wall where the majority of images were along the lower part.

That worked for her.

She positioned her hands and began moving from the direction the birds, a lizard, and a woman faced. This sounded like a story about a woman who had followed a man who betrayed her.

Casidhe stood upright and looked around the rest of the room. She had a sinking feeling none of this was going to help.

*"Hellooo," called in a deep voice.*

Was that Daegan?

The center of the room rose three steps up in a circle. Light glowed above the top step from somewhere below.

She climbed the steps and looked over the edge.

Daegan stood forty feet below on a narrow walkway with piles of bones all around below him. "Ya need to come down here."

*To a room full of spirits?* she mused silently. "Did you find somethin'?"

"Yes."

Damn, she knew he'd say that. "How do I get there?"

"I took steps down here, but I cannot return that way."

"Why not?" She squinted trying to see, but while lights were illuminated around the inside of the circle she stood up upon, only one light glowed down near Daegan.

He stared up with his face in shadows. "A wall formed after I passed through to this spot. I do not wish to go farther without ya."

Well, that sounded better than sending her down a separate hallway. She tried to give him credit for being right in that they had been able to search more. "What do you want me to see?"

Yep, she was stalling, but she asked a valid question.

He pointed at something in front of him, but beneath where she stood. "'Tis a column with more carved images of what ya read before. One appears to be a dragon."

"Okay, but how am I goin' to get down there?"

He smiled. "Ya jump. I shall catch ya."

"What the ... ? Hell, no. I'm not jumpin' into a hole. If you miss, I break my neck or my legs."

"'Tis the only way down and beyond from this point. I shall not miss. Show some grit."

# CHAPTER 11

CASIDHE COULDN'T DECIDE IF DAEGAN was nuts for expecting her to jump or if she was crazy to be considering it. When she climbed the three steps circling the center of the room, she found a two-foot wide ledge to step up on. That was fine for looking down into the fifteen-foot-wide hole to where Daegan waited below on a walkway.

Not for taking a literal leap of faith.

He had come through when they had been in dangerous situations before but asking her to step off a ledge and drop forty feet to where he would catch her tested her already shaky trust.

Was she really going to do this? "Do your kinetics work yet, Daegan?"

He frowned at her. "No. I do not need kinetics for this. I wish to be done with this place as much as ya. Toss your backpack first."

She stood there, staring at what could be the worst decision of her life. A far worse one than coming here, but that hadn't actually been her decision. Of course, telling her to throw her pack down had to be meant to give her comfort he'd catch her.

She unsnapped her pack, then secured all the pockets and swung it just past the edge and let go.

The pack seemed to fall forever, but he snagged it out of the air and grinned, placing the pack behind him.

All well and fine, but her body weighed more and did not come with straps. If he grabbed her arm, he'd pull it out of the socket. Maybe even pull off her arm if her dead weight yanked her down.

"Luigsech?"

He lost all his good points by calling her that again. She was allowing him to mess with her mind and had to stop it.

Looking over one last time, she said, "Get ready."

She inched closer, wishing a ladder would appear. A rope, sheets tied together, anything.

He held his arms out.

She pushed off and lifted her legs straight out in front of her up so he could catch her before she landed.

Then she took a literal leap of faith.

Air rushed past her. Fingers brushed her arm.

She reached out. Caught nothing. *"Nooo!"*

Her body smacked water. Made a huge splash. She sank, then she beat her feet and pinwheeled her arms, fighting to the surface.

Spitting out water and gulping air, she shouted, *"Dammit, Daegan!"*

"I am here."

She paddled her feet to hold her head above water and looked up to find a wooden ladder built into the walkway.

"'Tis simple to climb out," he said as if that were freaking encouraging.

Adrenaline sent her scrambling up the ladder. She snarled, *"You said you could catch me!"* Swatting wet hair off her face, she slung her hands back and forth, shaking off water. "What the hell?"

"Ya fell too far from the walkway. I was prepared." He stood there with a surprised expression as if she should have realized the error had been hers.

What?

She looked above her head at the lip she'd stepped off of and down to where she fell. Piles of bones were visible fifteen feet beneath the surface of crystal-clear fresh water.

He extended his hand toward her stomach as if to tug her soaked shirt down from where it had bunched under her breasts.

"Don't." She uttered that single word in a tone warning severe consequences if he failed to obey.

She could do without his help right now.

He offered, "Ya shall dry quickly in this place."

Mr. Helpful all of a sudden? She ignored him to look around.

At the end of the walkway stood a column, which went straight through to the bottom where bones were piled against it.

More hieroglyphic images she was beginning to feel she'd seen her whole life by now.

Daegan lifted her backpack.

"Give that to me." Her tone warned him not to argue.

"I thought ya might like some help puttin' it on." He held the pack where she could slide her arms into the straps.

Thankfully, they did not touch skin to skin. Her energy might attack his with the mood she was in.

"Test your gift on the column when ya are ready. We shall not hurry," he said in a nice voice full of understanding.

Guilt tapped at her for overreacting like a shrew, but she knocked that aside, too. She had been willing to leap off a forty-foot drop, thinking he would have snatched her from the air the way he had her backpack.

Clearly, he'd been more concerned over the safety of her backpack.

Did he sound guilty about letting her fall? Not even.

With the backpack buckled, she walked to the column. He stepped up beside her, crowding the narrow space where she had to stand.

Closing her eyes a moment, she turned to him. "I can reach everythin' on the column. You are in the way."

"I want to be here in case ya need help."

"You sent me off on my own to search a different passage then told me to jump forty feet and failed to catch me. I'm good."

"I told ya—"

She shoved a hand in his face. "Just stop."

He backed away, silent as a stone.

Her heart winced. This was the man she'd given that damaged part of her to, believing he would mend the ripped pieces. She'd believed he felt for her what she felt for him. She tried to hang onto her anger, but it was a thin cover for the hurt bruising her insides.

Shaking off what she could not change, she got busy with the hieroglyphics actually carved into the column. No relief or paint this time.

This was a confusing grouping of words, but at least the gold symbols floated up. She struggled to figure out the meaning, but nothing made sense.

Not until she finally hit upon the image of a man with a dragon head and the name Mulatko rose off the surface in gold letters.

Turning to the silent Daegan she'd put in time-out, she asked, "Is this what you saw as a dragon?"

He shook his head, his stubborn expression letting her know she'd ticked him off. She had no issue with that.

Searching the images, which stopped at her knees, she said, "I don't see a full dragon shape."

"Ya must move for me to point it out."

She stepped back and waited.

Daegan circled the column to the back side. She thought the small images had stopped halfway around. When she stepped behind the column, Daegan pointed at the obvious large image of a dragon. A fierce creature with dark eyes filled with death.

"I see. Yep, that's a dragon."

When Daegan said nothing more, she angled her head to him. "I just did not see it at first."

He shrugged.

This was going to be the longest trip of her life.

When they got out of here, she was done. She would find a place to call home and nurse her wounds while recreating her life and future.

She scratched her head, surprised to find her hair dry already. So were her clothes.

Not much humidity in this place considering water flowed through it. Was the water from some system left by the ones who built all this?

Daegan walked off to the end of where the narrow walkway opened to a larger landing. He stood patiently next to yet another dark passage. She could swear that had not been there when she first stared in this direction.

Would he include her or just go off on his own again?

Sounding as short on patience as her, he asked, "Are ya comin'?"

Why, why, why did it sound as if she was the one being

difficult when she'd been so glad to see him in Galway she'd gone along with everything he wanted to do?

Maybe that was the trouble.

Maybe it was time for her to take the lead.

She strolled over and walked right past him, entering the next dark hole first. It remained dark longer than she'd expected. When it became obvious no tube lights were going to come on, she dug out her LED light and kept walking.

Deep in the plain-walled tunnel, she stopped and listened. "Daegan?"

She turned around as a door shut.

Was he serious?

She started back toward that door and stopped.

Screw it. She'd get to the end of this tunnel and probably find him there with a new discovery. He seemed hell-bent on one-upping her. So much for teamwork.

This tunnel turned at an angle then went the same distance as the first part, maybe a hundred yards.

At the end of this one, she stepped out into a bizarre setting of tall trees with thick trunks and fat green leaves. An oak tree? Wild grass and multicolored wildflowers grew knee-high.

She waited for the unknown to hit her between the eyes. This did not fit the locale if they were beneath a pyramid or other ancient structure in an Egyptian desert.

Could they be in a realm?

Just when she had accepted they were underground and might find a way to escape, she lost faith. The last place where she and Daegan had been in an alternate world, he'd crashed out of it with satyrs chasing them.

This didn't feel as if they could find a glass wall to crash through at some point.

When nothing attacked her, she walked through grass, moving toward a narrow stream where clear water tinkled over smooth rocks.

Her mouth was dry as a desert.

The last water she'd fallen into had appeared to be fresh water, maybe even drinkable ... except for the bones. Ick.

She couldn't trust putting anything in her mouth from this

place. Glancing around, she shouted, "*Daegan!*"

Where was he?

How could he just take off in another direction without saying a word to her? She glanced over at where she'd come from. The hallway had disappeared, replaced by a more woodsy area.

The stream cut through the land and faded away in both directions. Not the most realistic.

"There ya are," Daegan called out. He stood on the opposite side of the stream about fifty feet away.

"Where did you go?"

"I saw an openin' and thought to look into it."

"You could have told me," she snarled, too angry to even try for a professional voice. She had to stop showing him how he scrambled her emotions.

He stepped forward, face contorted with confusion. "I feel ya are capable to venture on your own. I hold your skills in great respect. We both ended up in the same place. I do not understand the problem."

She'd had it. The time had come to straighten things out. "Is this attitude about what happened in the mountains?"

Cupping his chin around his beard, he seemed to give her words serious thought, then shrugged. "I think ya make too much of such a time. 'Tis behind us."

Damn him. Her eyes burned with tears. Now he was making light of it. Must be nice to wipe away any feelings he had for her. She couldn't seem to manage a cleansing of her heart like he had. What a disappointment.

She lifted her chin and told him, "You are not the honorable man I met."

He acted appalled. "When have I not behaved with honor?"

She couldn't point out anything specific she'd call dishonorable, but this was not the man she had grown deeply attached to and had wanted for her own.

Stupid her, she still wanted him. What had happened?

"Perhaps ya should keep searchin' alone, Luigsech, and I shall do the same. Seems ya are put out with me. We will accomplish more this way."

She was once more Luigsech to him. "Tell me this, Daegan.

Did you ever mean what you said that day when I woke beside you in Tristan's hotel room?" She could barely breathe through her tight throat. Hurt balled in her stomach, but he'd made a vow. If he backed it now and talked to her, they had a chance.

He smiled, a broad happy look with his arms spread out to each side. "I mean what I say at the moment I say anythin'. Ya cannot hold me to words spoken in a bed forever."

She wrapped her arms around her stomach and bent over, trying not to break in half. Tears she'd tried to hold back dripped freely.

He'd shaken her trust by not calming down after the meeting in the mountains and coming back to talk to her.

But now he'd truly destroyed any hope of trusting in him again.

The sound of something large moving through the woods behind her raised hairs on her arms. She wiped her eyes and lifted up as the land on Daegan's side changed to a stone-tiled floor matching the ones inside the structured areas.

Tall pink walls now stood behind him. One with sculpted images. A door appeared with that same imposing dragon on it.

She took a step forward.

The stream deepened and widened in an instant, turning into a river that curved and moved quickly, leaving her trapped on this side.

Panic over the possibility of not surviving shook her out of her heartbreak.

Daegan angled around to find the wall and door. He shouted over his shoulder as the river began churning and still growing wider. "This may be the way to Mulatko!"

He sounded thrilled, ready to take off again.

She yelled at him, "Do you not see me stuck over here? How can you do this to me, Daegan? How can you leave me here?"

His shoulders dropped with what appeared to be a long sigh. Shifting all the way around, he cupped his hands and called out, "I have tried to be honest with ya even though ya betrayed me. I have not mistreated ya. I am tryin' to find this Mulatko and plead for a way out of here. Can ya not sit for a minute?"

*That was it!*

How had she been so convinced of his honesty in the past?

How much more agony did she plan to put herself through? Her very survival had depended upon Daegan in this place, but where had he been at times?

Actually, she'd been closer to getting killed by following *his* advice and directions.

No. More. She would not listen to him or keep fighting to stay by his side any longer.

"*Go!*" she yelled. The ground on her side of the water shifted with the undulating river. She backed up and grabbed a tree trunk.

Another sound, a growl this time, came from deep in the woods getting closer to her.

She tore her eyes from the river to catch Daegan entering the damn door without a look back.

Should she try to leap over the river and follow him?

The river's edge encroached more in her direction as a loud howl rocked the woods.

No. This was her time to stand on her own.

The river had grown to fifteen feet across and now buckled with choppy waves as the current flowed faster from left to right.

Besides, even if she could reach the door Daegan entered in time, she'd likely only be disappointed again.

Just as she had that thought, the door vanished, leaving solid pink sandstone wall.

If they were no longer a team, then he could find his own way out of here. She'd been able to read most of the hieroglyphics so far. She'd keep going to find Mulatko, get the onyx fist holding a pulsing red center, and maybe even the grimoire volume, then find a way out.

That sounded like a plan.

If she managed all that, she'd take everything with her, but from here on out her first priority would be escaping this place any way she could.

# CHAPTER 12

"*ADRIANNA!*"

What was that sound? The humming energy had returned, but she could have sworn she heard her name.

She'd been falling slowly into a dark place, tired of fighting the pain and her future inside Witchlock. Her heart had slowed to a thump, pause, then another thump.

She'd failed Witchlock and her friends.

"Please, Adrianna. Open your eyes."

Was that Isak? She turned her head toward the sound.

"She moved. *She moved*!" Isak shouted.

"You still can't touch her yet." That sounded like Tristan, who followed up with a softer request. "If you can hear me, Adrianna, open your eyes. You're in an energy field. I'm thinking we shouldn't touch you."

Really? She forced her eyes open. Her lids felt as heavy as lead coverings. Pain riddled her body. She breathed slowly, then blinked and focused.

She could see a blurry image of Isak and Tristan.

Isak was crying.

Her chest squeezed. That man never broke. But seeing her hurt had done something awful to his insides. Tears burned her eyes at watching him.

Her heart started beating a little faster. Was she really alive? She didn't know if she could get out of this energy ball if that was all she had left of Witchlock.

Would she live if she managed to escape?

"What do you need?" Isak asked in an agonized sound.

Whatever she did, she could not harm another being. "Go away."

"What? *No!* I'm not leaving you." Face covered with sweat-streaked dirt and bruises, there was a man who went chest-deep into every battle.

She tried to smile at Isak, but her lips were cut and swollen. "I mean back up. I'll try to get out. Might not go well."

Tristan understood because he said, "She wants some room to work, Isak. Sounds like she's going to try to break out of that energy shield. If that's Witchlock, this could get dicey."

Isak looked torn beyond belief, but with a tug from Tristan, they backed away. Tristan moved Isak behind a thick tree trunk and found one for himself as a shield.

Hope had every cell in her body waking up.

They all hurt as if joined in a support group unable to heal, but she wanted to live and pain would not stand in her way.

Swallowing down her hesitation, she managed to lift the hand she'd always carried Witchlock in. She felt a curl of energy wrap her wrist and hand as she opened her fingers until her flat palm waited to be filled.

Taking a deep breath, she coughed and clenched her teeth. Had she broken a rib? Once her breathing eased, she said, "Please come to me, Witchlock."

The humming ceased again.

Holding her hand steady took raw determination. Her body trembled from the strain. She clenched her jaw, forcing her shaking hand to stay open, a blatant plea for Witchlock.

Energy began spinning quickly around her.

Uh oh.

She closed her eyes against the bright glow. Power whined as she felt the sphere moving faster even as she stayed in one place.

Then a pop sounded.

She dropped, landing hard on her back. "Ow."

Peeking one eye open, she looked at her hand and started laughing and crying hysterically. "*Witchlock!* You survived and kept me alive." Her bright energy ball whirled in a happy white orb above her palm, perfectly round. She could feel a thin stream of energy flow from her hand, up her arm, and to her chest.

Everything came into focus. Trees and grass had never looked so good.

Footsteps ran forward, then a body slid on the ground next to her. On his knees, Isak stared down with a flood of hope covering his face. "You're alive." He breathed out the words in a sound of awe.

Tristan appeared above her with a big grin. "How ya doin', witch?"

Before Isak could take offense, she answered, "Not my best, gryphon, but better than I probably should be."

Isak dipped his lips and lightly kissed her forehead. A tear dripped on her face. He lifted back up and used a thumb to gently wipe it away. His voice shook. "I thought I'd lost you."

"I'm still here, but I'll be moving slowly."

A frown crept into Tristan's face. "How bad are you injured?"

She hated to admit this in front of Isak, but she had no choice. "I think I broke a rib and I ... can't move my legs."

Isak said nothing, but his face whitewashed. In a flash, he switched into the man who led black ops teams to battle nonhumans. No fear. All confidence. "I have the best medical resources at my fingertips. I can air vac you out of here in seconds."

"Your doctors and medicine won't help me, Isak," she whispered gently.

"*Yes, they will!*" he argued, demanding the universe give him what he wanted.

"My body is only partly human. I can heal, but I will need help that humans can't provide." She glanced up at Tristan. "I'm thinking Lanna and Garwyli."

"I am, too."

"*No!*" Isak shouted at Tristan then turned back to her. "Why can't your majik energy heal you?"

His pleading broke her heart. She did not want to put him through more hurt. "Witchlock has been through a lot, too. If not for Witchlock, there's no way I would have survived at all."

"I don't want you going somewhere I can't be with you." Isak sounded pitiful.

Hearing her big warrior's heart breaking destroyed her.

He *could* be with her in Treoir, because Daegan and Tristan would make that happen, but she needed to do this on her own.

Healing this much was uncharted territory for her.

It might go horribly wrong.

She glanced at Tristan who had cocked an eyebrow in question, then focused on Isak. "No one would deny you to go with me, but there is nothing you can do while I'm in Treoir. I'll heal faster and better with Lanna and Garwyli. They will use their incredible power on my legs and spine. Your men, your mom, the Beladors, our allies, we all need you here. If you go with me, I'll be worried about not recovering fast enough to get you back here, which will slow my healing."

He sat back on his knees and cupped his head.

She'd given him the one argument he couldn't counter. He would never stand in the way of powerful healing that could save her.

Heaving a hard breath, he said, "Okay. I ... I want you healthy and happy. It's not about me."

She closed her fingers to hide Witchlock then moved her hand slowly to touch his face. That was the only arm working at the moment.

He moved his head to her and curled his hand carefully around hers.

She hadn't wanted to die without talking to Isak again after their bad breakup. She'd been granted that wish and would make good on it when she could. "Thank you for finding me. Let me fix my body and energy, then I'll be back to see you."

He swallowed and pulled himself together. "Tristan, can you teleport Adrianna without hurting her?"

"Yes."

Isak leaned down and kissed her cheek, then her hand he tucked close to her body. He stood up. "I'll be here waiting for you. I'll come to you if you need me. All you have to do is send Tristan and I'll drop whatever I'm doing."

"Thank you, Isak."

Tristan said, "One question before I call Quinn to tell him what I'm doing. What happened to Sen?"

She wished she could give him that information. "I don't know. Tenebris had Sen hidden in another part of the realm or whatever."

"You were in a building near Atlanta," Tristan filled in for her.

"That makes sense. Tenebris put a huge Imortik in my path and vanished, expecting the Imortik to possess me. I had no way out but to turn Witchlock loose."

Tristan's eyebrows shot up. "Was that the explosion?"

"Yes. I don't know what happened to Tenebris or Sen."

"Got it." He asked Isak, "Need me to teleport you back?"

"No. Just take care of her. I'll call in a chopper."

"Will do." After a brief pause during which Tristan had probably called to Quinn telepathically, he squatted down and opened his arms apart then used kinetics to slide beneath her and lift.

Pain struck in multiple places, but she clamped her teeth tight. If she made a sound Isak would be yelling at Tristan.

She gritted through the pain until the world swirled out of focus, only letting out a moan. She trusted the gentle grip of Tristan's telekinetic power.

At least she'd left Isak thinking she would come back whole. Had Storm been there, he might have noticed how she hadn't exactly told Isak the truth.

If Witchlock could repair her body, it would have done so already.

# CHAPTER 13

NASTY BROWN HAIR HANGING TO his thin shoulders, a bright yellow Timmon walked straight for where Renata hung across a pole. She kept peeking through her lashes. Her breath caught when he slowed.

A whimper tried to climb that same throat, but she kept it in. She'd seen others draw his attention and die seconds later.

Not her. She'd remain silent until she had no choice. Her insides trembled at the possibility of what Timmon would do to her. She'd been a strong Belador once, ready to fight anything. Staying in this place for so long had rattled her.

Only a small part of Timmon remained. The Imortik master inside him had clawed away more control every hour.

She'd been in this building so long she'd lost track of time, but felt certain she was close to the moment when she would lose what little grip she held over her own being. Her insides groaned and ached from the Imortik presence overtaking her. The one she'd named Minos after the legendary, and evil, in her opinion, king of Crete. She'd spent the entire time here fearing the moment when she would lose all thought and control to the Imortik inside her.

There hadn't been room in her exhausted psyche to consider something worse.

Timmon's heavy footsteps came closer.

Not another sound reached her in this hollow building.

She wasn't ready for the glowing yellow master to turn her into a mindless killer.

He paused.

Tears burned inside her closed eyes. She struggled not to breathe or move. Her lungs cried for air.

Then his footsteps continued slapping the hard floor.

She allowed air to slowly hiss out from between her lips, but kept her jaws clenched to hold back a sob of relief.

Minos rose inside her. His eerie voice came into her mind sounding disappointed. *Why did the master not speak to us?*

She hadn't realized Minos had noticed the master at all and made a mental note to be even more careful. She replied in a robotic monotone, *I do not question the Imortik master. I do not wish to insult him.*

Minos shrank back immediately as if someone might notice *him* questioning the boss.

If she weren't so spent from dealing with this thing inside her, she would have laughed at being able to put fear in the abomination. Slowly, she turned her head to look down the right side and see what Timmon was doing.

He kept going until he reached a thin young man at the far end of the same pole her limp body had been draped over. The poor guy had messy, short hair and nice clothes, which were now ragged and dirty. Human. He hadn't been here long.

Timmon shouted in his screechy voice, *"Wake up, stupid!"* Then his alter ego, the true Imortik master, ordered in a smooth baritone, "Rise, Imortik! Prepare for your destiny."

Her skin crawled at the way the pitiful yellow male body began to brighten then lift off the pole. He slid down until his feet touched the floor, standing in a slumped pose as if a puppet waiting on his strings to be pulled.

He'd been here what felt like less than a day and the Imortik had fully possessed him.

"Follow me," the Imortik master ordered in a powerful voice.

Renata shut her eyes and kept her body limp.

She waited until Timmon's heavy footsteps and the shuffling of his latest zombie-like victim followed before she peeked again to be sure they were past her. Then she eased her head up a tiny amount to watch where Timmon normally stayed.

He'd been stomping back and forth in that open area she'd deemed the front of the building, talking to himself and shouting crazy things since his secret friend left and failed to return. The one whose image had been blurred during a visit since Renata had been imprisoned. That friend had compelled

Timmon to not speak his name, according to Timmon's one-sided conversations with himself. That guy kept deteriorating more each day.

Now that she thought about it, Timmon's lack of whining recently scared her.

She attributed that to the true Imortik master manipulating Timmon as the evil energy took over. Did the calmer Timmon now mean the Imortik master was closer to taking over completely?

What being was Timmon that the Imortik master had chosen his body?

Baritone-voiced Timmon told the bright yellow human, "It is time for you to defend my followers. Humans and nonhumans are killing Imortiks. You will join the great Imortik army."

The glowing human's arm lifted as if yanked up, hand hanging limp. "Yes. I will protect Imortiks."

Her heart sunk at those words.

That poor guy might end up killing someone he knew, maybe someone he loved.

She was so glad for Roberto to still be in South America and not in Atlanta. She longed to have a chance to tell her fiancé goodbye, but not if it meant risking his life.

One prayer had been answered to be found by Beladors, but she had not wanted them to be captured.

The two who reached out to her telepathically were very recent Imortik possessions and harder to overtake fully than humans. They entered this cavernous building just a few hours ago and still managed to hold some grip on their mind and body.

Whatever majik or power surrounding this building which had kept Renata from speaking telepathically to Beladors on the outside had not prevented telepathy from working between possessed Beladors in here. What a relief to hear the friendly voices of Gretchen and Kaiser in her head. She could only reply to them in sign language or Minos jumped up if she tried communicating telepathically.

Thankfully, Gretchen had understood sign language and relayed messages to Kaiser telepathically, allowing them a circular form of conversation.

*Renata!* Gretchen whispered urgently in Renata's mind. *Are you ready?*

Renata jerked her gaze across the space to meet Gretchen's anxious face. Then she swung her attention to Kaiser a few feet to the right of Gretchen on the same pole. He waited quietly, but his hopeful look spoke just as loud.

These two had linked their Belador power with her. The stronger hum of energy inside her lifted her spirits and gave her motivation to keep going. She couldn't physically jump up and battle anyone, but that didn't dim the thrill of possibly fighting back at some point.

Kaiser's calm voice came into her mind. *Stop worrying, Renata. We understand your concerns about being close to fully possessed, but we believe we can keep you from harming an innocent being once we escape. You have to trust us to have your back or none of us will have a chance to get out of this.*

She understood, but linking her power back to other Beladors meant everyone linked suffered the same fate. If one died, they all died. What if her Imortik finished taking over her body and she had no way to fight back?

Would that make the Imortiks in her two friends take over their bodies sooner than the normal two weeks for a Belador?

She sent a message to Gretchen. *Wouldn't you two move faster without me?*

"Act like a soldier and not a human noodle." Timmon shouted and marched around the human whose body jerked and twitched. His high-pitched voice indicated he was not entirely possessed. "You'll get killed the minute you meet the enemy."

His threat had zero effect on a human battling the malevolence inside him.

Gretchen called to Renata mind-to-mind. *No. We are not leaving without you. We do not leave Beladors. You're the only other one we've found in here and everyone has been searching for you. We can't help any of these victims if we don't escape.*

Screaming so loud the building shook, Timmon blasted power at the human. The body burst into blue flames so fast the poor human had no chance to even scream.

What exactly had Timmon been before his Imortik possession?

*Renata!*

She jerked away from that disaster at Gretchen's urgent call and gave a little nod in reply. She had to link with them if she could.

Trust them.

She opened her power and pushed it to her friends.

Kaiser twitched in reaction then moved his thumb up.

She linked with Gretchen, who smiled and sent back, *Atta girl. You can do this. We can do this.*

Heavy footsteps stomped Renata's way again. She didn't have time to lower her head and look limp.

Timmon stopped right beside her. She could feel energy wafting from him.

Minos shot up like an excited puppy.

Renata squeezed her eyes shut, wanting to be anywhere but here.

*"Rise!"* ordered the deep voice of Timmon's Imortik master.

She couldn't stifle a whimper and tried not to move, but Minos was expanding inside her, forcing her to lift up and slide from the bar.

Her knees tried to buckle from lack of use, but that blasted Imortik inside her pushed energy into her legs. Between that and the Belador power her friends had linked with her, she stayed upright.

Legs trembling, she focused on staying strong inside. Her body warmed from head to toe. She lifted a hand, staring at glowing yellow skin climbing her arm and a sob escaped.

They won. She would never see Roberto again.

Gretchen's voice filled her head. *Don't panic, Renata. We are here for you. We can escape and defeat these bastards if you don't give into the Imortik. Play along with the master. Do what he says until we find an opening to make our move.*

If Renata couldn't walk or perform her orders, she wouldn't last long. She'd seen what Timmon had just done to someone he deemed useless. She carefully lifted her fingers enough to send Gretchen the okay sign.

"Follow me." The Imortik master stepped away.

Before she could decide to move her feet, her limbs moved on their own. Annoyance slammed her. She told Minos, *I want to move my feet.*

She stopped walking.

Timmon turned around. His evil eyes alone scared her to her toes.

She got moving.

Minos had pulled back, but now said, *I am in control. We do what I want.*

This was one of those moments she had to win to hold any control. Her Imortik either didn't have the power to force her or wasn't aware enough to realize he could do it.

She calmly explained to him in her unemotional voice, *It is not time. If you try too soon, we will fail the master. Did you not see what happened to the last soldier he chose?*

*No.*

Really? Minos missed that? She went into great detail sharing how the master had become angry and destroyed the Imortik.

By the time she finished, two things had happened.

Minos withdrew further and she had reached the end of the aisle.

Her pulse cranked up.

Should she unlink from Gretchen and Kaiser before Timmon yanked all her control away? On the other hand, she'd made a commitment to them and couldn't back out now.

Timmon crooked a finger at her.

Walking three more steps, she faced him and did her best to keep a blank expression. She forced her body to straighten so she didn't look like the last puppet body.

"Show me what power you have, Belador."

She hadn't expected that order and rushed to think of a reply to deliver in a wooden voice. "What would you have me do?"

A dark countenance crossed Timmon's face. "Do you not accept your place, Belador?"

Oh, no, she'd already failed.

Minos snapped, *Call him master!*

She quickly repeated, "What would you have me do, *master*?"

Timmon's face relaxed into its standard unattractive state, but the dark voice belonged to the true master. "Better. I have allowed you more time than the humans and demons."

He said that as if he'd done her a favor when in truth the Imortik could not fully possess a supernatural being as quickly as a human or demon.

The master continued instructing, "You must prove yourself to be of value to my army. If you do not, I will choose a new host for your Imortik."

Renata swallowed at that clear threat. Make a mistake and he'd kill her right after he instructed her Imortik to jump into another body.

"Follow me," the master ordered.

She fell into step behind Timmon's glowing yellow body, watching his boots with her downcast eyes. Wouldn't a master expect a slave to not look at his face? She could play this subservient part if it meant escaping with her two friends.

He passed pole after pole on her right, then took a right turn.

Which row were they on? Was he going to choose another victim to add to his army today?

"Stop."

She did and lifted her gaze. She stood in the aisle where Gretchen and Kaiser hung limp over the same pole.

Renata struggled to keep her heart quiet, but panic set in. Her blood pressure skyrocketed.

The deep-voiced Imortik master announced, "It is time to see if you perform better than a Belador captured a week ago. He was unable to kill on demand, forcing me to terminate him."

Nausea raced up Renata's throat.

She glanced at her friends, who pretended to be asleep but had to be catching every word with their sensitive Belador hearing.

He kicked Gretchen's leg. To her credit, she remained limp.

Timmon's glowing face leaned down, but the master's eyes stared at her. "Kill the Belador and join my army or die painfully."

# CHAPTER 14

BLACK ENGULFED DAEGAN AS HIS body dropped fast at high speed. He didn't care what happened to him as long as he ended up with Casidhe.

Wind beat his skin. His cheeks flapped and his eyes were pinned open.

His body jerked sideways when the hole he fell through changed directions. How had that happened?

Where was Casidhe?

Had she been hurt?

Vicious wind lashed at him until he slowed then landed abruptly on a downward slant. His body slid for another half minute.

Then he shot out into more darkness.

He'd fallen enough during battles to ball up his body and prepare. He hit hard, rolling forward then sliding to a stop.

His arms and legs flopped open against the stone surface.

Dizziness brought on a bout of nausea he'd never suffered before. He lay still, forcing his breath to slow, waiting for his body to return to normal.

With each inhale, he picked up the woodsy scent similar to the one in the room with Amentet.

When he opened his eyes, he was still inside some structure, but no longer in full darkness. A dim light offered aid in seeing his surroundings.

The minute his head stopped spinning, his first thought was of finding Casidhe. Struggling to his feet, he rasped out, "*Casidhe! Where are ya?*"

Catching his breath, he strode forward and cupped his hands to his mouth. "*Casidhe!*"

Her name echoed ahead.

Nothing moved. No other sounds.

He slowed to take in his surroundings. Just a long narrow hall again or so it seemed. His senses were telling him there was more here than his eyes could see.

When he glanced behind him at where he'd been spit out, he found no opening in the solid wall or from the ceiling above. Whatever he'd traveled through was now hidden.

Had Casidhe come to the same place?

Rubbing his aching head, he cursed himself. He should have kept his hand on her arm. He should have made Zeelindar tell them more before agreeing to find the blasted fisted onyx stone and grimoire volume.

Hell, he shouldn't have brought Casidhe.

What if something horrible happened to her?

He couldn't lose her. He had to find her, hear her side of what happened in the Caucasus Mountains. He had to hear her voice, see her smile, touch her again.

The thought of losing her made him sick to his stomach.

Made him want to vomit until he got all the close-minded stubbornness out of himself.

Ruadh's voice came to him as if spoken in a barrel. *She had to read.*

*Ruadh! Are ya harmed?*

*No. I am trapped. We are trapped.*

Daegan's stomach hit his feet. When would he stop hurting the people he cared for who depended upon his decisions? *I am sorry, Ruadh.*

His dragon said, *You will save us.*

For Ruadh's trust in Daegan to remain unshaken even though Daegan might have once again imprisoned them warmed his heart. *I shall do all in my power to escape this place.*

*Find woman.*

Daegan paused in walking, shocked at his dragon speaking up for Casidhe. Ruadh placed a high value on loyalty and trust. His dragon had been just as angry as Daegan when he found Jennyver standing with Casidhe and Herrick.

What had happened for Ruadh's change of heart that Daegan had missed?

*Must go*, Ruadh said.

That ended any thought Daegan had to ask about Casidhe. He did have one question. *Do ya know if Casidhe is near us, Ruadh?*

*Not here.*

Disappointment pushed aside his moment of peace. Daegan had his work cut out for him and he had no idea where he was or what his next move would be. He started down the long walkway where small versions of those tube lights lit up as he approached and flipped off as he passed once the next light ahead glowed.

Just enough light for him to check every foot of wall, floor, and ceiling for any change.

At the end of the passage, the hall split into two directions.

He walked over to test the one on the left. He could see a short distance ahead lit up. Then he stepped over to the opening on the right, which seemed blurry.

He stuck his hand out to pierce the foggy dark.

His fingers hit a wall as solid as rock.

If Casidhe had come this way, she would have taken the left, correct?

But Ruadh said she was not here, as in not here now?

Daegan had to find his own answers. She could have been here at one point and gone in search for him, taking the left hallway.

Going on instinct, Daegan entered the tunnel. This one had square pink stone walls twice the width of his arms extended and twelve feet up to a flat ceiling.

No sculpted images. The occasional tube of glass brightened as he continued through the box-shaped walkway.

The air carried a musty odor, nothing woodsy or floral, just a very old scent one would find in place where people had not lived in a long time.

After walking a few minutes, the passage angled slightly left. The new section had double the width of the one he'd just walked out of and a ceiling twice as high.

Indented tomb rooms had been created along the left side of this space, each shaped as deep rectangles eight feet tall. Above the entrance to every tomb room, hieroglyphics had been carved on a flat area.

Different types of coffins surprised him. He would have thought they would all be similar. Some were gold and silver with black outlines and in the vague shape of a body. Two were long boxes with beautifully molded frames and gold details.

He took his time passing by each one, trying to make sense of the carvings above the openings and on the sides of the occasional box pedestal supporting a coffin. The next room held a long gray-stone coffin adorned with jewels and silver inset. Gifted artisans had crafted these final resting places as works of art. Carvings above the entrance to that one included a man with a narrow chin beard and a tall hat or crown.

After two more rooms, Daegan stopped dead at one of the gold, blue, and black coffins shaped as a large body and perched on a black stone pedestal.

He squatted to peer more closely at the bird design carved into the pedestal wall.

That was no gryphon or bird, but a dragon.

Standing up, he backed away and searched the carvings above the tomb entrance. The artist had created a row similar to the ones Casidhe had translated, but Daegan could read none of it.

Studying the tomb, he debated if he should touch the dragon on the base to see if anything happened. That might disturb another angry being.

He couldn't do this. He had to find Casidhe.

She held more importance than their initial search and could be facing a threat *right now*!

He tried to step away, to continue his hunt, but his legs would not move. A tingle raced along his neck, warning he had to be careful when control had been snatched from him.

Returning to face the tomb room, he moved close and lifted up until he could run his fingers over what Casidhe called a relief.

He wished she was here to snap at him for getting in the way or not wiping his hands before touching the ancient art.

Nothing came to him.

He dropped his arm and stepped back, feeling foolish to think letters would rise for him.

He did not have her gift.

Nor did he have her.

A longing to hold her swept over him so fast he doubled forward with the pain. Hands on his knees, he gulped in air. This was all a waste of time and had put Casidhe at risk.

He had to find her! Catching his breath, he lifted up and stumbled backward until his body met the wall. That movement gave him hope. He tried leaving this spot to keep looking for her.

His damned legs would not obey him!

What had prevented him from moving?

Ruadh groaned something.

*What?* Daegan asked. *What is wrong?*

More groaning.

Energy gathered in the air, swirling around Daegan and stinging his skin. He quickly went on alert. With a glance right and left, he found nothing amiss.

Then he brought his gaze forward again.

An abomination with the body of a man glowed orangish-brown, but with an unfinished head.

Black holes for eyes raged.

Daegan could not move as the filmy creature before him finished taking shape. Ashen smoke poured from the tomb behind him, boiling down to the floor and wrapping his legs.

Every shred of survival instinct warned Daegan to hold still and say nothing.

The tall human torso took final shape with a dragon's head covered in brown scales and spikes jutting out the top. All of the nine-foot body became solid, now covered with a silver robe. Smoke spread out around this being. Leathery wings sprouted from each side, batlike shaped with pointed tips, also covered in nut-brown scales. Claws curled from hands and toes on bare feet sticking out from beneath the robe.

Expecting a smoky scent, the hint of eucalyptus surprised Daegan.

The eyes lightened to ashen then changed to that of a volcano about to erupt.

From that hideous form came a smooth male voice fueled

with the force of ancient power. "Why are you here, dragon?"

Daegan drew a breath, flexing the tight muscles across his chest. He swiped a hand over his head, hoping he chose the correct words.

He'd never been led astray by giving the truth. "I have been sent to find Mulatko."

"I am Mulatko. Why did you waken me?"

His heart thumped with hard beats. He'd found Mulatko. If only he had Casidhe with him.

"I apologize for disturbin' ya." Daegan continued, doing his best to use Zeelindar's exact description. "I am tryin' to save my people and was told I must find ya to locate two things. One was described as brilliant onyx stone carved in the shape of a small hand closed around a pulsin' red stone."

Mulatko snarled and his image wavered out of view then back solid again. "I would like much to see the evil rock gone, but Amentet agreed to hold this safe for the rightful owner."

What was Daegan to say to that?

He had no idea who had placed the black stone here.

"You have no more to say, dragon?"

He placed a hand over his mouth, searching for any idea. When Mulatko began to fade, he shouted, "*Wait!* Please."

The figure stilled.

"I was sent here by an oracle called Zeelindar. She is the one who asked for the onyx stone."

Nothing happened for long seconds then Mulatko whipped forward, his giant dragon snout almost touching Daegan's nose.

Daegan did not flinch, though it took all his strength to remain in place. He held his breath, waiting for a strike.

Mulatko demanded, "What have you done with Zeelindar?"

Releasing pent-up air, Daegan explained, "I have done nothin' with her. She has given me aid in findin' missin' grimoire volumes."

"What grimoire volumes?" Red lava eyes churned.

"The Immortuos grimoire volumes."

Mulatko unleashed a long and loud growl of fury. His form expanded, growing into something unrecognizable. Fierce energy pushed against Daegan's chest until he struggled to breathe.

Daegan tried calling up his power to shove back, but the trickle he received might as well have been a stick trying to move a mountain.

"Stop," Daegan implored. "I have harmed no one."

"*Noooo!*" the thing called Mulatko screamed in his face. "I will not allow such an evil to thrive again."

Daegan felt light-headed. His eyes blurred. He needed air. Squeezing out each word, he said, "I ... am ... here ... to—" He drew hard for one last breath. It was as if his mouth had sealed shut except for a tiny air hole.

Daegan wheezed out, "—stop ... Imortiks."

He doubted his words would make any difference and it didn't.

Mulatko kept yelling and howling crazy sounds. The pressure continued and the being seethed, "No dragon would come here to release a grimoire volume!"

Did that mean this being knew where the volume was?

Daegan fought to stay conscious. "I. Must!"

Nothing changed. He could not hear Ruadh, who should be forcing his way out by now. Daegan expected to be crushed beneath the weight of Mulatko's power any minute.

Mulatko finally pulled back into his original shape. He withdrew his power.

Daegan sagged and gasped for every breath that ended in a fit of coughing. He had to appear strong even in the face of a greater power than his.

As soon as he had the strength, he straightened to his full height and shoved hair off his face. "I am not here to turn grimoire volumes loose on the world. Someone else has used one to open a rift."

Mulatko growled. "*Foools!*" His wings flapped and he shook his clawed fists at the ceiling.

"I agree, but 'twas not by my doin'," Daegan hurried to say, trying to gain an inch with this being. "I am huntin' the missin' volumes only to *close* the death wall and save all in the human world from dyin'."

Mulatko swung his head away, staring to his left.

Daegan turned, following Mulatko's gaze but saw nothing.

Now that the pain in his chest had eased and he could breathe normally, he had to think.

Could the grimoire volume the earth dragon shifter had been tasked with hiding actually be here?

During the silence, Daegan searched his mind for past conversations with Fadil. His friend had told him his father would not speak of his mother's people. Fadil felt there must have been something bad about them, which was why his father had taken his mate and moved far from her people. Daegan recalled clearly now that Fadil had been warned to never go to the country called Egypt.

Fadil must have known early on about why his mother traveled a great distance every year alone to visit the country called Egypt. Had he known if she was loved or hated here?

What Daegan guessed to be ten minutes in human time passed before Mulatko ceased ignoring him.

The being's dragon head swiveled back around to face Daegan again much as an owl's head rotated. "Amentet tells me the one who brought the onyx fist and pulsing red stone to create an oracle was evil. For Amentet's part in an agreement with this being, she decreed for Zeelindar to possess the seeing eye, thus creating a powerful oracle. This being lied to Amentet and broke her trust when he failed to honor his part of the agreement. For that reason, Amentet believes Zeelindar sent you for this onyx stone and has given her permission for you to take possession."

"Thank you."

Turning toward the coffin, Mulatko pointed at the dragon sculpture on the base of the pedestal. The dragon no larger than Daegan's hand disengaged from the smooth marble surface and took flight out of the tomb room. Once in the larger area, the dragon gradually enlarged to five times its size then flew down the dark hall and straight into a stone wall that swallowed the creature.

In less than a minute spent in silence, the small dragon emerged as if flying through a cloud and carrying a black object in its claws to drop onto Mulatko's open hand. With that done, the dragon began shrinking as it spun away to fly overhead and then into the coffin room.

Once the dragon made a last circle around the room, it dove and landed against the pedestal wall, tucking its wings to lean flat against the marble. In the next blink, the dragon had returned to a stone relief once more.

Mulatko tossed the stone to Daegan.

He snatched the round rock from the air. Heavier than it appeared and the size of an orange, the fist hummed with energy. He lifted it to eye level and was stunned at the red center pulsing bright then going dark repeatedly within the small hand.

"You shall leave and never return, dragon."

Daegan snapped his head up. "I wish to ask about the grimoire volume. Zeelindar said one was here. I need that volume to save my people, other nonhumans, and humans from Imortiks." He'd debated the whole time about a third volume still being hidden and would not leave without knowing for sure. If only Casidhe could be here to make a smart remark over his lack of faith.

What would it take for Mulatko to answer him?

Daegan persisted. "Zeelindar said once I received this carved stone, she would tell me where the grimoire volume is located, but she claimed it was here."

Mulatko's dragon eyes narrowed, a sure sign this being's patience would run out soon. "Hold the blood stone upon your palm."

Daegan extended his hand and opened his fingers until the fist-shaped black rock sat in the middle. He stared at the pulsing red stone. The red seemed to be liquid.

"Ask the oracle your question."

Not wasting a second to question anything, Daegan stared at the stone. "Zeelindar, please tell me where the grimoire volume is located in this restin' place of Amentet and Mulatko."

If staring intensely would make a stone speak, this rock should be spitting out words.

How long would Mulatko wait for an answer from the oracle?

What about Casidhe? If he asked, would this being send him to her?

Zeelindar did not appear in her astral projection, as he'd thought, but her voice called out, "Daegan?"

He lifted the sculpted stone. Was Zeelindar speaking to him

through this object?

The pulsing red center now swirled into motion as though whipped around by a frantic wind.

"Yes, Zeelindar. I am here."

The oracle sounded relieved when she replied, "For you to hear me proves you have possession of my blood stone and you stand in the presence of Mulatko, who protects the grimoire volume. The blood stone enslaves me. Please do not allow it to be harmed. You hold control of my life in your hands."

Shocked, Daegan said, "Tell me how to free ya and I will."

"You can do nothing until you and Casidhe depart with the grimoire volume as well as my blood stone. We shall talk then. Mulatko is an ancestor of the earth dragon shifters. The leader of the clan before you were born tasked Mulatko with hiding their grimoire volume and protecting the world from Imortiks. You and Casidhe must prove you are worthy of his trust for him to allow you to take the volume."

Daegan admitted, "Casidhe is not with me. We were separated."

All movement inside the stone slowed until the red center only pulsed again, reminding him of a heartbeat. Clearly, Zeelindar must be unhappy to find he and Casidhe were not together.

Unhappy did not come close to the gut-wrenching fear he endured at the possibility of not finding Casidhe in this place.

Daegan looked up at Mulatko whose burning red eyes narrowed in censorship.

When Zeelindar spoke again, she sounded sad and worried. "You *must* find Casidhe to be successful. *If* you are successful and find your way out, I will share how to locate the third grimoire volume."

*If?* The oracle had doubts of them even escaping. "Zeelindar?"

The stone said nothing.

"*Zeelindar!*" Was the oracle gone?

How was he going to convince Mulatko to give him the grimoire volume and return Casidhe to him? Daegan grabbed at his first idea and shouted at the rock, "What will happen to your blood stone if we are unsuccessful, Zeelindar?"

Still no words came from the stone.

Mulatko announced, "The stone would return to me until Zeelindar found another being to free her, though I doubt such would happen. Amentet became curious about the blood stone over hundreds of years ago after she created the oracle in exchange for the being who was to have performed a task for her. When he failed and broke their agreement, Amentet kept the blood stone as hers. As time passed, she spoke to Zeelindar, who explained how she'd been enslaved."

When Mulatko paused, Daegan came up with ten more questions but dared not say a word until he finished.

Reptilian eyes flicked away then back to him. "Amentet asked what Zeelindar wished to be done with the blood stone. Zeelindar predicted the day would arrive when she would send two beings, one a dragon, the other undeclared. Her emissaries would first request the blood stone and then ask for the grimoire volume I guard. Amentet understood I protected the grimoire volume and would not allow any to gain that power again. For that reason, Amentet left the blood stone in my possession, but she asked for no promises about handing over the grimoire volume or the blood stone, and I made none."

Daegan had a sick feeling in his gut this was going downhill quickly and he had yet to find Casidhe. He needed specifics, then would point out how sending him to Casidhe had to happen first. "What must I do to gain this grimoire volume?"

Mulatko angled his dragon head to the side. "Did you not hear the oracle explain how you must convince me you are trustworthy?"

"Yes, but—"

"Silence, dragon. The question requires a simple yes or no answer. I did not ask to hold a grimoire volume for the earth dragon shifters, but neither do I wish for those abominations to walk free again. You act as if trust is so easy to gain."

Daegan inched forward with this negotiation one careful word at a time. "We share the same view on the Imortiks. How may I prove I am trustworthy?"

"Why should I trust you when the woman who traveled with you does not?"

*Casidhe!* Mulatko's question knocked Daegan back.

How could he reply or argue when guilt tore at him like the claws on Mulatko's hands? Daegan had no one to blame but himself. Scared of the emotions she'd roused in him when he found her with Jennyver and Herrick, he'd treated Casidhe as an enemy.

He had to find her or he could not go on.

He'd stay here forever hunting her.

Love and panic exploded at a white-hot boil, shoving his concern for the damned grimoire volume to the side.

He had to stop this and gain control of himself for any hope of finding her. Struggling to drag the words out, he shouted "I beg of you to send me to Casidhe."

His plea made no impression on Mulatko.

Daegan frowned, recalled to his duty, but he would not find her any faster until he answered Mulatko's question. Neither could he lie. "I admit I do not hold her trust."

Admitting that out loud shamed him.

The dragon snout opened and lava smoldered deep inside Mulatko's jaws.

Time was disintegrating.

Daegan fisted his hands, fighting to stay calm in the face of failure. "But I was friend to the earth dragon shifters when they lived. Fadil of King Anasch was my *closest* friend."

Mulatko snarled, "If you lie, I shall keep you here as my servant for eternity."

*No!* Ruadh roared, pounding at Daegan. *Not again!*

Daegan could not allow them to be imprisoned in a place like this, not again.

They would never survive a second time.

If Mulatko held him captive, should Daegan try to call his goddess mother? Would she hear him if he stood inside another realm? If she came, would all of the beings resting here rise up and slaughter her?

Too many unknowns.

He straightened his back and offered, "How may I prove my words are true?"

"Take my hand and I will ask Fadil's spirit if he claims you as friend." Mulatko lifted a scaly hand with sickle claws.

Daegan had spoken honestly, but had Fadil died thinking they were friends after that last battle? He grasped the hand that clamped his in place. He couldn't pull away without tearing his wrist apart.

Dark energy pulsed. He could taste the rotten stench in his mouth, but he would endure if for no other reason than to find Casidhe.

Mulatko's eyes had blanked into solid white, then returned to a searing red. "Queen Anasch accuses you of killing her family."

Her accusation struck a raw nerve, especially after Skarde had told him this woman could not be trusted with the truth. "I did no such thing. Someone pretendin' to be the red dragon killed others and started the Dragani War. My family died as well."

Fire licked at his hand. He clamped his jaws shut refusing to show any reaction.

Mulatko's dragon head angled to the side and his eyes calmed to an ashen color. "You speak the truth. I should not be surprised by the woman's lie. Queen Anasch descended from the line of Jezebel, a descendant I prefer to not claim."

Daegan felt rewarded for holding his temper. Had Fadil known his mother's bloodline? Jezebel had been a horrendous woman. That might explain the adulterous behavior of Fadil's mother.

Daegan had only one hope. "What of Fadil's opinion?"

The large snout lifted with Mulatko staring up, then dropped until his glowing eyes met Daegan's. "Fadil claims you parted ways not friends. How do you answer, dragon?"

Daegan again fell back on the truth. "I admit we did not part ways on good terms. I still considered him my friend, but his people believed the red dragon had attacked them. Fadil was angry with me. I was captured before I had a chance to convince his clan, and other clans, my dragon did not attack them."

Could Mulatko sense Daegan's pulse racing? Any next move would depend upon what Fadil had said to Mulatko.

"Again, your words are true."

Daegan dropped to his knees and lowered his head with humility. "Is Fadil at peace? Is there any way to pass along how much his friendship meant to me?"

"His words came to me through a guardian spirit. I am not

here to ferry messages." After a pause, Mulatko admitted, "But I shall ferry this one."

"My thanks." Daegan felt a weight he hadn't known he was carrying lift from his shoulders. What had Mulatko meant by a guardian spirit talking between him and Fadil? Daegan had no time to find out as Mulatko released his hand and kept talking.

"If the woman comes to trust you, I shall allow you to take the grimoire volume with the understanding it shall be used to close the death wall and be hidden forever once more. If the woman will not trust you, then you shall leave with the blood stone and she shall wander through these tombs for the rest of eternity."

Blood drained from Daegan's face and his skin chilled at that possibility. He stood quickly. "I will not leave here without Casidhe! I ask only to find her."

"Turn and face your final truth."

With no pocket large enough for tucking away the onyx fist, Daegan carried it in one hand and spun around. What did Mulatko mean by facing his final truth?

In place of the solid wall which had been behind him earlier, a tall opening formed for one person to walk through.

He stepped through, shocked at finding a raging river and forest. Above was not so much a sky as an endless gray color. He searched quickly.

Casidhe stood on the opposite side of the river with her mouth open and staring daggers at him. Why?

Relief spread through him in a hot burst of energy. Daegan rushed forward shouting, "*Casidhe!*"

She turned her back and ran.

# CHAPTER 15

KLEIO AWAKENED WITH A START from her trance. Her hands trembled.

She blinked to clear her eyes and noted all the candles had burned close to the end. She'd been in the trance for six hours? Her body ached and her head throbbed as if she had been out of touch for days.

She slowly got to her feet, blew out the flames, and made her way to the bedroom area of her space on shaky legs.

Too many images flooded her mind.

She needed to sit and write it all down then sort through what she could remember. These more recent visions had come to her fast, much faster than before. She'd moved from one to the next, feeling as if she'd been physically slammed by so much nonstop information.

How could she realize her future, the destiny Janus expected her to fulfill, if she could not sort out those visions?

There had been snippets of scenes, then stretches of one thing after another with no obvious tie between them. That could not be correct.

Not based on divinations she'd received all her life.

Once she'd washed her face, she walked over to the open window where dark shrouded the mountains. A dash of moonlight danced across the peaks, separating them from the black sky full of stars.

She had little time to pull together all she'd seen and come up with a comprehensive explanation for Herrick.

Taking a seat at her small desk, she withdrew paper and pen to begin writing as fast as she could. Some notes were of a face without a name, some of a name without a face. A mixture of locations came to her, then a massive battle.

She never saw the end of the battle, but understood that losing would be catastrophic for the human world.

When her energy to recall images, conversations, and actions waned, she sat back to reflect upon the only vision which had come to her fully formed.

It was the most important vision, in her estimation, which had to do with Casidhe.

Kleio could share nothing about that with Herrick. He had proven he could not be trusted to make honorable decisions. This was why Janus had handed the reins to her to make her own decisions.

As she sat there, staring out the window, her soul became less burdened. She began to see her next path.

She must not rush this decision, for this path would be one she could not change once she took the first step. There would be no second-guessing, no going back.

The decision she'd been waiting on had revealed itself. Her body lightened as if half her weight had been lifted away. Such was the emotional load she'd been shouldering for a long time.

Life would change. She welcomed this change.

She hurried to freshen up and change clothes before heading down to see Herrick.

When she found him downstairs, he was finishing up a meal alone. Servants normally busy taking care of the castle could not be seen. She did not blame them. Who would want to listen to Herrick rant nonstop?

She waited close enough for Herrick to see her as well as sense her.

The dragon shifter wiped his mouth with a cloth napkin and slapped it down. "What, seer?"

"I have had a full day of visions, which took me a while to sort out."

"Are you prepared to tell me where Jennyver is?"

Always the same question without any remorse. Kleio said, "I searched *again* for Jennyver. She is still behind a veil of some sort, blocked from me."

Surprisingly, Herrick did not go off the rails about that failed vision. "Find Casidhe."

Kleio placed a hand on her chest, preparing for another rampage. Janus had tasked her to take the lead and decide who to inform and which visions to share. "I have nothing to share about Casidhe." This was only because she would not.

Jumping up, Herrick pounded over to her. "You are becoming useless! *Who has Jennyver?*"

Standing firm, Kleio lifted her chin to him, making sure he saw the lack of fear in her eyes. Janus would not have chosen a meek woman for this assignment. "You ask the wrong question."

That stumped him into silence.

She waited for him to work it out in his mind. He had to earn what she intended to tell him.

His control snapped so fast, she had no time to back away as his power whipped around the room. He destroyed chairs and ripped tapestries from the walls. He slashed an arm from right to left at the large dining table.

Everything flew off in all directions. The massive table rolled.

She hunched over, covering her head as she backed away fast. She yelled, "*Stop, Herrick!*"

"No. I. Want. *Answers!*"

Fury rushed through her on a tidal wave of adrenaline.

She stood up straight in the storm blowing around the room. Horns grew from each side of her head, curling back at first with the tips pointing forward. Her black hair sprung from the tie she'd used to pull it from her face, now fanning out across her shoulders. A headband of hammered silver wrapped her forehead

Her simple gray wool gown vanished, replaced by a shimmering black one of silk which flashed red when light hit the material. Lace armbands held a trailing cloak in place.

Herrick stopped, slack-jawed.

His gaze locked on her as she lifted her hands in front of her chest-high to grip the hilt of a large sword pointing down.

Beneath the hilt, a magnificent gold dragon icon glowed.

"Who are you?" Herrick asked in a low voice.

"I am the same seer who has informed and advised you for many years, but I answer only to the god Janus. He has allowed me to serve you. If you harm me, he will come for you. He has been tolerant during your recent loss of control and knows I am no meek female to accept your abuse for long."

In spite of finally showing signs of caution, Herrick argued, "Anyone would be angry in my place. You bring me nothing of value."

Maintaining her calm, Kleio replied, "The person protecting the red dragon's sister is also hidden by a veil."

"What is this form you take?" He waved his hand at her image.

"This is for you to realize not all things are as they appear. You underestimate everyone and expect them to treat you with respect, something you do not give in return."

Skin around his dark eyes sagged as if he had not slept in days. He complained, "You cannot tell me where Jennyver is or who protects her."

"Again, you have yet to ask the correct question."

He grabbed his head, staring down for a long moment before slowly raising his face to her. "*Who* took Jennyver?"

Kleio nodded. "Now, you ask the correct question." She closed her eyes, calling her energy back inside her to allow her normal human body to return.

She had made her point with Herrick.

He should not be so foolish around her again. When she felt ready, she opened her eyes.

Herrick's face had lost much of his anger, now wary.

"You asked who took Jennyver. A person who Brynhild has taken as a friend traveled to the mountains with your sister and spirited Jennyver away." Kleio withheld the name of Brynhild's friend. If Herrick wanted to know, he should ask.

"My *sister* did this to me?" For some reason that confused him. "Where is Brynhild?"

"I will tell you, but I want something first."

"I owe you *nothing!* We made a deal. You have had all you asked for."

"This is true and I will honor our deal, which I will remind you included that either of us could end this arrangement whenever we chose." She waited until realization flowed through his face. He knew exactly what she was talking about. "You agreed to those terms, because you wanted the ability to replace me with someone better, maybe younger, should you find a more powerful seer. You never considered that *I* might be the one who chose to leave first."

Sullen silence followed with Herrick walking around, gripping his hair as he mumbled.

Kleio would not give in on what she wanted, not now.

Sighing loud enough to wake the dead, he asked, "What do you want?"

Kleio's heart fluttered with hope for the first step of her new path. "I wish to be taken to the land of my family and given funds so that I may spend some time alone. After that, I may or may not return."

Lowering his hands, he turned to her, the great room in wreckage all around him. "Where are you going?"

Kleio shrugged rather than lie. "I will not require much in the way of funds."

Herrick hated giving up any control, but this was not his choice. "I have never heard of this family. You have withheld things from me."

She shook her head, amazed this man who had survived for so long failed to understand he had lost the ability to question her or make demands. "I have answered all of your questions. Perhaps you know nothing of my family because they did not matter to you enough to ask about them or if I might have wanted to see them once or twice over the years."

Shaking his head, Herrick complained, "How did I fail to choose people who would appreciate what I did for them? Is loyalty too much to ask for?"

She held her tongue. This dragon shifter did not want the truth.

All at once, the fight seemed to leave him, deflating the giant personality. "I agree to your terms. Where is Brynhild?"

Inside, Kleio smiled at the win, but outside she remained stoic and determined. "As soon as you drop me where I wish to go, I will tell you how to find your sister."

Then Herrick would have to deal with the unusual being who she believed had a romantic interest in Brynhild, a man of strange powers who needed Jennyver just as much as Herrick.

# CHAPTER 16

DAEGAN KEPT YELLING, *"CASIDHE, COME back!"* He raced toward the river, looking back to find the wall he'd passed through from Mulatko's tomb room had turned into forest.

He dismissed that, determined to catch Casidhe.

She ran like a wild woman along the bank of the river. What had happened? He'd been so happy to see her.

Why did she act as if she feared him?

Daegan clenched the onyx stone in his fist and angled to his left to stay close to the river. He spun his legs fast, following her from the bank on this side and searching for a spot where he could cross. The water bucked and rushed in the opposite direction. That powerful current would slow him in swimming across to reach the other side.

He pushed harder, begging everything his body could give him. He had to keep her in sight. How was she outrunning him with a backpack on? *"Casidhe! Stop!"*

He jumped over a downed tree and kept hunting for any chance to cross the river. Where had all this forest and water come from? Were they not still underground?

He bellowed as loud as he could, *"Casidhe, stop! Wait for me!"*

She didn't even slow down.

A loud howl broke free of the trees. Wolf? Or some other creature? The animal sounded huge.

At the moment, Casidhe jerked around toward the sound and backed up fast from whatever scared her.

*"Watch out!"* Daegan roared, trying to stop her from falling.

Fixated on that animal, she stumbled backward, missed a step, and fell into the river. He lost sight of her where the water bounced against boulders and a fallen tree.

Daegan kicked off his boots and dove into the river. He called to Ruadh. *Can ya shift?*

*No. Take the power.*

They didn't have much between them, but Daegan's single arm drove through the water fast. He had the onyx stone clutched in his other hand. He could gain little by digging that fist in to fight the current.

Her backpack bounced into view for a second far ahead of him.

Was she being rolled along facedown?

He wouldn't get to her in time. Not with one arm.

His gut twisted at what he had to do and hoped Zeelindar would forgive him. He released the stone and began fighting the undulating water with powerful strokes to reach Casidhe.

His body slammed into a boulder. He grunted and kept going. He had to be getting closer.

But he still could not see her head.

*Please don't drown*, he begged silently. The endless sky above turned dark with bruised clouds.

Lightning popped.

The backpack rolled over with half of Casidhe sticking out of the water. Her head lolled to one side.

*No!* The water pitched him against more rocks and changed directions to flow the way he was going. Easier to swim through, but that sent Casidhe away from him faster.

Thin branches from the top of a tree stuck out above the water with deadly broken tips.

Casidhe shook her head and started flailing wildly.

Her backpack hooked on a tree. Water slammed against her, burying Casidhe in wave after wave.

Daegan caught her and fought to yank the backpack free. When he did, the river dragged both of them forward.

Casidhe's sobs broke his heart.

"I have ya, lass. Do not fash. I shall get us out of here."

"Go away," she wailed.

Why would she say that?

He hooked an arm around the pack to keep her head above water. The rapidly rolling river sent them forward faster than

Daegan could swim. Water dropped away from beneath them.

They went airborne.

She screamed.

He clutched her and the pack to him with both arms. His side smacked a rock when he landed. A rib cracked.

Casidhe's head had gone under water with him, but he'd surfaced to find her still breathing. That was all he cared about. She could rant at him all she wanted about whatever he'd done to upset her as long as she lived.

Finally, the water quieted and moved slower. Floating on his back, he spotted a smooth bank up ahead. His rib burned with every move of his arm, but he stroked hard and paddled his feet, holding her against his good side.

When his knees hit sand, he stopped and caught his breath. Then he stood, hoisting the backpack and carrying it with her up on the ground.

Power Ruadh shared began healing his painful rib.

He set her down, but held onto the pack. "Let me help ya take this off."

She wrenched away and stumbled to her knees. "No."

"What is wrong with ya? Why did ya run from me and now refuse my help?"

"Oh, so *now* you want to give me a hand?" she snapped, unbuckling the straps. When she was free of the pack, she got to her feet and turned to him. "I'm *done* with you. I am not blindly followin' you any more or jumpin' off cliffs or waitin' while you go gallivantin' around."

Daegan stared at her, trying to figure out where his Casidhe had gone. "I did not do those things."

"Now you think to deny what you did? At least before you owned up to bein' a jerk." She shook her head, red-rimmed eyes stung by tears, not the water she'd been in. "You made it clear I should not take anythin' you said to heart."

Daegan walked around shaking his head, hoping something would come loose to explain all this. He turned on her with his arms crossed. "Tell me when I have done even one of those things or said such words."

Now, she pinned him with a look that questioned his

intelligence.

They stayed that way for a long stretch until she gave up the staring match, muttering, "I'll go through this one last time, then I'm done."

One last time? She spoke as if she'd been repeating herself.

Lifting a hand, she ticked off each point on a finger. "Did you not meet me in the room with two ways out and tell me to take one and you would search the other?"

"Send ya alone?" He struggled for words. "I would not do such a thing. I have not been in this room ya speak of."

Her jaw tightened and her lips twisted. "Whatever. This one will be harder to deny. Did you not stand forty feet below me in that area with bones and tell me to jump, that you'd catch me?"

"*Ya did not jump, did ya?*" he shouted. Shock washed over him. "I do not know who told ya to risk your life. 'Twas not me. I wish to find this person who pretended to be me and crush his skull."

Her eyes widened in surprise. Did she believe him?

Just as quickly, that sterling blue gaze narrowed. "One last chance. Did you go to Mulatko's area?"

He could not see anything he might have done wrong so he admitted, "I met Mulatko and—"

"*I knew it! Get away from me!*" She backed up two steps and turned to stride through ankle-deep grass. The forest would be next.

If she disappeared again, he might never find her. "Wait!"

Shaking her head, she kept moving. "I can't do this anymore, Daegan. You're makin' me crazy."

What in the devil had happened while they were apart?

He kept in pace with her, close enough to not lose her. "Please, do not run. Talk to me."

She wheeled, looking like an animal ready to attack. Her eyes thinned and her jaw flexed. "*Talk* to you? Is that what you said?"

He kept silent, fearing any word from him would give more life to the rage surging in her face.

She propped fisted hands at her hips. "How many times have I asked you to talk and you shut me down or blew me off?"

"I was wrong not to allow ya a chance to explain what happened in the mountains. 'Tis not well done on my part and I am livin' with regret." He had thought to have a quiet conversation with her, but everything inside him said he had to speak now or lose her forever. "We talked about givin' the other person a chance to explain after what happened when Queen Maeve lied to ya. I did not uphold my part."

His voice dropped off. He'd negotiated complex peace agreements with every powerful being back when his father lived, but finding the right words for Casidhe stuck in his throat.

More than any of those powerful people, Casidhe deserved his words and more from him.

"And ... I am sorry," he said quietly. He'd been a fool, sticking to rigid beliefs formed around battle and clans. Casidhe had never been a threat to his life or those around him.

She'd shown incredible backbone to be in this place with him and he had let her down.

She'd stilled, lifting up straight. Her mouth moved, but when no words came out she stopped trying. Her arms lost tension, falling lax at her sides and her lips parted.

The rage building only a moment ago had banked and turned into confusion.

He waited, wondering if he should say more yet. His heart pounded in fear of having failed her so much she had given up on them.

Her gaze drifted away and she wrapped her arms across her chest, cupping her elbows as if holding all her parts together. When she spoke, her words came out whisper soft, but carried the great weight of making an important decision.

"When I woke to find you next to me in Tristan's hotel room, you convinced me there was a you and me. That we would have a chance to figure out how to be together after we found the grimoire volumes. Seein' me with Herrick tested that vow and you failed. Words alone can't fix this."

He'd damaged something special between them in the mountains. It was on him to heal the injury he'd inflicted.

Daegan stepped slowly toward her. "I meant those words and they have been eatin' a hole in my gut since the moment I came to my senses and realized I had wronged you."

She angled her face with her chin up.

No acceptance in that expression.

This was a battle he had to win. To lose would cost him all he could ever wish for. "I allowed emotions to blind me when I saw ya with Jennyver in the mountains. I should have realized ya have never caused me or those around me harm. Ya could have turned your sword on me the first time we met, but ya helped me kill Imortiks. Ya have stood strong by my side. Ya came here not for yourself, but for me and those we can save." He reached for her shoulders, holding them gently. "I care deeply for ya, lass, and want to right my wrong. I want ya with me."

Tears streamed down her face.

He closed the distance and leaned down to kiss her.

She shoved a hand on his chest, stopping him. "I have hungered for those words, but they don't hold value now."

"Why?" Someone had made the situation between them worse. "Who was this imposter to have swayed ya against me?"

"The Daegan I saw here might have been someone created to trick me. He didn't act normal, even for you. But every time he let me down, I thought back on how you hurt me when you turned away from me in the mountains. How you sent Tristan instead of comin' to have a private conversation yourself. I was betrayed by Herrick. As deeply as that hurt, what you did cut me far worse."

He dropped his head. His chest ached as if he'd taken a barbed spear to his heart.

Casidhe's voice shook with emotion. "I care deeply for you too, Daegan."

He lifted his head, sure that hope pooled in his eyes, but she was not finished.

"I've been strugglin' since we got here. I wanted to be held and comforted by you, to be told we could do this together. You may be ready to offer that comfort, but somethin' is missin' for me. I couldn't put my finger on it until now. You shattered my trust when I needed you most so how can I trust what you say you feel for me?"

He saw no chance of fixing this, but even knowing so would still not stop him from trying. "I do not have an answer, lass. Ya said words could not repair the harm I've done. I have nothin' more to offer. My word has always been my bond. What would ya have me do?"

She wiped her damp face with her hands and squared her shoulders, taking two steps back and putting more distance between them. "You said in Galway to call a truce so we could work together. I agreed. I'm still willin' to hold up my end of that truce. I say we find the onyx carved fist with the red center then the grimoire volume so we can finish this."

Daegan hated what he had to admit now. "I had the onyx stone in my hand."

She looked at his two empty hands and shouted, "*Had?* What happened? *We have to have that first or no grimoire volume!*"

"I know. I lost the stone."

"Are you kiddin' me?" She slapped a hand over her mouth as if to stop the flow of angry words. She moved her hand to slide over her hair in an agitated motion. "*Where* did you lose it? We need to go find that stone right now."

"We shall not find it." His heart had lost the ability to care for losing anything other than her.

"How can you give up so easily, Daegan?" she demanded, her tone questioning his strength of character.

Guilt and anger balled in his throat at her disappointment and his obvious failure.

He'd fought to protect his people.

He'd fought to save the human world.

He clearly had not fought hard enough to hold onto Casidhe.

Unbridled pain tore at him, ripping him apart in a way he'd never be whole again, not without her.

He roared, "I had the stone in my hand when I dove in to save ya. I could not swim fast enough with one arm to catch ya and would not allow ya to drown. I dropped the damn stone and—"

She gasped, took two steps, and leaped into his arms.

He caught her. He would always catch her.

Her momentum sent them tumbling backward to the soft grass.

She kissed him with a madness Daegan understood. He'd missed her lips, missed her touch ... he'd missed her.

He clutched her close, his mouth reuniting with hers after too long an absence.

Time had no meaning. He didn't care if they spent the rest of their lives in this moment.

She grabbed a fistful of his hair, holding him to her with a possessiveness he savored. The storm calmed and he slowed his kiss, taking time to show her how precious she was to him. His hands shook with having her back in his arms.

No victory had ever felt as powerful or sweet as Casidhe forgiving him. He slipped his tongue between her lips to taste her. She sucked on his tongue and he tensed at how heat burned from her mouth to his groin.

When the frantic need slowed to sweet pecks and hugging, she shoved up off his chest. Damp hair curled around her face. Her lips were swollen from kissing him.

She stared at him, eyes wide in wonder.

"What, lass?" His heart pounded at a crazy pace.

She whispered, "You gave up that onyx stone to save me."

"Aye. I would do it again. I will always come for ya no matter what it costs me."

Her fingers glided over his cheek with the touch of a butterfly. "I can't believe you did such a thing when gainin' the grimoire volume depended on the stone."

"How can ya not?" He kissed her slowly, then held her gaze as a rush of emotions stormed his chest. "Ya own my heart. I trust ya and will never doubt ya again."

He lifted up to kiss her forehead. "I should have climbed through those mountains on my hands and knees to have your trust back." He brushed hair away from her glistening eyes. "I now know why I have lived two thousand years, why I had to endure bein' captured. 'Twas to find a lass with a mighty heart capable of carin' for a man riddled with flaws. I shall always come for ya. No sacrifice is too great to stop me. I would gladly give up my life to protect ya with only one request … to hold ya in my arms as I drew my last breath."

Tears filled her eyes. She sniffled and pulled in a shuddering breath. "I never got the chance to tell you about how I grew up with the ice dragon clan, but I want to share all of it. The only thing I need you to know right now is I never wanted you and Herrick to battle. Also, I would have teleported Jennyver out of there and to you the moment I discovered her had I possessed that power."

He moved to kiss her forehead, then her cheek. "I will hear every word ya wish to share. I shall make mistakes, but I promise to not hold ya accountable to what others have done to me in the past." He nuzzled her neck and kissed her ear. "I shall hear it all ... soon."

Her knees clamped tight against his hips. She shivered. "I, uh, can't talk and do anythin' else right now, Daegan."

"'Tis your choice, lass. I am fine to save the talkin' for later." He rolled her over, taking her mouth as a warrior after a prize. Between kisses, he said, "I'm thinkin' 'tis time to do some makin' up to ya."

Breathless, she demanded, "Touch me."

His honor rose up to shake sense in him. He wanted to let go of his control and make love to Casidhe, but took a look around. He was being selfish to want this now and not wait for a more fitting setting their first time.

He sighed, tired of always putting what he wanted last, but he would gladly do it this time for her. "'Tis not a proper place to take ya, lass."

She pushed up into his face. "Are you serious? You want to take a chance at waitin' with *our* luck? It's time to prove just how much you want to make up." She lifted her hips and rubbed against him.

The gods forgive him, but he could take no more. He eased her back as he sat up on his knees. The hard tips of her nipples pressed against her damp shirt. He ran his hands beneath her shirt, pushing the cloth up until his fingers touched her soft breasts.

She clutched his forearms. "Yes!"

He leaned down, taking a breast in his mouth to suckle while teasing the other one with his fingers. Her sweet body had him shaking with need. Her nails dug into his skin, pleading for more.

He raked his teeth gently over the taut bud, then licked the tip.

He loved the hungry noises she made and moved to the other breast, loving that one equally. He finally had this woman in his grasp and would not let go.

Never again.

He'd waited a lifetime for her with no idea she even existed.

Demanding little termagant pressed her hips up against him, moving with purpose, and driving him mad. He burned to drive into her heat, but he would not rush this. He kissed the smooth skin from her breasts to her stomach. He kissed, then nipped her and moved farther down to unzip her jeans, ridding her of pants and shoes.

Her panties went next.

He eased her legs apart to kiss her heat.

"*Daegan!*" Her legs quivered.

Hearing his name on her tongue drove his hunger to be inside her. Not yet.

Even then, he had to take care and not step over a line. With no idea if she could handle his dragon's power, he could not bond while making love to her. She could die.

Holding back would test him. He wanted this woman bound to him and him bound to her forever.

Bound in love.

He paused as that hit him between the eyes. He had truly found love.

She surged upward, grabbing his shoulders. "What's wrong?"

"Not a thing. Everythin' is perfect. Ya are perfect."

She made a tiny gasp then gave him a smile from her heart. For that smile, he would give all he possessed.

Her chest moved with a deep inhale and exhale. "You are mine. Don't dare think I will ever give you up."

His lonely heart sang with triumph.

"But if you don't get busy, dragon, I'm takin' over. I want to see you and touch you."

He sat up and yanked the T-shirt over his head then leaned down, watching her eyes burn with desire and removed her shirt. Thankfully, she did not have a bra as modern women often wore.

Standing, he shed his jeans, freeing all of him.

She took her time gazing from head to toe, then her eyes started back up, lingering at his groin. "Hmm."

He looked down. "What is this *hmm*? 'Tis plenty."

"That was an appreciative hmm, dragon. As for bein' plenty, you might have a bit too much."

Saucy wench. He grinned. "Nay. Ya shall see how well we fit."

Dropping back to his knees, he moved up to her bent legs and pulled her shoulders close. When they were nose to nose, he said, "I have somethin' I need to say first."

"Thought we were talkin' later." She poked his chest, pushing him back a few inches.

He lifted her finger and licked it then rubbed the wet tip over her nipple.

She grabbed his shoulders. "Hurry up and stop prolongin' the agony or I may change my mind."

"Ya lie and ya are not in pain, lass."

"Depends on your definition of pain." She gave him a sexy smile that would drop an army in its tracks just to admire her. That tart mouth added, "I'm tryin' to imagine what would be important enough to stop a man from acceptin' what I'm offerin'."

"'Tis a precious gift indeed." His heart felt too full. He had to say this first. "I find I love ya, lass."

Her fingers slipped on his shoulder. No longer smiling, she blinked, her eyes shiny, and stared at him for a long moment.

He leaned in and kissed her, sharing his heart with his touch. Battling day after day to keep others safe, he'd never had time to think of his own needs. Of finding a woman to love. Duty had always come first.

This moment belonged to only him and Casidhe, the woman his battered soul begged to keep. Every time he realized he could have her forever, all he'd suffered through to find her faded away, leaving only love.

She was his breath and life.

Casidhe broke the kiss, eyes filled with unshed tears. She held his face in her tender hands. "I never thought I'd find a man who I wanted to hear say those words. I love you, too. I want forever with you."

He stroked her cheek with his knuckles, still wanting her desperately, but he had one more thing to say. "'Tis as I wish as well. I shall take care to not risk bondin' to ya until we know your power. Even if we never find out, I vow ya are mine and I am yours for all the days ahead of us."

She turned her head and kissed his palm. When she came back to him, she sniffled with a watery smile.

That was the beautiful picture now burned in his mind.

Grabbing her shirt from the ground, she wiped her face and tossed it aside. "Grass is ticklin' my butt, dragon."

He laughed. His woman would always keep him on his toes. He stood and lifted her over his shoulder with her laughing madly. When he had clothes spread out, he brought her back to lay on the ground.

What a sight to behold with her hair spread out, perfect breasts rising with each breath, and her lips parted in anticipation.

Her tongue slipped from between her lips to wipe a damp streak over her bottom lip.

"Ya wish to kill me?" he asked, hard as a stone already.

"I wish to have ya inside me," she mimicked him.

"I am but a servant to your wishes." He lowered himself until he could kiss her, saturating himself in the wonder of this woman.

She reached down and stroked him.

His entire body clenched. "Lass! Take care. My want is strong and close to the edge."

Leaning up, she murmured in a husky voice, "I know you're a million years old. I'll take it easy on you."

Daegan would not allow a challenge to his virility go unanswered. He took her wrists in one hand and shoved them above her head. "Do not move these hands."

Her eyes flickered with excitement. When he released her wrists, she stretched her arms and clasped her hands.

He warned, "If ya move, I shall start over."

"You're givin' me incentive to move."

"We shall see." He lowered his mouth to her breast again, but no longer teasing.

Casidhe shivered and gasped. "Uhm, yes."

While he swept his tongue from breast to breast, he reached between her legs, passing one slow stroke of his finger through her damp heat.

That wiped all humor from her face.

"Please, please, please, don't stop," she wheezed out. Her arms bent as if moving back.

He paused and she whined. "Remember, lass, I shall start over if your hands fall below your shoulders.

She shoved her arms straight again, her body taut.

He licked her nipples and blew gently. She shook beneath him. Her hips moved as if hunting his hand.

Dredging a finger through her folds again, he slowed at one place, teasing slowly.

"Daegan," she breathed out. "I need ... can't do this anymore."

Oh, but he was nowhere close to stopping. He lifted off her breasts and she shouted, "No!"

Kissing his way over her smooth skin, he continued to toy with her folds. She made a noise that sounded close to crying, but her hands remained in place, now with a white-knuckle grip. He quickened the movement of his finger, dipping one inside her, then two, never slowing his pace.

She breathed fast as if panicked. "Now?"

"Nay." He replaced his fingers with his mouth and tongue.

"*Now!*" she shouted.

He would not waste a second answering her. He pushed her closer and closer, staying away from the spot that would send her flying.

"Please," she breathed out.

Time for mercy. He lapped at the tiny spot that held her captive.

Her body arched, then she called his name. He kept her there until her trembling body gave in, then he kissed her gently until she lay boneless.

Pulling her arms to flop along her body, she declared, "I'm done."

"Not yet," he promised, lowering his lips back down to kiss her heat and lap up her sweet taste.

"I don't think I can ... oh, yes, I can," she mumbled, tensing once more.

He could not torture her again for so long. She might call up her sword to use on him.

Sweeping his lips across her inner thighs, he brushed his fingers over her damp curls.

She sounded as if she'd run up a mountain, but that did not stop her from tossing out a new challenge. "Are you not able to do more? I can let you rest."

He dropped his head, laughing. He loved this woman beyond belief. He picked up her boneless body, bringing her to him as he sat up on his knees.

Holding her up until her legs flopped behind her, he said, "Ya could not hold your sword right now if ya had to defend yourself."

"Talk, talk, talk. I could hold *your* sword and make you beg for mercy." She gave him a lazy smile, overly proud of her taunt.

He lifted her up and lowered her until he pushed just inside her.

Her eyes flew open.

Now he tortured himself. It took all he could do to ask, "Do ya want me to stop?"

She gripped his shoulders and leaned close to whisper, "I want you all the way in."

She'd slayed him with words. The coil of energy in his core tightened as he slid inside her, feeling her heat wrap around him. He began moving and she met his strokes, fierce eyes locked with his.

Every muscle in his body tightened, holding back for her. Slow had been the plan until she leaned down and nipped his neck. "*More!*"

He gripped her hips, moving her up and down. The need to let go built fast. His thighs tensed.

When he lifted her up again, she locked her legs, stopping him from pulling her down without harming her.

"Lass?" He stared at her in shock, his groin screaming for release. "What 'tis wrong?"

If she wished to stop now, he would be the one begging.

"Just remember next time you tell me you'll start over it goes both ways," she warned in a siren's voice. Then she relaxed and dropped fast, picking up the pace.

He slammed hard into her, once, twice, then he surged, filling her until warm liquid ran down between them. Stars passed before his eyes from the power of his release.

She clenched and came right behind him.

When his vision cleared, he held her to his chest. Her arms were wrapped around him, her hands rubbing up and down his back as if to comfort him.

How long had it been since he'd felt anything of the sort?

Too long to recall.

She turned to kiss his chest.

He closed his eyes. This moment had changed his life forever. How had he lived so long without this lass?

Until now, he'd been existing, not living.

He shifted around until she lay on top of his wide chest, face-to-face with him still inside of her. He brought a hand between them, massaging her breast.

She sighed softly. "That feels incredible."

She'd sounded sleepy. He played with her nipples, not intending to press her for more. Left up to him, he would spend hours and days loving her, but then men had little sense when it came to staying away from the women they desired.

Snuggling against him, she sighed a happy sound. "You are so screwed."

"'Tis the truth, but why?"

"I want nothin' less every time we do this."

"Ya shall have it, but we shall be more creative once we have a suitable place to play." He had forever to surprise her with many different ways.

No sex had ever felt this powerful.

That was the power of sharing everything with someone he loved.

But it would be even more so if they could bond.

Her lips moved against his chest with slurred words as she drifted off. "Just as long as you love me."

"Always." Feeling weary deep in his bones as well, he yawned. They had to find a way out of this place, but they'd had no rest for too long. An hour would give them strength for what they faced next and for hunting an exit. She used his arm as a pillow and clung to him, soothing his need to keep her close. He wrapped his arms and legs around her, falling into a deep sleep.

Water woke him.

His hair was wet. He and Casidhe had rolled to their sides with her still in his arms. He lifted his head and looked toward the river, which had now come to them.

"Casidhe, get up, love. We have to go."

She came awake fast, pushed up on her side, then gave the river a second look. *"The water is risin'!"*

He was up with his jeans, then lifted her to her feet. He grabbed her T-shirt. "Hold your arms up."

She squirmed into the shirt and jerked around. "The backpack!"

Daegan lunged, dragging the pack from where it had started floating in the water. When he turned back, Casidhe had her jeans zipped, frantically looking around.

"What do ya need, lass?"

"Shoes. I think they floated off."

"It shall be fine. We may have to swim out of here."

Her face dropped two shades of color. "Swim to where?"

Daegan had shoved his arms into the straps on her pack, quickly adjusting the closures to fit him. "I do not know, but I see no point in goin' deeper in the woods when the land does not rise."

Casidhe glanced at the woods as if questioning his logic. "What about the grimoire volume? You said you saw Mulatko."

"He would not give the volume to me because I had lost your trust.

Her face fell. "I'll tell him I trust you."

Daegan caught her arms, pulling her to him as water flooded to his ankles. "Do not fash. I failed us when I had a chance to gain the grimoire volume. I do not think Mulatko shall speak with us now that I lost Zeelindar's blood stone. I regret that with my whole heart, but I would have regretted losing ya far more."

She leaned up and kissed him. "If you say swimmin' is our best option, then we swim."

There was his strong woman. He had to make sure she did not

stray. "Ya stay ahead of me so I can see ya. 'Tis not an order, but a plea."

"I will."

He took her hand and led her into the water. When it reached his waist, he waited for her to begin swimming then he followed. By the time they were in the middle of the stream, the land surrounding them changed from a forest to pink stone walls. A twenty-foot-tall ceiling replaced the gray sky. Tube lights glowed in spots above.

Daegan fought against the worry over how the water continued to rise and widen. The current picked up speed. Daegan had to swim harder to reach Casidhe being carried away like a leaf in a tempest.

Up ahead, the water bashed against a wall.

Would the river flow no farther? If that wall was the end of the river, would the water continue to rise until they drowned?

He powered up beside Casidhe and grabbed her shirt, hauling her back.

Her arms flapped around. "What?"

"Look ahead. We must slow down before the wall."

"Oh, crap." She spit out a mouthful of river. "I'm tryin' to kick my feet to slow down. The current is shovin' me forward."

Paddling his feet hard and angling around, Daegan dragged her to his side, turning his back to protect her from the wall. The backpack hit first, taking the brunt of the pounding.

Still the hit knocked the breath from his lungs. He hunched, trying to drag in air. His body spun, unable to slow the water's fury.

Casidhe's body whipped back and forth in the current. Daegan tightened his grasp on her.

The river dragged him along the wall toward a dark hole where water swirled into.

Daegan feared the shirt he clung to her by would rip free. He shouted, "Grab my jeans."

She fought against slaps of water and finally caught her fingers on the waist of his jeans.

They were riding a fierce current slapping them all around while still driving him to the hole.

Casidhe battled to stay with him.

He had one hand shoved forward to block for her.

A whirlpool yanked them into a churning spin, dragging them into a hole forming in the middle. He fought to keep her head up and grab gulps of air before water covered his head.

His lungs burned. His head broke free. He shouted, "Suck in air be—"

# CHAPTER 17

CATHBAD TELEPORTED TO A BEAUTIFUL setting filled with tall graceful oak trees, which had been in this grove for hundreds of years. He recalled when this had been a smaller forest north of Arendal, Norway.

He'd led druid meetings here, but not the dark druids.

Those encounters had been kept secret below Newgrange Mound.

He walked along, enjoying the crisp air, creating white clouds when he exhaled. Dawn had not broken yet, but the tinge of early morning light and quiet added to the sacred feel of this grove.

When he reached the circular area where no trees had ever grown within, Cathbad opened his senses. He picked up no major power.

Strolling out where the last bit of moonlight kissed the grass, he waited.

Lakyle, the youngest dark druid belonging to the conclave of *Dhraoidhean Dorcha Elite*, had shocked him by capturing Casidhe.

After hours of searching for her in Galway, Cathbad had found her hotel room where she had not checked out. He finally had to accept she was truly missing and Lakyle had her in hand.

Someone or something moved through the undergrowth on the far side, then Lakyle appeared in his robe.

Cathbad had clashed with the young druid, but only as what happened when anyone questioned his authority. He could be magnanimous. "I am impressed, Lakyle. Ya succeeded quickly. Hand over Casidhe."

Lakyle settled his hands into the pockets of his robe. "I request to be shown the mark of the Seanóir first."

How dare that young prick question his status as Elder. Cathbad made no move.

Lakyle explained, "My great grandfather was a dark druid under Ainvar. He once told me the mark should be offered free of any obligation."

Cathbad managed to stand calmly when his insides burned with the desire to strike down this arrogant druid. He could not. To kill another dark druid would place a stain on his aura forever and all other druids, even those not dark druids, would see it immediately.

He'd be an outcast among his own kind.

Unable to do otherwise, Cathbad gathered his power to him, pushing it out until Lakyle grunted and stepped back with fear, as he should.

Cathbad lifted his voice. "Ya question *my* word, do ya now?"

Lifting his chin, which revealed a prominent Adam's apple moving up and down his thin neck when he swallowed, Lakyle did not back down. "My great grandfather told me the next Elder in line receives the mark. I only wish to see yours. Is that a problem?"

The little bastard kept gnawing at Cathbad's patience.

He could make Lakyle regret his words and teach the fool some respect without killing him. Just as Cathbad lifted his hands to hit Lakyle with majik, the trees shook with lots of movement.

All the other dark druids walked out, taking places on each side of Lakyle.

Was this a coup?

Then Ainvar strolled out of the shadows.

Sweat broke out on Cathbad's forehead. This could not be. Since awakening from the deep sleep he and Queen Maeve had been in, Cathbad had searched across the world to determine if Ainvar still lived.

That's why he had needed the passage translated in the book he'd given Casidhe. She had his bloody book.

Stepping forward as the other druids bowed their heads, Ainvar said, "You took my place knowing you had no right to this position. You have broken your vows and deceived the

*Dhraoidhean Dorcha Elite.* You must pay."

Fighting back the edge of panic slicing its way through him, Cathbad warned, "Ya cannot kill me or ya stain your aura. Ya would be unable to lead."

Ainvar spoke a soft command.

The druids behind him raised their heads as one.

Lifting his arms to hold out wide, Ainvar said, "I want you all to observe how a true Seanóir should rule. I am not going to kill you, Cathbad. I would never harm a dark druid. I took a vow to lead and protect. You were about to attack Lakyle with your majik though."

"I did not touch him," Cathbad argued, though he was losing ground. He could teleport away, but he would be hunted. He had to come to a resolution here and now.

"You shall be cast out, Cathbad the Druid, never accepted back to any meeting of the conclave. No dark druid will lift a finger to aid you in any way. You have created many enemies."

Cathbad considered how powerful he'd become since awakening in this time in TÅµr Medb, which boosted his power during every visit.

Where had Ainvar been all that time? Ainvar had no realm and was not immortal. How had he even managed to remain alive this long? That majik had to cost him every day.

Feeling more confident, Cathbad boasted "Ya could not kill me even if ya tried, Ainvar."

Ainvar's eyebrows arched to go with his smirk. "Oh? How do you think you escaped Queen Maeve's monster outside Newgrange Mound?"

Cathbad's lips parted.

Pressing on, Ainvar said, "I have a bit of advice for you. If I were you, I would find a place to hide. You have proven to be untrustworthy by all who could offer you aid. Do not dare to exact revenge on Lakyle or any other of my flock. If you do, you will pay a price far greater than being tossed out."

The one mistake Cathbad could not make right now was to appear weak. He had underestimated Queen Maeve. He would not make that error with Ainvar if the druid wanted to battle.

With a hand signal to his followers, Ainvar turned to leave.

An action meant to dismiss.

Cathbad shouted, "Do not be a fool to walk away when we would be far stronger together, Ainvar."

Everything around him stilled.

No tree leaf moved. No small creature raced through the undergrowth. No bird made a peep.

The druids supporting Ainvar turned shocked faces to Cathbad, which quickly morphed into smiles. They started toward Cathbad, probably thinking to chide him.

Ainvar whipped around and roared with the sound of a hundred angry lions. *"You shall pay now!"*

Power lashed out across the opening. Druids behind Ainvar dropped to the ground, covering their heads.

Cathbad called up his power at the same moment, sending it charging across to meet Ainvar's. The energy clashed, exploding into a gale of booming power. Cathbad followed up immediately, pulling energy from his surroundings to drive a spell. He flicked his hands and gave life to words thousands of years old.

Giant jaws with glowing fangs appeared above Ainvar and chomped down. Thick black smoke boiled. Lightning bolts shot free, striking trees and flying into the skies.

Cathbad grinned. That was Ainvar's great power?

The shrill whistle of something coming from above yanked Cathbad's attention up as a hundred bolts from across the sky shot down at him.

Cathbad threw up a kinetic shield.

The bolts struck his shield, hammering him to the ground. More bolts blasted earth away. When he hit the ground, power drove up into his body, shooting free in different directions. He screamed in pain. His vision blurred. He wanted to reach inside and claw out the energy.

When the attack ended and the air calmed, Cathbad lay flat on his back, gasping for air and bleeding profusely.

His head flopped to the side.

Ainvar stood there untouched by fangs now stabbed into the ground all around him.

Druids scurried to their feet, quickly surrounding Ainvar in a show of support.

Ainvar walked over to Cathbad and stared down his nose. "You will not die today, but your power will not return fully, not while you are in this world. Your aura has been marked with a stain of the unworthy. You should still take my advice to hide. I will come for you one day, Cathbad. When I do, I shall lock you in my Ghost Castle for eternity. That is if Queen Maeve does not kill you first."

Cathbad could not form a word. His throat locked tight and his mouth would not move.

How could anyone have done this to him?

All his druids disappeared first.

Then Ainvar vanished.

Cathbad called up his power. Energy struggled, pushing against Ainvar's binding. *Bloody druid!* Clenching his teeth, Cathbad shoved power harder. His eyes bulged. His face twisted painfully. Blisters pricked his skin. He shook with holding the power in place so long.

A loud pop happened.

The binding broke away.

Cathbad rolled over and coughed up blood. Ainvar would pay, but not until Cathbad regained his power. When he did, that prick would finally die, but not quickly.

Struggling to his knees, Cathbad stayed there, heaving one breath after another. When his vision cleared, he tried to teleport away.

He reappeared only fifty feet away.

Nothing like this had ever happened to him.

Queen Maeve could indeed kill him.

He would eventually find Ainvar and take that bastard down, but right now he had to heal enough to teleport then come up with a way to kill Queen Maeve immediately.

He needed TÅµr Medb and could not enter as long as she lived. With her gone, the threat hanging over him now would vanish and he'd regenerate his powers in TÅµr Medb, plus have the warlock and witch army at his disposal.

Ainvar thought to crush him?

That dark druid had a weakness. Everyone did.

Cathbad would discover it and destroy Ainvar, too.

# CHAPTER 18

QUINN HAD TRISTAN TELEPORT HIM to the mountain shielding VIPER headquarters. With Sen no longer standing guard, Quinn felt the Tribunal would stay in session until their pet executioner was found.

"Call me if you need me," Tristan said, disappearing.

"This is Quinn of the Beladors," he shouted at the rock face. "I wish to speak with the Tribunal."

A deep voice answered, "Have you found Sen?"

"Yes and no." Let the trickster god chew on that.

Everything around Quinn blurred during the instant teleporting. When he could see clearly again, he faced the usual trio, as expected.

That annoying minstrel, Hermes, and Justitia, the unflappable goddess of justice, stood in their normal spots. She wore her plain robe and held the scales of justice. Hermes strummed his lyre. His hair stuck out from his skullcap above eyes dreaming of something other than playing a significant role here.

Loki, on the other hand, did not wear his standard Armani suit or the equivalent. A black duster fell to his knees. Horns stuck out from his head. His body had grown to half again the size of his human form.

Bad sign for Loki to shift into his true state.

No point in putting off the inevitable.

Quinn addressed all three. "We located Adrianna only because she used Witchlock to blast her way out of a building south of Atlanta where Tenebris had imprisoned her."

Surprise rippled across the dais. Loki's eyes narrowed. "You wish for us to believe this Tenebris had the two of them in a building within the human world?"

"It's the truth." Quinn kept his tone all business. "We thought from the beginning they might still be in the human world."

"Daegan indicated such," Justitia interjected. "He said someone with a gift for remote viewing saw Tenebris after he'd taken Sen."

Of course, all this group cared about was Sen.

Quinn moved on. "Yes, we have someone with that ability. We also have another person who helped us narrow down the location. We had teams all over the area when that building exploded. Many were close enough to be harmed."

Twisting his lips in a sour expression, Loki said, "You have yet to tell us anything about Sen."

"When we found Adrianna, she was two miles away from the blast and unable to stand. I sent her to Treoir in hopes the healers will be able to ... help her." No one on the dais showed any concern. Typical. Quinn continued, "Adrianna told us Tenebris had kept Sen separate from her. She thinks they might have survived the blast since they were not standing with her when it happened. Tenebris said Sen had warned him about Witchlock."

Hermes paused in strumming and sent an expectant look to Justitia. Her head swiveled to Loki, who asked, "Why would Sen give any aid to the being who imprisoned him?"

Quinn answered that for Sen. "From what Adrianna said, Tenebris had been torturing Sen. He executed the torture somewhere close enough for her to hear Sen, but she believes Tenebris had a healthy respect for her power and likely moved Sen somewhere. Had Tenebris wanted to kill Sen, he could have."

Loki's eyes literally boiled a bright white. "We want Sen found. What is so difficult to understand about that?"

Pounding in Quinn's head after the blast had backed off for a bit, but returned with a vengeance now. "We want him found as well. That is why I am here now. Please do not take any Beladors off the street. We need all of them to support the search. We have someone else who might be able to find Sen."

"Who?" Justitia asked.

"She is a gifted young woman in Treoir."

"How does she intend to help while within another realm?"

"Since being a child, she has been able to hold a personal

item of a missing person in her hand, which invokes visions or dreams of where to find that person. If you can supply something of personal value to Sen, I would take it to her."

At the lack of reply from anyone, Quinn pressed harder. "Even a hunting dog needs a scent to track. We found Adrianna by handing this same young woman a key ring Adrianna's sister had made for her."

What else could Quinn say? Nothing. If the Tribunal truly wanted to help, this was the moment.

Loki vanished and returned within a second. He held up a glass container as round as Quinn's hand and twice as thick. "Sen lives in a Spartan way. This is the only item that was not part of basic living quarters."

Quinn opened his hand. An iridescent flask-like container with a silver-and-black metal stopper, reminding him of a flat perfume bottle with a fatter hole at the top, appeared on his palm.

Closing his fingers around the container, he said, "Thank you." And he meant it. With Daegan gone, Quinn would take any break from fighting with the Tribunal and losing Beladors.

"If you will teleport me to—"

Before he finished his sentence, Loki had tossed him outside the mountain, dumping Quinn on his ass.

Aid from the Tribunal evidently had limits.

Quinn called to Tristan, who showed up quickly. Quinn fired off the top question on his mind. "Is Reese safe?"

Tristan frowned. "Of course she is. Between me, Evalle, Casper, and you, she's protected. Add Isak to that and you have a badass battalion watching over your baby mama."

Quinn gave him a tired smile. "I know. I just worry when she is not near."

Clamping a hand on Quinn's shoulder, Tristan said, "We all understand. What happened inside?"

Hitting the main points, Quinn filled him in. "I have this for Lanna to try to locate Sen."

Tristan lifted the pretty jar up to hold between him and the moon. "Is that a seed or pit inside?"

Quinn had not looked closely yet and took it back to study the content. "It does appear to be some kind of pit." He began to have serious doubts about Lanna getting anything from a pit in a bottle. "I am not entirely sure that Loki did not produce that so we would have no way to claim the Tribunal refused to help."

"That bullshit would fit Loki, but I'll take it to Lanna if you want."

"We have no choice to do otherwise. How is Adrianna?"

Tristan pinched his chin in a thoughtful pose. "Lanna and Garwyli are taking turns working on her. They said it would be a while before they knew anything definitive. I'll check on her when I drop Sen's pet seed off so Lanna can look at it when she takes a break from healing Adrianna."

Giving the glass container a long look, Quinn debated for a moment then handed it to Tristan. "I say we let them heal Adrianna as much as possible first then take a look at this. Does it sound as if they are feeling positive about Adrianna?"

Tristan averted his eyes. "They want to put her in a deep sleep to boost her healing."

"Is there an issue with that?"

Releasing a slow breath first as if he hesitated, Tristan admitted, "Garwyli was against it. He worries that Adrianna may fall in too deep a sleep that only her power can bring her out of. Lanna feels she can nudge Witchlock to wake Adrianna when the time comes."

Quinn had two immediate concerns. If Lanna failed to get what she wanted from Witchlock, she might try something dangerous and harm herself. If she did not bring Adrianna back, Lanna would carry that loss deep inside.

"I know what you're thinking, Quinn, but no one can manage Lanna. She was a force before she went to study under Garwyli. She's scary powerful now. We have to trust her not to hurt herself or Adrianna in the process."

True, but Quinn could no sooner deny his protective instincts for his young cousin than he could for Reese. "When you take this container to leave for Lanna, please include a note explaining it belongs to Sen and to only do what she can when she feels up to it. When you come back, we'll return to the team."

Tristan traveled so quickly, Quinn had no time to dwell on

anything very long. He was anxious to return to the blast site until Tristan altered those plans with new information.

"I moved the team before you called me here."

"Why?"

"Evalle received word the demons were popping up in midtown. With Isak's team better equipped to investigate the explosion, Reese wanted the chance to track down I-zubrrali."

Quinn slapped a hand over his eyes. "Of course, she did. The women in my life will put me in an early grave." Shoving his hand over his hair, he nodded. "Let's go."

Tristan held up a finger, an action that meant he listened to telepathy. Lines formed on his forehead when his eyebrows drew tight. He murmured, "Shit."

"What?"

"We have to wait for the team to stop. They're being chased by a helicopter gunship with the human military. Evalle said she and Casper killed an Imortik just as the helicopter came into view. It started firing at all of them."

# CHAPTER 19

MACHA FINALLY CHOSE TO FOLLOW the Scáth Force around Atlanta until they received word of the red dragon. So far, there had been no word by early evening in Atlanta. Once she'd found out all she could, she'd turn her attention to how to make the best use of that information.

While observing Queen Maeve's warlocks and cloaked from their view, Macha began to realize this group had no intention of trying to grab an Imortik.

They clearly feared the yellow monsters more than Queen Maeve, which said a lot. To intentionally disobey her orders would end with them dying in worse ways than most minds could comprehend.

Not hers. She smiled at the many inventive manners she'd utilized for ending a life with maximum suffering.

Erath had captured a troll earlier to interrogate for information on the Imortiks and grimoire volumes. That was taking too long and turning out to be fruitless.

Once Erath called it a day for the Scáth Force and she'd gleaned all she could, she would teleport away and wait in Mongolia for Queen Maeve.

That bitch believed she held the reins to the supernatural world.

Those reins would turn into asps to bite her. Queen Maeve would not live long enough to regret her foolishness.

Macha would take down Daegan first, if he flew into whatever trap Queen Maeve had set, and kill the crazy queen next.

Remove two thorns from her side. Then Macha would have no need to satisfy her deal with Loki.

If Daegan died immediately, he should not have time to call in his goddess mother. Once Queen Maeve died, there would be no one to prove Macha had killed Daegan and it would be easy to point a finger at Queen Maeve.

No one would care who terminated Queen Maeve.

Most supernaturals would hold a celebration.

Yawning from boredom, Macha swept a look around at the rundown buildings with broken windows and weeds growing in parking areas on the east side of the city. Homeless humans slept inside doorways. She could do without the stench of rotting food and bodily odors circulating.

Maybe that's why Erath and his team hid here. They hoped the strong scents would mask theirs.

A mild hum of energy approached. Someone cloaked.

She perked up. Who snuck up on the Scáth Force? There were no other supernaturals nearby. This could be interesting.

Erath finished interrogating a troll that had known less than a beetle. Would he release the troll?

One of his men pulled out a dagger and answered that question.

Macha wrinkled her nose at the new smell of troll blood. If not for remaining concealed, she would dispose of the body just to breathe clean air.

Energy built as the unknown cloaked one continued toward Erath and his team. This being had not concealed his or her energy signature the way Macha was currently doing.

Had that been intentional?

The warlocks finally turned toward the cloaked being, but they had taken too long to notice. Any being of power would have struck down the entire team by now.

Light shimmered around the being and the cloaking disintegrated, revealing Cathbad.

Why hadn't he just appeared without a stealth approach?

Still, this was far more interesting than Erath's activities.

Cathbad spoke first. "Erath. 'Tis good to see ya."

Erath made no motion to agree. "We are unable to speak with you, Cathbad. Our queen's orders."

"The same queen who sent ya to capture an Imortik?"

Macha moved closer. Had Cathbad been in the cemetery when she'd listened to Queen Maeve and her warlocks? If so, he'd clearly hidden his power there.

"How do you know of our orders, Cathbad?"

Point to Erath for asking the question Macha needed answered.

"I spent time in Oakland Park Cemetery and finally found one ghoul who was desperate enough to shake hands," Cathbad explained, then asked another question as if assuming control of this group. "Who has been killin' the Nightstalkers?"

Macha smiled at the mystery none of them could solve.

"We don't know and would like to identity the being screwing up everyone's intel," Erath groused.

Cathbad held himself erect and with confidence, but something had been off about his cloaking.

Had he realized his power signature had leaked out?

He spoke with authority when he told Erath and his group, "Ya do realize Queen Maeve is insane, do ya not?" He held up a hand. "I will not put ya on the spot by answerin'. Ya must know she has cut her deal with the Imortik Master."

Macha canted her head in surprise. Loki might kill Maeve himself if he learned that tidbit.

Looking decidedly uncomfortable, Erath tried to sound as if this was not news to him. "We know Queen Maeve has an understanding with the Imortik master."

"'Tis good to hear. If ya think this through to the final outcome, ya should realize she will no longer need any of ya, not even you, Erath, if ya figure out how to deliver an Imortik to her."

He'd stunned the entire bunch.

Sweat broke out on Erath's forehead. "That can't be true. She will always need an elite force." But he didn't sound convinced himself.

Cathbad scoffed. "Why? If the world is overrun by Imortiks and she shares control with the master, what would be your duties?"

Macha had always respected Cathbad's ability to manipulate, but these warlocks should not believe his words. If Cathbad still held a high place with Queen Maeve, Erath would not have said a word about not being allowed to speak to the druid. Even more significant, Cathbad would not be here trying to seize control of Queen Maeve's elite warriors.

Staying with Erath's team was paying off more than Macha

could have imagined.

Erath shuffled around in place and his men watched him with trepidation. They had to follow him.

Would Erath lead them off a cliff?

Cathbad held up his hands as if surrendering, which he had never done. "Very well. I came here to offer ya a chance to continue and thrive once ya are free of Queen Maeve, for she will not survive her scheme. I know for sure she has no way to deliver even one grimoire volume since I control the person who can find the missin' one."

Was that a lie or truth? Macha tapped a sleek fingernail against her chin.

Erath's rigid stance and loyalty began to deteriorate beneath Cathbad's announcement. The warlock looked at his men, probably wondering if one of them would hand him over to Queen Maeve then take his place while she'd slowly dismembered Erath.

Calling his men into a group huddle, Erath and the warlocks whispered back and forth.

When they broke apart, every warlock glanced around nervously. They should be concerned.

Queen Maeve could be standing nearby hidden by cloaking just as Macha had been doing all day. But that stupid queen had the ego of Zeus and believed herself invincible.

Dragging in a deep breath, Erath said, "We wish to hear your proposal."

Cathbad held back any wild laughter he might be feeling and addressed Erath as his own man. "I am quite proud of ya. I could not stand by and watch the best of TÅμr Medb, plus all the many warlocks and witches servin' that realm, be destroyed by a queen whose mind has been corrupted from reincarnatin'. I have watched her fall apart and lose control no matter how much I've tried to save her."

Macha covered her mouth to keep from bursting out with her own wild laughter at Cathbad The Nurturer.

Without missing a beat, Cathbad said, "When do ya expect Queen Maeve to return?"

Sounding more confident with this new direction, Erath held

back nothing. "She intends to return after she has dealt with the red dragon. She did not share her specific plans with us, but I felt she had a trap in mind to set in Mongolia. She said to listen for word of the red dragon there today or tomorrow. I don't know how to tell you where to find her."

"'Tis not necessary. I shall find her. I would not expect her to return." Cathbad waited as the men began to smile, sensing they'd chosen the winning side to join. "In the meantime, ya must hide until I return to tell ya she is no longer a threat to ya."

"I like the sound of that. Where should we go?"

Cathbad explained how Erath could enter a nearby MARTA station where city trains carried humans from point to point. By the time he'd finished, they had been given a way to find tunnels where Queen Maeve could not use her scrying wall to locate them.

Quite clever, actually. Macha found Cathbad's plan sound, but why did he need Queen Maeve's Scáth Force out of sight? Did he really believe he could kill the queen and take over TÅµr Medb?

She remained close by as Erath and his men snuck away, heading to the MARTA station.

Cathbad chuckled, happy about what he believed had been a perfectly executed plan. And it would have been if not for one mistake.

He assumed no one watched him.

Macha appeared in front of him.

He didn't move to react, but his face lost its normally tan and healthy look. "What do ya want, Macha?"

"For you to do me a favor."

His face rearranged into slightly surprised, mostly not interested. "Why would I do anythin' for ya?"

"If you don't, I will feel honor bound to share what I heard you and Erath discuss with Queen Maeve."

# CHAPTER 20

REESE RACED WITH EVALLE AND Casper down an empty Decatur Street, heading toward the Five Points intersection still a mile away. Bullets zinged all around them in rapid fire from a shooter riding the rails of a helicopter. She stayed in line between Evalle and Casper, who could leave her with their speed, but they wouldn't.

To keep up, she forced herself to run faster and zigzag when Evalle did. The effort to not throw up kept her focused and had nothing to do with her pregnancy.

She was not a damn runner.

Casper yelled, "Need to take a break, Reese?"

"No." Reese wanted to strangle him for making her talk. If she opened her mouth again, she'd lose the war to keep her insides from coming up.

Pumping her arms and checking over her shoulder every time gunfire erupted, Evalle yelled, "Hang the next left into Peachtree Fountains at Underground."

"What about humans?" Casper called back.

"Probably none around, but we'll avoid them. The chopper shouldn't fire if they see humans."

Shouldn't did not equal wouldn't.

Reese kept her mouth shut and breathed through her nose. None of her group would risk a human life even if they knew for sure the chopper gunman would stop shooting. With the way Atlanta and other cities across the country had curfews in place, not many humans were around to make videos or be in the way.

The sound of a helicopter flying back and forth to catch sight of them between trees and buildings howled closer.

Reese had no idea what Evalle planned, but she was onboard if it meant no longer being target practice.

Evalle took a hard turn to the left, not slowing a bit. When she reached the retail shops at street level of the area known as Underground Atlanta, she led them to run along the empty retail shops.

The chopper had zoomed overhead and could be heard coming back, but the shots had silenced for a moment.

Reese yelled, "They're headed this way again."

"Down here." Evalle stopped and pointed at descending cement steps.

Reese raced down with the other two following close behind her. When she reached the bottom and stepped out of the way, she dropped to her knees. Every breath hurt.

Evalle came up to her, not even breathing hard. "You okay, Reese? Did that hurt the baby?"

Reese shook her head and lifted a finger, begging for a minute to recover. When she could talk, she stood up and said, "I'm good, just don't run that much." She put a hand on her stomach. "Albert is fine."

"Albert will not do, love," Quinn called to her.

She jumped up as he reached her on long strides and willingly fell into his arms.

"Good to see you, too." Evalle made that jab as she walked past them and over to Tristan.

Reese pushed to the side to find Tristan. She smiled, still unable to say much more.

Quinn stroked her back. "Are you sure all is fine, sweetheart?"

She looked up into the eyes she wanted to wake up to forever and nodded again. "Yep. Just had to recover a minute. All is peachy with both of us."

Loud whomping circled outside.

When she had a chance to search her surroundings, she realized Evalle had taken them down to the original Underground Railroad, which felt like a very old partially enclosed parking deck or basement with cement walls. Rails that had carried the first trains to this city were now a level below new roads built above.

A vehicle could get in here but not a helicopter.

"We can't stay long," Evalle pointed out, destroying Reese's moment of safety. "If we don't leave, they'll send in the National Guard Hummers."

"Yeah, and I saw tanks earlier," Casper said.

Reese waited for Quinn to weigh in. This was his team and she frankly had no ideas.

Quinn kept an arm around Reese. He addressed Evalle and Casper. "Give me an update."

Casper jumped in first. "We were using Reese like a divining rod to track down demons—"

"I am *not* a divining rod, *highlander*."

Casper didn't really care for that other part of his body and sent her a quelling look.

She smiled, her point made.

"Anyhow, we were hunting demons and I-zubrrali while Reese *directed* us when an Imortik came out of nowhere."

Evalle added, "Quinn, there were four more Imortiks far behind that one. They stood in a group and watched like a coordinated unit. I think the master or someone is organizing those things."

"Bloody hell." Quinn sounded as if he could use twenty hours of sleep. "I'm thinking to take us all to my building not far from here where you can eat and rest."

Reese backed out of his arms. "Not yet." She glanced at Evalle and Casper, wanting a team decision. When they nodded, she continued, "We were closing in on I-zubrrali. I really believe we had him on the run because the demons were thinning out. If we stop for even an hour, he'll find a new place to set up business and we'll have to fight that many more demons to get to him the next time."

Quinn clearly did not like her idea, but he had agreed to not bench her as long as she wanted to stay on the streets. "I shall agree if we find him in an hour or less. After that point, you all need some downtime."

"That's fair." Evalle turned a look on Casper.

He shrugged. "I'm in no matter what."

Tristan said, "I can take you wherever you need to go while I'm waiting to hear from Daegan, but that could happen any minute. I thought I'd hear by now."

That last part had been filled with worry.

Where was Daegan this time?

Reese felt for the dragon king. Nothing would get better for him until they stopped the Imortiks.

"Where do you wish to pick up tracking the demons?" Quinn asked, his tone flat and not thrilled at all.

Casper explained how they'd been moving from the parking lot at Trader Joe's in Midtown toward Piedmont Park when they killed the Imortik-demon. "We followed from there over to Hill Street before it reached Memorial Drive when the helicopter showed up."

Tristan listened intently. "Where do you want to teleport to?"

Before Quinn could pick a place farther away, Reese suggested, "Let's go back around Hill Street to where we picked up the helicopter. Maybe the human military will be busy here hunting us after we disappear."

Evalle clarified, "That's a good plan. If they aren't there, we work back toward Trader Joe's and see if we can pick them up again."

Casper nodded.

Quinn grumbled under his breath, but told Tristan, "We'll link with you to save your energy."

"Good idea."

Linking Belador power with Quinn and Evalle, Tristan teleported them really fast. He landed them behind one of the closed businesses along Hill Street on the eastern outskirts of the city.

Reese's eyes adjusted to the darkness quickly. She had no idea how Tristan managed to teleport to a great spot, but his local skills were a testament to how familiar he was with this city.

While Quinn and Casper discussed a plan for covering a large area, Evalle walked over to Reese and pulled off her dark sunglasses. Bright green eyes glowed. She whispered, "You don't have to risk your life every minute. We're all proud of what you're doing, but we don't want anything to happen to you." She held up a hand to stall Reese's reply, adding, "Let me narrow down what I mean. Your safety is of utmost importance to all of us, but I have not seen Quinn as complete in a long time as he is around you. He was in a dark place for a while and it took a lot to pull him out. So please, don't gamble with your life when you have this much power around you."

Raking fingers through her hair, Reese listened and didn't make her usual denial that this was any trouble. The last two days had been tough for her and everyone. "I hear you, Evalle. I'm not taking any unnecessary risk, but I want Quinn and all of you not to fight an army of demons, plus the Imortiks, plus a rogue black ops group lead by a wizard, plus human military just doing their jobs. The only part of that I can truly help with is stopping I-zubrrali."

"Okay, champ. We'll run as long as you can handle it, but we won't think less of you when it's time to stop." Evalle shoved her sunglasses back in place and stared above Reese's head. "Good talk. Let's kill some demons."

Reese laughed. "I agree, but we need to get Quinn onboard before he shuttles me off to the basement of his secret building for his teams."

Quinn strode over to them with Casper and Tristan. "Since Tristan may have to leave at a minute's notice, I'm putting him behind to watch our backs. Before leaving, he'll send a telepathic message to alert us. I'll take Reese with me. Evalle should stay with Casper so we will all be informed."

Heat buzzed inside Reese. "My demon attractor is spooling up."

"Time to rock." Evalle stomped her boots, releasing blades.

Casper said, "I'll wait until I see them to let out my crazy half."

Grady appeared out of thin air, but his body failed to completely turn solid. "Ya'll got a mess goin' on."

Evalle turned to her favorite Nightstalker. "What are you talking about?"

"I been tryin' to get answers on that Tenebris. He was seen near Sweet Auburn Market and didn't look too good, face all jacked up on one side. Like he done jumped into a fire fight with no water hose."

Evalle explained, "Adrianna used Witchlock to blow her way out of a building. She was being held here in the human world.

No one knows what happened to Sen and Tenebris."

"I didn't see no sign of Sen, but no one gonna miss him."

Reese urged, "Hate to interrupt, but demons are headed our way."

Evalle rushed ahead. "Can you find out where Tenebris might be staying?"

"Naw. That's the problem. Some bein' is shakin' hands with Nightstalkers, then killin' 'em."

Curses flew all around. Evalle took her cap off and settled it back into place. "I have to go, Grady. Do not shake with anyone. I'll put the word out and see if we can find out who's destroying Nightstalkers. I'm sorry. I know these are your friends."

Grady nodded, his eyes red-rimmed. "Go on and get done. I'm glad that witch is safe." He faded to nothing, blending with the dark night.

Tristan asked, "Still feel the demon energy, Reese?"

She had stood calmly paying attention as the energy changed. "Yes, but now my energy is acting strange the way it has every time I-zubrrali shows up."

All eyes turned to Quinn.

He had a kicked-in-the-nuts look.

Reese felt bad. She hated being the boot that kicked him. She started to give in to what he wanted when Quinn said, "Break into two teams with Tristan at our backs like we discussed. Stay in sight of each other. The first one with a visual on I-zubrrali calls out immediately."

With the team in agreement, Reese started forward, keeping track of how her energy acted.

Damn if Casper hadn't aptly described her as a divining rod. When this was behind them, she'd let him know she conceded his point.

She and Quinn moved from behind the building then weaved their way between structures on this side of the road.

Evalle and Casper had crossed the narrow street and mirrored them.

Tristan was somewhere behind, but he could zap himself forward in an instant if anyone called to him.

When Reese broke out into the opening, she scoured the

area for any sign of demons. I-zubrrali must have incredible control to keep his monsters away from her when they had to be foaming at the mouth with the urge to drain her.

Quinn turned to observe Evalle and Casper. Reese had her back to him, searching the area ahead where she could see farther down Hill Street beneath streetlights. It would be easier in daylight.

She took two more steps forward to look past a closed restaurant to see if her churning energy would strengthen.

A hand came out of nowhere to latch onto her and yanked her to the left.

She put her foot out, stopping her body from sliding, but she was losing ground.

Quinn was there in an instant. He clamped his hand on the one holding her and yanked it forward with a roar. *"Let her go!"*

A man tumbled into view, broke free of Quinn to roll, then came up on his feet lithe as a trained gymnast. An extremely attractive male with golden hair and searing green eyes. He wore jeans and a straw-colored Henley pullover.

"Who the hell are you?" Quinn demanded, stepping ahead of her.

Tristan appeared instantly. "That's Joavan, a Faetheen who tricked me and Daegan into helping him."

Joavan sidestepped and vanished as if walking behind an invisible wall.

"What was he doing here?" Tristan asked. "Don't trust that bastard for anything."

"He stuck his hand out from some cloaking and grabbed Reese." Quinn sounded rattled. He already worried about her hunting I-zubrrali and now this.

Reese wanted to calm Quinn. "I shoved my foot out and stopped him. I'm guessing he was trying to pull me into his cloaking."

Tristan had a different take on it. "Best I can recall, Joavan doesn't cloak himself so much as he travels by entering his home world and coming out somewhere else. That makes me think he was trying to pull you into his home world."

"Why?"

"My first thought would be because of your remote viewing ability." Tristan lifted his hands in surrender. "Daegan has an amulet that Joavan wants, but Daegan needs it to close the death wall when the time comes, according to a druid named Ainvar. The druid also happens to be Joavan's father and they hate each other. Joavan could have been observing us when you found Adrianna."

Reese swallowed hard. She had said she would take no unnecessary risks, but it sounded as if her being exposed at all was a risk.

"I'll stay closer to keep watch," Tristan said in a comforting voice.

"Thank you." Quinn nodded, then stilled for a few seconds. "Evalle called to say they've spotted a demon." He turned on Reese. "I promised to not smother you, but I need you to stay close to me. I was almost too far away when I realized what happened."

"I understand." She consulted her body. "I don't feel the scrambled sensation that calms quickly, which I normally do when I-zubrrali is around. I hope he didn't slip away."

Quinn said nothing, which indicated his disagreement.

Back on the trail of demons, she and Quinn angled toward Evalle and Casper who were now slightly ahead and reaching Hill Street.

By the time Reese and Quinn reached a spot on this side of the normally busy thoroughfare, Evalle and Casper watched her, waiting for an indication of where to go.

Reese still felt the constant churning she got when demons hunted her. The only thing she knew to do was keep moving forward to maintain a strong energy reaction.

She mused, "It feels like I'm chasing the demons instead of the other way around."

"Any suggestions?" Quinn asked.

"Not really. I think we should go that way, based on what I'm picking up." She pointed out her new direction.

"Lead on, sweetheart."

Reese did as he suggested and continued the chase, which took them closer to Memorial Drive. If they had to go past that point, they'd have to cross the interstate.

When Reese made it to Memorial Drive, she looked to her left. "The power is stronger to the east. It's like they hopscotch around."

"Evalle is calling me." Quinn paused then said, "She has an idea, but I am not wild about it."

"What is it?"

"There's a nightclub in that direction called the Iron Casket, which is owned by a nonhuman named Deek D'Alimonte."

"How does that help?"

"He's a centaur and likely has no tolerance for demons."

That was news to Reese, but this was Evalle's stomping grounds. "Okay, what's the plan?"

"Evalle is calling Deek to alert him we're headed his way tracking a group of demons and asking him to help."

"Will he?"

Tristan appeared next to them. "Evalle told me what she's doing. We have a fifty-fifty chance Deek will be in the mood to kill something besides us."

Heh. Reese said, "I'm still following the demons instead of them chasing me. That makes me think I-zubrrali has to be managing them."

"Which way?" Quinn asked.

Heading east, she struck out on this side of Memorial Street while keeping an eye on Evalle and Casper over on the opposite side.

At the sound of a helicopter flying toward them, Quinn grabbed her and dove between two buildings. From what she could see, Evalle and Casper had done the same. Tristan should have no trouble staying out of sight.

As soon as the whomping sound faded, she dashed back out, sure Quinn would stay close. Hurrying ahead, she made it two blocks down the street when the sensation in her chest disappeared. "*Damn!*"

"What's wrong, sweetheart."

"The demons are gone. I feel nothing. That's just ... crazy."

"Let's keep going. I can make out Deek up ahead in his parking lot. Perhaps he was around during the last Imortik outbreak and could share something useful."

Curious to meet a centaur, Reese squinted. A great big guy with black hair and a body of muscles stacked on muscles easy to see with no shirt, stood in front of a shiny nightclub called the Iron Casket. The gleaming metal and crystal-looking decorations glittered like bait for a Fae.

Wait. *Iron* Casket? That sounded like a death trap for a Fae. She'd have to get the story on that place later.

Quinn lifted a hand to catch Deek's attention. At the same moment, Deek jumped around, looking to his left. Then to his right.

The large man started walking toward them.

Stopping, Quinn wondered aloud, "What is he doing?"

Glowing yellow beings emerged from each side of the nightclub.

Deek began jogging faster.

Evalle and Casper ran across the street to join Reese and Quinn.

Tristan appeared next to Quinn. "What's Deek doing? He can teleport."

"I don't know, but don't interfere," Evalle warned. "You know how he gets when he's pissed off." Her words sounded backed by experience.

Deek yelled, *"Runnn!"*

# CHAPTER 21

RUNNING AS FAST AS SHE could again, Reese rethought her desire to meet a centaur if it meant dying with him. "Doesn't he have powers?"

"Oh, hell yeah," Evalle muttered staying with her. "Don't dare try to tell him what to do."

Quinn slowed and turned, which meant everyone else in the group did the same. He tossed out, "I'm wondering if Deek needs help. With Tristan, we can always teleport away if it comes to that."

Tristan said, "True."

Deek hadn't turned on any super speed, just remained about fifty feet ahead of Imortiks now falling into order like a military troop. The monsters must have thought Deek could not move any faster. They picked up their pace to a full run. Some were possessed trolls and a couple demons, but others looked like humans dunked into fluorescent yellow.

Wearing only a pair of dark pants and barefoot, Deek raced up to Quinn's group, looking like a Spartan warrior character Reese had seen in a movie. Wild black hair fell around his teak-brown face. Glowing eyes burned with crazy warlord bloodlust. He lacked only a spear and shield.

The warlord had better do something quick.

Imortiks barreled forward at full speed like a pack of wolves following the scent of fresh blood.

Deek turned to the monsters and roared, *"Never cross my land!"*

That was it? Reese looked at Quinn, who didn't back up a step.

Power rushed around, almost choking her.

The crazy warlord shifted into a huge horse from tail to neck.

The rest remained as the upper body of a human looking Deek. The centaur's horse part reared up and came down hard, blasting holes in the pavement.

Chunks flew like shrapnel.

Quinn covered Reese's head. She pushed to the side to see what happened next.

The ground buckled, rolling away from Deek, stopping only when a sinkhole large enough to swallow two dump trucks opened up.

Unable to stop their momentum, Imortiks fell in one after another.

Screams and cries burst from the hole.

It was over in seconds.

Reese couldn't speak. She hurt only for the humans who had not been saved.

Tristan asked, "Can they get out?"

Deek's hooves stepped around until the scowling centaur faced him. "I would be a moron to have opened a hole from which they could escape and rise again. They are burning as we speak."

Tristan lifted a finger in salute. "Gotcha."

When Deek stomped back around, he raised arms of cut muscle, holding them out toward the hole and called, "*Ignis. Mors. Adolebitque in aeternum.*"

Piles of buckled land shifted, filling the hole, then kept moving and smoothing out until everything appeared as if nothing had happened.

Reese couldn't translate Latin. Her best guess was, "Bury the yellow bastards and clean up the landscape."

Evalle folded her arms across her chest and moaned.

Quinn grabbed his head.

"Oh, fuck," Tristan groaned.

Reese swung around in front of them. "What's wrong?"

Taking a shaky breath, Evalle said, "Two of those Imortiks called out telepathically as they fell. They were ... Beladors."

Reese squeezed Quinn's arm. She had no words to ease their loss. They had to stop these Imortiks soon.

Fighting to regain his composure, Quinn said, "One shouted

his name and I recognized the voice of another. We shall inform the families. Those monsters *must* be stopped!"

The centaur waited quietly.

Tristan suggested, "Maybe the connection to their master's control snapped as they entered Deek's pit and that's how we heard them."

"Very likely," Quinn agreed. He lifted his gaze to Deek. "Thank you for your help."

Deek nodded. "Stay off my land." He trotted down the road then entered his parking lot and shifted back to a fully dressed man wearing a classy suit.

"He won't keep helping us?" Reese asked. "He could kill lots of Imortiks at one time."

Casper hooked his thumbs in his jean pockets. "We are very fortunate Deek didn't toss all of us into that hole. He rules that piece of land like a separate country. Not even the Tribunal messes with him. The only reason his parking lot is empty of customer vehicles is because he chooses to keep his club closed right now. It has nothing to do with human or supernatural laws."

"Casper's right." Evalle's gaze tracked Deek as he entered his building. "Tristan teleported me away from a battle one time and I accidentally landed there. I thought Deek was going to kill me or keep me imprisoned for life."

Appalled, Reese asked, "Could he do that?"

All four said, "Yes."

She wanted to know more, but energy churned in her chest. "We're hot with demons again."

Everyone prepared for a potential threat.

Quinn asked, "Which direction?"

"Give me a minute." She turned away from Deek's nightclub and took two steps then shifted back around. Her energy spun wildly. She pointed. "That way."

"Toward Deek's place?" Evalle sent Reese an are-you-kidding look.

"Yes, but I'm thinking we'll go way past there. If I-zubrrali was watching, he would be foolish to mess with Deek."

Taking the lead with Quinn at her side, Reese struck out at a what she considered a good pace, walking a number of blocks until they reached Boulevard.

The pull of energy strengthened to her right.

She waved a hand, directing the team to turn south, which would allow them to walk under the interstate and stay better hidden from the helicopters. She noted a few bars had lights on. Rap music floated from one along with the aroma of barbeque.

Her mouth watered. She'd like to go to Quinn's R&R building in downtown, but not until she found I-zubrrali.

Heat swirled in her abdomen. She rubbed a hand over the firm area, not quite a bump. "Hang in there, Junior. We're going to kill that bastard."

Quinn squeezed her shoulder, letting her know she had his support no matter what they faced. The fact that he hadn't suggested a ridiculous name for their baby indicated the depth of his worry.

She wanted to end this tonight and hoped the hour she'd agreed for giving up the hunt would not run out before she found her bastard father. She had a plan in mind for taking down I-zubrrali. Quinn would lose his mind if she told him, which was why she kept her strategy secret.

Once they passed under Interstate 20, she felt so much demonic energy she had to catch her breath.

"Reese?"

She lifted a hand, indicating she was fine. Quinn did not push her for more.

They entered an area where no vehicles traveled and no one walked along the street even though it was not really late at night.

This area of the city felt abandoned, though that was not true. Humans were tucked in tight at home, staying off the streets until the military could save them from nonhumans.

The military could only kill a massive number of Imortiks by dropping a bomb large enough to destroy Georgia, but that would still leave many more monsters running free.

Not a solution.

Taking a quick left, Reese walked deeper into an older community. New homes built seventy years ago and older were now part of a poorer area, but the tidy yards and maintained structures showed pride and love.

Dogs howled from several different places.

She slowed on a sidewalk in front of a row of houses, sick at heart. "I think the demons are in this neighborhood," she whispered to Quinn while tilting her head to indicate an area between two houses. "Forcing us to fight in a human residential location would so fit a monster like I-zubrrali."

"The humans will likely remain locked inside, especially at night."

"Let's hope so." She waited until the rest of the team joined them. "I'm going to keep moving toward where I feel the demons might be congregating based on how they're agitating my power, but I expect that to change when we encounter I-zubrrali."

Casper asked, "You think he's here?"

"Demons would be all over me long ago if he were not. I think he has been leading us to this spot, so yes." Reese shook off the trepidation climbing her spine. "Normally when he shows up, I feel nothing at first as if the demons disappear, then my energy just goes crazy. The second I sense I-zubrrali is around, I'll tell Quinn so he can alert all of you."

"Think we should fan out, Quinn?" Evalle asked, staring at the modest homes where few porchlights burned.

"Yes, but not beyond sight of each other."

"Understood." Evalle waved Casper to follow her.

Quinn and Reese turned between the houses.

She assumed Tristan took up the rear again.

A dog inside a home Reese passed, barked and lunged at the window. She jumped away.

Quinn grabbed her arm to keep her steady.

What kind of badass could she be if a dog startled her?

Ready again, she moved deeper and kept going through wooded yards, climbing fences, squeezing through thick landscaping. She crossed a two-lane street in the same neighborhood with houses on each side.

After passing through to the other side of the last row of houses and a narrow barrier of trees, she came upon the rear parking area of a business with a two-story building.

Barking and howling followed.

She'd managed to wake up the whole neighborhood without finding one demon. When she reached the middle of the parking lot, her energy quieted.

She waited for the weird change she should feel from I-zubrrali, but it never came. "Damn!"

"I take it we've lost the demons and their leader," Quinn commented in a calm voice.

"Yes." She glanced to her left where Evalle and Casper were sneaking around twenty yards away, easy to see with overhead lights brightening the empty parking lot.

Tristan popped into view. "I heard from Trey that the team in Athens needs to be brought to your building in Atlanta. They have injuries. Trey is calling in a healer to meet them."

She fluttered a hand in frustration. "No reason to hang around longer, Tristan. I lost the demons."

"Sorry." Tristan waited on Quinn for the final word.

"Thank you, Tristan. We have it from here." When Tristan disappeared, Quinn waved over Evalle and Casper.

The pair made it to within forty feet of Reese when that chaotic energy began to stir inside her. She whispered, "Don't move."

Quinn stilled and must have called to Evalle telepathically as she and Casper stopped immediately.

Three demons raced out of the wooded area behind the neighborhood they had just left and three more boiled over the top of the building.

They were being attacked from the front and back.

Evalle shoved up a kinetic wall at the ones coming from the woods while running with Casper to join Quinn and Reese.

Quinn's kinetic barrier faced the building. He yelled, "Ready to attack?"

Reese had already spooled up a strike in her hands. "*Yes!*"

He lowered the shield and she took out two demons running side by side. The blast struck between them. Stinky dust filled the air. Quinn hit the third one with a kinetic right cut. That one hit the ground, but didn't die. Quinn pointed at a stack of cement blocks, lifted one kinetically, and sent it flying.

The block smashed the demon's head. More dust.

Looking over her shoulder, Evalle had dropped her wall. Casper was gone. In his place that highlander swung a sword, cleaving two demons in half, one behind the other. Dust flew in a windstorm generated by the wide blade.

Evalle had her dagger in hand. She ran at the last one the woods had belched out, flipped in the air and landed on its shoulders, knocking it backward.

The demon was fast and lunged up to grab her throat.

She shoved the dagger deep into its chest and pulled up hard, ripping the demon open. A dust cloud engulfed her.

She waved her hand across her face, coughing as she backed up to the group. "Everyone okay?"

"We're good." Quinn still sounded worried.

Reese asked, "What's bothering you, Quinn?"

"Why only six demons? Not that I wish for more, but this was almost too easy and unlike I-zubrrali."

"I don't know but I don't feel him or demons." Reese had to face the fact her hour to find that bastard was pretty much up.

"Let's go home," Quinn announced, very likely reading her disappointment and taking his opening to put her somewhere safe. "The shortest path is back through the neighborhood. I'll call for a car to meet us at Boulevard where we peeled off to enter the neighborhood."

Adrenaline still pumped as hard as disappointment through Reese. She should have gotten I-zubrrali tonight. Something kept niggling at her that this had been her only chance. She had nothing to base that upon but her gut.

They reached the last street they'd crossed running through the neighborhood. Reese had been lagging behind with her thoughts and Quinn had allowed her space. That man knew her so well.

She heard a huffing sound and stopped. A beagle trotted toward her on the sidewalk to her left.

With all kinds of predators willing to eat someone's pet, Reese paused. Her big mutt was safe in Treoir.

Over to her right, Quinn stopped. "Reese, the dog is fine."

Behind the dog, a girl of four or five years ran calling, "*Come back, Skipper!*"

"Shit. Let me grab the dog and hold it for her." Reese headed for the mutt that sprinted away as she reached for the critter. It ran between two houses. She considered chasing the pet.

A woman screamed, *"Lily!"*

Reese forgot the dog to rescue the child for her mother.

Reese could hear Quinn far behind her, muttering, "This night will not end."

A young woman ran down the steps of the house, shouting louder. *"Lily, come back!"*

Alarm climbed Reese's spine. She ran for the child, calling out, "I'll stop her."

When she got close, the child disappeared. Reese turned to see if she'd missed the little girl in the dark.

A hundred feet back, Quinn was heading her way. He took off faster. *"Look out, Reese!"*

Evalle screamed, *"Runnn, Reese!"*

Casper flipped into his highlander.

All three of them raced toward her with their super speed, but the moment slowed into sluggish seconds.

She spun around to face I-zubrrali ten feet away, grinning.

I-zubrrali shoved a hand pointed over her shoulder and shouted, "Fall down!"

Wrenching her neck, she watched Quinn, Evalle, and Casper's highlander hit the ground fifteen feet back. No one was moving. They had to be alive. Please be alive.

Reese swung her gaze back to face I-zubrrali.

This would be her only chance.

He stood there, confident as a brick wall ready to smash an insect that dared to fly into it. He'd played her by messing with her energy to convince her he was not near then creating the illusions she'd chased.

Rolling her hands around each other, she balled up energy. "You die now."

An Imortik-demon shot from the darkness and shoved its clawed hand inside Reese.

She made a wheezing sound, unable to breathe around the pain. The Imortik-demon struggled to gain purchase in her body.

I-zubrrali ordered, "Get away from her. *I am your maker!*"

Nothing slowed this demon possessed by an Imortik, not with its hand clutching her energy.

Reese cringed. The glowing monster shook with excitement.

I-zubrrali shouted words she couldn't understand.

The Imortik-demon was yanked backward.

It flew to I-zubrrali's open hand. He shook the yellow demon by the neck. "I told all of you. *I want the baby!*" Then he smashed the abomination headfirst against the sidewalk.

The sulfuric stench of the dust singed her nostrils.

Reese clutched her chest, heaving painful breaths.

"Bring me the baby and all pain will end," the bastard said, as if telling her he had cookies for her.

Tears burned her cheeks. She forced her legs to move. The power she'd felt before had waned with that attack. "You killed my people."

"No, I didn't." I-zubrrali frowned at her.

"Prove they live or I'll kill this baby myself." She put her hands on each side of her abdomen. Junior's heat surged to her hands. She hoped that meant he understood she only bluffed about harming him.

"When I have the baby," I-zubrrali clarified.

"No." Reese shook her head. She hurt everywhere, but sidestepped away into a yard where she could turn to keep an eye on I-zubbrali and Quinn. "They aren't moving."

I-zubrrali rolled his eyes. "You have been the most difficult child." Stepping up until he was even with her, he whipped a hand at the three on the ground.

Quinn lifted his head and shook it. Evalle and Casper began moving, too.

Relief smacked Reese.

When they all stood, Quinn rushed forward and slammed up against an invisible wall. He beat on it. "Touch her and I will kill you!"

Something grabbed Reese's shoulders and dragged her backward.

I-zubrrali cut his head around. "No. *She is mine!* What is wrong with you miserable Imortiks?"

The yellow monster stepped into view and growled a demonic sound, then dove inside her.

She arched, squeezing out a painful sound. Agony ripped through her. Nausea crawled up her throat. Her body shook and vibrated.

The Imortik-demon yelled in her head, *Stop fighting.*

*Never.* She called up her energy.

The monster inside howled and clawed at her, not giving an inch.

I-zubrrali screamed his special words again at the demon part of the Imortik, demanding it release her.

From the first touch she could tell this Imortik-demon had been stronger than the last.

Demons appeared all around them. Hundreds.

Striding to her with supreme confidence, I-zubrrali roared in a deep voice, "*The baby is mine!*"

Miserable, disgusting being. She called up her energy before she blacked out from pain and balled her trembling hands.

When I-zubbrali stepped close enough to reach for her stomach, she jabbed a hand into his chest, burying her hand to the wrist.

Shock rode his face.

Surprised her, too, but it might be due to the Imortik trying to gain purchase in her. No way. She'd kill his maker and take out two monsters with one fist.

Energy charged through I-zubrrali and bloomed around her arm, bright yellow Imortik energy. She screamed at the burning sensation ravaging her skin and muscles.

I-zubrrali shouted, "*Stop!*"

He thought to defeat her with only a word?

She grinned with insane madness overtaking her. Her arm began to feel as if it joined to his body.

Oh, no. She did not want to be connected to him any more than she wanted an Imortik-demon inside her trying to grip her energy.

She called up more power and clamped her other hand across I-zubbrali's face, driving her fingers into his skin.

He screamed as if his balls were being dragged over hot coals.

There was the sound she wanted.

They fell to the ground, but she fought to free herself and finally wrenched away.

I-zubrrali lay on the ground screaming. Flames erupted in one eye, then his chest burst open with fire. His hands burned. Both legs incinerated from the toes up. Blood poured from his mouth thick as hot lava, scalding his skin. His death was slow and agonizing to the very end.

Everything he deserved.

She sat there, dragging in one breath after another. Her body shuddered from the strain.

"Junior?" she whispered fearfully. Heat circulated in her abdomen.

Tears burned her eyes.

She stood, feeling invincible. Her insides had calmed.

No demons in sight and no I-zubrrali.

When she checked on Quinn, he stumbled forward, free of the barrier and hurried toward her. Then stopped short with a look of horror.

She fist-pumped. "*Yes!*" Why wasn't he still moving?

Quinn's face crumbled, wracked with pain.

Evalle rushed up beside him. With one look at Reese, she started crying. That woman never cried.

Quinn walked forward.

Casper ran up and grabbed him, shouting at him, "*Don't!*"

Quinn fought him like a mad man. "*LET ME GO!*"

"Quinn?" Her voice broke. Reese looked at her fist and arm.

A shimmer of yellow rolled over her skin and grew into a bright glow.

Then caustic power exploded inside her.

# CHAPTER 22

DAEGAN'S LUNGS BEGGED FOR AIR in the vicious whirlpool still dragging him down. He had no chance of releasing Casidhe while she clung fast as a barnacle to him.

How long could she hold her breath?

His chest ached and she was so much smaller.

Pressure kept their bodies forced together as one, diving deeper and deeper. Then he was yanked sideways and flipped around.

Formidable spinning water drove him forward in a whirling tunnel. His lungs were close to giving up.

A mighty wave grabbed hold and shot them up as a double spear in the air.

Daegan gasped for breath. He tried twisting to protect Casidhe, but little could he do to soften the blow of landing like a giant boulder hitting the water.

The blow knocked his head around. Stars flew through his gaze. Dazed, he sucked in a mouthful of water.

Power calmed and Daegan's body popped up to the surface. Casidhe had lost her grip on him.

He choked and spewed water, then looked around, lunging to grab her still body. He wrapped an arm around her chest, holding her head up.

Moonlight danced over gentle ripples.

He searched for a bank and started swimming toward it. *"Lass!"* He caught another breath. *"Casidhe! Can ya breathe?"*

His knees raked across the bottom. He dropped his feet to the ground and turned to lift her in his arms. Struggling to move his exhausted legs through the water, he fell to his knees on the sandy bank, lowering Casidhe's limp body.

She wasn't breathing.

"*Nay!*" He'd seen someone saved in Atlanta by breathing air into the body, but that person hadn't drowned. Daegan took a deep breath and bent down, blowing gently into her mouth. What else had that human done?

He recalled the healer pushing on the unconscious person's chest.

Careful not to crush her bones, Daegan made the same motion six times, then two more. Sucking in air, he blew into her mouth again. Nothing changed.

Daegan dropped his head back to stare at the heavens and roared, "*She is mine. I want no other. I beg of ya do not take her from me! Where are ya, mother, when I need ya.*"

Energy spun through his body and into his hand on her chest. Her power reached up to tingle against his.

He leaned down and began to breathe his energy into her plus push it gently through his hands carefully holding her head.

When he blew his life into hers again, her energy buzzed stronger against the pads of his fingers.

He pleaded in a whisper, "Come back to me."

Casidhe jerked up and away from him, spewing water everywhere. He held her and pounded her back carefully. When her stomach had no more to give up, he pulled her against him, shaking hard. His next breath shuddered.

He could have lost her.

Coughing, she clung to Daegan's arm. "What happened?"

He dropped his head to hers. "Ya scared me. I wished we had bonded so if ya had not survived, I could have followed ya."

She hugged him tight, her arms trembling. "I'm sorry I scared you. I can't hold my breath underwater for long."

"I am glad ya came back to me." He hugged her, so damn glad to have her against his chest. He would not let her out of his sight again, not put her at risk.

She stilled then pulled back, looking around. "We're outside? Above ground?"

"Aye." Once he had her sitting next to him and breathing, he was in no hurry to call Tristan or anyone else. He had no grimoire volume or blood stone.

He needed this time with her, just a few minutes.

She raked her hands through her hair, then gave up trying to do anything with the wild curls he loved.

She said, "I should feel bad about failing at our plan, but ... I am so glad to be here with you."

"As I am with ya, lass. I shall explain to the oracle and offer to do whatever I can to free her."

"What do you mean by free her?"

Daegan explained how the blood stone held Zeelindar's freedom.

Casidhe nodded. "She basically told me she was trapped, but that's even more horrendous. I'll help too if she comes up with a new plan."

Daegan would not sleep well knowing he left a woman in bondage. He would lose more than sleep if Casidhe stepped away from him before he could have her safe in Treoir.

Casidhe leaned over and kissed him. He dipped his head to her, always wanting more. After a moment, she tilted her head, gazing out over the river and stilled. "Daegan?"

He felt her tense. "What, lass?"

"Do you see what's floatin'?"

Squinting to focus, something round lit by the moon floated toward them then a soft wave tossed it up on shore.

The black ball had a throbbing red center.

Daegan lunged forward and snatched up Zeelindar's blood stone.

He couldn't believe the stone had followed them. Moving back next to Casidhe, he offered it to her.

"*This* is Zeelindar's blood stone?" She lifted the onyx fist, eyeing it with anger due a rock holding a person's freedom.

"Aye. I would never have thought to see that again. If we are to leave with only one item, I would rather it be a way to free the oracle. We shall just have to find another way to stop the Imortiks."

"I agree. I felt bad for her after she gave me a verbal smackdown for whinin' over you not talkin' to me. I have my own flaws, dragon." She smiled over at him, sharing in the joy of one battle won.

"'Tis trouble I caused." He kissed her forehead.

"Sweet dragon," she murmured. "So how does this onyx fist work?"

"Zeelindar said once we returned, she shall explain how to help her. She also said she would tell us how to find the third grimoire volume, but she may not since I failed to gain the second one."

"*We* failed to gain the second one. We share the good and the bad now."

His heart rippled with happiness. He used kinetics to lift the ball above Casidhe's open palm.

Her laughter tinkled. "You have some power back, eh?"

"Aye. I may have enough to teleport a short distance if a threat arose, but I shall still need to call Tristan soon to take us home." He paused on the word home.

What would home be without Casidhe?

Empty. Nothing.

He would discuss where she planned to live and not tell her she would go with him. She became prickly when he wanted to ensure her safety and he failed to discuss such things. He grinned to himself, looking forward to more days of testing her patience. That brought out her warrior side, which he adored.

More days of everything. He wanted her close by to know she was safe at all times and to continue filling a gaping hole he'd had inside for too long.

After lowering the blood stone back to rest on her palm, he glanced around, making sure no one snuck up on them. "Ya still think we are in Egypt?"

"I'll bet we are and this water is the Nile River."

He knew nothing of this land of Fadil's ancestors and wished his friend had shared more in the past.

Something as wide as his two hands floating in the water glowed with an array of colors.

Daegan had been through enough surprises for one day.

"Let's move back from the river." He stood, picked up the backpack and dropped the blood stone inside, then reached for Casidhe's hand.

"Why?"

"'Tis somethin' floatin' this way and it glows. I have seen ya too close to dyin' to watch again. We must back far enough away to be safe. I shall teleport if we have no other choice."

With his help, she scrambled to her feet and they ran fifty steps.

He gently moved her behind him.

She stepped around the other side. "Stop it. I'm not drownin'. We're a team. Don't make me call up my sword."

Daegan snorted at his headstrong woman and waited silently with her as the glowing object neared the shore.

When the water flipped the mysterious object in the air, the glow changed to a golden orange color as it landed hard in the sand. One corner protruded.

He said, "Stay here and I shall take a look."

"Not a chance." She took a step, determined to get there first.

He jumped ahead, pain in his leg from the venom showing up for the first time in a while. He ignored that and grumbled at her for not listening only to receive laughter in return.

When Daegan leaned over to pull the object out of the sand, Casidhe shouted, "*Stop!*"

Hand yanked back, he waited.

"It's a box with the same markings on the top as the other grimoire volume we found." She grabbed his arm, excitement bubbling off her.

Daegan lowered his head to get a better look. He used kinetics to move sand off the flat bronze surface.

He stared in awe. "Mulatko gave us the grimoire volume. I did not truly believe another one remained hidden until now." His leg throbbed, which made sense as the venom had not bothered him while inside the underground chambers.

He turned to Casidhe with a crooked smile. "Mulatko must have known I earned your trust back before we left."

She hugged him and his world tilted with a deep joy. He kissed her on the head, then had a troubling thought.

Would this box bring Imortiks running to them?

"'Tis time to go," Daegan announced abruptly.

"Really?" she snuggled closer. "The minute we leave here we have no privacy and our world returns into chaos."

"True, but I fear Imortiks comin' for this box."

She backed out of his arms fast. "Sold me with that."

A gust of wind stirred the water. Sand blew around, stinging Daegan's exposed face, chest, and arms. Another unexpected thing. He'd had enough of Egypt.

Casidhe swatted hair off her face and stared past him with a wary look. "Let's grab our stuff and teleport."

"What 'tis wrong?" He glanced over his shoulder to find sand being moved by some energy, not a gust of wind.

"Think I need my sword," she said quietly, her gaze still locked on whatever had the sand moving.

"Sit down," a voice ordered as the oracle's astral travel image came into view.

Daegan remained standing with Casidhe. "We wish to speak with ya, Zeelindar, but this grimoire volume may bring Imortiks to us all."

"You and the grimoire are shielded within my power."

He couldn't argue with that, but still felt wary. If an Imortik showed up, he hoped the oracle's cloaking held strong.

Zeelindar came fully into focus. Though still translucent, her upper body appeared the same as before in a human shape, then formed into one long shape from the hips down.

Once Daegan and Casidhe sat cross-legged facing the oracle, Zeelindar paused her swaying back and forth. "You were successful with Mulatko."

"Aye, but it would have aided me to know I had to convince Mulatko that Casidhe and I trusted each other to receive this bronze box," Daegan said, still not happy about how close he could have come to losing Casidhe. "We were separated and I might not have found Casidhe again."

Giving him a pinched look, the oracle said, "Why would you think such a thing? Mulatko had to test you both to know you would be worthy of *his* trust. You could only prove such apart from each other."

"That explains the fake Daegan I had to deal with before the real one showed up," Casidhe grumbled, which pleased Daegan.

He never wanted her to think he would behave so dishonorably.

In looking back, they had both battled to survive that place and now had the grimoire volume in hand, as well as the blood stone. They had come through a gauntlet to have faith in each other again, now stronger than before.

Zeelindar continued, "You have both proven to be trustworthy more than once. I wish to thank you for all you have done."

Daegan had pulled the backpack to him to dig out the blood stone and stopped. "I did not honestly believe we would find a second grimoire this time, but now that we have, it begs the question of how many are in Atlanta."

"One. There has always been only one."

That meant someone was lying. Daegan had to think on that. "How do we find that last one?"

Casidhe leaned forward. "And how do we call up the death wall?"

Zeelindar told Casidhe, "A single volume might answer one or more questions, depending upon the volumes you have."

Daegan finished digging out the onyx rock. "We have your blood stone, Zeelindar."

She became very still as he lifted the small fist clamped around a pulsing stone.

He asked, "Is the red in the center your blood?"

"No. It holds my heartbeat."

Lowering his hand to prop on his knee, he glanced at Casidhe before sharing what he knew. "Mulatko said an evil bein' brought this to Amentet to turn ya into an oracle."

Casidhe drew in a sharp breath, but kept quiet.

Zeelindar nodded, sadness shrouding her face.

"Mulatko also said how this person broke a pact with Amentet, which is why Amentet retained possession of your stone."

"Yes." Zeelindar added, "Amentet is not always considered a kind being, but she has been fair with me for hundreds of years."

Casidhe asked, "Hundreds?"

The oracle nodded.

"What a horrible thing to happen to you."

Zeelindar said, "Horrible is knowing there is no end. You hold the end of my slavery."

Again, Daegan offered, "Then tell us how to free ya."

"My master must crush the stone himself before he dies. To find a way to make that happen will not be easy to accomplish."

"Who is the bein' you call your master?" Casidhe asked.

"He has had many names over the centuries, but you know him as Ainvar, leader of the dark druids."

Casidhe's mouth opened with trying to speak, but she snapped her lips shut. She looked up at Daegan. "The book Cathbad gave me is called *Before Ainvar*."

He frowned in surprise. "I have met this druid."

Casidhe had not been with him. "Really?"

"Yes. Remember when Tristan took ya to Atlanta from Spain? Tristan and I then traveled with Joavan to Ainvar's Ghost Castle in another land."

"Got it."

"I know of this," Zeelindar said, interrupting their conversation. "Ainvar and Cathbad are at odds, but Cathbad is no match for Ainvar at the moment. Soon, Ainvar will need a new way to rebuild the power in his Ghost Castle where he spends years at a time to continue his miserable life. The castle is fading daily."

"It appeared strong when I visited," Daegan interjected.

"Had it been at full strength, you and the gryphon would have died there."

That chilled his blood. "How can we force Ainvar to break this stone and save ya?"

Zeelindar weaved back and forth. This time her forehead creased with some concern where in the past she had remained peaceful looking. "Ainvar will manipulate any move you make once he realizes you have the blood stone."

Daegan silently groaned at the idea of tracking down Joavan to ask him to help find Ainvar. "I know of someone I can ask to point me at Ainvar, but we parted on poor terms. Do ya have an idea how we can find Ainvar when he is not in the Ghost Castle?"

"You do not need Joavan to find Ainvar," the oracle answered, proving she knew more than Daegan would ever realize. "You possess the one thing Ainvar needs to power his castle."

Thinking back on all that had happened, Daegan lifted his head quickly. "The amulet?"

"Yes. He will come to you before you are able to close the Imortik death wall. He must not allow you to drain even a drop of the amulet's power."

Daegan had faced many challenges, but being prepared made the difference in victory. "Once I return to Treoir, I shall carry the blood stone and the amulet with me at all times to be ready when he comes for the amulet." He realized Zeelindar had skirted the original conversation. "If ya shall share who holds the last grimoire volume, we are ready to gain it and close the Imortik wall."

"I will tell you how to find the third volume once you free me."

"Ya just said we have proven ourselves trustworthy," Daegan argued.

"And you are, but I must know for sure I will not be left in this life forever. You hold my only chance to escape."

Casidhe slumped. "Is there anythin' else we should know about freein' you?"

"Ainvar is a vicious opponent with many enemies. If he dies before the blood stone is crushed *by his hand*, I will never be free. He will not stand by and allow you to close the death wall with that amulet. When you force him to crush the onyx stone, he must die immediately after."

# CHAPTER 23

BRYNHILD PROUDLY HAULED A LARGE trunk filled with gold and jewels she'd won in battle. She should have received her share of her father's hoard, but Herrick had to be squatting on that.

"*Umph!*" sounded behind her.

She chose a spot for her trunk to sit then stood, turning to take in the massive space, which swallowed her hoard. Satisfaction bled through her.

And contentment she had not expected to feel. This home and hoard room gave her a renewed desire to add new treasures. She had a great amount of gold and jewels, but a dragon could never have too much.

Another grunt sounded behind her.

Looking over toward the entrance at the upper level, she asked, "Do you need help, Joavan?"

He stumbled down the steps with smaller boxes, copper dishes, and gold chalices in his arms. "No." He placed the pile near the steps, grumbling the whole time.

Let him complain. She was no happier with him. He'd boasted he would bring her one of Daegan's people who could find her sword, but returned from his trip to Atlanta with no one.

"I swear I can hear you criticizing me in your head," he said, standing with hands on his hips and irritation dripping from his lips.

"If that were so, you would not be here now and most likely not alive," she quipped.

"Always with the threats." He looked down, shaking his head. "I did my best to grab that woman with Quinn. She is always surrounded by powerful people. They almost got *me*."

Did he want sympathy?

He would wait a long time for such an emotion from her. "It does not change that I still have no way to find out who took my sword."

"Probably that deceitful Cathbad."

She lifted a shoulder. "Perhaps. I wish to know for sure."

He strolled over to her, talking the whole way. "I have traveled constantly, taking you between the mountains and here with my power to move your hoard. Is it too much to expect you to appreciate my efforts?"

"Do not whine, Joavan. It is unbecoming." She thought he would reply with one of his clever comments, but he remained sullenly silent. She sighed to herself. Men. "Yes, I do appreciate getting my hoard away from Cathbad. There. Are you happy now?"

Swerving away from her, Joavan studied the wine barrels stacked against the wall. "I would need a new definition for happy. I have tried to befriend you and ally with you for each of our goals." Stepping over there, he leaned against the barrels with his arms crossed. "I enjoy a challenge, but I am not one to crawl and beg. Perhaps I was the only one who believed we had an alliance."

Neither would she beg or crawl, but she did not want to lose Joavan.

*Because of his skills*, she quickly reminded herself.

That was all. She had been alone before.

Still, she imagined moving forward without Joavan and didn't care for the empty feeling. She entertained a thought of finding another man, one who would satisfy her, but her only choices were humans.

They were no match for her even as an occasional companion.

Joavan kept his gaze on her as if he saw this as a point of commitment or not. No, he was not foolish enough to expect her to be a mate because he was no more interested in that than her. She had an idea of what bothered him. He had become weary of her keeping him in the dark on so many things.

She had never considered growing close to anyone beyond family, but she had no loyal family still alive. She would have to build her own clan.

Joavan could be a powerful partner, just as he'd offered.

Striding across the distance to him, she watched as his face gave nothing away. Difficult man, but a male falling at her knees would have bored her in seconds.

Reaching out, she ran a finger from his cheek and down around his strong jaw. She was not ready to share all her thoughts, but felt she had to give him something. "I am not easy to be with. I have never spent so much time with anyone who is not family."

A single eyebrow lifted slightly at that.

She'd surprised him?

"You have been exceptionally helpful, teaching me how to live in this new world, Joavan. I do have much to thank you for and I do still wish for our alliance." She never apologized to anyone, but could give him words he needed. "I want you to stay."

Time ticked slowly by in her mind as she waited to see if she had salvaged this relationship or if it was time to strike out on her own.

Again, that empty feeling slithered through her at being alone again. She refused to think it was solely about losing Joavan's ... partnership.

He straightened away from the barrels.

She smiled, enjoying her win.

Instead of kissing her as he normally would, he angled to the side, walking toward the steps. "That is good. I am in the mood for Boeuf Bourguignon. You will love what I prepare."

Stifling a laugh, she gave him the win. "Beef stew sounds delicious."

"Do not make it sound so pedestrian." He was the strangest man.

Once she finished sorting out her treasures, she lifted the last piece and placed it in an honored position.

Joavan came striding back into her treasure room. He didn't slow as he took the steps down to the lower level.

Gifting him with a smile, she asked, "Could not make up your mind what to cook?"

His serious expression never changed. "I have important news."

"Oh?"

His sly smile grew. "I have had my network watching for the red dragon. He has surfaced. Once I have regained enough power, we will go to the mountains in Mongolia."

"How far away? Show me this place."

Joavan tapped his phone, opening a map. "We are here." He pointed then moved his finger. "Kharkhiraa Mountain range is here."

"His red dragon has been sighted there *now*?" she asked, gritting her teeth at Joavan acting so casual.

"Yes, but there is no rush, dove. This proves we can track Daegan."

She strode to the steps.

Joavan's voice took on a menacing edge. "Where are you going, Brynhild?"

Climbing the steps, she turned at the top with her hands on her hips, taking a stance. "You know exactly where I am going and what I have to do."

His hand gripped the phone so tightly it creaked. He shouted, "We had a deal! If you kill Daegan, I will never get my amulet back."

"I will make him tell me where it is before I cut his throat."

"No! Daegan would never tell you that and you know it."

Her dragon banged and growled to get out. Brynhild tightened her muscles, holding firm.

She would not be denied the red dragon's death this time. "We will find a way to get your amulet!"

Joavan's face deepened into a dark red. "Walk away now and I will not be here when you return."

"Do not ever threaten me."

"That is no threat. That is a vow."

She held his glare for a second then turned away, heading for the ledge for her dragon to take flight.

Joavan would be here. Where else would he go?

# CHAPTER 24

A STRONG, ICY WIND BUFFETED THE peaks of Kharkh-iraa Mountain range in northeastern Mongolia, holding Macha's long deep auburn hair off her shoulders. She wore a barguzin sable fur coat over her modern clothing.

She had a fondness for silk shirts with full sleeves. The deep blue one she wore today a perfect match for her tan wool slacks.

She'd preferred gowns while in Treoir, clothing that demanded respect as much as her power, but gowns were cumbersome in war.

"Ya believe to take Treoir again, eh?"

Shifting a narrowed glance at Cathbad in his dark brown fur cloak and matching cap, she considered ignoring him. They had a simple agreement. She would aid him in killing Queen Maeve and he would give her the name of the woman working with Daegan who could locate a grimoire volume.

A woman Daegan would come to rescue, according to the druid.

Macha dismissed the druid's question with a statement. "Treoir has always been mine. I will have plenty of time to deal with Daegan once Queen Maeve is gone. You need only do your part today."

Cathbad had teleported here, but it had taken him longer than her travel when they departed from the same location. He had a power issue he would not admit.

"Do not hesitate to teleport me away once this is done," he reminded her. "I tapped a great deal of energy right before I saw ya in Atlanta. I would have waited another day had ya not needed to do this now."

She found his predicament amusing.

The powerful Cathbad the Druid negotiating for her help.

"I will teleport you away from here, but you are on your own getting into TÅµr Medb." He'd tried to negotiate that outcome.

Macha didn't care how he found his way to TÅµr Medb. Even after watching that crazy queen die, Macha would not trust the bitch not to return to TÅµr Medb in some form. The woman had disgusting necromancer skills.

Wouldn't Queen Maeve love to have Macha at her mercy in a hostile realm?

Never happen.

Macha had not lived this long without thinking through every possibility. She'd wanted to know one thing. "Why did you and Queen Maeve go into a deep sleep for all those thousands of years when you were both already immortal?"

The druid didn't answer at first, then seemed to decide the truth no longer had to be hidden. "Three different oracles saw our deaths. We knew each other well and had joined up to battle at times, but we crossed paths at the third oracle. Queen Maeve had already looked into a way to fake her death, but I pointed out the flaw in her plan, which would end with her bein' captured and tortured. Neither of us wanted that, so we began brainstormin' how to defeat death. We believed even some immortals would be killed over two thousand years."

Macha had hoped to never see either one of them again. At least one would be out of her way today. If Daegan's red dragon did show up, he might even kill Queen Maeve for her, but Macha would not risk killing Daegan here.

Cathbad could not be trusted. That druid would use knowledge of who killed the red dragon to betray her at his first chance, which would be as soon as he regenerated his full power.

Cathbad twitched. "I believe I see a giant red beast flyin' in the distance."

So Daegan *was* here?

How had Queen Maeve known he would show up in these mountains?

"Time to move closer." Macha teleported both of them to a ridge below where the dragon flying in the distance could see Cathbad.

Early morning sun peeking over the mountains reflected off

shiny red scales.

Macha murmured, "You're crazy like a fox, Maeve."

"Crazy like a rabid fox." Cathbad stomped snow off his fur boots. "We still have to find her."

Macha cloaked herself and lifted off the mountain, floating around to watch the dragon. It took a wide arc and flew back this way. The giant body and massive wings defied the laws of this world's gravity by staying aloft. The spiked head looked to the left as if choosing a place to land.

Then the dragon descended.

Macha returned to where Cathbad walked around shouting, "Where are ya, Macha?"

She remained cloaked, pushing her voice out. "Do be quiet."

"Do not disappear without tellin' me."

She'd been tolerant until now. Drawing power to her, she sent it out across the ridge, knocking Cathbad on his ass.

He slid toward the edge, tossing kinetic stabs to slow his body down. "Dammit, Macha!"

Lifting a finger, she crooked it and he stopped moving. She would enjoy toying with him more, but one day he would seek retribution. With another crook of her finger, Cathbad's body shot forward and up until he stood on the snow.

"I do not answer to you or anyone else, Cathbad. We have a business arrangement. You are not my peer today with so little power. Do not try to order me around again."

He brushed snow off his fur coat, cheeks red with fury. "Fine. But I wish to be done with this as much as ya do."

Ignoring him, Macha noted, "We should teleport over there where the dragon landed next to Queen Maeve."

Twisting around, he squinted. "Ah, that's where she is."

Without waiting, she teleported them and cloaked both of them before reappearing.

Queen Maeve cooed to her dragon, "You are delightful, *Cúpla Dearg.*"

*Cúpla Dearg?* Red Twin.

Now that Macha had a closer view, that winged beast barely resembled Daegan's. She gave the queen credit, though. Everyone thought this being only crazy, which she was, but this part of her fit the crazy-like-a-fox description.

Queen Maeve sent her pet flying again.

Macha still could not believe what she'd discovered about that pseudodragon.

Had Cathbad known? Speaking of him, she no longer wanted that druid breathing the same air inside her cloaking as her now that Queen Maeve was alone.

Macha wanted Queen Maeve worn down before she tangled with the bitch. "Time to go, Cathbad."

"I will in just a moment."

No, he would leave now. Macha stepped away from him, drawing her cloaking close as she did.

Exposed, Cathbad looked over his shoulder, eyes burning hot blue.

Macha enjoyed his panic. *That's right. This is your part, druid.*

Queen Maeve spun around, rising into the air as she did. "What are *you* doing here, druid?"

"I came to offer a deal for ya to have a grimoire volume."

Golden hair changed to pale blue and danced in the wind, flying all about her youthful face. "That does not explain how you are standing on this mountain."

"Ya are not the only one with scrying abilities." He crossed his arms and spoke to Queen Maeve confidently as if he still possessed all his powers. He had better have enough to battle with his old partner.

"Do ya still want the grimoire volume or not?" Cathbad demanded, sounding as if he had little patience.

Queen Maeve descended to the ground. "You lie too much, Cathbad. I have no reason to believe you anymore."

"Ya are one to talk, dearest. The last time we met, ya unleashed a monster to kill me."

She studied him. "It *should* have killed you. How did you escape?"

"I should tell ya and allow ya to try again? I think not."

"Where is the grimoire volume you offer for barter?"

"I shall show ya when we have an agreement." Cathbad's voice remained strong.

Macha had her doubts. He tread on dangerously thin ice with

a giant shark waiting beneath the surface. One wrong step with Queen Maeve might end with him in pieces.

Making a show of looking around, Cathbad asked, "Are ya alone?"

Macha considered striking him down where he stood. That was not how they agreed to do this. Was he trying something underhanded?

"You just now teleported here?" Queen Maeve asked, her words wrapped in suspicion.

"Of course. I am not fond of snow and cold, as ya know."

Queen Maeve didn't agree.

Macha believed that was a lie. Was Cathbad testing Queen Maeve's memory or trying to confuse her? And why would he ask if she was alone?

Queen Maeve lifted her hand in the air without looking over her shoulder. *Cúpla Dearg* had been gliding around and made a sharp turn, flying straight for this ledge.

As the beast approached, waves of majik spun off its body. What had Queen Maeve created? The beast landed and stepped up beside her, lifting its giant head above her to stare at Cathbad with glowing red eyes.

"Call your beast down, woman. Make me fight another one of your creations and I will not give ya the grimoire volume."

Macha paced back and forth.

Cathbad had just made it more difficult to kill Queen Maeve. He was supposed to draw her close enough with a fake grimoire volume, a bronze box Macha had created, and hold it out with two hands. Then he would tell the queen the grimoire volume called in Imortiks if she did not grasp it with both hands.

Macha knew what the original grimoire volumes should look like and to not touch the bronze boxes, but Queen Maeve had not been a part of stopping Imortiks in the past.

Once Cathbad drew Queen Maeve in close and convinced her to use both hands to hold the box, Macha would call for the power in the box to attack.

Posionous majik would rip free, streaking up the queen's arms like black vines, tangling and bonding her hands to the Trojan gift.

Queen Maeve could spew power, but not fast enough to survive Macha bringing her force against the crazy queen.

That brought Macha back to *Cúpla Dearg*.

Had Cathbad kept his mouth shut, that pet would still be flying. The more she studied the beast, the more she noted power seeping out.

She could probably kill the fake dragon as well, but she'd rather not battle something Queen Maeve had created with no idea what she faced.

Queen Maeve began shaking her head. "Something is not right. You would not be here if you had the grimoire volume."

Cathbad changed direction by asking, "Do ya truly think the red dragon will come here? Ya should not be takin' your pet out right now."

She smiled and lifted a hand. *Cúpla Dearg* lowered a spiky chin close enough for her to stroke the wide jaw. "Daegan will come and *Cúpla Dearg* will show him what a truly majikal beast can do."

"Or Daegan will find out ya started the Dragani War and nothin' will stop him from makin' ya pay."

"I do hope he finds out." Queen Maeve smiled with innocent pleasure of the truly insane. "I want him to know he was bested back then in more ways than just being captured."

"Do ya not worry another dragon shifter will come for ya?"

Grinning as if he'd suggested a child could destroy her pet, she said, "What other dragon shifter, druid? They all died. Every dragon shifter king believed he was more powerful than us. The red dragon most arrogant of all. Even the ice dragon shifters had five children and they failed to survive thanks to us."

Cathbad quickly corrected her. "Not us, but you."

"As if you did not know what I was doing with this wyvern, druid?" She stopped stroking her pet's chin. All of a sudden, Queen Maeve stilled with her head angled as if she listened to something in her mind. "Enough of this. Show me the grimoire volume or leave."

Macha leaned forward. Had something just transpired between those two? Had he spoken to her telepathically?

"Very well." Cathbad reached inside his coat.

Macha prepared to unleash the majik bound to the box, then leave Cathbad to face Queen Maeve *and* her glamoured wyvern. The box carried enough power to maim.

From nowhere, a brilliant silver-blue dragon burst into view.

An ice dragon.

Macha teleported above all of them to the next peak.

The ice dragon landed hard, blowing snow off the ledge in a wave. *"You killed my family!"* came out of the dragon's mouth.

Queen Maeve teleported on top of her dragon and it pushed off, falling quickly until flapping its wings to lift.

Launching off the ledge to fly after the wyvern, the ice dragon had more wing speed.

Queen Maeve could teleport herself, but could she teleport her huge pet at the same time?

At one time, Macha would have said yes, but she had no idea how much Queen Maeve's power had corrupted with her fall into insanity after the reincarnation.

The wyvern tried flying in loops and darting to each side.

That beast did not possess the flying skills of a true dragon. On the next short turn, the wyvern dove to get away.

Diving right behind, but faster, the ice dragon blew an avalanche of ice down on Queen Maeve and her wyvern.

The wyvern began to spiral down.

Queen Maeve's screech started small and grew to a bellow as she exploded the ice in a brilliant burst of light.

Cathbad had backed up fifty feet, yelling, "Cloak me, Macha. Where are ya?"

Macha considered leaving him exposed, but she had questions for the druid. She cloaked him, but did not teleport him to stand with her. If he could not clear his tracks, anyone could follow them to where he now stood.

Queen Maeve had flown low out of view.

All of a sudden, her wyvern lifted above the ridge, flapping slowly. Queen Maeve shouted, "I will find you, Cathbad, and I will kill you slowly then bring you back as my puppet."

The wyvern's glamour had patches falling apart in areas, but it turned and flew straight up fast then vanished into a cloud that had not been there before. In the next second, the cloud disappeared.

Macha had not been sure until today that Queen Maeve had started the Dragani War. Cathbad had known. She should thank them as she'd benefitted by gaining full control of Treoir, but she wanted to strangle that deceitful Cathbad right now.

Queen Maeve had wanted Treoir and the spoils of King Gruffyn's castle. While Queen Maeve had received Daegan's other sister in their deal with King Gruffyn, she had no way back in the early days to gain Treoir without Jennyver or as long as Macha lived.

For a long time, Macha had believed Queen Maeve had poisoned King Gruffyn and captured Jennyver, but after imprisoning Daegan, the queen never made a move to take possession of Treoir.

Then Queen Maeve and Cathbad dropped out of view.

No one could tell Macha what had happened to Jennyver. The best she had figured, Jennyver died when her father's kingdom had suffered the final dragon attack.

Macha could have gone after her but the woman had wanted to be at her father's bedside. Besides, Jennyver's children became the new heirs of Treoir along with Macha once no more immediate family lived.

If only Daegan had died in TÅµr Medb.

A loud crunch below pulled her from her thoughts.

The ice dragon held its wings wide. Fury burned in the blue reptilian eyes. The beast roared, *"Where are you, Cathbad?"*

Macha took in where she'd cloaked him. The druid had managed enough power to clear his tracks. He was not entirely defenseless.

In the next instant, the dragon began shrinking until it shifted into Brynhild, a daughter of King Eógan. She wore fur-and-leather boots. Battle armor with her family's blue and black crest from long ago covered her body. The one thing different was Brynhild's long blond hair had been chopped off. She wore it very short in the style of today's human women.

Macha had not been surprised like this in a long time.

Brynhild stomped and roared curses. She shouted, "You lying bastard. I know you're here. You would not go until you knew if I died. That wyvern pretended to be the red dragon when my family lived and *you knew it!* You and that bitch started the Dragani War." Her voice dropped low. "And you did *not* save me. You *stole* me from my family while I still breathed! They needed me. Now you hide like a coward, but I have ways to find you. One day, when you have no idea I am close, my dragon shall bite off your disgusting head." She shifted and flew off, vanishing immediately.

She could cloak her dragon?

Macha teleported down to the ledge. She uncloaked Cathbad.

He opened his mouth.

She nailed it shut.

His eyes bulged.

"You thought to use me today." She ignored his shaking head. "Did you think I would not realize you were speaking to Queen Maeve telepathically? You changed your mind once you arrived and realized Daegan was not here. What were you saying to convince Queen Maeve to take you back inside TÅµr Medb?"

His eyes glared, but also exposed how she'd caught him.

"You were the fool today to think you could have teleported away with Queen Maeve to her realm and used that box I created to kill her where she holds the power." Macha shook her head at him. "Such a fool to cross me and now you have a dragon after you."

She snapped her fingers and the nails disappeared, leaving blood oozing from the holes.

"You bitch!" he shouted. "I was doin' no such thing."

"Save your lies, Cathbad. I had a feeling you have issues with your power. I should have seen this sooner. If you speak of my being here, the nails will return again the moment you finish a sentence. Give me back the box."

Once he'd handed it over, he spoke quietly. "I will explain all. Ya misunderstand what happened today. We were both here. Ya should keep that in mind."

She laughed. "You will say exactly nothing to anyone. What do you think Loki and the Tribunal would think about you keeping an ice dragon shifter alive all this time?"

"We can still do this."

"You owe me, druid. Bring me this woman who Daegan cares for and who can find a grimoire volume or I will inform Loki of the ice dragon still living."

Cathbad scrambled to fix the problem. "Take me to Atlanta and I will share many things ya do not know."

"Find the woman and I will find you." Macha knew all she needed. She teleported away. Alone.

# CHAPTER 25

ZEELINDAR HAD DISAPPEARED AS THE eastern sky began lightening in advance of dawn.

She'd dropped a difficult decision in Daegan's lap.

How would he manage to free the oracle and not commit murder? While he cared nothing for Ainvar or Joavan, he would not strike down someone in cold blood.

"What are you goin' to do, Daegan?" Casidhe asked while she shook sand out of her empty backpack then reloaded it with her belongings.

"I do not know. I shall think on this. I feel we must free Zeelindar from being a slave to Ainvar."

"But you can't just turn your dragon loose on him."

"Aye." He was thankful Casidhe understood his hesitance. To take a life without reason, regardless of the being's past sins, would be dishonorable.

She stood and hooked her arms in the backpack.

"I shall carry that," Daegan said.

"If I recall correctly, you need your hands to deal with transportin' the grimoire volume. I can carry the blood stone in my pack."

Daegan stepped over and cupped her face, kissing her. "I wish we did not have to go back to the chaos, as ya call it."

She lifted up and her lips ignited a fire in him to have her again. Her energy sizzled and danced with his. Against her sweet mouth, he said, "We should steal a few more moments."

Pulling back, she cocked an eyebrow at him. "You're stallin'. Not that I don't agree, but I want all of this grimoire stuff done so you and I can have our time to see if we fit."

He reached behind her, yanking her bottom against him. "We have proven we fit."

She chuckled. "You know what I mean, dragon." Her eyes twinkled, but her voice held a deeper meaning. "I don't even know what power I possess or what exactly I am. Once this is all behind us, you could help me research. I know dragons can't bond with just anyone."

His heart swelled with love for his caring mate. "Ya shall *never* be just anyone to me."

"I want to be *everythin'* to you." She put her fingers on his lips. "Before you say more, listen. Our energy likes each other. I want to not just be with you, but to bond with you."

He dropped his forehead to hers and sighed. "I want that as well, but I shall never risk your life. If my power is too great, it could kill ya."

"I know. That's why I'm sayin' I am willin' to wait to go the next step until I know for sure what that will be."

Where was his hotheaded termagant when he needed her ready to rip off her clothes and spend another hour in each other's arms?

Tristan's voice came into Daegan's head. *Hey, boss? Can you hear me?*

Everyone worked against him.

He told Casidhe, "Tristan is callin'. I shall bring him here to teleport us."

She kissed him slowly and he gave in, stealing another minute. Then she backed away and crossed her arms. "Call in Air Tristan."

Daegan sent word to his second-in-command.

Tristan appeared immediately. He looked at the two of them and around at the water then the grimoire volume in the sand. With a grin, he said, "I can't wait to hear this story."

"'Tis good to see ya, Tristan."

"Me too, Tristan." Casidhe stood back.

Tristan's gaze shifted to her and his voice changed to polite. "It's good to see you as well. I'm glad you're both safe. I'm sure you played a role in getting that grimoire volume."

"She did." Daegan wanted to say more, but Casidhe was not comfortable yet with her place next to him until he could declare her as his mate. He could do so without actually bonding, but she would feel lacking in front of his people.

"I'm guessing you two had a chance to talk."

Daegan nodded at Tristan. "She is all to me."

Casidhe smiled at his declaration.

"Good to hear." Tristan dug into his jean pocket and produced a small rolled up paper the length of his hand. "Trey got a call from Luigsech's—"

"'Tis Casidhe, not Luigsech," Daegan softly corrected.

"Oh. Got it. From Casidhe's hotel. The woman said a crow delivered this. It has Casidhe's name and is sealed with wax. The woman feared keeping it in the office with all the supernatural things going on." Tristan said that with sarcasm and handed the tiny scroll to Casidhe.

While she stepped aside to open it, Daegan told Tristan, "We shall share our story about findin' this grimoire volume as soon as we have time. We are goin' to Treoir." Daegan would be able to keep Casidhe safe there.

Casidhe finished reading the paper, rolled it up, and put the scroll in a pocket on her backpack. When she lifted her gaze to him, she had a blank mask in place.

He felt a wave of worry from her. His heart dipped at the conflict in her face. What could be wrong?

Swallowing, she walked over to join them. "I'm not going to Treoir."

Daegan's jaw muscles threatened to snap from clenching them so hard. He wanted to start ordering everyone to do what he needed, but that was not the way to handle any of this. He tried a new tactic. "I wish for ya to be somewhere safe, lass."

"I can keep myself safe."

"What was in the note?"

Her eyes implored him to understand. Her mask lowered just enough to show him her pain. This was important to her. "I will share all as soon as I can, Daegan."

How could she think to go anywhere alone now? "I wish to have Tristan teleport me to wherever he takes ya."

She pressed her lips in determination. "I do not want to be followed by anyone. I have somethin' I must do on my own."

Tristan became quiet as a stone.

Daegan forced words out in a calm voice when he wanted to rail. "I could send ya to Treoir against your will, but I would not treat ya that way. I want to be at your side because ya wish to have me there."

"Oh, Daegan." Her voice cracked. She squeezed her eyes shut, but tears spilled out anyhow. When she opened her red-rimmed eyes, she squared her shoulders. "You said you trusted me."

His chest tightened until he fought to breathe. Every painful draw into his chest built more pressure until he squeezed out, "I do trust ya, lass."

"Then allow me to leave."

"Why?"

"I'm goin' to find out who I am."

# DIANNA LOVE

# TREOIR DRAGON
## CHRONICLES
### OF THE BELADOR WORLD
## BOOK 9

# CHAPTER 1

"YA CANNOT GO WITHOUT ME." Daegan crossed his arms with his feet dug into the Egyptian sand and prepared to do battle. His heart slammed with every beat. He could not let her out of his sight.

Not the woman who would be his only mate. "I could live without bondin' but I cannot breathe without ya in my world."

Casidhe caught her bottom lip, looking vulnerable from his words, but his warrior shook that off. Before he could say more, she matched him in attitude and folded her arms, jutting up her chin in defiance. "What about trustin' each other's decisions?"

He trusted her and needed to not jumble his words this time. He had to win this battle. He feared never seeing her again if they did not stay together.

"Has nothin' to do with trust, lass. I trust ya with my life. Has to do with ya bein' safe." Once the Imortik threat was over, which was more *if* than *when*, he would be fine with her out of his sight.

But he would not lie to her or himself.

Tristan stood off to the side, his gaze bouncing back and forth.

Rare for him to not have something to say, but Daegan's second-in-command knew when to talk and when to stay out of harm's way.

Tristan was in no danger from Daegan, but Casidhe and her temper combined with an ancient sword were another story. She would not swing at Tristan's neck but Daegan's friend could be injured if she missed Daegan's throat.

She narrowed her gaze, not a bit of the sweet woman he loved showing. "I do not want to hold you up, Daegan. I'm bein' considerate, dammit!"

"So am I!" he roared.

She roared right back, "Not really."

Tristan snorted.

Daegan glared at him then tried to make peace. "I cannot perform my duty while wonderin' if ya are safe, lass."

She walked around, spewing a frustrated sound, and shoved her hands into her hair. When she came back to him, she made an obvious effort to sound reasonable. "What if I said my errand would go faster without you?"

Cocking an eyebrow in challenge, he asked, "Do ya speak the truth?"

She kicked sand and grumbled under her breath. "I have no idea."

"Do not forget that I need ya to read the grimoire volumes if we find them and 'tis possible for ya to do so." Yes, he was grasping at any reason to keep her from leaving.

"I won't be gone a full day." She held her hands up in surrender. "I don't want to slow us down from stoppin' the Imortiks either."

Daegan stepped over and put his hands on her shoulders. "I do wish for ya to know the truth of your past. Travelin' shall be faster with Tristan. If we all go together, Tristan and I shall watch for any threat so ya may accomplish this duty quickly. Please do not ask me to watch ya leave with no idea ya shall be safe."

"Where do you need to go anyhow?" Tristan asked.

She flicked a look his way. "To Galway."

Daegan's chest muscles began to loosen with the first sign of Casidhe giving in. He did not want to rule over her, far from it, but he had not been lying when he said he could not function while constantly wondering if Imortiks, demons, Cathbad, or some other threat found her.

She might defeat an Imortik or demon if she was attacked by one at a time, but even that might go very wrong.

The faster he could send her to Treoir where she would be protected when he could not be at her side, the sooner she could begin to decipher these grimoire volumes.

His plan was expedient and logical, but his stubborn beauty sometimes took exception to his ideas.

"If I say okay this *one* time, do not think it means you can have your way *every* time," she warned, glaring at him.

"Understood." Yes, he was smiling, but he hadn't been this happy in a long time. Maybe never.

His chest relaxed. He turned to Tristan. "I wish to have the new grimoire volume over in the sand put away in Treoir."

"You got it, boss."

Casidhe stepped over to lift her backpack. "I'm thinkin' we'll keep the blood stone in here."

Daegan took the pack from her hands.

She wheeled around on him. "*I* am wearin' it!"

Prickly woman. He would prefer to carry the load, but instead he lifted the pack with the straps hanging free. "I merely wish to help ya."

"You aren't foolin' anybody, dragon," she muttered, sliding her arms into the looped straps and stepping out of his grasp. She groused out, "Thank you."

*Do not laugh*, Daegan warned himself. But he found her need to be nice even when angry adorable. He found everything about this woman amazing.

Most of all that she cared for him.

Tristan used telekinetic power to lift the bronze box from where it had stuck in the sand to float above his palm. "What's a blood stone?" he asked.

"'Tis the way Ainvar enslaved the oracle. Zeelindar shall never be free until the stone is broken by his hand."

Tristan's jaw dropped. "I didn't see that one coming, but it doesn't surprise me. She probably waited for someone who could help her to come along."

"She actually did wait specifically for us." Casidhe turned as she finished snapping the buckles. "It's a long story, but you need to know one thing for watchin' Daegan's back. Ainvar will be comin' to get the amulet from him, accordin' to Zeelindar."

"I thought Joavan needed the amulet," Tristan said in Daegan's direction.

"He does, but now we know why Ainvar took the amulet. He requires a tremendous amount of power to keep his Ghost Castle operatin', which provides him with energy to keep livin'. Accordin' to the oracle, Ainvar does not want the amulet used for anythin' like closin' the death wall and risk diminishin' the power he can withdraw from it."

"I'm all in for keeping that amulet away from him," Tristan agreed. "This world could do without scumbags like Ainvar. Okay, I'm going to Treoir to get this thing off my hand." He disappeared.

Casidhe stepped up to Daegan, shoving her annoyance in his face. "We need some guidelines. You can't just have your way all the time."

He caught the backpack straps on each side of her chest and tugged her to him.

She opened her mouth to lash out again, but he lifted her up on her toes and covered her lips with his. He intended to kiss the fury right out of her. She turned warm and willing. Would he ever lose this need to have her close, to see her smile, to just know she existed?

Never.

She gripped his hair, holding him in place.

There was his fiery female.

He never wanted to douse that fire. Not when he looked forward to a future of sparking her temper just to enjoy when they could spend hours naked making up. He moved a hand to unsnap her jeans and slip his fingers inside.

Her lips crushed harder against him and her body tightened as he toyed with her folds. He had little time, but his lass was more than ready. She tensed and groaned her release against his mouth.

Thankfully, they stood alone on this shore.

When he'd milked her release for all she had to give, he zipped her pants and finished the kiss that started it all.

She still had his T-shirt wadded up in her fists when she weaved away from him. Her rosy lips were slightly swollen and thoroughly loved.

Morning light reflecting off the Nile River behind her shined a halo around her head. His angel.

He glanced at movement far down the river to the left. A boat came into view.

His termagant could barely stand and looked tipsy from too

much ale, but even that did not stop her from challenging him. "That all you got, dragon king?"

Hell no. He'd thought to relax her and managed to do the very opposite to himself. He adjusted his jeans, grunting in pain. "I promise ya more when we are alone, but Tristan shall return any moment."

Her eyelashes fluttered. She stepped back, looking around with deep pink cheeks. "Cut it out. You think I'll forget about you gettin' your way, but I won't. I mean it when I say we need rules."

Tristan appeared as she spoke the last sentence. "What rules? We don't need no stinkin' rules."

Daegan didn't understand why that was funny to Tristan, but he laughed.

Casidhe took them both in. "You don't even know what that means, do you, Daegan?"

"'Tis funny. Nothin' more to know."

"Argh! It's a line from a movie."

Daegan shrugged. "'Tis fine by me."

"Never mind," Casidhe snapped. "I need to get movin'. I want to go to my hotel room first to shower and change clothes. Alone. That is *not* negotiable."

Daegan sighed. He knew as he stood here that winning the battle to join her on this trip would come with a cost, but he would not worry about tomorrow's troubles today. "'Tis an excellent idea. We shall eat as well."

"Everyone ready?" Tristan asked, his eyes on Daegan.

"We should link and save your energy." Daegan sent his power to Tristan, who grunted.

"Got it, boss."

Daegan caught Casidhe's hand in his, expecting his prickly woman to snap at him. He did not want to lose her even during teleporting and didn't care what that said about him.

She glanced over with happy eyes and winked at him.

He shook his head, sure that he would never know what to expect from her.

Everything blurred, but they traveled quickly.

The skies outside the hotel window were dark when he

expected sunlight.

Tristan commented, "I hear rain drizzling."

Standing inside this room, Daegan recalled how angry he'd been just a day ago when he believed Casidhe had betrayed him.

Trusting did not come easy to him, but he would take care with her trust from now on. She had every reason to be just as wary to open her heart to him. That she had showed the strength of character to move past those who had wronged her and his poor judgement humbled him.

Tristan walked around the beds to the window and moved the sheer curtain aside. "I see a couple places I could pick up some food." He walked back to where Daegan waited as Casidhe dug through her backpack, yanking out clothes and a small bag in a hurry. "Do you two have any preference for a sandwich, pizza, whatever?"

Lifting upright, she shook her head. "I wasn't hungry until you mentioned it. Now I'm starvin'. I'll take anythin'."

"As shall I," Daegan added, standing to the side of the bathroom.

"I won't take long. Don't forget to cover your glowin' eyes before goin' out, Tristan." Casidhe hurried into the bathroom and started the shower running. She used her foot to push the door shut.

Tristan adjusted the dark sunshades that appeared on his face, then stepped over next to Daegan. "Thanks for the shades. I won't make it back for twenty minutes in case you need to *freshen up*," he teased in a quiet voice, laughing all the way out the door.

Daegan grinned at Tristan's ability to read his mind. Without another thought, he teleported into the bathroom and shed his clothes.

# CHAPTER 2

REESE STARED IN HORROR AT her hands and arms, begging for the yellow glow not to be real. But it was easy to see in the dark after midnight.

"Grab Quinn. *Stop him!*" Evalle shouted.

Hearing his name was the only thing that could drag Reese's gaze from herself.

Quinn jerked and fought, bellowing like a trapped animal. "Let me go to her!"

Evalle had jumped in front of Quinn and shoved up a kinetic wall Quinn pummeled with his own kinetic power.

Casper's highlander form had Quinn by the shoulders, yanking back and losing ground.

Tears poured down Reese's face.

Quinn ordered, "Move, Evalle! I do not want to hurt you."

"You can't help her, Quinn," Evalle pleaded, her arms starting to bend from muscle strain.

He backed up and ran, shoving kinetic hits down at his feet, which allowed him to catapult over Evalle's barrier. She dropped her arms, spinning to watch him fall and tumble on the ground.

Shaking her head, Evalle ran to him with Casper close behind.

Quinn got up, limping as he turned to Reese. This man never showed emotions when he had to lead, but he'd abandoned leading anyone to get to her.

Evalle shouted, "*Reese! Please* stop him."

Forcing herself to stand up straight, Reese backed up with both hands out front. "No, Quinn."

He kept coming.

"*Nooo!*" she screamed at him and scrambled until her back hit the wall of a house. "*Please stop!* For me."

He'd made it within several strides of her and struggled to not keep moving. Arms hanging slack at his sides, face wrecked with agony, he pleaded, "Don't leave me here alone. I can't do this without you."

She couldn't face her future without him either, but to bring Quinn along would hand the Imortiks a hell of a catch. "I'm not going anywhere, babe, but you can't be with me." She sobbed out the last part and covered her face with her hands.

"Reese?" Quinn whispered her name, his voice quivering.

She would have plenty of time to dwell on her misery and lick her emotional wounds. Quinn needed her now. Lowering her hands, she sniffled and wiped her eyes.

She had to look hideous, lit up like some creature for Halloween.

After a couple short breaths, none of which calmed her, she said, "Hear me out. I will stay in Atlanta and learn what I can about Imortiks to give all of you and Daegan a chance to figure out how to save everyone."

The Imortik inside her said, *No one is saving you from me. You are special. So am I.*

She answered it in her head. *Shut the fuck up, Dickweed.*

*What do you mean by dickweed?*

*I'm not your mama. Figure it out since you're so special.* She ignored her inner beast and told Quinn, "Please don't come near me until then. They would likely kill me to get to you." That should make him keep a reasonable distance.

Quinn sagged. His lip trembled.

Seeing her powerful man broken by this made her crazy. She wanted to rip open her body and yank this monster out.

Her stomach suddenly warmed. Junior?

That sensation of a tiny life hanging in there gave her something to help Quinn. She tried her best to smile. "Junior is still with me."

His face crumpled. He covered his mouth as tears poured from red-rimmed eyes.

Reese looked to Evalle. "I will take care of myself. You must keep him safe."

Biting her lip to hold back the obvious emotion racking her body, Evalle nodded as if she understood Reese meant to keep

Quinn safe from himself. He wouldn't intentionally injure his body, but in his present state of mind he could be reckless.

Clearing his throat, he shoved both hands through his hair, ending up with an even wilder look. "Where will you be?"

As if Reese had that answer? "I'll stay in the city. This ... thing inside me isn't ruling my actions." She silently added *not yet.* "I'm thinking Piedmont Park might be a good place to stay near."

Changed back to his normal form, Casper had said nothing until now. "Would you feel better if we found a place to, uh, *secure* you?"

Quinn's face lifted. "Yes, I could do that for you. It would be comfortable and safe."

That might be the best idea. She said, "Maybe—"

Her nosy Imortik cut her off. *Lock us up and the master will send an army to free me.*

Could her dickweed be special after all? Or was he lying?

Stepping forward with hope spreading across his face, Quinn said, "Maybe what?"

She really hoped she could prevent this monster in her from forcing her to hurt someone. If it showed that ability, she would find a tree or pole to cling to until a Belador found her before the humans did.

"Maybe we'll do that if I feel this thing starts to take control, but for now I want to stay free to help." Reese gave him as much hope as she could.

Evalle had frowned the entire time during their exchange. She locked her gaze on Reese, wanting more.

When Quinn dropped his head, Reese shook hers at Evalle and mouthed the word, *Later.*

Nodding, Evalle walked up to Quinn. "We will put word out for every Belador in the city to watch for Reese and give her any aid she needs."

He picked up his head. "Yes. We shall escort her to Piedmont Park."

Dickweed bragged, *They won't be with us long. There are six Imortiks heading this way.*

That piece of garbage inside her had just threatened Quinn

and her friends. She had to protect them. "I'm going to Piedmont Park later. The thing inside me has other Imortiks nearby and wants to meet them. If I fight for control, it will try to harm me or one of you."

Quinn looked like he could not take one more blow.

Reese did the hardest thing she'd had to in a long time. "I will see you soon, Quinn. I love you and so does Junior." Without giving him a chance to react, she spun and ran between the houses, then raced away into the night.

Shouting broke out with Quinn yelling something she couldn't understand. It sounded as if Evalle and Casper struggled to hold him back. She had to get far away.

She wove this way and that, covering the first mile in several minutes.

Evidently she was now a runner with Imortik superpower.

She could no longer hear her friends.

Only the sound of her heart shredding.

*Where are you going?* her monster asked.

*I haven't decided yet.* She kept churning her feet and dipping into stretches of trees and undergrowth. Hard to hide from humans and other nonhumans when she was bright as a fluorescent glow tube.

*The master wants to see us.*

Reese slowed to a walk, shoving branches aside and pushing her legs through the underbrush. She wanted to test this thing inside of her. *Your master doesn't even know I exist.*

*Oh, but he does. He sent me out looking just for you after Imortiks observed you sitting at an explosion site and using majik to find someone.*

The scary part of that was realizing the Imortiks weren't all mindless monsters taking over bodies. Some had cognitive ability. She had to pass that information on to the teams.

Giving her monster a dismissive sound, she said, *For crying out loud. That's almost a parlor trick, but you probably don't know what I'm talking about.*

Dickweed said nothing.

*Not so smart after all, huh.*

She kept going and casually explained, *On occasion, I can*

*find someone I've met before, like that woman I saw not too far from the explosion. I'd met her recently.*

*Ah, that will suffice the master's needs,* her monster said in a giddy tone. *You know the person the master is hunting.*

Her stomach fell.

She wanted to throw up.

The Imortik master wanted her to help him find a friend.

# CHAPTER 3

IN THE MIDDLE OF CHAOS defining her life, Casidhe hummed. Why? Because she could stand under rushing hot water to take a shower and wash her hair.

Talk about simple pleasures.

If only her mind would shut the heck up about where she had to go next.

Did Kleio really know where to find the ice dragon chronicles?

If she didn't, Casidhe would accept what she knew about herself and let go of hunting her origins until she and Daegan finished finding all the grimoires. If they didn't stop the Imortiks, would the truth of her blood line really matter?

No. She wanted to be with Daegan every step of the way battling the Imortiks.

If they lost, she'd be with him to the end.

Hooks on the curtain rod screeched across the metal bar when the plastic sheet was snatched open.

Casidhe squealed and backed up to the wall opposite the shower head, covering her tits. "Oh, shit, Daegan. Don't scare me like that."

"'Tis a good thing ya shall have us with ya to prevent anyone else from scarin' ya so easily." He stood there with every carved inch of him gloriously naked and a wolf's grin on his face.

Her gaze dropped to what had him so proud.

She arched an eyebrow at him.

Stepping into the blast of water and yanking the curtain back in place, his gaze never strayed from her. He trapped her against the wall between his hands on each side of her face.

"You are entirely too full of yourself, dragon."

Leaning down, he kissed her solidly, then again. His voice rumbled deeply with his need. "I would prefer ya to be full of me."

Casidhe mumbled against his lips. "Tristan might be back in minutes."

"I have it on good word he shall not return for quite a bit." Daegan's eyes glittered with mischief.

"You're both a pair of rogues." To be honest, she was up for getting into trouble with Daegan. Tristan's first sign of accepting her being with Daegan again warmed her heart, too. She slid her arms around her dragon shifter's neck and eased up to kiss him.

His erection thumped her stomach.

She warned, "This time, I want all of you."

"Ya should not say such when I am yet to be inside ya, lass." He kissed her cheeks and neck.

"Do I have to do everything?" She bit his ear.

He growled and hooked a hand under each leg, lifting her against all that delicious muscle. With the determined look of a warlord prepared to raid a castle, he used his erection to tease her until she dug her nails into his shoulders. "Now, now, *now!*"

If not for Tristan returning soon, she might not have gotten her way, but Daegan eased her down and she kept taking him. He picked her up and down, setting a fast pace.

She loved how being with him felt natural and right, loved him being deep inside her. Together as one.

She kept her eyes glued to his smoldering gaze even as her body coiled then broke free, sending shock waves through her. Daegan came right behind her, clearly very ready since that moment on the Nile. His muscles had tightened with the strain of waiting, but he pulled off a power struggle with his body until he could hold back no longer.

She hugged him, squeezing her thighs until his knees bent, but her dragon shifter would not fold. He had her secure in his arms. She had never felt so safe or wanted.

Curled around him, she turned her head under his chin. "We do fit."

"I had no doubt, lass."

"We're gonna have to work on your lack of confidence."

He laughed. For someone who had exited the world two thousand years ago and returned today, Daegan was quick to catch on to teasing.

He moved inside her.

No way. She lifted up to look at him.

He had that cocksure look of a man who could do anything he pleased.

She regretfully reminded him, "We still have to shower."

"Ya made the choice." Then he proceeded to wash her so thoroughly he left her wanting more.

How could she be both relaxed and pent-up again? She snatched the shower curtain back and stepped out. Searching for a towel, she located one on a shelf below the sink.

When she bent forward, he caught her around the waist with his arm, stopping her from going farther. "What are you doin'?" she asked breathlessly.

"Followin' your orders. Put your hands on the sink and do not let go."

Okay, that turned her nipples into hard little beans.

Her pulse ratcheted up, but she did as he said, staring into the mirror at his body behind her. Every inch of him was carved muscle and power. Nothing turned her on faster than the heat burning up his gaze.

"I can't promise not to move if you touch me," she warned in what she hoped sounded sultry. She had never felt sexy in her life, but Daegan brought out a hidden side of her.

"I shall do more than touch ya," he promised in a deep voice.

"You are the most demandin' ... uh." She arched when he reached around and gently massage her breasts. Large fingers moved through her folds.

She gripped the edge of the sink tighter.

When had sex ever been fun?

Since falling in love with a two-thousand-year-old dragon shifter with a body hotter than an Adonis. Daegan would never complain her getting too hot during sex.

He entered her and her womb tightened.

The world faded away to just her and Daegan as he loved her with every touch. Her mind and body splintered again but with him this time.

And he held her safe. Always there for her.

As she would be for him if her legs ever functioned again.

Once he had thoroughly wrung everything she had to give, he held her boneless body against him. Then he lifted her up and stepped back in the shower, cleaning both of them quickly. She should grumble at him for once again doing whatever he pleased, but when he sat her on the sink and towel-dried her hair, she fell a little deeper in love.

Smiling the whole time, he paused to kiss her.

She was the worst slug.

She draped her arms over his shoulders. "If I don't dry myself off, we'll be here for hours."

"I shall lower ya if ya can stand."

"Don't sound so smug, buster." When he lifted her from the sink, she made a point of taking her time sliding down against him.

He groaned, grasping her shoulders and setting her back. "Ya are a wicked lass. I cannot wear jeans if ya keep that up."

Laughing, she took the towel and started drying her body.

The door to the hallway slammed. "I'm *baaack*," Tristan sang out, as if Daegan did not possess supersonic hearing.

"Be out in a minute," she called out. When she took in Daegan's predicament, she thought back on when she'd saved him by suggesting he picture using his considerable body part on Queen Maeve. "I told you how to fix that one time."

Daegan frowned in confusion then horror snapped across his face. "Do not speak those words!" Then he cursed.

She pulled a long-sleeved T-shirt on and stepped into her jeans, glancing over. "*Annnd* it worked again."

Able to now wear jeans and a dark-green pullover, Daegan groused, "I shall need Garwyli's healin' to cleanse my mind of that visual. I beg of ya, do not mention it ever again."

"I won't need to if we have more time in the future."

"'Tis a constant thought for me as well," he muttered with disappointment.

Dressed but barefoot and noticing Daegan had boots, she said, "Shoot. I don't have shoes."

Socks and boots identical to the last pair she had worn covered her feet by her next breath. "Thanks. You can be pretty handy."

"Mouthy wench." He kissed her quick then opened the door for her.

She refused to feel embarrassed at walking into the room with Tristan knowing what they'd been doing. They were all adults and Tristan had played a role in Daegan showering with her.

The smell of pizza hit her and wiped away any thought except eating.

Tristan had open pizza boxes spread out over the dresser with plates, napkins, and six bottles of water.

"You nailed it." She grabbed her plate, loaded pizza on it, and took a bottle of water with her to one of the two beds. Sitting cross-legged, she attacked the food without any grace.

Daegan sat on the side of the same bed, facing Tristan, who had taken a seat on the other bed.

Not a word was said as they all chowed down.

Fed, freshly showered, and totally loose from incredible sex with Daegan, she was ready to get moving. She hadn't wanted to drag these two along with her in case her trip took longer than she hoped. But Daegan had a point. She would be constantly watching for Imortiks, demons, Cathbad, and anyone else who thought she was of value.

Gathering her garbage, then picking up Daegan's and Tristan's on the way, she piled it all into the big white bag the food had been in.

Tristan stood up. "I'll take care of that." He and the bag left, then he returned in seconds.

She had a serious case of envy over teleporting.

Daegan stretched as he stood, his face less tense than it had been for too long. She gave herself a mental pat for being the reason he seemed rested and smiling today. The sleep they grabbed in the underground world had helped as well.

"Where to now?" Tristan hadn't asked any specific person, but Casidhe was the only one who could answer him.

"We're going to meet Kleio."

Daegan joined them. "Who is this woman?"

A small trickle of hope squeezed through the sudden tightness in her chest. "Kleio is, or was, the seer at Herrick's castle."

Daegan and Tristan exchanged tense looks.

# CHAPTER 4

"YA TRUST THIS WOMAN?" DAEGAN finally asked, disrupting the silence.

"At one time, I would have said no," Casidhe admitted. "I thought for the longest time she didn't like me because she never encouraged me to remain at Herrick's castle. I've since come to learn she had tried to protect me over the years and she was the one who guided me to find Jennyver. Kleio was bound by an agreement she made with Herrick a very long time ago, which allowed him to be in charge of what she could or could not share of her visions with others. She went against him to stand up for me and point me in the right direction at the risk of his retaliation."

"What does she want with ya now?" Daegan asked, sounding sincerely curious and not as suspicious.

Casidhe had wanted to tackle this on her own, but she would not deny how nice it was to have Daegan's support and a chance to rebuild her friendship with Tristan. With that in mind, she laid it all out for them, including details she just had not had time to provide.

Running her hand over damp hair to hurry the drying process, Casidhe continued, "In all these years, Kleio has never before left the castle and lands except for trips to find specific herbs with Herrick takin' her there and back. She sent the note to the hotel that Tristan brought me."

"Delivered by a crow?" Tristan asked.

"Yes. Herrick's clan had an elaborate message system. He allowed no technology. Kleio preferred usin' a crow due to the bird's high intelligence."

"Is she like Zeelindar?" Tristan frowned, clearly trying to sort it out in his head.

"Not exactly. Where Zeelindar is an oracle who probably manipulates different energy to see into the future, she has not been human for a long time and holds serious power. Kleio is human, for as much as I've seen, but she once commented that Herrick did not rule her. I asked what that meant. She serves a different master by choice, one I feel might be otherworldly, who *allowed* her to be Herrick's seer. Kleio sometimes sees a glimpse of the future, but more than that she seems to put her finger on exactly what is happenin' with anythin' related to Herrick and the ice dragon clan specifically."

"What does she have for ya now?" Daegan asked in a calm way, but he paced in the small area as he listened.

"Kleio's message said she knew how I could read the ice dragon chronicles, which would answer the question of who and what I am." Casidhe had the note tucked inside her backpack and wanted to cling to the small roll of paper for fear of it vanishing.

Daegan stopped walking and turned to her with honest excitement. "That would be wonderful. How do we find this Kleio?"

"The note said she had Herrick drop her off in Dublin because she did not want to risk him findin' out where she was goin'. She told him she would visit family, which she did that first day. She had plans to spend last night in a bed-and-breakfast in an area called Howth, not far from Dublin. Startin' there, she is leavin' me notes like breadcrumbs to find my way to help me elude Herrick if he stuck around to watch for her or me, but she believes he has to return to his castle quickly."

Shaking his head, Daegan seemed disappointed. "I have no idea where this Howth is, lass."

Tristan had been listening with his gaze pinned on the window. He angled around to face both of them. "Let me look it up on the map." He dug out his mobile phone and tapped several times. "This bed-and-breakfast place seems to fit. Here you go, Casidhe."

She smiled at Tristan for using her first name as opposed to calling her Luigsech. Another sign of his acceptance. She studied the map. "That's the name she wrote in the note."

Tristan informed Daegan, "Howth is basically on the east side of Ireland, straight across from us. Outside is clearing up but the guy at the pizza place said a hell of a storm just blew through here heading east."

"The weather may aid us in hidin' our arrival, but 'tis still mornin'," Daegan pointed out.

"That shouldn't be a problem," she announced, having pulled up the weather on Tristan's phone. "Pizza guy is right about the storm cuttin' across Ireland. Looks like we'll arrive in the middle of it slammin' Dublin."

"'Tis helpful, but there are always eyes about," Daegan persisted. Then again, he had teleported far more than her.

She lifted a finger. "Hold on. The map shows a lighthouse and indicates it's temporarily closed. Tourists will likely wait for the weather to clear before comin' out. And, temporarily makes me think they could be refurbishin' the lighthouse. There's a narrow two-story buildin' with a flat roof connected to it."

"Technology can be helpful sometimes, boss."

Daegan grunted.

Tristan moved around to take a look over her shoulder. "That should be less than a mile to the place she gave you."

"Here ya go." She handed the phone back to Tristan. She had awful luck with any mobile phone lately.

"You ready, boss?" Tristan shoved the phone into his back pocket.

Daegan called up hooded rain ponchos for all three of them. "I am now." He stepped close to Casidhe, tucking her hair inside the hood and holding her gaze with his.

She got it. He was showing his faith in her decision-making and that he was willing to meet Kleio. Her heart did a little jig at the look in his eyes. If she could bottle this feeling warming her from the inside out, she'd call it Pure Joy and include a warning the contents were addictive.

They landed on the rooftop in driving rain.

Daegan blocked the worst of it from her by stepping around to face her while water bullets struck his poncho sounding like they were under attack.

Tristan shouted, "Ready to go down to the ground?"

Daegan pulled her close. "Aye."

The jump took seconds, but the rain stopped hammering her immediately. She opened her eyes and stepped out of Daegan's embrace.

Water flew at them and bounced away.

She liked the safe zone of being cloaked, but asked, "Don't you think someone will notice water bouncin' off us?"

"I see no humans or activity to make me think they are here. When we are close enough for humans or any other bein' to see us, I shall drop the cloakin'."

"Sounds good to me." She took off at a fast pace, knowing those two would stay with her and not push her to keep up. She had walked, ran, and biked a lot when living at her cottage. She could keep up this fast jog for a few miles.

It seemed like forever since she'd been to her cottage. Since then, she'd lost everything she thought mattered to her and found out how wrong she'd been.

Having Daegan at her side was the only thing that mattered now. She had been hurt by Herrick and Fenella, but she survived their betrayal.

She would not survive losing Daegan.

The sooner they got this done, the faster they could return to Atlanta and stop the Imortik invasion.

Running in a normal way and not to escape death felt good in spite of the storm. Still, an elite runner she was not.

She covered the narrow strip of land from the lighthouse and harbor to the mainland of the peninsula, then passed a restaurant and pub. Once there, she followed the map in her mind until they were able to take a left turn onto a street past quaint homes and gardens.

When she neared the bed-and-breakfast guesthouse, she slowed to catch her breath.

Tristan and Daegan searched their surroundings. Neither one was out of breath, dammit. Not much to see beyond thick shrubs taller than her that bordered the entrance.

When she could speak, she asked, "Any chance you could conjure up an umbrella?"

The handle to an open black umbrella appeared without Daegan pulling his gaze from the road they'd taken.

Now she could push the hood back and wipe her face before knocking on the door, but she had a feeling something was off. "What's going on, guys?"

Tristan glanced at Daegan, said nothing, and kept sweeping a look over everything.

"The venom stings a bit now as it has when I have been around a grimoire volume. 'Tis not strong, but I do not wish to linger longer than necessary."

Sting probably meant Daegan's leg ached a lot. "You think a grimoire volume is *here*, Daegan?" She doubted it. Based upon all they'd gone through to find two, that would be too easy.

"Nay. I fear we may be attractin' Imortiks. We must hurry and not draw them to the humans."

"Crap. Let's go." She strode quickly past the shrubs then past gardens showing off verdant landscaping and flowers blooming in neat beds. What had probably once been the home of a large family had weathered shingles and a brown roof. A large porch allowed Casidhe to climb the steps and drop the umbrella to sit on the wide wood flooring.

She knocked quickly on the wood part of a door with a cut-glass center.

It took a minute for someone to open the door. "Goodness, come in. 'Tis bucketin' down out there." A tall woman with a cap of gray hair and wearing a full-body calico apron held the door. The toasty interior of the house smelled of fresh bread.

The woman lifted her head to look past Casidhe. She had a light and happy voice. "I'm Inez. Those two be with ya?"

"Yes, but they don't wish to come in and drip on your floor more than I'm doin'. I won't be here long." She paused then pushed straight to the point of her being here. "I'm sorry to disturb you, but someone left a message here for me. She visited a day ago."

Inez held herself erect like a schoolmarm with unwavering attention and not as open as she'd been at first. "Who might ya be?"

"My name is Casidhe Luigsech and the woman who sent me here is named Kleio." Casidhe suffered a blast of panic. She'd never asked Kleio her last name.

"How would ya be knowin' ta recognize the note?"

Casidhe had only one answer. She moved her hand inside her poncho then reached into her backpack, pulling out the rolled note. It still had the seal, though broken.

She handed it to the woman and hoped that would suffice. This inn keeper had not asked for photo identification.

Kleio probably said not to trust anything printed by a machine.

Inez took the note, inspected it as thoroughly as any homework had ever been reviewed, then she smiled. She reached in the pocket of her apron and withdrew an identical-looking rolled missive.

Letting out a long sigh of relief, Casidhe thanked her and hurried to read it before stepping outside again. When she finished, she rolled it up and realized she had no way to tip the woman. "I have no cash with me, but I promise to return at some point and pay you for your help."

"No, ya will not. This Kleio gave me a gift no money can match." Her pretty green eyes glistened. "My fifteen-year-old granddaughter disappeared three years ago and is the only family I have after my son and his wife were killed in an accident. I have searched nonstop and would have paid anythin' ta find her." She reached into her apron pocket and withdrew a tissue, dabbing her eyes. "I had an important dinner meetin' last night I had ta attend. It meant a lot ta my business, which has kept me sane, but Kleio warned me ta stay home. She told me my granddaughter wanted ta come back but had no money and even less faith in bein' welcome."

Casidhe really needed to go, but she could spare a minute to find out what happened after this woman had given her the note. She nodded to encourage the woman.

"I was quite shocked and struggled ta decide what ta do until Kleio explained the girl had tried ta call me twice but hung up when the machine answered. I wondered how she could be knowin' these things."

*Welcome to my world*, Casidhe thought with amusement.

"Kleio said my granddaughter would only call one more time. I truly questioned her but finally stayed. I had ta know so that is how I was here ta take the most important call in my life."

She clutched her throat then said in a thick voice, "I had a friend close ta where my granddaughter hid in an empty buildin' who went immediately ta pick her up for me. I am here now only ta give ya this note, then I'm leavin' to get my baby girl." She cried a bit, then waved Casidhe on. "Kleio said do not tarry. Off with ya."

"Congratulations about your granddaughter and thank you for helpin' me."

Happy for this woman, Casidhe opened the umbrella and rushed out in the deluge.

"Did ya find a note?" Worry lines crossed Daegan's forehead.

"Yes. The note from Kleio said to meet her at the home of the ice dragon clan."

Tristan's face fell. "She's sending you *back* to Herrick's castle?"

"Nay." Daegan had that knowing look on his face. "We go to the home where Herrick grew up. King Eógan's castle." He nodded in the direction of a spot between two monstrous shrubs. "We shall not be seen teleportin' from over there."

Clasping his fingers around Casidhe's arm as soon as they stepped between the thick greenery, Daegan told Tristan, "Link with me and I shall direct our teleportin'."

That was the last thing she heard before she went through a blur of colors and light. When the swirling stopped, wind whipped around her and lifted the umbrella from her hands, sending it tumbling for the cliff's edge ten feet from where they stood. Water rolled and bashed rocks below.

Tristan pointed a finger at the umbrella, using his kinetics to bring it back.

"Thanks." Casidhe snagged the handle from the air, wrapped it up, and snapped the closure. She shoved it inside her backpack so Daegan wouldn't have to call up another one.

At least the rain had not come this far north. The sun steadily climbed, sending warm rays down even through the mist clinging to this coastline.

When she looked around to find the castle, her backpack strap slipped from her fingers.

She stood in the midst of ruins with crumbling walls and no

roof to shield anything.

Her chest hurt with disappointment. "Are you *sure* this is where Herrick and his family lived?"

"Aye, 'twas King Eógan's castle. A grand one at the time."

She caught the sadness in Daegan's voice. He really had not wanted war among the dragon shifter clans.

Tristan shoved his sunglasses up on his wind-blown hair. He walked a few steps away and took a slow look as he turned around. "I know you hated seeing people use your father's castle as a tourist location, boss, but this has to be worse."

"Agreed. I have no thought of how we shall find anythin' here."

Casidhe picked her way through the rubble, searching for Kleio. She took care not to fall or step into a hole. When she'd gone far enough to see up and down the coast as well as the land leading away from the ocean, she turned around and went back to Daegan.

What if something had happened to Kleio?

That woman had not been out in the world for most of her life.

Tristan continued meandering around and pausing to touch parts of the stone walls still standing.

Casidhe felt the need to give Daegan and Tristan everything she had so they could decide to leave when they wanted. "Kleio said she'd be here every day for a month if that's how long it took for me to arrive. I may have missed her and be wastin' a day of time."

"'Tis not late mornin' yet, lass. Unless she slept here, she would need to travel from a village to this spot."

"Yeah, I guess so, but ... this is disappointin'." Even if Kleio was here, how would they find any chronicles?

"Come." Daegan turned and headed for the cliff's edge.

She followed until she stood next to him. "Okay, what?"

Daegan pulled her in front of him with her back to his chest and wrapped his arms around her. He drew in a deep inhale and let it out slowly. "Breathe, lass. We must allow this woman time to arrive. Until then, close your eyes and envision what life in this castle might have been like long ago."

She shut her eyes. It took some time, but she finally let go of the thousand things worrying her. She heard birds flying overhead and the wind whistling at times. She imagined eating in a great hall much like Herrick's but one filled with happiness. Her hair flicked around her face and she allowed the tickling, content to just be in the moment.

"We have company," Tristan called out.

Casidhe had to shake herself from what turned out to be a moment of meditation. Daegan swung her away from the cliffs, then walked with her to where Tristan stood on the far side of the ruins facing inland.

In the distance, a small charcoal-gray Land Rover with dried mud on the body bounced over the uneven ground making its way to them. After a few minutes, the vehicle pulled up and parked. The driver said something to his passenger then nodded.

Kleio emerged from the passenger side and waved to the driver as he turned around and began bouncing his way back.

During Casidhe's few visits to the castle, the seer had normally worn simple wool gowns.

Seeing her in dark pants, a cream-colored knit top, and black boots seemed so modern in contrast. She wore a red cape that fell to her knees. Her black hair was not in her usual severe bun or long braid, but drawn back into a ponytail that fell to her waist. Curly black locks escaped to blow around her face.

Kleio had never worn makeup that Casidhe could recall and didn't today, but this Kleio looked younger and happier than the one she'd known for so long.

"Hi, Kleio." Casidhe hurried to introduce everyone. "This is Daegan on my right and Tristan on my left. Guys, this is the woman I told you about."

"'Tis good to meet ya," Daegan said, and sounded as if he meant it.

"Nice to meet you," Tristan followed up.

Kleio did a double take when she noticed Tristan. "Your eyes are ... bright."

He grinned. "They glow. It's standard equipment with the Alterant-gryphon package."

"Very nice." Smiling at each man, Kleio said, "I thank you for keeping Casidhe safe and bringing her here today. I did not know she'd have the ability to teleport or I'd have started out earlier."

Casidhe noted, "I wouldn't have made it until tomorrow otherwise."

Now that they were all together, Daegan pressed Kleio. "Ya believe Casidhe shall find records in these ruins?"

Kleio angled her head either thinking about something or recalling her vision. "Yes."

Tristan and Daegan startled, both glancing at the carcass of a once vibrant castle then at each other.

"Not to be rude, but how would something written have survived and still be in this place?" Tristan asked.

"This is my first visit. I wish to see the land as we talk." Kleio checked every face, then turned to her left and began picking her way toward the cliffs. "I am assuming you told them what I am, Casidhe," she said, not looking back.

"Yep. They know."

With a simple nod, Kleio said, "I had multiple visions between when you left and Herrick bringing me to Ireland. We all have duties and little time to perform them. For that reason, I will only speak of the dreams about you and discovering your origins. In my vision, you traveled here and found the ice dragon chronicles, which answered all your questions about Shannon and how you are connected to the ice dragon clan."

Chill bumps lifted along Casidhe's skin and she was not cold.

Could there really be a set of ice dragon chronicles? Here?

When Kleio reached the cliffs, she peered out over the ocean then her gaze lowered to the majestic crashing of waves over boulders and rock piles.

Daegan stepped up with Tristan beside him to follow her gaze. "What do we search for, seer?"

"A large stone or group of stones shaped as a turtle provides the first hint for locating the chronicles."

Casidhe tried to make every rock and stone out to be a turtle but failed. "I don't see it."

Kleio turned to her. "If this stone was simple to find, enemies would have located the history of the ice dragon clan."

"I understand, but Herrick never mentioned the ice dragon

chronicles to me the whole time I trained to be a squire."

Kleio chuckled. "That does not surprise me. From comments Herrick made over the years, I believe he and Brynhild shared a dislike for what they both considered nuisance work better left to those beneath them. I have never known Herrick to keep *any* records over the time I spent around him, which leads me to believe he had not in the past." She paused, forehead wrinkled in thought. "In my early days at the castle, I pointed out how a daily journal would be helpful in keeping track of all his trips of hunting for Skarde."

Daegan had been leaning forward with his hands on his hips, staring at everything. He lifted away from the edge and asked, "How was he searchin'?"

"Back then, he made routine trips once or twice a week, flying in dragon form over uninhabited lands and during storms to call telepathically to Skarde." She shrugged, seeming to not understand Herrick to this day. "He knows you have his brother so he has no reason to hunt now."

"Ya do not think he follows ya here?" The first sign of suspicion crept into Daegan's voice.

Casidhe hoped she had not made a mistake coming here. The last thing she wanted was for Herrick and Daegan to battle again in any form.

"No," Kleio said without hesitation. "I was careful about traveling and I am fairly certain he had to return home as soon as he reached Dublin so he could fly under the cover of darkness."

"Why would this be if he no longer is tied to his lair without Jennyver there?" Daegan crossed his arms and turned to her while Tristan walked farther down the cliffs searching the water.

"I thought he would be free to fly more often as well, but I have noticed a slight aging in him. I wonder if the land and castle contribute to his living so long."

Casidhe jumped in. "Sounds like what Skarde said, Daegan."

"True."

Shock widened Kleio's eyes. She asked Casidhe, "You spoke to Skarde?"

"Yes. We had to make a stop in, uhm, where he's stayin'." Casidhe sliced a look at Daegan.

He told Kleio, "Skarde is in the Treoir realm where we are keepin' him safe. There is nowhere for him to go at the moment and he is not happy with Herrick."

Kleio took her time choosing her words. "That is too bad. Herrick is not stable right now. Seeing his brother might be good for him."

"Not really." Casidhe picked up the conversation. "Skarde had a close friendship with Jennyver. He's furious about what Herrick did to her."

Kleio tried to speak and quit.

Casidhe laughed, covering her mouth and nose to keep from snorting. "Don't take this wrong, but I have never known somethin' that you did not already know."

Pink tinged the seer's cheeks. "You did surprise me. I only had a vision of Skarde being unhappy with his brother. I can see how my having visions must have been annoying at times."

"You have no idea, but that's in the past." Casidhe grinned, glad to not carry that baggage anymore.

Anger took too much energy.

"*Hey! Come here!*" Tristan called out.

Casidhe took off running. She heard Daegan following close behind. Kleio would have to catch up.

When she reached Tristan, she looked where he pointed. "What? Show me."

"Just wait."

Daegan put his hands on her shoulders, leaning past her. He didn't say anything at first until a rolling wave blasted the rocks and cliff wall, then the water washed back.

As it did, Daegan confirmed, "'Tis a turtle shape."

"*Where?*" She stuck her neck out even more.

"'Tis deeper below the surface, lass. Ya may not be able to see the shape as we do. My dragon and his gryphon possess sharp sight. If we were flyin' now, we would have seen it sooner."

"What he said," Tristan murmured. "Now what?"

Kleio caught up to them, breathing hard. "Give me ... a minute." She held a hand over her chest. When she caught her breath, she watched as Daegan and Tristan pointed down and explained where to look.

Fat clouds passed in front of the sun before the next big wave. That's when the surface became more translucent without the reflections and Casidhe caught a glimpse. *"I see it!"*

"I do, too." Kleio stepped away from the edge.

Casidhe turned with Daegan and Tristan, all of them waiting for the seer to share the next piece from her vision.

Kleio hesitated then said, "This may not make sense, but I think you have to travel from the turtle toward the room where the chronicles are located."

Words escaped Casidhe. Did this woman not realize that turtle formation was at least twenty feet or more below the surface?

Tristan scratched his nose, cutting his gaze at Daegan who stood between them.

Daegan lifted his chin, looking out to sea. Casidhe had noticed how his face had been clean-shaven after their shower. It would be nice to have that kind of majik.

"Are ya sayin' King Eógan hid the history of his clan beneath the water, seer?" Daegan asked.

"I'm sharing what I saw. I know it to be true, but I can only share the details that came to me."

Trying to help Kleio, Casidhe asked, "What else was in the vision? Can you describe the room or what the chronicles looked like?"

Daegan interjected, "I do not know if 'tis the same for other clans, but only family may access our chronicles."

"Well that leaves me out," Casidhe muttered.

Where Kleio had been understanding and comforting when Casidhe had needed it during her last visit to Herrick's castle, the seer's voice sharpened now. "Did you not take possession of Shannon's sword?"

"Well, yes, but—"

"Did you not also call up armor to cover your body?"

"I'm not sure how I did that," Casidhe admitted, wishing she could depend on it happening again.

"My point is that the sword would *only* go to family."

Casidhe had put off thinking about Skarde's words but couldn't dodge them now. "Skarde said the two swords created for him and his twin, Shannon, were struck at the same time.

Their mother imprinted their hands on each other's sword as well as their own. They could lift each other's weapon to protect one another, but no one else in the family could. He said only a descendant should be able to claim Shannon's sword, but he was certain Shannon had no children."

No one spoke as Kleio closed her eyes and let her arms fall loose at her sides. Her eyes moved back and forth behind her closed lids.

When she opened her eyes, she didn't have an encouraging look. "I might be able to discover more with time, but nothing comes to me at this moment. I believe without a doubt you must find the chronicles for any answers."

Tristan's tawny hair flew all around. "You didn't answer Casidhe's question. Do you have any details about the specific place we're looking for?"

Staring at nothing in particular, Kleio said, "Everything was dark at first as I moved through the vision. Then light glowed from some point, I honestly do not know what caused the light, and Casidhe came into view." The seer closed her eyes and kept talking. "The interior was primitive with three steps carved of stone, which Casidhe climbed. Then the room brightened more and ... a cave." Kleio blinked her eyes and focused on Casidhe. "You were in a cave, but I do not think it was Herrick's. I believe it to be here."

Casidhe stepped around to face Daegan. "What if the turtle is pointin' to a cave openin' on the face of the cliffs?"

"Any dragon shifter flyin' around or members on a ship close enough to see the cliffs would find it," Daegan said, dumping cold water on her hopes.

"Knew that would be too easy." Casidhe lost hope she'd been clinging to only moments ago.

"Do not give up, lass. I have an idea."

She lifted her head slowly, trying to determine if Daegan was just doing his best to cheer her up or if he knew something others here might not. "What are you thinkin'?"

Looking over his shoulder, Daegan took his time answering. When he returned to face everyone, he didn't sound happy when he explained, "The cave might require enterin' from the sea."

Casidhe's lips parted. "You think we have to dive down and hunt an underground cave?"

"Not ya. Me."

"How do you plan to do that?"

Tristan stared up at the sky. "Tell me you aren't planning on shifting out here, boss."

"'Tis the only way. My dragon can dive for longer than I am able."

"What about my gryphon?"

Daegan shook his head. "We do not know if yours is able to dive for long periods. If I find it, I shall return to make a plan."

"Which will include takin' me with you when you go back, *right*?" Casidhe emphasized. She didn't like the idea of an underwater cave, but she had been the one to bring Daegan here and had survived the flood underground in Egypt.

"I doubt I shall be able to touch the chronicles myself, so yes. First I wish to ensure 'tis safe."

Kleio spoke up. "We may have another hour until the local tour group swings by these ruins from what my guide said. I convinced him to leave me because I knew the tour would make a stop here around noon to feed their group."

"We need to hurry," Tristan pointed out.

"I have not seen an airplane or boat the entire time we've been here," Daegan said, taking off his shirt. "'Tis only one way to do this quickly." He turned toward the sea and shrugged out of his jeans then leaped off the cliff.

Casidhe lurched forward and screamed, "*Noooo!*"

# CHAPTER 5

L ANNA WASHED HER FACE AND grabbed a towel to dry her skin. Her eyes were gritty. She'd been awake too long, but Adrianna needed constant healing.

Garwyli's strength continued to dwindle, but he'd stepped in and sent Lanna away.

If only the old druid could benefit from being here in Treoir the way Beladors did, but no. She could push longer with Adrianna if he'd just allow her.

Still, she should rest. Her power had to regenerate too, but as tired as her body was she could not calm her mind enough to sleep.

Adrianna's injury was tied to Witchlock.

Lanna felt certain of it, but she had to first go through all the steps Garwyli had taught her and was still coaching her on. Someone's health, especially Adrianna's ability to walk again, could not be taken lightly. Lanna had been learning to hold back her first inclination to jump in and fix someone based on what she believed to be the problem.

She could see how Adrianna would test her tendency to be impulsive. Healing had come fairly easily to her on injured animals the guards had found and brought to her. While this was a realm controlled by the Treoirs, the animals were from the natural world and allowed to live normally.

That meant Lanna had healed a bird with a broken wing, a rabbit with puncture holes from a large dog or wolf bite, and a chicken unable to lay eggs.

The hen had only needed to be held and cuddled for a while.

Lanna explained to the guard whose family owned the chickens that he should find a child in their group who would give the chicken some extra attention.

The guard thought she was joking until she failed to smile.

He came back two days later to tell her the chicken was producing again, and he'd found a young girl who loved feeding and caring for his flock.

Now Lanna smiled. Life in balance. Taking care of the hens also gave the girl something to feel proud about.

Adrianna required an entirely different level of healing.

Finished freshening up, Lanna headed for the solarium. She might relax enough there to take a nap on the window seat. When she entered, she found a package on the cushion next to the window.

She lifted the brown paper wrapping.

A note from Tristan had been taped to it.

He explained that Quinn had gone to Loki to inform the god about the explosion, then finding Adrianna, but that she had no idea what had happened to Sen or Tenebris. To keep Loki from stroking out, Quinn ask for something personal of Sen's for tracking him.

The glass object inside the paper was Sen's sole personal possession, according to Loki.

By the end of the note, Tristan said Quinn did not want to take any energy or time away from Adrianna and that Sen could well be in another realm by now, if he even survived the explosion.

In other words, Quinn wasn't asking for her to rush to send him word. He understood how much Adrianna needed her and Garwyli.

Sitting on the cushion, she considered if she should unwrap this or not.

She'd always thought of Sen as a potentially dark being simply because of how he'd mistreated Evalle so many times and tried to kill Storm one time. Sen hadn't been much nicer to the others, but he'd put forth extra effort to make Evalle's life miserable.

Would this object burn her fingers? That had happened once before with a lock of hair belonging to a powerful dark priestess.

Staring at the package would not answer her questions.

She peeled away the top of the paper to find a round, but flat-shaped, glass as wide as her palm and with a metal stopper on top. The stopper had a strange design carved into the metal she could not identify.

The glass had hundreds of cuts, giving the exterior a similar look to a cut diamond.

What had this container been used for?

Light flowing through the window at her back struck the iridescent glass when she held it up, sending shards of brilliant color all over the room.

She had to remove the rest of the paper still creating a safe barrier between the glass and her hand to know if she could even touch it. She took a deep breath and discarded the brown wrapping entirely.

Energy warmed her hand.

Nothing terrible so far.

She should wear gloves when handling unknown objects, but that would prevent her from tapping her power to learn anything.

Lifting the lovely container high again, she turned it until she could see inside. It held a dark wooden-looking oval chunk bigger than her thumb and with ridges.

When she tilted the bottle, the chunk slid around.

What was that?

Exhaustion had sometimes been better for handling an object than being fresh when her mind could be jammed with too many thoughts.

She sandwiched the glass between her hands and closed her eyes. The glass warmed again against her skin. Not a surprise, though it did make her wonder if Sen was truly dark or ... a damaged being. She returned her focus solely to the container.

Some objects with a lot of energy would warm, especially if this had been gifted to him by someone important.

The same warming had happened when Lanna held Adrianna's key chain. Her sister's emotion had been wound through the fine detail in threads woven around the key chain.

This flask-like glass should be valuable in finding Sen.

But who had given this to him?

As she held it, she followed Sen around VIPER headquarters where he paused and rushed to the entrance. He stood as if waiting on something then opened the mountain wall. Beings appeared as if they had teleported there. Maybe he had teleported them, since that's what Quinn had said was Sen's duty during the Imortik problem.

Demons and Imortiks appeared and rushed Sen.

She clutched the ball tightly watching as he fought to kill demons piling on him. The Imortiks clamored to beat off the demons to reach Sen and looked even more dangerous. She would not want to face those yellow monsters.

Sen moved his arm and teleported to another place, somewhere underground with a wide hallway.

He'd brought the Imortiks with him and opened a wall to a simple room with no furniture. Sen pointed a finger and sent the first Imortik flying into the room and closed the wall to solid again.

He turned and stood there as an Imortik came out of hiding and attacked him.

Then the vision blurred.

Lanna tightened her hold on the glass.

An image flickered of Sen howling and fighting the Imortik. Sen's face came back into view. He beat the Imortik down with hits of power, but the monster clawed Sen, ripping open a deep wound.

He yelled as if a hot iron had been driven through his chest. Slapping a hand, he blasted the Imortik with power. It exploded, turning into dull yellow ash.

She hadn't heard specifics on fighting an Imortik, but that seemed to work. Had that Imortik been a Belador? If so, Daegan had made an agreement with the Tribunal that possessed Beladors had to be locked up in VIPER headquarters, not killed.

While Daegan and many others did not like dealing with Sen, the dragon king would not judge harshly when someone fought to survive.

Again, the image faded away.

Dropping her head forward, Lanna wanted to yell at the glass. Losing her temper with items of power never went well so she drew in another slow breath and kept trying.

More blurry images passed through her mind, then a woman teleported into the area where Sen lay bleeding. She held a gold set of scales like the kind used to weigh objects. Lanna had heard about a goddess being in the Tribunal meetings with Loki who wore a white robe and a blindfold.

This woman had to be Justitia, the goddess of justice.

Sen groaned in agony. In the next moment, Justitia teleported him to a room with two elders in gray robes and said, "Sen has been injured badly. Heal him."

She disappeared.

Then nothing again.

Lanna pressed her hands harder against the glass until the surface made red marks where the glass tips dug into her skin. She relaxed her hold.

What had happened to Sen?

Opening her eyes, she lifted the pretty flask, turning it again. The wooden piece inside now floated in the middle, spinning slowly.

Was that a peach pit? It sure looked like one, but why would Sen have a peach pit in a container that reminded her of a large perfume vase with a fat stopper?

Why had the vision ended?

Would she be able to figure out more if she held the peach pit in her hands? She put her fingers on the metal stopper and could hear Garwyli in her mind making an *ahem* sound.

If he stood here, he would warn her against rash decisions.

Everyone finally respected her ability and wanted her help. If she assumed wrong and made a mistake with this glass container, her impulsive action would set her back.

Garwyli might be so angry, he'd make her start part of her training from the beginning again when she wanted to move ahead from what she had already learned.

She was too close to possibly begin lessons on teleporting a farther distance than from one room to the next.

Garwyli had paled when she shared how she had managed that much on her own.

He would not show her anything new unless she proved she was gaining control of her emotions as well as her majik. She studied the peach pit longer, still sure if she could only hold that pit she'd learn more.

Was finding Sen worth the risk of Garwyli's displeasure?

Quinn had not been in a hurry.

Sen would not help anyone.

Still, she itched to know what the peach pit would share.

# CHAPTER 6

CATHBAD HAD SCOUTED OUT THE best place for this meeting. He had one chance to get it right and walk away alive.

How had his life come down to this? He would face a future in exile if he failed. He wouldn't survive without a realm.

With so much attention on downtown Atlanta, Kennesaw Mountain National Battlefield Park northwest of the city fit his criteria of little foot traffic and a lot of open space. Fearful humans were staying home.

Daylight was still a promise with the sun yet to rise above the eastern horizon. Gun powder residue from a recent Civil War reenactment clung to the grass and trees. Why did humans enjoy reenacting a civil war?

He'd held his cloaking in place, but the hour of the meeting was upon him. Dropping his shield, he stepped twenty-five yards across neatly trimmed grass.

A few clouds floated in the solid blue sky.

Some might think this a good day to die. He agreed if it was not him.

Macha appeared in a shimmering wash of crystal flecks that floated around her then gently disappeared.

"Macha."

"Where is the woman?" Macha's face gave away nothing, not even her deep hatred.

Cathbad kept his voice conversational. "She is here. I have her cloaked nearby. I want proof ya shall teleport me to TÅµr Medb when I hand her over." He could now teleport into TÅµr Medb under his own power, but not as long as Queen Maeve remained in the realm.

In other words, not until she was truly dead, never to rise

again.

"You wear on me, druid. That was not our deal. You owe this to me for failure to uphold your part in the mountains."

"Nothin' worked out for either of us." He held his arms open. "We underestimated Queen Maeve's power."

Macha made a noise of disbelief. "Do not include me in your assessment. She is losing all control and falling apart, unable to maintain her shape. While she is likely far more powerful than *you*, she is no threat to me."

He lifted one side of his mouth in disregard. "Sounds as if ya are still intent on killin' Queen Maeve. Regardless of what ya claim, I would warn ya to not underestimate her. Ya have had to hide in your mother's realm after the incident with Daegan takin' over Treoir, where Queen Maeve has her own realm."

Now Macha allowed her fury to slip into her seething gaze.

He pretended to not notice. "Plus, Queen Maeve also has been forced to remain in her realm continually while the Tribunal barred her from enterin' the human world. Ya see now how she disregards the Tribunal rule since the Imortiks showed up. Nothin' stops her from goin' wherever she wishes. I believe she is becomin' unbeatable."

Macha sneered, "I find myself more bored than usual."

"I shall be happy to uncloak the woman who belongs to Daegan if ya agree to give me what I ask for."

Macha eyed him as one would a slug and gathered energy to her, ready to battle. "I am not negotiating with you again. Your power is of no value to me. In fact, what happened to your aura? What stained it?"

Pissed at her bringing up the insult placed by Ainvar, Cathbad did an outstanding job of reining in his temper. "Ya say ya do not need me, but I have the woman who I know possesses the ability to bring Daegan in faster than ya can. Just be reasonable and I shall uncloak Casidhe, then ya can take her and ambush Daegan when he shows to negotiate for her freedom."

"I am done here, druid! I have my own plans, which do not require the assistance of a lesser being."

He'd had enough. "Very well, ya shall have all ya wish for." He pointed at a spot to the side of Macha.

Queen Maeve appeared, standing fifteen feet tall and covered in pieces of her tattered gown. Her human form had warped to a giant. Gray and brown matted hair sprung from all over her misshapen head. Claws curled at the tips of long fingers. She opened her jaws to screech and fangs filled the opening.

The crazed queen roared, "You think to kill me and Daegan? I shall find him today and turn him into my dragon throne again or maybe just compel him to take me to Treoir. Then I can rule *both* realms." She dropped her head back and laughed insanely.

Macha stared for a second, then white-hot rage wiped away her surprise.

Cathbad stepped back, hoping he had bet on the best horse for this battle.

Macha lashed her arms at Queen Maeve, striking with blasts of energy as she floated up to eye level with the huge monstrosity. Queen Maeve had been incredibly beautiful at one time, but that woman was forever gone.

Every strike from Macha smacked Queen Maeve's head and chest. The queen stumbled back with smoke sizzling from holes now oozing blood. Before Macha could release another round of hits, Queen Maeve opened jaws two feet wide and bellowed a curse, which shot out as black foam shrouding Macha.

Thick black froth began wrapping tighter and tighter, changing into heavy cables around Macha. She shoved her hands between two thick strands and forced them apart, breaking free but wobbling in the air.

Without hesitating, Queen Maeve followed up with raising both fisted hands and striking a vicious blow straight down on Macha, knocking her into the ground.

Macha hit hard, blowing a hole in the ground with earth flying.

Cathbad smiled. So far, so good. He'd found the Scáth Force's leader and told him to pretend he was still loyal to Queen Maeve and to deliver a message to her.

To stroke her ego, Cathbad admitted he'd made mistakes in the past, but he knew who held the power. As a way to make amends, he informed Queen Maeve of Macha's plans to kill her to prevent Queen Maeve from capturing Daegan before Macha could kill him.

As Cathbad had intended, his message riled the insane queen to the point she came to meet him and agreed to a deal. He would help her kill Macha then give Queen Maeve the woman called Casidhe who could bring Daegan to Queen Maeve.

In return, she would allow him back into TÅµr Medb.

As if he'd actually enter that realm while Queen Maeve still lived? No.

She still accused him of stealing Casidhe from her library, which he hadn't done. He reminded her he could have cloaked the woman and himself had he wanted to spirit her away.

Once she accepted his words, they planned out this battle.

He hoped Macha damaged Queen Maeve enough for him to finish her off since he did not possess Casidhe.

Macha called up a storm of spikes to rain down on Queen Maeve. That would have been a brilliant idea if Queen Maeve had not immediately covered her skin with steel scales. She swung her huge arms and hands wildly, swatting the spikes away.

Macha had to dodge the ones knocked at her.

Cathbad dropped to the ground when three came flying at him. They stabbed deep into the ground and a tree trunk behind him.

That had been too close.

He truly had no idea just how powerful Queen Maeve had become as the madness had taken over her. Now would be a good time to cloak himself, but she'd warned him if he failed to remain in sight she would hunt him down and rip his limbs off one at a time.

Standing here and risking his life around those two was not wise but necessary. He needed the power of TÅµr Medb to replenish his power to his original state of greatness.

Ainvar would eventually come for him.

Cathbad had to be ready at any moment.

Macha began teleporting in and out of view, attacking from unexpected locations. Her evil smile just as confident as Queen Maeve's distorted one.

Could Macha actually kill the crazy bitch?

Macha popped into view with a burning spear and stabbed

Queen Maeve in her back. Macha held the spear as Queen Maeve's arms flapped back and forth trying to reach her. When Queen Maeve jerked around, Macha flew around too. The spear was melting scales, then the spear stabbed deep.

Cathbad couldn't believe what he was watching.

Macha laughed hysterically. More of a cackling scream. Had she pierced Queen Maeve's heart?

Did either of those two even possess one?

Standing bent over, Queen Maeve howled and shoved her hands at her chest in pain.

Cathbad started cursing. This would be a disaster.

All at once, Queen Maeve arched up, holding the end of the still-flaming spear in both hands. She ripped the spear forward, dragging it through her body.

Macha stopped laughing and cocked her head in confusion.

Wily like a fox, having yanked the spear free, Queen Maeve tossed it to the ground and spun around. Her eyes boiled red. She cursed and flung empty hands in attack.

Macha appeared unconcerned and blinked out of sight.

In that second, Queen Maeve grew half again as big.

Cathbad hadn't thought that possible.

When Macha appeared again with energy wrapping her hands shoved up to attack, she had to bend her head back to face her opponent.

Queen Maeve flicked her hands at Macha, but this time two monstrous black wraiths flew from her long fingernails, howling and engulfing Macha.

The demonic-sounding wraiths locked onto her body.

Macha teleported. Within a second, she returned, yelling a spell in an ancient language Cathbad hadn't dared to use in a long time.

The one time he had, the spell had backlashed on him. What was she doing?

Queen Maeve's hands blurred, turning into the tail of the wraith. She snarled awful sounds.

Helicopter blades beating the air alerted Cathbad military were headed inbound. He could not stop this. Not while one still stood.

Macha finished spewing her spell.

The wraiths wrapped around her burst into flames, burning her body. She screamed more from fury than pain.

Flames raced along the stretched wraiths all the way to Queen Maeve's hands and backlashed across her body. She howled. Her giant body whipped back and forth.

Hummers forged across the ground behind him. A tank pushed through trees on the far side of the wide lawn.

Three big black military helicopters swarmed overhead.

Cathbad turned to flag the Hummers. As soon as someone in fatigues stepped out, he shouted, "Ya cannot take out one without takin' both. If ya kill them right now, ya shall all die and blow apart most of this state."

The big human with a fierce scowl and followed by a team of his armed men ordered, "State your name."

Cathbad knew this Isak Nyght but pretended otherwise. "I am tryin' to help stop Imortiks." These humans would not know he lied.

Queen Maeve and Macha fell to the ground in a loud blast, sending debris flying.

He and the soldiers ducked.

The black wraith shriveled into smoke. Queen Maeve shrunk to her normal size looking like something dragged through a bombing.

Macha struggled to her feet and pointed at her adversary. "You will die soon, bitch."

Queen Maeve moved slowly and held her head high as she sat up. "Ready for another go?" She flipped a hand at Macha, striking her with a black-and-red lightning bolt.

That single attack was enough to knock Macha to the ground.

With both hands covering a huge hole in her chest, Macha wheezed out, "*Dagda!* Come for me."

Queen Maeve turned a face of wrinkled skin and burned scalp to glare at Cathbad.

Silver light shot all around Macha in a glowing fortress, then her body lifted into the glow and disappeared along with the fortress.

She'd called Dagda, powerful leader of the *Tuatha Dé Danann*, to rescue her?

Cathbad hadn't expected anything that drastic, which meant she would not be seen again for a long time. That would give him time to rebuild his energy, but only if Queen Maeve died.

"Allow me a moment to save lives," Cathbad said while holding up a hand to Isak, who still had a nasty weapon pointed at Queen Maeve.

The same kind every one of his men had trained on her.

He was not sure they could kill her or he'd step back and let them have at her.

Cathbad walked over to her, speaking softly. "I saved ya from this human military. They were about to blast ya to pieces." That should gain him all kinds of rewards.

She hissed at him and the crowd, then vanished.

The bitch left him?

Isak strode up. "What was that all about? And you still didn't identify yourself."

Cathbad held his temper in check when he wanted to unleash his power on easy human prey. "I am the one who has been givin' aid to Daegan in findin' the grimoire volumes. 'Tis all ya need to know about me. As for those two, just be thankful neither one decided to destroy everyone out here."

He cloaked himself and walked away. Let them think he'd teleported.

Macha would kill him if she could, but for her to call Dagda to save her was as serious as it got with that goddess. She would not be back in the near future, maybe not for a long time.

Queen Maeve had failed to hold up her end of their bargain. She could not be trusted for him to enter TÅµr Medb where she would be even more powerful.

He paused and stared up at sunlight playing between the trees. His power waned. Ainvar would come for him. His stomach roiled and his body shook at the thought of facing that bastard again before he regenerated his power in TÅµr Medb.

Based upon what he saw today, he truly had no idea how to kill Queen Maeve.

# CHAPTER 7

DAEGAN HAD BEEN IN THE midst of shifting when Casidhe's scream reached him. He waited for Ruadh to finish forming and arc upward with powerful flaps to sweep across the water. Ruadh's chest and legs barely missed a sharp boulder.

*Well done, Ruadh.*

His dragon sent back, *Easy.*

*I know ya do not care much for divin', but we must find this cave if 'tis under the water.*

Half a mile out, Ruadh banked around sharply, heading for the cliffs.

Daegan intended to send a telepathic message to Tristan about calming Casidhe, but the lass now stood at the edge with her feet apart and her hands shoved on her hips.

There was his warrior.

He hadn't meant to frighten her. When he returned, she'd tear into him about not informing her first, but it only meant she cared. His heart had never been so full of happiness. One day, she would know what to expect of him and him of her.

Once Ruadh had picked up speed closing in on the cliffs, they dove, hitting the surface at an angle. Water exploded around the big body with wings now tucked. Ruadh used both tail and paddling to move forward.

Daegan continued speaking telepathically with Ruadh. *We must find the rocks shaped as a turtle.*

His dragon wasted no time in scouring the sea floor, which turned out to be far deeper than Daegan had thought. They approached a pile of rocks near the cliffs. When Ruadh lifted up, they floated beneath the surface but above the turtle shape and angled to face in the same direction.

Daegan saw nothing at first.

A fish almost as long as Daegan's human body swam by and straight for the wall below the cliff.

The fish disappeared.

Ruadh moved forward slowly. A black hole began to take form. Small fish raced out of the void.

Daegan said, *Appears to be a hole, but we do not know how far it goes or how narrow the openin' shall be.*

*Turtle points at hole*, Ruadh replied.

Hard to argue with that, but if they had to shift underwater for Daegan to teleport to the surface it would have to be fast. He could be too deep down and too far into the hole to swim out in time to breathe again.

Debating only wasted Ruadh's air.

Daegan said, *Take in all the air ya can then we shall dive.*

Floating up, Ruadh stuck his head out long enough to fill his lungs and expand his chest, then dove straight down. They entered the black hole, moving forward as fast as Ruadh could go.

What if they ran into a wall or had to dive deeper in another hole?

Daegan quieted his mind. He could not help his dragon by worrying about the unknown. Ruadh possessed unusual instincts Daegan had trusted since day one.

Ruadh slowed and leaned to the right, then turned upward and began to climb steps.

Were these the steps Casidhe had to climb?

Still moving through darkness. Ruadh's head broke the surface. His dragon heaved, expelling air and sucking in more, having shown no sign of distress.

Daegan said, *We need room to shift. I cannot see how much space is in here.*

Ruadh's body rumbled.

Daegan watched through his dragon's eyes when Ruadh blew a slow stream of fire straight up.

The large cavern had plenty of room, which should not surprise him since this had belonged to dragon shifters.

Once Ruadh climbed two more steps and stood, water rushed off his massive body. They shifted. Daegan stood waist-deep on the top step his dragon had reached. Unwilling to clothe himself yet, he called up a flame to float on his open palm.

Light glowed over a wide area above the water. It took a moment for him to figure out how to reach the landing by testing which way to step across an underwater walkway.

He made it to the point where he stood on stone flooring three steps below the platform and called up more flame.

The cavern grew even bigger as light searched out the walls.

Gold and silver poured from chest after chest. More dishes, mugs, tables, and instruments were stacked and piled. He stood in King Eógan's treasure room. Light glinted off jewelry, so much jewelry.

The queen must have planned to share much of this with her daughters and the mates of her sons.

None of which ever happened.

Daegan hurt for the king and his family. Skarde, Brynhild, and Herrick should come to claim their part of this hoard.

If they could meet without bloodshed.

For all that had been hidden in this cavern, he saw nothing of chronicles, but he also doubted a wise king would make locating the family history easy.

Daegan considered testing his teleporting ability, but if he failed he'd put everyone in danger trying to find him.

He called out, *Tristan?*

*I'm here, boss.*

*Try lockin' on where I am and linkin' with me. We did this before. It should work.* Daegan sent his link to Tristan.

He felt a surge of Tristan's energy. Good sign. Then his second said, *I think I've got you.*

*Ya must be sure, Tristan, or ya might not survive.* Daegan would like one day not to put the people he cared for in danger to perform their duties and help him.

*I'm on it.*

Daegan felt the draw on his power as Tristan teleported.

"*Whoa!*" Tristan yelled, splashing into the water. He came up sputtering and shoving hair off his face, then spun until he saw Daegan. He blinked out of sight and reappeared next to Daegan, dripping water.

"Ya cost me a year or two of life," Daegan groused, holding the flame in his hand so Tristan could see. "'Twas fortunate ya landed on water."

"Yeah, the location was a little murky in my mind. I just focused on getting to you." Tristan looked around. "Wow. Is that someone's hoard?"

"Aye. Appears to be King Eógan's." Daegan clothed himself in jeans, boots, and a T-shirt then called up a mental image of where he'd left Kleio and Casidhe. "Think ya can teleport us to the cliffs?"

"Should be simple after making this trip one way. Ready?"

Daegan nodded.

They returned to the cliffs arriving behind where Casidhe stood with her hands still jabbed at her hips and telling Kleio, "I'm gonna strangle him when he returns."

Standing quietly, Kleio stared out at the open sea. "I still say he knew what he was doing. He just did not explain it to you."

"He should have."

"What if you were battling something with him, Casidhe? Would you stop to tell him every action you had to take?"

"She would not," Daegan answered.

Casidhe jerked around and lost her footing, arms waving to keep from falling.

Daegan teleported to her and caught an arm around her waist. "Ya seem to have a nervous twitch, lass."

"Only around you," Casidhe smarted back. "If you'd tell me what you were doin' and stop sneakin' up on me, I wouldn't be standin' here guessin'."

"I did not know what I would find down there," Daegan said, intentionally trying to throw her off track.

"You know I'm talkin' about you divin' off this cliff."

He sighed hard enough to ruffle her hair. "My dragon and I have done such many times over the years. 'Twas not somethin' to mention."

"Did you locate the cavern?" Kleio asked anxiously. She had her hands clasped in front of her.

Casidhe stepped away from Daegan to face him with a similar expression of concern.

"My dragon did. 'Tis a large cavern beneath this land." He would say nothing more of the treasure. Casidhe might trust Kleio, but Daegan would rather wait until Skarde could come here before Herrick or Brynhild might raid the entire hoard.

Casidhe's lips parted. Her eyes rounded in awe. "You really found it?"

"Aye, lass. Just told ya."

"Can you take me?" Her voice had dropped to whisper soft. She stared at him as if he'd conquered an entire army.

He felt ten feet tall and ready to slay anything for her. "Tristan and I shall take ya down."

Kleio smiled, clearly happy for her vision to be proven true.

Casidhe grabbed her backpack.

"Ya do not need that, lass," Daegan told her.

"I never know. It's been handy more than one unexpected time." She pulled out the umbrella and handed it to Kleio. "You might need this at some point and it's in my way."

Kleio accepted the gift, holding back a smile.

"She's got a point about the backpack, boss." Tristan's clothes had dried in the wind.

Daegan caught Casidhe's arm. He'd noticed the venom lightly throbbing in his leg a few times. Not the strong burn as when Imortiks were around but enough to not leave anyone alone.

He told Tristan, "When we teleport down, I want ya to return up here. I do not wish to leave Kleio defenseless."

The seer slashed a surprised look his way then dipped her head in a nod of thanks.

This time, Daegan and Tristan teleported to the spot where they had departed, but without the benefit of light.

"Call me if you need me." Tristan vanished again.

Daegan released Casidhe and she reached out to grip him. "Don't move without me."

"Be calm. I shall provide light." He opened his palm, bringing up a large flame. "Do not fash over the flame this time. It harms none."

"I'm not complainin'," she told him, walking toward the steps and stopping. "Wow. That's incredible."

"Yes. I wish to keep this secret until Skarde is able to visit so his brother and sister do not come first and take all of it."

"I'm not sayin' a word." She turned to him before climbing the steps. "Herrick is supposed to have his own hoard in his cave behind the castle. He never wanted for money the entire time I knew him. I think he's added to it over the years. I saw him show up with bags of shiny goods. No tellin' where he got all of it."

Daegan would not point out how that had been the life of dragon clans, Vikings, and others back in the day. "Where do ya think to look for the chronicles?"

That snapped her back into action. She hurried up the steps, walked a few feet, and turned. "This feels like what Kleio said about me walkin' up three stone steps with light comin' from behind. I'm not sure what to do next."

Daegan started to follow her and had a sensation he should not. He offered, "I mentioned my family chronicles. We must use our power to make the chronicles appear and to find the tomes we wish to read."

"Okay. I don't really have that kind of power."

"Are ya sure?"

She gave him a droll look. "I think I'd know."

"Ya did not know ya could call up armor," he pointed out.

She nibbled on her thumbnail, eyes narrowed as she stared at nothing. "I actually sent Herrick flyin' backward when he came after me."

Daegan's energy boiled with his swift anger. The flame shot straight up.

"Hold it, Daegan." She had her hands out as if to calm him. "He didn't touch me. But I had a moment when I made up my mind he was not goin' to make me do anythin'. That's when I called up the sword and it flew to me the first time. The armor covered my body and I made a defensive shove, which worked like I had kinetic power. But I haven't done that since."

He calmed his breathing. The flame shortened but remained bright enough to light the cavern. She did not want him slaying everyone who had wronged her. He could agree as long as none of those who had dared to threaten her ever crossed his path.

Returning to what she had to do, he suggested, "Sounds as if ya only had to *believe* in your power to take over the sword and use kinetics. Try usin' your power to search for the chronicles. As long as nothin' tries to harm ya, I shall stay here. I sense my dragon shifter power might interfere as 'tis from another clan."

"I guess that's as good an idea as any." She did not sound confident.

"When Tristan had to find his way teleportin' here, he said he thought he had my location. I told him he had to be sure or he might not survive."

She'd stilled, listening intently to him.

Daegan shrugged. "I believe ya shall succeed if ya believe ya have the power. 'Tis somethin' no one can explain about energy, majik, and power as it manifests differently for each of us. One thing I do know, doubt leads to failure where confidence and belief lead to success. Take your time. I shall be here. "

Her face changed from unsure to calm determination. Her shoulders came up and squared. She gave him a sharp nod and turned to face the center of the room.

He waited silently as she moved around the upper level, walking over to run her fingers over the treasures.

Was she looking for inspiration?

She lifted a goblet that glowed from the flame, smiled, and returned it to the pile.

Once she'd circled the room, there was no obvious place to go from there. Walking slowly, she made her way to the center and wove her fingers together, then clamped them on her head.

This might not work after all.

Should he have used different words? Something that would not have loaded her shoulders with more burden? How was she to find something only a dragon shifter descendant could locate?

Daegan could stand here for hours if that was what she needed, but the longer he waited the more he realized he'd made a mistake to push her.

She lowered her arms first to her sides, then she dropped her chin and closed her eyes. Her breathing calmed.

He'd give her a few more minutes, then call her down so they could teleport out to ask Kleio more questions.

Casidhe lifted her head. She extended her arms in front of her with her hands clasped. She began to turn slowly, going around once, then twice. On the third turn, she opened her eyes. Her sky-blue eyes glowed like sparkling diamonds.

Then energy swirling slowly now spun faster with her in the middle.

She disappeared.

Daegan's heart slammed fast in his chest. "Casidhe!"

# CHAPTER 8

POWER RACED AROUND CASIDHE, GROWING into a crystal-blue so bright she squinted and lifted a hand to shield her eyes.

What was happening? She closed her eyes to center herself as Daegan had shown her when staring out over the ocean.

Something tugged on her energy. She opened her eyes as the energy drew her into the cerulean tornado.

Feeling a little terrified, she worked at not resisting. She had to trust that she was supposed to be here in this moment. Her body felt light as if she might float off the floor of the cavern.

There was no floor.

Where was the cavern?

Daegan would be okay, right? What if he tried to reach her after she disappeared? He said the ice dragon energy prevented him from climbing the three steps.

If he rushed up them to find her, would the energy kill him?

Her heart thumped madly in her chest.

No. Stop obsessing. Daegan had lived longer than her and knew enough not to test that energy. He trusted her to find her way to the chronicles. She trusted him to remain safe.

He would be okay. She wasted time and energy stressing over the unknown.

All she could see were powerful threads spinning around her, as if she stood in the middle of a cotton candy machine. So far, nothing had bound her body or hands.

Tendrils peeled off from the inside of her blue cone of power, floating toward her when she would have expected them to be flipping wildly with the speed of the tornado.

She started to reach for the tendril then pulled back.

She had no manual on what to do inside here.

More tendrils waved at her.

What the hell?

She hadn't come this far to wig out now. She lifted her hand slowly and inched her fingers toward the closest tendril, surprised when the bright blue wisp did not meet her partway.

Once she had her arm fully extended, she pointed one finger.

That must have been the right idea.

A tendril gently latched onto her finger, wrapping around and around. She smiled, delighted to get something right.

Then the tendril tightened.

"Ouch." She tried to pull back, but the fine thread did not give or even stretch into a straight line.

A monotone female voice commanded, "You may make a request, but know this, by your touch you swear to never betray what you learn here."

Like she had a choice?

Who was talking?

Casidhe stuck to obeying the order. "I agree and request to read the ice dragon shifter chronicles."

The voice did not answer and the thread let go.

What had she said wrong? She tried again, "I request to read King Eógan's family chronicles."

Everything around her changed, replacing the blue energy cocoon with a circular room forty feet across. Wooden shelves eighteen inches deep and at different heights covered the entire circular wall surface. Some held thick tomes but the high shelves at least thirty feet up from where she stood had been filled entirely with scrolls.

Did that indicate the oldest information would be in the scrolls on top?

If so, that would mean the last of the chronicle entries should be on the lower levels within her reach.

All well and fine, but one circular shelf appeared to hold a hundred books as well as scrolls.

To read all those alone would take weeks.

Casidhe quietly asked, "Are you still here?" Her breath formed a white cloud as if the temperature had dropped severely, but she felt no cold.

"I am ever present," the smooth female voice replied.

"Is the journal, or journals, belongin' to Shannon, daughter of King Eógan, here?"

"No journals."

With another glance at the amount of books and scrolls, Casidhe had to start at the most obvious place for her search. "I would like to read the last of the ice dragon family chronicles to be added to the library."

Movement at her right drew her around. A thick book with a dark-blue leather covering and a tooled design of black and silver slid from a shelf and floated to her. She opened her hands and the book stopped before reaching her.

The voice said, "No one may touch the chronicles except the immediate members of the ice dragon family."

That would be Brynhild, Herrick, or Skarde.

"I understand."

Moving again, the book paused right in front of her waist-high.

If she couldn't touch it, how would she move pages?

She'd recently flipped pages unexpectantly with her translating power and lifted two fingers on her right hand. She swiped them above the book from right to left.

Nope. That would have been too easy.

"I would like to start at the last entry and work backward," Casidhe suggested.

The cover flipped open, then pages flew by.

She caught glimpses of neat text and images, but nothing she could identify so quickly. When the pages stopped three-quarters of the way in, text written on the left page had been finished on the right.

That perfect handwriting made her think a female may have written the words.

Careful to move her fingers slowly to hold an inch above the page, Casidhe had to shove her left hand in her pocket to prevent herself from automatically reaching for the book.

Would this even work?

She waved her fingers from left to right, starting at the top of the left page. Gold letters flowed up as she passed over the words.

The joy of seeing her gift working made her laugh with delight.

By the time she finished this part, she'd confirmed the words had been written by the queen. The queen had feared for the lives of her children and king. The ice dragon clan possessed the greatest number of dragon shifters at the time, but the queen had feared the red dragon's ability to war.

At the same time, the queen noted she was not convinced the red dragon could be behind the attacks. She'd met the young man when Brynhild had been offered as his mate once her daughter came of age.

Daegan had been polite, saying while he was honored by the offer, he did not intend to take a mate for many years. He suggested Brynhild decide for herself when the time came and he expected King Eógan and King Gruffyn to always be allies.

Regardless, Herrick had ranted for days about killing the red dragon for insulting his father and ruling the island.

Casidhe shook her head at Herrick. Daegan had shown great consideration for Brynhild while Herrick saw insult to the king.

Daegan had insulted no one.

The queen's last words were, *As time nears for battle, I pray hourly to end this madness. All I can see of the future is darkness and rivers of blood. The king prepares for the Dragani War, though he admits to me he feels there is much unknown about this war. He sent word to King Gruffyn for them to meet. The slaughtered messenger's body returned slumped over his horse.*

*All of our clan are ready to strike down the red dragon.*

*I see no hope to prevent this bloodshed and fear this to be my last entry.*

Casidhe needed to read the page prior to this one. She stared at the page she wanted to flip. In her mind's eye, she saw her fingers move the page.

Just like that, the page turned.

Had she convinced the bodyless guardian to trust her?

Probably not since the power in this library could likely wipe her out should the guardian become angry.

The new pages told more of leading up to the last moments before bloodshed. There were two different handwritings. One more masculine. Probably the king.

Her gaze caught on a line of text referencing Shannon. She slowed down to reread. The queen had ended a paragraph and skipped down to add a line all by itself, which said, *Shannon delivered a sealed letter to me, asking for the king or myself to open the letter upon her death. I am sad for any child to believe her days may be coming to an end and encouraged her to hold onto her faith. She smiled at me and repeated her request to grant her wish. I gave my word. If the king falls, I may likely fall with him. For that reason, I grant the family member who reads this chronicle permission to open her letter. I feel it is of grave importance to her.*

Focusing her mental energy, Casidhe flipped the next page.

A graying envelope stood caught in the seam between pages. She brushed her fingers above script on the papyrus without touching it.

*For The One Who Wields Lann an Cheartais* had been written on the front of the envelope.

Casidhe gasped and paused with her hand positioned to snatch up the letter. No threatening moves. "I request to read the *For The One Who Holds Lann an Cheartais* letter."

"To do so, you must possess *Lann an Cheartais,*" the voice dictated.

Just pulling the sword out might not work if Casidhe had to prove she *possessed* Shannon's weapon.

Drawing in a deep breath, she let it out slowly, releasing the tension that had been building in her chest.

She could do this. She had to do this.

The chances of finding Shannon's journal were dismal at this point.

Turning her outstretched hand to the side to avoid damaging the book, she commanded in a firm voice, "Come to me *Lann an Cheartais.*"

Her blade whistled free of the sheath and flew over her head to pause in front of her. She gripped the hilt and said, "Behold Shannon's sword, which I carry with great respect and honor."

"The letter is yours," the disembodied guardian voice declared.

Really? She could take it?

Keeping her questions to herself, she replaced the sword in the sheath and reached for the letter, careful not to touch the chronicle pages.

Energy sparked when her fingers clamped over the letter. She lifted it up. Tiny stars showered and floated away from the thick envelope.

She broke the red wax seal with trembling fingers and removed three crisp pages folded in half.

Her heart pounded wildly. This could be the moment she found out who she was and how she possessed Shannon's sword. Had Shannon decreed a being with enough power could take it or only a descendant?

Casidhe swallowed, ready to find out and fearful at the same time. She'd believed over the years that she had truly been part of Herrick's clan. That fantasy crashed and burned.

Her hands were shaking too hard. She held the letter against her chest and closed her eyes.

Skarde had been Shannon's twin. Everyone knew how close twins were and he'd sounded adamant that his twin sister had birthed no children.

Casidhe had to be realistic.

It was time to stop clinging to a fantasy and accept reality. She'd never admitted it out loud, couldn't without humiliating herself, but she'd wanted to be a descendant of purpose. To be more than an accident of fate born with a fairly simple power to translate books and thus a default recipient to claim the sword.

Much as she loved her ability to translate words, compared to beings who could teleport and use kinetics, her gift came in way last.

She had Daegan and a future.

That was enough.

Ready to read the letter and accept whatever direction the words sent her in, she pulled the letter away from her chest, her mind calm. Opening the folded sheets, she raised two fingers on her right hand to scan the text, listening to Shannon in her mind.

*I am sad to leave my family, but the day my mother or father read these words I will no longer live. I endured to do my best as a child of our powerful dragon shifter clan, happy to raise my sword alongside our clan and my family to defeat enemies.*

*I fear many clans have been tricked, ours included. The red dragon has never attacked a clan. King Gruffyn's son holds the power of a demigod by an unknown goddess mother, one powerful enough to gift King Gruffyn with a dragon shifter unmatched in power. I say this knowing every one of our dragon shifters are exceptional.*

*Daegan of King Gruffyn strived for peace all his days.*

*I hold him in high regard. For many years in my youth, I wished to have been chosen as his match.*

Casidhe pulled back. A rush of jealousy brought about her ire. This had been two thousand years ago. Still, she didn't like any woman thinking to catch Daegan's eye.

Shaking her head at herself, Casidhe kept reading.

*Brynhild, the one who never longed for a mate and children, was chosen instead. If my father is reading this, I wish you to know I understood. She was both the firstborn daughter and a powerful warrior. Their union would have produced highly gifted children had Daegan not refused the match.*

*I still laugh at how Brynhild quietly threatened to kill Daegan if he thought to mount her, then raged at his rejection. My sister has always been a strange one.*

*Yes, I am dithering about finishing this, but I must admit something to you both which pains me for many reasons.*

*Mother, I have always held your advice to my heart. Your words never sent me astray. I must admit I failed to adhere to an important warning and paid a price.*

Casidhe's heart quickened with curiosity.

*You recall the year I left to travel. Skarde became quite angry with me, but I needed to discover who I was on my own and what future awaited me. You were the only one who withheld complaint. I thank you for smiling and wishing me well.*

*By my second week of flying, I had observed a few tribes in different lands. I found no dragons but many interesting animals. I flew in dragon form each day then slept in human form at night. While flying over blue water that rivaled the color of our seas, my dragon followed the line of white sand spilling into a forest of huge trees with palms. Not a forest as any I had ever seen before.*

*My dragon glided low. We watched large fish beneath the surface and smaller ones darting in the shallows. We had been searching for a larger animal for my dragon to feed upon.*

*A wyvern burst from the thick forest and attacked us.*

*I was shocked. Why would a wyvern attack a dragon?*

*And why had I not sensed this beast sooner? Majik had to be involved.*

*We battled, but the wyvern had attacked from below, striking my dragon's belly and ripping apart a large wound. My dragon flew beautifully and buried the wyvern in ice.*

*I believe the beast to have been crazed. The strange gray eyes were more dead than alive.*

*My dragon had ended up out over the bay and struggled to fly to the bank. Had we shifted, I would have been too injured to survive the swim. By not shifting, my dragon risked sinking to the depths before healing.*

*We barely reached the sandy shore. My dragon collapsed. Everything became black. I do not know how long we slept, but when my dragon awoke, we were in the middle of the lush forest.*

*A tribe of humans with painted faces and arms surrounded us as my dragon awakened. Each held a deadly spear.*

*My dragon's chest wound had been sewn closed with a heavy cord.*

*When my dragon jerked around to stand, the natives backed away and pulled up their spears for attack.*

*I was not sure we could fly away before being stabbed in the unhealed wound by every warrior.*

*A man appeared suddenly wearing a tunic, flowing pants to his ankles, and white cloth wrapped around his head. I thought he had teleported, the same gift Daegan possessed.*

*The natives fell to their knees at once showing respect to this leader.*

*So many things I wish to say about that time.*

*I admit I am once again darting around the entire story. It is written in my journals. You have my permission to read those.*

Having completed a page, Casidhe slid the first one to the back of the stack. Had Shannon included how to find her journals in this letter? Casidhe kept reading.

*No longer am I able to avoid my shame. I spent a month with this man, a jinn. I close my eyes, sure you are shouting at me, Mother. You warned me, but we both know fate is fickle with a mind of its own.*

*I had a child by this man.*

Casidhe squeezed her eyes, which were filling with tears. Emotion flooded her, clogging her throat. This had to be confirmation that Shannon, an ice dragon shifter, was her ancestor. Sure she knew the ending, Casidhe hurried on, anxious to read every word.

*This is where I have traveled whenever I requested time alone over the years.*

*Skarde took my absences to heart, so sure he had wronged me in some way. Please tell him the truth and lighten his heart. I was never unhappy with my family. I love you all, even Brynhild who refuses to show her feelings and Herrick in his hardheaded way.*

*I gained a promise from my mate, Chaakir. If I should fail to arrive for my annual visit, he must deliver our child to meet my family. I ask of you to show them both love. You do not have to announce who they are as this mating will surely embarrass you, but I wish you to know my child and the man who holds my heart. I wish for my child to inherit my journals.*

*I did not want to admit this while alive and live each day with the disappointment in your eyes.*

*I have never known the mind of a coward, but I believe cowardess to be failure to act when possessed by fear.*

*I do not believe the love I shared and baby I birthed as a failure but a choice. Father chose you and loves you. You said jinn males could not be trusted, but you would not say all jinn males were unworthy had you known my mate.*

*My mate believes our precious little girl shall be jinn but not her descendants. He was told by a prophet he would birth a child of two bloods who would live as a jinn, give birth to one daughter and two boys, then live until gray hair covered her head. One female descendant from each generation after would be born with an unusual power.*

*This made me smile before he explained how one child would rise from rags to call upon a sword no one else could wield, the only one to possess this weapon. I asked him to describe what the prophet said of the sword. He spoke every detail of my sword though this prophet had never seen my blade. I left my sword with Skarde each time I traveled.*

Heart pounding loud in her ears, Casidhe carefully read each following word through blurry eyes.

*I wish for you to gift my child with this letter so she will know my mate's words and mine to her below.*

*Beloved child of my heart, your father and I love you very much. If I am not the one to hand you this letter, I no longer live. You must pass along these words to females in every generation. The one who calls my sword to her shall possess the power of both bloods. She shall not unlock all her gifts until she bonds with a mate. There is nothing more powerful than a bond formed of love. If she bonds with a jinn, she shall become a very powerful jinn, one who shall lead. Such a choice would unlock far greater power than most jinns have ever experienced and bestow her with gifts beyond imagination.*

*If she bonds with another powerful supernatural, her jinn powers shall grow no stronger and she shall become something different. The descendant who takes possession of my sword may think to become a dragon if she bonds with a dragon shifter. The prophet claims this is not possible. Should she choose any other supernatural than a jinn mate, the outcome could be monstrous and deadly.*

Casidhe's lips parted.

She didn't want to die.

She didn't want Daegan to die.

What if she became a monster and killed him?

# CHAPTER 9

BRYNHILD'S DRAGON LANDED ON THE wide ledge jutting out into the hollow mountain range surrounding the entrance to her new home in France.

This had turned out to be a perfect place for her.

She had Joavan to thank. He had been so angry with her. Perhaps he would be cooking when she surprised him with the news Daegan still lived.

That should soothe his bruised ego.

Then she would bring back his laugh with robust sex.

Shifting to her human form and dressing casually, she sauntered down the hall and through the gated entrance.

With one deep whiff, she knew no one cooked.

Joavan could not be gone.

She continued on to her hoard room, her footsteps on the stone floor loud in the stillness. She would search for rugs soon to soften the sounds and begin putting her touch on each area, making this truly her home.

When she reached her treasure room, the emptiness hit her in the chest.

He was truly gone.

All alone, she could admit to herself the ache in her chest had never happened before. Nor had she felt this deep loneliness before meeting Joavan.

He had really left her.

Yes, she'd annoyed him, but she often annoyed him. Had he not realized she would help him find his amulet?

Her conscience had rarely been offered a voice in the past when she believed her actions in war were justified, but now it had plenty to say.

Evidently, she had not given enough consideration for what

was important to him. Grudgingly, she admitted she might have been too focused on her needs to hear his.

Her conscience brought up another point. If she'd killed Daegan, Joavan might have had to wait too long to find the amulet.

Again, she nodded as she walked deeper into the larger area of the treasure room.

Why did she have to feel bad about all that when she was already beating herself up over her tarnished honor? In hindsight, killing Daegan would have been a grievous error for many reasons.

First and foremost, she would have killed a man who had not harmed her family as she'd believed. That would not have been retribution, but a slaying.

In being so determined to take down Daegan, she had broken Joavan's trust.

The most surprising part of all that was how much it hurt to not see him again. She missed his laughter already. She missed his warm touch even more.

"Do not be foolish," she snapped at herself for acting like a weak woman. Men were easy to find. She understood the world better and would survive without him.

She squatted in front of one stack of gleaming gold family pieces, lifting a chalice with a dent. She smiled at remembering when she'd made Skarde angry enough to throw it at her and miss, striking a corner of the stone wall. She'd kept it in her hoard, not because it was any more valuable than other chalices, but for the memory.

Skarde had always been the peacemaker, too nice by half.

She'd wanted to see what it would take to rile him up. Her even-tempered brother could turn into a monster when pushed hard enough.

For years afterward, she showed him respect by not crossing that line again. Of course, she still poked at him. That was her nature. He would glare at her and she'd laugh.

Then he'd laugh.

Such a small thing to remember, but her chest felt heavy with the loss of that laugh. She had always expected to be part of a large family with all the bickering and laughs.

Sighing, she placed the chalice back down.

It felt strange to be alone, no longer one of five.

As for Daegan, had she succeeded in defeating his red dragon, she would have fallen deep into despair. It would have happened the moment she learned the truth about a wyvern pretending to be his red dragon when she could not reverse that action.

With this new knowledge, she would find a way to regain her honor.

To do so would take some serious thinking.

Standing up, she picked through pieces and sorted them according to where she would have shelves built to store everything. The time dragged by with her listening to every sound, determining it was not Joavan returning.

No! She would not think about the smooth-talking Faetheen!

She reached the end of three small stacks and found her shield leaning against the wall. How many times had she lifted her shield and sword without a thought before flying into battle?

Holding her hand out, she called out an order in her native tongue.

The shield flew to her hand, pausing in front of her, waiting for her fingers to curl around the handhold. Memories flooded her of standing tall with her family to protect their people and send an enemy running. She squeezed her fingers tighter, suffering a pang of longing to have her original life back. To feel the warmth of her mother's love and her father's respect. She swallowed hard, pushing down the emotion threatening to buckle her and kissed her shield.

If only she could call her sword to her the same way, but she'd tried again in different places. Her sword would come to her no matter where it rested. Something blocked her weapon from obeying.

She struck a pose and moved the shield back and forth, feeling the urge to battle again. No one could wield her sword except her.

Where was her beloved *Lann Saoirse*?

She suddenly stopped.

She knew how to find her sword.

# CHAPTER 10

CASIDHE CAREFULLY GRIPPED SHANNON'S LETTER, still processing what she'd learned. She was absolutely Shannon's descendant, an ice dragon shifter descendant.

This was the time to dance around celebrating over learning so much about herself.

She might be more excited if the letter hadn't put a cloud over choosing to be with Daegan. He hadn't wanted the two of them to bond without knowing if she could accept his power.

She had been willing to risk that danger only because she believed her and Daegan's powers were drawn to each other, but to risk turning into something that might kill Daegan? That was worse than becoming a monster.

She could not bind him to her until she knew more about her power.

How could she have come to this point only to face a more crushing decision?

Daegan would be anxious to find out what she'd learned.

She'd need time to digest the letter's information.

Until she could find Shannon's journals or research jinn history, the *real* history written by jinns and not someone who filled in empty places with wild guesses, she could not bond with Daegan.

Damn. Damn. *DAMN!*

This was to be her moment of truth, not a bottomless well of new mysteries.

She folded the letter and placed it back inside the envelope, then hesitated to just stuff it in her backpack. What if the chronicle guardian took offense?

But the voice had given her the letter.

Screw it. Casidhe found a safe place for the letter in a pocket.

Lifting the backpack into place and buckling up with fresh confidence, she asked the bodyless chronicle guardian, "Would it be possible to move these chronicles to another place on King Eógan's land?"

"No."

Okay, then. Maybe Daegan could bring Skarde here soon and he might shed light on what had happened to Shannon's journals. The most realistic answer was the journals had burned when the castle fell.

Time to get moving. "Thank you for allowin' me to read the chronicles of the ice dragon family." She had figured out to be precise with her words and acknowledge the family often.

When the guardian voice said nothing in response, Casidhe nudged with, "I am not sure how to leave, but it is time for me to go. If you would—"

The room began to slowly spin.

What was it with supernatural energy that could not allow her to finish a damn sentence? Oversized powerful egos.

She shouldn't think negative thoughts when she had yet to find her way back to Daegan.

Holding her arms across her middle, she remained still as the spinning picked up speed and formed into a light blue cone of power once more. No threads reached out to her, but neither did they slap her out of the living snow cone.

Pale blue threads changed into sparkling white and blue as if she had been molded inside a diamond now spinning beneath the sun.

Nothing new happened.

Why hadn't the guardian told her how to exit this whirlwind?

Casidhe took a step back, then another, and the outer wall surrounded her.

She backed up again and the glow shrank to the size of a small campfire.

"*Casidhe!*" Daegan bellowed.

She spun around.

He still remained on the lower level, but he was not the calm man she'd left before entering the library shielding the ice dragon chronicles. She'd never seen panic in his face. He tried to hide the emotion, but he'd been worried.

She had to walk across the wide upper level to reach the steps to him. "What?"

His eyes blazed with relief. "What have ya been doin' all this time?"

"I'm sorry, Daegan. Did you think the blue energy harmed me?" Hurrying down the steps, he met her at the bottom.

She didn't get a chance to speak before he locked her in his arms and held her firmly against his chest with his chin on her head. His heart thumped furiously.

This feeling of being wrapped in love was worth whatever it took to find all the answers. She wanted forever in this world and the next with Daegan, but not if bonding turned her into something hideous.

When he eased his hold and lowered her to the floor, he did not release her. He cupped the back of her neck, his big fingers pushing up into her hair. "'Twas only a moment of blue energy, then it vanished with you."

"Oh, wow. Uhm, how long was I gone?"

"Last time I spoke to Tristan a few minutes ago, he said an hour and a half had passed."

"Huh. Felt like ten minutes." She ran her hand over his beard and stroked his cheek.

Now that he had her in front of him, Daegan caught her hand to kiss the palm. "Did ya find out anythin'?"

What could she share that she'd learned and not lie? "The ice dragon chronicles are massive. When the energy settled down, I stood in a library type of place, completely circular and really tall. It has this female guardian."

"Is she a goddess?" Daegan's hands moved to her shoulders, rubbing gentle circles at the tops of her arms.

"Just a voice. No body or holographic image, but she controls the chronicles. Once I knew how to ask questions correctly, she brought me the chronicle with the last entry. I figured that might be the most pertinent right now. I only read the final pages. That's where I found a letter from Shannon specifically left for the one who possesses her sword."

His face relaxed as he listened intently. "What did she say, lass?"

"A lot of things. I need some time to absorb it all, but she had a child." Her skin rippled with chills again at speaking those words out loud. Her smile felt crooked but full of joy. "Skarde did not know he had a niece."

Daegan's face split with a huge grin. He gripped her shoulders and leaned down giving her a kiss that reached her toes. "Ya are her descendant?"

This was where answering got dicey. "Yes, but I have inherited strange blood. It's not as simple as havin' dragon shifter blood."

Frowning, he lifted his head. "What do ya speak of?"

"She mated with a jinn. Because of the jinn blood she carried along with dragon shifter blood, her first born was expected to be jinn. I need to find jinn records referencin' this child to know more about the descendants. Shannon and her mate kept their relationship secret. Based on when the chronicles ended, I don't think her mother or father ever met the child, but Shannon had wanted that to happen. Her letter had been sealed and slipped into the chronicle pages to be opened by her mother, father, or a family member upon her death."

Casidhe's shoulders lifted and dropped with a long breath. "I'm thinkin' they died with her so none have read this letter before me."

Daegan pulled his hands back and threaded his fingers and cupped his hands behind his head. "Do ya know more of your power?"

"Not exactly. I have to read the letter again and possibly discuss it with Skarde. He might be able to help me understand Shannon's words better."

"Ya have the letter with ya? The guardian allowed ya to leave with it?"

"Yes, but the chronicles can't be moved. She said the letter was mine, which I took to mean it was not part of the chronicles."

Daegan stared over her head, blinking slowly. "I would have to bring Skarde here for him to read the chronicles."

"True, but the good news is that as long as we can access this cavern, he can read them. He didn't know where they were so Brynhild and Herrick might not know."

Daegan shook his head at that. "Does not make sense. How would Skarde, Brynhild, and Herrick find the chronicles once their parents were dead?"

She'd had the same question in the back of her mind while traveling here. "I thought about that and think Herrick might know the location. Based upon what I know of him, he never cared for the chronicles or accurate information about your family passed down by the Luigsechs. I am not a blood Luigsech, but I never knew who actually birthed me. For now, I'll take what I learned today and begin to build my own history."

Lowering his arms, Daegan smiled at her. A sweet, welcoming smile. "I have felt your distress over sortin' through lies about your past. There shall be time to hunt for more once the Imortiks are gone. I am hopin' the venom in my body shall leave when the Imortiks are forced behind the death wall. When that happens, I shall take ya wherever ya wish to go to research."

Stopping the Imortiks hung over any hope for a future.

She stepped up and hugged him around the waist. "Thank you for comin' here with me. I would never have found this cavern." She kissed his chest and pulled her head back to look up. "We make a good team."

"Aye, we do." He took his time kissing her, running his tongue past her lips to engage hers.

Her energy spun and tingled across her arms then buzzed between them, reaching for his.

When he pulled back, he unlatched the buckles on her backpack. "Ya have carried this long enough. I do not care to see ya bearin' the weight, though I know ya are capable." He eased her out of the straps and adjusted them to loop his arms through.

She turned, taking a last look at the gleaming treasures. "You want to take a closer look before we go?"

"Nay. The energy does not allow me to climb the steps."

Another indication she truly possessed dragon shifter blood. Why couldn't she have been born a dragon shifter? That would have solved any bonding problem between her and Daegan.

"I spoke to Tristan," Daegan announced, pulling at the straps to settle the backpack. "A group of tourists came while ya were within the energy and are just now fillin' vehicles to depart."

When Daegan and Casidhe teleported to the cliffs with Tristan's aid, Daegan addressed everyone. "I know ya have questions. We must leave soon. I feel the venom burnin' more. We may be drawin' in Imortiks."

Kleio's eyes flared with fright, then she calmed just as quickly.

Casidhe realized Kleio had stayed when she'd originally mentioned leaving with the tourists. "Are you ready to return to where you're stayin', Kleio?"

"I settled my debt this morning at the local inn. I have all I own in a bag beneath this cape and am heading to be with family."

Daegan stepped up to ask, "Where would this be?"

"The Isle of Man. I am from a family of fishermen and gifted women."

"We shall take ya there if ya are ready."

A smile lifted her face from calm to joyous. "I would deeply appreciate this."

"Tristan?" Daegan glanced over his shoulder to where Tristan stood sentry watching their backs.

"I'm ready when you are, boss. I saw it on the map when we were hunting this place." Tristan walked over with his phone out for Kleio. "I've made the island as large as I can. You need to point out a place for us to arrive unnoticed."

"It is simple." She studied the small island between Ireland and the United Kingdom. "This spot where sheep graze this time of year. I will be happy to walk from there to my family's village."

Casidhe took Daegan's hand. She did not have to, she just liked the way his face softened when she touched him.

Kleio had been spot-on about where to teleport.

They appeared on a hill above a smattering of sheep in the gentle valley beyond. Casidhe hadn't expected to feel such a loss at saying goodbye to Kleio and waited as the seer thanked Daegan and Tristan.

Kleio seemed hesitant to leave. She told Daegan, "I am here because Janus, the god who gifted me with the ability to see around me what others are not able to view, had recently tasked me with a mighty duty. I have followed his guidance since a very young age. For the first time in all these years, he placed my future and that of this world in my hands."

"How could he lay all that on you when you were livin' in the middle of nowhere?" Casidhe couldn't decide what to do with her hands now that Daegan had the backpack. She crossed her arms.

Kleio huffed out a laugh. "At first, I had a similar thought. I felt empowered and overwhelmed at the same time. At our last meeting, he said *'Your vision will change your path and your path will change the course of the human world. The world will either survive what is coming or burn into eternity.'* Through meditation and looking internally, I realized what his words had truly meant."

Sweeping a look at all the expectant gazes waiting on her next words, Kleio explained, "It was not complicated. I had visions of Jennyver being in Herrick's lair. I knew then I had to take a different path than the one influenced by Herrick's decisions. In taking this new path, I had to stand against Herrick to show Casidhe the truth, which had been hidden from her and all of us. In doing so, it forced Casidhe to take a stand. I feared I had made a huge mistake until I saw you call up Shannon's sword in front of Herrick and watched what I believe had been her armor form around your body."

Casidhe's skin prickled at that memory. She rubbed her arms. "In that moment, I felt I had lost everythin' and decided I would rather die standin' than live as his servant." Daegan's arm snaked around her shoulders, pulling her to him. He kissed the top of her head.

He was showing how proud he was of her in spite of how they'd parted ways that day in the mountains.

Kleio nodded with a grand smile. "Yes, that was an incredible moment. In giving aid to you, I also found my inner strength and broke the chains of complacency. That power is what allowed me to discover the last part of my path, which led me to meet you at the ice dragon castle ruins."

Tristan had watched the seer as every word spilled from her lips. "Wow, that's huge."

"Yes, but my duty is complete. I have changed my path and my path changed the course of the world with Casidhe recognizing her powers and her past as well as partnering with the red dragon. The fate of the world depends upon all of you." She looked to Daegan. "Your sister is still alive and safe. If the world survives, so shall she. I have had no visions informing me of where she is now, but her future shall be placed in your hands at some point."

Casidhe hugged an arm around Daegan. "We'll find her."

He seemed unable to speak and just nodded.

Tristan's fingers twitched against the side of his jeans as if he wanted to get moving.

Casidhe asked Daegan, "Do you think Kleio and her family are in danger here from Imortiks?"

He frowned at the question. "I do feel venom in my leg, but 'tis just there, not throbbin'. Still, it would be wise to inform your people to be careful."

"Thank you, but we are safe," Kleio assured them with the confidence of someone capable of knowing what lay ahead of her. She took Casidhe's hand, squeezing it gently. "Trust your heart and your ability to make the right choices. You are far stronger than Herrick ever realized. His loss for being so blinded by only what he wanted."

"Thank you for everythin'." A lump of emotion formed in her throat and her eyes burned.

With a smile and nod at the men, Kleio struck out, walking happily down the slope toward the sheep. An easy breeze toyed with the hem of her cape.

Casidhe envied the seer for her peace and going to live with her family, but this woman had given her the tools she needed to find her own peace and family.

"We've got a problem, boss."

She flipped around at the urgency in Tristan's voice. "What's goin' on?"

Tristan grimaced when he explained, "I just heard from Trey that Quinn is in bad shape."

"How was he injured?" Daegan asked.

"Not a body injury. The last I saw of him was not long before you called me to Egypt. The team was using Reese to find I-zubrrali, who led them into a trap with Imortiks and demons. The Beladors dealt with that then Reese didn't feel I-zubrrali anymore. Quinn was taking the team to his downtown building, so I went to help another team Trey had called me about. Evidently after I left, I-zubrrali showed up again. I don't have all the details, just the bottom line. An Imortik jumped Reese and now possesses her."

Daegan cupped his head, pain clear in every fine line of his face. "We must find her and take her somewhere safe."

"Right now, Evalle needs us. She told Trey that Quinn is having a meltdown. They can't stop him from going out to hunt for Reese. She's keeping two Beladors on him around the clock, but she's afraid the team, Quinn, or both are going to be harmed. We all know a sane Quinn does not want that to happen."

"What can I do to help you, Daegan?" Casidhe asked gently.

He lifted his head and what she saw in his face physically hurt. "Would ya go to Treoir to start readin' the grimoire volumes we have, but promise to not touch them?"

She couldn't refuse him this. "Of course, I will. Let me take my backpack."

He quickly released the buckles and shrugged out of it, then put it on her, resetting everything to fit her.

She didn't know when she'd see him next and mentioned, "I'd like to talk to Skarde again at some point, but only if you're okay with my speakin' to him."

"I am fine with ya speakin' to anyone in Treoir ya wish." He glanced at his right-hand man. "I shall wait for ya here, Tristan. Please introduce her to Lanna and Garwyli, who shall make sure Casidhe has all she needs."

"*Wait!*" Casidhe shouted. She felt like a foolish young woman, but she was young after all and had done her share of foolish things recently, so she might as well own it.

"What, lass?"

"This." She hugged him, holding tight against the tension turning his body into a stone statue. She did not let go until his muscles eased and he wrapped his arms around her.

He kissed her, taking a simple touch from wonderful to

amazing, then kissed her forehead and her hair. "Thank ya. I miss ya already, but I shall return soon."

She nipped his lip and smiled up at him. "We're gonna win this, Daegan. Take care of your people. I'll wait in Treoir, but I'll come to you at a moment's notice if you call. I'm here to help."

"Good lass."

"Why aren't you comin' with us then leavin' for Atlanta from Treoir?"

Daegan's gaze strayed. "I shall contact Trey to find out everythin' I can while Tristan is gone. Then we shall move more quickly in Atlanta."

She didn't believe him, but she would not fight him. Maybe he wanted a few minutes for himself to sort out his thoughts. If no one else would grant him that, she could.

That was reason enough to not argue.

His reluctant hands released her, then he nodded at Tristan.

Her last vision of Daegan before the world lost focus was of him standing with arms crossed, legs apart, ready for whatever unholy battle he had to face next.

# CHAPTER 11

CASIDHE BLINKED AT THE DARKNESS, expecting sunshine in Treoir, but this realm did not function according to the human world. Still, lights shining on the castle and illuminating the grounds spreading out before her presented a breathtaking image.

"I'll introduce you to Garwyli," Tristan announced and started to walk off.

She quickly said, "Tristan? I know we're in a hurry and don't want to delay you."

He looked over his shoulder but did not turn. "But?"

In three quick strides, she caught up to him. "We can talk and walk, right?"

"Sure."

Ugh, were they back to one-word answers? She wanted to clear up any issues he had with her right now. "I got a chance to explain everythin' to Daegan while we were in Egypt."

Tristan lifted his hands. "What Daegan does is none of my business."

"*Dammit!*" She had wondered if Tristan had only encouraged Daegan to take a shower with her for Daegan's benefit, which would not do. She wanted Tristan to understand she would protect Daegan with her life, too. It would have been nice for Daegan to have had time to inform Tristan of how she and his boss had worked out their relationship so they could have a real one.

She'd been right to give Daegan the one thing he couldn't ask his people for, alone time to think.

Tristan stopped suddenly. "What's wrong now?"

She jumped in front and turned to face him. "What you think *does* matter to Daegan, *and* to me."

That surprised him. "Why?"

"Because you're as close to him as a brother, which I'm thrilled about. I don't want him fightin' the world alone. I will do my best to help every way I can, but it's more difficult for him if there is conflict between us."

"I've been nice to you," Tristan argued, but he clearly still had reservations and all his politeness would not hide those.

"Just tell me what it is you want to know and I'll answer your questions, but don't act like this doesn't matter."

Tristan said nothing and stared off past her.

She could be just as stubborn, but she didn't want to be since Daegan was waiting on Tristan to return so they could go help Quinn.

Tristan released a soft sigh. "If Daegan thinks you're all in with him, that's fine as long as you are." His jaw flexed before he continued. "I can't take another front-row seat to watching what happened to him when he thought you had betrayed him to the ice dragons and with Jennyver. I understand it was not what any of us thought, but it was agonizing to see Daegan gutted that way."

She heaved a deep breath. "I understand. You have no idea how seein' the disappointment and hurt in Daegan's face that day in the mountains cut me as much as hearin' him say he never wanted to see me again."

Tristan at least grimaced at that reminder.

Not finished, she said, "Daegan and I had agreed to not jump to conclusions, but he did. I don't hold it against him, not now, but we cleared the air and made a commitment to each other in Egypt. I am willin' to fight monsters to protect him and hold onto what I feel for him with all my strength. I just do not wish to fight you and cause him more pain."

Tristan scratched his head. "Fair enough." He took his time forming his next words. "I can wait to hear the rest of the story at some point. Based on what I saw on that sandy beach, he clearly cares for you and trusts you *again*. I am willing to do the same once more, but that's all. If you ever betray him again, I will drag him away from you. That being said, if he has decided you're his, then we will all support his choice."

A rush of relief shook her. "Agreed." She extended her hand. "Shake on it."

He laughed, breaking the tension, and clasped her hand.

Before he could release her hand, she covered his with her other one and leaned in. "I give you a vow that I intend to protect Daegan and care for him in the way that will make you proud."

"I would say you don't have to, but that would discount this conversation." A big fat grin broke across Tristan's face. "Thank you. Now, we need to get moving."

"I'm ready."

Tristan strode forward with faster steps. As he neared the castle, guards stood with weapons ready until they saw him and lowered their swords.

They watched her with suspicion.

Stopping abruptly, Tristan took in every guard's face. "This is Casidhe Luigsech. She is here as Daegan's guest. Please pass that through the ranks so everyone will know."

Every head dropped in respect.

She hadn't earned their respect yet, but she intended to with her translation skills. She smiled and said, "Nice to meet all of you."

Tristan hurried up the steps and opened the tall doors.

She rushed to catch up, walking into Treoir-freaking-castle. *Try not to gawk like an idiot*, she reminded herself. Talking had always been her go-to safeguard when nervous. "Sounds like things are a mess in Atlanta."

"It's bad, but Daegan will also struggle with you being away from him." Tristan didn't turn his face to her but she caught a smirk.

Grinning at how nice it felt to regain her friend, she teased, "It'll be good for him to miss me the way I already miss him." Then she chose her words carefully. "Daegan is everythin' to me, Tristan. I mean it when I say I will work hard here and do all in my power to protect him, even from himself."

Tristan had slowed before reaching a door six more steps down. "What do you mean by that?"

"Daegan has yet to figure out he is only one man. He is determined to carry the weight of protectin' the world on his shoulders. We can all help him, but he won't rest until we stop this Imortik invasion and none of us will have a life until then either."

"It's who Daegan is."

"I know, but ... " She thought on what Daegan had to face next. "I met Quinn once. He was very nice to me and clearly a good friend to Daegan. Who is this person Reese?"

"Quinn is a friend and more. He is the Belador Maistir for North America, one of the most powerful and level-headed Beladors I've ever known. He's falling apart because he had to watch Reese, the woman carrying his baby, get possessed by an Imortik."

Casidhe grabbed her throat. "That's horrendous. I'm sorry for him. That's unimaginable." She had to send Tristan on his way. "Remember what I said about Daegan tryin' to do this alone. He trusts you completely. I know he'll listen to you if he needs to step back to survive. Please watch over him."

"I will."

The door opened and an old guy, like older than dirt, with long white hair and a grizzly white beard to his chest, stuck his head out. "Ya bringin' her in or not?"

Tristan let out a sigh under his breath and walked over to address the old codger. "This woman is Casidhe—"

"Luigsech. I know, I know."

"Do you know why she's here?" Tristan countered in a testy voice.

"Of course. She is ta translate the grimoire volumes." Garwyli glanced over at her with sharp blue eyes, an odd contradiction in the wrinkled face. "Come along, lass."

Casidhe had been feeling really confident until now but had to force her feet to move. "Bye, Tristan."

"Good luck."

Why would he say good luck? She paused. "What did you mean by—"

He disappeared.

Stop stalling. She spun around and stepped into the room where the old guy stood on the other side of the door, eyeing her as if he had the ability to open her mind and pull out whatever he wanted.

"Hi." Stupid opening since she'd already met him and he knew who she was plus why she was here, but that had been the only word to escape her brain.

"Save yar worryin'. I shall not harm ya." No smile supported his words.

She stepped closer to him. "If you'll show me somewhere out of your way to sit and read, I promise to be quiet."

He shook his head. "Nay."

Her heart jumped around, trying to decide if she'd foolishly stepped into a dangerous situation here.

The door behind her opened. *"You are here!"*

Casidhe turned quickly to face the young woman she'd seen standing with Daegan in the mountains. The same one she believed had controlled Skarde with majik.

This young woman could not be twenty, walking forward with her blond curls bouncing and a welcoming smile. She extended her hand and spoke with an accent from another country, maybe the Ukraine. "I am Lanna. You have met Garwyli. He is grumpy today."

"I am no such thing," the old geezer grouched.

That's all it took for Casidhe to relax her shoulders and shake hands. "I guess everyone knows who I am."

"Not all, but many will by the end of this day. Are you hungry or thirsty?"

"Water would be nice."

The old guy snapped, "'Tis on the table."

Casidhe looked over to find a silver metal pitcher with rivulets of water running down the side and two mugs of water poured. That had not been there a moment ago.

Lanna picked them up and handed one to Casidhe. "Do you know Garwyli is druid?"

"Nope." Casidhe kept drinking, anything to avoid speaking too much now.

"His majik is much strong. Mine will be one day."

Placing the cup back on the table, Casidhe thanked Garwyli, who finally smiled underneath all that white beard. Casidhe said, "From what I saw in the Caucasus Mountains, you have plenty of power."

Lanna's smile held no ego or boast but more like a cat hiding a secret. "Thank you." She waved her arm toward the back area of the room, which seemed to be a dark gray fog. "We shall read books."

Casidhe could see no wall. As she started forward, she glanced at the table. The pitcher and glasses were gone.

Evidently, the druid was a neat freak.

With Lanna as her guide, Casidhe strolled out of Garwyli's imposing presence to the rear of his territory where the dimness began to lighten to a white mist. As Lanna stepped closer, the mist cleared away, revealing a massive library.

Casidhe stepped inside and stopped to absorb everything.

Light glowed from above now, but there were no skylights, just the feel of a softly lit dome hovering above the room. Wow. Had she died and gone to a booklover's heaven? Surrounded by an endless supply of books was a balm for her tired soul. A smile welled up in her and burst out in a silly grin.

"It is magnificent, yes?" Pride flowed through Lanna's voice.

"I have no words for it. My soul loves books."

"I did not read so much before coming here. Now, I must have time every day to read or I will be grumpy like Garwyli."

"*I am not!*" Garwyli shouted from far behind them.

Casidhe laughed, holding her belly. The rest of her tension fled, leaving her comfortable.

When had she laughed so hard?

Not since the days of being with Fenella, who had betrayed her.

Remembering her once-friend cast a shadow over the moment until Lanna touched her arm and said, "I am told all happens for a reason. We must accept rainy weather with sunshine."

Without bringing up what had hurt Casidhe so badly, Lanna reminded her of the balance in life. She'd lost what she'd considered her life when Herrick betrayed her, but she'd gained Daegan and all those connected to him.

"You're right, Lanna. Today is filled with sunshine."

Lanna led her through the aisles, explaining different scrolls and books, then walked past several aisles to a new area.

Pointing, she said, "This is library Tristan delivered for you. No one touches these books." Lanna gave her a guilty glance. "I lie. I touched books to find you for Daegan, but I put them back."

"You and Garwyli are welcome to read any of my books," Casidhe assured her.

"Wonderful! Now is time to open grimoires." Lanna walked briskly until she reached an open area with cushy chairs perfect for hours of reading. A round knee-high stone and glass table sat in front of the chairs.

Casidhe removed her backpack to place next to the chair she took and waited. Shouldn't they have gone to where the grimoire volumes had been placed?

"We must not touch volumes," Lanna warned, settling in the other chair. "Not until we know for sure if they will harm us."

"Okay, but where are they?"

Holding both hands above the table with her palms down, Lanna closed her eyes and whispered something too quiet for Casidhe to pick up.

A hushed sound blew across the table, then a bronze box she recognized appeared.

Whoa. Casidhe had been in the presence of majik many times, but had a feeling she was only observing a sliver of what power resided inside Lanna.

Serious concentration painted Lanna's face as she moved her hands while whispering words. The bronze box squealed as the heavy seal around the lid cracked, allowing the lid to elevate up and over to sit on the table.

Next, a stack of chopped up sections of a scroll floated up and out of the box to rest in front of Casidhe.

Lanna studied the position of the papyrus sheets and frowned, then called upon her majik again to move the sheets away from Casidhe, though still in her line of vision.

Next, the powerful young woman used her finger to lift a sheet and float it down in front of Casidhe. She grinned and slashed a look at Casidhe. "Garwyli will be proud. I learn to isolate majik, not use all at one time."

"Was that a problem in the past?"

Lanna admitted with a hint of guilt, "I was in basement of

giant building in Atlanta one time with humans captured by bad beings. They threatened me, my friends, and humans. I did not control emotions then and building shook with thunderstorm in basement. I could have buried us." She gave an impish grin. "I am much better now."

Casidhe's mouth opened with a silent *oh*. She had met so many beings with different powers and gifts since that infamous day when Daegan broke into her cottage.

No, he had teleported in. That seemed like a lifetime ago when it had been just under two weeks.

As Lanna watched her expectantly, Casidhe realized the woman waited for her reaction. "I bet Garwyli is havin' a field day trainin' you." She smiled to show Lanna she meant it as a compliment.

"I do as he instructs each day, but he sometimes stops early with headache." Lanna chuckled. "I think he tells me that to tease me."

"You definitely have a unique relationship. Let's see what's in this first box," Casidhe said, turning her gaze down to the yellowed papyrus. It had a dry woodsy scent. With a quick glance, she confirmed she could decipher nothing without her gift.

But would her gift work if she did not touch the pages with one hand at the same time as she had been forced to do with another book and the Egyptian hieroglyphics?

If she did touch the scroll sheets, would they burn her hand the way the bronze box had the first time?

When Lanna had everything set, she turned to Casidhe with expectant eyes. "We must all play parts when time comes to close death wall, but we must know what to do. I tried to read script." She shook her head slowly. "I have much majik, but I cannot read these words. We need gift you have had since birth. We need you."

No pressure there.

Casidhe pushed all her focus to the pages. Lanna and Garwyli knew about her gift, which saved her from explaining.

What if she failed?

How would they stop the Imortiks?

Casidhe forced her left hand down on the cushion she sat upon to keep from moving her hand out of reflex and lifted two fingers on her right hand.

Energy rose from the pages.

# CHAPTER 12

CATHBAD WALKED WITH SOME PAIN, but he would heal completely once he figured out how to kill Queen Maeve so he could take over TÅµr Medb.

His diminished power would regenerate far faster in that realm.

But he had enough power to follow Lakyle through the dark streets of the young druid's small community outside Dublin.

So many new structures in parts of Dublin, but what appeared to be older sections still had a feel of times past, though badly decayed. Bronze historical plaques along the way noted fascinating details from the time Cathbad had been in a deep sleep with Queen Maeve.

That idea had not turned out as he'd planned.

The cobblestone path he walked upon now had carried many travelers in the past, though still passable.

Cathbad had not come here to sightsee but to find out when he was expected to die.

Lakyle was slower than a snail and had taken far longer to pick out vegetables from a nearby farmer's stand than any woman cooking a meal. Cathbad shook his head at himself. He should have found a way to prevent that one from returning to another dark druid gathering. Had the young druid teleported or opened a bolt hole to travel to Newgrange Mound?

Neither mattered at this point, only what information Lakyle would tell him.

Cathbad waited at the last corner before crossing to the three-story brick apartment building where Lakyle lived. How very mundane. Lakyle would have made a better human than a dark druid.

In the next minute, a light glowed in the windows of a unit on the second floor. Lakyle passed by two of them with bags in his arms, likely headed for the kitchen.

Cathbad searched around in the dark night to find a spot out of view.

He wanted no one to exclaim at his sudden change in appearance.

Once he had himself glamoured into Ainvar's likeness and wore a dark-blue robe with a hood, Cathbad practiced Ainvar's voice.

Satisfied, he walked quietly across the street.

The robe drew attention, but in this darkness few people wasted time hurrying past him.

The entrance had a key code to unlock the door.

Cathbad checked that no one was close by and teleported to the other side of the door. He took the creaking wooden stairs to the second floor and turned left to the apartment. This had to be the one facing the corner where he'd stood observing.

He listened with his ear against Lakyle's door. The young man was chatting to someone who did not answer. Must be on his phone.

Cathbad gathered his power quickly. This last part would drain him greatly. He had to hide his aura since he could not emulate Ainvar's and his had the stain. Sweat rolled down the back of his neck as he quietly cast the spell to shield him without hiding his physical image.

He had no way to be sure it worked until he stood in front of Lakyle.

Only one chance to leave with what he needed.

After dabbing sweat from his face, he tugged the hood forward, keeping his head better hidden. Then he teleported to the other side of the door, pretty sure no furniture would be right in front of the entrance.

The apartment had no more personality inside than Lakyle. Drab furniture, gray carpet, a battered desk sat in the corner with a computer. The chair in front of it had cost a few coin.

Lakyle's high-pitched laugh cackled in the kitchen.

Cathbad moved forward silently until he stood in the middle of the living room.

"I think I have that book. Let me go check." Lakyle talked as he exited the kitchen, almost running into Cathbad.

Lakyle jumped back, eyes round as two fists and mouth stuck open. He yanked the phone back to his ear. "Got someone at the door. I'll call you back." He thumbed the phone off and lowered his hand, his entire body shaking.

That reaction still did not tell Cathbad if the glamour and aura shield worked.

Lakyle dropped his gaze and spoke with deep respect. "Seanóir. I'm humbled by your visit."

Relief swept through Cathbad with the speed of a wildfire and whipped up his anger just as quickly. He should not be standing here worrying about his appearance and dark druids should be bowing to him.

Cathbad shifted into the role of Ainvar, who believed himself to be a fatherly leader over the dark druids. Not one of the current dark druids had truly known Ainvar. Lakyle's ancestor may have revered Ainvar, but any druid who followed the dark druid leader thousands of years ago would not be so quick to think of him as fatherly. Those who had seen what a barbarian Ainvar could be to harvest any energy for dark majik took care around him.

Cathbad had no issue with Ainvar's methods, only that the prick never died and had managed to keep his presence hidden.

Using Ainvar's voice, Cathbad said, "I am exceptionally pleased for young blood in the dark druids. Our kind is a select and small group of great power. You have impressed me thus far."

Gloating, Lakyle smiled for a second, then a serious mask fell over his down-turned face to hide his prideful look. "Thank you. I am in your service at any hour of any day."

"This I know. I am visiting each of you. I must be assured all of you are prepared."

"Yes, Seanóir, I am ready."

Cathbad needed details, such as when Ainvar intended to attack him and how. If he could not get inside TÅµr Medb soon, he'd need a way to defend himself against Ainvar's personal strike force.

Not even Ainvar would want to go up against his own group of dark druids. Cathbad said, "You must know your role so well you are able to execute with precision even in your sleep and you must arrive *exactly* on time."

Nodding, Lakyle said, "I swear to you I have spent every waking minute going over the plan. On my honor, I will arrive in the national park in America precisely at daylight. I will immediately gather my power, then wait for your command to execute my part. I understand that each of us must act without hesitation or the plan will fail."

Lakyle lifted his gaze cautiously. "I will not ever be a weak link. We will slay the red dragon and return the amulet to you. We will all benefit from the amulet's power of life and be stronger for it. With you as our leader, we will rule the human world."

Cathbad's next words stalled in his throat.

He was not at the top of Ainvar's list to attack? Not that he would foolishly complain, but he'd only hoped to find the time and location of his impending battle for survival.

This visit had produced so much more information.

The leader of the dark druids intended to take down Daegan for an amulet.

What amulet?

He'd been so taken aback, he'd allowed Lakyle too much time to stare at his form. "Uhm, Seanóir, please do not think me rude, but do you realize your aura is not present?"

Cathbad almost snapped at the young druid. He caught himself and fell back into character of pretending to be Ainvar by infusing his tone with a pleasant lift. "Of course I do. I go many places this night and must keep my presence hidden. I intend to train every one of you on how to shield your aura for covert occasions."

Lakyle's gaze changed to one of adulation, so much that Cathbad might drown in it if he did not move this along. "Your dedication is exemplary, Lakyle. We thrive under the cover of darkness where others tremble. You have practiced well. Tell me exactly how you plan to reach the location for our great victory. A few had the correct location but would have arrived a hundred feet too far away. We must be precise in all things."

Adulation moment over, panic spread over Lakyle's face before he stammered out his travel plan and destination.

Sweat pebbled on his forehead as he waited on confirmation or condemnation.

"Ah, Lakyle, I would say this was a wasted trip since you are truly prepared and have the exact details, but it was worth the time to have a private moment with you."

Air expelled from Lakyle's tense body until his shoulders dropped, relieved to have been correct. "Thank you, Seanóir. I will hold this moment dear and count the minutes until I stand with you in battle."

"Until then." Cathbad teleported out to the foyer at the entrance just as a woman opened the door and squealed.

Sounding American, she recovered to snap, "Who are you?"

Returning to his normal speech, Cathbad said, "Ya frightened me as much as ya scared yourself. I am a man of the cloth. I am leavin' from comfortin' one of my sheep who lost a family member."

She yanked her purse strap back to her shoulder from where it had fallen. "Sorry about that. It's just I did not see you inside the glass door, then opened it and there you were."

"'Tis understandable in the evenin' and with my wearin' a dark robe. I must be on my way to another home."

"Oh, sorry." She backed out and held the door for him.

Human women could be of use after all.

As he blended into the shadows, Cathbad considered everything Lakyle had said, especially about the amulet providing a life power. Did Ainvar need new power to continue his pseudo-immortality?

If that happened, Cathbad would never be free of him or Queen Maeve.

An idea grew in his mind, one with great risk, but he had no other option.

This would be his only chance at survival.

If his plan succeeded, he would have all he wanted for eternity.

# CHAPTER 13

*KILL THE BELADOR AND JOIN my army or die painfully.* The master's frightening words echoed through Renata's head, shocking her into dead stillness.

Renata used all the control she could dig up to not yell that she would not kill anyone.

Definitely not her two Belador friends listening to this sickening conversation.

"You will not kill?" Timmon asked in his own voice, but with enough warning to pull a whimper from deep insider her.

She'd rather deal with Timmon. She clamped her lips shut until she could speak like a good little possessed robot. At least Timmon was speaking in his whiny voice and not the deeper sound of the Imortik master possessing his body.

Even one word from the master's voice would send fear clawing up Renata's spine.

Her personal Imortik presence, Minos-The-Idiot, shouted in her head, *Why do you make the master wait?*

She silently sent back, *The master expects us to make good decisions. To do so means not spitting out the first words that come to mind. If you make me insult him, we will both disappear, just like that weak human he destroyed.*

Minos had no comeback but did not withdraw all the way.

Hoping she sounded unemotional, Renata lifted her chin in a show of false confidence. "I am confused. I thought we were to protect Imortiks."

Timmon, aka the master, stood beside her saying nothing for a minute.

She would not be tricked by his silence, a tactic to make others, especially uncomfortable beings, start rambling.

"You are correct, but I have two new Beladors who are

dispensable. To fully possess them as you are would require time I may not have."

Oh, no, what now?

She pushed her fears aside to think strategically as she'd been taught back during her early days as a Belador. She'd already made it this far with the encouragement of her Belador friends, Kaiser and Gretchen.

No going back now.

Taking in enough air to get this said in one breath, Renata acted surprised. "You do not know how a powerful Belador controls those below him or her? We have Maistirs in charge of thousands of Beladors for that reason. I am a Maistir in training." She hoped her friends didn't snort in laughter at that empty boast. "Even with these two possessed, I should still carry the power to direct their actions. It is the reason Beladors have been so powerful for many years, but to be honest, few outside of our people understand how our hierarchy works."

Gretchen and Kaiser had pushed her to throw in with them by linking power with each other to find a way to escape. She hoped they were onboard with her seat-of-the-pants planning.

"Look at me," Timmon ordered.

Renata shifted around immediately to obey. She hated to give him what he wanted, but a good job of acting was key to pulling this off. "Yes, master?"

Timmon's voice remained higher than the true master. "Show me this control."

"How many Beladors do you wish me to use for a demonstration?" She wondered if he'd admit holding more than three Beladors in the building. How would they free any others?

"You know there are two in this aisle, yes?"

"Yes."

"Direct the one closest to you to follow your orders."

That would be Gretchen, whose body hung across a thick pole running from the front to back of the building. Her arms fell limp past her head.

Renata took two steps toward Gretchen and stopped. She lifted a hand in her friend's direction. "Wake up, Belador female."

Gretchen didn't even twitch.

Sweat formed at the back of Renata's neck. She kept her hand outstretched without moving and drew soft breaths. She needed to keep her heartrate calm.

Gretchen's eyes opened. She blinked several times and slowly turned her head toward Renata with an angry frown in place. Her gray eyes narrowed with so much hate, Renata had a moment of worry.

"Who calls me?" Gretchen demanded in a gritty voice in desperate need of water.

"As your Belador superior, I do," Renata replied. "Stand and prepare for duty."

"I will not—" Gretchen's mouth shut as her body stiffened and began dropping backward off the pole. She dropped the last few inches and stood there, shoulders hunched. "What is ... happening? I want—"

"*Silence!*" Renata ordered, cutting off Gretchen's next words. The female Belador stared in surprise at Renata, who had a moment of real concern. Was she actually drawing that reaction from Gretchen with her new Imortik energy?

*Tell the master I am here and ready*, Minos ordered, breaking into her thoughts with his sullen voice. He clearly wanted to run the show.

Renata had figured out how to slap Mr. Brown Noser into line. She sent back, *Again, I warn you we have one chance to serve the master. If he wanted to speak to you, he would have. But if you're willing to accept the blame, I will tell him what you said.*

*No.* After that one-word reply, Minos withdrew deeply this time.

Finally. What a pain he was, but at least her Imortik was not dominant. Renata shoved her mind back on the plan and hoped she wouldn't end up getting her, Gretchen, and Kaiser killed.

When the master said nothing new, Renata decided to sell this idea more and really hoped Gretchen was in there somewhere.

Lowering her hand to her side and keeping her gaze on Gretchen, Renata asked, "What is your name, Belador?"

"Athena."

Renata almost laughed at the confirmation Gretchen was still here and knew exactly what Renata was doing. Athena had been a war goddess. Unlike her hot-tempered brother, Ares, who fought like a madman, his sister had been revered for her strategic ability when it came time to battle.

Perfect.

"Are you prepared to do your duty, Athena?"

Now speaking in a calm and compliant voice, Gretchen nodded. "Yes. I will execute your orders."

Renata turned to Timmon, who seemed to be watching in fascination. She explained, "My Imortik and I have bonded fully. My powerful Imortik allows me power over these Imortik possessions as well as their Belador bodies." There, she threw a bone to Minos who she felt smile. Ick. Sticking to the script she kept making up as she went, she asked, "What else might I do for you, master?"

That last question tugged the master's attention from Gretchen and brought back Timmon in his own voice. "I want you to lead a unit to protect beings possessed by our Imortiks. Three new Imortiks leave each rift every day at this point. More will escape as rifts in the world continue to open and widen."

Oh, hell. How many rifts were in the Atlanta area alone?

She couldn't ask without drawing the wrong attention. Instead, she nodded with a solemn expression of hanging on his every word.

Timmon's face lost stress lines, replaced by a smug look. He really enjoyed being treated as the top of the food chain even if the powerful Imortik master inside him actually ran the show. She could always tell if the master took over.

Timmon's voice would change to a much deeper tone.

"Do you wish me to take both Beladors? We are trained to work in units of three for the most productive outcome." Renata never glanced away from Timmon. She wanted to convince him he owned her. She could bide her time for a chance to smash his disgusting face into the ground.

That image lifted her spirits.

Timmon seemed torn. Did he worry the master would not approve of his decisions?

Renata made herself stand very still when she wanted to fidget and tap her foot at Timmon, more a slave than she was.

"No." Timmon crossed his arms. "Leave the male."

"Of course." Renata barely got that out. Her throat thickened. She wanted to cry. How could she and Gretchen leave Kaiser? "Where is the best place for the two of us to start?"

"We are belowground. I shall take you up to the surface. A recent rift opened near Piedmont Park in Atlanta. You will go there first."

She was still in Atlanta? *Don't think about it!* Timmon was powerful. He might pick up a change in her pulse.

But she couldn't deny her excitement. She and Gretchen could contact Beladors and send them here to save Kaiser and the others.

Walking back to the front area, Timmon waited on her.

Renata stayed in character, telling Gretchen, "Follow me."

"Yes."

Moving in an unhurried way, Renata stopped within six feet of Timmon. She did not want to get any closer than necessary. Gretchen followed, pausing to stand next to Renata with her eyes facing down.

Timmon started walking away, grumbling to himself.

No, no, no. If the master took over this could get complicated. In fact, she and Gretchen might not be able to leave.

"*I've got this!*" Timmon shouted with his hands up in the air as if he spoke to someone. He turned around to head back.

Renata shoved her gaze down, too. Anything to show a sign of deference to him and the master.

Stopping to rub his head, Timmon said, "I *am* doing my part. I can't if you keep taking over me. We're supposed to share. That's what ... *shit!* I hate my cousin! I can't even say the name. That asshole compelled me to not use names, probably because I would have created a new curse with that one's name by now." Timmon's eyes glowed fluorescent yellow. "I should still contact her," he muttered to himself, falling off into looney land again.

What female was he talking about?

Timmon became still. He argued, "Two is plenty. Why?"

He must have been convulsing because his feet moved oddly, then he started breathing hard. "I will do it."

Renata glanced over at Gretchen's hand. Her friend slowly

composed a thumbs-up sign, then she relaxed her fingers.

If Gretchen thought they were okay, then Renata wouldn't panic.

"Call up the male Belador," Timmon ordered.

Renata did her best not to sag from relief. She nodded, lifted her head, and walked stiffly back to Kaiser, performing the same orders. When she returned, he walked behind her without speaking.

"We are ready to protect Imortiks," Renata offered.

Facing the exit again, Timmon walked and complained, "No. You made a deal with my cousin. You can't take over until the wall is open. You're draining too much of my energy when we fight."

Renata would feel bad for anyone else to sound so exhausted and disappointed, but clearly Timmon's cousin, who could be male or female, had abandoned him.

Who was the woman Timmon kept threatening to contact?

Standing erect and sounding less beaten down, Timmon nodded. "Yes. I can handle this." He paused, looking over his shoulder.

She affected the attentive student face but remained silent. The less she said, the better chance she had to not screw up.

"We'll go upstairs now." Timmon led the way.

The minute she got out of here and out of sight from Timmon, maybe she could reach out to Beladors. She, Kaiser, and Gretchen could take off running as soon as Timmon disappeared.

Freedom had never meant as much as this moment.

She could call Roberto.

She could find out about Devon.

She could—

"I will stay with you for today until I feel you are able to implement my orders and kill those necessary to be taken down," Timmon informed her without looking back.

Scratch her first plan.

She could do nothing with Timmon sticking close to her except wait for the moment his master took over and demanded she kill someone.

# CHAPTER 14

SMOKE ROSE IN MULTIPLE PLACES from fires across downtown Atlanta in midafternoon as Daegan appeared with Tristan on the rooftop overlooking Woodruff Park. The sound of people yelling and screaming filled the air, then shots from a weapon peppered right after.

Below, human National Guards were holding back a mass of citizens shouting curses about nonhumans hunting humans. Some were armed with weapons and others carried swords. A few had ventured out with nothing more than hand-painted signs declaring nonhumans had to die.

Did these humans think to go up against a supernatural with a sword or sign?

"That sucks." Tristan peered over the edge. "I hope Isak has some line of communication happening with the human military."

Daegan feared for the lives of all humans. "These people are not safe out on the streets. What happened to the curfew?"

"Don't know, boss. I'm guessing the military is spread out thin with supernatural and Imortik activity in other cities, and they don't want to hurt humans who aren't attacking other humans."

"Let's step back before we're spotted. While we appear human, better to stay out of the way when we cannot offer aid." Daegan reached out to Trey telepathically as he found a spot with a view of the street. *I am near Woodruff Park where a human mob is up against their military force. I see no sign of Quinn or his team.*

Trey replied, *That's because he had to move out when the military rolled in. He said he was headed to Piedmont Park. Imortiks were sighted there.*

*Any specific location in the park?*

*Quinn didn't say, but I don't think he's there yet. Stand by. I'll find out where he is.*

Daegan shared what he'd discussed with Trey.

Tristan had been staring up as a helicopter flew over quickly. "Got it." He watched until the helicopter was no more than a moving blur. "That chopper had a strange insignia on it."

"Why was it strange?"

Bringing his gaze back to Daegan, Tristan squinted. "Didn't appear to be Atlanta PD, US military, or even from Georgia. In fact, I'm not sure it was from this country."

Trey's voice jumped into Daegan's mind. *Quinn isn't at Piedmont Park yet.* Trey gave him directions, which Daegan relayed to Tristan.

"That's not far from the Georgian Hotel where I have the room." Tristan suggested, "We can teleport to the room and take off from there."

They did and teleported from the hotel to a secluded spot on a side street. From there, they reached a secondary road paralleling Peachtree Street, which had too much military traffic. Tristan claimed to have used this route often in the past and figured Quinn would do the same to avoid running up against the crowds and the National Guard.

Even here, the rumble of heavy engines and angry shouting clouded the air.

Daegan had been striding along quickly when Quinn flashed into sight two blocks up, clearly weaving his way from shadow to shadow along a street with houses.

Calling telepathically, Daegan said, *Quinn, we are right behind ya. Wait up.*

Quinn had just ducked out of view but stuck his head out from the corner of a building, looking back.

Oddly, the two Beladors who seemed to be with Quinn were a block behind him. As Daegan and Tristan caught up to those two, they filed in behind.

Daegan took in Quinn's haggard face and filthy shirt with wrinkled pants, none of which belonged on Quinn's normally put-together appearance.

What could he say to start this conversation and not sound critical?

Quinn saved him from figuring that out by speaking first. "Did your trip go well?"

"Aye. A challengin' trip, but we are back and alive." Daegan hesitated to say anything about the grimoire volumes out in the open. "I am very sorry about Reese."

"Thanks, but she's not dead yet. I have full faith in forcing the Imortiks behind the death wall and saving all of our people." Quinn tried smiling, but his face had forgotten how.

Daegan would not diminish that hope. He intended to do all in his ability to save his people, which included Reese, Renata, Devon, and the others. "We are movin' closer to this goal all the time. Ya should take a break and rest. Tristan and I can step in to help."

"I'm not ready to stop." There came the powerful man who had stood as the Maistir when Tzader had to stay in Treoir.

"Walk with me, Quinn," Daegan said and stepped away. He telepathically told Tristan to keep the other two back.

Quinn fell into step. "I know what you want to say, Daegan, but I've got to find Reese and bring her back to stay somewhere safe until this is done."

"I understand. In your shoes, I would do no less. My concern is ya are exhausted, which means ya may make a mistake to either harm yourself or one of the Beladors with ya."

"I've ordered those warriors to return to Evalle, but they told me she's taken over as Maistir and her orders stand. Bloody hardheaded woman."

If not for how serious the situation was, Daegan would have smiled at Evalle spinning the tables on Quinn by assuming responsibility.

He was damned proud of her.

"Send the men away, Daegan." Quinn shoved his hands in his pockets and stared ahead. "You know I don't want them harmed and I am not coming in."

What could Daegan do?

If he ordered Quinn to stand down, it would break his friend even more. Plus Daegan had been telling the truth. Had Casidhe been possessed by an Imortik, he would be doing all in his power to find her and keep her safe even at risk to himself.

"I shall not interfere with ya huntin' Reese if ya allow those two Beladors to remain close to ya so ya can work as a team. 'Twill limit the danger to all of ya. They shall watch your back and know the risk of bein' on patrol. When ya believe they need rest, then I ask ya to have Evalle send in two more to take their places. Can ya do that for me, Quinn?"

His friend's sad smile had a little more life this time. "Sure. I may even stop during the change of guards and grab a few hours to sleep."

Daegan did not believe his words, but Quinn had sounded sincere. He might surprise everyone when exhaustion overtook him. "Do ya have our people lookin' for Reese, too?"

Quinn stopped and turned to him. "No. I did not wish to use resources for myself."

"'Tis not just for yourself. Our patrols should be keepin' an eye out for any of our people just in case the ones missin' are not imprisoned somewhere. Ya should have Trey update the list of missin' Beladors and allies to include Reese and send images to every patrol. We do not want to attack an Imortik-possessed Belador or ally."

Rubbing the back of his neck, Quinn looked up. "You're right. We should have been doing that. I think we decided they were all captured by now, but here I am out hunting one person." His weary gaze tracked to Daegan's. "I'll tell Trey. He'll know where I am at all times if you need me."

"If I knew what Tristan and I could do this very moment, we would join ya. As it is, I must continue my hunt for the information we need."

"Absolutely." Quinn extended his hand. "Thanks, Daegan."

"Ya are welcome. Be careful, friend. I need ya." Daegan raised a hand, signaling to Tristan to bring the other two forward.

Once Quinn was on his way with his guards closer, Daegan told Tristan, "I cannot stop him now and face him at the end if he does not find Reese again."

"Hey, I get it. Just hope he doesn't get jumped in the meantime."

Daegan nodded slowly. "I must find Evalle."

"What's up with her?"

"Accordin' to Quinn, she claimed to take over as Maistir and sent those two Beladors to shadow Quinn. They would not listen to his order to leave and overrule hers."

Tristan's eyebrows climbed high on his forehead. "Da-yam. I'm impressed."

Daegan smiled. "As am I. She needs me to declare her the Maistir for her to hold the power necessary to rule our North American Beladors."

"You think she'll keep the position?"

"Aye. Quinn shall be in no condition to take over again with Reese an Imortik. If we figure out how to close the death wall and hopefully save our people, I am not so sure she shall survive. She has demonic power, which may work against her. If she does survive, Quinn needs the time left to be with her when 'tis time to give birth. I do not envy facin' that knowin' the child shall not live."

Tristan's grim sigh shuddered out. "There's no good ending to any of this for them. He loses her to the Imortik or she survives and they lose the baby."

"'Tis why I believe we should not expect much of him from now on. He has been an exceptional Maistir and cared not about Evalle takin' over now. I believe he was glad for it."

Tristan took a moment, appearing deep in thought. "She's ready to do this, but she may tell you she only claimed the title trying to rattle Quinn back into sanity. Storm will be the other hurdle. He'll be the first to admit she's qualified, but he's not going to give in easily on her taking so much on her shoulders even if she agrees."

Daegan considered the move he was about to make, which could not be temporary. Beladors faced unimaginable challenges everywhere. Those here in North America needed someone strong they would respect and follow.

Evalle would make a powerful Maistir, if she agreed.

If not, Daegan's only other choice for the role would be Tristan. That choice would severely impact Daegan's hunt for the third grimoire. Also, he knew in his heart Tristan had no wish to be a Maistir.

Daegan considered going to Evalle, but the streets were practically empty here with nothing going on due to businesses being closed. "Let's find a place for teleportin' in and out."

He strode along the narrow road until he found a deep separation between two closed business. "I wish to speak with Evalle here. Teleport her to me if she is able to leave what she is doin'."

"Will do, boss." Tristan stood silently for a moment then nodded. "Trey's hunting her. He said she was around Five Points when he heard from her ten minutes ago. I'll go there first."

With Tristan gone, Daegan turned to enter the alley.

Three steps in, Joavan appeared. "We have unfinished business, dragon."

# CHAPTER 15

REESE RAN INTO SMALL POCKETS of Imortiks while trying to avoid the master. She only managed to remain free because she had figured out her Imortik could not push her to do anything physically unless she called on her demon power.

At those times, she'd had to fight him for control of using that power.

She'd given up trying to move through downtown Atlanta at midday with military and angry humans when not presented with abandoned streets. She'd headed east of the city just for a new direction. Skulking along Virginia Avenue, she dodged over to a box for collecting donated clothes and dug to find something that would stand out.

The bright red T-shirt advertising a bar should work. She removed her shirt and pulled that one on and wrinkled her nose at the musty smell. She had a plan for when she saw Quinn again.

She'd like to think she could turn her back and leave him for his own good, but she couldn't. Not any more than Quinn could walk away from her and Junior.

But she had to come up with a way to make her being possessed easier for Quinn.

Back on the street, she had made it to a narrow strip of land with a few trees that had served as a small park for local families to bring kids and pets.

Four glowing Imortiks stood beneath the shade of a wide oak tree, not even trying to hide.

Dickweed inside her got excited. Its nasty voice seeped into her head. *I feel our master near.*

*Shut up,* she sent back.

*You do not hold the power,* Dickweed crabbed at her.

Talking mentally to it, she said, *Let's consider your situation. I have the body. You jumped on for the ride. I have the demon power and will turn it on an Imortik if you keep harassing me. So who's the bitch now, huh?*

As she shut down her Imortik, she angled around, sneaking up closer to the four Imortiks.

A tall skinny guy told a woman next to him, "You will kill the next human to arrive."

"Yes, master."

He was the master? He couldn't see the woman's fear flash with her facing away from him, but Reese saw it. The male and female behind that woman looked just as unhappy.

Huh. Reese scooted around until she could watch for a human to show up. It only took a few minutes before a homeless man wobbled down the street.

The Imortik master ordered, "Kill that one."

Before anyone could race out to fulfill his demand, Reese got to the man first and shouted, *"Runnn! A demon is after you!"*

It never failed to amaze her how certain words drove immediate motivation. The man ran straight across the street between two buildings.

Reese turned around grinning.

The Imortik leader shouted, "You two Beladors, bring that one to me!"

Beladors? Oh, crap.

A male and female, both of which had not been excited to kill that old guy, came charging after Reese with gusto.

Yikes. They thought she was an Imortik, which she was, but not one out here killing anyone.

She turned and raced away. While she had a new speed level with the Imortik inside her, she was not Belador fast. She dove between a building and a roll-off dumpster.

Yuck, what an awful smell.

When the two Beladors ran past her, Reese leaped out. "Hey, you two!"

The female Belador turned and shoved her hands up with a look of death in her eyes.

Reese yelled, "Stop! I'm an ally of the Beladors. I'm with Quinn."

The male had outrun the female Belador and hurried back to stand with her.

Lowering his hands, the male asked, "*Reese?* Is that you?"

"Thank goodness." She walked up to them, but the female still had a wary look.

"Yes, I'm Reese. Who are you?"

"I'm Kaiser and this is Renata."

That stopped Reese short. "*Renata?* One of the first captured? I can't wait for Quinn and Daegan to find out you two are still alive."

"There is ... another Belador." Renata sounded choked as her hands fell to her sides and her body convulsed.

Reese backed up. "What's wrong?"

Putting a hand on Renata's shoulder, Kaiser filled in Reese. "Renata is close to the end of the two weeks for being fully possessed. She's battling to hold onto free will and her Imortik tries to take over when she's distracted. We had to leave another Belador with the master."

"I saw the other woman." Reese's heart dipped at that news. "How do we free her?"

Renata finally stopped moving erratically and pulled herself together. "If we go back without you, we will likely die. If we bring you with us, we put you in great danger."

Reese appreciated the thought, but that still did not solve their problem. "We have to do something."

While Kaiser and Renata told Reese all they knew about Timmon, who indeed was the master, the physical struggle for Renata to keep her Imortik from taking over showed in the strain on her face.

Renata clenched her teeth and trembled. "If we don't go back, I'm sure the master will kill Gretchen. She's like Kaiser, not possessed long enough to lose all free will."

"Renata? You need help?" Kaiser held his hands out trying not to touch her again.

Curling her fists white-knuckle tight, she shook her head. "No. He will not win after all I've been through to escape that master, but I give both of you permission to use your power on me if I say I can't stop him or if I am unable to communicate at all." Her head jerked to the side. She keened in pain then twisted until she faced forward.

Reese fought nausea over watching what almost two weeks of possession had done to this woman.

Kaiser asked, "What are we going to do? We can't leave Gretchen."

"I have an idea," Reese asserted. "We aren't far from Piedmont Park where Beladors always have a patrol due to activity there. Let's go there."

Renata worried, "I don't know if we can speak telepathically to a Belador. I tried as soon as we got out of where he'd kept us and it didn't work."

"Mine either," Kaiser confirmed. "Our Beladors may kill us first."

Wanting to give this woman some encouraging news, Reese put on a positive front. "You two are going to hide. I think many of those Beladors are hunting for *me* so I have the best chance of not being attacked."

"Why are they hunting you?" Renata asked.

Kaiser replied, "Because Reese and Quinn are a couple and Reese is carrying his baby."

Renata started to cry. "You can't let them have your baby."

Explaining Reese's complicated pregnancy situation would help no one. She scoffed. "I just killed a monster who wanted my baby. No one gets a pass for touching this child. Keep the faith, you two. Daegan will find all the grimoire volumes and force the last of these bastards behind a wall, then we'll all be saved." She didn't believe that ending was possible, but it was worth every word to see hope spread over Renata's expression.

As the crow flew, Piedmont Park couldn't be a mile.

When they reached the park by carefully skirting patrols, Reese pointed out a spot for Renata and Kaiser to hide in the southern half and made them promise to wait for her to come back.

Reese moved through the trees heading for the north end of the park and came upon a familiar black jaguar moving fast toward her, probably drawn by the demon power she carried.

Storm had been born with different demonic capability.

She held up her hands, sure Evalle's mate would recognize her, but the jaguar snarled and launched at her.

Terror drove her voice high, "Stop, Storm. *It's me, Reese!*"

Something invisible hit the jaguar right before claws and fangs reached her, pummeling the huge black jungle cat sideways in a roll.

Quinn came out of the shadows on a dead run, yelling, "*Storm! Don't hurt Reese!*"

The jaguar stood and sidestepped, as if dizzy from the blow. He shifted to human. "Reese? Hell, I'm sorry."

"Yes. I'm ... this. But the monster doesn't fully control me so far. It seems to be strongest when my demon power rises up."

"Please shift back, Storm," Quinn said, stumbling to a stop and clearly not happy about Reese talking to a very naked Storm.

She had no complaints. Quinn was the only man for her, but Evalle had just as hot a mate.

Storm returned to his jaguar form and stepped forward, his dark gaze tracking from Reese to Quinn.

Reese snapped around as Quinn started for her. "You can't come near me."

He stopped, though his struggle hurt to watch. His handsome face had aged in the last twenty-four hours. He declared, "I will save you somehow." Red lines streaked his eyes like a confused road map. Dark circles shadowed beneath his bloodshot eyes. He was killing himself slowly.

Her heart bled at hearing his determination to save her when he had to know that was not possible. She'd thought being a demon magnet was the worst life in the world, but in a matter of seconds, a yellow monster changed her perception of life. She wanted to snap her fingers and go back to dealing with her demon energy.

At least then, she could have still been with Quinn.

Quinn took another step forward and Storm's jaguar moved to intercept him. "Back off, Storm. You would do the same if this had happened to Evalle."

The jaguar dropped his head and stepped back, then hit Reese with an imploring look.

It was up to her to keep Quinn safe.

She tried to talk him through this. "Please, Quinn. I am terrified of you being possessed. I can't live with them getting their hands on you." She caught sight of two men running up behind Quinn.

"*Sir!*"

Quinn swung around and snarled, "Stay back. Don't get within fifty feet of me and watch out for *other* Imortiks."

Not happy, they nodded and retreated, but stopped more like thirty feet away. Probably ready to protect their Maistir from her.

When Quinn swung around to her, he had no anger, just bald pain on his face. "Please come with me so I can put you somewhere safe until we stop these Imortiks."

She would not make him admit there was no way to save her. Instead she said, "I'm the best asset you have right now. The monster inside me can't make me go to the master. I'm in no danger from Imortiks as long as I stay free."

Storm's gaze swept to her with a look that said he'd heard the lie.

She wouldn't acknowledge the black jaguar when Quinn hadn't caught the way she'd brushed off an Imortik threat at this point. She would be fine if no one on either side took her down. "If you'll tell Isak I'm out here, he'll help keep the military from taking a shot at me if they know who I am. That's why I found this red shirt in a pile of clothes at a collection box."

Quinn's clothes were wrinkled and dirty. He hadn't shaved since she last saw him. His blond hair stuck out everywhere as if he'd been trying to pull it out in fits of madness.

The reason she'd come looking for Beladors struck her during the glum silence. "I need your help to save some Beladors captured by the Imortiks. I found Renata."

Shock overrode everything in Quinn's features. "Renata? You did?"

"Yes. She's teamed up with two other captured Beladors that haven't been Imortiks very long. The master thinks Renata is fully under his control and has assigned her to take the other two out as a three-person hit squad."

Quinn's eyes sharpened with intelligence that had been hiding behind his fall into deep grief. This man needed a mission, something besides trying to protect her from an impossible situation.

That's why she was also better out here being productive.

"What do you need us to do?" Quinn asked, sounding more like the man she missed desperately.

"I've got Renata and Kaiser hiding nearby."

"Kaiser was captured? I hadn't heard."

"Yes. I think he was teamed up with a woman named Gretchen. She was captured at the same time."

"We have teams out actively searching for all of them." Gaze tracking back and forth over the area, Quinn asked, "Where are they?"

"Not far. The three of them were together with the master until I heard that monster order Renata to kill a human. To save her from having to prove she would or not, I ran into the opening, sending the human running. The master ordered Renata and Kaiser to bring me to him."

That jerked his attention back to her. "What were you doing exposing your presence?"

"Don't you dare get an attitude with me, Quinn," Reese snapped. She'd been living on the edge since becoming a yellow beacon running the streets.

The two Beladors with him looked at her as if a chihuahua had threatened a rottweiler.

She ignored them. "I have control of my body. The Imortik, which I've named Dickweed, gets involved when I need my demon-fighting power."

Storm's jaguar smiled at what she'd named her inner monster.

Quinn held up a hand to stall her answer and told Storm, "Evalle called to me and asked for you to meet a team near the Fourth Ward. They've got a demon cornered and could use your help. We shall be fine."

Storm nodded and took off, blending into the landscape more than a massive predator should be able to pull off. That one had majik on top of being a Skinwalker.

Reese explained, "The Imortik seems to be wrapped up with my power more than any other part of my body, based on what Renata and Kaiser told me about theirs. As for later on ... " She hesitated, trying to be gentle with Quinn, but this situation allowed for no easy answers. She shrugged. "I don't know what will happen. I'll worry about that if anything changes." She hated having to put her terminal life out there so boldly, but Quinn had to accept that she didn't expect to prevail with this situation.

"How's my boy?" he asked in a gentle, but heartbroken voice.

Damn him. Three words and she wanted to fold at the knees. Holding back the emotion she could not deal with right now, she said, "He's fine, but he's ready to roll, too."

Quinn's eyes gave away his desire to say more.

She backed up a step, breaking him free of his tangled thoughts. Straightening to his full height, he asked, "Very well, what shall we do?"

That was her man of action. She waved, "Follow me to where I have those two hidden so I can tell them the plan."

"Which is?" he asked.

"I'm thinking if the master is still standing only with Gretchen, we can yank Gretchen free and kill him." She paused in thought. "I wonder what happens if we kill the master?"

With a grim smirk, Quinn said, "I guess we shall find out."

# CHAPTER 16

CASIDHE'S PULSE CLIMBED AS GOLDEN letters began to lift off the page of the first grimoire volume.

Lanna gasped. "It is true. Your gift is amazing."

Smiling at the powerful young woman, Casidhe said, "I take that as a high compliment comin' from you. I won't forget seein' you with Daegan in the Caucasus Mountains. Impressive."

Blushing, Lanna admitted, "I am learning much from Garwyli. I had lots of power when I came to visit. He teaches me how to use specific energy. My power grows as I am better student, but ... I am not always best student." She sighed heavily. "He will tell you I sometimes make rushed decisions."

Casidhe stopped reading and laughed. "I love it. Someone else that drives these powerful men crazy." She lifted her palm and Lanna immediately brought hers up for a high-five slap, chuckling as she did.

"Now you must tell me what you read," Lanna said, her energy flowing calmly around the area.

Returning to her task, Casidhe began reading the first few pages then paused. "This sounds as if we definitely have the first section of the grimoire. It reads like a daily journal of the sorcerer's discovery process, which would be enlightenin' and fascinatin', but we need specifics about dealin' with the Imortiks. I would normally take a week or longer to go through all this. Let me flip fast until I feel like we are past the development stage."

"I agree."

Casidhe slashed her fingers across from right to left in the air and pages turned easily. She'd stop, translate enough to know she had not read to the part she needed yet, then continue on after sharing what she'd found.

Hours later after skimming areas and the occasional interrogation from Lanna, who did not try to disguise her curiosity, Casidhe sat back.

She stretched her arms up, releasing tight muscles from leaning forward so long, grumbling, "I prefer books."

"I will hold page in air for you, yes?" Lanna suggested.

"Thanks, but no. We're at the end of this volume and I think we're just reachin' the part where he and the female Fae worked together to create the Imortiks. I wonder if we'll have to reverse engineer what he did to undo an Imortik or if he planned ahead and created a kill switch."

Lanna sat back, face earnest as she had a thousand-yard stare in her eyes. "If we do not figure out answer, I know Fae who might know something of this Fae."

"Oh?"

Returning to Casidhe, Lanna said, "Yes. She is half sister to very strong white witch. They cared for me after ... uhm, after bad time with evil sorcerer."

Casidhe's heart clenched at the thought of anyone harming Lanna, but she asked no questions. If Lanna wished to talk about her experience now or later, Casidhe would listen. After their time chatting today, she had figured out that Lanna had a deep loyalty streak and wanted the people she cared for to be safe and happy.

Pushing a smile into place that sat alone on her face, Lanna added, "Yes. Fae very nice to me. She does not trust many and we must not ask favor, but she will answer my questions if we must ask about Fae."

"Excellent." Casidhe sat up, ready to start on the second grimoire even though she needed a mental break.

"You will stay with Daegan, yes?" Lanna asked with no hesitation over such a personal question. "You have power as great as his."

Casidhe would never take insult. This young woman had a heart as big as the Treoir realm, but being reminded of Shannon's letter hit her in the stomach. She mumbled, "That's a hard question to answer."

"Is not difficult," Lanna argued politely.

Oh, to have that innocent confidence again. Casidhe had learned better now that she knew so much more. She could destroy Daegan, and maybe others important to him, if they bonded. Nausea climbed her throat. Fighting against the fear, she shrugged. "It is sort of complicated. I'm a descendant of Skarde's twin sister but not just dragon shifter blood."

"That is wonderful." Lanna clasped her hands and stared at Casidhe as if she'd said she'd found the key to the universe.

If only.

Casidhe had yet to find wonderful, not when Shannon's letter had ripped her happy future from her grasp.

"That explains why Shannon's sword comes to me and allows me to possess it, but I'm more of an unknown entity. Definitely not a dragon shifter."

Shoulders slumped, Lanna frowned.

Lanna took everything to heart and wanted to find an answer to suit her immediately. Garwyli had probably been tested sorely by figuring out how to forge all that raw power into an operative vessel.

Lanna would likely never fit into any box.

The world and those around her had to accept who she morphed into by the time she finished her training.

That thought would make Casidhe smile if she weren't trying to climb out of her pit of anxiety.

"I would like to hear more." Lanna probably believed with enough pieces she could move them around in her mind and end up with a satisfactory answer.

How could she quiet Lanna's curiosity without revealing what she had yet to tell Daegan? Casidhe decided to switch the conversation around. "Daegan fears he'll kill me if we bond without knowin' my power level. I can't allow that to happen to him. He's been alone a long time and carried so much grief from past losses. I don't want to be one more person he feels responsible for losin' any more than I wish to die."

She didn't want to be the greatest danger to Daegan.

Lanna hissed out a sigh. "We must find way for this bond to work. Daegan will never be happy unless you two are united as one."

Casidhe marveled at how Lanna was such a fixer. This powerful being who might be nineteen or twenty wanted people happy around her and seemed determined to have her wishes met. If wishes were boats, Casidhe would own a fleet. "Daegan and I may not be meant to bond."

Just saying those words took her breath.

She kept her tears sucked in, determined not to cry when her heart was bawling. She had to get this out or burst from holding it inside. "I don't know what I might turn into if we bond, Lanna. I have no control over that."

A serious expression settled over Lanna's face, then she shook her head. "I cannot say all I see in visions and dreams, but I know Daegan will bond to a mate. He will not feel at peace unless he knows his mate's power is joined with his so he can find her and protect her at any time. So that he can stay with her while alive ... and after."

Well, crap. Casidhe did not want some other woman mating with him just because she didn't have enough power or would turn into a monster and kill him.

What the hell kind of deal would that be?

Also, the only way Daegan would take another woman as a mate would be if Casidhe died. She knew that without question. He might then consider a match with a dragon shifter for the future of Treoir, but Brynhild was the only one around and she hated Daegan.

Were there other dragon shifters still alive?

Who knew? Definitely not Casidhe. She hadn't known Daegan and Skarde had actually lived for all these years.

Then Brynhild showed up.

There might be another female dragon shifter living secretly.

Nope. Casidhe had to figure out what would happen if she bonded with Daegan. Soon. Her head throbbed with too many questions and too few answers.

Lanna stood up. "I am tired and must be here to learn all I can. Brina, warrior queen of the Beladors, allows me to use sunroom. We should take break and eat."

Had this intuitive young woman read her mind or guessed that Casidhe needed to walk away for a few minutes?

Eyeing her with an intense look, Lanna said, "I do not read minds. Maybe one day, though. Your face has many questions. You must trust yourself to make right decision."

"I hope so." Casidhe had more doubts than confidence, but she planted a smile on her face and stood.

Lanna sighed quietly. "You smile but are crying inside. It is okay to cry outside."

A tear escaped in spite of Casidhe's battle to hold them back. She wiped it away with a finger and nodded then needed to change the topic. With a glance down at the grimoire volume in piles, she asked, "Do we need to put this away?"

"No. Is fine. No one comes into Garwyli's area without his knowledge or permission."

That was good to know. Casidhe had no idea how long she'd be here or when she might return to Treoir once she left again. She lifted her backpack. "If we have time, would it be possible to visit Skarde?"

Lanna had walked off and returned. "Have you met Skarde?"

"Yes. Daegan took me there when we came here to pick up the grimoire volume for meetin' with an oracle. You didn't see me because Tristan went into the castle for the grimoire volume. I did ask Daegan about talkin' to Skarde and he said yes."

"I must hear this story," Lanna said, clearly surprised. "I am glad to take you to Skarde."

"Thank you. I have a letter I must give him from his twin sister."

Lanna's pretty eyes crinkled with delight. "He has been so sad. That should make him happy."

Casidhe had thought many times about his reaction and happy wasn't the one that came to mind.

# CHAPTER 17

AFTER RESTING ENOUGH TO GENERATE a substantial amount of power he could use for only a short time, Cathbad went to retrieve his Scáth Force. He teleported into the underground railway area between two downtown stops for Atlanta's metro transit system. During his time running interference for Queen Maeve and researching information for his own benefit, he'd located the entrance to a series of hidden tunnels called *Maze Mortis.*

Civil War ghosts resided there and controlled passages at times opening new ones and shutting off current hallways, thus the name that translated into Maze of Death.

After sending Erath and his men to hide in the aboveground transit tunnels from Queen Maeve's scrying wall, Macha had shown up unexpectedly.

She'd heard him tell his Scáth Force where to go. Between that and fear Erath or one of his men might have broken ranks and run to Queen Maeve, Cathbad caught up with them hours later. He'd teleported them into the *Maze Mortis* where no nonhuman, not even a ghoul, would enter without good reason.

Macha would never lower herself to go there. She'd thrown a kink in his initial plans, but he'd almost outwitted her and Queen Maeve at the same time.

Who would have thought that wacko queen and her wyvern were so powerful?

Cathbad could not go back to his life before.

Queen Maeve had to die.

Ainvar, too.

Macha's death would be a nice bonus.

Cathbad studied the walls of the transit tunnel as he walked, avoiding the tracks. How many trains could be running in the middle of the day with no downtown travelers around?

He found the unmarked entry point for the maze. The ghosts hadn't been hostile with him when he'd teleported in the last time, but the ghost energy down there climbed higher than any power he'd ever encountered with mere spirits.

On his last trip, he'd had just enough time to take in the long hall leading from the entry point to deeper inside the maze. It was decorated with nineteenth-century furniture, rugs, and paintings, all of which could change in a blink.

If he'd sent the Scáth Force to hunker down in the basement of an abandoned building, Queen Maeve might have still found them.

His Scáth Force should have been comfortable in the large room he'd found down the first hall, which had carpet and sitting furniture.

With no subway trains passing through this very minute to see him, Cathbad teleported to the other side of the wall and found himself in a ten-foot-square box.

What had the ghosts done with his men?

He called out, "I am here to take my men with me." He hoped leaving his Scáth Force with these ghosts had not been a mistake.

The wall in front of him now blocking what had been a long hallway the last time disappeared, revealing an even longer passage stretched out a hundred feet with small chandeliers hanging every twenty feet.

His Scáth Force team were pinned against the walls on each side with their arms above their heads as if shackled, but the shackles were invisible.

"What did ya do to anger the ghosts?"

All five sets of terrified eyes slid sideways to Cathbad.

Their mouths were shut tight.

Cathbad held his forehead. When he got his hands on TÅµr Medb, he would not come down to this hellhole ever again.

He'd met no specific ghost, but he'd seen them flash in and out of sight when he'd brought the men here and left them with plenty of food and water.

He fought the urge to roar at the spirits, instead asking in a polite tone, "What may I gift ya as thanks for allowin' my men to stay a bit?"

Erath's eyes changed from fear to incredulous.

Cathbad thought that one would be the first to realize he could not simply demand their return. This place held too much energy to risk using his majik. That had been the whole reason he'd known they'd be safe.

Cold air rushed through the space and set a chandelier tinkling.

A ghost wavered into view. Tall, scrawny, and dusty. A soldier's cap sat flat on his head with a dark brim. His sunken eyes had bluish shadows and whiskers sprouted over his face. Suspenders on his khaki uniform held up his pants. The boots had likely walked hundreds of miles every day.

Cathbad waited for the spirit to make the next move.

Opening a mouth with rotten teeth, the spirit roared, "Bad men must go."

Not that Cathbad agreed with the ghosts assessment, but he wanted expedience over a battle of words. "I am here to claim them. I did not realize ya would take offense at their presence."

"They used black majik to make beds."

Cathbad glared at Erath, whose gaze dropped. Cathbad could understand, but he had warned them to stay quiet and out of sight. Erath should have known better.

The ghostly soldier was not done. "They tried to bed our women."

Cathbad might kill the Scáth Force himself for stupidity. This soldier appeared human because these ghosts had been here long enough to rule this space, but he'd warned Erath to not draw attention.

"You stay with them," the soldier said.

Cathbad's gaze snapped to the crazy spirit. He thought to imprison a druid? No longer polite, Cathbad dropped his voice to one of authority. "I am willin' to take my men and leave. I shall not stay under any circumstances. Ya would not like what happens if ya think to force *me*."

No response might mean he'd gotten through to the crazy solider.

The men fell from the walls, landing hard and falling to their knees with groans.

"Five," the soldier said.

Cathbad cocked his head at the ghost. Five what?

"Four."

"*Get up men!* We must leave," Cathbad ordered, not sure what the ghost had in mind once he ran out of numbers. "Now! Unless ya wish to stay!"

"Three."

Realization flooded their gazes. The men pushed up and limped quickly toward him.

"Two."

Cathbad needed them on this side of the ghost. He didn't trust trying to teleport with the ghost between them.

The last man rushed past the ghost as the soldier said, "One."

Cathbad teleported, hitting a wall of invisible sludge. He called up power he couldn't afford to expend for long, pushing to drive through the impediment.

He yelled a curse that should blast through anything.

The invisible sludge softened.

Cathbad and his men shot into the subway tunnel with a bright light heading for them. He barely teleported to a new spot before the train hit them.

Humans seeing them vanish was a small concern right now.

When he reappeared inside the terminal where people waited for their trains, the stale-smelling area was empty with the exception of two homeless men. One had curled up in a corner and the other one stood staring at a support column with black marker scribbles on it.

Erath stepped up, face blanched white. "We do not want to go back there, Cathbad."

"Neither do I." Cathbad took stock of his ragged group. "Ya stay and all the others must find a place to hide on their own for a bit."

"Why not me?" Erath asked, his voice suddenly very suspicious.

The men circled around behind Erath, a clear show of support. Cathbad would have time to gain their loyalty if any of them survived, including him.

He produced a stack of twenty-dollar bills and handed it

to Erath. "Give that to your men for food, but they must find somewhere quickly and underground or Queen Maeve shall locate all of ya with her scryin' wall."

"Understood." Erath handed the money to the one who appeared to be his assistant. "Why am I not to go with them?" he persisted.

"Ya must take a message to Queen Maeve for me."

Erath's mouth opened like a fish. He tried to speak and ended up shaking his head.

"She will not kill ya, Erath, if ya tell her all I have to say. To begin with, tell her ya and your men were imprisoned in the *Maze Mortis* and ya escaped."

"I don't know if I can lie to her and still live, Cathbad."

"Stated properly and with confidence, 'tis not a lie." When Erath did not look convinced, Cathbad added, "'Tis simple. Ya either work with me and deliver my message for the chance at a long and happy life or ya walk away and live a short but torturous one once she finds ya."

Looking beaten to his knees, Erath gave in. "I hope your message has something in it to cheer her up."

"This message shall redeem ya in her eyes and leave her ecstatic." Cathbad grinned to bolster Erath's shaky resolve.

Cathbad only hoped Queen Maeve allowed Erath to live long enough to speak.

# CHAPTER 18

DAEGAN HAD BEEN TELEPORTING SHORT distances across Atlanta from late morning through afternoon so he and Tristan could split up to check on the Beladors. Evalle had not let him down, accepting the role of Maistir, but she needed some help beyond Storm who kept her cloaked from the sun.

He still had to take a break. He was slowing down significantly. The venom in his leg felt like claws digging into the muscles.

The Imortik energy flooding this city should have turned the air yellow.

He teleported to the familiar rooftop near Woodruff Park where he and Tristan often met up with each other and with other Beladors.

Daegan could not understand the humans in the street below and in other parts of Atlanta. Some feared nothing or did not believe supernaturals existed.

Regardless of the reason, leaving the relative safety of their homes would get them killed with what currently slithered through this city.

The human military continued to pour into different locations. Daegan had to find Isak to learn where he and the Beladors, plus their allies, stood with the human military.

Daegan swept a look over the tan uniforms of the National Guard, then his gaze stuttered on a small unit among the soldiers.

Huntsen, the leader of the men who had imprisoned Daegan in France, stood with ten men in their familiar black uniforms.

Why were they here?

Tristan questioned the image on a helicopter earlier. Had that been one of Huntsen's?

That man would not be on the side of supernaturals.

Had Joavan, pretending to be one of Huntsen's men as he had

when Daegan first met him, sent Huntsen's group to increase chaos ripping this land apart?

Joavan had said nothing about that when he showed up while Tristan had gone to find Evalle.

Daegan struggled with his decision to hold back from Tristan what he'd discussed with Joavan, but Daegan needed Tristan to act naturally when the time came.

Tristan's voice came into his mind. *Hey, boss. You're not gonna believe who wants me to give you a message.*

*Who and what message?*

*A young scrawny druid waited outside Trey's house until Trey spoke to him. The druid wanted to find me. When I showed up to meet the guy, he said Ainvar had a message for you. That piece of garbage, Ainvar, is willing to hand over the third grimoire volume to you in trade for the amulet. He claims he was lying about you needing the amulet to close the death wall. He only said that to ensure you would not hand it back to Joavan before Ainvar had a chance to make this trade. He also wants a book he claims is his that he has learned Casidhe possesses. Said she'll know which book.*

Daegan knew what he wanted to do but took his time in replying. The only thing throwing him out of step was Ainvar wanting the book. Daegan had negotiated a future deal with Joavan, one he could not mention to Tristan yet.

Tristan had every right to distrust Joavan and Ainvar.

So did Daegan.

He trusted Tristan with his life, but Daegan played a dangerous game and had been expecting Tristan to bring him a message only about the amulet. That was why he'd needed Tristan, who held Ainvar in the lowest regard, to act naturally.

He also believed his second-in-command would understand once Daegan revealed all to him afterwards.

Tristan was as wise about strategy as any other.

Daegan had the amulet with him but had never expected to bring a book. He told Tristan, *Go to Casidhe and bring the book with ya.* He gave Tristan his location and asked, *When and where does Ainvar wish to meet?*

*That's the kicker, boss. The meeting is five this afternoon in Stone Mountain Park. That's eighteen minutes from now. I checked with our people and all human access to the park has been barricaded or marked with a minimum ten thousand dollar fine for being caught inside any state and national park in Georgia to limit security resources. People are still showing up sometimes but not many.*

Tristan clearly would not be kept from this meeting.

That was fine. Tristan would teleport away if Daegan ordered him to do so.

Daegan instructed, *Retrieve the book from Treoir and return to pick me up from our rooftop where we observe Woodruff Park.*

*I'm on it.*

One minute passed, then another. Tristan was taking longer than Daegan expected with so little time to make this meeting. When Tristan appeared, so did Casidhe with a book clutched in her arms and her backpack on.

"I tried, boss, but I would not risk hurting her."

Daegan turned on Casidhe with anger building from fear of her even being in Atlanta. "Ya cannot stay! Give me the book and return to Treoir."

"When are you goin' to learn that orderin' me around doesn't work?" she shouted back. "Tristan said you had fifteen minutes. Every word is cuttin' down that time."

Tristan interjected, "Almost twelve minutes now."

Before Daegan could speak again, Casidhe said, "I need you to listen for one minute. Ainvar's name popped up in the second grimoire volume. So we need to be careful to keep him away from the volumes just in case. My second point is this book is titled *Before Ainvar*. It reads like an autobiography." At Daegan's frown, Casidhe quickly explained, "Like it was written by Ainvar, which is my guess. I scanned a lot for anythin' significant or referencin' the grimoire volumes."

Daegan spoke up, drawing a narrowed look from her. "Joavan made a comment that Ainvar did not want to close the wall. I took that to mean Ainvar had no interest in helpin' the human world, but now I wonder if he may have had a hand in openin' the rift."

She shrugged. "I still can't say yes or no about that because the grimoire volumes did not point to him as bein' part of the original grimoire plan. The sorcerer behind all this had heard of Ainvar's search for immortality. In the first grimoire volume, the sorcerer journaled notes about how he intended to make some deal with Ainvar. That may be the only reason Ainvar is mentioned, but it doesn't preclude Ainvar bein' involved."

Tristan and Daegan exchanged quick looks.

Casidhe crossed her arms. "What's goin' on?"

"I was approached by Joavan," Daegan started. "We have reached an agreement I have no time to explain." Daegan sent a quick telepathic message to Tristan. *I am sorry I have not told ya all yet, but I shall.*

*No worries, boss.*

"You intend to trust that Faetheen?" Casidhe's voice jumped with every word.

"Yes. I *must* take the book with me."

She had a staredown with Daegan.

He growled at her.

She answered with an evil smile. "I'm goin' to the meetin'."

"Nay!" Daegan's stern reply sounded final to him, but the lass had a stubborn streak as wide as an ocean.

"You are *not* in charge of me, dragon king."

"This human world is more dangerous by the day."

She flipped a hand casually. "We can argue all you want, but you're only wastin' minutes. How much time do we have left, Tristan?"

"Seven minutes."

Giving him a quick nod of thanks, she made her position clear. "I am goin' with you. For one thing, I may have to translate somethin' in this book. You can't do that without me."

Daegan could send her teleporting back to Treoir, but that would only crush the trust they had begun to build. His voice rumbled deeply. "If ya give me the meanin' of the words, I do not need ya there."

Casidhe quit arguing.

Daegan knew what she was doing. He could bluster all he wanted, but he would not force her to stay anywhere she refused to be and she knew this.

Silence fell over the group heavy as a lead blanket.

Daegan's eyes glowed silver. He should not attempt to intimidate her, but she could not go to this meeting. He didn't even want Tristan there based on what Daegan expected.

As if anything intimidated this lass? Casidhe called up her power and her eyes glowed an unusual green, but not as light colored as those on an Alterant-gryphon.

Tristan stepped back.

She blinked her glow away and glanced at him. "What?"

"If you two explode, I want to be far enough back not to get my eyebrows burned off."

Growling out an angry sigh, Daegan conceded. "She shall go with us."

"If you give your word you will not teleport me away without my permission." She tilted her chin at him, daring him to argue.

"Ya are an infuriatin' lass."

"Glad you're startin' to realize what you signed up for." She grinned at him, walked over and lifted up to give him a kiss.

He could have stood there as a cold statue, but her touch had an effect no other power held over him. He caught the back of her head with his hand, holding her close with little pressure. He kissed her hard, then lifted up. "Ya cannot have what ya want every time with a kiss."

She patted his cheek and stepped back. "That has yet to be seen. I'm ready to go when you are. Tick-tock, boys. We need to move it."

# CHAPTER 19

CASIDHE HAD GRASPED DAEGAN'S ARM just before teleporting to a massive lawn leading up to the historic Stone Mountain east of Atlanta. The half-round bald mound of granite and other minerals displayed historic carvings above the lawn and lake where laser shows were held during summers.

She'd been to Atlanta only once and had spent that time inside Tristan's hotel room. While waiting on Daegan to arrive, she'd read about this historical location where the massive lawn often bustled with activity and people enjoying picnics on blankets.

One day, she'd sit on a blanket and picnic with Daegan.

Not today.

Quiet clung to the air scented by the smell of grass and trees. Nature seemed unconcerned with Imortiks.

Tristan appeared immediately on the other side of Casidhe.

"How many minutes left?" Casidhe whispered out the side of her mouth to Tristan.

"Three and a half, assuming Ainvar is on time."

"What else can ya tell us about the book?" Daegan asked softly, his head turning from side to side, keeping watch the same as Tristan.

With so little time, Casidhe condensed what she'd learned. "As I read *Before Ainvar*, I began to realize the title had not meant so much the world before Ainvar in general as it did his view of the supernatural world prior to him becoming a legend in his own mind."

Daegan's lips tilted with almost a smile.

She hurried to explain, "I reviewed the part Cathbad had originally wanted me to translate, which was Ainvar talkin' of bein' unwillin' to accept only one lifetime to rule the dark druids. He went in search of how to live forever, which ironically meant leavin' his dark druid group on their own a lot. Others stepped in as the Seanóir, which translates into Elder. He dedicated his life to trackin' down every person and scroll he could find which mentioned anythin' about Gilgamesh, a giant Nephilim who ruled Uruk thousands of years before Ainvar's time and had searched for immortality."

"I heard of Gilgamesh and that he sought immortality, but not that he had succeeded," Daegan said.

"It's a long story I'll tell you at some point, but Ainvar found part of a tablet from a scribe beneath Gilgamesh who shed some light on what Gilgamesh had learned. Ainvar also located unusual beins' of power who pointed him in different directions. The bottom line is Ainvar decided he needed a vessel, which would hold majikal power from which he could visit to regenerate his power, sort of like how you and Beladors heal faster and regenerate power faster inside Treoir."

Not taking his eyes off the setting where light diminished faster as the sun dropped from sight, Tristan murmured, "So Ainvar's Ghost Castle is like a battery recharging station."

"Not a bad analogy," she agreed. "But I think Ainvar has to supply his castle power in some significant way so he can draw from the natural energy inside as he needs it. The thing we have to keep in mind is that Ainvar spent a great deal of time in hidin' over the last thousand years. He had other oracles who told him the Imortiks would arise again, which is one reason he trapped Zeelindar to have as his perpetual oracle. She confirmed that the Imortiks could force the world to its knees. He has waited a long time to rule everyone. He found that he had to limit the times away from the castle when the power began to wane. If he needs the amulet, his castle is low on energy, which means he's desperate. After a lifetime of defeatin' death, he will stop at nothin' to gain the amulet. More than that, I fear he may have a way to take control of the Imortiks."

Out of the twilight, a small glow of light shined just above the ground a hundred feet in front of them.

Daegan told Tristan, "Keep an eye behind us and I shall deal with Ainvar."

Swinging to face in the opposite direction, Tristan said, "Got it."

"And do whatever 'tis necessary to protect Casidhe above all."

Casidhe argued, "No, Tristan. Cover Daegan's back."

Tristan said nothing, which meant he would not accept her words over Daegan's order.

The light continued to grow until it reminded Casidhe of a giant oval light bulb as tall as Daegan. When the pulsing glow became static, a man emerged, allowing a halo of light to surround him.

"I take it that's Ainvar," she whispered.

"Aye. 'Tis time to hand me the book."

"No."

"Unlike Tristan, Ainvar shall not hesitate to harm ya seriously to gain the book, lass. If that occurs, all negotiation is off and we battle to the death."

# CHAPTER 20

HAD DAEGAN REALLY BROUGHT THE Luigsech woman here?

Cathbad grinned from inside the cloaking allowing him to stand on the side of the lawn leading up to Stone Mountain's carved face. He didn't trust Ainvar to be any closer than two hundred feet away even while cloaked.

Anticipation sent his heart tapping furiously.

The cloaking he'd spent a load of majik on in advance of this meeting would protect him from eyes, noses, and anyone who could lift a power signature.

With another look, he sized up Casidhe again, surprised by this unexpected gift.

Cathbad rubbed his hands together, excited beyond belief. Just the fact of those two still being together at this point meant Daegan would battle anyone who tried to harm her.

Erath had not returned from delivering the message to Queen Maeve, which gave Cathbad indigestion, but he would just have to sit and wait.

If this failed, he had nowhere to hide from Ainvar.

# CHAPTER 21

CASIDHE DEBATED ON HANDING OFF the book to Daegan. Not that he couldn't have it to negotiate with, but the minute she released the book, she had no doubt he'd have Tristan teleport her away.

That would leave Daegan alone.

Ainvar teleported to fifty feet away.

Eleven men appeared around her, Daegan, and Tristan, spread out in a circle to encompass them and Ainvar. Each of the men opened his arms and lifted his hands above his head.

That couldn't be good.

Daegan murmured, "Hand me the book. I need ya safe."

"No, and don't you dare send me away. I'm not givin' up the book until I know you're both goin' to be safe. Those other eleven men might be Ainvar's guards."

"Dark druids," Daegan corrected. "They are not human."

"Whatever they are."

Daegan used telekinesis to yank the book from her hands to catch with one of his. "Now, Tristan."

"Dammit, Daegan!" Her body tugged up, then left, and right.

Tristan ground out, "Can't teleport."

The power pulling on her vanished. Not being able to teleport was bad, but she would not leave Daegan and Tristan to face this bunch alone.

Anger and worry warped off Daegan. "Ya should not have come, lass."

"Well, I'm here. Let's do this and walk away from it alive."

Tristan spoke over his shoulder. "I think the druid group surrounding us created some sort of dome to keep us in, which is preventing teleporting and telepathy, because I tried. We aren't walking away until Ainvar and all of them are dead or all of us." He took a breath and added, "Don't think I haven't realized you didn't want me here *either*, boss."

"We shall discuss this later if we are all still breathin', but no, I did not want either of ya here. I have made a gamble and did not wish it to include your lives."

"Tough. We're here to make sure you live." Casidhe tilted her chin toward the druids, done with arguing.

Daegan lifted his voice, "I am here as ya requested, Ainvar. I am not feelin' so generous to give ya anythin' when ya trap me and my people."

"Ah, Daegan, you are a most worthy opponent."

With her hands now free, Casidhe held them loose at her sides and widened her stance.

She had her sword in her backpack and believed ... okay, hoped, her armor would show up again if she called forth her sword to do battle.

She had to be able to fight an enemy alongside Daegan. What kind of mate would she be for a dragon shifter if she couldn't hold her own in the supernatural world?

Mate? She could not bond with Daegan until she knew what she'd turn into or if one of them would die.

Ainvar called out, "Hand over the amulet and book, Daegan. I will allow you and your friends to leave."

What a big fat lie, but Casidhe kept that to herself. Daegan would not believe this dark druid.

Daegan took his time answering. "I only need the amulet to close the death wall. After that, ya and Joavan can argue over it."

Casidhe tracked the direction of Daegan's gaze, which moved quickly from right to left with the mountain face always in view. With that narrowed area to keep tabs on, who or what was he searching for?

"I had hoped to keep this peaceful, dragon." Ainvar's voice took a decisive dip into evil.

Joavan appeared just outside the circle of druids. The Faetheen looked panicked.

Ainvar became rigid and turned. "What are you doing here?"

Joavan's voice was dulled by whatever dome of energy the

druids had created. Joavan slapped a hit of power at the dome, not disturbing it one bit. "You will not leave here with the amulet, Ainvar."

"You cannot break a power dome formed by the conclave of *Dhraoidhean Dorcha Elite,* though you are welcome to drain your energy trying."

Daegan groaned under his breath. "'Tis not goin' how I expected."

A wild war scream ripped through the air.

Casidhe gripped Daegan's arm at the sight of a glowing red dragon appearing to fly off the top of Stone Mountain and head for them.

Even Ainvar lost his arrogance. He swung around, manifesting a white staff. A clear orb sat on top. The black adder inside the orb had red eyes and curled back, ready to strike. Energy drifted from the staff in waves. Ainvar began shouting out words that sounded like a spell, a curse, or something worse.

She dropped her backpack and called up her sword.

*Lann an Cheartais* flew from the sheath and into her hands. Armor flowed over her from head to toe. Her power flashed with energy.

Tristan's whispered, *"Wow!"*

Daegan and Tristan shoved up kinetic fields.

Ainvar tossed his hands forward and up. Shards of energy shot from his fingers, smashed against the inside of the dome, and spread like a lightning rod of fire.

The flying beast flew kamikaze style straight into the dome. Brilliant red light flashed and power exploded, knocking the dragon-like creature back.

Something was not right about that dragon.

The dome wobbled but held.

Casidhe doubted anything could pierce this dome. "Queen Maeve is flying that dragon thing."

"'Tis not a dragon. She used that beast to start the Dragani War!" Daegan bellowed. His head enlarged and his bones made hideous breaking noises, then he stalled in midshift, grunting with strain. He finally pulled back, unable to change into his dragon. That giant sword she'd first seen at her cottage appeared.

He gripped it with one hand.

Veins stood out on his neck and muscles bulged beneath his shirt.

Queen Maeve's beast flew in a tight circle and came back again.

Ainvar shouted, "More power for the dome." Then his voice became inhumanly deep when he ordered, "*Zeelindar! Come forth!*"

His druids began chanting in response to his order.

The dome changed from clear to tinted with a dark mist, but not so much to prevent Casidhe from seeing outside where Joavan had backed away. His panicked gaze switched from the dome to Queen Maeve.

Inside the dome, Zeelindar appeared in her astral travel form, shouting, "*Stop, Ainvar. Stop!*"

Ainvar told her, "Use your power to help kill the dragon and his people. *I must have that amulet!*"

The oracle's eyes churned red and white, then her mouth opened. She sent no power flying, instead pleading, "They will give the amulet to you if you don't kill them."

"*You lie!*" Ainvar became more unhinged by the minute. "I want it *now!* You must do as I command!" The dark druid ignored Queen Maeve so certain she could not breach his dome.

Joavan ran back and forth a few steps as if waiting for a chance to do something.

What? Why was he here?

When Queen Maeve's beast dive-bombed for another attack, Joavan cupped his hands around his mouth and shouted at her.

The hag scowled at Joavan, but at the last moment, she pulled the beast's horned head straight up in flight before hitting the dome.

As the reptilian body dropped down, sharp claws ripped over and over.

Daegan shouted, "We cannot kill Ainvar. Stay here. I shall stop him and break this dome." He ran forward to attack.

"*No!*" Casidhe ran with him, sure that druid would strike Daegan down with some spell.

She pulled her sword back to swing for the neck.

Reputations were everything after all.

Enraged, Ainvar shoved both hands at them, flinging Daegan and Casidhe backward in the air. She hit Tristan's back. He made an umph sound, but didn't fall forward only because he was pushing power into his kinetics.

The eleven druids shouted, *"Seilbh a ghlacadh ar chumhacht!"*

Casidhe's feet flew out from beneath her. Her back hit the ground, knocking the sword from her hand that flipped up and dropped perfectly next to her leg.

She felt something clingy and invisible fall over her body. "Daegan, what's goin' on?"

"'Tis a spell. They have us pinned beneath a net to take possession of our power."

She could barely lift her head and turned to Daegan on her left. Tristan was on her right. She couldn't move the rest of her body. "How do we get out of this?"

Ainvar screamed, *"Give me the amulet or you shall stay there until you die. 'Tis not a nice death!"*

Two of the druids cried out as if stabbed.

Casidhe lifted up enough to see Queen Maeve's beast flapping hard and ripping into the dome with steely-looking claws as long as Casidhe's forearms.

What kind of flying creature could that be?

Ainvar had jumped around at the sound of his druids and pushed power harder to stop Queen Maeve's claw-machine from breaking through.

More of the eleven druids groaned and whined.

Queen Maeve began growing larger and morphing into an unbelievably grotesque shape. Her fingernails lengthened to ten inches long. She lashed at the dome with her beast.

Joavan looked even more worried. Why?

Visible cracks fingered across the dome from the ground up between each of the eleven druids. One large chunk burst apart in a loud boom. Sizzling pieces shot everywhere.

Casidhe closed her eyes and ducked her chin. When she opened them, Daegan was growling and lunging against his restraints. Tristan did the same.

Queen Maeve thrashed Ainvar with blood-red lightning

bolts, zinging his head and arms. He raged, his arms and hands whipping everything he had at her.

The crazy queen's greater body size became top-heavy and slid to the right. She fell off her beast.

Every muscle in Daegan's arms and shoulders were taut with pushing against the netting. Lines burned through his clothes, creating crisscrossed wounds over his body and limbs.

Casidhe could smell burned skin on him and Tristan. The netting smoked where it struggled to burn her armor.

Daegan finally said, "I shall convince Ainvar to free us in exchange for the amulet. When I do, Tristan shall teleport you away with him."

Casidhe and Tristan both shouted, "*No!*"

Zeelindar wailed, shouting above the noise. "I can't protect myself, Ainvar. Leave so I can go."

Ainvar only cared about trying to save himself and gain that amulet. Clearly, this was a do-or-die situation for him.

Casidhe worried aloud, "If Ainvar dies now, Zeelindar will never be free."

Tristan gasped, "If we don't break this power net, we're gonna die."

They needed more power. Casidhe searched her brain for an idea and came up with one. "You two link."

"We already have, lass," Daegan gritted out. "We do not have enough energy to fend off this many dark druids with their power united as well."

Queen Maeve vanished, then came back into focus. She looked down at herself in shock.

Had she cloaked herself and it failed?

The mad queen unleashed a wild scream a demonic monster would envy.

A line of netting touched Casidhe's wrist and hand. She clenched her teeth to beat back a cry of pain. The net would eventually chop their bodies into pieces.

Tristan let out a long miserable groan, gasping, "Is it time to call your mother, boss?"

Daegan spoke past tight muscles flexed in his jaws. "If we do not break free soon, I may have no choice, but she could turn all of this much worse."

That was hard to imagine. Casidhe's world was ending second by second. She, Daegan, and Tristan needed power now. She would never be with Daegan here or in the afterlife because she had feared bonding.

All her choices came down to a single one. Bond and face maybes or don't bond and die without ever seeing Daegan again.

A calm fell over her.

If she had to die today, she would not die a coward.

She twisted her face to see him and announced in a proud voice, "I love you, Daegan. If we had lived, I would be with you any way I could. Bond with me so I won't lose you in the next life."

Daegan tried to turn to face her and got one eye on her. "Lass, my power could—"

"Kill me?" She gave him a watery smile. "Without you, I am dead anyhow. If you're willin' to risk the unknown of my blood, I'm just as willin' to take that risk to save all of us or end up with you forever." She couldn't think about the third alternative of turning into a hideous beast, but if she did, she hoped it would be powerful enough to kill Ainvar.

She would accept any personal outcome if it saved Daegan and Tristan.

Queen Maeve and Ainvar were having a screaming power match. Sweat poured off his druids, who were fighting to keep their knees locked.

Eyes filled with love, Daegan's voice boomed, "Casidhe Luigsech, descendant of Shannon of King Eógan, and my one love, I ask ya to bond with me as my mate."

Voice trembling, Casidhe quickly replied, "Daegan of King Gruffyn, dragon king of Treoir, and the only mate I shall ever want, I accept your bond."

Tristan cut in, "Hell of a time to make me a best man."

Power surged from both of their bodies, gathering around them and balling into a spectacular silvery red and blue glow that burst forth, expanding as it filled the inside of the dome.

Casidhe gasped at the gut punch of energy that rushed through her unlike anything she'd ever felt.

Daegan roared a victorious shout.

Tristan yelled in pain.

Crap. He had already been linked with Daegan. Had she killed Tristan?

Eleven druids buckled and fell to the ground, writhing and crying out.

Casidhe felt the net clinging across her armor snap and the tension lift from her body. Her armor hissed from burn stripes and her hands had blisters from being seared, but the rest of her had not been singed.

With the power dome failing, a disgusting stench of burned limes tainted every breath.

She sat up in time to see Ainvar smack Queen Maeve's beast with a flaming ball of energy, knocking the creature to the ground. When it landed, the red glow vanished, leaving behind a badly scarred and burned wyvern with demonic red eyes. Its wounds oozed black blood, smelling as bad as sewer stench.

The giant monster that had once been Queen Maeve pulled her arm back where lightning bolts sparked from her fingernails. She lashed forward, slapping the whip across Ainvar.

He howled at the strike, which slashed wounds in his face and chest, then grabbed the sparking whip. Hands smoking and smelling of burned skin, he yanked, breaking the whip.

Queen Maeve looked at her empty hand and teleported to her creature still laying on the ground. Cloaking covered them then failed again.

Growling through her fangs, she gripped her beast with shaking arms. They vanished. She must have managed to teleport them both.

Zeelindar shifted her vision to Casidhe and Daegan, mouthing the words, *I'm sorry.*

Joavan shot past fallen druids into the now-defunct dome as if he had rockets for feet.

Ainvar turned to watch the Faetheen. The druid moved slowly and looked as if he'd walked out of a nuclear blast. His face was covered in blisters and blood soaked his ripped robe.

Not so smug now, was he?

But the leader of the dark druids still carried plenty of hate to generate a sneer. "I still have enough power to kill you, Joavan."

Joavan skidded to a stop in front of Daegan and Casidhe, then produced a sparkling multi-pointed star upon his palm. If one of the wildly expensive glassware companies could produce that, they'd own the market forever.

Then she realized what he had.

His crystal shielded a necklace.

Joavan sounded smug when he said, "Daegan could not give you the amulet. I am the one who holds this treasure, Ainvar. I am here to show you how much greater I am than you. You should run! The minute I return with this, our people will hunt you as your power fails and punish you for your crimes. I am the only one who can break this container to free the amulet."

Casidhe would have thought Joavan had more survival sense. How did he get the amulet from Daegan and why risk coming here to taunt Ainvar that way?

Ainvar's eyes grew huge and yellow-mad as a rabid dog. Using majik, he yanked the star from Joavan with one hand and called up his staff from the ground with his other hand.

Joavan looked horrified. *"Do not dare break that!"*

"Never think to order me." Holding the iridescent star in his hand, Ainvar slammed the head of his staff down, smashing the star.

When the sparkling object shattered, the pieces paused six inches out then disintegrated, revealing the crushed blood stone. A thick smell of copper filled the air as blood ran through Ainvar's fingers.

His face flipped from anger, to horror, to agony, every expression as satisfying as Zeelindar's surprise and joy.

Before Ainvar realized what was happening, Joavan called up a sword and raced toward him. The Faetheen swung his blade fast in a horizontal sweep and yelled, "This is for all your crimes against my people!"

The blade took Ainvar's head off, dropping it at Joavan's feet. He lifted the bloody head and shook it at the eleven druids. "You are enemies of the Faetheen!"

Every druid vanished.

Casidhe lunged at Daegan who pulled her to him, holding her

tight. His body shook.

She sniffled. "I was so afraid I had put you two in more danger. I would never want you to be harmed because of bein' with me."

The noise and smell of battle fell away as Daegan ran his palm over her face. "Long ago, I was offered an arranged marriage to gain a powerful ally for our kingdom, but I declined. My father understood and told me if I ever found the mate of my heart, I must be willin' to fight for such a love no matter what tribulations might arise."

He drew in a deep breath and on the exhale said, "With one look into your eyes, I am willin' to go to war."

Game over. Casidhe started crying against his chest.

Daegan hooked an arm around her.

Tristan moved around on his knees then slumped into a sitting position. "Am I caught in your bond?"

Daegan laughed. "Nay. Ya are safe."

Casidhe caught her breath and lifted up, wiping her face. "I did feel your link."

Tristan sounded sincerely surprised. "Really? I was so busy watching whatever you two were doing to bond, that your power hit me like a double-fisted punch to my solar plexus. But I'm good now."

Casidhe felt a sharp pain in her middle.

Not now. She couldn't do this in front of everyone. Daegan would see her differently forever. She called her power forth and clamped down hard against what moved inside her.

Daegan tilted his head at her. "Are ya in pain, lass?"

"Not really." She smiled weakly. "That was one heck of a battle."

"Daegan and Casidhe," Zeelindar said, pulling both their gazes to her and saving Casidhe for the moment. The oracle's holographic form wavered in front of them. Tears streamed down her face.

Rising first, Daegan gave Casidhe a hand to help her up beside him. Tristan stood as well.

Casidhe smiled the biggest smile she could find. "You're free, Zeelindar!" In spite of everything, joy wrapped her heart at realizing she and Daegan, with Joavan and Tristan's help, had helped free a woman from centuries of bondage.

"I have no words to express the relief I am experiencing." Zeelindar's form wavered and the mist dissipated until she slowly became solid, looking more as a real person than any time Casidhe had seen her. The strange lines on her face and body vanished. The filmy clothes were replaced by a white flowing shirt, long dark brown skirt, and sandals on her feet.

Joavan's sword disappeared. He snapped his fingers and a bag large enough to hold a pumpkin appeared. Dropping the head in it, he spoke to the bag. "My mother and king deserve your head."

Joavan slung the strap of the bag over his shoulder and came striding up to Daegan's group.

Casidhe eyed the bag uneasily. The bottom had turned red but did not drip blood. Ew.

Nodding at the Faetheen, Daegan said, "Thank ya, Joavan." Then he explained for everyone, "Joavan came to me to discuss the amulet. We reached an agreement if he would help us with Zeelindar's blood stone." He slashed a glance at Tristan. "I shall explain all later."

"That's fine, boss. You probably wanted me to react naturally to Ainvar, which I did."

"Ya always show your intelligence, Tristan, and never fail to amaze me. Thank ya." Returning to Zeelindar, Daegan said, "I wished to fulfill your request, but I could see no way to convince Ainvar to crush your stone."

Casidhe recalled Daegan also saying he would not take a life without reason. He would have had plenty of reasons today, but she was glad for Joavan to have avenged his people and saved Daegan that duty.

Zeelindar hung on every word, nodding as he spoke.

Daegan continued, "Joavan came up with a plan, which should have been simple had Ainvar not locked us inside that dome."

Not to be left out, Joavan stepped in next. "I glamoured the blood stone with a cover Ainvar would not hesitate to fully crush, which would break the blood stone. To kill him afterwards was an obligation to my people for the great harm he wrought."

When the men quieted, Zeelindar said, "You have all blessed

me by removing Ainvar's curse. You fulfilled your part of our agreement. I shall tell you how to find the last grimoire volume, Daegan. You must bring the other two volumes as close as you can to the rift. That will be the place the greatest number of Imortiks have escaped around. The volumes are pulled to each other to become one again. But you must not do this until you are ready to call up the death wall."

Casidhe flinched against her muscles twisting. "What do you mean by ... call up the wall?"

Zeelindar frowned at her, but replied, "When the grimoire volumes were separated, the beings present combined their powers to stop the Imortiks. Their joined power brought a wall from beneath the ground, which opened and words from the grimoire forced the Imortiks behind the wall. This is all I have to share. Now, you must find the words in the grimoire volumes for how to control the Imortiks."

Tristan asked, "So are you saying we need the beings who closed the first death wall present to tell us how to call up the wall again?"

"You must have at least one person who participated or observed the event to instruct you."

Casidhe had her arms crossed to hide the way her fingers were digging into her biceps to hold back the shooting pain.

Daegan was not just asking this time when he said, "Where were ya injured, lass? Ya are in pain."

"Nope. Not injured," was all she could say.

Zeelindar pinned Casidhe in place with her serious gaze. "Do not fight the change. This is not death but the result of your decision."

"I know," Casidhe wailed, gripping her middle.

Daegan's face paled. "The bond. Is the *bond* hurtin' ya?"

"No. I'll explain ... when we leave."

His silence did not mean he agreed. Daegan would allow her a few minutes, no more. Casidhe wanted to get away from everyone. Changing the subject, she asked Zeelindar, "What now for you?"

"I finish my life as I should have when I was first human. Do not forget that you must be present to read the third grimoire volume, Casidhe. Two dragons and a goddess are required. A sacrifice of a very powerful being must be chosen by a goddess to seal the death wall."

"Sacrifice?" Casidhe's voice thinned.

Zeelindar began to fade. She looked at her hands and arms as they became transparent.

Casidhe cried, "Oh, no! I'm so sorry."

Zeelindar's face shined with happiness. "Do not be sorry. I go home to be with my family. Long ago, I left a letter with someone who passed it down through future generations. It is to be delivered to my descendants when I fail to make my annual astral visit to the person holding the letter. I have waited long for my family to know the truth that I never abandoned them. Protect what you have." Zeelindar continued to become more and more transparent until she turned into a blur of green light that floated away on the wind.

Joavan watched the green light until it disappeared. "Ainvar will no longer threaten my people. Do not forget our agreement, dragon. Time is not my friend."

Daegan confirmed, "I shall not forget. While time is not your friend, I shall claim ya as mine."

Joavan's eyes widened with surprise and appreciation. He nodded, took a step, and was gone.

The sound of helicopters approaching rattled Casidhe. Her body shuddered with more pain. She gasped out, "Daegan, I need to get out of here."

"Not until ya tell me what is hurtin' ya."

"We have seconds before this goes really bad!" she shouted at him.

Tristan's power reached her and they teleported away with her doubled over.

# CHAPTER 22

As the world came back into focus inside Treoir realm, Casidhe dropped to her knees on the soft grass, groaning.

Daegan fell beside her. "Tell me what must be done!"

She struggled to squeeze out the words while gripping her stomach. "Shannon's letter. I found out I could bond with a jinn and be a powerful jinn." She sucked in air, heaving it out. "I would never be a dragon even if I bond with a dragon shifter." She panted, caught another breath, and said, "To bond with any bein' other than jinn means I might end up ... a monster or ..." She screamed, *"Get away from me! I don't want to kill you!"*

"Nay, lass. Do not say such. I shall not lose ya!" Daegan shouted at Tristan, *"Bring Lanna and Garwyli!"*

Stuck in her own personal hell, she whispered, "I gave the letter to Skarde. He might ... ow, ow, ow." Her body was trying to break apart. "Daegan ... I do not regret bondin'. I wanted you to live."

"Not without ya, lass. I love ya more than life itself."

She tried to smile but it probably looked closer to an animal being clawed into pieces. "I really thought we'd have more time this way."

"Do not say such things."

Lanna dropped down on the other side of Casidhe. "I am sorry, Casidhe."

"Not your fault." Casidhe's body seized hard. She stared at Daegan. Just one more look at the man she loved.

Garwyli shouted with a lot of voice for an old codger, "Release what is inside ya! Do it now or ya shall not live!"

"Nay!" Daegan told Tristan, "Bring Skarde!"

Again, Tristan zipped away.

Casidhe's back bowed until she lifted up on her fingertips and toes. She screamed, unable to hold back against the pain eating her up.

Daegan pleaded, *"Lanna! Garwyli! Do somethin'!"*

Garwyli held his hands above her and roared, "Ya shall not deny yar destiny! Release yar beast!"

Skarde and Tristan appeared as Casidhe stood as if yanked up by her hair. She looked at Skarde, hoping for any sign that he knew what was happening.

His face crumbled. He trembled with his fist at his mouth.

Not what she was hoping for.

Still screeching at the top of her lungs, she finally accepted defeat and let go. Her body began pulling and twisting. Bones snapped and muscles stretched. The pain. She had to be dying. She started to black out, but whatever had taken over her body held the reins and continued to reshape her.

At the sound of loud snapping, she felt her back break open.

When she could breathe again and see, she stared down at shock riding across every face.

Lanna's face had turned the color of snow.

Garwyli seemed more curious than anything.

Tristan's eyebrows were high on his forehead and Skarde stared for a moment then ... began smiling.

What did that mean?

She finally looked for Daegan, the one reaction she feared seeing the most.

His beautiful gaze scanned her up and down with awe. What a strange reaction to a monster. Not really. Daegan would never make her feel bad about something she couldn't change.

Daegan's lips didn't move but she heard him talking.

*Is this what ya hid inside, lass?*

She wasn't sure if she could speak in this form and thought, *I have no idea what I was hidin' inside, Daegan.*

His eyes widened. His voice came back. *Ya heard me?*

*Yes. How bad is this? I must be ten or twelve feet tall.*

Daegan's lips lifted and curved until his grin could not stop growing. He shouted, "Ya are fifteen feet at least in height and a magnificent creature. Open your wings for us."

Wings? Had that been what broke free from her back? She wasn't sure how this body worked. She thought hard about flapping her wings.

She felt wings moving and her body lifted.

She could fly? But she wasn't supposed to be a dragon.

Everyone below cheered. She could see the castle with guards watching in surprise.

How did she land this body?

She thought hard about slowing the wings until her feet hit. Or did she have paws?

Daegan turned worried. "Is time to shift back to your human body, lass."

Crap. How did that work?

Garwyli stepped up and called out, "'Twill be simpler after ya practice. Close yar mind ta distractions and bring up a vision of yar human form. Be calm and yar other half shall be calm."

How would he know? He was a druid.

But he'd sounded confident, which might be just to convince her she could do this.

She tried to change by force of will and started breathing too fast. Like panic fast.

That didn't work. The longer she couldn't change, the more it scared her.

Daegan's voice came to her. *Calm your mind and body, lass. Do as Garwyli tells ya. He has healed many of us for centuries and knows the body even if he does not shift.*

*Okay, I'll try to relax.* That's what she needed. To hear and feel Daegan inside her.

Closing her eyes, she focused on her human form and how she'd felt standing on that cliff's edge with Daegan. She'd fallen into a meditative mood then and ...

Her body began changing again, shrinking, bones shortening, and muscles pulling tight.

*This hurt, too!* She held her groan inside, sure it would sound really loud. So much was going on with her head and body, it took a moment for her to realize she stood in her human form.

The one she *knew* Daegan loved.

When she felt his arms around her, she let go of her anxiety, feeling weak as if she'd just climbed a mountain. With no skills to do that either, she'd be as amazed to have survived that as she was having lived through shifting.

He whispered, "I cloaked ya right away. Ya had no clothes at first, but ya shall now."

Thank goodness Daegan had hidden her naked body from everyone.

A pink T-shirt formed around her upper body, then jeans covered her legs. He must have decided he liked her barefoot.

She drew in a deep breath and stepped back. "Were you tellin' the truth? I'm not hideous?"

"Nay." Daegan admitted, "I have no idea what ya are, but ya have wings with the head and body of a hawk. Your feathers are the color of autumn and your head is dark gold with black about the eyes."

"She is Hawdreki," Skarde announced next to them.

Everyone had gathered close by now. Casidhe turned to Skarde, glad for Daegan's arm wrapped securely around her waist. "What is a Hawdreki?"

Skarde studied her as he spoke. "When you gave me my sister's letter, I was ... hurt. I thought we were close enough to share all, but I never pushed Shannon to reveal her secrets. Perhaps that allowed us to remain so close." His hands were folded together, arms hanging at ease in front of his body. "I was chastised by Herrick and Brynhild for not wishing to war as they did. Shannon and Noreen felt I should journal. I seemed to please no sibling, but I enjoyed reading what others wrote more than laboring to understand my own thoughts."

Casidhe could appreciate trying to figure out her thoughts some days.

Continuing in a soothing voice, Skarde kept his attention specifically on Casidhe. "Shannon and I had long discussions about our family, how we were dragon shifters and also possessed jinn blood. As I saw you today, I realized she had not been speculating but telling me something important not long before she died. She spoke of what would happen if one of us mated with a jinn and had a child. I reminded her our mother had warned about choosing a jinn as a mate."

Daegan's hand moved from Casidhe's waist and rubbed up and down her arm as if he could feel her heart thumping wildly.

"Shannon would not tell me where she discovered the things she shared or why it would matter to any of us, only that I had to promise to remember every word should I need such information in the future. The letter pained me only because I miss her desperately and wished to have helped her carry that burden. That is when it all came together in my mind."

Casidhe said for the benefit of those around, "I was gifted this letter as a descendant of Shannon. She mated with a jinn in secret and birthed a child, who was believed to only be jinn. A prophet told her and her mate a female descendant would one day take possession of Shannon's sword, which I did when I faced a furious ice dragon shifter."

Skarde asked, "Herrick?"

An angry rumble came from deep inside Daegan.

Chuckling, Casidhe said, "Yes, it was Herrick, but he was not prepared for a pissed-off woman. The sword came to me and Shannon's armor shielded my body, then I knocked him on his butt with my power. That power comes and goes I think because I'm not confident in it yet."

Poor Skarde. He was happy, yet sad, too.

Tristan, Lanna, and Garwyli's eyes remained on Casidhe, likely realizing shifting was not unexpected, only the result. Casidhe said, "To sum all this up, had I bonded with a jinn, I might have become a powerful jinn. The letter also warned if I bonded with any other bein', includin' a dragon, I might turn into a ... monster."

"'Tis why ya tried to hold back," Daegan commented.

"Yes."

"You did not possess all the information," Skarde said. "I knew after my conversation with Shannon, I had to find out more without pointing a finger at her. I foolishly thought at the time she had found a jinn male and was trying to decide if she should take him to mate. I never guessed she had already done so or birthed a child by him." Skarde's eyes were distant as he continued. "I went to our mother, who I knew would not suspect *me* of choosing a jinn as I had shown no serious inclination toward choosing a mate at that time. To be honest, my heart was taken."

Casidhe's heart softened toward Skarde for his deep interest in Jennyver.

Daegan's fingers tightened on her arm, but not painfully. She had a feeling Daegan had not come to terms with Skarde's adoration of Jennyver, especially with his sister still missing because of Herrick.

Skarde glanced at a bird flying by, then shook himself back to the present. "My mother enjoyed discussing ancestorial information among other things. When I spun enough story to slip in my question, I asked her about a child of such a match. She smiled at me and said, 'You may shield her secrets and I will share what she does not know.' I laughed. My siblings and I believed we were so smart as we grew. Then with a few words, she reminded us who held the knowledge."

Lanna had been somewhat patient, though shifting her weight from foot to foot. "Is Casidhe from line of Hawdreki shifters?"

Garwyli rolled his eyes and whispered, "Patience, child."

Sighing loud enough to reach all ears, she nodded.

Skarde gave Lanna a polite smile of indulgence. "My mother explained about Shannon's female descendants as Casidhe just shared."

"Female?" Casidhe asked.

"Yes. My mother claimed if Shannon had a child with a jinn, her power descendants would be females and many centuries would pass before one possessed her sword. The next step would be bonding. Mother said she knew of a legend that the descendant of a powerful dragon shifter bonded to a jinn would produce a Hawdreki. She held out hope one of her five children would be that child with every birth."

"Why?" echoed around the group.

"Because my mother was descended from the *first* jinn, an immortal being. She had expected to die as soon as she birthed the one to become a Hawdreki. When that did not happen, she warned all of us to not mate with a jinn. She had grown up around many deceitful ones and feared such a mating. She hoped my twin would not rush into anything, having had a dream that Shannon would not live to see the first anniversary of her only child's birth. I told her I truly believed Shannon had not mated yet, but I would speak to her. Mother said she hoped so, then said a Hawdreki shifter would be more powerful than a dragon shifter."

Casidhe had hit overload and slumped against Daegan.

She was not a monster or dying. She could shift into a Hawdreki, whatever that looked like, and fly. But she honestly feared trying to shift again any time soon.

That had been terrifying.

In spite of feeling overwhelmed, she asked, "Was there anythin' else?"

Skarde seemed reluctant to share more, but he'd come too far to stop now. "My mother said legend held the Hawdreki would live a long time if she did not die of her own choosing."

Daegan did not like one word of that. "Casidhe would not take her life!"

"I did not say such a thing, Daegan. I said unless *she* died by her own choice. If you think about it, you will understand."

Maybe she *had* reached her limit. Casidhe said, "Thank you all for bein' so supportive when I truly did not expect to survive this change. I feared havin' to live far away and alone as a monster if I did survive. I know in my heart you would not have been unkind to me no matter what I turned into. I don't know everyone well, but I hope to get to know you better." She swung her attention to Lanna. "You did nothin' wrong for tellin' me your honest thoughts. You can't take responsibility for somethin' that is only my decision."

Lanna nodded. "Thank you. I still learn how much to say."

Garwyli tossed the young woman a tired look as a grandfather might over a bright student unable to sit still in class.

Would Daegan want her to live here in Treoir?

Casidhe should have asked Daegan about the future, but life together still seemed so far away.

Of all the things she had to worry about, her mind went back to Zeelindar's last words about the death wall closure requiring the sacrifice of a powerful being.

Daegan had been birthed by a goddess.

She was descended from a jinn god.

Before she had time to think that through, Daegan became very still. He announced to her and Tristan, "Trey has called to inform me Loki wishes for a meetin' immediately. Loki said it has to do with the fate of our Imortik-possessed Beladors still in VIPER lockdown."

"Freakin' Loki can't ever help," Tristan groused.

Daegan shrugged. "I have the feelin' somethin' has changed by what Trey passed on. He said Loki had not demanded my presence but merely informed me there is now a short window of time to protect my people."

"I'll go with you," Casidhe offered.

"Nay. Loki may allow Tristan, but no more, to enter the Tribunal with me. I have no idea what is goin' on."

She turned up that stubborn chin. "We agreed you would trust me to make my own decisions. I am a Hawdreki. I'm still havin' trouble acceptin' that, but it's beside the point. I have power to protect myself and stand with you to fight."

Skarde, Lanna, and Garwyli waited nearby, all happy to listen in.

Daegan tossed Tristan a look, which his second caught onto quickly and walked over to talk to those three snoops.

Then Daegan tugged Casidhe another thirty feet away.

When she stood in front of him, his intense gaze took her breath away. It was as if he couldn't take his eyes off her.

The impact of what they'd done finally sank in.

"I am in awe of our bond," Daegan said, his voice thick with emotion. "As if 'tis not the most precious gift ever, ya can also shift into a Hawdreki and fly with my dragon."

"What does your dragon think?" Casidhe suddenly worried about someone else close to Daegan not accepting her.

"Ruadh is very pleased. He is happy in a way I have never sensed before. He speaks with few words, but each one was heartfelt."

"Ruadh?"

"Aye. The only one who knows his name beside ya is Tristan. I keep it secret. Spells are cast with true names in our world." Holding her face in his hands, he said, "I do not know what these changes shall mean for the future or children, but to hold ya forever 'tis all I could wish for. Anythin' else shall be an unexpected blessin'."

She hadn't thought about children, but she'd love to build a family with this amazing man. Still, just as he said, if they only had each other, that would be enough for her as well.

He continued, "I do not ask ya to stay here because I doubt your power or skill in battle. Skarde claims ya may be far more powerful than me."

Her face warmed with a blush. "I am not claimin' that, Daegan."

"Oh, but I shall and be proud to lift ya high to the world and declare ya as the most magnificent mate of all times."

She blinked hard. "Don't you dare make me cry and ruin all my badass points," she muttered, swiping her eyes.

Stepping up close, he laughed and hugged her body, which formed against his as if they'd been made together then the mold broken.

He whispered, "We were always meant for each other. After two thousand years of bein' captive then freed in this new world, I believed I would spend the rest of my days alone. Then ya came along full of fire and beautiful in so many ways. Now I realize the fates had chosen the perfect woman for me and I had only to be patient until they placed ya in my path. I shall be forever grateful no matter how long it took to find ya."

He lifted her face to his and kissed her deeply.

This right here was all she'd ever hoped for. The mere thought of losing him and all they shared terrified her.

She kissed him, holding onto this feeling. She would not lose him unless she had to walk into a fire to keep him alive.

For him, she would face anything.

He brushed a hand over her hair, which had to be scattered from the shift alone. "Another reason I wish for ya to stay here while I make this one trip is for ya to learn about shiftin' in a safe place. I would give very much to stop the world from movin' forward so I might be here with my dragon to help ya, but I must go quickly to protect our people."

He said *our* people.

She had gained even more from this bond.

She lunged up, wrapping her arms around his neck and he caught her to him, swinging her around. She did not want him to leave. So many beings and monsters were out to kill him. When he finally released her, she said, "Do not be gone long or I will find a way to the human world."

He pecked a kiss on her forehead. "I have no doubt. I have learned my lesson of underestimatin' ya."

"Good." She'd put on a strong front for him. She wanted him to be confident while gone to face Loki with no distractions.

Daegan walked them back to Lanna, Skarde, and Garwyli. "I shall not be gone long and wish for ya to arrange whatever Casidhe may need."

"The lass shall be fine, Daegan." Garwyli slanted a look at Skarde. "'Twill be good for her ta have Skarde share his knowledge of shiftin'."

Skarde looked absolutely shaken. "You will allow me to remain out here, Daegan?"

Tristan cocked an eyebrow at Daegan, waiting for his decision.

Trust had to be earned and shared. "Aye, 'tis a good suggestion. I only ask if ya shift that ya stay here close to Garwyli and Lanna."

"I wouldn't dare fly away, Daegan." Skarde's normally solemn face lit up with a grin.

"Ya have my appreciation for givin' Casidhe aid. She is your family, too, after all."

Skarde shifted his stare to her. "Shannon's descendant. My niece."

Family. Casidhe's heart could not hold any more joy. These people all looked at her as if she were truly family. She would do her best to earn their respect.

Daegan stepped over to Lanna, quietly asking, "Have ya had any luck in huntin' for Sen with the glass thing Tristan brought ya?"

"Not really. I saw where Sen was fighting Imortiks inside VIPER, but nothing from when he and Adrianna were captured. I will keep trying." Lanna sounded more troubled than disappointed.

"Thank ya." Daegan had kept his voice nice, but Casidhe was starting to know him better. Had he needed information on Sen for Loki? She'd heard pieces about him and Adrianna being captured but not why Sen was important.

She waved at Daegan right before he and Tristan teleported away.

Casidhe spent the next half hour changing from human form to Hawdreki, then back. She didn't quite have the knack of pulling clothes to her as fast as Daegan, she discovered in the most embarrassing way.

Each time she looked up, Garwyli and Skarde averted their gazes.

Not Lanna. She grinned and shouted encouragement.

When her shifting began to slow down and take more effort, Casidhe announced, "I am becomin' tired."

Skarde told her, "You don't want to shift that many times so closely anyhow. Twice in a day can be a lot."

"Oh. How could I change so many more times here?"

Garwyli's thick white eyebrows lifted. "Treoir allows ya more power than in the human world."

"Really? Why?"

"Daegan's powers ta heal and change benefit by bein' in this realm as he is of King Gruffyn's immediate family. Our Belador queen and her descendants in Treoir give power ta our Beladors as well. Through the bond ya share with Daegan, ya also benefit when here."

Lanna's face had become closed. "Yes. Is wonderful to have."

Garwyli caught her eye and gave her some look that made Lanna shrug. "I say nothing more."

Casidhe wanted to be ready the minute Daegan returned. She announced, "I am not a pro at shiftin' yet, but I think I can do it when called upon. I would really like to freshen up and maybe grab a bite of food while we read more of the second grimoire volume."

"Yes." Lanna acted as if Casidhe had just solved her problems, but Casidhe did not believe the lighthearted look on Lanna's face. She could feel worry trickling from the young woman. Maybe she'd find out more in the library.

# CHAPTER 23

THE WOODS WERE UNNATURALLY QUIET when Daegan and Tristan arrived outside VIPER headquarters in the North Georgia Mountains.

Normally Sen would be the one to open the wall by using his power, but no one had found him. If Daegan were pressed to guess, he'd say Sen had not lived through the explosion Adrianna barely survived.

Tristan had asked Garwyli about her while Daegan had spoken to Lanna. Adrianna could not walk yet. He had to find the time to see her himself then be the one to inform Isak of how much she could heal.

Reese might not make it back to Quinn.

Beladors faced the end of the world as they knew it if the Imortiks won.

The losses kept piling up.

Daegan called telepathically, *Loki!*

In the next moment, Daegan and Tristan teleported into the Tribunal.

That same too quiet hollow feeling outside hit Daegan again in this realm.

Loki slumped upon a throne. Alone on the dais.

"Where are the other two?" Daegan asked, though he could do without Hermes.

"Everyone is gone." Loki tapped his fingers on the arm of the golden throne outfitted with black cushions. "You must take your people."

"We still have to force the Imortiks behind the death wall." Daegan would make sure his possessed Beladors were safe, but more than that he wished to return them to their original bodies. The goddess Justitia missing bothered him the most.

"As I understand it, I must have a goddess involved to call up and close the death wall."

Loki stared at him for long seconds. "You aren't hearing me. You have lost, Daegan. There is no way to call up the death wall, put Imortiks behind that wall, or close it. Without Sen, I have no way to keep VIPER operating."

"Ya cannot just pull up stakes and leave. This is the future of the entire human world." Daegan throttled his desire to knock some sense into this irritating god.

"Oh, please, tell me something I don't know," Loki smarted off.

Tristan glanced over and lifted his shoulders.

Daegan understood. They had to find a goddess regardless of what was going on with Loki. "Where is Macha? She should be willin' to help us."

Loki sat up straight. "You are joking, right?"

"Nay. She has an investment in her followers, too. She should have been here the whole time helpin' us locate the grimoire volumes."

Loki stood and paced, laughing under his breath. When he paused, he turned to Daegan. "She came here, claiming she would find a grimoire volume, then failed because she was so determined to kill you."

Manipulating deities. Daegan should have known those two had been conniving behind his back. "Ya must have promised her somethin' for the grimoire volumes. What treasure did she walk away from to kill me?"

Cocking a sly eyebrow, Loki said, "If she had delivered even one volume and provided the name of the being who started all this, you would have failed at your agreement with the Tribunal, true?"

"Aye."

"Based upon that outcome, you would have had to speak the name of your mother." Loki called up a glass of wine. "We told Macha if she succeeded before you, she could be present when you announced the identity of your mother. Somewhere along the way, the idea of making it appear as if someone else had killed you and her gaining rule over Treoir again tempted her more than learning your mother's name. From what I heard, she tried to kill Queen Maeve before that batshit queen could capture you again. Evidently, Queen Maeve has gained a great deal more power from her insanity. She wounded Macha bad enough for Macha to call upon Dagda to teleport her away."

Tristan blew out air that sounded like a soft *wow*.

Walking back across the dais, Loki made a clicking sound with his tongue. "Everyone was too busy trying to capture or kill you to be of any real help."

Tristan muttered under his breath, "Freaking crazies."

Daegan nodded in agreement, then told Loki, "And it sounds as if ya and the rest of the Tribunal were too busy makin' deals behind my back to worry about the Imortiks."

Loki raged and grew another two feet. Horns shot from his head and his suit disintegrated, replaced by a billowing long black coat. Thunder rocked the realm and wind blistered the air. "I have spent more time here than any other deity. Do *not* think to point fingers at me. I did *not* open the rift."

Hair flew around Daegan's face, but he stood rigid against the power wind with arms crossed. "'Tis not the entire truth. Ya come here more to entertain yourself than anythin' and now ya leave when ya could do some good."

"All of the Tribunal deities have pulled back," Loki shouted. "No goddess will leave a realm unless the Imortiks are stopped. Justitia figured out who Tenebris is. A demigod who enjoys the protection of a powerful pantheon. Tenebris likely took Sen to his home realm."

Daegan held so much disgust for this group. "Deities enjoy all the attention and devotion they receive, but when 'tis time to aid humans and less powerful nonhumans, ya all turn tail and run."

Loki did not explode with indignation as expected. He shrugged. "Based upon what I've heard happened with closing the first death wall, all three grimoire volumes will be needed in Atlanta where the first rift appeared to do it again." He took his time, walking past the throne as he spoke. "Immortals do not wish to be around with so much supernatural power in one place. This is not the same as two thousand years ago, Daegan, when supernaturals were careful about traveling to one location where others might be."

Daegan had nothing to gain from Loki. "Ya called me here about my people. What did ya mean by a small window of time?"

"I am releasing your possessed Beladors from lockdown."

"Nay! They shall be fully possessed or very close in days."

Loki stared up for the count of three then dropped his head with a sound of disgust. "What I've been trying to tell you is that I have no idea when or if a Tribunal will form again in this realm." He stopped quickly. "Did your person find out anything on Sen from the glass container I sent with Quinn?"

"Not yet. She is still searchin'." But Daegan had serious doubts if Lanna could find Sen at this point.

"That settles it."

"What are ya sayin'?"

"Tenebris sent word to Hermes to deliver a message to the Tribunal. He correctly saw Hermes as the least threatening one to contact. Tenebris is livid about the witch blowing up his hidey hole in Atlanta. Evidently Tenebris enjoys the human world. Anyhow, he lost interest in keeping Sen once Adrianna used Witchlock. Tenebris now demands we deliver Adrianna in exchange for Sen."

"Nay!" Daegan pushed back. "She is healin' in Treoir and no one is to touch her."

Lifting a shoulder in a sign of not caring, Loki went on. "That's your choice. I will be gone by the time he and his pantheon show up to destroy everything in sight. I asked for twenty-four hours but received no reply. There is no telling when he will return. That is why you have to retrieve your possessed people now. I'm leaving as soon as this meeting ends. With Sen gone, there is no one else to teleport your people out of here. They would be stuck until they died. I am fulfilling our agreement."

Daegan thought on it and came up with only one answer. "When we teleport outside the VIPER mountain, allow me one minute, then send the possessed Beladors to me there."

"I can do this."

Loki must really want to be done with this to offer aid at all. Daegan told Tristan, "As soon as we leave, I shall take control of the Beladors while ya contact Quinn. He said he had a place to hold Reese if she would come in."

Tristan shrugged. "I hope he has enough room."

"We shall make it work." Daegan had to find a goddess, but the selfish beings were going to hide. "I hope every goddess who refuses to give aid shall remember they had a chance to make a difference."

Amused now, Loki suggested, "You could call your mother."

Daegan found nothing humorous about using that option. How could he risk it when his father had warned him time and again to never utter her name. He'd even said Daegan might be better off not calling her even if that was his only hope for surviving.

"Then again, she might be of no use," Loki added. "I wasn't there the first time Imortiks were put down and think you need someone who was present because so little is known. No one wished to write down details. Better that no one knew how to open or close the wall beyond what is in the grimoires. That means you won't have all the information when the time comes. You do know what duty the goddess performs, don't you?"

This was not a time to play ego games. Daegan kept silent.

"It's quite simple. As I understood it, the body of a powerful being is needed to close the wall. Last time, the Fae female who had partnered with the sorcerer to create Imortiks had been joined with the sorcerer as one body by a goddess. She then used that dual body as a sacrifice to form the gates for the death wall, evidently locking the Imortiks behind it. If the gates still exist on the death wall, I have no idea what role a sacrifice plays this time."

Tristan rarely spoke in the Tribunal, but asked, "Who was *that* goddess?"

"I could not gain her name, though I did try."

Loki would only have done so for the power of holding that information.

Daegan thought back on what he'd been told. "While traipsin' around to find grimoire volumes, I recalled hearin' the Fae escaped and the dragons dealt with the sorcerer to close the wall."

Loki's eyebrows lifted in an arrogant way. "You must realize deities create false narratives often to blur history, especially about Imortiks."

"Why would they do such a thing?"

"To hide the fact a powerful being must be sacrificed. A number of goddesses know the truth of what happened long ago. Would you want to be the goddess who tells another being they were chosen to be sacrificed?"

"Of course not, but what of the bein' who opened the rift this time? Same as the sorcerer, that person should face death for all the lives destroyed and make a legitimate sacrifice," Daegan argued.

Again, Loki laughed and not with any humor. "Even if you find the being who opened the rift in Atlanta, that person may not possess enough power required in the sacrifice to force the Imortiks behind the death wall and bind it shut. The goddess chooses the sacrifice, which may end up being someone you know. You will have no say over her choice. Now, do you understand why all the goddesses have left? They neither want to make that decision nor be selected as the sacrifice."

# CHAPTER 24

REESE MADE QUINN AND THE two Beladors with him wait while she went to retrieve Renata and Kaiser. She snuck into the dark area close to the graffiti-covered bridge in the park and waved her two new friends out into the open.

When they both reached her, Kaiser had a grip on Renata's arm. Tilting his head at Renata, he said, "She's okay, just has moments when her Imortik tries to take away her control."

"Understood." Reese took two steps farther out to wave Quinn and his group over, then quickly explained who was coming in.

Kaiser had a moment of panic but managed to stand firm.

Reese could appreciate the fear of being killed. She was at risk if she ran up on a Belador unaware of her relationship with Quinn or a human military group that might blast anything yellow.

Quinn strode up, eyes going to his possessed Beladors. "I am so happy to see you both. If I could hug you, I would, but we'll work on freeing you first." Speaking with the authority of a man who had led powerful Belador warriors for a long time, he shifted gears to strategy. "We must move covertly back to the Imortik master and figure out how to grab Gretchen."

Kaiser said, "I can speak to her telepathically, but I just tried to reach out to you telepathically and it didn't work. Both of our Imortiks are in the early stages. Once we're close so I can be sure not to distract her or expose that she's communicating, I'll find out what's going on."

"Excellent."

Kaiser gave Quinn specifics on where he'd left Gretchen and the master.

Reese stayed next to Renata and Kaiser, leading the way. Quinn kept his people ten feet back as Reese had requested. He hadn't liked hanging back, but she'd reminded him how she and the other two possessed beings had no control over an Imortik jumping from one of them to Quinn or his other two Beladors.

As they neared the area where Gretchen had been left, the sound of demon blasters erupted.

Kaiser shouted, "*No!*" and ran ahead.

Quinn's harsh voice came out low. "Do not engage, Reese."

She could not let Kaiser go in alone. She caught up with him when he slid to a stop behind a tree.

Two human black ops individuals with demon blasters were approaching the spot where Reese had expected to find Gretchen and the master.

Four yellow bodies were sprawled on the ground, not moving. The two men with weapons crept forward toward the bodies.

Out of the corner of her eye, Reese caught Quinn and his team twenty feet to her left behind cover.

Kaiser said, "Gretchen is alive. I just talked to—" He stopped speaking, his gaze suddenly tense.

The two humans stepped up to look at the Imortik bodies.

"*No! It's a trap!*" Kaiser called out.

One human jerked around to face Kaiser, lifting his weapon. At the same moment, two translucent Imortiks flew up and into both of the men. Weapons dropping from their hands, the two men grabbed their heads.

The master came to his feet as if lifted by invisible arms to watch those two as they became possessed.

Reese whispered, "Tell Gretchen, this is her chance to run. We have people to protect her."

Kaiser nodded, staring intently at his friend on the ground. She quietly got to her feet and tiptoed a few steps to the side then disappeared.

The Imortik master was shouting at the two humans clawing at their bodies. "You think to kill Imortiks? Watch how we deal with puny humans."

He grabbed the face of each possessed human and their bodies shook from whatever energy he drove into them. When he let go, the bodies flopped to the ground, burst into flames, and the stink of sulfur floated to Reese.

With those two dead, the Imortik master called over his shoulder, "Come here, Belador. You must hunt your friends."

Gretchen was no longer there to obey him.

The master turned and howled, "*Traitors!*" Then he faced forward again, his skin color growing into a blinding yellow and pulsing. He lifted his voice, "Your friends must be here to save you. *Imortiks, come to me!*"

Something grabbed Reese's middle and yanked. She shoved her foot forward, fighting the pull.

Kaiser groaned and wrapped his arms around the tree.

Renata started forward with long strides.

Reese tackled her to the ground, which held Renata back, but exposed both of them to the master.

His unholy gaze snapped around to where she'd landed.

Quinn stepped out, pointed at both blasters on the ground, and used his kinetic power to make them fly to his two hands.

The Imortik master slammed a fist on the ground, sending it rolling toward the trees.

Reese stood up and balled her hands around each other, calling up a load of her demon power. Dickweed shouted in her head, *Do not harm the master!*

Oh sure, that would stop her.

Quinn flipped a blaster to another Belador and said, "*Attack!*" They had to jump over a wave of ground. Trees cracked and broke, falling to the ground with a thunderous noise.

Two blasters unloaded on the master, but that freak teleported away.

He reappeared next to Reese and grabbed her by the neck.

With her demon power humming, Reese shoved a fist of energy into the master's gut before he could leave with her.

His mouth rounded in shock. He clutched his hold around her neck tighter. Stars flew through her vision.

Kaiser kicked at the master who ignored him. Renata tried to get up, but Reese had a foot still pinning her down.

She shoved more demon power into her fist. The master's eyes turned black. She shouted in his face, "*Die, you miserable dog!*"

Dickweed screamed in her mind to stop.

Her head wanted to explode.

The master's fingers fell away. Then he vanished.

Her shout must have cut through the blaster noise. Quinn was there a second later. *"Reese?"*

She held up a hand, wheezing past her raw throat. "I'm good. So is Junior." She removed her foot from Renata's back and reached down to lift the woman. "I'm sorry, Renata."

"Thank you for saving me." Renata got to her feet then her body twisted into an impossible shape. She yelled, "Ahhh! I don't know if I can fight this thing much longer."

Reese gripped her shoulders, holding on as Renata whimpered and her body unwound. "You can do this, Renata." Reese turned to Quinn. Her heart squeezed at the agony and longing in his face before he looked away. She had to drag him out of his dark place. "Do you have somewhere safe for your Beladors, Quinn?"

He snapped around, red-rimmed eyes serious. "Yes. I—"

Gretchen staggered into sight with one hand in the air and the other over her chest. Her clothes were shredded and blood had splattered her face, but her smile was brighter than her sour yellow glow.

"It's me," Gretchen wheezed out, collapsing next to Kaiser. *"D-don't shoot!"*

Kaiser released his hold on the tree and hugged her. "You're safe."

Reese released Renata who had herself under shaky control again.

"Thank you all for freeing me." Gretchen turned to Renata. "We wouldn't be here right now if you hadn't taken that risk so we could escape."

Renata's haggard appearance fit her having been a prisoner of war with a monster. "I'm glad. I thought we would all die when he ordered me to kill an innocent person."

Reese stepped between those three and the others. "Quinn, we need you and the Beladors to back up. I know you didn't mean to get so close," she lied.

Gretchen broke free of hugs and gave a head nod to Quinn. "Good to see you, Maistir. She's right. Stay back. We don't know what these things in our bodies will do. They might jump from us to someone else like what happened to those two humans.

The Imortik master holds no value of human or nonhuman life, only if a body is a worthy vessel for an Imortik."

"We did see that sickening display," Quinn noted.

Renata spoke up. "But how did you escape the master, Gretchen, when Kaiser and I were struggling to not go back to him?"

"I would have been right there with you had I not felt his hold on me break. What happened?"

Quinn explained, "Reese used her demon energy to hurt him."

Sweat ran down Kaiser's face. "I was hugging a tree, but my grip was slipping. Thanks."

"You're welcome." It wasn't as if Reese had done something special. "I had no idea if that would even work, but we use the weapons we have."

Handing off the demon blaster to his other Belador, Quinn asked, "What can you three tell us about the master?"

Kaiser shook his head, looking to Renata, who had been possessed the longest.

"I think he's waiting on some partner to show up again and he despises his partner," Renata shared. "His Imortik has been slowly taking over his body and his partner convinced him to do this."

"What's the partner's name?" Reese asked.

"Don't know. The non-Imortik part of the master is called Timmon, who talks to himself a lot and whines that his partner compelled him so he can't even share a name. When I saw them meet one time, the partner's image was blurred and could be male or female. That one is definitely the leader. Timmon got stuck as the Imortik master and hasn't been happy about it the whole time." Renata's face and neck muscles tensed. "Timmon called this partner his cousin ... *oh, shit, he's got me again!*" Her fists shook and every muscle in her neck and shoulders tensed.

Reese grabbed her hand. "We're here." Her fingers were getting crushed between Renata's Belador strength and the monster inside her.

As Renata once more came back to them, she gasped and struggled for every breath. "Timmon ... he fought his Imortik and ... uhhhh." She spoke through clenched teeth, forcing out the words. "He ... kept threatening to contact some female, but ... " She took in deep breaths until she could finish. "His partner warned him to not dare call her or she'd make things worse. I think ... I think the Imortik inside Timmon has taken over at least ninety percent." She dropped to her knees as if merely talking was taking a toll. "Timmon's voice changes from high to deep when the Imortik is in charge."

Kaiser had crumbled to the ground next to Renata. All the possessed beings waged an internal war. It hurt Reese to watch and not be able to help them.

Listening closely to Renata, Kaiser said, "I wonder who the female is? They all have to be nonhumans and probably powerful ones."

"Oh, that's right." Renata stared thoughtfully, looking as if a light wind would knock her over. She whispered, "Timmon said something about being a demigod."

Sounding appalled, Quinn asked, "How could a demigod end up possessed by an Imortik?"

Kaiser offered, "Based on his incoherent ramblings I heard, Timmon claims his partner tricked him. Maybe it's a female love interest."

"Yes," Renata breathed out in agreement.

"Like kissing cousins?" Reese suggested in a dark tone. She would believe anything about that monster.

"With a demigod, who knows?" Gretchen lifted a shoulder to shrug and even that movement looked stiff.

"Do any of you know what Timmon or the master is planning?"

Gretchen piped up, "I do. I was actually glad when Renata and Kaiser did not return, because I wanted them to escape." She gave them a caring smile. Then she nodded at Reese. "The master said once Renata passed the test of capturing you that he'd have her lead his army to break all Imortiks out from behind the death wall."

"Bloody hell," Quinn murmured. "Did he say when or where this would happen?"

"No, but I'm thinking soon since this sounded like the only test he had planned for Renata to return. Also, while waiting for her, the master commented that he had other Beladors, but we didn't see any. He seemed to think if Renata could control us, then she would be the perfect head of his army."

With a sweeping look at all his people and Reese, Quinn said, "Renata, Kaiser, and Gretchen, would you like me to place you in a safe holding area?"

Of the three possessed Beladors, Renata was the most drained looking, but admitted, "Not yet. I want to help stop them for as long as I'm able."

With a quick glance at Gretchen, who was shaking her head, Kaiser concurred, "Not us. We've worked as a team for a long time in Europe. We can help rescue other Beladors, or anyone else for that matter, by getting close to the master. We've been possessed less than twenty-four hours. Demons and humans are overtaken pretty much immediately. We just need you to put out word to the Beladors to not attack us because we can only speak telepathically to other possessed Beladors."

"I'll arrange for that right away," Quinn confirmed. "You will need something like Reese's red shirt to help our people and allies identify you from the enemy Imortiks."

Reese frowned and slumped. "Damn. That master will be looking for a red shirt now that he's seen mine. We need a new ID tag."

Quinn pinched his lip in a thoughtful expression. "I just spoke to one of my people who is bringing ballcaps for all of you. Each cap shall have the first initial of your name on the front in a specific shape but different colors against a dingy white background. I hope to have them majikally spelled to give off a glow only our people can detect. The hats will appear well-worn rather than new."

"That's a cool idea," Reese agreed. "As soon as we get the hats, what's next?"

"We go Imortik master hunting," Quinn declared in the calmest voice, but Reese knew that man up and down.

He was ready to kill.

# CHAPTER 25

"I HOPE GARWYLI SHALL HAVE AN idea of how we might close the death wall without a goddess." Daegan hurried through the castle, having just teleported back to Treoir with Tristan.

"Isn't it just like a bunch of gods and goddesses to bail on us when they could actually do something useful."

"True. I wish I knew of at least one goddess who had been present the first time they dealt with Imortiks. I hope Casidhe shall be able to tell us more as she reads the grimoires." He didn't even lift his fist to knock as he approached Garwyli's area.

As the door opened, the old guy asked, "What has ya worked up, dragon?"

Daegan waited for Garwyli to enter ahead of him and followed with Tristan closing the door. "I shall save ya all the annoyin' details, but I saw Loki. Everyone in the Tribunal has abandoned the human world for the protection of their own realms."

"Does not surprise me." Garwyli leaned hard on his cane, walking to the chair he always preferred.

"He claims no goddess shall help. If we cannot close the death wall without a goddess, 'tis a problem." Daegan preferred to stand and pace around as he spoke. "Loki told us the goddess has to choose the bein' to sacrifice."

Garwyli tapped his fingers on the top of his cane. "I admit, I did not know this about the goddess."

Of all the things Daegan had to be concerned about, that one stood out. "He said the sacrifice must be a powerful bein'. Is someone's blood used to open or close the wall? I shall not condemn anyone to die for this wall."

"That I cannot answer," Garwyli admitted. "I believe ya shall need the last grimoire volume to reveal more details."

Tristan hadn't moved an inch while he watched the druid intently. "Loki said last time a goddess had joined the bodies of the sorcerer and Fae who created the Imortiks together to form one powerful body for the sacrifice."

Garwyli sat back with a puzzled expression. "I believed the Fae had been spared, but as I think on it, I can see how a goddess might have wished ta make them both pay. We must find out how important havin' a goddess shall be. Is there another way ta bind the wall? If they only needed a goddess to join those two bodies together, ya may not need one for closin' the wall, but if Casidhe finds out differently ... that shall be a problem. Macha claimed to have been present last time, though I have no idea if she played a role or merely watched, but I would not trust her."

Huffing out a sarcastic laugh, Daegan shared what Isak had passed along via Evalle about that goddess. "I do not expect Macha to return any time soon. She fought Queen Maeve and suffered serious injuries, according to an eyewitness. Besides, she would only raise a finger to kill me."

"'Tis the truth of it." Garwyli's face wrinkled even more with a fierce frown. "Lanna and Casidhe are in the sittin' area of the library. Young people! I never had such an area before, but Lanna would not be quiet until I gave her chairs and such."

Daegan stole a look at Garwyli. The druid still moved slowly and sounded tired, but he held much affection for Lanna. "Tristan, check on the gryphon village. Call anyone back from Atlanta who is still on patrol. There is nothin' they can do as we draw near to dealin' with the death wall and I would prefer them to patrol here. I shall recall everyone who is not with our immediate force there."

If his order had surprised Tristan, it did not show on his stoic face. "Will do."

"Thank ya, Garwyli." Daegan started for the library in the back when the druid stopped him with words.

"I know ya must have Lanna with ya when the time comes, dragon, and ya shall protect her all ya can, but she shall not stand by if her friends are in harm's way. Ya must find a way ta prevent her from harmin' herself."

"On my word, she shall be safe." Daegan strode away, out of ideas and almost out of time. He was prepared for how the misty barrier functioned, which had appeared to be an empty space during a previous trip to the old druid's library.

As soon as he crossed into the massive room with rows of bookshelves, the smell of old leather, papyrus, and Casidhe's scent filled him.

With that one breath, he felt whole. His shoulders relaxed, but he would not be fully at ease until he could ensure her safety from Imortiks.

When he found her and Lanna, the two had their heads together, murmuring over whatever they'd discovered.

Casidhe's sweet profile made his heart skip a beat. He wished to leave them both here where they would be safe. The minute he did, he would not be welcomed back by either. He would deal with their wrath if he could stop the Imortiks without them. They both wished to fulfill their duties.

He'd made an agreement with Casidhe to trust her and he always wanted her to know he believed her to be his equal.

Skarde had declared her more powerful.

That made Daegan smile. He headed to them. "What have ya learned?"

Casidhe jerked and slapped her forehead. "Must you always scare me?"

"'Tis said to be surprised as ya are comes from a guilty conscience."

Lanna had her elbow on her knee and chin propped on the palm of her hand. Her blue eyes crinkled at his teasing.

"I have a clear conscience, dragon," Casidhe claimed. "You just like to catch me unaware."

Aye, he did, but would not admit such.

Lanna sat up. "We have learned more, but need third grimoire."

Daegan went for what he had to know now. "Does it say we must have a goddess?"

Casidhe shook her head, offering a sad, "No, but these grimoire volumes are the sorcerer's journals. Entries are about creatin' the Imortiks. It does sound as if he intended to have a plan for stoppin' them if they got out of hand, but I won't know until I read the last one. I'm not really expectin' to find details for how to handle closin' the wall since that fell to the dragon shifters and goddesses. Makes sense why we need a goddess who had been involved last time."

Lanna stood and gave Daegan a stern warning. "You hold too much inside. You will not be able to stop Imortiks alone."

"I know this, Lanna."

"Your head knows, but your heart does not wish to risk any of us."

Having followed the conversation, Casidhe jumped up and strode to him. "Don't even think to leave me here."

"'Tis the truth I wish to battle with my dragon and spare all of ya, but I cannot do this. I need ya both."

Lanna didn't smile triumphantly. Instead, relief flowed across her face at Daegan's admission that he needed everyone's help to win this war.

Casidhe, on the other hand, smiled. "Thank you for not fightin' over this."

"I do not know why we need two dragons, but ya and I are the closest we come to meetin' that need. I considered bringin' Skarde, but ... he has not been in this new world at all. He would be overwhelmed and either end up dead or harmin' someone unintentionally." That still did not ease Daegan's concerns over Casidhe being here. "Have ya shifted enough to feel ya can do so when the time comes, lass?"

"Yes."

Lanna didn't look so sure, but neither did she counter Casidhe's words.

Tristan's voice came into Daegan's head. *Boss, I just heard from Quinn. Sounds like the Imortiks might be heading to where the death wall will appear.*

Hearing those words punched Daegan in the gut. He had to leave now and take these two with him. *We shall meet ya on the castle steps.*

*I'm going there now.*

Daegan wiped a hand over his mouth, hoping this would not be a mistake. He would likely make mistakes but did not want to fail either of these women. "We leave in ten minutes. Ya must have a safe way to carry the grimoire volumes."

Lifting a finger, Lanna said, "I spoke to Garwyli on this. We do not need the bronze boxes that weigh so much, just the sheets of papyrus. Garwyli has plan. He has one box. I will take this one to him now." She pointed her finger at the pages lying in two stacks and returned them to the bronze box and floated it out ahead of her.

As he watched her leave, he didn't notice Casidhe closer until she'd leaned into him with her hands on his chest. Tension which had kept him twisted in knots now eased. He lowered his chin to her head and held her to him, regretting the minute he had to let go.

She kissed his chest. "I know you don't want me there, but I do not want you there either. Once we put an end to these Imortiks, then we can ... plan a future." Her voice had drifted off.

He pulled her away from him and dropped his head down. This was the time to give hope he didn't feel. "Then we shall spend a great deal of time far from everyone." He lingered on a kiss, worried every time he touched her if it would be the last one.

Lanna called out, "I am ready."

Casidhe sighed. "Show time."

# CHAPTER 26

DAEGAN WENT ON IMMEDIATE ALERT the minute he, Tristan, Casidhe, and Lanna appeared during twilight in a wooded area of Piedmont Park.

For a major public park, this one was eerily silent with the sun having just set.

Before supernaturals were exposed to humans and Imortiks roamed the land, this area would normally have been filled with people walking pets and playing with small children this early in the evening. Between the curfew and fear of the unknown, humans had either left the city or were secure at home.

If Imortiks succeeded, humans would never have a safe haven again in this world.

Tristan stepped out of the cover first. "I had Trey send word to Isak you wanted to talk to him."

"Good."

The whomping of helicopters in different directions and loud truck motors replaced Atlanta's normal traffic sounds.

Lanna started to follow Tristan.

Daegan hooked a hand on her arm. "Stay here." He stepped ahead of her and turned to face the women. "Ya both promised to do as I *asked.*" He emphasized the word *asked* so Casidhe would not get her feathers ruffled.

She had feathers to ruffle now.

"I only wish to see if people are here," Lanna replied in defense of her action.

"Nay. The only ones we may see shall be Beladors, other nonhumans, both allies and enemies, as well as human military. Ya must keep an eye around ya at all times. The Imortiks are continuin' to pour into the city. Right before we left, Garwyli said the numbers might grow if Imortiks escapin' through other rifts besides the first one are now bein' called to Atlanta. I have many reasons I wish to have both of ya surrounded by guards, but we do not have enough Beladors. If ya need one more reason to take care, keep in mind how we may not succeed if any of us make a mistake such as allowin' an Imortik to take ya."

Finally, a healthy level of fear climbed into Lanna's face.

Casidhe respected the danger of Imortiks, but now that she had evolved into a Hawdreki, Daegan had to make sure she understood she was just as vulnerable as Lanna.

"Here he comes," Tristan announced, lifting a hand, signaling to a black Hummer.

Isak's driver jumped the curb and drove straight to them.

Tristan said, "Park management wouldn't like that, but with the war we're fighting in this city, that will likely be the least of what gets damaged."

Isak stepped out from the passenger side, one hand cupped against an ear. He uttered a brief reply then lowered his hand. Little changed on this man, who stayed fully ready as a soldier. He wore what Tristan called black cargo pants and a tactical vest with a matching T-shirt beneath, which strained to hold in Isak's powerful body.

A rear passenger door opened and out came Senior Agent Huntsen from France.

Daegan thought he'd never see that man again after Tzader aided Daegan in escaping Huntsen's lockup. Nothing of the annoying man had changed from short hair similar to the National Guardsmen around Atlanta to a face with deeply carved lines reminding Daegan of pets called bulldogs. Unlike the guards here, Huntsen wore a black shirt and pants. Beady eyes too dark to reveal a color tightened with one look at Daegan.

Isak spoke first. "I have teams spread out over the city and ready to move as soon as they know where to go."

"I think we should—" Huntsen started.

Isak cut him off with a slice of his hand. "This is *not* France. You have been given ally status *with* restrictions. You can talk after I finish. Understood?"

Huntsen had no trouble understanding, but he clearly did not like anyone treating him as a foot soldier.

Daegan had little time to spare. "I intend to call my Belador teams together and form one unit to follow the master leadin' an army of Imortiks. I have seen ya stage your people in the most effective way. I wish for our strengths to compliment one another's."

"Are you working with nonhumans, Nyght?" Huntsen asked in a voice reeking of disgust.

Isak's jaw muscle jumped.

Daegan lifted a hand, asking for him to wait.

Tristan had stepped away and turned his back, shielding his gaze when the Hummer showed.

Daegan wanted him here. "Tristan?"

"Yeah, boss?"

"Join me." Daegan watched Huntsen's face change from angry to shocked to wary. Before the human could say another word, Daegan powered up his voice. "Do not speak or ya shall regret the consequence."

"Listen here, weirdo."

"*Lanna!*" Daegan had no doubt she'd understand what he wanted.

She stepped forward.

Huntsen smirked at her as if she were a joke.

She smiled, lifted her finger, and spoke softly.

His mouth clamped shut. He grabbed at his lips, eyes terrified.

She told him, "Please listen to Daegan and Isak. When Daegan and Isak wish you to speak again, I will free your mouth."

This guy stared at Isak with a deranged look.

Isak sounded beat down when he sighed in Huntsen's direction. "I tried to tell you we have nonhuman allies and protectors watching over the humans. Shut up and learn something." He nodded at Daegan. "This one is the dragon king of Treoir, another realm from our world. Tristan is a Belador and shifts into a gryphon with his own set of powers. You met Lanna and she gave you a *tiny* glimpse of what she can do. I'll let Daegan finish the last introduction."

Daegan stepped aside for Casidhe to join them. "This is Casidhe, my mate and a Hawdreki shifter."

Isak's eyebrow shot up. "Congratulations. I look forward to

finding out what a Hawdreki is when we have time."

It might be boasting, but Daegan didn't care when he said, "She shifts into somethin' beautiful and deadly with wings. I am told she may be more powerful than me."

Casidhe's cheeks pinked. She sent him a quick glance that scolded him for embarrassing her, but he knew she appreciated his words filled with pride.

Huntsen's ruddy skin lost another shade of color with each introduction.

Daegan told him, "The man who came to retrieve me at your buildin' is another powerful Belador. What ya do not understand is that Beladors have lived among humans for thousands of years. Our people are in law enforcement, medical, teachin', and every other type of duty in many countries. They took a vow to protect humans long ago and many are married to humans. No other force in this world is as strong as ours or as dedicated to the innocent. But ya must understand we have innocent nonhumans as well."

Huntsen quieted, his eyes glued to Daegan.

Daegan had no idea what that look meant, and didn't care, as long as the man did not get in his way or harm his people. He filled Isak in on all he knew about the grimoire volumes and how they expected to draw in the third one. "We have the first two grimoire volumes sealed in a bag shielded with majik in hopes to not pull in the third one until we are ready. This may all turn into a bloody battle."

"Copy that."

Daegan took those two words as an acknowledgement.

Evalle called out from beyond the Hummer, "Hey, hold up. I'm coming."

When she arrived, Daegan introduced her to Huntsen. "This is our North American Belador Maistir. She leads all of our forces on this land and her word is final. She is also capable of shiftin' into a gryphon."

Evalle fingered her dark sunglasses, lowering them to reveal her bright green gaze. "Hi, there."

When Huntsen said nothing, she asked Daegan, "Is he mute?"

Lanna answered, "Yes. He would not stop talking. Daegan

asked for silence. Congratulations on becoming Maistir."

Huffing out a grumble, Evalle said, "Thanks."

It had taken some work to convince Evalle she was ready, but she understood more than most how Quinn could not return any time soon. To hear her accept her new position in front of everyone without qualifying it as temporary was exactly what Daegan needed. She made him proud.

He turned to Isak. "I asked Evalle to take a team and stay with ya so that we shall be able to communicate immediately."

Huntsen narrowed his eyes, staring at Daegan as if he didn't understand.

Tristan filled him in. "We also communicate telepathically."

"That's a good idea," Isak admitted. "My men are all on comm units, but it gets confusing for your people sometimes."

Evalle rolled her eyes. "He means I don't use the correct radio jargon when I speak."

"From what Casper told me, you don't have radio etiquette either," Tristan said in a lighthearted tease.

"True that." Evalle shrugged.

Huntsen crossed his arms and amped up his glare at Daegan and Isak.

Daegan instructed Huntsen, "I shall have Lanna free your mouth if ya are willin' to discuss this as an ally. If not, ya shall be teleported into Isak's ride."

"Agreed," Isak confirmed.

Lanna lifted her finger and whispered again.

Huntsen watched her suspiciously, then opened his mouth, moving his jaw to stretch muscles.

Isak asked, "What's the verdict?"

"I'm willing to hear what you have to say, but I want to be able to give my honest feedback," Huntsen pointed out.

"Let's try this, Daegan." Isak had the look of a man whose patience had been smashed to bits.

"First, ya must know when not to shoot. Killin' the wrong supernatural could mean destroyin' the one hope humans have to survive, and they shall fall first to an invasion of Imortiks," Daegan started, watching Huntsen struggle to remain quiet. "The only way for the human military to destroy Imortiks is to use powerful weapons across the entire land. Even then, ya would kill many innocent humans and still lose the war."

Huntsen asked, "Why?"

"Because Imortiks would continue to escape through rifts openin' all over the world. There is only one way to save this world from Imortiks. We must force them behind a death wall and close that wall forever."

"Where is this wall?"

Casidhe asked, "If I may?" When Daegan gave her a quick nod, she shared, "I also have a gift for readin' ancient text. I have been translatin' the first two grimoire volumes."

"What's a grimoire?" Huntsen actually sounded interested.

Lanna cocked her head at Huntsen as if he were a strange being. "Simple explanation is book of majik. This one is much more. A powerful sorcerer and Fae joined forces to create Imortiks. This grimoire was his journal. When last Imortiks were put behind wall, grimoire was broken into three parts. Three dragon shifter families from two thousand years ago each hid a volume. Someone found one volume and used majik to open rift but cannot open death wall to free all Imortiks without the other two we have."

"Excellent explanation, Lanna." Casidhe continued, "We believe the third volume will explain how to stop Imortiks. The sorcerer who created Imortiks might have had a way to control or even destroy them if he needed to, but that was not in the first two grimoires."

Frowning might be Huntsen's natural expression. He wore it so well. "So you do know how to destroy the Imortiks?"

"Not yet. We must locate the third grimoire volume." Daegan appreciated what Zeelindar had told them of how to find number three, but with all he knew at this point, that would be the most difficult to obtain. It wasn't as if the person holding the last one would allow the grimoire volume to join the other two without interfering.

Probably sensing Daegan's concerns, Casidhe interjected, "When we have the third volume, I'll read it as quickly as I can to locate the information we need."

Huntsen asked, "When did this all originally happen?"

Casidhe gave Daegan a sideways glance, waiting on his reply.

"'Twas before I was born." Daegan found simple worked best with this annoying human.

"For Pete's sake, when was that?" Huntsen grumbled.

"Two thousand years ago."

Huntsen swallowed hard, tried to talk, then couldn't seem to find the words.

Isak did not allow Huntsen to say more. "Moving along, that's the gist of what we're doing. I don't want fifty questions about all this from here on. Ask me anything pertinent to whatever we are doing at the moment and you can stay with my people."

"Plus me," Evalle piped up, her face revealing amusement with Huntsen's dilemma.

Daegan drove home Isak's point. "Stand with us and ya shall gain nonhuman allies, a value of which ya shall soon realize."

While Huntsen still suffered from his brain not feeding his mouth, Isak said, "I'll make this easy for you. I've had many years of running operations to locate nonhuman predators. The top of our government knows me and sends projects my way when they need special help. Nonhumans are not a new subject for them. As I stepped from the Hummer, I received orders being sent to the National Guard and other military teams here that I am coordinating and taking the lead on human and nonhuman defensive forces. You're either onboard or heading back to France immediately."

"I may regret these words, but I'm in and my men will follow Isak's lead. I need to know how to deal with situations like this in my territories." Huntsen's gaze skipped from face to face as if gauging reactions to his words.

"There's an idea," Casidhe snapped. "Learnin' about who you're dealin' with before you toss a dragon shifter into your prison and threatin him. Make that mistake again and we will *all* show up at your door."

When every person around Daegan nodded, including Isak, Huntsen said not a word.

Daegan was still angry about Huntsen snatching him off a cliff in Spain and forcing him to leave Casidhe alone. But he took immense satisfaction in her words.

She would make a formidable leader should he fall in this war. Isak grunted a sound of acceptance.

Quinn's voice entered Daegan's head. *I'm in East Point with Reese and a group of possessed Beladors. We've been following the Imortik master. He's leading an army of Imortiks somewhere and gaining Imortiks as he goes. What do you want me to do?*

# CHAPTER 27

D AEGAN TOLD ISAK AND HIS people of Quinn's location. Tristan always seemed to know when Daegan needed help with details and called to him telepathically. *East Point is southwest of the city.*

Without pausing, Daegan tipped his head at Tristan, thanking him while he finished his thoughts. "Quinn wants to save Reese at all costs, which I understand, but I need to keep him away from the master and I believe Reese would support me on that. An Imortik with Quinn's mind lock ability could be used as a weapon against everyone. Quinn would not want that to happen. I shall take Casidhe and Lanna to meet up with him, then inform Evalle of what we do next."

Tristan did not ask about his role. He knew he would be at Daegan's side throughout all of this.

Isak took a minute thinking then said, "I'll send teams to strategic positions on each side of Quinn's current location. We'll be able to move in faster from there when you give the word. I'll keep helos in the area but prevent them from flying over the Imortiks until it's time to attack. Depending on the terrain when the two teams arrive, we'll try to put snipers with demon-killing loads up high."

Evalle put her phone away from where she'd been texting. "Storm and Casper are up to speed. They're covertly tracking a pair of Imortiks northwest of the city and said those two just did an about-face to head south. That could put them on track to reach the master at some point."

Tristan asked, "What about the human National Guard we know is here and special operatives in the city? Are they just here for surveillance?"

"No. I know all the players here on our side." Isak addressed everyone. "I have my top people attached as a communication connection for military special operations units we need in active roles. The National Guard is to push humans back from these areas and do their best to prevent any dangerous outbreaks of citizen chaos. People are afraid, which we all understand. The National Guard is best suited to protect the locals, even from other humans."

"Good thing." Evalle shook her head. "Some idiots thought this would be an opportune time to loot businesses and homes. The National Guard shut that bunch down quickly."

Isak's steady gaze never wavered. "Yep. I've made it clear to the powers in charge that once this is over they need to meet with your representatives, Daegan. Going forward, this world will continue in chaos unless we come to an agreement on both sides. Nonhumans are officially out to the public. If you can stop this Imortik invasion and show humans whose side you're on, they'll be more open to having talks on how to move forward. If not, there will be nothing to talk about."

"'Tis well done, Isak," Daegan praised. "I sent word out days ago that *any* nonhuman found attackin' a human or nonhuman shall be killed. There are no second chances or excuses when we have informed those in our world to stay away from the southeastern region, specifically the Atlanta area, if they are not a member of our teams."

"I like it." Isak glanced to his left. "Huntsen? Ready to roll?"

Without speaking a word, Huntsen backed away from Daegan and his people, gripped the rear passenger door handle, and jumped in.

Isak would normally take off at this point, but he hesitated. "Is there word on Adrianna?"

Lanna offered him an encouraging smile. "She had bad injuries. We put her in healing sleep for long time."

"She's in a coma?"

"Is like that, but this sleep heals better when body is not struggling. She is awake now and ... ready to continue."

"I don't mean to sound unappreciative, but what does that mean? Can she walk?"

Daegan had the same concerns but knew his people, Lanna

especially, would inform him once she and Garwyli knew what they would be able to do for Adrianna.

"Adrianna is strong. Witchlock is powerful." Lanna took her time choosing her words. "She does not walk yet, but I am full of hope. Garwyli and I work to heal her all day. I left him at her side. Adrianna smiled and asked everyone to be safe."

Daegan admired the way Lanna had given hope without saying for sure if Adrianna would be able to walk again. He felt sick at the possibility a woman they all called friend, and one Isak cared deeply for, might not regain that ability.

"Thank you. Please send word to me when you know more."

"Yes. I promise."

Coming from Lanna, that was a vow.

Isak and Evalle turned toward his vehicle. With a quick hand signal from Isak, one of his men exited the rear passenger door on the driver's side, leaving it open.

Evalle stopped walking. "Isak, I know you mean for me to be close by inside the Hummer so we can communicate, but I'm more useful outside. I have faster speed, telekinetic power, and can sense nonhumans coming our way."

That admission brought on another jaw-drop moment for Huntsen, who had opened his door with his ear cocked to listen.

"Copy that." With a new hand signal, Isak's man returned to the vehicle.

Isak climbed into the front passenger spot, slammed the door, and rolled down the window. All the doors closed and every window dropped at the same moment.

As the Hummer's headlights flicked on, Evalle stepped up on the running board next to Isak's seat and grabbed a handhold just inside his door.

Once the Hummer departed, Daegan linked with Tristan then asked him to gain Quinn's exact location and teleport their team to him.

They landed in the outfield of a small baseball park off Kimmeridge Drive in East Point, Tristan informed Daegan.

Daegan told him telepathically, *I wish to leave Casidhe with Quinn until we need her with us. Quinn shall want to track Reese, but I fear he might rush in when he should not or use his mind lock, which is just as dangerous to him and others. Go along with what I say.*

*Understood, boss.*

Quinn emerged from the dark woods bordering the field with two Belador warriors close behind, which pleased Daegan to see. Reese walked slightly behind him then three more glowing yellow beings trailed behind.

"Wait here for me," Daegan announced, holding his people in place.

"How about I go, too?" Tristan pushed with urgency. "It would be even worse for an Imortik to jump you."

"Yes." Daegan blinked out of sight then reappeared quickly, now standing twenty feet from his former Maistir. "What is goin' on, Quinn?"

"These Imortiks are all our people." Quinn turned to his group. "Renata is back."

Daegan hadn't felt weak in the knees in a long time, but losing Renata that day when she had been so close for him to grasp had haunted him continually. "Renata?"

She stepped forward with a woman and man on each side, each holding onto one of her arms. She had lost weight and her dark eyes sagged with exhaustion. It hurt to think of what she'd endured, but Daegan would not give up a moment of seeing her still alive.

Sniffling, Renata brought up a trembling smile. "These Beladors are Kaiser and Gretchen, who came to help from Europe. My control is shaky at times because of how long I've been—" She jerked, her back arching until she stood on her toes keening in pain. She shouted, *"No! Shut up!"*

Daegan started for her.

Quinn threw a hand up, his face struggling to hide his own agony for Renata. "She has moments when the monster tries to take full control, but she has managed incredibly well in spite of everything. Kaiser and Gretchen will keep her safe. They have only been possessed a day."

Kaiser explained, "We react differently. I sometimes think I'm losing to the monster, but as long as I don't pass out I can manage it."

Gretchen added, "Pretty much the same for me. Our Imortiks can't seem to speak to the master telepathically, but the master can call us to him if we don't have a way to hold back."

Frustration rolled off Quinn. "I offered to put all four of them in a safe holding place where our people would protect them, but they wanted to stay free to fight."

Daegan had to tear his gaze from Renata. "I am very proud of ya all. We have two grimoire volumes and have learned how to call the third one in with those two when the time comes. We shall only have one chance to force Imortiks behind the death wall, but 'tis all we need." He sounded more confident to himself than he had before now.

Quinn shared everything Renata had told him about the master taking over the body of a demigod called Timmon and that Timmon had a partner who could not be identified.

"Is the partner male or female?" Daegan asked as he heard Casidhe and Lanna walking up. He knew they would not do as he said, which was why he'd made a decision about those two before coming here.

Renata answered, "The partner was blurred the one time I remember them talking. I could not discern anything more about that one. Even the speech pattern sounded odd."

Lanna asked, "Is this partner or master in control?"

"At first, I had the impression the partner might be the brains of the group, but the Imortik taking over Timmon's body is becoming more powerful."

Daegan needed strategic information. "Do ya think this master heads to the death wall spot, Quinn?"

"We were following them east of the city when he called out for all Imortiks to come to him. I have to assume that means the ones in this city, not across the world. Reese hurt him badly with demon power, then he teleported away. We had given up and were heading back toward Atlanta when we had to hide. Imortiks were coming out of different places, all headed south and moving as if they were sleepwalking. We followed and found ways to move around them until we ran close to the big group the master had amassed. He was headed this way."

"Quinn, I wish to speak to ya for a moment."

If Beladors surrounding Daegan thought his request strange since he could have used telepathy, they had been wise enough to withhold their thoughts.

Some things had to be discussed in person.

Leaving his two guards and the others, Quinn hurried to catch up to Daegan's long strides. "What do you need, Daegan?"

When he felt far enough from sensitive ears, Daegan still kept his voice low. "I am pleased to find ya not possessed."

Quinn lowered his gaze and admitted, "I have not performed as one of my position should for our Beladors, which was why I handed my control over to Evalle."

"I have informed her she is now to be the new Maistir goin' forward."

Lifting his weary face, Quinn's eyes held a spark he'd been missing. That could be due to finding Reese. "Evalle will perform well. I am not rogue, Daegan, just ... needing to be with Reese for as long as I can."

"I understand but I have a need only ya can perform at this moment if ya shall agree."

"Whatever you ask."

"It requires allowin' Reese and the other three to lead the way to the master and to help us understand what he is about. I fear he shall open the death wall without us bein' prepared to stop him."

Squaring his shoulders, Quinn said, "We are all at your service."

"Thank ya. I know I can always depend upon ya. I wish for ya to keep those two Belador guards and Casidhe here."

"We should be with you to help," Quinn argued.

"Casidhe shall be needed to read the last grimoire when we are ready to close the wall. Ya as well. I cannot do my duty while watchin' over her and Lanna. They are both powerful, but I feel Lanna shall offer more aid in locatin' the last grimoire. I shall protect her with my life. Casidhe is now my mate. I trust ya to protect her the same way."

"Your mate? That's ... terrific, Daegan." Quinn uttered those sincere words then seemed to become lost in his thoughts.

Seconds swam by as Daegan waited to see if he'd have a

mutiny on his hands.

Lifting his tortured gaze to Daegan, Quinn said, "I understand. Just promise me you will call me in. With no idea how this ends, I need to be with Reese."

Daegan did not want Quinn near the master, but neither would he keep Quinn from Reese if this was indeed the end. "I shall. I understand your need just as I wish to have Casidhe close to me."

When Quinn excused himself to explain the plan to Reese and the three Imortik-Beladors, Daegan waved Casidhe over.

She took immediate offense to being left. "Why not take me with you to watch your back?"

"We do not know what the master's partner is about and Isak's people can do only so much." Daegan held her gaze with his pleading one while he quickly whispered more to convince her. "I need ya to protect Quinn. If he stays with Reese while we hunt the master, I may be unable to protect him from bein' possessed. The master could throw a more powerful Imortik at him as Tenebris threatened to force on Adrianna."

"Ah. I see."

"I would prefer ya to not be even in the human world, but I shall send Tristan when the time comes to bring ya, Quinn, and his guards. Ya are the most powerful warrior I can leave with him, but do not mistake this to mean ya should take risks. I trust ya to use that wise head to be careful and safe. Much as I wish to lose no one, I cannot live if anythin' happens to ya, lass. If ya must shift, take care to avoid flyin' with human military jets ready to shoot anythin' in the air not human."

"I understand. I know I'm not invincible."

Daegan gave her lips a soft kiss. "We should find out somethin' soon. Do not become anxious waitin' on us. If ya have a question, have Quinn or the other two Beladors call out to Tristan. I fear Quinn becomin' impatient first. Watch him."

"Don't worry about me, Daegan." She adjusted her backpack. "I have more weapons than I've ever had and I want you to come back to me, too. Got it, buster?"

He chuckled and answered in kind. "*Got it*, lass."

"Now you're learnin'."

Lanna had been creeping closer as he'd spoken to Casidhe. He finally lifted a hand, waving her in.

She'd approached silently, not always a positive thing. "What is plan?"

Daegan explained everything to Lanna that he'd told Casidhe. "Ya shall stay with us to be prepared for when to call in the third grimoire volume."

Lanna eyed him the way Storm would when he lied, but she did not possess that gift. He hoped.

He had twisted the truth with her, Quinn, and Casidhe.

Quinn would protect Casidhe to keep both of them far from the master and Imortiks until Daegan knew exactly what was to transpire.

Casidhe would protect Quinn and become better acquainted, which would help when Daegan brought them to him. He told Quinn the truth about teleporting him to be with Reese when the time came to deal with the death wall.

He'd also told Casidhe the truth about needing her later and keeping Quinn safe.

The last of his flock Daegan had to protect from herself was Lanna. As long as he kept her between his body and Tristan's, she would be safe.

Daegan remembered Casidhe had the two grimoire volumes in her backpack. "I need the papers, lass."

She turned her back to him, allowing Daegan to pull the unusual sack from her backpack. Garwyli had created the bag to appear soft, but it was actually firm to the touch. He'd added a strap. The old druid swore the grimoire pages would be safe.

Daegan handed the bag to Lanna who looped the strap across her body as if wearing a purse.

That left his hands and Tristan's free for defending against a threat.

When Quinn returned, his group followed.

Reese called over, "Everyone who does not have their own personal Imortik riding shotgun, you really must stay back at least ten feet. Even farther is better, because we can't control our Imortiks if one of ours tries to make a leap between bodies. While Imortiks exiting our bodies might sound like a good idea, we don't want to watch someone else become possessed, especially not any of you. We've also observed those previously possessed dying when Imortiks leaped out of their bodies."

"Thank ya, Reese." Daegan swung around, taking in the landscape. "Which way do we head to track the master?"

Reese pointed southwest.

"Take your three and wait over there," Daegan told Quinn. "I know 'tis hard to separate from Reese, but I give my word to teleport ya to her soon."

Quinn wore what Tristan had once called a kicked-in-the-nuts look. Daegan longed for the day all of his people would be safe and happy, especially those standing in this area who had been through so much.

Daegan felt just as sick about not keeping Casidhe close to him, but that would not be the safest place. Quinn was too distracted to keep himself safe and would abandon all sense if he thought Reese was in danger.

Casidhe might say she knew she was not invincible, but she had just gained the ability to shift into a powerful form. Daegan would have preferred for Skarde to tell her she would be more powerful than a dragon shifter *after* the Imortiks were gone. Until Casidhe learned how to use her gifts in a battle and could shift in seconds, she was vulnerable as well.

Daegan waved Reese on to lead the way, then he and Tristan followed with Lanna between them.

They had covered a half mile, coming across two Imortiks heading in the same direction. Daegan discussed it with Reese, who had a suggestion.

She and her three possessed Beladors joined those two Imortiks.

Once he could see that the foursome appeared safe around the Imortiks, he moved Tristan and Lanna to the left side.

Reese had taken up the right side of the Imortik group, talking to the first two to keep their attention on her.

Following the Imortiks was not so simple as Daegan had to maneuver around buildings and over backyard fences with dogs barking to keep pace with her.

Tristan would wait and teleport Lanna with him once Daegan

made it over obstacles to continue walking.

An explosion stopped them all in their tracks.

Daegan called to Evalle. *What caused the explosion?*

Evalle sent back, *We were attacked by that rogue group I ran into when we were hunting the demons. Palaki, the wizard leading them, showed up with a small army. I took off to determine what was hunting us. He saw my eyes and ordered his men to kill me. Fat chance of that when I can use my kinetics and Belador speed. Then they began blowing up our roads. Two homeless people hidden under a canvas were hurt and sent to the hospital. Isak and I believe that Palaki activated a trap for nonhumans. I told our Beladors to stay back until they hear from me. Isak was pissed off. He sent out one of his badass teams with orders to arrest any they could and neutralize those that resist. Let you know more when I do.*

Ending the conversation, Daegan filled in Tristan and Lanna as they pushed hard to catch up to Reese's group.

Lanna whispered, "Is faster to teleport."

"True, but not safe if we don't know who might be standing there when we land," Tristan replied.

"Yes. I will remember this."

When they found Reese again, Daegan held his arm out to prevent Lanna from moving. They had entered a thick grove of trees. Atlanta had parks everywhere, but this one hid a large section of ground in the middle clear of any vegetation.

The master and his yellow horde slowed as they reached that open area.

Daegan swung around looking for a place to observe. He pointed at a water tower, nodding at Tristan.

As soon as the three of them teleported to the walkway circling the middle of a giant ball, Daegan called up a cloaking wall in front of them to hide behind rather than being fully surrounded by the shield. He'd been pushing his powers too much and needed to hold some in reserve with the venom stabbing all up and down his leg.

"So many," Lanna breathed out as the master stopped in the middle of the dirt patch. Yellow glowed bright in the dark where Imortiks filled in all around him.

Tristan gripped the handrail. "There have to be at least a hundred Imortiks already."

Daegan wondered out loud, "Could this be where the death wall shall appear?"

Lanna squeezed closer. "We do not have enough information. Even with third grimoire volume, we need goddess. Not just any. Must be one from last time to show us how to close wall."

Daegan agreed, but it wasn't as if he could snap his fingers and convince even one deity to step in, much less finding one with Imortik experience from the past.

He hated to put any more of his people in danger, but he trusted the ability of his warriors. "How far is Quinn's downtown buildin' from here, Tristan?"

"Eleven or twelve miles."

"Evalle has thirty Beladors waitin' for her word to leave. If she does not need them at the moment, I shall bring them here in case this is where the death wall appears."

"I can teleport probably five people at a time," Tristan offered even though it would deplete his power.

"Nay. We have no need to hide our supernatural powers from humans right now. At the speed those Beladors are able to run, they should be here in minutes. We shall have to return to the ground to meet them." Daegan cleared the move with Evalle, who said she'd send out the order to meet him at the north edge of the park.

Once Tristan had teleported them down to the ground far enough away for the Imortiks to not see or hear them, Tristan asked, "Is there a plan?"

"Aye, but not a good one," Daegan admitted. "I have no idea how strong our people shall be against that many Imortiks and we must find our three Beladors with Reese before battlin'. Once Reese's group calls to any other possessed Beladors and we are able to pull them out, we shall open the bag Garwyli made for the two grimoire volumes Lanna carries. That should call the third grimoire to us. Before that point, we shall have surrounded the Imortiks with a kinetic barrier. Between my majik and Lanna's, I feel we have a chance to form a ward of some type to hold them in and allow us to free up our warriors."

"Yes, we can do this." Lanna had grown quieter by the moment, but Daegan sensed no fear rolling off her. She seemed only to be paying close attention, ready to give aid.

A supernatural presence approached too soon for it to be the Belador team.

Daegan, Lanna, and Tristan flipped around at the same time to face the being.

"Show yourself," Daegan ordered, sure the being was cloaked.

Brynhild appeared with her hands on her hips and fire in her steely blue eyes.

# CHAPTER 28

C ASIDHE HADN'T COMPLETELY ACCEPTED DAEGAN'S reason for leaving her with Quinn, but then she could see how compromised Quinn had become.

Who would blame the poor guy?

They'd been talking a bit. She now knew Reese carried his baby and could not deliver a live child due to the demon energy inside her.

Quinn kept moving in circles as if trying to mentally break free from Daegan's request.

To Quinn, those words had been an order but given in an understanding tone. Quinn paused and studied her. "Daegan would not have left you here unless he believed you were powerful enough to protect yourself. I don't mean to insult you or Daegan, but I have advised my warriors against linking our powers. I want to know for sure just how safe you are if we have to battle Imortiks."

Casidhe gave him an understanding look, but she didn't get what he was talking about. Tristan and Daegan had linked more than once to teleport. They would likely link again to battle.

Why would it be a problem for these men when linking meant a surge in power?

One of his men called Dirk must have seen the question on her face. "We avoid linking when we battle unless we have no other option, because if one dies, we all die. The link is a double-sided blade."

She kept her shock hidden but had a new set of questions for Daegan. What had he and Tristan been doing linking so often? Sure, that gave them more teleporting and battling power, but ... it *doubled* their chances of death.

When Dirk had begun speaking, Quinn paused to listen then

pushed at her again. "This brings me back to why Daegan left you here. I am pleased to have you with us, but I find it odd that Daegan would leave his mate here with us. That he would not think himself far superior at protecting you."

Was Quinn saying Daegan left her for Quinn to protect?

That was backward. She was here to protect Quinn.

She would not make assumptions and end up right back where she and Daegan were at odds again. "Daegan has not had time to share somethin' we only recently learned."

"Oh?" Suspicion still hovered in Quinn's voice.

"I do have powers I'm just beginnin' to understand and learn how to call upon, but I did not know until recently that I am a descendant of the ice dragon shifter bloodline."

All three sets of eyes gaped at her.

Quinn stepped closer, speaking in a hushed voice. "You're a *dragon* shifter?"

"No."

"Ah. I did not think so or you would have shifted when we first met you near Galway."

She kept her amusement tucked inside. "Just because I am not a dragon shifter does not mean I am defenseless."

"True, but you will still need us to protect you."

Quinn really thought he was protecting her. Evidently, Daegan had spun that story to give Quinn a good reason to stay back.

But if Quinn and his two guards ran into trouble while they waited, those men would put their lives on the line to keep her safe. She needed to show them she could pull her weight in a battle so no one had to be unnecessarily hurt.

The men stood within ten feet of her.

She'd noticed how if she moved, they kept her in their circle. "I have somethin' to show you, which will explain why Daegan is fine with leavin' me here."

Curiosity piqued in Quinn's understanding gaze, but he really did not believe her.

Unlatching her backpack, she handed it to Quinn. She could show him the sword later. If she called it up now, she still had no idea if the armor would show up every time, plus the sword would only be in her way.

He took the backpack and hooked it over his shoulder, frowning.

Maybe this would surprise him in a good way and lighten his mood.

"I need to step over to these bushes behind me."

"I would rather you stay in view," Quinn argued, taking on a tone that he'd likely used often when directing his warriors.

"Give me one minute. You'll be able to see my head the whole time."

More frowning, but she ignored him, hurrying behind the bushes to strip out of her clothes. She did not want to stand naked in case her shift took too long.

When she pulled the T-shirt over her head, Quinn shouted, "*Casidhe!* What are you doing?"

She laughed and called up her Hawdreki. The first bone that popped crushed her smile. It took her a full minute to make the change, but she finally stood in front of a speechless Quinn and two googly-eyed Beladors.

Could she talk to Quinn telepathically?

She tried, heard no reply, and just opened her wings wide. That felt good after all the stretching and breaking.

Quinn found his voice. "What the devil are you?"

Swinging her big Hawdreki head around, she could see the tops of some trees and buildings in the distance.

An explosion sounded between her and where they'd parted ways with Isak and Evalle. Smoke plumed. She quickly called up her human body, shrinking as fast as she could, but not nearly as fast as she had in Treoir.

Now she understood the difference in power that Garwyli had explained. While she dressed again, she kept an eye on Quinn and his men.

They had all turned in the direction of the explosion.

Pulling clothes on hurt because her muscles had not formed all the way back to normal, but she couldn't linger. With her shirt on, she picked up her jeans to step into, wishing she could dress faster. Another pair of jeans formed on her legs. Awesome. She rolled up the old pair, put on her shoes, and stepped out from the bushes.

"Looks like some explosion happened back near downtown."

Quinn glanced around as if he'd forgotten her. He repeated, "What the devil are you?"

"A Hawdreki. I'm told I may be more powerful than Daegan, so don't panic about me if danger shows up."

"That bloody *liar!*" Quinn bellowed.

"What's wrong?"

"He left you here to force me to stay back. He didn't need me to keep you safe and away from where he was going."

She stared away from him, putting together all the pieces. Had Daegan misled both of them? She opened her mouth to rant about her mate's overprotective audacity and the world blurred.

Colors spun around her.

Who the hell was teleporting her and where was she going?

# CHAPTER 29

DAEGAN STEPPED AHEAD OF LANNA, leaving Tristan to watch their backs as he faced Brynhild. He warned, "I would not allow my dragon to kill ya when we battled at the cliffs, but ya should not expect mercy today. I have come to realize all but one of your clan are my enemies. Leave now if ya wish to live."

Brynhild showed no signs of anger or aggression. She spoke in a calm voice. "I have learned you did not start the Dragani War."

Her statement shocked Daegan to his toes. What had happened to change her mind? Was she telling the truth?

"Therefore, you did not kill my family," Brynhild concluded. She held her head high as she explained, "I was born into an honorable family and upheld my father's beliefs. We allowed no one to harm ours without making them pay. He was a great king who never acted with bad intentions. He would have been disappointed had I killed you based on lies. I am not proud of having tried. I am here to regain *my* honor. My brother, Herrick, will have to make reparations himself over his unforgiveable actions with your sister."

Daegan had expected nothing of this sort to happen any time in his current life and definitely not now.

Tristan spoke to him telepathically. *What do you want to do, boss?*

*I wish I had an answer for ya. Allow me a moment to speak with her.*

Without giving any indication of accepting her words, Daegan said, "While I am glad for a second ice dragon shifter to realize I did not start that war, why do ya come to me now, Brynhild?"

"Who is the other? Skarde?"

Daegan dropped a curt nod.

"He was never much for war." Brynhild smiled for only a moment before returning to Daegan. "Had Skarde and I been closer, we might have figured out the truth between us. I recently saw the imposter I believe started the war. Queen Maeve flies a wyvern she has glamoured to appear as a red dragon and poured majik into it, making the beast an extension of her power."

Daegan could do no less then admit what he knew. "I saw this wyvern today and should have suspected her sooner. She caused all of us unforgiveable losses."

Brynhild wore her hair much shorter, which gave her a different appearance as well as the bone necklace. The armor with her family's colors and insignias covering her body differed from Casidhe's.

Could that be due to Casidhe's mixed blood?

Standing tall in spite of the embarrassment in her voice, Brynhild said, "I feel Cathbad aided Queen Maeve to start the Dragani War or at the very least knew what she was about and concealed her actions. Either way, that druid is as guilty over his part in the war as he is for capturing me when I fell during battle. I believe he may have taken me down with his majik."

"That makes sense. After smellin' a burned lime scent her majik left behind at our last battle, I now know she killed my da."

Tristan snapped his fingers. "That's the Noirre majik."

"Aye." Daegan relaxed a tiny bit. "Tristan told me of how Cathbad locked ya inside a frozen pond in a mountain lair."

"True." She angled her head to look at Tristan. "I am glad we escaped. I am sorry you had to bite off your hand."

"Not as sorry as I was to do it," Tristan returned in a brittle voice. "I'm with Daegan on wanting to know why you're here *now*."

Allowing a brief nod of acknowledgment, she said, "I have spent time gaining information. I do not have much, but I was told you would need two dragons to deal with imprisoning the Imortiks. I will help you in return for clearing all past actions by me only. I do not speak for either of my brothers."

Daegan hesitated to accept her offer, which would mean he

could send Casidhe back to Treoir. Until now, Casidhe had been the closest to a second dragon as he could provide.

He also did not want to pass up the power of a second dragon. He told Tristan mind-to-mind, *What do ya say about acceptin' her offer of aid?*

*I'd like to toss her off a cliff with her hands tied, but I also believe she's telling the truth. One thing I came to realize about Brynhild is that she is in your face with whatever she thinks. If you want to accept, I can work with it.*

Lanna huffed out a sharp breath. "I hate when you talk in minds!"

Brynhild broke out laughing. "She is the small powerful being you had in the mountains, yes?"

"*Yes!*" Lanna answered before Daegan could.

He explained in a stern voice, "Lanna, when in a war, 'tis not considered rude to have private conversations. If ya wish to aid us in this war, I need ya to accept sometimes Tristan and I must speak telepathically."

She glanced up at Daegan with guilty eyes. "I understand. I am not upset."

That was not the truth, but she had pulled her young claws back in and sounded more mature.

Addressing Brynhild, Daegan said, "Thank ya for your admission. Takes a strong person to strive for peace, somethin' we all once fought for and must do so again. I accept your offer as does Tristan."

Brynhild gave a regal nod this time. She walked over to join them.

Daegan caught her up on the basics of what they were doing and pointed out the Imortik group growing larger. "The master is talkin', but I cannot hear him."

Lifting a hand with the palm facing out, Lanna closed her eyes and whispered something.

Daegan lifted a finger to his lips, asking for silence from Tristan and Brynhild.

When Lanna opened her eyes and lowered her hand, she announced, "Master has called Imortiks to surround and protect him as he opens death wall. He will release *all* Imortiks."

Tristan started to curse, glanced at Lanna, and instead said, "Now we know what the master is up to."

Brynhild noted the setting. "I have flown around this city to search out these beings and found a few more but not so many in one group."

Lanna warned, "Must be careful. Jets attacking dragons."

"Not mine. I can cloak my ice dragon." Brynhild's lips lifted in a smile of pride.

"That is wonderful," Lanna praised.

Daegan changed the conversation. "I have Beladors comin' here to help contain these Imortiks. We hope to do so before the master makes the wall appear and releases even more."

"How do they do this wall?" Brynhild asked.

"We are not sure yet," Daegan admitted. "We have yet to find the third grimoire and hope that shall answer our questions. As ya mentioned, we do need at least two dragons. We must also have a goddess who was present when the last death wall was closed, plus Lanna, who is as powerful as ya stated."

Lanna inserted, "Casidhe, too. She must read last grimoire."

Daegan had to admit Lanna was correct. Brynhild filled the role for a second dragon, but no one else he knew could read the last grimoire. "Yes, Casidhe has a rare gift to translate any text," he told Brynhild. "The only goddess I know of who was involved in the past is Macha, but she was badly injured fightin' with Queen Maeve and is gone, plus she is no ally."

"Macha is not much loss," Brynhild claimed. "Cathbad and Macha have been scheming together. Cathbad said he would help trap you so Macha could kill you. Then he called in Queen Maeve, double-crossing Macha."

Daegan asked, "Why would he go against Queen Maeve?"

Lifting a finger to speak, Brynhild said, "I spent too much time with Cathbad during which I came to understand he wishes to return to TÅµr Medb, but he and Queen Maeve are in conflict. I do not believe she will allow him to return. To me, this means he plots to kill Queen Maeve and rule TÅµr Medb alone. Cathbad would not risk his own life when he could pit Macha against Queen Maeve."

"Sounds about right." Tristan stretched his neck back and

forth. "None of these beings are of any help."

"'Tis true." Daegan had become weary of dealin' with all of them. "I tried callin' to Justitia, but even the goddess of justice does not answer my call for aid. Both Loki and an oracle stated the goddess who joins us must select a powerful bein' for a sacrifice to close the wall."

Brynhild gave a small laugh of disbelief. "That would require someone such as Queen Maeve who would care nothing about the consequences of condemning a supernatural to be a sacrifice. It would be fortunate if she were around and the grimoire words forced her into the position of sacrifice."

"That's the best idea I've heard," Tristan admitted. He told Daegan, "We're running out of options and time. If the master calls up the death wall, we have two dragons and Lanna, but no goddess. Is it time *now*?"

Brynhild gave Tristan a confused look. "What do you mean?"

Daegan explained, "He asks if 'tis time to call in my mother to help us."

Now Brynhild caught on. "Ah! The goddess whose name you have never revealed. Why do you keep it secret?"

Moving low branches out of the way, Daegan explained he'd been forbidden to do so. "To be honest, I would hesitate to call her just to save me. That might place every person around me at risk of death should she deem those deaths as the simplest way for me to survive."

Brynhild cocked her head at him with a surprised expression. She agreed, "We must find a way without that goddess. Maybe no goddess. They are all most untrustworthy in the best of times."

"Daegan, come look." Lanna squinted at the tree thicket where yellow glow spiked between trees and limbs like a million giant yellow fireflies. "I think time must be close."

Taking a long gaze at Imortiks of all shapes and sizes cheering and hooting around the master, Daegan considered his next move. Many of those were demons. Had Reese's group found any more Beladors? How fast would the wall show up? He wished to send Tristan for Casidhe, but he did not possess the third grimoire yet. Until Casidhe had a role to play, she and

Quinn would only be at greater risk here.

Daegan's heart squeezed with worry, but he had to trust his friend. Quinn would allow nothing to happen to Casidhe, just as he knew Daegan would watch over Reese.

Daegan told his group, "Keep an eye out for Reese and our three possessed Beladors."

"Possessed Beladors?" Brynhild questioned.

Tristan explained about them while Daegan spoke with Evalle telepathically. She had called to inform him of the Belador support team closing in on his location and that she'd chosen one called Lorcan to lead them. That warrior had arrived with one of the international groups. From within the mixed bag of Beladors Evalle had sent Daegan's way, she felt Lorcan had the most experience to lead.

Daegan informed his team, "The thirty Beladors we are expectin' should be close. We must move a short distance more to prevent alertin' Imortiks to their arrival."

Backing up, Brynhild asked, "Why would Imortiks come to this location?"

"I do not know for sure, but am thinkin' they know the actual place the rift first opened. 'Tis supposed to be the same place the death wall shall appear."

Keeping himself between Lanna and the Imortiks as they backed away, Daegan reminded her, "I respect your power and skill. Please respect my decisions and obey any order as I shall not have time to explain in the midst of battle."

"I will, Daegan. I know this is dangerous and do not want to make mistake for someone to be harmed."

"Good lass."

With a greater separation from the Imortik crowd, Daegan reached out telepathically to Lorcan. *I am Daegan. Evalle has sent ya to me.*

*Yes, dragon king.*

Giving Lorcan instructions, Daegan hoped Lorcan knew how to bring the Beladors forward quietly. He should have realized Evalle would send them with specific instructions. As the first warriors snaked through the surrounding area silent as ghosts, Daegan was impressed.

One man as tall as Daegan lifted up and raised his hand. All the warriors stood together behind their leader.

Daegan extended his hand. "'Tis nice to meet ya, Lorcan."

Stepping forward, Lorcan shook firmly and briefly bowed his head of thick black hair cut short. "I am honored to fight alongside you, dragon king."

Daegan introduced everyone, then he described where the Imortiks were gathering. "This appears to be where the master shall try to open the death wall. To do so, he must have the last grimoire volume, which we believe he possesses. We hold the other two, which should call his volume to us. I have no idea how that works. Our plan is to surround these Imortiks and form a solid wall first with kinetics, then Lanna and I shall make it stronger with majik."

"I understand." Lorcan stood ramrod straight and just as determined looking as the rest of Daegan's team.

Daegan turned to Lanna with his hand out.

She sighed and slipped the strap over her head and off her shoulder. "I thought I would hold papers."

"I have dealt with the first two volumes enough to know the third could burn ya severely should it fly to ya." He took the strap in his hand, holding the bag in front of him. "Now ya can open the flap."

Losing her irritation, Lanna became focused. She had watched Garwyli seal the bag with a spell. She placed her hand on the loose covering at the top and spoke the words Garwyli had taught her.

Gold light spilled from inside the bag.

Lanna lifted the flap, tossing it back to reveal the grimoire sheets glowing as if coming to life. "I did not expect papyrus to glow."

Daegan hadn't either, but it wasn't as if any of them knew what to expect.

Evalle called to Daegan. *Heads up that Isak is moving in forces close to where you are in case you need help.*

Daegan started to say he would give the order if he needed Isak's help, but instead replied, *Good. We shall began buildin' a kinetic wall around the Imortiks. I shall inform ya as often as I am able, but I leave any decision for usin' Isak's force up to ya in case ya see somethin' I do not.*

She remained silent for a stretch then said, *I'm on it.*

After passing along his discussion with Evalle to his group, Daegan instructed, "Teleport to a high spot, Tristan, and find out if more Imortiks are comin' in from any direction."

"Be right back."

Lanna's attention had not strayed from the grimoire bag. "Why does third one not come to us?"

"It may not show up right away, Lanna. Also, the third volume may not come if the master, or another bein', is able to control its movement."

While Tristan was gone, Daegan went over his two-step plan with Brynhild and Lorcan.

Lorcan remained quiet until Daegan finished, then agreed. "It is a simple plan. Those are the best."

Brynhild shrugged. "I see nothing to complain about." She slashed her gaze at Daegan. "I will stand with you, Tristan, and Lanna?"

"Aye. That shall offer the greatest protection for all three grimoire volumes when the last one comes to me."

Lanna had her arms crossed and a vexed glint in her gaze, but she did not argue or demand to do more than he asked of her.

She would be even less happy in a moment.

Upon Tristan's return, he began counting off what he saw. "Isak's forces moving close to us include military tanks, a stream of Hummers, tactical equipment, and rocket launchers. I saw four heavily armed helo groups in the air hanging a little ways out. That was only the obvious equipment. My bet is the landscape is filled with operatives moving around we won't see until they're needed."

Daegan thanked him, then spoke telepathically to Tristan as he pretended to move his attention around, searching the grounds. He first laid out the two-step plan he'd already given the group, then added, *I need ya close, but I also need Lanna protected every minute. Garwyli has impressed upon me that Treoir and our people must have her for a long time. He states she shall be a far greater gift to all of us than him.*

Tristan's gaze moved to Lanna, who did not see his surprised glance with him standing slightly behind and above her. *I hear you, boss. I'll keep her safe.*

*I know ya shall*

Tristan changed the topic. *Have you heard from Casidhe or Quinn?*

*Nay. I take that to mean they both believe the reasons I gave them to watch over each other. I told Evalle where they are and she is sendin' ten additional warriors to remain out of view and protect them.*

With Lanna close to keep her as safe as possible, Daegan joined Brynhild and Lorcan. He snatched a twig from a branch and squatted down to draw in the dirt as he spoke. "This is the group of Imortiks. Form the men in a wide circle out here, Lorcan. Ya shall stand on one side of this circle and I on the other. When 'tis time, we create a united kinetic wall and move toward the center, but do not link powers."

"Yes, dragon king."

As Daegan and his Belador army snuck around the Imortik master's area, Tristan kept Lanna between the two of them. Daegan had hooked the bag strap around his neck with the bag in front of him.

Daegan waited to give Lorcan the order to engage their kinetics.

Reese, Renata, Kaiser, and Gretchen rushed over behind Daegan.

Whispering from behind, Reese said, "We didn't find any more Beladors. All these beings seem to be demons entirely overtaken by Imortiks."

Daegan cautiously replied, "This makes killin' all of them easier."

Tristan, Brynhild, and Lanna did not react, but Beladors close to him startled. Daegan sent a telepathic message to Lorcan and his warriors that none of these four were to be harmed. They were his people.

His warriors quieted.

"Is Quinn okay?" Reese asked.

"Yes." Daegan had not had time to call Quinn telepathically

and was not sure he could reach Casidhe's mind with his, but Quinn had not reached out to him either. He had to trust both of them and the Beladors Evalle had sent to watch over them in secret.

Still, he had a driving need to go protect Casidhe. If he showed up unexpectedly, she would be angry at his lack of belief in her abilities. She wanted him to trust her and treat her as an equal.

The farther he stepped away from her, the more he found it damned difficult to stick to his agreement because he cared so much.

As soon as his team had the master and Imortiks imprisoned kinetically, he would protect Lanna as she used her majik, then Tristan could bring Casidhe and Quinn here.

Daegan cleared his mind of all except stopping the Imortik master from unleashing a horde of monsters in the human world.

Sending out a telepathic signal to power up kinetics, Daegan stepped into view of Imortiks along with his Beladors. They all had their hands up. The kinetic wall formed immediately, meeting his power on his left and right.

Quiet dropped over the Imortik crowd.

The master, now standing on something that raised him a head above his followers, swung left and right, clearly not believing what he saw.

Lanna stayed behind Daegan, but not far. She whispered, "Ward now? I must run around perimeter to pull ward together."

"Not yet. We need to move in closer first and tighten the circle to allow them as little room as possible to move. 'Tis harder to break a barrier with little room to move."

Yellow beasts began shouting and waving fists at them.

The master pointed a finger in Daegan's direction and raged from the center of his followers. *You shall all bow down to me!*

Reese said, "That deep voice is the actual Imortik master speaking."

Daegan telepathically told Lorcan to move every Belador forward slowly. The bag of grimoire papers began to swing back and forth across his chest, then stopped on his left and tugged around his ribs. The blasted things had some strength and were pulling in the wrong direction. He could not yank them back while he held up his part of the kinetic wall.

As they all took steps forward, Daegan sensed Lanna becoming agitated. "Lanna, why are ya becomin' upset?"

She didn't deny it. "Something wrong. Master not right."

Daegan tried to figure out what she meant, but blasters sounded to his left.

Evalle called to him, *Isak's men caught two Imortiks heading for the pack you're surrounding.*

The Imortik Master yelled a string of unintelligible words at the ground as if he demanded something.

Was he calling up the death wall?

"*No!*" Lanna cried out. "*All wrong!*"

# CHAPTER 30

DAEGAN TORE HIS ATTENTION AWAY from the Imortiks growing more agitated and louder by the moment for a second. "What is all wrong, lass?"

Panic slid over Lanna's face when nothing had disturbed her until now. "Third grimoire not coming to us. Two volumes you hold try to reach missing one. They pull in wrong direction. When Casidhe read grimoire volumes in library, none say master in control first time. Imortik master created to lead followers to heed sorcerer's rule."

Tristan argued, "That sorcerer died."

"*Yesss*," Lanna stressed. "Master is here because rift was opened in Atlanta. Who opened rift?"

Daegan thought on what Lanna said. "Maybe the partner Renata told us about."

"*Yes*! That is leader," Lanna stated with authority. "Why is he not here?"

Ten Imortiks broke off from the crowd and rushed Daegan, slamming the kinetic wall hard.

The master pointed at Daegan and demanded, "Bring me that dragon!"

Tristan groaned from the body slam against his kinetics and put more muscle into the shove, knocking Imortiks back. He squeezed out, "Do you think the person who opened the first rift and is Timmon's partner, cousin, whatever, also stole the third volume from VIPER's vault?"

Lanna lifted a finger "Yes. This."

Daegan could not take time to debate who was in charge of the Imortiks. More yellow monsters rushed the wall all the way around. Why would they be here with the master yelling about calling up the wall if this was not the place?

Beladors slid backward in two places.

Hating to do this, Daegan sent out a telepathic order to link. The response was immediate and powerful. *"Now!"* Daegan ordered and pushed forward, growling as his people kept committing all their power. The Imortiks fell back, falling on each other and stumbling to get away from him, as they should.

Demonic Imortiks turned rabid and ripped into each other.

The master railed, *"Obey me! Do not fight amongst yourselves. We must call up the death wall and free all of our followers. Kill all but the dragon."*

That one order had the Imortiks returning to zombie state and scrambling to reorganize as they came for Daegan.

But Lanna had been correct.

Daegan did not know enough yet to stop Imortiks and it wasn't as if those monsters were going to wait for him to gain it all.

He began to understand what had Lanna shaken.

He might not know everything, but this did not fit what he'd been told either. Still, he couldn't do anything else until he enclosed these Imortiks. Misgivings about what that master might be doing changed his mind on keeping Lanna here.

The barrier could break.

Daegan said, "Tristan, teleport Lanna to stay with Casidhe and Quinn until we need all of them."

"No, Daegan," Lanna said, not shouting or emotional. Her voice vibrated with anger and power. "I must be here. If you send me away, I can teleport short distances on my own. I will return." Then she added, "If other Imortiks in city do not find me first."

She'd bring Quinn and Casidhe back, too.

The master raised his hand then slapped it down toward the ground. "The death wall calls to me. We will overrun the dragon's puny border."

# CHAPTER 31

DAEGAN HAD NO WAY TO stop the master from flooding enough Imortiks at the wall to pour over the top of their kinetics. When that happened and one Belador died, they'd all fall while linked.

Maybe that master had the last grimoire volume hidden from view. He had no idea, but why was the bag holding the other two trying to cut a groove in his chest and side?

Brynhild dashed away. Where was she going?

He heard the sound of a dragon roar, then screams. It ended quickly then she returned. "More Imortiks. Now dead."

Had those slipped past Isak and Evalle?

Reese shouted, "The master is calling us to him. We're staying back in a group to hold our ground."

Daegan shouted, "Aye." Then he told Tristan and the closest Belador on Daegan's other side in their minds, *I am unlinkin' to protect Lanna. Take my spot.*

He dropped his hands and the kinetics closed together quickly.

Lanna's lips flattened. "Please do not send me away, Daegan. I have had visions. I *must* be here."

He placed his hands on her shoulders, meeting her gaze straight on. "I am not sendin' ya away, but askin' ya to wait here until I know what we are dealin' with. If the last grimoire does not come to me while I hold these two, there is no reason to put ya at risk. We do not know enough about why the master is here or why his partner is not here. I agree with ya that somethin' is not right."

She bobbed her head in acceptance, blond curls with black tips bouncing. "Is fine."

He kept his hands in place and whispered a quick request from his majik, then backed away. He could see her, but no one else could through the cloaking he had formed around her.

Lanna squinted her eyes and stuck her head forward. Fury flamed in her face. She started shouting and pounding against the cloaking.

Not a sound escaped and nothing moved.

He had placed more than a cloaking spell around her. He'd formed a second defense, which would repel anyone or thing that came close to her.

The ward would last no more than six hours.

If he and the Beladors had not succeeded, Lanna would then be able to escape with her ability to teleport even a small amount.

Before that happened, he would have called in Isak and every other option he had to get her and the others to safety.

The kinetic barrier his people had formed was shrinking slowly, but he had a bad feeling and decided to move ahead to the second step in his plan even though he had not found the last grimoire volume. The bag remained plastered against his side as if the grimoires were looking in the opposite direction of the master for the last one.

Evalle called to Daegan. *Isak thinks we need to move ahead to break the Imortiks into groups.*

That was Daegan's second step. *I agree. Once our Beladors break apart, I shall let ya know.*

*I'll be ready*, Evalle said.

Daegan sent his message to both Tristan and Lorcan. *We shall now begin to unlink ten Beladors from the large circle and squeeze Imortiks into one small pod at a time. When that one is set, the next starts right away. My group shall move in last to surround the master with the Imortiks closest to him.*

Returning to his spot to relink with his warriors and hold up his part of the kinetic barrier, Daegan told Brynhild the plan.

She replied, "I wish I could use my power with yours, but I am ready for anything else."

As the Beladors sheared off on Daegan's right and left, herding Imortiks into their round pods with kinetic power, the master shouted, "*Now!*"

Daegan's group had not enclosed the master yet. Had he just made the wrong move in the Imortik master's game?

# CHAPTER 32

LANNA SHOUTED, "LET ME OUT, Daegan." She should have given him all her visions, but Garwyli had warned her over and over if she did not understand a vision she should not share it freely.

He'd explained that as she grew stronger, everyone would take her word as carved in stone. That was a huge responsibility. She kept pounding, but Daegan had done more than lock her in a ward.

He had powerful majik, too.

She closed her eyes to avoid staring at the smudged images outside this ward. Had he thought she would not be able to handle blood and injuries?

If he knew the horrors she'd been through, he would not be so worried about shocking her.

With her eyes closed, she recalled a recent vision of Daegan turning to see an enemy coming at him. But where had he been when she had this vision? She had yet to figure that out, which was why she'd been mature and kept it to herself.

Now she wished she'd been her impulsive self of the past and warned him.

Still, any warrior in battle should expect someone to attack his back. That's why many fought back-to-back in large groups.

When she opened her eyes and squinted, she could see Daegan's circle of Beladors separating. Why?

The dull sound of helicopters flying nearby came through.

This would be a good time for telepathy.

If not in a ward, she could teleport. She had plenty of majik but no way to communicate with any of these people.

Her vision kept banging around in her head.

The Imortik master demanded his followers capture *the*

dragon. Had he seen Brynhild too or had she been hidden behind Daegan?

As Lanna studied what was going on, the Beladors formed three circles. She had not seen that in her vision. She closed her eyes and suddenly saw Sen's twisted face.

Why? What was happening to her visions?

He was screaming.

She opened her eyes, heart jumping around in fear.

Who hurt Sen? What did that have to do with Daegan fighting the master?

Reaching inside the light jacket she'd pulled on before leaving Treoir, she pulled out the thick flask-like transparent container with the peach pit inside.

Glass should not prevent her from gaining insight from the pit, but this iridescent holder was no simple glass.

Should she open it?

Garwyli would ask, "Why now? Because it's the middle of the morning or a sunny day or because a bird flew past?"

Embarrassed at that reminder, she returned the flask to the inside pocket of her jacket. She was sorry for Sen being tortured, but she could not help him at this moment.

Daegan needed her.

Shouting erupted. Was Daegan in trouble? She could see his back but did not know if anything attacked him.

Drawing in a deep breath, Lanna said, "I do this now, because Daegan is in danger, Garwyli. If he dies, they all die."

She called up her power and shoved her fingers into the cloaked warding and cried out in pain. Tears streamed down her face. She kept pushing and broke the first layer. It cracked and shattered.

Heat seared her hand and wrist. She could not stop now. Drawing harder on her internal energy, she pushed again. It felt as if the power peeled skin off her hand and wrist.

She sobbed and kept going, calling up a spell to break through.

Energy exploded in a flash. She grasped her injured hand to her stomach and stumbled forward, managing to stay on her feet.

Nothing was attacking Daegan.

Why had she believed he was in such danger?

Reese yelled, *"Look out!"*

Lanna turned to face a surge of Imortiks coming out of the trees toward the backs of Daegan and his team.

Ambush.

That had been her vision.

# CHAPTER 33

CRAZED HOWLING AND HIGH-PITCHED SCREAMING noises from the Imortiks would leave anyone deaf, but even more so for Daegan, his Beladors, and other nonhumans with sharp hearing.

His men strained to hold the tighter circles around groups of Imortiks. His kinetic barrier pinned in the largest bunch and their master.

The master had begun slamming powerful hits against the Belador kinetic wall.

But he had not called forth the death wall.

Did he need his partner?

Did the master even have the last grimoire volume?

Daegan sent word to Evalle that Isak could stun the Imortiks in the two smaller circles which did not include the master.

Whomping of incoming helicopters approached.

Above all the racket, Daegan heard Reese shout, *"Look out!"*

To his horror, the next words came from Lanna. "Imortiks ambushing from behind." He twisted to look over his shoulder to where Lanna stood there facing off with a wall of yellow monsters.

His heart hit the ground.

Daegan yelled at his Beladors to hold tight. He teleported to Lanna and Tristan showed up next.

Loud now, a helicopter, with armed soldiers sitting in the open sides, fired on one group of Imortiks, getting most. They swung around lower.

Tristan cursed. "The master is pulling the helicopter down."

Men were yelling. The blade noise changed to a sickening metallic squeal, then the helicopter crashed close enough for Daegan to feel the explosion.

He shouted, *"Ya need to leave now, Lanna!"*

"Do not teleport me away!" she shouted back with power belonging to a dragon. "I must be here. If not, people will die! Do not make me live with their deaths."

He had to keep her safe, too. How could he do that and explain later if his people were slaughtered?

Lanna shoved her small fingers forward, shouting Latin in a voice bulging with incredible power. Her body shimmered with energy. But one hand was bloodred as though the skin had been scalded.

The first row of Imortiks crumbled.

Beladors shouted behind Daegan. Lorcan's voice came into his mind with orders for the warriors, *"Your line is broken. Unlink!"*

More human military roared overhead. Blasters fired in rapid succession.

Isak had warned Daegan not to shift into his dragon or the human military would take him out after what happened with Macha and Queen Maeve's battle.

Daegan shouted at Brynhild as she raised her hands, "Do not shift. Humans fly with weapons to shoot you."

She held out a hand and called up energy and forced cold air to surround Imortiks. More fell with eyes frozen open but were not dead.

Daegan and Tristan battled Imortiks still coming at them from different sides.

The master appeared between them and the ambushing Imortiks they'd been holding off. With one hand, he hammered the kinetic wall Daegan and Tristan held up.

Energy crackled in the air.

Explosions rocked the ground behind Daegan. Beladors fell one by one, struggling to stand again.

Oyster-gray clouds overtook the dark sky, quickly shifting into a metallic silver color and shrouding them in low light.

Lanna could not stay longer. Daegan would not place her in more danger on the chance she might save others. He called out, "Tristan, tele—"

A bright yellow dust cloud engulfed him, smothering his

words as he choked.

The master shouted, "Do not attack. Form around me!"

Daegan blinked to clear his eyes and coughed, choking on the dust. Lanna, Tristan, and Brynhild were all hacking, surrounded by the yellow cloud. Imortiks were overrunning his Beladors. Two monsters paused to dive into Beladors. Then those newly possessed Beladors followed the crowd of Imortiks bypassing Daegan, Tristan, Brynhild, and Lanna to obey the master.

The rest of his Beladors fell where they stood, still breathing, but unable to battle. Imortiks formed behind their leader and out from each side.

Daegan forced words through his dry throat. "Tristan, for the love of all 'tis holy, teleport now with Lanna."

"I already tried and can't teleport."

Lanna lifted a face filled with determination, even now trying to help him. "Do not blame yourself no matter what happens. We must all be here to fight."

While Daegan admired this young woman standing strong with them, he would never be able to face Quinn or live with himself if he lost her.

He took in the line of Imortiks jumping around and jeering. Renata, Kaiser, and Gretchen were crawling through the line on each side of the master, who would likely kill those three for being traitors.

Ruadh battered Daegan's insides. *Burn enemy!*

With human military being the lesser concern, Daegan agreed with Ruadh and tried to shift. All he got for his trouble were daggers of pain through his chest and limbs.

Inch-thick roots shot up from the ground around where he stood and wrapped him from ankles to knees. He shoved a power hit at the roots, willing to take any injury to his legs.

Not one root broke.

Lanna, Tristan, and Brynhild were just as trapped, but Lanna quietly spewed a string of Latin. That made the roots around her legs smoke, but nothing more.

"I am sorry, Daegan," Lanna said in a shuddering breath. "I did not understand my vision was ambush."

"Shh. Be calm, Lanna. 'Tis not your fault. Focus on freein'

yourself and escapin' if ya can. Teleport if ya are able."

A tear ran down her cheek. "My power like mud. Does not move."

Tristan asked in a strained voice, "Can you shift, boss?"

"Nay. Not even my dragon can force the change." Daegan grimaced at the tiny claws digging into the skin on his legs. He ignored that as he had the Imortik venom with him for every step.

The Imortik master called out, "We shall gain three powerful beings! You three may take the two women and the male with glowing green eyes." He pointed at three Imortiks, the largest of his group who appeared anxious to possess anything. Their empty eyes sharpened and became crazed. They opened mouths filled with fangs and shouted strange sounds.

Daegan had never been held captive by panic, but neither had he felt helpless to save those he loved while standing so close to them. He tried calling out to Trey, then Quinn, anyone who could send help.

No one replied.

How had he failed Lanna, Tristan, the ice dragon, and all his people this way? He had let down those so important to him again.

At least Casidhe and Quinn were safe.

That had been a good decision.

The Imortik master enjoying his moment of power continued running off at the mouth about how no one was his match as a demigod. That his army could not be stopped.

A military soldier raced out from where he must have been hiding and blasted the closest Imortik but not with the weapon set on stun.

That Imortik exploded.

At the same moment, the Belador lying closest to that end of the Imortik line grabbed his chest and screamed, then ceased breathing.

Daegan bellowed, "*Stop you fools!*"

Clearly annoyed at the interruption, the master had killed the Belador. He flicked a hand at the soldier, who lifted in the air and fell, hitting head down. His limbs limp as his lifeless body dropped.

Returning to his moment of euphoria, the Imortik master shouted, "I have done much in this demigod body, but once I control a dragon and gryphon, we will rule this world from the air!"

No, this could not be happening! Daegan heard Tristan's heart pounding louder over Lanna and Brynhild's frantic heartbeats.

The Imortik master shouted as if he spoke to the world, "The time has come to show the red dragon who is most powerful!" He pointed at Daegan. "You will serve as the sacrifice to open the death wall."

"Boss, no!"

Brynhild shook her head. "We must stop them."

Lanna sobbed silently. She had clearly used all the words she knew to save them.

Daegan tried reaching out to Casidhe, *I love ya, lass. Do not hunt for me. Stay safe.*

She didn't reply!

He had to find her. He loved her with all his body and soul. His life couldn't end this way with never seeing her again.

The master started marching forward with his three Imortiks literally slobbering at the chance to dive into powerful bodies.

Daegan would die to save all his people and allies. He was not being given that choice.

He'd sworn on his honor to Garwyli he would do all in his power to keep Lanna safe.

Tristan, his Beladors, and Brynhild deserved better than to end this way.

Nobody here deserved to end up an Imortik slave.

He took one last look at his ragged group, battle worn, bloody and on the verge of death. Yet they still remained defiant, ready to take their last breath with him.

The master smiled in victory as Imortiks closed in within twenty feet of Daegan.

Daegan's stomach clenched with a damning decision.

He had only one weapon left.

Daegan held his arms out and opened his hands palms facing up then shouted, "Deniela, daughter of Tiamat and Apsu, and mother who birthed the red dragon, I call upon ya to please come to my aid."

# CHAPTER 34

WHEN CASIDHE FINISHED TELEPORTING, SHE blinked a couple times to clear her eyes. Taking in the land shrouded in a strange twilight around her, she tried to figure out what the heck was going on.

Such as who the hell had teleported her.

She started walking forward and ran into an invisible wall, face-first. "Ouch." Cloaking? No. A majikal cage.

Just to be sure, she rushed in another direction, hitting the undetectable wall with her fist this time.

But in this direction, she saw Quinn suspended upright a foot off the ground. With his arms clamped against his body, he appeared to be wrapped. Even his cheeks were smushed.

Horror-filled eyes stared at her.

She trembled and her teeth chattered. Shock was taking over.

Fires stoked up from the ground fifty feet in front of her.

To fight off panic, she turned to look around for some sign of where she stood.

Monuments, statues, and headstones stuck up from different locations a short distance away.

She banged her brain to figure out what she was looking at, because it felt familiar. She tried calling out to Daegan. *It's me, Casidhe. Quinn and I were teleported somewhere. I'm trapped inside some kind of majik.* She waited. *Daegan?*

He couldn't hear her.

She and Quinn were on their own.

She glanced at Quinn again, cringing at how bad he looked. His skin was turning a pale shade of dirt that scared her. Why was she in this enclosure and why had Quinn ended up wrapped up like a burrito to hang on a tree?

She kept turning around and around. Who had put them here?

Movement on her right drew her gaze. People were walking in slowly as if in a trance. Adult men and women. They all had the same blank expression. She twisted to her left and more emerged, stepping around headstones and statues.

All humans.

Frustration made her crazy. "What do you want?" she shouted as loud as she could.

No one answered.

Quinn's gaze never left her. She mouthed the words, *So sorry.* She must have caused this by shifting and someone saw them.

"*Hear me!*" a voice finally said, but there was no body. The sound flowed in and out of her enclosure as if the land itself had given life to the strange swirling sound.

Was it male or female? She needed to hear more.

"By the powers infused in this grimoire volume, I call up the altar as servant to the death wall."

Altar?

Casidhe froze, recalling Zeelindar's words. *A sacrifice is required to close the death wall.*

Would one also be required to open it?

What about the other two grimoires? Weren't those needed? The voice could be male, maybe, she didn't know. Was this the master? If so, why not show himself?

Where was Daegan and his people?

She turned to face an empty stretch of land, leaving the monuments and headstones at her back. Dirt and rocks rumbled then the ground broke apart in front of her.

The earth belched out a black granite structure eight feet long, three feet wide, and four feet tall. Soil sprayed away, showering the humans still entering the area, who didn't notice in their zombie state.

So much for her theory of needing all three grimoire volumes to make anything happen.

Dark clouds formed overhead.

Was water required for this sacrifice?

Quinn suddenly fell free of his binding. He shook his head to clear it and pushed up to his feet in a rage. "Daegan will destroy you for touching this woman!"

A giant hand with three claws appeared in front of Quinn and slashed across his body.

Was he going to be the sacrifice?

No!

Casidhe screamed, "Leave him alone!" She tried to call up her Hawdreki. Muscles cramped. Bones bent but did not break. Blood ran from her nose. Too painful. She bent over with her hands on her knees, sucking in air.

Quinn held his middle and made it to his knees, weaving. "I'll tell Daegan."

He'd spoken as if answering someone, but she hadn't heard a question.

Then he disappeared.

She looked at the empty altar. Her knees shook.

She had power dammit, but where was her sword? In fact, where was her backpack? She'd given it to Quinn before she'd been teleported away.

Energy settled around her. She didn't move, holding her breath.

All of sudden, her body flew up in the air and over to the altar where she landed on her back. Her wrists and ankles were pinned down by a force.

Oh, hell. This was happening. She screamed, *"Nooo!"*

# CHAPTER 35

EVERYONE FROZE AT DAEGAN'S SHOUT for his goddess
mother.

Tristan's jaw went slack.

Lanna's eyes bloomed with surprise.

Turning slowly to him, Brynhild's gaze held respect.

Daegan swallowed, heart ramming his chest as he waited for
something to happen. Anything. Had he not used the correct
words to call the goddess?

Did she even remember giving birth to him?

Would she show up angry and kill all of them?

Or would she never show up?

The Imortik master stared at Daegan with his forehead
furrowed in concern. Evidently just the name of that goddess
alone had been enough to delay the master's triumphant moment.
The Imortik demigod gazed up at dark clouds for the third time
as if the sky would open and a threat would fall through the
strange darkness.

His Imortiks stared up as well.

When nothing happened, the master seemed to draw in a deep
breath of relief. He pointed at Daegan. "You lie. I know the story
of your birth. She is not com—"

The master clutched his chest. "*No!*" screamed Timmon. "*It
wasn't me! It was my cousin!* I was possessed! Kill the master,
not me … *pleeease* … " His eyes popped out of his sockets and
hung against his cheeks. Blood spewed from his mouth, nose,
and ears.

Imortiks facing them fell to their knees in pain and agony.
They flopped over like fish out of water gasping for air, dying as
they made hideous noises.

Then every one of them, including the master, burst into

flames and disintegrated.

The roots around Daegan's ankles began shrinking and slithering back into the ground. He checked the others and all three watched the ground as they too were freed.

As Timmon disappeared into flames, Daegan had a brief moment of sympathy for what appeared to have been a weak and vulnerable being manipulated by a more powerful one.

But he would not regret the death of the Imortik master.

His mind went to the innocent Imortiks. What of Reese and her three? What about the two Beladors just possessed?

Had he already taken innocent lives by calling to his mother? He struggled to be thankful for those saved, but how could he face the loved ones of those who had died?

A heavy ball of guilt landed hard in his stomach.

Would the time ever come where he did not lose those he had sworn to protect?

The silver storm clouds had not changed, growing a more ominous gray by the moment.

Tristan murmured, "Is any of this a good sign, boss?"

"I have no idea. Ya know I have refused to call her every time until now. I would die for all of ya, but I could not stand by and watch ya killed or possessed with even one small chance to save ya. I only fear the warnin' my father gave me about how callin' my mother came with a price."

Lanna asked in a hushed voice, "What price?"

"'Tis the question I cannot answer."

A dazzling display of violet light speared through an opening in the clouds directly overhead. The hole widened and the light shot straight down like a glowing highway to the blood-splattered arena where the master had just stood.

Next came a regal stag carrying a woman in a shimmering gown, which changed from green to blue and back. Sparkles danced around the lavender winged stag adorned with gold horns and thick black fur from chest to neck. Her stag's hooves barely tapped the illuminated pathway with wings flapping softly until its first two hooves stepped onto the ground gracefully, then it tucked the elegant wings.

Not even the air dared to move.

Standing fully on the ground, the stag dipped low to its front knees, allowing the woman Daegan guessed to be his mother to dismount.

As if Deniela could not teleport? An inconceivable thought. Her dark hazel eyes blazed with gold and silver specks.

She stepped off her beast and stood six feet tall.

Black hair fell in long sheets. She swept a long drawn-out look over everyone until her gaze parked on Daegan. She spoke rapidly in a language he could not understand.

Daegan felt eyes on him, but he had been given no instruction on how to communicate with her should they ever meet. Clearly, his father had been confident this would never occur.

With no better way to reply, Daegan said, "Thank ya for answerin' my call and for destroyin' the Imortiks."

Was there any hope she might have destroyed *all* the Imortiks spread across this world?

Probably not, but that would be nice.

Deniela angled her head, studying him with a confused look on her exquisite face. She lifted pearl-white fingernails on slender fingertips to her temples and closed her eyes.

Her fingernails changed color to blue, then green, and finally silver.

He could see no resemblance to his face. She had smooth skin a shade darker than his and what he'd heard called an aquiline nose with a noticeable bridge. Her round eyes were outlined in black, which she did not need with her thick lashes.

Most nonhumans would not be so bold to risk closing their eyes around unknown beings, but Deniela had proven she was not someone to attack.

In less than a minute, she lowered her hands and spoke English in a smoky voice with a strange accent. "These were not so difficult to kill, but they are as locusts. More shall follow."

Just as Daegan had expected. She hadn't taken all the Imortiks out.

Tristan spoke to Daegan telepathically. *I don't know much about the history of gods and goddesses, but your mother sounds Persian maybe. Wasn't Deniela's mother, Tiamat, one of the original Babylonian deities and pretty freakin' evil?*

Daegan sent back, *Yes. I wish I knew more about Deniela, but 'twas not a conversation my father cared to have more than once. I have heard over time things such as Tiamat blamed a god named Marduk for Apsu's death. Tiamat believed Marduk would kill her. Before that happened, she gave Deniela the duty to make Marduk pay if he succeeded in her death and took over to rule. I have no idea if that happened and wish to say I expect Deniela to be a lovin' goddess, but I have never lied to ya.*

Lanna hissed, "*Shh!* Show respect."

A slight frown toyed with Deniela's face as she searched the grounds. "Why are Imortiks free? Do none of you realize what abominations they are?"

Now released from the master's hold, Daegan sent a quick message to Evalle warning Isak and human military to not attack or approach.

And definitely to not go near Deniela.

He replied to his mother, "Yes. We are aware of the Imortik danger. 'Tis why we are tryin' to stop them. I hold two of the three grimoire volumes but have not found the third. The person who stole that one intends to release all Imortiks." Based upon her question, he assumed she knew something of the Imortik history, but she kept asking questions.

"Why are any volumes out in the human world?"

"'Tis a long story. I had to locate these to force Imortiks now runnin' free all over the human world behind the death wall permanently."

"The word permanent no longer serves a purpose in this language when the last death wall has not remained closed."

He would not argue words with her. "Still, 'tis my duty to find the last volume to remove Imortiks from this world."

"You are in the wrong place at the wrong time." She smiled and tapped her cheek. "I just drew that saying to me from this time. I shall keep it."

Holding tight to his patience, he asked, "What do ya mean? Do ya know where I *should* be?"

She moved around gracefully, as if taking in the landscape of a kingdom. "I did not realize the human world had changed so." Then she seemed to catch his question. "You have no sacrifice for closing the wall and it is unwise to tamper with that wall. A significant crack might wake the ancient one."

What the devil was she even talking about? "I am far more concerned with savin' everyone in this world than wakin' anyone."

She gave an exaggerated sigh. "You must hope he remains asleep. His mother prefers it that way."

Daegan could appreciate someone sleeping his life away to avoid an annoying mother.

When he would not engage again, Deniela returned to the original conversation. "As for closing the wall, you may be too late. The person who possesses the third grimoire has acquired a sacrifice."

Daegan's pulse jumped. He had the sick feeling he'd made a grave error. "Who has the third grimoire?"

She almost wrinkled her brow with a frown but stopped in time. "I must think of his name. There were so many children over the years."

Another minute stretched forever while Daegan lost ten years off his life waiting.

Before she could come up with a name, Quinn appeared suddenly at Daegan's feet. He bled from three wounds slashed across his chest.

"*Cousin!*" Lanna cried, falling down next to him. She put her hands on his chest and started whispering frantically through her tears.

Daegan dropped to his knees. "What happened to ya?"

Reese raced out of the woods, screaming, "*Quinnn!*"

Deniela whipped around at the intrusion, her hand coming up quickly. "*Blink and you die! First you will provide answers.*"

Daegan teleported to stand in front of Reese, forcing her to stop. "She is *not* a demon."

"I thought you wished to *kill* Imortiks." His mother sounded very disappointed in his action.

"Any demons and Imortiks that have not possessed a human or Belador body. I believe if we can force Imortiks behind the death wall, we shall also find out how to pull the possessed energy from humans and nonhumans. There are three possessed

Beladors behind me in addition to this woman who must not be killed."

"Five," Reese corrected. "We grabbed the two Beladors who were just possessed."

"Thank ya." Then he told his mother, "Every one of them is precious."

Deniela allowed a delicate wisp of air to slip out between her lips, which still managed to carry power. "I do not understand you, Son." But she lowered her hand.

Relieved, he told Reese, "Please allow me a minute and I shall call ya to Quinn."

She squeezed out a tearful, "Hurry."

Daegan teleported back to Quinn. Again on his knees, he lifted Quinn's head. "Tristan shall take ya to the healers."

Quinn grabbed Daegan's arm. "No. We must go now. He's going to make Casidhe a sacrifice to open the death wall."

"Who?" Daegan demanded.

"Sen. He has the last grimoire volume."

# CHAPTER 36

GASPS RAN THROUGH THE BELADORS when Quinn announced that Sen held the last grimoire volume *and* Casidhe.

Lanna had never witnessed anything like this woman Deniela and her stag, but if that goddess did not hurry up and help them find Casidhe, Lanna would take a gamble to find Sen herself. First she had to heal Quinn, but the wounds were not closing at all. Blood continued to seep out.

Still kneeling beside Quinn, Daegan shouted, "Sen is behind all this? I shall kill him for touchin' Casidhe. Tristan—"

"Who is this Casidhe?" Deniela asked with impertinence.

"My mate," Daegan said in a tight voice, anxious to leave.

Quinn gasped out, "She changed into her Hawdreki to show me she could protect herself and us. I think Sen saw her."

"You should keep that one alive, Daegan," Deniela commented as if suggesting what to eat for his next meal. "He speaks in a purposeful way."

Daegan laid his hands on Quinn's wounds with Lanna. She shook her head, her throat closing up at the thought of losing her cousin.

Quinn's eyes rolled up in his head.

Reese sobbed.

Lanna begged the dragon king, "Please save him."

Daegan sent a beseeching look up at Deniela. "This man is important to all of us and a demigod has injured him. Can ya give him aid?"

"I hear nothing for centuries and now you ask for one thing after another."

Lanna glanced at Daegan who should not have to choose between saving Casidhe or Quinn.

The dragon king's voice boosted with power. "I do not have time to waste. If ya shall not help, say so now."

"Were you taught no manners?" Deniela complained.

"My *mother* was not present to give such lessons," he snapped in a louder voice.

She waved a hand over Quinn and his wounds began to heal faster. "Go then. Perhaps you shall be more pleasant in the future."

Lanna grabbed Daegan's arm. "Cousin is breathing. Wounds are healing."

Daegan stood. "I apologize for bein' terse. I am in quite a hurry. Thank ya."

But his mother was not done. "Just what is a Hawdreki?"

Daegan closed his eyes as if he battled to keep from shaking the breath from his mother. "I shall explain the next time we meet."

Quinn groaned as he struggled to move. "Help me up."

Daegan and Lanna brought him to his feet. Reese raced up close. Lanna lifted a hand at Reese to stop her. "He lives. Please do not touch."

"I won't. Just keep healing him, please." Reese's devastated face glowed and she kept a hand over her stomach.

Now that Daegan felt Quinn would survive, he asked, "Where is Casidhe?"

"Oakland Cemetery. Take me with you," Quinn pleaded. "I can still fight."

Lanna hurt to watch Daegan's agony with trying to save everyone.

Reese started forward. "I'm going, too. So will the other five. You might need us."

Deniela placed fingers lightly at her throat, appearing curious and entertained. "You have a most unusual following, my son."

"Aye, and every person here is important to me. Thank ya again for your aid. Forgive me for leavin' abruptly, but my mate needs me. *Tristan!*"

Lanna shared his anxious need to reach Casidhe.

Deniela seemed amused. Tiny sparkles gathered at the corner of her eyes.

"Let's link and do this, boss."

In the next moment, Lanna appeared and searched around her.

Daegan and Tristan stood with Brynhild, Quinn, Reese, and their Imortik-Beladors among vaults in the middle of Oakland Park Cemetery. No Deniela, though, or the other Beladors.

Where was Sen? Where was Casidhe? Had Daegan and Tristan teleported them to the wrong place?

Quinn looked around. "This is not the place! He told me I was in this cemetery and to bring you."

Daegan took off running with Quinn, Tristan, Brynhild, Reese, and five Imortiks racing to keep up.

Was Sen playing games? Lanna would have a better chance of supporting Daegan and saving Casidhe if she knew more.

Digging inside her jacket, she pulled out the glass flask Loki had given Tristan for her to use to find Sen and yanked the plug from the top. She flipped the container over and dumped the peach pit into her hand. Now for some answers on the being they were going up against.

Sen had clearly lied about being captured.

Holding the pit sandwiched between her palms, she closed her eyes and began seeing many images. So many flew at her, she couldn't sort through them fast enough. "Too fast," she whispered to herself.

Where was Sen?

She focused on one image that paused long enough for her to see Sen calling up the death wall and gasped.

"Where did you find my peach pit?"

Lanna's eyes snapped open.

She stared up, unable to speak past the terror flooding her.

# CHAPTER 37

DAEGAN COULD FEEL CASIDHE REACHING through their bond, but he could not hear her in his head. He raced toward that pull, terror unlike anything he'd ever experienced gripping him and blurring his vision.

The bag of grimoire volumes Garwyli had created tugged him forward by the strap around his neck. These two volumes were going toward the third one.

Not the other way around as he'd thought.

"Boss, *look out! Humans!*" Tristan powered his legs to stay with him.

Daegan barely missed mowing down a group of adults walking slowly as if asleep but with their eyes wide open. He wove through the sluggish bodies, leaping over headstones and dodging tall statues until he reached the area at the east end of the cemetery with a large grassy area and trees.

Sen stood on a wide pedestal of marble ten feet in the air. He clutched a wad of yellowed papers in his fist.

Those had to be the third grimoire volume.

Casidhe had been stretched out upon a slab of granite sitting upon a base. Two demonic-Imortiks stood guard at one end of the altar.

She twisted her neck, her beautiful eyes round with terror, and screamed, "*Daegan!*"

"*No!*" he roared.

Sen stopped whatever he'd been saying and looked up. "There's my pain-in-the-ass lizard."

Daegan strode forward. "Free her."

Wearing a mean smile, bright red T-shirt, and jeans on his six-and-a-half-foot-tall frame, Sen had the same facial and physical appearance of any other human out there. But his power flooded the area and his eyes were no longer blue.

Two white orbs stared out from his face.

Sen pointed to the middle of the mass of humans and ten demonic-Imortiks appeared, immediately turning on the innocent beings.

Daegan called up his Belador sword to cut down the closest Imortik.

Tristan shouted, "I'm teleporting humans to Piedmont Park and telling Evalle to handle it."

Reese and Quinn fought their way past panicked humans to blast an Imortik with Reese's power and Quinn's kinetics.

Saliva dripped from the fangs of the two demonic-Imortiks standing guard over Casidhe.

Daegan had to get to her.

Bloated clouds like puffy pewter shapes began drifting together above him as if called in to drown out the sunshine.

Sen lifted the grimoire volume sheets and began shouting as he read.

Garwyli's grimoire bag yanked away from Daegan's neck, breaking the strap and disappearing.

Casidhe sang out, "He's callin' up the death wall to open it!"

Daegan glanced up at Sen as the demigod's grimoire papers vanished in mid-statement. He did not hold the bag with the other two volumes either.

Sen looked all around him, then across the field of people where Tristan kept sending them away, and Quinn continued protecting humans along with their five Imortik allies.

Daegan teleported up to Sen's pedestal and swung his sword.

Sen blinked in and out of view, missing a serious wound by the thickness of a hair.

Daegan paused abruptly in mid swing.

Sen popped into view.

Releasing his swing, Daegan connected with Sen's arm a second before the demigod teleported far to Daegan's left. He teleported right behind Sen.

Calling up his own sword, which sizzled with dark majik, Sen attacked the moment Daegan appeared, but Daegan had been ready and ducked.

Then Daegan struck. The clanging of their weapons grew louder than the melee going on. Daegan's sword locked against Sen's, pulling them face-to-face.

"You will die this time, dragon."

"If so, I shall ensure ya lead the way."

# CHAPTER 38

C ASIDHE STRAINED TO LIFT HER head from where Sen's majik had her pinned down on the granite.

Daegan fought a teleporting Sen.

Everyone else battled to kill demonic-Imortiks and protect humans. But more humans kept filing in, walking like zombies.

Sen uttered a curse.

Casidhe whipped her head back around in time to see a bloody slash on Sen's arm before he teleported off the pedestal and beyond the end of her feet at the end of this stupid altar.

Daegan teleported off the pedestal, staying with Sen.

She pushed at the power holding her captive, groaning at the tight wrap. She growled like a crazed beast and called up more energy until the bond made a loud cracking sound.

Sitting up, she searched for Daegan. He and Sen were teleporting. When Daegan appeared with Sen again, two swords clanged back and forth with brutal strikes.

She couldn't help anyone bare-handed.

She saw no backpack on Quinn, which meant he'd left it at the last place they had been together. Standing up on the granite, Casidhe held her hand above her head and shoved power into her voice. "Come to me, *Lann an Cheartais!*"

The demonic-Imortiks guarding her turned and leaped.

She whipped her hands down and shoved energy forward fast.

Her power struck them both, sending them flying backward and skidding into two humans, knocking them off their feet.

The Imortiks were so fixed on her, they got back up and stalked forward, jaws open and claws out.

She stuck her hand up in the air again. *"Come on, dammit!"*

A whistling noise behind her sounded like a jet approaching, but not exactly.

Those two Imortiks picked up speed, coming back.

Was that keening whistle a jet after all?

With the first Imortik three steps away and claws pulled back to swing, a grip slammed her open hand. She swung low and across.

Timing was everything.

A yellow head walked into her blade and went flying like a well-kicked soccer ball.

Imortik number two stopped, watched, and dove at her. Armor covered her body before her next move. She whacked at the Imortik. It dodged and grabbed her ankle to yank her down.

She slashed the arm off the one clutching her, sending that Imortik off howling. "*Yes!*"

Joavan appeared in front of her. "Here. The last grimoire volume. Call up the death wall." He shoved papyrus sheets at her. She took them and he vanished. She could hold the sheets?

But she had to keep her sword with her. What would Shannon have done? Believed in her power and her armor. Casidhe held the sword pointed up. "*Lann an Cheartais*, return to a scabbard on my back."

She opened her hand and the sword zipped above her head and pointed down. "Shit. I didn't mean—"

Diving, the blade shushed past her head and entered a scabbard she evidently now possessed. If she survived, she had to spend some time getting to know this sword and armor.

Daegan and Sen still battled. Too much blood was flying.

Lifting the pages in one hand, she flicked fingers on her other hand across the lines, trying to ignore the battle with humans screaming, Imortiks jumping into bodies, and her friends bleeding.

That damned one-armed demonic-Imortik came back snarling and stuck its other hand out to grab her.

She swung her booted foot, hitting it squarely in the face.

The head split open. It fell back, landing on a human woman who fainted.

Okay, then.

Hurrying to read to the last pages, Casidhe began speaking the words, which shocked her. She'd always been able to read any text to herself and speak the translation out loud. This was new.

She shouted every syllable of each word.

Could the stupid wall even hear her?

The altar shook. Casidhe sidestepped to keep her balance. Way down on the other side of where Daegan and Sen battled, the ground buckled. Daegan had blood all over him.

How much was his?

She started gasping for air. This was not the time to hyperventilate! Mentally slapping herself, she sucked in a deep breath. She had to hurry and get rid of these monsters.

More shaking and rocking interrupted the ones that battled closer to her as they tried to stay upright.

An earthquake was breaking up the ground across the cemetery land.

Piles of dirt and debris blew up out of the ground behind Daegan and Sen.

Then a sonic boom sounded.

Round iron posts with sharp metal thorns jutted up and began rising from the ground. Thick bones that could have come from dinosaurs were cross members. Tall oak trees were knocked out of place, crashing everywhere. As the obsidian structure climbed to fifty feet tall and a hundred feet wide, two gates held together by a black and silver chain as thick as her leg hissed with energy.

Bright yellow fingers stabbed out between the poles, then haunting faces appeared which no longer possessed any humanity.

Clanging and howling behind the gates started up and grew into a cacophony of horrific noises.

Sen stopped, looked at the tall structure, then saw Casidhe. He teleported to her altar. Daegan teleported behind her and threw a kinetic wall up between her and Sen.

The evil demigod teleported back to his pedestal and ordered, "Humans, march to the gates and prepare to join my army."

In spite of all Tristan's teleporting efforts and her friends battling, there were still a lot of humans. Casidhe understood what Sen was doing. He had called humans here to use as host bodies for the Imortiks.

Daegan put a hand on her shoulder. "I may have only one short teleport left in me. I'm droppin' the kinetic wall to save energy. I want ya to join Tristan. I do not want Sen to harm ya."

"I've been kickin' butt up here. I'm not goin' anywhere."

Loud thunder boomed across the dark skies. Golden light shot down, spearing the altar and washing across them both.

"Maybe my mother is returnin'." But Daegan didn't sound convinced.

"You called your mother here?" Hope strangled Casidhe's next breath.

"Now to choose a guardian for my followers!" Sen announced.

A massive lightning bolt shot down.

Casidhe went spiraling to the ground in a fast teleport.

The bolt struck Daegan. He arched off the altar. Veins thickened over his body and face. He yelled a frightening sound. Brilliant gold light encompassed his body.

Tristan shouted, *"No! Sen is a dead man!"*

Casidhe lunged forward, but Tristan and Quinn caught her arms and pulled her back. She roared, *"Let me go, damn you!"*

"We can't save him if we all go up there," Tristan said, sounding panicked and trying not to. "Does Sen have *all* the grimoires?"

"No. I have the last one." She only cared about getting to Daegan. She shouted, "Sen is turnin' Daegan into an Imortik guardian! That must be the sacrifice to open the wall. *We need to save him!*"

With power boiling around him, Sen lifted off the pedestal and ordered, *"Imortiks attack!"*

Yellow monsters spilled from the woods, running toward humans too shocked to know what was happening.

Tristan looked like he was snapping a whip as he flung Imortiks at the black gates. He lifted his middle finger as they hit. *"Good thump!"*

Brynhild had been battling in her human form. She shifted into her ice dragon and launched over the top of the Imortiks to unload ice on them, taking down over half.

Casidhe called up her sword. As she grasped the handle, she

realized Sen was doing nothing to stop Brynhild or any of them. He had both hands pointed at Daegan while calling out the same type of words she'd spoken.

Was he using what he'd remembered from the one grimoire volume?

Casidhe pushed past humans and attacked Imortiks, slicing and jabbing her sword to clear her way. She had to get to Daegan.

She dipped down and jumped up to the altar.

Daegan's body levitated off the altar before she reached him. His body tilted horizontally and turned until he faced the death wall.

He struggled to break free, but his body kept floating toward the gates.

"No! You can't have him," Casidhe screamed. Daegan had teleported her away before the lightning bolt could strike her, sacrificing himself.

Grinning with unbridled happiness, Sen called out, "You see, Daegan, I never planned to *kill* you. I had a higher purpose in mind. I knew you would come for her. You walked right into my trap. You have the honor of opening the death wall gates. You will become my Imortik-dragon, the guardian for eternity, a far worse punishment than death."

Casidhe shoved her sword into her new scabbard and yanked the pages from where she'd stashed them inside the front of her armor. She hurried to frantically read how to counter Sen's move and shouted the phrase she believed would do it.

Daegan flipped over to face her. Agony etched his face. His elevated body continued to glide backward toward the gates.

She wrenched her head to glare at Sen. "Stop it, you monster!"

"Daegan chose to be the sacrifice." Sen's white eyes glowed with madness. "If you do not allow both of us to continue so he can open the gates, you condemn him to eternity as the gatekeeper when his body joins with the structure. Then he'll live in the underworld forever."

She had less than a minute before his body touched the wall and read faster. Nothing would stop this except him becoming an Imortik slave to Sen.

Tristan teleported under Daegan and tried jumping. Whatever

force Sen held over Daegan rebuffed Tristan's attempts. He teleported to Sen who knocked Tristan thirty feet away to land in the sea of humans.

Quinn, Reese, and the Imortik-Beladors still tried in vain to save the humans but there were so many Imortiks.

No one could save Daegan.

Not in the next fifteen seconds.

Daegan deserved to live.

He would do anything to avoid ending up an Imortik monster killing innocents and his own people.

Casidhe gripped the sheets, twisting them in her fist and shaking at losing Daegan. She shoved the papyrus sheets into her armor and made a decision to use her only choice for saving Daegan.

She yelled at Daegan, "I must stop you from touchin' those gates. I'm sorry and I love you." Reaching fast over her head, she drew her sword and sent it flying at Daegan.

The blade buried into his stomach.

# CHAPTER 39

DAEGAN'S BODY JERKED WITH THE impact of the sword stabbing through him. He stared at it, unable to speak. Then he fell to the ground, hitting hard and rolling to his back with the sword sticking out of his stomach.

Pain blinded him.

Sen cursed and screamed, repeating what he'd said to send Daegan to the death wall gates as if he could pull off what Tristan called a do-over.

Daegan had been stabbed in battle before but not with a sword filled with jinn majik. The jinn mother of the ice dragons must have bespelled this blade.

He could survive dragon-shifter majik.

Not this.

Casidhe raced up to him and yanked out the blade, then dropped to her knees to cover the wound gushing blood.

She was bawling her eyes out as blood ran through her fingers. "I'm so sorry. I'll find a way to save you. I could not let you become bound to that gate for eternity."

Tristan appeared next to her, his voice furious. "What did you do?"

All the Imortik-Beladors and Quinn circled Daegan's body standing apart and lifting their hands to hold a kinetic barrier. They were protecting Daegan from Sen. It wouldn't last long. Brynhild's dragon landed hard on the side where her dragon could stand over them and face Sen. Her dragon roared.

Daegan put his hand over Casidhe's bloody ones. "Do not fash, love. I thank ya for this gift." His voice was weakening when he explained to Tristan, "My mate had the courage to save me from bein' imprisoned forever."

With suffering deep in his tear-filled eyes, Tristan said, "I'll take you to Treoir to heal."

Daegan did not want to say goodbye to either of these two, but he had to tell them the truth. "Treoir cannot heal this wound. The sword is of ancient power."

Casidhe moaned. "What have I done?"

"Do not regret the throw, love." He wheezed. "Your sword 'tis the rare weapon here that could have ripped me from Sen's condemnation. 'Tis a chance I could shift and heal, though not much of one. I am still caught in Sen's web of energy. If ya move me, I shall die even faster. I feel the venom inside me flowin' through my entire body now."

Still pressing hard, Casidhe hung her head, gasping for air. "I would have taken the sword to myself if that could have saved you."

Tristan pleaded, "Call your mother again!"

Daegan's heart pummeled his chest. "She is gone."

Power struck the ground, blasting earth everywhere.

A bright explosion hit behind Casidhe.

Daegan tried to move and fell back.

"I got this, boss." Tristan jumped over to bolster the kinetic wall protecting Casidhe and Daegan from Sen firing off blasts. "That bastard has lost his mind."

"Ya must get Casidhe and Brynhild out of here. Sen shall realize any minute that he has two more of powerful descent to use for sacrifice."

"*No!*" Casidhe wiped her eyes on her shoulder.

"Lass," Daegan urged, struggling to speak.

She leaned down close and said, "I have nothin' left to live for without you. I will *not* allow you to go to the next life without me."

Daegan's voice shook with emotion. "I love ya more than ya can ever imagine. Do not dare risk your precious life."

"If Sen manages to get away with this, he'll have to face my Hawdreki." Blood continued oozing through her fingers.

A tower of energy flushed across the land.

Daegan strained to his side to see what was happening.

Casidhe twisted around, her hand still on his wound.

All at once, Daegan couldn't move his body, only his eyes. He could breathe. He rolled his eyes down to his wound where the blood had stopped in midstream from the gaping hole.

He tried to whisper. Not happening. No telepathy.

Everyone in the clearing had been frozen in place except Sen, who stood upon the pedestal with his arms crossed. He glowered at a spot on the ground in front of him.

Energy wavered back and forth then settled until a woman came into view. Lanna stood next to her.

What the devil was Lanna doing with this strange being?

He'd thought Quinn had her somewhere safe.

When Lanna turned to look at Daegan, so did the woman.

Not much taller than Lanna's petite stature, the woman had skin the color of snow with red lips and black hair piled in soft shapes on top of her head. She wore an odd headdress that seemed to be vines with pinkish-peach-colored flowers woven with gold and red strands of material. The ankle-length, dark-red dress she wore had deep sleeves at the wrists and a black sash around her small waist. Simple sandals covered her feet, but she was no simple supernatural.

Her quiet pale-blue gaze appeared young. Anyone looking deeper would know she had lived for many centuries.

Daegan would guess a deity, but what was she doing here?

The woman and Lanna turned back to Sen, who had waited for her to speak. So out of character for him.

"What have you done, Senkereh?"

Sounding annoyed instead of worried, Sen shrugged, "I did my time with the Tribunal. They've disbanded. I am *free* and *I* intend to rule all of the Imortiks."

"You have not changed in the past one thousand years." The woman made that statement as though pondering her words at the same time.

Sen laughed, a sound filled with menace. "You don't think so? I figured out how to open rifts for the Imortiks, shut down the Tribunal, and I'll now rid this world of worthless humans as soon as I open those gates."

She took her time with each word she spoke. "Timmon's spirit came to me before he passed. My nephew's soul was severely damaged. He told me how you tricked him into being possessed and how he feared your retribution if he called me for help. I must now inform my sister of losing her child and that Timmon's spirit shall wander alone in the afterlife for more years than you have lived."

Shrugging, Sen said, "My cousin knew what he was getting into when he agreed to become the Imortik master. It made him feel important."

"And Tenebris? I was told he returned home badly burned by a witch's majik. I would not have thought that possible."

Sen showed no remorse. "He came to me asking to be involved in whatever I planned to do once I got free of my slave time. He thought it would be fun to screw with the Tribunal. That one is *not* on me."

The woman made careful movements as she spoke, clearly in no rush. "This death wall was to never be opened again."

Daegan would have frowned if it had been possible to move his facial muscles. She didn't sound terribly concerned but more like she wanted to catch up with a friend. Daegan took in everyone from Tristan and Casidhe to Quinn, Reese, and the others. They were all stuck in the position they'd been in right before this woman arrived. Even Brynhild who had shifted back and been in the process of clothing herself wore a shirt and partial pants.

Sen walked away from her as far as the platform on his pedestal would allow, staring up as he did. He turned back to her with his hands hooked at his hips. "This is not your battle, *Mother*. Go home to the safety of Mount Kunlun and let me be. You have tortured me enough."

Mother? She had to be a goddess to produce a demigod. A supernatural of lesser powers would not have been able to show up and freeze every living thing near her. Daegan wanted to hope she would help them, but even his own mother took little interest beyond his initial call for aid.

Sounding unhappy, as if her child had only behaved poorly, Sen's mother said, "You hold no regrets even now for taking the life of your father. No mother wishes to kill her child. That is why I gifted you to the Tribunal for the chance to make amends and gain knowledge." Her soft voice shielded her emotions.

"You thought I'd learn from *fragile* humans who are *beneath* me?" Sen snarled. "Unbelievable. You shouldn't have chosen a human to mate and should thank me. I fixed that embarrassing mistake for you."

When his mother spoke this time, her voice lifted with a push of power. "*You* were the result of that mistake," she reminded him. "Thankfully, he had more children before you came along to end his life. You could have been as great as his descendant Genghis Khan, but you never possessed the humility or mercy of the greatest leaders. You care only for yourself even now and have shamed all of us on Mount Kunlun."

Dropping the casual tone, Sen became very serious. "Look, we had an agreement. Once I did the time with the Tribunal, I could live as I pleased. You have to stick to *your* part of that deal, too. With the Tribunal disbanded, I am technically free and you no longer have a hold over me, *Mother.*"

Based on that exchange, Daegan now held less hope of closing the death wall.

Without addressing his comment, his mother turned to Lanna. "Who did you say is capable of reading the Immortuos Grimoire?"

Lanna twisted around and pointed at Casidhe. "She has gift to read anything and has read the first two grimoire volumes."

Daegan didn't want that woman to get near Casidhe. Sen's mother had not proven herself an ally.

Sen proved he could power up his voice even more than his mother had and roared, "*Do not dare interfere in what is mine!*"

Returning to face him, his mother continued conversationally, "You have your freedom, Senkereh. Now that you have exercised such freedom, you belong to the world again. As such, you are subject to the rule of this world. I am not interfering, but performing the same duty I was called upon for when the first death wall had to be closed. I would be performing this duty now even if you were not here."

His mother glanced at Casidhe and said, "You shall read the text now."

That freed Casidhe, who fell forward from being in midturn. She looked at Daegan.

The woman said, "He does not bleed until he moves again."

With no other way to communicate, Daegan hoped she could see the love and worry in his eyes.

Casidhe nodded and stood to face the woman as she pulled the third volume of grimoire pages out of her armor.

Sen shouted a curse and shoved a blast of energy at Casidhe.

*Nay!* Daegan strained to lunge up and protect her, but he couldn't move.

Casidhe dropped the pages and slapped her hands at Sen, blasting the energy back to knock him off his feet.

He teleported in the middle of the fall and returned to the pedestal, confusion ruling his face.

Lifting her hands, Casidhe looked at them as if they belonged to someone else, shook her head and muttered, "I want to wake up from this nightmare." She picked up the pages Sen must have realized he could not steal from her, especially with his mother standing there.

In a clear voice that cut across the silent land, Casidhe began reading out loud in the original language. She read the last page to herself and stepped around to face the wall and shouted a blur of unintelligible words.

Behind her, Imortiks began lifting from bodies and floating to the wall.

"Stop! You can't do this," Sen roared. "I just called in every Imortik in the world to this spot! You're screwing with my plan!"

His mother ignored him as he tried to stop filmy Imortik energy from reaching the wall. The bodies jerked up and down before passing Daegan.

Sen's mother lifted a hand, which evidently blocked Sen's power.

Hundreds of yellow bodies poured into the area from every direction. The translucent beings kept moving.

Sen started howling with laughter. "What am I thinking? I already know the words to open the wall and bring every Imortik back plus hundreds of thousands more. Have your fun. I can play this game all day."

Casidhe flipped around to face the woman.

Still standing there, Lanna sent Daegan a wan smile but she

did not appear harmed. He hoped not. How had Lanna found Sen's mother?

Daegan's body sizzled with a change. Yellow mist escaped from his thigh in a long stream, heading for the gates.

Casidhe had not seen that while facing away from him. She told Sen's mother, "Sendin' the Imortiks and their energy behind the wall is all I can do. I'm not sure how long they will remain. The pages read as if this must all happen quickly. As the only goddess here, you—"

With the lift of a delicate hand, Sen's mother requested silence. "I am aware of my duty." She swept around to face Sen.

The demigod lost his smile, now so angry his fists shook at his sides and muscles bulged beneath his skin. "You done? Hope you had fun. All you managed to do was delay the inevitable."

Without turning away from Sen, his mother began explaining, "During the first time of closing the death wall, we called for dragon shifters of two different clans to unite their powers and create the gates for this wall. The same two used their powers to close the gates. This time, two dragon shifters of different clans shall unite their powers once again to close the gates. I request the red dragon and ice dragon shifters to stand together."

Daegan felt his body released from her hold.

Brynhild rushed over and offered him a hand. Casidhe stood on the other side, both lifting him to his feet.

Casidhe studied his wound. "You stopped bleedin'."

"Ya pulled the Imortik venom from me." Daegan smiled at her and leaned to kiss her.

Sen's mother interrupted his kiss when she continued dictating everyone's moves. "Both dragon shifters face the gates unaided."

Casidhe glared at the woman's back, but Daegan hobbled around, gritting his teeth. He felt lightheaded from the blood loss. He silently asked Ruadh for more healing power. His dragon made noises that sounded as if the woman had muted him.

Daegan told Ruadh not to worry. He could stand for now.

Sen's mother said, "Each dragon shifter shall point a finger toward the gate and touch fingertips." She paused and asked, "You do have *Cearcall na Sìorraidheachd*, Daegan, correct?"

Brynhild asked, "What?"

Daegan answered, "'Tis an amulet."

"Joavan's amulet?"

"Aye." Daegan called up the amulet from where he'd kept it on his being with majik and looked over his shoulder. "I have the amulet."

Nodding, Sen's mother continued, "Loop the amulet over your fingertips and onto your wrists. You two shall speak the words to close the gates together and send the death wall back to the underworld where it shall remain."

Sen teleported in front of Daegan and Brynhild. "You didn't really think I was going to let her get away with this, did you? I indulged her too much over the years, but you *can't* kill me and she *won't* kill me."

Daegan wanted to turn Ruadh loose on Sen, but that was not an option at the moment.

Brynhild had the same issue. She could only seethe without changing.

Sen reached for the amulet and disappeared before touching it.

Daegan glanced over his shoulder. Sen's mother had sent him back to his pedestal and pinned his arms to his sides. Plus his mouth had been slammed shut in a crazed smile which did not fit with his fury. Sen stared at his mother as if he could blast her head to pieces with his mind alone, which he might be capable of if not for being locked in place by her power.

Daegan could feel his stomach wound closing up. The pain eating his insides told him he was far from healed or surviving yet.

Casidhe stepped around to his side, holding her papers again.

He handed the amulet to Brynhild to reach out to loop it over their wrists better than he could at the moment. With that done, he allowed his fingertip to touch hers while both of them pointed.

The second their fingers touched, multiple strands of red and blue energy streaked out, weaving together into a thick rope before striking the gates. The energy quickly spread out like jagged roots on a tree and crawled over the entire surface of the gates.

Casidhe said quickly, "I'll read a chunk of words then you two repeat it at the same time. Okay?"

"Aye." Daegan nodded.

"Yes." Brynhild didn't move.

Starting with a shaky voice, Casidhe focused so hard on what she was doing her words began to smooth out. She waited only long enough for Daegan and Brynhild to recite what she'd told them.

When Casidhe had nothing else to say, Daegan glanced over to see that she held the last sheet. He could not move without breaking the line of power he and Brynhild were feeding the gates.

Casidhe looked around at Sen's mother. "That's all I have. What now?"

His mother said, "Hold the papyrus sheets upon your palm."

Returning to face the gates, Casidhe did as told, holding her palm out with the pages.

They disappeared.

Daegan glanced to see the pages land in the hands of Sen's mother, who said, "Place the other two grimoire volumes on your palm now."

Casidhe said, "I don't have—" then made a surprised gasp.

Daegan cut his gaze over to see two more piles of papyrus sheets on her palm.

All of those vanished.

Daegan checked and Sen's mom had all the grimoire volumes.

Holding the sheets upon one hand, Sen's mother addressed her son. "You speak the truth, Senkereh. I cannot kill my child. You earned your freedom and now wish to rule the Imortiks. I shall grant your wish."

Brynhild howled, *"We have been tricked!"*

# CHAPTER 40

CASIDHE HAD REACHED THE END of her rope. She felt turned inside out and now Sen and his mother were going to screw everyone? "If this goes any worse, I'm gonna shift into my Hawdreki," she warned Daegan.

"Wait until Brynhild and I are able to separate this connection," Daegan replied over his shoulder.

Brynhild added, "I think we try to break apart and see what happens."

Casidhe had her doubts about that working without harming them. "Let's listen to see what his mother does before we make our last-ditch effort in case it kills us all."

"You have dark humor," Brynhild complimented.

She thought Casidhe was joking? Strange ice dragon shifter. Wait, was Brynhild her aunt?

Sen's mother began to grow in size, but not hideously as Queen Maeve tended to do. This woman was still petite-looking and soft, but a twenty-foot-tall giant now.

Lanna stepped away, staring up at Sen's mother who began speaking in a formal way.

"As *Wang Mu* Niang Niang, Queen Mother of the West and mother of Senkereh, I choose Senkereh to become the eternal gatekeeper of the death wall."

The same golden lightning bolt struck Sen showering him in golden light.

She must have released the hold on him. Sen's face warped wide, then taller, as his body began to lose its muscular definition. Clear blue eyes replaced the white orbs.

For the first time, his voice dropped to a frightened whisper. "Don't do this. I'll come back and—" He screamed as his body stretched and thinned. His voice reduced to a squeal. While warping out of shape, his body flew to the gates and his back slammed against the thorn posts.

Blood ran freely from his body.

Legs, arms, and torso kept stretching to reach the top and sides of the gates. His face became flat and then all of him merged with the structure until the only moving part was blood tears running from his eyes.

The earth shifted and rumbled, then the structure began sinking down until the ground had swallowed it.

Daegan hated watching anyone end up where Sen had. Casidhe had saved him and his dragon from an unimaginable eternal end.

When the top passed out of view, the ground everywhere shifted back to normal with grass growing where it had been and trees lifting from the ground as roots snaked deep again.

Power that had been crackling from Daegan and Brynhild to the gates snapped back to each of them.

Brynhild lifted the amulet off their hands and gave it to Daegan.

"Thank ya, Brynhild. Ya have proven your honor well today."

She gave him a smile and short nod. "It feels good not to carry the burden of hate any longer and to have gained an ally."

When Daegan turned to stand next to Casidhe, Sen's mother stood before both of them. She addressed Casidhe. "You would have made a grave mistake to battle Sen for the sole purpose of following Daegan in death."

Casidhe tried to lift a shoulder, but while the armor had some flex, shrugging seemed not as easy. "It was a calculated risk. I will die eventually. I did not want to wait seventy years to join Daegan."

Daegan's big hand reached for hers. He squeezed her fingers, letting her know he hadn't agreed with her plan either.

Speaking as if instructing a simple child, Sen's mother explained, "Daegan is a demigod and dragon. He would heal once the Imortik influence left his body."

Casidhe conceded, "True, based on all of this having worked out."

Ignoring that statement, Sen's mother continued in the same

tone. "You are Hawdreki, a descendant of the formidable first jinn. You could not have prevented Senkereh's last attack had you not been *his* equal." She told Daegan, "All three grimoires are inside the wall with Sen's body."

Daegan stood stronger by the minute, but blood began trickling from his wound. He gritted out, "What if Sen finds a way back?"

"I am now the only one who can call the wall up and remove him." With that said, Sen's mother vanished. Everyone could immediately move again.

Casidhe took a look at Daegan's wound and called out, "No! Come back. He's not healed."

Daegan dropped to his knees. His dragon began to show life inside him. He would try to shift soon.

Deniela appeared and stared down at him. "How have you lived so long? You are quite careless, Son."

Raising a gaze lacking tolerance, Daegan didn't even speak. He could not perform a word battle with her.

"Please save him," Casidhe begged.

"Move aside."

Casidhe jumped back, hands twisting with worry.

Tristan stared down anxiously but said nothing.

Deniela pointed at Daegan's bloody stomach. The bleeding stopped and his skin began to mend.

He saw stars when he stood this time, but Ruadh should be able to heal him from there. Trying for polite, he told his mother, "Thank ya again."

A screeching sound flew into view overhead.

Queen Maeve rode that glamoured wyvern again.

"Who is that and what is she riding?" Deniela asked.

He groaned. "'Tis Queen Maeve. She is the one who locked me in TÅµr Medb for two thousand years and wants to capture me again. 'Tis said she has developed an ungodly amount of power, especially when riding her beast."

"This day will not end!" Casidhe said, sounding ready to kill something. "It may be time for her to meet a Hawdreki."

"No, lass. Do not go up. Ya saw how Queen Maeve's madness has turned her into a deadly opponent. She has poured majik into her wyvern and it makes her more dangerous."

A shearing sound in the distance filled the air.

Queen Maeve's glamoured wyvern circled around high above them, showing off, then angled down to dive right at Daegan.

The high-pitched whistling became louder as a jet flew into view like a giant silver arrow. It released what Tristan had told Daegan was a rocket.

The weapon hit Queen Maeve and the wyvern. Power pulsed and expanded in a huge ball of fire and energy, rocking the jet as it passed, but the pilot pulled his craft under control.

Deniela watched with amusement filling her face. "What possible reason could she have to pretend a wyvern is a red dragon? Someone should tell her there is only one."

The flaming ball of Queen Maeve and her wyvern landed on the nearby railroad tracks, missing houses.

Tristan muttered, "Black witch down, form a perimeter."

Someone nearby snorted a laugh.

Deniela angled her head to Daegan, eyebrows drawn tight. "Your people are strange."

Said the woman who was making Daegan nuts. "They grow on ya if ya are around them long enough."

Tristan grinned. "You gonna make it, boss?"

"Aye. 'Twill take some time, but I feel my dragon sendin' healin' energy through my body." He had not paid a terrible price for calling his mother as his father had warned.

Casidhe had been standing with the oddest look on her face.

"What troubles ya, lass?"

"I just thought on what Sen's mother said to me. Was she tryin' to say I have the same power as a *demigod*?"

Daegan thought back on that moment and felt a burst of joy. "Aye. I believe she meant not just power, but perhaps ya shall live a long time with me. Ya should finish your research."

"Are you serious?" Casidhe asked with no small amount of awe.

A woman screamed, then Lanna yelled for help.

Daegan teleported Casidhe, Tristan, Brynhild, and his mother, he thought, but she was not there when he landed next to Lanna.

Quinn knelt next to Reese who was hugging her stomach and keening. She screamed and burst out crying.

# CHAPTER 41

QUINN PLEADED, "WHAT CAN I do? What do you need?"
Reese was panting. "I don't know. Renata, the humans,
everyone who lost their Imortik was dancing around, but not
me." She let out a low guttural sound like an animal being cut
open.

"Is it the baby? We can go to a hospital."

"Not with what I am." Reese rolled over on her side, face
blanched.

Daegan said, "We shall take her to Treoir. Tristan and I can
teleport."

"No, please," Reese whispered. "Let me just lie here."

"No, I won't lose you," Quinn argued. He looked up at Lanna.
"Can you help her?"

Wiping her eyes, she said, "I do not know." She went to her
knees and her lip trembled. "I will not like if I harm baby."

"I'm sorry, Lanna, I shouldn't ask something like this of you."

Reese reached out and grabbed Lanna's hand. "When the
Imortik pulled out of me, it felt like he took half my insides
with him. Can you tell if the baby is ... you know."

Nodding, Lanna said, "I will look."

Daegan got down with Lanna. "If ya want, I can try healin'
her, too."

Taking a deep breath, Lanna said, "Maybe. I must feel for
... problem first." When Reese released her, Lanna pulled up
Reese's shirt and placed both of her hands on her abdomen.
Lanna dropped her head and stayed there for the longest time.

Veins that had been raised along Reese's muscles relaxed and
smoothed out. She started breathing better.

Quinn watched Lanna with hope broadcasting through every
breath.

When Reese finally uncurved, she drew a deep breath with eyes on Quinn. "Guess I'm back to my norm."

He smiled at her, but Daegan could see the fear still in Quinn's face.

"You are not same," Lanna announced.

Reese lost her smile. "What are you talking about? Did I ... did I lose the baby? I would be bleeding."

"Baby is fine."

Relief whipped around the group.

Lanna sniffled. "Bad energy gone. Baby is happy."

"I know." Reese started nodding. "I'm glad the Imortik is gone."

"Demon energy gone."

Reese sat up with Quinn supporting her back. "What?"

"Imortik liked your energy."

"Yes."

"I think when Imortik bonded to your energy, it pulled demon energy out when Imortik sent back to wall. You are ... free."

Reese reeled, whispering, "It's gone?" She shouted, "Wait. I feel heat!"

Tristan asked, "You're in heat?"

Quinn sent him a threatening look. "The baby generates heat."

Lifting his hands, Tristan stepped back and grinned at Daegan when Quinn looked away.

Reese stopped talking excitedly and asked in a low voice, "Does this mean I'm human now?"

Lanna shook her head. "I do not think so. Try remote viewing for Quinn. He has stayed at your side."

Reese closed her eyes and started describing what Quinn had done hours ago before they joined up again, then stopped and opened her eyes with a sheepish grin. "I still have *that* gift."

Quinn hugged her to him and kissed her forehead. "Every bit of you is a gift to me."

Letting out a sigh as if people were not paying attention, Lanna said, "You have much more. You have no demon power but still have baby."

Quinn and Reese turned to her. Quinn asked, "What are you saying, Lanna?" His voice held a warning to not give Reese false hopes.

Lanna would not be intimidated. "You should see Garwyli to check for healing, but I think baby is safe and strong. You have no demon power to hurt baby. I would not say if I did not believe very much, but I am looking forward to holding Phoedra's baby brother." Lanna teared up in spite of her smile.

Everyone cheered.

Daegan clapped Quinn on the back. "Ya shall have to come up with a final name at some point."

Evalle walked up. "I'd call him Hammer. Just give him a nickname right off the bat."

Taking a shuddering breath, Quinn told her, "Lanna believes the baby will live."

Daegan rarely saw Evalle speechless. Behind her, Storm walked up smiling then gave Reese a double take.

Reese glared at him. "Don't you dare say I still have demon energy."

"No way. You don't have any demonic power registering."

Evalle told him the news. Storm shook Quinn's hand and congratulated both of them. He added, "I think Lanna's right. If the baby lived through all that with the Imortik and the demon power getting pulled out, he is one tough little boy."

"He can play with Feenix when he starts crawling," Evalle offered. "Just don't bring any silver toys or silver binkies."

"Why?" Brynhild asked, having stood back to observe.

Tristan supplied, "Feenix is Evalle's pet gargoyle. He's two feet tall, has a lisp, and eats anything silver. Lug nuts are a favorite."

"This is most interesting." Brynhild seemed relaxed with the group.

Evalle gave Storm a glance then announced, "Once we help the human law enforcement get the city settled down and debrief everyone, Storm and I will host a meal at our building."

"Debrief?" Tristan asked. "Look at you talking Isak's lingo."

"He won't give me much credit for one word." She laughed.

Daegan saw Isak with his men, which was how Evalle had ended up here. He told Brynhild, "Ya should meet some of our human allies."

She followed him over.

Isak's men glanced her way then gave her a second look.

Brynhild lifted her chin, clearly enjoying the male admiration.

Daegan said, "Thank ya for all ya did to protect humans and nonhumans, Isak."

"You're welcome. It was a team effort from both sides. Huntsen didn't like it, but he doesn't have to. He'll come around or be left out of any future events. Our men are working with the local authorities to help the humans who were caught up in it here today. We took out Palaki and arrested the men we managed to keep alive. Their heads are screwed up."

"We must unite the protective nonhumans with the humans in some way," Daegan said.

"That's going to happen now because of the humans here today," Isak confirmed. "They're still terrified and we both know that predators still exist, but I heard some of them talking on the way out about how they never knew these threats existed and admitted that good supernaturals saved them. I've already heard from the press about wanting interviews."

Daegan cringed. "I am not the bein' to interview."

With a tired grin, Isak saved him. "As your new Maistir, Evalle wants her people to be safe and for humans to like the Beladors and their human families. I think she's going to be your poster girl."

Tristan caught up to them. "Even with glowing green eyes?"

"She talked to a couple leaving here today who asked if she was a nonhuman. She dropped her dark sunglasses and smiled big for them. They stared a minute then asked for a selfie. It won't be perfect, but we have to start somewhere."

"Cool." Tristan glanced at Daegan then Brynhild.

Daegan said, "I am sorry, Brynhild. I want ya to meet Isak Nyght whose company created blasters for dealing with nonhumans."

She had begun smiling then frowned.

"For killing demons," Isak clarified, glaring at Daegan who found his embarrassment amusing.

That should remove any doubt about what a bad idea it would be for Daegan to do interviews.

Isak shook hands with Brynhild. "What exactly are you?"

Daegan answered, "She is an ally of the Beladors and a powerful ice dragon shifter of King Eógan's dynasty."

"Is nice to meet you," Brynhild said in her sultry voice, no doubt boosting it for more male attention.

Tristan rolled his eyes but chuckled, too.

Isak became serious, asking, "Keep me posted on Adrianna, please."

Daegan offered, "Would ya like to teleport to Treoir? I know ya do not care for travelin' that way."

"I would fly on the back of a half-dead goose if Adrianna needed me, but I'll wait until she asks to see me. I just want to know she's healing." As if that was too much emotion for Isak right now, he said, "Good meeting you, Brynhild. When things are calm, I'd like you to come shift for me to photograph. I'm building an archive of our supernatural allies. If they know what you look like in both forms, they'll protect you, not attack."

"This is good. We will talk soon."

Isak gave a finger salute and took his men with him.

Evalle and Storm headed out.

Daegan saw Casidhe with Reese and Quinn. He was done with people and wanted to take off his mate's armor. Immediately.

Joavan appeared behind Brynhild.

# CHAPTER 42

D AEGAN WAS ACTUALLY GLAD TO see the Faetheen. He wanted to get everyone off his back before he left with Casidhe. "Joavan. I have been expectin' you."

Brynhild wheeled around as if Daegan had yelled to watch out for an attack.

Joavan shook his head. "Do not trust her. She lies."

Brynhild bristled. "You are one to talk. You hold his sister."

That accusation stiffened Joavan's profile. "We have reached an agreement. His sister is being cared for by the best of our healers. He shall see his sister soon. How interesting to see you standing here when you failed to kill him after many tries."

Daegan closed his eyes. Brynhild and Joavan had been together and now had issues?

Embarrassed to be called out for her actions in front of Daegan, she leaned in with her hands fisted. "I have discovered the truth. The red dragon did not start the Dragani War or kill my people. I came here to stand with him and fight the Imortiks. I have regained my honor, which is more than you can say. You are only here for your amulet."

Sounding disgusted, Joavan said, "Yet again you do not have all the information. I intervened to save an oracle who was helping him find the grimoire volumes. And who do you think snatched the grimoire pages from Sen today? Huh? Think they just floated away?" He lifted his chin at her surprise. "You have made many mistakes and one was to turn your back on me. I would not trust you if you were tied up."

Brynhild snarled, "This is not a time to fantasize of sex, which will never happen again, *Faetheen*."

Joavan's face turned deep red.

Daegan's stomach was still healing and he desperately wanted

Casidhe in his arms. "*Enough!* 'Tis not the time to have a lover's squabble."

Joavan sneered, "She is not my lover."

"I would not touch this one with gloves," Brynhild muttered.

Daegan would never get out of here until he dealt with both of them. He told Joavan, "Brynhild and I were just finishin' up our discussion. Might I have a moment with her? Then I am most anxious to complete our agreement."

"As a gentleman, I will wait over to the side and allow you privacy."

"Thank ya, Joavan."

Brynhild narrowed her eyes at the Faetheen as he walked away.

"Now, Brynhild. I am most thankful to have had ya here today. We would not have closed the wall without ya."

For Daegan, she smiled. He knew very well the show of happiness was more for Joavan's benefit.

"Ya also gave me insight on Cathbad, Macha, and Queen Maeve, though we no longer must worry about her," Daegan said. "I shall be happy to help when ya need somethin'."

Shifting around to further shield her words from Joavan, she dropped her voice and admitted, "I do have a favor to ask."

"If 'tis within my power and ya do not ask me to kill anyone or go to war, I shall grant this wish."

She smirked. "It is not so dire, Daegan. I merely need something found when I return to share more."

"Tell me what ya search for and I shall do what I can until then."

"No. I have someone to see right away," she said, glancing away for a moment. "Your people deserve rest, then they will be fresh for this hunt."

He extended his hand. "I look forward to helpin' ya. I hold ya in high respect as a dragon shifter with great honor. I am thankful we shall be allies. Would ya like to see Skarde?"

"No. I only want to find something that belongs to me."

"Very well. Be careful flyin' until we have worked things out with the human military."

"I will." She gave him a half-hearted smile and turned, taking a couple steps toward Joavan. "I would like to speak to you."

Joavan vanished.

Pain whipped across Brynhild's face for a second. She recovered to grumble under her breath, shift into her dragon, and disappear as quickly with her cloaking.

Daegan could hear the dragon's wings flapping fast. She was in a hurry to leave.

When Joavan appeared again, Daegan pulled out the amulet and dropped it into the Faetheen's hand.

"Thank you. I do not want you to doubt me but as I told you, I need this amulet to retrieve your sister. I will return quickly."

Nodding slowly, Daegan showed the trust Joavan had gained.

In several moments, Joavan reappeared.

Daegan stood up straighter, his heart beating fast at finally seeing his sister again.

Reaching to his side, Joavan gently pulled Jennyver into view.

Her pretty red hair flowed in waves and she had the deep green eyes Brina had eventually inherited.

Jennyver took one look at Daegan and dove at him. He caught her and spun her around, feeling as if he'd conquered the world by getting her back. She let out the sweetest laugh, which turned into a quiet sob. When he lowered her feet to the ground, he held her a bit longer, stroking her back as he would a bairn.

He also noted she had on a very nice gown and shoes suitable for a princess.

Her face glowed with a healthy color. Daegan struggled to hold back tears of joy himself. "'Tis good to see ya, Jennyver. I wish ya had not gone through so much to end up here and I shall never thank Herrick for what he did to ya, but I intend to cherish every moment of havin' ya in Treoir. Ya have family waitin' to meet ya."

"Joavan and his people were very kind to me." She turned and hugged the Faetheen, surprising him. He hugged her briefly then released her to stand with her brother.

She told Daegan, "It has been quite a shock to be in this world. His people helped me to ... " She looked to Joavan.

"Decompress," the Faetheen supplied. "Just as men returning home from a long battle need time to settle their heads back into feeling normal."

"Thank you," she told him with deep sincerity.

Daegan felt just as thankful. He had no idea how he would have handled bringing her into this world and explaining all that had happened. "I thank ya for the care your people gave Jennyver."

Joavan sighed deeply. "I felt everyone had wronged me, except Jennyver. I put her with my healers and swore on my blood that if they cared for her, I would return the amulet. I have kept my word. You have kept yours, Daegan. We are no longer enemies."

Before Daegan could say another word, Joavan disappeared.

# CHAPTER 43

BRYNHILD FOUND HER WAY BACK to the Caucasus Mountains flying while cloaked. Moonlight shed over the quiet mountain range, making the snow glow around her feet. She'd pulled furs and boots to her human body.

Nothing stirred far below in the valley this late at night.

How long would it take for Herrick to step outside the ward so she could have final words with him?

She might be able to cross into the ward, but she preferred to not alert him of her presence first if she touched the ward and could not pass.

When she'd first escaped Cathbad, she'd been lost with no idea where to go. She had never considered coming here. This castle of her ancestors had been designated for the oldest ice dragon sibling, Herrick.

Also, she'd been determined to find and kill Daegan.

To find him, she had to be in the human world. Learning the truth and no longer carrying the poison of hate soothed her battered soul.

Having a home offered her solace, too. She hadn't realized she'd even wanted a place of her own until Joavan had found a perfect one.

Where was Joavan?

Could he not come back to yell at her?

She tried to convince herself she was furious when he refused to speak with her, but the ache of his rejection could not be extinguished by any other emotion.

Her chest felt empty as a hole in a tree.

Blustery wind swept a dusting of snow constantly around this ridge high above where Herrick's castle hid. How much longer would she have to wait?

She did not wish to waste her breath speaking with him, but he had dishonored their father's legacy and deserved to hear her thoughts. She had lost honor with Daegan but had earned back the right to hold her head high again.

Herrick had treated her as garbage to be tossed aside.

Joavan had stopped supporting her by leaving.

Daegan had accepted her as his equal.

She could not go back in time to fix past mistakes, but she could move forward with new knowledge. Her father and mother had been wise parents. She had trouble believing they'd committed her mistakes to gain their wisdom, but perhaps everyone learned in the same way.

Daegan deserved credit for not retaliating against her when he would have been justified, such as when he found out about Herrick holding his sister captive.

How could Herrick have kept a woman in stasis all that time only to use for trade?

Brynhild breathed in a deep breath of the chilly air, held it for a moment, then released the air. She must begin to heal herself from the inside out.

Even with the deep hatred she'd carried for Daegan over thousands of years, she would never have taken it out on his sister. Her father would be ashamed of how Jennyver was treated.

Herrick had always been a self-centered bastard, so sure of his position. She had never criticized his battle skills, but he had made bad strategic decisions at times. He'd rage at her when she'd find a flaw in his battle plan and pointed it out.

His head had been too great in size to accept anyone else's ideas, and never a woman's.

She growled, disgusted with so many egregious errors along the way, hers included.

She would never change who she was, but losing Joavan had shaken her. She regretted the day she'd flown away from Joavan to kill Daegan, which she'd failed to even do and then found out her plan would have resulted in murder.

All that misplaced hatred cost her Joavan.

He'd helped her find her footing in this new land and she had let him down. No wonder he went to Daegan to work out how to get his amulet, upholding his commitment to his people. She had no one to blame for her poor judgement except the woman in her mirror. She was easily as intelligent as any man, more so than some. From this point on, she would take a breath before reacting as a start.

Once she finished with Herrick.

He deserved her wrath.

It was now up to her to prove the ice dragon clan had believed in honor. Every member of King Eógan's clan had been proud to belong to such a dynasty.

Clearly, Herrick had not.

A giant blue and silver dragon flew out of the ward heading away from her.

She tensed, prepared to shift, but her new plan to think before she reacted kept her feet planted. A griffon vulture appeared right behind Herrick, flying hard to keep up with the dragon.

Should she deal with Herrick in dragon form or confront him when he returned?

Movement below caught her eye.

A middle-aged man, whose wiry muscles came from honest labor every day, passed through the ward on the rugged ground, heading across the valley. He carried a large pack on his back and a walking stick in one hand.

Maybe she would follow this man until he returned and take hold of his arm to pass through the ward. That way, she could wait for Herrick in the comfort of his castle.

A woman emerged next, also wearing a backpack and pulling a rope tied to a goat with bags slung on each side as a saddle. Then another woman with a child. A man herding four sheep followed.

She studied the stream of people leaving in single file. Not one made a sound and all moved as quickly as possible.

Was Herrick's clan leaving him?

While watching the humans plod forward as fast as they could move, Brynhild realized how Herrick could at least pay for the way he had dishonored her.

She shifted and flew down to the valley, landed in their path, then uncloaked her dragon.

The tribe of people stopped all movement.

She returned to her human form. "I am Brynhild of the ice dragon clan."

The man leading them stood firm. "We can no longer live with Herrick. He has broken mentally. We fear him."

"Where will you go?"

He hesitated.

She explained, "Had I wished to kill you, none would be standing now. I am not happy with my brother. He has lost honor."

Nodding, the poor man almost crumbled with relief. He started explaining where many of them had family in a place called southern Russian. She flew him there first, realizing it was not so far by dragon, then returned to take all the others.

Daylight had come long ago and many hours had passed with the sun moving to its zenith by the time Herrick returned to his castle.

Brynhild sat in a chair near his hearth. She'd passed through the ward with no trouble, but he had likely set it for family never expecting *her* to show up.

Only Skarde.

In the end, Herrick had simply not cared.

His loud shouting outside indicated he had discovered people missing.

The heavy door slammed open.

He pounded toward her, having clothed his body in furs and leathers of when they'd lived thousands of years ago.

She still marveled at being alive in this era. Herrick had the only key to a long life by using the majik of this castle, but it had never been meant for immortality.

Whatever had happened to him in the past week had clearly aged the parts of his face not covered by a thick beard.

He took one look at her and bellowed, "What are you doing here?"

She stood, now wearing her armor. She wanted him to see her as she had been when they had once battled side by side. "You have brought great dishonor on the house of King Eógan. Our father would be ashamed of your actions."

Herrick would never admit her strike had hit true, but his eyes flashed with hurt. To hide any emotion, he snarled, "You are not one to lecture me."

"I have made my own mistakes based on what we believed long ago. Then I discovered the red dragon did not start the Dragani War, which you had me convinced he did. Still, I take responsibility for my actions. I made amends and am now allied with Daegan, just as mother and father had once wanted."

"You are the one who brings shame to our clan!" He stomped closer. "The red dragon killed many of our people."

"No." Calmly standing her ground, she explained, "We were fooled by Queen Maeve, who had glamoured a wyvern and gave it exceptional majik. I saw this wyvern with my own eyes and heard her admit to starting the war because she hated Daegan and likely all dragons. Once she had Daegan imprisoned in TÅµr Medb, she allowed the war to continue, pitting dragon clan against dragon clan until we wiped each other out, forcing those who survived to go into hiding. We lost our entire world for a lie."

He must have heard the truth in her words to have become so silent.

She was not finished. "Your people abandoned you. They said your mind was broken and they feared you."

His mouth opened. "They're gone?"

"Yes. I made sure they reached their destination safely and gave them a way to alert me if anyone put them in danger. You do not deserve a clan who loves you. You do not deserve to live after committing the heinous atrocity of holding Daegan's sister captive in your lair as nothing more than a trinket. That is your sin to carry. You do not deserve family. I will not be back."

She walked out with him standing alone in his castle, shifted into her dragon, and flew out of the ward. With her dragon cloaked, she took her time heading home, to the home she became more attached to with each return. She felt lighter than she had in a long time, but she would be alone as well.

With no idea how to find Joavan, she could not fix the damage between them.

She swallowed hard, flying slowly to delay returning home where the kitchen Joavan had enjoyed cooking for her would be painfully silent.

# CHAPTER 44

D AEGAN CHECKED ON JENNYVER AGAIN, having settled her inside Treoir castle. Brina had almost fainted when she found out Jennyver lived. She'd grabbed his sister and hugged her for the longest time, then began chatting as fast as the words could leave her mouth when she was not crying.

Jennyver smiled more and more. She would find her way in this new world just as he had.

Tzader had welcomed Jennyver back to the castle, stating she had only to ask for what she needed. Brina couldn't figure out what to call a woman so close to her age who should be her many times over great-grandmother.

Jennyver solved it by asking everyone to use her first name.

When Daegan paused at the door to the sunroom, his heart doubled in size at the sight of Brina and Jennyver holding the twins.

Also admiring them, Lanna looked up with an expectant gaze at his presence.

Daegan nodded. She'd waited long enough.

Standing, Lanna announced, "I must go."

Brina looked over to Daegan. "Uncle, are ya not comin' to play with the bairns?"

"Jennyver shall eventually tire of holding them. I shall return then."

Lifting a tart chin his way, Jennyver said, "These two may be tall enough to carry me around before I tire of holding bundles of sweetness."

He laughed. "Casidhe and I shall return later."

"Where is the lass?" Jennyver asked, indicating Casidhe.

"Flyin' with Tristan's gryphon."

Lanna walked past him without a word, impatient for him to

get moving. He followed her to Garwyli's quarters. She barged in and announced, "Please come walk with me."

"Do ya think I wish ta exercise?" Garwyli grouched at her.

The old guy looked worse than he had the last time Daegan had seen him. His gnarled fingers could barely hold onto his walking staff. His once-bright eyes were dull and watery.

But Lanna would not be denied. Holding back tears making her eyes shine, she went over and put a hand under his arm, gently saying, "If you come with me now, I will not bother you to walk again when you do not wish."

"'Tis not one of my wishes at all." When she would not give up, Garwyli patted her hand. "I shall make this last walk then ya shall listen ta my final instruction."

Lanna bit her trembling lip, took a breath and said, "Yes, I will do this."

Garwyli gave her a long look, one that questioned if she was sincere. Even with her help, he struggled to rise, leaning hard on his cane. "Do not take long. I wish ta see the bairns."

"I promise to be brief."

Daegan had difficulty watching the druid limp forward with Lanna keeping him in her grip, but he would not offer additional aid.

Every man deserved his dignity.

As Lanna finally reached the door to the hall, which Daegan held open, she said, "I want to speak privately with you and Daegan."

"Why can this not happen here?" Garwyli was usually not so abrasive with Lanna, but Daegan would be no happier facing his own last days.

"I do not ask for many things, but this I want," Lanna stated firmly.

Once outside the door, Daegan teleported all three of them to the hall where Garwyli had opened a hidden door in the wall and shown Daegan his private garden.

Garwyli became angry, snatching his arm from Lanna and muttering, "'Tis nothin' left here." He glared at Daegan. "Ya agreed ta protect her even from her own foolishness."

Lifting a hand in supplication, Daegan said, "I have made

good on that promise. As ya told me, druid, Lanna is her own person. She wishes to visit in the garden."

Mouth open then closed, Garwyli sounded hurt. "Did ya tell her about it?"

Daegan shook his head.

Lanna waited patiently.

Spitting mad, Garwyli ordered, "Ya promised ta not waste yar power."

Lanna said, "I have not broken promise and will always protect my power. Please open wall. You have never brought me here. I wish to enter with you."

Garwyli's shoulders drooped. He lifted a trembling finger and created an opening, but to do so drained him.

Daegan cringed. Had this been a mistake? Lanna had convinced him this visit would lift Garwyli's spirits and he'd trusted her.

With the opening in place, Lanna did not touch the druid.

Garwyli limped forward ten steps in his pitiful hunched over form. He paused and lifted his head, crying out, "What have ya done?"

Daegan had not known what to expect, but compared to his last visit, the garden had changed drastically.

Lanna followed him in and walked past to stand before Garwyli when she spoke. "I did not break my promise. Casidhe has much power, maybe even demigod. I used majik and she gave power as a gift to you. She is just as thankful to be here and for all you have done to help Daegan or she might never have met him. I am ... " She swallowed and finished in a shaky breath. A tear ran down her cheek. "I am very thankful for all you have shown me. Without you, I would not be growing into my power and learning how to make wise decisions."

While Lanna spoke, Daegan marveled at the lush scenery that appeared to have burst forth with new life in days instead of months. Even as he watched, a bud on a plant opened, turning into a magnificent pink flower.

That his mate had done this with Lanna filled him with pride.

Stepping closer to Garwyli, Lanna's tears flowed freely. "There is plenty power here to keep you healthy much longer while I have chance to live my life and still train. I miss people I care about in Atlanta, but I will come always and spend much time to become better with my majik. I need you here to guide me for years."

Garwyli began to stand straighter by the second. When he could find his tongue, he said, "Ya are strong enough ta be the druid now, but ... I have felt guilt over stealin' yar life."

Lanna hugged his shaking shoulders. "I have learned much. No one, not even you, can steal what I do not hand over. I know who I am now. You gave me this gift." Pulling back to wipe her eyes, she said, "Now you will be here to teach me until I am ready to make Treoir my last home. This will not be soon, but I make a commitment now to return when I am ready. I want Daegan to hear my words and trust me to do what I say." She hugged Garwyli again and the old guy dropped his cane to hug her back.

His gnarled hands did not turn into young fingers, but they no longer twisted up and now showed strength.

Daegan pushed words past his thick throat. "I thank ya, Lanna and Garwyli. My father would be so proud to see everyone here today."

Garwyli sniffled. "Go on, Dragon, and see yar mate. Ya worry too much over yar flock. Lanna and I shall be out soon. I wish to sit and speak with her not as a student, but a peer whose company I relish."

Lanna smiled brightly. "I am still student. I am ready to learn teleporting."

Garwyli groaned, "Ya shall make me crazy, lass."

Daegan laughed, walking out to the sounds of Lanna talking excitedly and Garwyli grunting in response.

Treoir would have the old druid for many more years as well as Lanna's formidable powers.

Once outside, Daegan hunted Casidhe and found a surprise first.

Skarde and Jennyver walked across the wide grounds leading away from the castle.

When Daegan explained to Jennyver about Skarde being here, she'd adamantly refused to see him.

Daegan had never thought to stand up for any ice dragon again. He took time to share many things Jennyver did not know, which included how Skarde had been willing to kill his brother over what had happened to her.

She made it clear she was still angry at ice dragons but decided to face Skarde in his dungeon with Daegan at her side. Skarde had surprised Daegan by being gentle and understanding as she yelled at him, cursing the lack of honor among his kind.

After expelling all that energy then leaving with Daegan, she'd asked that Skarde be allowed out of the dungeon.

That had been a simple request because Daegan had already given Skarde his freedom to show Casidhe how to shift into her Hawdreki and fly. Skarde had chosen to keep the dungeon as his personal place to reside for now.

The ice dragon had proven he was trustworthy.

From where Daegan stood atop the steps, those two walked an arm's length apart, but they were talking as they strolled.

Maybe they could help each other heal. Daegan would not help Jennyver by hovering as a mother hen.

She was his father's daughter. She was strong.

His gaze finally found the person he'd been looking for.

# CHAPTER 45

CASIDHE WAVED AT DAEGAN AS she strolled out of the woods with Tristan and the rest of the gryphons behind her, all of them now in human form. Belador families who had lived here during the Imortik problem were spending the last day in the realm relaxing before they returned to the human world by choice.

Warriors and guards were taking shifts so everyone could enjoy eating a meal on blankets.

Daegan teleported to Casidhe and pulled her into his arms as if they hadn't seen each other for years instead of hours. She loved every touch and would never take one moment together for granted.

This man could kiss the socks off a nun.

Lucky for him, she was no nun.

Cheering roared around them, the only reason Daegan slowed the kiss to sigh and admit, "'Tis damned inconvenient to have so many around us at times."

She gave a deep belly laugh. "Oh, it totally sucks to be so beloved."

He nipped her ear. "My mouthy termagant."

Daegan turned to the crowd with Casidhe snug under his arm. "I have been remiss in introducin' my new mate to only those I ran into. Please meet Casidhe of Treoir, Hawdreki protector over all our people, humans, and allies."

Another cheer filled the air.

"You're embarrassin' me," she complained quietly.

"Ya shall survive." He squeezed her then continued for the crowd. "I shall travel in the upcomin' months to meet all of our Beladors and their families, plus strive to develop friendly relations for us with humans. It shall not be simple and many shall not accept us at first, but with time I long for peace in all forms. Thank ya each and every one for the sacrifices ya have made and standin' strong in the face of impossible odds. We have all proven there is nothin' we cannot overcome together."

With that, he set off an even louder roar.

She led him past well-wishers to where she found the spread that had been laid out just for their dragon king and his new mate. She had only ever hoped to belong, to be wanted, to be part of a family.

She'd received a greater family than she had ever expected and a mate to share her life.

Now she really had a life.

Daegan was correct. Merging with humans in the same world would come with difficulties, but she would be at his side to do her duty for their people.

Glancing over at the castle, Casidhe paused to take in the couple walking toward them, each carrying a baby.

Rich auburn hair had been braided and piled on Brina's head. The pretty Belador warrior queen had a shapely natural body and wore a mint-green gown trimmed in gold. Her smile jacked her from pretty to gorgeous.

Every set of eyes on the tall Treoir king walking alongside her held equal admiration and love. Tzader kept a protective glance on Brina and his babies even among hundreds of warriors who would give up their lives to protect them. His smooth brown skin matched his warm eyes. His bald head and body cut with muscles bulging beneath his white shirt made for a fine mate and leader.

They made it no farther than the first blanket when every woman jumped up to surround them and the babies.

Daegan noted, "'Tis good of them to bring the bairns out to visit."

Finishing up her thick sandwich, Casidhe took a swig of what Daegan had told her was the best of grog. If men had been out for days battling in the heat with nothing to drink, this probably tasted good. She'd have him supply wine soon.

She took in all the happy faces. "I would have enjoyed meetin' Renata's fiancé if she had been ready to bring him."

"'Tis not easy to explain what we are to humans, but she shall have a long time to do so. For such a fierce Belador, she became shy when askin' if we wished to be invited to the weddin'."

"I would love to go!" Casidhe had snatched a piece of fruit, waving it as she talked.

"I told her we would be honored and hugged her, plus I asked that she take plenty of time off for her weddin' and honeymoon. Devon offered to join her when she returned home to watch her area so Renata could be with her fiancé. I offered to send someone else, but Devon refused. He said spendin' time there until she returns from her honeymoon shall be like a vacation after what he just went through." Daegan studied the grounds with a thoughtful expression before smiling at Casidhe. "I have learned of this honeymoon thing married humans do. Sounds fun."

"It does." She could not steal him away for such a trip with so much going on, but maybe down the road. "I wish Evalle and Storm had managed to come, but she said their small gargoyle missed them." Casidhe couldn't wait to meet Feenix.

"Aye. We shall have another group of Beladors visit Treoir soon to enjoy a break. Perhaps those three shall make that trip, though Evalle seemed content to remain in Atlanta for a while to aid Isak with the media and other human relations. In fact, she pointed out we needed to continue runnin' patrols to keep supernatural predators from takin' advantage of a limited Belador force in the city." Daegan picked up a napkin and wiped his mouth. "Tristan shall make her job easier once he returns as the liaison between Beladors and humans."

"I think he's excited to spend some quality time with his lady, too." Casidhe had enjoyed talking to Tristan when he took her to the gryphon village and introduced her around. His sister had come running up to hug him, then immediately gave him a hard time about not taking her for the final fight with Imortiks.

Tristan ignored her rambling to ask what she had been doing.

Casidhe might have envied the bond between Tristan and his sister, but she was surrounded by many sisters.

She also had Jennyver, who was just as new to this place as her.

Tristan came up. "What happened to your mother, Daegan?"

"She left before I could speak with her. I shall try to find her again at some point to make sure she knows how much we all appreciate what she did."

Casidhe smothered a chuckle. Daegan had been so exasperated with his mother he hadn't really minded when she disappeared without even saying goodbye.

He shrugged, looking up at Tristan. "I feel Deniela has returned to her realm where she—"

"I am here, Daegan."

Quiet dropped across the picnic area.

Daegan tensed. He had clearly not realized his mother could enter Treoir without his help, but then Deniela was far older than the majik it had taken to create Treoir, according to what he'd told Casidhe.

Daegan stood and faced her. "Hello, Mother. I am glad ya visited." He announced who she was to the group.

His people smiled back tentatively, seeming unsure of this woman's presence.

Add Casidhe to that list.

Brina and Tzader watched Daegan, probably waiting for him to call them over. Daegan would not want to drag this out any longer than required to show his appreciation.

Deniela glanced around with a pleasant expression, though not exactly a smile. When her gaze dropped to Casidhe, she asked, "Is that the Hawdreki?"

Casidhe did not care for the condescension in that question.

Evidently, his mother struck a raw nerve with Daegan. In a tight voice, he said, "Please meet my *mate*, Casidhe, who is also a magnificent Hawdreki." He had reached for Casidhe's hand while speaking, bringing her up to stand.

Taking her time to reply, Deniela asked, "Was not that Brynhild a dragon?"

Many sitting on blankets sucked in a breath, including Tristan.

"I have introduced ya to my mate, Mother," Daegan said, speaking each word with emphasis. "Do ya not wish to welcome her to the family?"

Crap. Casidhe would have liked a chance to discuss this first and not draw Deniela's full attention. The goddess might zap her just to free up Daegan for a female dragon.

Screw being frightened. Casidhe was pissed off.

Deniela lifted an eyebrow as if she'd heard Casidhe's thoughts. Had she?

"Welcome to Daegan's family," Deniela finally said, and everyone released their breaths.

It was not lost on Casidhe that Deniela only welcomed her to Daegan's family, but that was all she needed. Once Deniela left, Casidhe would have Daegan all to herself.

Daegan cleared his throat and showed what a gracious man he could be by ignoring his mother's slight. "I am glad to have the chance to properly thank ya for comin' to our aid to defeat the Imortiks and mendin' my body until my dragon could. I feared ya had left before I had a chance to speak when not battlin'."

Deniela cocked her head at him. "I am happy to have come. I find the human world far more intriguing than in the past. To be specific, I saved you twice and healed your friend Quinn. I count three gifts so I shall stay three times as long."

Eyes blinking with confusion, Daegan finally got past being stunned to ask, "How long shall this be?"

Chuckling as if to herself, Deniela stated, "I do not believe such a span of time can be calculated."

Now Casidhe sucked in a breath. That goddess was staying?

Completely at home and pleased with herself, Deniela waved him away. "Finish your meal, Son. I wish to enjoy the festivities."

Brina stood, calling out, "Please join us, Deniela."

Casidhe would thank Brina later herself. Daegan had shared all that had happened with Brina and Tzader for them to become mated as king and queen of Treoir.

"'Tis time to leave," Daegan said abruptly, clamping Casidhe's hand more securely in his. He strode away so fast she had to run to keep up but didn't mind.

She wanted some alone time with him, too.

After passing through a grove of trees, she realized where he was taking her. The gryphons had landed in this area with her. After shifting into human forms, they dressed in clothes, which had been delivered by a Belador who had picked them up from the gryphon village. Tristan had arranged that so everyone could fly unencumbered.

The minute Daegan was in the center of the clearing, he turned to her. "Shift. We shall fly."

"I need a minute to pack up my clothes before I go. I haven't gotten down callin' up clothes yet."

He dropped his head and kissed her. "Ya shall not need any for days where we are goin'."

Her hormones went into overdrive. Game on. She grabbed her shirt and ripped it wide open and shucked off her clothes in record time, then shifted.

Daegan blasted much more quickly into his red dragon. He waited for her Hawdreki to hop and take off first. Once she was airborne, his dragon launched into the air, flying ahead of her. Then his magnificent red dragon led her higher than the gryphons had flown, gifting her with a breathtaking view of Treoir, which went forever in all directions.

This was her future, a life she could never have imagined.

Daegan's voice came into her mind. *I love ya mate and have never known happiness as I do now. I have a place for our honeymoon.*

Her Hawdreki let out a cry of victory. Casidhe sent back, *I love you more, dragon.*

# CHAPTER 46

CATHBAD WALKED THE HALLS OF TÅμr Medb. He'd kept tabs on Daegan and his people in Atlanta all the way to Oakland Cemetery. Watching that display of power had him shaking until crazy Queen Maeve thought to capture Daegan after he survived Sen.

Shaking his head at all that transpired, Cathbad continued wandering. He should feel victorious to rule TÅμr Medb, but that bitch Queen Maeve had killed the entire Scáth Force and found a way to lock him out of her scrying wall.

He had not experienced hate so deep since Ainvar stained his aura. It would require a miracle to remove the stain.

Warlocks and witches bowed to him as he passed through the halls, but no respect showed in their eyes even though he'd saved them from a mad queen.

To be honest, a jet piloted by a human had performed the deed. Cathbad was glad after realizing Queen Maeve had become nigh indestructible.

But he now had the red dragon, an ice dragon, and the Tribunal as his enemies. The Tribunal would form again, but perhaps in a different way. Deities could not keep their noses out of the human world, especially Loki.

TÅμr Medb would be here when Cathbad was ready to spend more time, but he needed to get away. With his renewed power, he teleported to the mountains where he hoped to find Brynhild's family tray missing from her hoard in the cavern.

Hunting her down and claiming her hoard once he disposed of her would give him something pleasant to anticipate. He was not one to mope around and this deep ache felt too close to moping.

Inside the cavern, he took stock of everything. The pond

no longer had chunks of ice floating on the surface. His gaze drifted to the far wall.

That bitch had removed every piece of her treasure.

He grinned at finally having a positive come from all the misery he'd been through.

She'd left the chair, bookcase, and lamp intact probably to thumb her nose at him.

He strolled past the water and crossed the wide cavern to stand where the tray had been. Her taking it would have activated the tracking majik he'd placed on the tray. But as he neared where the tray had been, he noticed a piece of parchment chest high against the stone wall.

There were no words on it.

Had someone left that in place with majik?

He tugged the parchment and it came loose with no problem.

Words began scrolling across the surface in neat strokes, which read:

*Your spell on the ice-dragon platter was not so difficult to locate and disarm. Stay away from Brynhild.*

No signature, but Cathbad added one more unknown enemy to his list. He shook his head. Could he not receive a break?

The cavern shook when something heavy landed outside on the ledge.

Cathbad rubbed his hands together and started grinning.

Brynhild had not left that note, which meant she had returned. With his renewed power, he would bring her to heel. He spun to face the opening where moonlight had been dusting the entrance.

All light vanished as the dragon thumped heavily entering the cavern.

A tingle of concern climbed his spine.

Brynhild's dragon was quite large but had never shook the cavern as the walls trembled now.

Growling with each step, a dark shadow slid over the pond then paused. A black dragon with tattered wings and scars across its chest ducked through the entrance and stopped in front of the pond.

Cathbad couldn't breathe.

Black eyes turned on him. Massive dragon jaws larger than any he'd ever seen opened and roared, *"Never enter my lair!"*

Fire blasted from its jaws.

Cathbad teleported in flames.

D EAR READERS –
Developing and writing this series has been one of the most challenging projects I've attempted since crafting my first book. I started writing this two years early so that I could release the books close together because of the cliff hangers. I know what it is like to wait on a continuing story.

I want to thank you so much for your enthusiasm as each new story was unveiled. I always want to hand you my best and truly appreciate that you came on this ride with me. I do plan to write more books in the Belador™ world (after I let my whimpering mind rest a little, lol).

Additionaly, I want to thank all of you who have gone out to post reviews. Those are a great help to readers and authors.

No story becomes a book unless the writer is motivated to put those words on paper.

Knowing you are all out there waiting on more stories keeps me motivated.

Thank you!

Dianna

# MORE BOOKS

*Thank you for reading my books. If you enjoyed this story, please help other readers find this book by posting a review.*

To be notified of all future releases, please join Dianna's newsletter at https://authordiannalove.com/connect

**For SIGNED PRINT copies** of Dianna's books visit www.DiannaLoveSignedBooks.com where you can also preorder new books.

**The complete 9-book series of Treoir Dragon Chronicles in ebook and audiobooks**
Treoir Dragon Chronicles of the Belador World: Book 1
Treoir Dragon Chronicles of the Belador World: Book 2
Treoir Dragon Chronicles of the Belador World: Book 3
Treoir Dragon Chronicles of the Belador World: Book 4
Treoir Dragon Chronicles of the Belador World: Book 5
Treoir Dragon Chronicles of the Belador World: Book 6
Treoir Dragon Chronicles of the Belador World: Book 7
Treoir Dragon Chronicles of the Belador World: Book 8
Treoir Dragon Chronicles of the Belador World: Book 9

**The hardback print versions of Treoir Dragon Chronicles**
Treoir Dragon Chronicles of the Belador World:
Volume I Books 1-3
Treoir Dragon Chronicles of the Belador World:
Volume II Books 4-6
Treoir Dragon Chronicles of the Belador World:
Volume III Books 7-9

*Note: Hardbacks can be ordered/preordered signed and personalized from www.**DiannaLoveSignedBooks**.com

**Reviews on Belador books:**

"…non-stop tense action, filled with twists, betrayals, danger, and a beautiful sensual romance. As always with Dianna Love, I was on the edge of my seat, unable to pull myself away."
~~Barb, The Reading Café

"There is so much action in this book I feel like I've burned calories just reading it."
~~ Goodreads

"…shocking developments and a whopper of an ending... and I may have exclaimed aloud more than once…Bottom line: I really kind of loved it."
~~Jen, top 500 Reviewer

"DEMON STORM leaves you breathless on countless occasions."
~~Amelia Richard, SingleTitles

"...Its been a very long time since I've felt this passionate about getting the next installment in a series. Even J. K. Rowling's Harry Potter books."
~~Bryonna Nobles, Demons, Dreams and Dragon Wings

"As much as I am impatient for each installment these stories are so worth the wait." ~~ Rosemary, Goodreads
"This adventure win or lose is going to change things for Evalle and her friends. Brava Ms. Love for another fantastic ride."
~~ In My Humble Opinion

# AUTHOR'S BIO

*New York Times* **Bestseller Dianna Love** once dangled over a hundred feet in the air to create unusual marketing projects for Fortune 500 companies. She now writes high-octane romantic thrillers, young adult and urban fantasy. Fans of the bestselling Belador™ urban fantasy series now have a new Treoir Dragon Chronicles of the Belador™ World spinoff. Dianna's Slye Temp sexy romantic thriller series wrapped up with Gage and Sabrina's book–Fatal Promise–perfect for bingers! She has a new League of Gallize Shifters paranormal romance series. Look for her books in print, e-Book and audio. On the rare occasions Dianna is out of her writing cave, she tours the country on her BMW motorcycle searching for new story settings. Dianna lives in the Atlanta, GA area with her husband, a motorcycle safety instructor, and with a tank full of unruly saltwater critters.

Visit her website at **www.AuthorDiannaLove.com** or
**www.DiannaLoveSignedBooks.com**

# A WORD FROM DIANNA...

IN ADDITION TO THOSE I mentioned in the dedication, I must always thank Karl, my wonderful husband and partner in this journey. He is the greatest gift in my life!

Nothing happens without a good team. High five and a big thank you to Candace Fox, Leiha Mann, Kimber Mirabella, Jennifer Cazares, and Sharon Livingston Griffiths, who are so supportive in many ways.

I am so blessed to have an awesome early review team – they keep rocking big time! Kate Tilton coordinated the review team and much more throughout this series!

I could go on and on, but I keep hearing "write faster," so I'm jumping back into my cave.

CPSIA information can be obtained
at www.ICGtesting.com
Printed in the USA
BVHW041345220621
609602BV00011B/17/J

9 781940 651125